This book is mainly dedicated to Heather Best for protecting this story when my computer crashed. She was the only one who had it, as I lost three hundred pages in the process. Because she was a dedicated reader, I was sending her pages at a time to read over. I owe this book to her.

I also want to acknowledge my family and friends who supported my talent, as weird and bold as it may be at times. My mother, Rhonda, Aunt Judy, Cousin Kelly and the Govro family, my father, Bobby, and the Cornell side, Dorothy Fleischmann, a lifelong friend full of encouragement and support, Mary Tresch and family, everyone at Southwest Medical Center, OB/GYN Inc, and Barnes and Noble in Crestwood.

My husband, Chad, and children: Drewan, Lailah, and Baby Chad.

To my friends Niki Cambron and Michelle Frix.

I could ramble more names, as I know so many of you want to read your name in my book. Well, this is for you, too. Dawn Cornell, Danielle Frix, Sheila Webb, Ashley & Justin Webb, Ann, Jeremy and Jen Dorner, Carol R. (This is for you, too, Rettinger).

Last but not least, let's give a shout out to Kelsi Connell...

And to Rocky Sanford and family, you are in my heart. This is for you, too.

I hope I make everyone proud.

Foreword

My thoughts drifted along a fine line, somewhere between the darkness and a dream world. The sea of confusion soaked deep into my cerebral tissues and hemorrhaged my reality. In other words, I was in a coma.

I lay lifeless in Cheriton Hospital, hooked up to a respirator and I.V bags. I was finally able to crash my adrenaline and find peace within myself. To my own dismay, nevertheless, I was condemned to my mind, unable to reach out and worsen my body with more toxins.

I was left to explore my mind, go to the depths of my memories. They weren't dreams in sequence, or full dreams, at all. My memories were more like visual disturbances, flashes of faces and feelings that I didn't want there in the first place. My head had gone into a graveyard, digging up memories that lay beneath the ground. Ones that I hadn't thought about in years.

I was to relive the past, repeatedly, with the emotions charging my body. As my brother flew through the windshield, screaming his last breath to the end, I couldn't close my eyes, as I did when it happened. Visions of sexual awakenings aroused my senses, yet babies cried their way into my arms. Faces of many laughed into my ears, haunting my every silent breath. I was trapped to witness and feel everything that I had avoided while life took place outside of my body.

I couldn't expect them to understand me. I couldn't expect anyone to love me. I wasn't able to possess the happiness that I felt as a child. I was warped into knowing things, feeling awful, wicked things within me. No, I wasn't innocent and naïve. What I did, what I felt when the needle pricked my forearm well...it was a pleasure that I couldn't escape. Even now, as I lay in my head, heroin danced in my dreams, pricking my every thought.

And, so, life must go on. Recovery may be near, but who am I to accept the challenge? I am a mere son of an invisible father, a raccoon with no home. I lead nowhere, with nothing, yet, struggle to live.

We may as well start where we left off, where I am swept away to security, and my new-found brother, Binderman, is heartbroken.

Chapter One
Binderman

Within seconds, I leaped over several cars and stumbled to my brother's side. It felt like hours getting to him. Every second counted. The world froze beneath my feet. I was standing in the middle of the world's cemetery, as if the human race had been decapitated. I was alone.

I practically ripped the door off of its hinges. He fell out onto my chest, blood everywhere. His body was limp and dangling against me. He was dead. My brother was dead. With his eyes half open, glazed and blank, his mouth parted. The blood poured like a waterfall.

Not him, not Cardy, anyone but Cardy could die. I didn't care. My breath had stopped. I was hyperventilating. My chest ached. My heart was beating too fast. I had tremors. I was panicking. My eyes were wide pouring my own waterfall.

I screamed "help," But it was too late. "Help my goddamn brother, stupid motherfuckers!" all the vehicles slowed to watch, but no one wanted to hand me a cell phone or call an ambulance. They may have already done this, but I didn't care. I wanted everyone to stop and help me. They had to.

I glared up into the sun as it shined into my eyes. I blamed God. Cardy was supposed to live and walk away from this. He was my brother, my only fucking brother. *God if only now, make him wake up. Make him okay. I needed him. You have my mother, you stupid son of a bitch, you CAN'T have him!*

With my cheek to his cheek and his blood all over me, I slapped him. I pounded his chest as blood poured more. This can't be happening to me. He doesn't even know I exist! He'll never understand that he had a better brother than Jeff.

I clung to him as if I was dying. Everyone stared. I cried. I screamed and moaned and gritted my growl at everyone. I rubbed his head. I gathered his hands and held him, rocked him. He was my baby brother. He was my life, my blood, my whole destined existence.

If you let him live, I'll change. I swear on my mother's grave, I'll change and make everything right. I'll never cheat, again. I won't party. I'll step away from Cardy and let him get help. I promise. Please, hear me, now. Don't you fucking abandon me. I'll go to church. I'll fucking pray, every night. I know you fucking hear me, God.

I was going into shock. I couldn't feel a thing. I can't…I can't…I was losing reality. I was convulsing, going into a seizure or something. As paramedics pulled me aside and gave me a mask to breathe in, I fought to stay with Cardy. I wouldn't let go of his hand. It took five guys to hold me down. Finally, a paramedic gave me a shot and I was out.

The crash spun in my head, repeatedly. It was a visual cycle of Cardy's body, spiraling in front of me. His blood tainted me. I saw it on my arms and my hands. I felt the warmth, the smell. I was frozen to that moment that he fell onto me, lifeless. He wasn't breathing. His eyes were dead.

I couldn't help him. I didn't even think of CPR. I couldn't think, period. I was shocked. I turned to ice. My baby brother was in my arms, needing me in the most fatal way, and I couldn't help him. I failed him. I failed myself.

"Bin, are you alright?" My father's voice sprung me to look up. I was in a hospital bed, in the emergency room. I didn't know how long I had been out, or if they pronounced Cardy D.O.A.

I cried, harder. I couldn't speak. I couldn't stand. All I could do was sit up, reach out to him. He rushed to my side and gave me a long hug. I hadn't hugged my dad in years. So, I held on, too desperate to care about pride.

"What happened, were you in the car? Did you hit your head?" His hands rubbed the back of my head and his eyes searched for evidence of my bruises. I had none.

"He's dead, dad. He's dead. I tried to save him. I tried." I mumbled, still staring at the tile. I couldn't feel my feet. I couldn't feel the bed underneath me. I felt dizzy and out of my body.

It wasn't the first time I had felt like this. It was déjà-vu, all over, again. The feeling took me back to a time where I had lost the most important person in the world. It was the time I had lost my mother. I couldn't see passed today. I couldn't move on with my life.

"You're talking about Christopher? Son, look at me." And he forced my cheek over to stare into his blue eyes. He was a man that I once looked up to. A father, by all means, who took it upon himself to teach me what becoming a man meant. However, that man that I stared at today was someone that I didn't know. I had lost that connection with him.

We were strangers.

"Christopher is in critical condition. He's in the I.C.U as we speak." His eyes met mine with concern. He was full of questions that I knew. By calling him, I meant to answer them, but, now, under the circumstances, I had no intentions of telling him the truth. I needed time.

"So, he's alive? He's not dead?" My arms began to shake with hope. Cardy wasn't dead, he had a chance. Maybe…I had saved him.

"Son, Bin, I need to know that you're okay. What happened?" His strong grip had me by the shoulders. It brought back many memories of him holding me down when I used to throw fits. His hands were still strong, still able to knock me out if I misbehaved.

He was a strong man, indeed. At Six foot four, he was a man of dignity and strength. He was well respected, from the business sense, to a man of honor, bearing the Sox name that it entitled. The Sox had a long history of wealth, with many trades fit to suit anyone in need, my grandfather, the Architect and real estate owner, to my grandfather's father, a defense lawyer who backed up criminals in New York City, better known as hit-men.

That's where the money came from. Sometime, back in the day, my great grandfather had scored big on some of the bigger names in show business and crime. He headlined many papers, winning case by case with his know how. Well, I respected him, anyways.

"Dad, I'm fine. It's Cardy. He lost control at the bridge and hit an oncoming truck. He's lucky that his car didn't fly off. It almost did." The scene replayed in my head, visualizing the car hoods as I trampled over them.

"You weren't in the car? Why is there blood, why are you in here, then?" He tugged at my shirt collar, at the blood that stained maroon on my skin. My hands were covered in Cardy's blood, our blood that we shared.

"It's Cardy's, fuck, aren't you worried about him? Don't you give a flying fuck about your goddamn son, dad? He's yours, start acting like it!" I pushed into him so I could stand. Fuck this crazy bullshit. I wasn't about to sit here as if I was in need of a doctor.

He pulled me back and looked me over. His eyes wondered all over me, until he decided to say more with another hug. "I'm so glad you're okay. I thought it was you. I wouldn't know what I would do if I lost you."

I didn't hug back. I sighed. "That's how I feel about Cardy, dad. I need to see him." I was about to head out through the curtain in the emergency room when he stopped me, once again.

"Dena is with him. He'll be fine. Bobbi's in the waiting room, she's worried sick. She said it's all over the news. I need to know what you said to him and if anyone else knows." He went straight into more bullshit. He was more afraid of the publicity that Cardy would bring, rather than his second son dying.

Challenging him, I shoved into his chest. "No one knows, motherfucker, if that's all you care about. I've been through hell with him, dad. I'm the only one who fucking cares about him. Dena could care a fucking less about Cardy. She kicked him out into the streets when Jeff died. I'm all he's got. If I were you, I wouldn't let that fucking bitch near him!"

"And what the fuck am I supposed to do? She's his mother. We had a deal, and if you wouldn't have messed it all up, everything would have been fine. I don't understand why you had to stick your goddamn nose in it in the first place. How the fuck did they end up Pierre?" He was clueless to everything. I didn't know where to start.

"Dad, they've been in Pierre. They were here, first. I've been friends with his brother since I was twelve. I didn't stick my nose in anything that I wasn't forced to be a part of." I didn't like our reunion being based on the sole purpose of his arrival about Christopher's secrecy.

"What do you mean they've been in Pierre the whole god damn time? She was supposed to stay in Cheriton, where she belongs! That's why I moved you kids there, to get away from her damn kids!" He was on fire over nonsense.

"You got to be shitting me! You said we moved because you couldn't stand the sight of the house mom died in! You're a piece of shit, you know that?" And I walked out, ready to leave him and my inheritance behind. Fuck him, he was a no good lying bitch of a father.

He rushed after me too scared to cause a scene worth preventing. "I moved you kids to Pierre because I had to. She threatened to take him to your mother, but your mother…" My mother couldn't stand the thought of his late nights out. My mother wouldn't stand the fact that he was cheating on her. My mother committed suicide because of his sorry ass. I could have finished that sentence with so many endings. My mother was a saint and didn't deserve to put up with his stupid ass.

"She was in Pierre, first!" I fumed, heading to the information desk for the whereabouts of my brother.

He jerked me around and got in my face. "How long have you been dealing with him?" It was still about the secrecy. It was still about keeping Cardy hidden.

"Fuck you." I wanted to spit at him. I wanted to kill him, more like it. Instead, I walked past the receptionist and into the waiting room for my sister. I nodded at her and she bolted to my side. I held onto her wrist so we could both escape my father.

"Binderman Joseph, you better not walk out of those doors, I'm telling you what! I will write you out of my will as fast as your footsteps!" He threatened me as if it would bring me to a stop. If he thought that all I cared about was money, then he never knew my ass.

"What's going on, why is dad so mad? What did you say to him?" Bobbi's eyes were already tearing up. She knew that any time our father was around, shit could go either way. I wasn't about to stand by and let shit simmer. I never did when he came home. I told it like it was and that's why he never came. He couldn't face the fucking truth.

"Don't worry about it. We're going home and locking all of the doors. Don't let him in, I doubt he has a key." I pulled her along, making sure that she didn't look back long enough to have regrets. We were walking and we needed every step ahead that we could get.

"Yeah, but where is he going to sleep? We can't keep him out of his own house, Boo." She liked to avoid certain situations. She liked to bump heads with me if she could prevent a conflict of interest. It was annoying.

"I don't give a fuck. He thinks he can walk back into our lives and keep Cardy away from me. That isn't happening, not anymore." I huffed on, ready for our long hike through Cheriton and Casa. My stupid ass didn't bring my wallet for cash for a cab. My stupid ass ran out of the house after Cardy without taking my phone. This entire night was fucked up.

"Does Cardy know?" Her eyes gazed into mine. She was such a little girl in dire need of protection. She was always looking for my opinion, my point of view. I couldn't see her going anywhere without my directions.

"I told him, but then he crashed. I don't know if he was in his right mind to remember." I forced Bobbi behind some bushes at the entrance of the hospital. My father was close by as he called our names. He was frantic. I didn't know if he was scared of losing us, or scared of my anger and what I might do to get back at him.

That was OUR deal. If I would shut my mouth long enough, say forever, maybe, then I could use his money at my convenience. Back when I threw it in his face when my mother died, I had become a loose end. I knew of his affair. I knew how to bribe him and control him. He didn't like that power, so he shut me up, anyway he knew how.

"Cardy's going to make it, right?" Bobbi squatted on her knees and asked me something I didn't know for sure how to answer.

"Yeah," I lied, praying that God had heard my screams. It was in God's hands, now, and he better make it right.

"Fuck this bullshit." I felt like a coward taking my sister away from him. We shouldn't have to walk home.

Redirecting my thoughts, I turned around. I stepped into view and had it out with him. "Dad, why did you come home?"

He was out of breath from running. He stopped and inhaled. "Because you called me."

"Bullshit, stop lying to me, dad! You came home because you were afraid that people would know about Cardy!" I blocked the intersection of the parking lot. Cars couldn't get through to the other side and I wouldn't move, fuck them.

"I came home because my fucking son was crying!" His chest rose and fell with his voice. He bent over with his hands on his knees. When he stood, he grabbed his chest. I didn't want to cause him to have a heart attack, so I eased up.

"Cardy is my brother, whether you like it or not. It's my choice to have him around me, not yours. He doesn't have to be your fucking son, but he's MY brother. Bobbi's on my side, too. She wants him around." I glanced back at Bobbi for a head nod. She wouldn't get involved, but the least she could do is nod in agreement.

He sighed a heavy groan. "Just get in the fucking car and we'll talk about it on the way home. I've had enough of yelling for one night. I'd like to get settled into the house, maybe sleep on it awhile. We need to get everything out in the open and see where we stand. I need a cup of coffee, that flight was exhausting, this whole night is hell on my blood pressure." He bitched and bitched until we neared his silver Cadillac. It was a car that he kept at my grandmother's house, too scared to let me near it.

I stared out of the window for a piece of solitude, but he wouldn't rest. "Let's get one thing straight, Christopher wasn't meant to be. He was a mistake that never should have happened and his mother and I came to terms with an agreement. He wasn't supposed to know about us or anything dealing with us. She gets a check in the mail that's more than enough. I do everything that I can for that boy. Hell, I wasted more money on that kid that I did my own two. It's not right that we give him more. Is that why he's here, for more money?" He had it all wrong.

I bit my tongue from lashing out. I didn't want to cause an argument. "I hung around his brother, Jeff, J.D. We're in the same grade. Cardy started coming around us, wanting to hang out with us. I couldn't tell him no, dad. He was in the car when his brother died. I was the one who pulled him out. I took him to grams and grams told me what to do with him. If you want to pin shit on anyone for anything, then blame grams, 'cause she told me to bring him home."

That night was something that I wanted to forget, but it came back to me in dreams. I knew it came back worse for Cardy. If it wasn't for J.D's death, I think Cardy would have made it out, okay. He wouldn't be in this fucking position to start with.

"Grams told you to bring him to MY house? Why on earth would she do that? What did Dena say?" He was confused.

What he didn't realize was that Grams had another grandson. She missed out on his childhood as much as I missed out on a brother. He was our family, our blood. Why wouldn't she want our family united? Why didn't he ask himself this question?

"Dad, it's all twisted. You're avoiding the point. The point is that YOUR son, Christopher, is in that fucking hospital dying. You need to be a father and make sure he's alright. I did my part, it's your turn. I don't give a fuck if you spent ALL our fucking money on him, you owe him. He needs you." I jerked myself into the seat and crossed my arms. I refused to say more.

"Daddy, Cardy treated me like a sister. He watched out for me. The least we could do is watch out for him." Bobbi's voice came from the back seat, all soft and sweet. She wasn't used to getting between our fights. She kept to herself. To hear her opinion, not directed from one of ours, was rewarding to listen to. Bobbi was growing a back bone.

My father blew smoke out of his mouth and threw his cigarette to the curb. He didn't say one word to Bobbi. He knew he was wrong, and he knew that Bobbi didn't speak up for herself. Maybe, if at all, he would listen to his daughter. I didn't care. I wanted Cardy to be safe and alive.

When the car stopped, I retreated to the kitchen. I rushed off before welcoming my dad back into the house. I was met by Angie, whom I had forgotten was at my house when the shit popped off.

"Holy fuck, hide! My dad's home! Where's Devon?" I rushed around to get any of Devon's things out of sight. The last thing I needed was a lecture on babies when I was concerned about Cardy's survival.

"Your dad?" Angie was clueless to anything that included my dad. She was surprised that I was letting my guard down and reacting in such a frightened way.

"Trust me, not tonight." I warned, rushing her into the guest bedroom where I had stashed her in the beginning. Devon was asleep in his playpen. "You can sleep here, tonight, but don't come out of this room. If you hear us yelling, don't move. Keep him quiet, whatever you have to do. If he starts screaming, you're gonna have to leave. I'm sorry. I'll tell you all about it, later." I kissed her cheek and was about to shut the door.

"How's Cardy?" She whispered, trying to get a glimpse of my father as she peered around me."I saw it on the news."

"He's alive, but I don't know. Wait up for me." I shut the door and rammed into Bobbi.

"What's in there?" She tried to push passed me to see for herself.

"None of your fucking business." When she wasn't pleased with that answer, I admitted the truth. "It's Angie, alright? She's in there with Devon and we need to hide them from dad. I don't feel like getting into this shit, right now." I was defeated. Nothing I could do to keep anything going right.

She raised her eyebrows in surprise. She knew I didn't usually spend time with Angie, and it added to her curiosity. When she didn't ask why she was there, I rolled my eyes. "Alright, fuck, I'm talking to Angie; we're not going out, if that's what you want to know. She's been here for a few days. Now, go keep dad away from this door." I shoved her in the other direction and rubbed my head in exhaustion. How the fuck did all this happen to me?

I back tracked to my first plan and headed for the kitchen. I opened the freezer door and took out Tequila. Thank God for this shit. I poured it into my mouth and sat on the bar stool. I drank it until it was gone. But, it didn't stop there. Oh, fuck no. I opened another and another until I was out of Jose Cuervo. I went on to Jack Daniels and drank my world into oblivion.

By the time my dad returned to the first floor, I was drunk off my ass. I don't know if he saw me drunk before, or not. I didn't remember the last time he was home.

"Oh, Jesus Christ, Binderman." He sneered, staring at the bottles on the counter next to me. I only smiled.

Instead of lecturing me on alcoholism, he joined me, straight from the bottle. "We're two lost souls swimming in fish bowls," He laughed, tilting the Jack up to his lips. That, we were, I almost forgot how much of an alcoholic he could be when he put his mind to it.

Chapter Two
Basia

"What do you mean, I can't see him? I'm his girlfriend!" I stomped at the receptionist desk of Cheriton Hospital. I glanced over at Darron as he held onto Jasmine. We were both there to stand by his side. Hatred had subsided for the time being.

"We have court orders not to permit anyone to visit Mr. Deburke. His mother has just issued the documentation. I'm sorry. You may want to call your attorney." The thin lipped lady didn't even give me eye contact. She busily typed on her computer with better things to do.

I slammed my hand in front of her face for her undivided attention. "I don't HAVE an attorney. This is his daughter. I need to see him, immediately. I want to know his status; I need to know if he's okay. Will he make it, or will he die without anyone permitted to SEE him?" I didn't have time to be polite. This was, seriously, a matter of life or death.

"Miss, I'm going to have to ask you to leave, or you will be escorted out. I'm sorry for the inconvenience that Ms. McPherson has made." Her name tag read "Flora." Her hair was cut short, above her ears, dyed blonde. Her makeup was way too much cover-up and her nails were fake. I didn't like this lady.

A light of hope sprung in my head. "I don't know who Ms. McPherson is, maybe there's a mistake. His mother's name is Dena, Dena Deburke." I leaned on the counter and smiled. Darron was getting impatient with Jasmine as she hung herself over his arm. She wanted to get down. She was about to throw a fit.

"Nope, says here that his mother's name is Dena McPherson, maybe YOU made a mistake." She rolled her eyes and lifted the receiver to call security.

I don't know why this lady was giving me a hard time. I wasn't doing anything wrong. I only wanted to know about Cardy's condition. Channel Five said he wasn't breathing when the ambulance reached him, but the paramedics were able to get a pulse. They were reviving him on the way to the hospital.

I needed to know more.

"Well, can you at least tell us if he'll make it, please? We came all the way from Pierre by taxi. He's my best friend." Darron shifted Jasmine up to his hip, back in place, but she gave out an awkward shriek. It made the people glance at us in annoyance.

She stopped typing and hung up the phone. She leaned over her keyboard to whisper. "I can't give out that information, I'm sorry. You'll have to get an attorney or talk to Ms. McPherson. The restraining order is in place." At first, before she sarcastically acted like she cared, I thought she was going to tell us a room number, maybe tell us he's breathing on his own.

"Come on Darron, this bitch is on my LAST NERVE!" I jerked him by the arm as we stomped to the front doors. I didn't, usually, say curse words. I didn't, usually, get angry at innocent people, but, today wasn't the day to fuck with me. Cardy was dying and I was helpless to do anything about it.

Outside, I threw my arms into the air. "What are we supposed to do? Why did Dena get a restraining order against us? Why is her name changed? What is going on? I need to see him, Darron!"

He shoved Jasmine into my stomach and stepped back. He had enough with her tantrums as she cried louder to make him take her back. "I don't know. I don't understand anything. We need to talk to Kyle, maybe he knows more. Maybe he can get information from Boo. I bet Boo knows everything."

"I'll talk to him, myself. I don't need Kyle to be my messenger. I'm not afraid of Boo. It's all his fault why Cardy is in this position in the first place! If he hadn't put him on drugs, then Cardy wouldn't be going insane and trying too hard to be someone he wasn't! I'm going to give Boo a piece of MY mind!" I confidentially admitted.

I couldn't believe that Boo had led Cardy to his death. I hope he was feeling all the guilt in the world. I hope he's satisfied in his accomplishments. Wait until I see him, we're going to have it out.

Now, all we could do is wait, and pray that God had some heart left in him to preserve Cardy's life. I couldn't imagine losing him. I will never forgive myself if he was gone. I should have stayed by his side, no matter what the cost.

Chapter Three
Cardy

My eyes ripped open to bright stabbing lights. It was so bright that my vision blurred with confusion on where I was. I couldn't make out much more since my head and body was being restrained. Panic took over.

Everything was loud and ear piercing. Voices rushed around, circling my thoughts with a wave of indecision. A tube was shoved down my throat gagging me. My mouth was dry and tight. I felt sick. I had a headache that was throbbing in the back of my head as if the nerves in my neck had been dead, and now, waking up.

Why were there white lights hovering above me? Why were there worried tones in everyone's voices? I tried to shift, jerking to see, but the wires, the tubes, the machines held me back.

Oh, I was in a hospital. As the dreamy fog began to lift, my mind was able to distinguish, more of reality. Something was wrong with me. Something had happened to me. A clue didn't linger. No triggering thought formed in my head. I was lost.

As my eyes grew wide with fear, more worry set in. not one face stuck in my memory. My name had vanquished. My family, my life, all had vanished with my memory. What if I had brain damage? What if I was paralyzed? Maybe, I was stuck in my head. What if it was for eternity? Would they pull the plug on me? Could they do that? Am I dying?

"Mr. Deburke?" A man's soft tone drifted towards my ears. It was deeply accented, maybe Italian or European. He wore a white coat and name tag, which meant he was the doctor.

"Uh," I groaned with all my might. I parted my lips to speak, but speaking was harder to do. *Please, let me communicate to this man.*

"Christopher?" A woman's shriek of panic poured over me. Fresh tears and small fingers formed over my cheeks. I tasted the salt drip into my mouth as she cried. Christopher, Christopher, who the hell was Christopher?

Oh no, do I really have amnesia? Why didn't I know that name?

"Baby, you're awake!" She clasped her hands over her face. It was such an old face. Her eyes were sad and droopy. Dark circles held firm ground to her white complexion, so, hollow. She had wrinkles at the seams. Her cheekbones sagged down like a waterfall of skin. Her lips pierced, unintentionally, as her age grew tired.

"Good news, son, your vitals are improving. You're obviously, awake. I just need to ask you a few questions, Irene? Irene is going to take out that tube, for a minute." His pocket pen gleamed into my eyes. I squinted away. I couldn't take another bright beam.

Seconds later, the tube was out, leaving me scratchy and sore. I stretched my lips apart, then, together, again. I stuck my tongue in and out. God, I hate cotton mouth. Did I have a sore throat, too?

"Fingers, how many?" The guy raised up his hand. The lady who knew me looked on, impatiently. She seemed eager to touch me, hold my hand.

"Three," I mumbled. I wasn't stupid, I could count. I just needed a few minutes to collect my right mind, that's all. I hope. If I had one little trigger, I'm sure I could recall my entire lifetime.

"Do you know where you are?" He scribbled on his clipboard. I heard the pen glide over the paper right above me. The pen clicked closed and he slipped it in his pocket.

"A hospital." I stretched my head up, and then from side to side. I attempted to massage my neck with my right hand, but the I.V in my wrist prevented me. I ran my eyes over the needle imbedded in my skin. I noticed the welts running up and down my arms. A small sore caught my attention. It was on my forearm. It looked as if a drill had dug into me. That was weird. I followed the tubing up to the bag, but my vision wasn't clear enough to read the labeling. The doctor and I met eyes, again.

"Do you remember what happened?" He seemed nice enough, patient with my delay in response, as I searched the room for an answer. I ended up shaking my head without a clue.

"Okay," He glanced back at the lady with sympathy and continued, "You see, Christopher, you were in a terrible accident, a car accident, head on collision. Luckily, you had air bags and it saved your life. You've had some head trauma…swelling, increased pressure in your brain. It may take you a few weeks to remember some things. It's usual with head injuries. We'll follow up with more scans." He stopped to flip through a folder.

"Fractured your collar bone, broke some ribs, a pulmonary contusion, broke your nose…your C.T's showed increased intracranial pressure, but, thankfully, it subsided with our treatment. The only thing for concern is your blood work, but, we'll get you up and walking before we get into that. Let's think positive." He went into explaining that intracranial pressure was the amount of fluid in my skull. I had hit my head on the driver-side window pretty hard, causing brain swelling. The increase in pressure was due to the swelling.

I may show signs of memory loss, temporary changes in personality, headaches, and possibly seizures. He wasn't sure. As he went on, I focused in on that lady. She was…she was…

"Mom," I reached for her hand. My hand was weak and shaky. Clear adhesives were forcing my limitation on how far I reached.

She was pleased that I recognized her. She gripped my hand and brought it to her face. How could she get so old, so quickly?

When the moment was over, she withdrew her hand. She sat up, properly. "You're in bad shape." It was opposite of what the doctor had just said.

"Well, let's get him on the right track before we start talking negatively." Dr. Garcia suggested closing the folder. The doctor gestured for Irene, the nurse, to accompany him outside in the hallway.

"Mom," I said, again. It felt like years since I had seen her. I couldn't get over the fact that she had aged, so graphically.

"Oh, honey, I should have never, if I knew, I could have changed…God, I'm just so happy that you survived. There was a time where I thought that 'this was it', my son is dead. I'd never get to see you, again." She rambled with her tears falling. She was so nervous. I didn't know if she was weary of my condition, or scared to be near me.

"Here, let me sit you up." And she pressed an automatic button on the bedside until I was upright.

"What happened to me? I don't remember any of it. I can't tell you my name, let alone, anything else." I was getting a weird sensation. Nothing made sense. It was awkward to see her, even though she was my mother. It felt like years since I was aware of things, rather than two weeks being in a drug induced coma.

"I...I don't really know. I received a call to rush to the emergency room. I was told that you were in a car accident and might not make it. The wreck was on the news. I saw the car. It was so awful, I mean, just by the look of it, I was certain you were dead. My baby, dead on that gurney." She dazed off, as if she was reliving the horror.

I tried to recall it, but I had nothing. "Who called you?" Maybe, a name would trigger something.

She rolled her eyes, as if it annoyed her. "Your father." She didn't say more. What was the deal with him? Her ring finger was bare. She wasn't married. Was there a divorce? Who was he?

As embarrassing as it was to admit, I had become a child, dependant on his mother. She was all I knew. I had no memory. I was a lost boy, waiting for the day to walk and interact like a normal human being. I refused to let her out of my sight. If she tried to leave the room, I would hold onto her, any part of her, so she would stay. I was afraid that if she would have left, so would the rest of me. My reality was gone. My past was buried.

Day by day, I was getting my personality back. The first thing to recover was my temper. I was easily frustrated by everything. When it was time to eat, my mom rushed me to shovel it in. All I could think about was the cold chills I was getting. Sure, I was starving, too, but the room was too cold and drafty. I felt naked in this stupid gown. I had goose bumps up and down my legs.

After Irene gave me a heated blanket and turned the central air off, I picked up the spoon. I had a bowl of chocolate pudding in front of me. I liked chocolate pudding, but my damn hand was shaking as if I had Parkinson's disease. It was pissing me off. The first bite fell off of the spoon and landed on the edge of the tray.

With a couple more times of trying, I forced the spoon steady with my other hand, too. I guided that motherfucker towards my mouth, feeling stupid for using both hands for support. As irritated as I was, I ended up sliding the damn tray to the floor. It was a reflexive gesture, an angered one. It had shocked me as much as it shocked my mother. My damn temper was taking over.

My mom didn't say anything. Instead, she went digging into her purse and found some gum. She handed me Juicy Fruit. I chomped on it, taking my anger out on the gum. I watched my mother clean up the chocolate mess on the floor. The flavor temporarily satisfied my taste buds and calmed me down. It was as simple as that, gum. I was like a child, happy that, for once, it had been that simple.

As I chomped and chewed, I held out my arm, first, to watch it shake with tremors. Then, I noticed the pink welts, up and down my skin. That sore, I didn't know if it was from the crash or something else. It looked like something else. I scratched it, repeatedly.

My mom glanced up and immediately began yelling at me. "Cardy, don't DO that!" THAT name had more impact. That name fit me. I searched the room for more information to hit me. Cardy Deburke, that's who I was, but what else?

I tried to obey my mom and ignore the itching that just so happened to spread everywhere now that I was told to stop. It was getting worse. "What IS this shit?" I raised my forearm up to my face and surveyed the edges. It wasn't a complete circle. It was a gash, like something had inserted itself in there. The scab was dark and thick, maybe from a syringe when I had been in the emergency room.

"You tell me," Her face was firm as if she was blaming me for the damn thing.

My attitude adjusted to fit her remark. "I don't fucking know! Why would I know?" my language was automatic and I didn't mean to cuss at her. I sighed, deciding to ignore everything that was probing me to understand. Instantly, I KNEW it wasn't from the crash. It was from something else, something more into my past. I kind of didn't want to know, anymore.

"Cardy, your tests are all screwed up. I don't mean that they're wrong. I mean that they're all filled with drugs. The doctor can't believe that someone your age would be into all that stuff. So, I wouldn't doubt that your head's all messed up from that, not the accident." the lady was snapping at me like she had a right to. I didn't care if she was my mother or not, I was offended that she was accusing me of doing drugs.

"So, you're saying that I did this to myself? I'm a fucking junkie? Unbelievable." I sneered. I ran my fingers over the welts. "Then, what's this?"

"Cutting marks," Her head tilted at me as if she knew it all.

"Cutting marks, I'm a fucking junkie and I mutilate my body, now? That's bullshit." I grabbed the railing to stand. Immediately I got dizzy and lightheaded. I fell back against the mattress. The room spun out of control. I wanted to puke and heave. Fatigue took over and then, I wanted to sleep.

My mom gave up the argument and rushed to my aid. "Slow down, Cardy, you can't get up and expect to walk around. Lay back, rest. I won't bring up the past, again. Starting today, you're a new guy, man, actually." I caught her eyes doing their own surveillance.

She sat down in the arm chair next to me. She placed her purse in her lap and began rooting in it, again. Out came her car keys, her cell phone…cell phone. Something sparked a thought. Impulsively, I snatched it from her and flipped it open. My fingers punched in numbers, too fast to recall in sequence.

My mother jerked it back in annoyance. She closed it. "What are you doing? Who are you calling? You are in a hospital for Christ's sake."

I was puzzled. I didn't know what I was doing, either. It was spontaneous. I had a number in my head for just a second, now it was gone. No name came to mind. "I don't know, mom, I don't know." I laid there with confusion. Blankness filled my head I had nothing to think about because I had nothing to start with. All I could do is listen to the machines, the beeps, and the footsteps in the hallway. And sleep, I could sleep even though I had been in dreamland for two weeks, now.

I drifted off easily and peacefully. But, my dreams weren't as nice. I felt myself falling into the unknown, naked and fearing for my life. I heard screams from my past chasing me, nipping at my earlobes like vampires on a blood feast. I fell and floated into the blackness that surrounded me. Familiar voices flapped by me, with laughs and giggles and sobs. I knew that I KNEW everything. I knew all of their names in my dream. I repeated them in the air, feeling the words fade off of my tongue. As I dropped into a black hole faster and faster, the scenery switched into a road. I was in a back seat. The speedometer reached the limits, breaking off into the wind. I was soaring down the street. Voices were getting louder, hurting my ears. I wanted it to stop. The screams transformed into a ringing sensation as the fear escalated. I felt like I was dying. I didn't want to die.

JEFF.

I sat up with the bright lights blinding me, again. My heart was racing. My breath was short and fast. I felt like I had just ridden the Tilt-a-Whirl at a carnival, dizzy and off-balance. I wanted to vomit. As I grabbed for my mother, I did hurl.

"Nurse, doctor?!" My mom panicked. I looked around, searching for the names that lingered in my head until the nurse approached.

"His blood pressure is increasing, his heart rate is up. Vomiting, hmmm, Dr. Garcia?" And she ran to get the doctor.

I wiped the tears from my eyes. I felt like my head was smashed between two rocks. I couldn't help but moan. I held my mom's hand for comfort as the nurse slipped a needle into the I.V. My tremors relaxed and my head went numb. I was off to another nightmare, with less physical response from my body.

Chapter Four
Binderman

A silhouette stood in front of me. Someone lifted my head. I knew her, but fuck, I couldn't think straight. I was sick to my stomach and didn't want to move from the kitchen floor.

"Boo," She sighed, as if I was more trouble than I was worth.

I only groaned in reply. I had a splitting headache and my stomach was tossing. I shouldn't have drunk so much, last night. What time did I stay up to? Who knows…

"Can you help me, Bobbi?" The girl's voice called out to my sister, who must be nearby.

I laughed at her idea of moving me. They couldn't lift me if they wanted to. I waved them away and slouched back into position. I zoned in on the floor so I could concentrate on sleeping.

"Boo, you're getting germs on you." Bobbi smirked, hoping it would send me into miraculous sobriety. She knelt and gazed into my face. I smiled, drunkenly.

"Get the fuck away from me." I forced out the words.

"Do you want Devon to see you like this? Do you want him to grow up and become an alcoholic?" Angela, that was her name. Her motherly tone was getting on my nerves.

"Dad just left to bring back breakfast. I told him you wanted a nice big juicy steak with all the fat still hanging on it, maybe with sausage gravy and bacon, too." Bobbi was pissing me off. She knew what she was doing and I didn't like it.

I was a vegetarian. I didn't eat fucking meat. She knew that. I gagged with the image and curled up on my side. I didn't want to move, no matter what they did. Sure, the ceramic tile was hard and cold. Sure, I knew germs were under me. Sure, fucking sure, fucking sure, but, I couldn't go on about my day.

Life sucked.

Moments later, I was hit in the head with a plastic bottle. A small laugh trailed, with Devon's face appearing in my sight. Where the fuck was Angie?

"Angie!" I angered, trying hard to shove him away from me without hurting him.

"What?" She sighed and picked Devon up as he climbed all over me. He had just turned one and already getting into shit. "Maybe if you were on the sofa, he wouldn't be able to reach you." She had a point.

I'll move, a little later. I had no motivation to get up or crawl. She'll just have to keep him out of the kitchen. Maybe she should leave. Yeah, leave me alone.

Soon enough, the front door opened and slammed shut. My dad was home. What was Angie doing out of the room? I was too messed up to explain myself.

He came straight to the kitchen and stepped over me. "Sleep well?" He joked, bastard. "I didn't know what to get you, so I got what I would get if I had a hangover."

Oh, no.

Bobbi stood beside him and giggled, brat. "Binderman's a vegetarian, dad. He doesn't eat meat. He's not manly like you are." She was asking for it, wasn't she?

"A what? Seriously, Bin, get the fuck up and eat." He made it sound like it was a normal every other day, living life like nothing big was going on.

My brother was dying.

I grabbed the bar stool and pulled myself up. Luckily, the bar stool was mounted to the ground, or I would have slid to the floor. I leaned on the counter for support and stared at my family. "Where's Angie?" I eyed Bobbi.

"Her mom picked her up a few minutes ago. Her mom came home this morning. You know, you were supposed to take her home yesterday so she could be home when her mom showed up." Bobbi was saying a bunch of words that I could care less to hear.

So what, Angela may have needed to go home, yesterday, I didn't give a fuck. It was her choice to stay here with me while her mother was in Florida, not mine. I only agreed. It wasn't like I knew this shit would happen. If I knew, then I would have kept Cardy closer to me. He wouldn't have had time to get to his car.

"I don't give a fuck." I cocked, sliding into the seat. I dropped my head to the granite and closed my eyes.

"Don't talk to your sister that way." And he buttered some toast. His plate was full of nasty ass shit, gravies and pig and cow and…disgusting. I closed my eyes, again.

"Boo, look," Bobbi smiled, biting a piece of sausage in half, letting some of it fall out of her mouth. She hadn't done that since I was in ninth grade. I didn't understand the deal with her. Ever since my father walked through that door, she had turned into the bratty little sister I had to deal with, before.

"That's enough Roberta. Why are you calling him that name?" My father had missed out on everything, right down to my nickname that I had since I was twelve.

Teesa gave it to me. She said that people called their boyfriend or girlfriend that and I had thought it was hilarious. When she started calling me it, the name stuck. Everyone called me by that name. It was better than being called by my father's name.

"It's his nickname, daddy." Bobbi's voice was childish. She was regressing or something. I didn't like the impact he was doing to her.

"Well, a lot of things are going to change around here, starting now." He opened his napkin and laid it across his lap. I guess he wanted a family breakfast together.

"Says who?" I mumbled through my arms. I couldn't stand to smell the food. Nevertheless, I couldn't force my body to leave the kitchen. I hadn't had a hangover like this since New Year's.

"I say, Binderman. How come when I checked my accounts this morning I am about nine hundred thousand dollars short? Can you tell me where all my money went to?" He paused for me to swallow, yet I couldn't respond. I wasn't prepared for his arrival…far from it. He continued, "How many cars did you purchase? I counted five vehicles out there, four of which I never permitted you to buy. And why is the Chevelle out of the garage?"

"Fuck," I sighed. I wasn't about to explain shit. If he didn't want me to spend his money, then he shouldn't have given me the cards.

"This is an outrage! I come home, find my son drinking his life away, wasting my hard earned money on stupid cars, with a stupid nickname as if he's in a *gang*, what the hell is going on around here? You bring Christopher into this house, the house looks like at tsunami ran through it, what *else* do I need to be told about?" He turned the family breakfast affair into an all out debate.

"I can't take this shit right now, dad! Cardy is dying, don't you give a fuck?"

I forced myself to stand, swaying from the liquor and balancing my body towards the doorway. I was running away from the shit I knew was wrong.

"Is he the one to blame for everything? Because I'm not talking about Christopher, Binderman, I am talking about my *goddamn* money. I am talking about your future!" He pounded his fist against the countertop and waited for my explanations. Bobbi withdrew, like she loved to do.

"Fuck my future, dad. You're not hearing me! My *goddamn* brother is in the fucking hospital, dying! I was the only fucking one who saw it happen. I held his fucking body in my arms, dad. Money, future, cars, the house, all that shit is SHIT, dad, it's not important." I leaned against the doorway, holding my head. It was pounding with his loud voice. I couldn't take this shit. I wasn't used to him being home.

"Not important? Not important, Binderman, what I give you kids is *not* important? You better figure out your priorities, this instant. I can take it all away from you and then we'll see if it's important or not. And those cars are going back. You can keep the Expedition because I like it, but the rest, they're going back. The Chevelle is going to your grandmother's and this house will be spic and span by the end of the week, do you hear me?" He thought he could step into our lives as if he left yesterday.

"Just go back to Brazil or France, or wherever the fuck you came from. I don't know why you think you can stay away for six fucking years and walk back in here and be a father. I don't give a fuck what you do with the cars." I made it to the sofa and fell over the arm rest. With my head on the cushions, I tried to block out anymore words.

He decided to disturb me. "I was not away for six years, Binderman. Get that through your head. When your mother died I was right by your side. Don't you fucking forget what I did for you, I had to cope, too, you know. I didn't leave the country until you were sixteen. You know I was promoted. I may not have been home enough, but, I was around. You saw me." He stood above me like a giant.

"Leave me alone!" I screamed into the cushions. I couldn't believe that my life had twisted around to be like this. One day, everything was going as planned. With a blink of an eye, my life sucked.

"Binji," I felt him take a seat next to me. He placed his hand on my shin which made me tense up. I didn't want him touching me. "I can't go back to Holland."

"Holland, you were in Holland, where at in Holland?" I uncovered my face only for a second.

He laughed before he spoke. "Amsterdam."

"Bullshit," I mumbled. My father was not in Amsterdam. I refused to believe him. For one, Amsterdam didn't need a cop bringing down bad guys. It was legal to smoke and drink at an early age. Shit, I wanted to go there, myself. It was every teenager's dream land.

"I quit my job." He admitted.

I turned around to meet his eyes. "Why, because you had to come here?" I figured he would stay, then. He loved his job more than he loved his damn kids.

"No, I quit a year ago. I couldn't take the pressure. I got held up in Amsterdam. You can never tell a day from a month, there. I was drunk from the time I set foot in the place until you called me. I needed a wakeup call, thanks." He smiled a strange smile, one that I took as a stranger's. I didn't know the motherfucker.

"Why didn't you come home?" His reason to stay away from Pierre wasn't for the sake of his job, then. It was to escape reality. I knew that, why didn't I believe myself?

"Why do people do anything that's wrong?" He let his question linger in my head too long. He couldn't follow up with anything more. I didn't have the patience to listen to bullshit.

"Fine, dad, go back to Amsterdam and drink to your death. Make sure you exclude me out of your will 'cause I could care less about money." I made myself climb the mountain of the stairway to my bedroom.

"I'm staying Binderman. You can bet on that, son. After what I saw today, I don't think I'll ever leave this house. I have a lot of mistakes to fix!" He yelled it after me like it was something I wanted to hear.

Nah, dad, you have that backwards. I FIX shit, not you. You can't do anything, right.

Chapter Five
Cardy

I decided to stand and walk to the bathroom. Standing was a job within itself. My legs were like jell-o and I had to hold onto furniture for support. I was confused about everything. My mother couldn't answer the questions I had. My mother didn't want to, or something. So, heading to the bathroom, I wanted some time to think by myself.

With a little guidance from my mom, I was in the bathroom. It was smaller than I had imagined. The shower stall was so close to the toilet that I could stretch my legs into it if I sat down. The sink was awkwardly sticking out behind the door. I didn't appreciate the loud ventilation fan that turned on with the flip of the light switch.

I eased my way to the toilet lid just to ease my knees. My muscles were stiff. My joints ached. My head began to pound again and if I stood back up, I might get dizzy. I felt it coming on. I held my face in my hands and worked on a memory.

The sore on my forearm bothered me. I touched it, again. It was a weird reminder that I shouldn't recover the past that I had somehow crashed out of. Somewhere in the back of my head, I *knew* that I knew. Was I prepared to remember?

Then, I noticed the mirror above the sink. I was curious to see what I looked like. Did I have bruises or scars? I pulled my limp body up against it, stared into my reflection. A stranger stared back at me. Who was I? The person in the mirror didn't belong to me. It didn't connect with me. The person was someone else, someone from my past, someone I feared to see, again.

I had my head wrapped, white gauze around my forehead. My lips were chaffed and my skin color was as white as a sheet of paper. I looked pathetic and malnourished. I resembled a street rat crawling from a sewer that begged for some crack in the middle of the night. I *was* a junkie.

I stretched my eyelid and let go. I slapped my cheeks. I moved my head from side to side. Was I going crazy? Maybe I had brain damage. I lifted my top lip and viewed my gum line. I needed a toothbrush. Damn, I needed to bleach my fucking teeth. When was the last time I did that? How come I remember doing that at the dental office?

I stuck out my tongue. It was dry, so dry that I had a line straight down the middle of it. I turned the water on and splashed my face. *Wake up, dammit, wake up.* Only, it wasn't *my* voice I was hearing. It was someone else's.

I couldn't get up enough nerve to piss because the catheter taken out had left me sore. It burnt as I stared down at it. At least, I had it. I wasn't paralyzed from the waist down or anything. That was a plus.

When I returned, my mom had a bag of peppermint candy. "Here,' she offered. I took it knowing that it was the least I could do since I couldn't brush my teeth.

When I brought the hard candy to my mouth, however, a powerful whiff of peppermint danced into my nostrils. It was a welcoming turn on for some reason. It triggered something. I saw a flash of skin, tan skin that smelled like candy. I could remember, ugh…I didn't want to think about sex, right now. My shit was in pain. I had to shrug it off. It was a stupid thought. It wasn't something to recall with my mother, that's for sure. Was I really only seventeen? Did I even have sex?

Of course, I did. The thought of it wouldn't get out of my fucking head.

Similar situations would occur for the next few weeks. When I saw Gatorade, I was magnetized to it. I didn't feel the need to drink it, I just stared at it. Something was calling out for me to remember. When I ate peanut butter cookies, it, too, caused a reaction in my thoughts. The smell, alone, was something from my past. Cheese pizza swam in the backwaters of my mind. I *knew* it wasn't my choice in pizza. It belonged to someone else, someone I had been close to from my past. I didn't understand why certain sights and smells triggered reactions the way it did. It only added to the frustration of putting a finger on my memories. I was left with none.

My physical reactions were hard to deal with. I'd get headaches with severe pain and tremors. My stomach would clench and I would want to hurl. The room would spin. Dr. Garcia said it was from the drug withdrawal. Soon,

I would be off of the Methadone, and it may increase. I didn't remember being a Heroin addict, but the withdrawal symptoms were proof enough.

My nightmares were always the same, though. Car crash after car crash invaded my dreams. I may have had different scenes and people involved, but there was always a car crash. Sometimes, a lake of blood stood before me. Sometimes, babies would be screaming. I couldn't make out anything that was real. The dreams didn't help me figure out who I was or what I was about.

My mom continued to stay with me. She helped me piece together my childhood. I remembered all that stuff. I recalled Jeff and my dad. I knew our house and my room. I knew all the sports and activities that I was into. I really missed skateboarding.

Nevertheless, she refused to help me with my teenage years. She said what I didn't know would do me some good. She hoped that I would never recall that time in my life. I had the possibility to start over and not have the craving to be a junkie.

The doctor said I may never recall the few weeks leading to the crash. Whatever was said or done was lost, forever. He said with time, I should restore the rest of what I couldn't recover. I was headed down the right path. My Cat scans were improving. My blood work was good. I had a chance towards full recovery.

Maybe my mom was right. Maybe by not remembering, I was able to go on with my life and have a new beginning. Somehow, I knew it was the only way. It was my own thinking that prevented me from the past.

I knew that I was into drugs. I knew that whatever I had done was erased for the safety of my sanity. If I could keep it out of mind, then maybe I was fixed. I knew that much.

My deep dark secrets that lurked when I slept was buried. I knew there was an evil part of me trying to escape, but if I shrugged them away, then I was given a new life, a life outside of Pierre.

It was worth trying.

"Mom, these are Jeff's." I pulled out a couple of sweat suits that read our last name down the sides. They were custom made. I remember when he bought them. I was in eighth grade. He came home and showed them off. He said all of his friends were doing it. I thought it was stupid.

"I figured they should fit you. If you don't want them, I'll toss them in the charity pile. I didn't know your size. In fact, I think you're bigger than Jeff was at seventeen." She had eased up around me. When she first approached me she was nervous. Now, after a few weeks of being around, she was herself, again.

"The nurse said I was Six Two." I slipped the sweat pants on and stood. Jeff was shorter than me, but because he wore his pants bigger than he was, they fit.

"Yeah, and she said you were a hundred and fifty pounds, too. You need to start eating, appropriately. I don't know how you stayed alive. You look like a stick." She admired my stance and smiled.

We were on good terms. It felt good.

She frowned and sighed. "Jesus, you look like your father." She tightened her grip on her purse as if it annoyed her.

Confused, I sat back down. "I look nothing like dad." My dad was short and stocky. He had brown hair and brown eyes. I was exactly opposite of him, if you ask me.

"No, your real father. I mean, you have always favored his side, but, now, wow…it's like staring at him all over, again." Why she would chose to bring him up was beyond my understanding. I didn't have a real father that existed. My real father was dead to me.

I ignored her comment and decided not to pursue the possibility. I didn't want to know about him. I had a dad named Jebb. It was enough.

I was being discharged, today. I had the paper work to leave and everything. The only problem with that was that I was going to court. I wasn't going home.

"You know what I want? I want a fucking Big Mac and fries. I'm tired of this hospital shit." I tied my shoes and stared down at them. They were the ones I had come in with. They were Jordan's, something I wouldn't dare put on my feet.

"Stop cursing, so much. I didn't raise you to have such a filthy mouth." She eyed me, suspiciously. I think she was afraid that I would resort back to a time I couldn't remember. In contrary to her belief, I wasn't about to. I liked who I was.

"Sorry. What's going to happen, today? What do I have to do?" My nerves were on edge. I was going to court for God knows what and getting a sentence for God knows how long. She knew the details and wasn't about to inform me of them.

Another nerve racking problem was that I had been thinking about a cigarette since I woke up this morning. I saw the squares in my mom's purse, so, I knew she smoked. I needed to get up enough nerve to ask her for one.

"Cardy, let's just go there and see what happens. You apparently don't have your license. It was revoked for a year, for some reason. You missed your court dates, got a warrant, and now, you wrecked your car into a Diesel. The man decided to sue you for his hospital bills. Your test results clearly point out that you were under the influence. Your father has already talked to the judge, so I hope they worked out a deal. You're lucky to have a father who can pull strings. You might be looking at some time in jail, so, be prepared." She didn't want to go into detail. It was the part where she was hopelessly helpless for me.

"Jail? Mom, I don't want to go to jail! Can't you take me away? We can skip town or something. Don't make me go! I'm seventeen, mom." My simple life was going down the drain. I didn't know what I was looking forward to outside of the hospital, but it was especially not jail.

"Honey, your father knows what he's doing. His other son has been in and out of that courtroom I don't know how many times. He knows the judge pretty well. I'm sure it's not jail time. You might have community service or something like that. I just want you to understand that everything you do has a consequence. If it's jail time you get, then that's what you get. You have to serve your sentence. It's not up to me. If was as easy as running away and hiding, trust me, I would. It's time to face the fact that what you did was wrong." She stood by the doorway with her purse under her arm. She was more than ready to face my consequences.

"You should have never kicked me out!" I stormed off of the bed and was shocked by that memory. She had left me, abandoned me. It was all her fault.

"Excuse me? Cardy, this is not the time to go blaming other people's mistakes. I know mine, do you know yours?" She stood ground, ready for an argument. She realized that I knew more than what I was telling her. I don't know where it had came from, but I knew more than what I was telling myself.

"Yeah, mom, sure. Let's get this shit over with. I wanna move on with my life." I hurried down the hallway into the unknown. That memory had left me cross. She had kicked me out and I was left to defend for myself at fifteen. I didn't know where I went, but it was all because of her lack of parenting.

When we hit the outdoors, it was refreshing. The sun was beaming bright and the wind was a warm breeze. God, it felt good to feel the wind. The sky was blue and peaceful. It was a better day to go skateboarding rather than a stupid courtroom.

"I want a cigarette, gimme one." I held open my hand. I wasn't about to ask nicely. I deserved it.

She huffed, but fumbled to open her purse. "I don't know why I'm letting you do this. It better not be for the worse, you hear me? First, a cigarette, then pot. God knows what else." She was angry at me for recalling her status at the time of Jeff's death. We all had made mistakes. Let's fix them.

"Here," And she handed me a lighter. It was the first time my mom had witnessed me do it. She looked on amused.

I held it between my lips so easily. I was a smoker. I couldn't give up smoking if it was the last thing I had to do to recover. I needed that relaxation. Once a smoker always a smoker, I was set on believing that for my own nerves.

"You feel better?" She sighed, heading to her car.

No, I felt lightheaded. The cigarette brought a rush of dizziness before it could calm me down. Maybe it was a bad idea to smoke. I had just recovered from a head injury, confusion taking up my time. I should have tried it when I was sitting down.

"Mom," I yelled after her. It was a shame that I had to depend on her for so much. I stopped in my tracks and bent over on my knees. I wouldn't drop the cigarette.

"Oh, Cardy, come on." She rushed to my side and stood me up. She balanced me to the car.

She drove the same maroon Taurus that she had drove a few years, ago. I knew that car, well. She placed me in the passenger seat and strapped the seat belt around my waist. I laughed as she hadn't done that since I was in third grade.

"I got it, I got it, come on, now." I shoved her out of the car and shut the door. I inhaled the cigarette deeply, letting the nicotine take over my lungs. Okay, I felt a little better. I still didn't want to go to court.

"Just be prepared, that's all I'm saying, okay? I love you. Remember that.

I have done all that I could do to make amends with you. I didn't mean what I said that day, Cardy. I hope you know that. I expected you to dart back in that doorway the next day. When you didn't, I called everywhere for you. Darron told me where you were. I stopped calling because you went home." She started the car and took off slowly.

"That doesn't make any sense, mom." I held the back of my head and smoked on. I scoped out Cheriton as we drove down the long narrow roads to the Court House.

"It doesn't matter. You're with me, right? We have each other. That's all that matters. I won't ever leave your side, again. We're in this together." Something told me that I was glued to her for my entire lifetime.

When we pulled up to the stone tower of a building with liberty statues posted as guardians at the entrance, a scene was taking place. Cop cars had their lights flashing and parked sideways. Some police men were forcing a lady in heels from the staircase. She fought back, spitting and kicking until one of her heels fell off onto the ground.

"Jesus Christ," My mother mumbled, knowing that we had to walk through it all.

The lady was in a mini skirt. Her long legs stretched out as she tried to kick them. She wore a red halter top that matched her red lipstick, bright as fuck. She was obviously a stripper or hooker. I didn't know which of the two.

"She looks familiar." I gazed on as her blonde crop of hair revealed her face. If I didn't know better, I had met her, before.

"Well, unless you went to street corners or strip clubs, I doubt you know her." My mother assumed that I didn't have the capability to surround myself in such filth.

"No, I think I know her." (I think I had sex with her.) My memory went into overtime as the stripper's hands had been all over me at one time. Yeah, I knew her. I had tasted her bubblegum on my sixteenth birthday.

"Cardy, get real, *that* is a hooker. Why on earth would you…" Her mouth closed as she assumed the truth. Her little boy wasn't a little boy, anymore. I had sex with a stripper, once and many times, ago.

I laughed at her reaction. I blew out smoke and tossed my square to the curb. "It's no big deal. I didn't know-know her, if that's what you think. I didn't even get her name." I opened the door.

"Jesus, Cardy," She watched the lady get shoved in the back seat of the car. I didn't know what she was doing or why she was arrested, but I didn't care, either. I bet she wouldn't remember me.

"I think you need to be tested for AIDS." My mother concluded following me out of the car.

I stopped and stared over the car hood. I met her eyes. "I don't need to be tested for AIDS, mom. I'm sure they did all that in the hospital." I laughed some more as her facial expression was full of fear.

"No, I doubt they thought of that. You went in with a head injury, not an STD check up. I can't believe you would stoop so low with that...that skank. I hope you wore a condom, at least. You *did* wear one, right?" I recalled all the times my mother followed Jeff to his room, lecturing the facts on condoms and diseases.

"Yeah, mom." Although, I didn't remember to that extent.

"Jesus, Cardy, I can't believe you turned out this way. I had better plans for you. You are worse than your brother." She said it nonchalantly, but I took offense.

"I am *not* worse than Jeff, mom, trust me. He was all over the place. He didn't know what he was doing at all." I recalled a time where Jeff fell into my bedroom. He got up, pissed on my dresser, and fell into my closet. When I yelled at him, he fell on *me* and threw up on my rug. No, I wasn't like Jeff at all.

"Let me ask you something, why are you here, today? You think that driving doped up is safe? You think Jeff used Heroin? You think Jeff...let's just drop this. It's going nowhere. You have to have a clear mind in that court room," She pinched her lips tighter and walked up the staircase as the cop cars drove away.

"I'm not like Jeff because Jeff is dead." I mumbled. She heard me, but didn't respond. Jeff wouldn't be here trying to fix shit. He wouldn't want to change the way he was. He'd walk right back into his bedroom and snort up his cocaine. No, I wasn't like Jeff at all.

Or was I?

Chapter Six
Basia

I couldn't take care of Jasmine, anymore. I was a useless body, condemned to my mattress, captive under black comforters and suffocated under stone pillows. Cardy's crash had torn me to pieces. I couldn't be a mother, not anything.

I cried for a week. When I couldn't cry, I held my breath, hoping it would be my last. If Cardy was dying, so was I. I felt to blame. If I had been around more, if I had paid attention to him, maybe then, maybe he wouldn't have been so depressed to depend on alcohol. I didn't know why he crashed, or what he was on, I just knew it was something. It was something that could have been prevented.

Darron took care of Jasmine. He brushed her hair, gave her a bath, turned on her movies, and woke up through the night to her teething. I wasn't available. I was in a space of silence. I never wanted to see the light of day, again.

I felt like God had deserted us. He punished us for the sins that we had committed. He cast darkness over me so heavy that I even considered selling my soul to save Cardy's life.

I laid around for hours on end, going over the details of Cardy. He didn't deserve the lifestyle that he was put in. he was such a lost boy, couldn't see the path of righteousness. He had it all, and lost it all.

I waited for the phone to ring, a call to tell me that he was dead. Every time it rang, I held my breath. I listened to the tone of Darron's voice.

Darron kept in touch with Kyle, who kept in touch with Cardy's friends. It was a direct line to his status. Cardy's condition was critical. He was in a coma. He didn't have brain damage, but he was in a coma. His body was weak. The drugs had a huge impact on his recovery.

I pictured him circling his head, trying to get out, but couldn't find the light.

Death lurked above, waiting and pacing around to attack him. I prayed even then to God, hoping that he wouldn't shun me out.

God, hear me now, if never again, I need you to give Cardy the strength to recover. I need you to fill his heart with love and let him forget the horrible terrors that he has endured. I don't care if he hates me, or he forgets me. I don't care if I never see him, again. Just make him better. Let him survive and feel happiness.

And, God, if you hear me, tell my mother I love her and I miss her. I need her, too. Forgive me for my sins, for I have been avoiding everything in my life. May Jasmine love me, even though I have not been a good mother to her.

Forgive me for asking you for help, for I am weak. I do not deserve your love, but you are all I have. Please, do this for me, for Cardy, for Jasmine. She needs to know her father, if nothing else.

Cardy is a good person. He needs to know that. You know that, why is his life so hard? What is his purpose in life?

God, if you hear me, please, send him my love. I appreciate anything that you can do.

I was desperate. Deep in my heart, I wanted to die. The only thing keeping my alive was Cardy and Jasmine. I lived for them. If I lost Cardy, I pray that I had the strength that Jasmine needed from me. I prayed that I would not want to commit suicide.

Chapter Seven
Binderman

Nothing mattered more to me than my brother. And, there was nothing I could do to help him. Dena, his mother, had a restraining order against me. My father tried to explain that she had one on everybody, but that shit didn't matter. I took it personally.

She saw me as a threat to him. She thought I was to blame for his behavior. She thought that I would disrupt his rehabilitation and cause more pain. Maybe, she was afraid that he would see her as she was, a no good whore that kicked him out in the first place. I may have some influence in his thinking, so she thought.

She only wanted him because he was a priceless piece of ownership. He was worth more than her entire family and their generations to come. Cardy didn't know it, but he sat on billions. Being blood related to me, he had the right to everything that my father, and his father before him, possessed. I'm talking about estates all over the world. A million dollar industry was at stake, here. He had bank loads of cash. Not to mention, the trust fund that is at his disposal when he's eighteen. He didn't know it, but Dena did.

Dena didn't love him. Dena never did. She was a crazy bitch that my father should have never fucked with. If she kept Cardy in need of her, she could sweet talk her way into my father's money, my money. I couldn't let that evil bitch use my brother like that, not anymore. She had used him long enough. He was mine, now.

But, what could I do? I was already arrested twice for being within a hundred yards of Cardy. She had security guards posted up outside his room. Nobody was allowed in. nobody was allowed to call. My father had access, but he was a stupid son of a bitch that refused to visit him. Sure, he fit the bill because I made him feel guilty, but, visitation was something more. It was something he wasn't ready to do.

Dena thought she was smart, letting him pay for everything and nestle her way closer to Cardy. Keeping my father on good terms with her stupid ass, she could weasel her way into his life, again. She could bribe him, like before. She could use her conniving ways to provoke him into anything. And, I wasn't about to let that happen.

My dad wanted me to stay out of it. He was still afraid that she would ruin him. He didn't want to get to know Cardy and didn't want me to bother with him. Bullshit. There was no way in hell that I would listen to his weak ass. I fight for what's mine and Cardy had more of my blood in him that he did of Dena's. It was obvious in his appearance. He looked just like me.

"Dad, you have to see him. He looks just like us, here, look at the pictures." I was half sober for once, trying to calm down on that shit. I hadn't been sober since the day Cardy had the accident.

He pushed passed me and grunted. He refused to look at him. It pissed me off.

"You can't run from him, anymore, dad. He's a part of us, a part of me. Just look at the Goddamn pictures." I yelled after him, throwing the photographs in his face. A bunch of them were of Cardy when he was drunk, but, that's how it went. A camera never got the other stuff. Fresca only took pictures when she was tipsy, herself.

He sighed, tired of hearing about the son he wanted to forget about. He gave me a look and bent down. He picked up one picture and stared at him. It was the first time he had seen him since Cardy was five years old.

"Huh," He half smiled. He shoved the photograph into my stomach and walked away. It wasn't enough.

I ran after him. "Dad, he looks like me, doesn't he? We're like twins. Even Fresca said so." The thought of Fresca hadn't entered my mind since that motherfucker said that he fucked her, Goddamn it.

I didn't know if it was true, or not, but I wasn't about to ask her. If she ever admitted that shit, I'd go crazy. I couldn't look at her, anymore. I hadn't seen the girl for about two months, no call, or anything. That was unusual, since the bitch came crawling back, any other time.

"Yeah, Bin, he looks like you. It's not news to me. I knew that shit when I first saw him. I knew that boy looked identical to you. That was why it was so important to keep him away. It was proof enough to your mother. That would have been all she needed to see. It doesn't matter, she found out, anyways." He opened the freezer and took out a bottle of Vodka.

I remembered that day like it was yesterday. I had come home from school and she was crying on the staircase, waiting for me. I tossed my book bag down and asked her what was wrong. She said we were leaving my dad, for good. She had our bags packed and in the car. She wasn't going to confront him, but I insisted.

We waited for Bobbi to come back from ballet and then, we were going to leave. She wouldn't tell Bobbi why we were leaving, but, we had to go. My father had outwitted her, however, and came home early. He begged for her forgiveness and she buckled.

She was never the same. She knew of Christopher and my father's affairs and was never right in the head, again. He had driven her crazy, so crazy that she decided to kill herself.

"His mother has asked me to help her out, financially. Can you believe that nonsense? Where did all that money go? Hell if I know." He sipped the Vodka before pouring it in a glass of ice.

"Then, do it. If you won't, I will." I checked the freezer for more alcohol, but was disappointed to find nothing. Great, I had to get the fucking stash in the basement freezer. I was running out and didn't care to call anyone to supply me. Sure, I could ask Cody for his I.D, we looked identical, too. But, I didn't feel like talking to that bastard. He was still pissed at me for fighting Dewey and trying to fuck Mikayla, his girlfriend.

"Give me your wallet." He held out his hand as if I would comply.

"Why?" I didn't expect him to be serious. He couldn't possibly take away my credit cards. What the hell did I do to deserve THAT shit?

Nothing.

"Because I asked for it, Binderman. I want my cards back. I am nine hundred thousand dollars short and you haven't showed me one thing that was worth shit. I want my money back, or my cards. This shit stops, now." He was fucking serious. My father was fucking serious as fuck!

What the hell was I going to do?

"No, not unless you pay for Cardy, you help his ass, then I'll do whatever the fuck you tell me to do. Until then, fuck you." He had bribed my ass long enough. It was MY turn.

I dashed off to the basement and closed the door after me. That asshole probably didn't remember where the basement door was. I headed towards the deep freezer, behind the staircase, and sat my worried ass down in a wooden chair. I took out one of my last five bottles of Tequila and gulped it. Fuck, when this shit was gone, I'd have to resort to J.D's extra supply of Jack Daniels. After that, I'd have to use Brian's Yeager and Fresca's stupid ass lemonade. Life wasn't fair.

My basement wasn't as big as the rest of the house. It was a small cellar. The ceiling was short enough to hit my head on. The beams had a good twenty years worth of spider webs, and I knew there were crickets down here. I heard them, sometimes.

This was the place that I had taken girls to when I was younger. I smiled at that thought. When my father was upstairs, doing whatever he did in the library, J.D and I would rush the girls down here to feel them up.

Teesa was the first girl that I was with. Cardy didn't know it, but she was the girl that I had lost my virginity to, also. We were thirteen, barely hitting puberty. Neither one of us knew what we were doing, but we managed to do it. That's why Teesa was so special to me. I had an obsession with her since I met her.

God, those years were great. It was a time when I had the world in my hands. I could have done anything and everything and it wouldn't have mattered. I was a child, able to get by with murder if I wanted to.

Teesa.

I decided to give her a visit. I hadn't heard from her for a few months. She was probably going back out with Roger. She liked to bounce from him to me like that. I didn't understand why she had a thing for his broke ass, but, what the hell. With Fresca out of the picture, I needed to occupy my time with something, why not her?

I scrambled to my feet and climbed the wooden stairway. Where were my keys?

She lived in Cheriton, now. As much as she bounced from guy to guy, her home life was the same way. She was never stable. Sometimes, she lived with her aunt in Pierre. Other times, she ran back to her father in Cheriton.

Teesa was loaded just like my family. She may have been a whore without dignity, but, her childhood was spent with violin lessons and horse stables, just like mine. We came from the same school, St. Paul Academy. She had transferred so many times back and forth, that the school board, finally, wouldn't accept her back, saying her grades weren't good enough. Whatever. They saw her as an embarrassment to their community.

I had house keys to both her places in Pierre and Cheriton. I bet Roger didn't have that access. Teesa favored me as much as I did her. We were a team, where one had on-going issues, the other was there to redirect their troubles. Therefore, it was time that I told someone about Cardy being my brother.

Her house was dark, but it usually was. Her father was a seventy year old man, unable to get up out of bed unless someone helped him. He suffered from Emphysema and some kind of cancer. It was a bad condition for both him and his daughter to deal with.

I headed around back and unlocked the door. She wasn't expecting me, but I knew she was home. It was a week day and she didn't dare disturb Roger on a school night. He had enrolled in some trade school and worked during the day. He was too busy for her ass, if you ask me.

I passed the million dollar kitchen with actual work stations for a chef. Her father once owned a restaurant in New York and had his equipment transferred here when he was first diagnosed with cancer. Back when he was able to move around, he would show Teesa a few recipes. The girl could cook if she set her mind to it.

I followed the hallway to her bedroom and onto her bed. She was asleep. Her pink satin sheets were wrapped around her fully clothed body. Her makeup was still on with the glitter smearing down her cheeks. She was naturally beautiful, but she was obsessed with makeup.

I crawled in next to her, kissing her ear as I spoke. "Baby, wake up, it's me."

Startled, she jerked up and slapped me across the face. She smiled when she realized who she hit. Her fingers reached out to rub my face since I hadn't shaved in about two weeks. I doubt she had ever seen me this scrubby.

"What's going on?" I think she may have thought the worse for Cardy, since I didn't make house calls unless I was in need of a good talk. Ha, a good something. Teesa and I was cool like that. What I couldn't tell Fresca, I was able to ramble on to Teesa, since she wasn't my girlfriend.

"Nothing, I just wanted to see you." I kicked off my shoes and slid under the covers, ready to lie next to her to fall asleep.

"Is Cardy alright?" She turned to face me, all the while keeping her fingers glued to my stubble. She was amazed that I had let go of my appearance.

"He's okay, I guess. I don't know. I can't see him. His mom has a restraining order against everyone. I'm not allowed to visit." I smiled, lightly, and kissed her nose. I was thankful that I was there. I could melt away from the pain and try to live a little.

She sat up, abruptly. "That sucks." She had more on her mind. I could tell that she wanted to say something else, but was waiting for the right time.

"Where have you been?" I tugged on the buttons of her pajamas, ready to undress her.

"Boo, I can't…a lot of things have changed. I need to talk to you. I'm glad you came over." She wasn't in a playful mood or in any normal mood at all. I didn't like the damn serious tone to her. Teesa wasn't serious. It wasn't her nature.

"About what?" I sat up, too. She was probably going to tell me to back off, since she was with Roger. She DID get like that, sometimes. I hated it. She was mine and he knew it.

"About everything. I hadn't been coming over because of this." She forced her left hand into my view. My mouth tightened.

On her ring finger was a fucking diamond ring. The motherfucker had proposed to her ass or something. I stretched out her arm and held it up at her. "What the fuck is this, Teesa? He wants to marry you? You want to marry him? What the fuck is this shit?"

I was appalled that Roger thought that he could just take over my broad and make her his. She was MINE. I'm going to kick his fucking ass. Nah, I'm killing his fucking ass. I sat on the edge of the bed in anger. Life *really* fucking sucked.

"He asked me because of the circumstances, Boo. We *have* to." She stretched out her long body and rose up her pajama shirt. She patted her stomach to insinuate something worse. Oh hell, no.

"You're fucking pregnant?! Why didn't you fucking tell me this shit, Teesa? How do you know it's his? How do you know it's not mine, or Cardy's…or whoever else you fucking slept with?! Come on, Roger? You can't marry Roger. You can't have a kid!" I felt like I had left a nightmare and walked into a horrible extension of one. My life was getting worse by the minute.

She fumbled for words. "I tried calling you, Boo. And it's not yours. It doesn't matter who it belongs to. Roger wants to marry me and make it *his* kid. He knows that there's a chance that it's not his, but he loves me."

I found myself biting my nails, harder and harder against the cuticles. I was in deep thought on how to kill Roger. I wasn't thinking right, anymore. Roger had to go. Teesa had to have an abortion and I had to clean up my fucking hell hole of a life.

Somehow.

"Roger doesn't love you, Teesa. He wants you because you're mine. He wants what I have." It was a logical explanation. I couldn't see how that bastard could fall in love with someone who couldn't keep her pants on around dick.

"No, you're wrong. Boo, you have Fresca. You'll always have Fresca. I have no one, Boo. I love you, too, but, Roger loves me for me. He doesn't call me for a booty call, he calls me to tell me about his day. He comes over to take me to the movies. He wants to spend time with me. He doesn't just want me when he wants me." She made me sound like a fucking asshole.

"Come on, Teesa. You can't just break it off with me. What if I told you that I wasn't with Fresca, anymore, would that change shit? What if I took you to movies and shit like that? What if I wanted to marry you, would you change your mind with Roger?" I didn't want to lose her, too. I was getting desperate to have something familiar in my life, no matter what the cost.

"Boo, it'll never work out. You know that. I can't trust you, I'm sorry. I have a baby to think about." She tried to touch me, again, but I stood up.

I was beyond angry. "Yeah, that shit might be mine! Teesa, come on, think about it! Roger can't do shit for you! He can barely keep up on his rent, let alone a fucking kid! Don't do this shit to me!" I tried to keep my voice down in respect to her father, but it was hard to do when all I wanted to do was scream at her.

She scrambled off of the bed to approach me. "It's not yours. The last time we had sex was New Year's, remember? I hadn't seen you since then. I'm not that far along. I'm sorry, Boo. We have to grow up sometime, right? Let me be with Roger."

"That's bullshit, Teesa. If it's not mine, then I give a sixty percent chance that it's Cardy's, which means I have a fucking say in the matter!" I fought the tears that had been fighting their way into my life since the whole fucked up situation came.

"And when do you have a say in Cardy's matters?!" She was ready to argue, which was a first with me.

"Since he's my fucking brother, motherfucker!" I turned as the tears came pouring faster. This isn't how I expected it to go. I wanted to tell her my issues and have her tell me things were going to be alright. She was supposed to do that shit.

"You're kidding!" Her eyes widened with the possibility as her hands went over her mouth in shock.

"Fuck it," I gave up. Fuck Teesa, fuck Fresca, fuck my dad, fuck the goddamn world. I kicked her door open and rushed out to hide my fears.

If I didn't have Teesa, or Fresca, or Cardy…who the fuck did I have?

I hated my life.

Chapter Eight
Cardy

"Mr. Deburke, we are here today, to go over the facts of your case." He shuffled some papers in front of him, adjusted his small glasses, and glanced up at me. He was a stern man, with deep wrinkled lines on his cheeks. They sagged like a bulldog's, yet, thinly. How could I take someone seriously, if all I paid attention to was his jowls?

He had taken favor to my mother and me, welcoming us to his office, rather a large court room with too many empty chairs. His office was the usual mahogany desk and bookcases, family fishing pictures with the camouflage vests and fishing rods. Above the door entrance, a good size bass was mounted with pride. He was a fisherman, a woodsy-type guy.

By habit, I leaned back in the chair. My mother quickly shoved my shoulder to straighten up, which, I did. I couldn't concentrate. My eyes were all over the walls and my hands couldn't be still. I sat on them for a while, then shifted in my seat. What the hell…get on with this shit.

I wasn't nervous, anymore. I was anxious. I didn't want to be still. I didn't want to sit in silence as he read over the reports. I didn't know what to say. I tried not to cough or sigh or anything, as it would be disrespectful. It was hard to do.

"What is wrong with you?" My mother whispered, crossly. It made her tense up, scared that it would cause the judge to dislike my behavior, maybe, take it the wrong way.

I bounced my leg and crossed my arms. I wiped my chin and scratched my neck. I didn't know what was wrong with me, either. It seemed like eternity before he decided to clear his throat.

"Mr. Deburke, I see so many young people throw their life away, nowadays. They come in my court room, promise to be good, and then, I see them within a year's time. They feed me a bunch of nonsense about not making ends meet by flipping burgers. They con me into believing that five dollars an hour isn't enough money to buy diapers, which force them to sell drugs. And, by selling drugs, they ingest them, and so forth. You see my point." He stacked the papers together and sat them neatly back down in front of him. He was stalling or thinking, I didn't know the difference.

"Your honor, has my son been in trouble with drug dealing, because I wasn't aware of this..." She turned to me as if I had a lot of explaining to do.

I shrugged, racking my empty head for clues on whether I was some notorious drug dealer. Beats me.

The judge, Judge Calhoun, appropriately smiled. "No, I was using that as an example, forgive me. Your son is here because of possession of a controlled substance. He had driven under the influence of a controlled substance. He has been a danger to our streets and our children. He's failed to appear in court, he has been in an accident, luckily that he lived through. I was told by his father that given the circumstances, he's been through a rough two years. It doesn't give him permission, or does it give him an excuse for his behavior and MUST pay for his consequences. On any given day, I would sentence him to a long stay in the county correctional facility, probation, and community service. He would have a long list of classes to take and so forth. However, Mr. Deburke, I have come to an agreement. It's not a light one." He pulled his glasses off and set them aside. He rubbed his forehead in disbelief.

"Son, I am hereby sentencing you to twelve months of rehabilitation at Safe Haven. This program is the best that money can buy and one of the best treatments in the country." He sighed it out like he was going to regret it.

This wasn't *his* plan of action, I could tell. It was the best that my father could persuade. Maybe, it was the only thing my father could persuade out of Judge Calhoun, I didn't know.

Twelve months meant one year. One year in some sort of rehabilitation place seemed rather extreme. Wouldn't being in jail involve less time?

"What kind of rehab are we talking about? Safe Haven sounds like a crazy ward. I'm not insane, if that's what you're getting at. What's my other options?" I leaned forward, straightening out his bronze name plate that faced me.

He watched me, cautiously. He gathered the all ready together documents and laid them out. He glanced down, assumed to be reading them and spoke. "Safe Haven is not a mental institution, Christopher. Safe Haven is a highly recognized estate in New York that has possibilities for youths, such as yourself, to redeem your inner strengths and withstand the society around you. In other words, Safe Haven is exactly what it says, a safe institution for troubled teens committed mostly by their parents to undergo some sort of change. Some patients in there have minor criminal records such as petty thefts. Parents look to the staff to redirect their criminal minds to a more positive outlook. Then, there are ones, such as yourself, who have dealt with drugs in your past that get a second chance to choose your paths. I, personally, prefer this method, rather than a correctional facility, where young adults begin to hate society, and when coming out of such nonsense, get back into the daily routine of whatever put them in there in the first place. Let me help you consider this…you *have* no other option."

His words were metaphors that painted a pretty picture for parents. His idealization was irrational. Safe Haven was a building that took parents' problems away, hiding them for a future time. I didn't believe one word that came out of his mouth, nor trusted him.

I glanced over at my mother, who seemed pleased and enlightened by his theory. I was left alone to abandon all hope in my future. If I was to be institutionalized for stupid shit that I did, which, in my opinion, wasn't *that* bad, then, I wasn't going to go nicely. They were going to work for my time there. I wasn't about to abide by their rules and be happy with any outcome. I don't know, I just didn't want to go, period.

My mother gave me a teary-eyed hug and questioned the conviction. "And who is going to pay for this program? Does the state pay for this kind of stuff?" I sneered at the thought of it. Let's not think of my feelings, let's think about the money wasted out of her pockets.

"Ms. McPherson, Christopher's father has generously accepted the tuition fee. That is one less thing you have to worry about. He wants only the best for his son and would like to see his full recovery." He folded his wrinkled hands and leaned back in his chair. I could have sworn that the old man wanted to take a nap.

"Bullshit," I mumbled under my breath. My mother nudged my elbow to keep my mouth closed. What I wanted to know was why the hell did he call my mother by her maiden name?

The judge perked back up and continued. "Safe Haven is known for their strict consistency policy. Christopher will follow a routine, whether it be of his choice or theirs, he will pick out his courses and work on his education. He will not be released unless he abides by their pre-requisites for graduation. Ninety percent of the children do not relapse. It is a pleasing statistic, we couldn't ask for more."

I guess I would fall in the tenth percent, then. I couldn't imagine the place if I tried. I saw a prison with bars, a bunch of retards in front of the television set, laughing to "I Love Lucy" re-runs. I saw white walls and medicine cups, restraints and electric chairs. A bunch of psychologists would be brainwashing me with cardboard paint splatters, somehow, hypnotizing me into changing the world. I saw a cult, fit for everyone else, but not me.

"Is this a high school? Can he accomplish his goals within the twelve month period, or will they hold him until he meets the acquirements?" My mother was asking more detailed questions than I could think of. They were important ones, and I tried to pay attention, biting on a pencil that I somehow, managed to find in my hand.

The judge swiveled his chair to the back wall and opened a file cabinet. After many pounds from his palm, he managed to slide it out. He skimmed through some hanging folders until he came to one he liked. He grunted and withdrew it. He turned back around, handed it to my mother. "This is the pamphlet. I don't have many, since I can't expect the accused to find the money to pay for it. It's a privately owned business that is well respected, yet, the government won't allow it to be state funded. It's a shame because it does wonders with our children."

"Thank you, thank you so very much, Judge Calhoun. I appreciate you doing this for my son. I don't know what we would have done if he was sent to jail. I don't think he would be positive...again, thank you." She was all up on his nuts and it disgusted me.

"Just make sure I don't see him in here, again. I will be pleased in knowing that Safe Haven has helped him." He shook her hand, tried to shake mine and walked us out of his office.

"Oh, this is good news, Cardy. I can't believe he was so nice to you. I mean, you heard him say what would have happened if…" I walked ahead of her so far that she had to cut her own self off with words.

"It's ridiculous, mom. What the hell is that place? Why do I have to go? I'd rather go to jail. I'd probably get three months in or something. It's not fair.

When do we have to be there?" I stopped in the lobby and held out my hand for a cigarette. She knew what I wanted and retrieved them.

"The paper says tomorrow. It's in New York, so we have a long drive to deal with. We should probably get going. Thank god you don't have to pack. We wouldn't make it. We can stay in a motel when we reach the border." She was full of hopes and dreams and many in-between's.

I, on the other hand, wasn't thrilled. I lit the cigarette, incinerated most of it quickly, and stood on the steps, arguing my case. "What if we have car trouble, or can't make the dead line to be there? What if something happens and it doesn't work out? Why do I have to be there tomorrow when I just got out of the Goddamn hospital?"

"Settle down and stop using God's name in vain. That's probably why you're in this position in the first place. You need to be praying more, I know it. And, what was wrong with you back there? I haven't seen you like that since…you haven't been taking your medicine, have you? When was the last time you took it? Was it back when you lived with me/? No wonder why you're acting out. You can't help it. You need your medicine. Oh my gosh, it makes perfect sense. I was told by your doctor that if you stopped taking it…" She rambled more nonsense.

"Mom, stop it. I don't need any medicine. I'm perfectly fine." I decided not to say anymore in fear that it would lead to more of her political, medical, theoretical, and hypothetical bullshit. She was good for it.

"Well, I'm going to call your pediatrician and get a prescription. We'll stop by the pharmacy and pick it up. You can't make things better for yourself if you're not calming down enough to accept them." She was a mother, alright. She thought she had to start from scratch with my A.D.H.D. it was double the bullshit.

"I'm calm, don't you see me calm? I have a cigarette, it's all I fucking need!" I raised the second square up to her face and smirked. I got in the car and withdrew myself. I sat on my hands, trying not to adjust the air vent, or turn on the radio, or change the stations, or flip the visor up and down. She didn't have power windows, so that was a plus.

"You had to get that from your father." She shook her head in disbelief.

Chapter Nine
Binderman

I couldn't go home. I left Teesa's and drove as fast as I could to end the goddamn headache I was getting. All of this shit going on was making me sick to my stomach. Teesa couldn't be pregnant. And, if she was, she shouldn't be marrying Roger for the sake of it. Nothing seemed real.

Cardy was in the goddamn hospital. Teesa was knocked up. My father was home with plans to kill my future, and Fresca fucking broke it off with me. What the fuck else could go wrong? I could think of many other things, and I tried to tell myself that shit, but it wasn't working.

Cardy could be dead. Teesa could be knocked up by ME. My father could have stayed in Amsterdam, drinking his life away, without a care about us. And, Fresca, well, I didn't know her fucking deal. I wasn't about to figure her out. I had too much else to worry about.

I sped into Pierre and dialed the only number that popped into my head. Foster Bryant's.

"What's up with you, dog, where you at?" I slowed down, recalling all of the damn car accidents that my people had been in from drinking. I wasn't about to be another statistic in Pierre. That shit needed to stop.

"I'm at my brother's crib, come through if you want. We're just chilling, playing Madden." Foster sounded like he was smoking an 'el, the way his voice went in and out.

"Cool," I made a u-turn.

Seth was Foster's older brother, twenty six to be exact. Seth was the biggest drug dealer in the northern part of Pennsylvania. He did some time in Pittsburgh Prison and now, thought he was the shit. He had little gang bangers running dope errands from St. Paul to Pittsburgh, it was idiotic.

I didn't associate with Seth, that much. I didn't respect someone who did wrong shit to the wrong people and loved doing it. He was a conniving back stabbing motherfucker. As ironic as it was, his father was the sheriff of Pierre.

It always seems to go that way. My father was part of the D.E.A. For my four years of high school, I sold drugs to kids in my neighborhood. Ironic, yes. Parents seem to over look the fact that their kid could be at play with the same shit that they try and keep off the streets. Maybe, just maybe, kids do it because they can.

I knew a lot about drugs. My father went hard to work at keeping me informed on the four types of drugs and their effects. I was more informed than most kids at twelve. I knew what I could do and shouldn't do. He should have told Cardy.

The problem with information, nevertheless, is that it is useless if a child *wants* to do it. B.J, my father, could preach all he wanted about marijuana. He could make me eat as many cigarettes as he wanted to. B.J could lecture and explain and hope to brainwash me into the sobriety that he wanted me to adhere to. BUT, I wanted to experience what I wanted to experiment with.

It doesn't mean that my father wasted his precious time in preaching. No, in fact, I held it important. After my years of experimentation, I would have enough sense to walk away. I'm not talking about heroin or cocaine or anything more addictive than budd. I wasn't stupid enough to mix myself up in that shit. That shit was scary. I blame and applaud my father for teaching me that it was scary.

Before all this mess took place, I had a plan I was following.

My high school years were mapped out at fourteen. I was going to have the time of my life. I wasn't going to be tied down and discipline. No, I was going to rebel and party and fucking fuck the shit out of bitches. I was, as everyone called me, "The Prince of Pierre."

I had an image to uphold.

But, now, I was twenty. What the hell was I going to do, now? High school was the past. My college attitude wasn't around. At first, Brian and I had planned on going to the same college on a football scholarship and maybe going pro. Yeah, that was a fucking dream wasted. Brian was in boot camp.

I wasn't prepared to think about my future. I had Bobbi and Devon and Cardy to think about. My senior year was actually a blur. I had spent another year doing nothing with myself. Ah, fuck it.

I pulled in front of the apartment complex. The appearance wasn't too shabby, as Pierre didn't accept "ghetto" images in their town. The place needed some tuck-pointing done and a good paint job, but other than that, the apartments seemed fairly kept.

It was the inside that worried me. I hadn't been inside this dump since my junior year, when I scored my last cocaine bag before getting it from my cousin, Cody. I didn't do it, but, I sold it.

It was a four family complex. When I walked into the front entrance, the grey carpet was worn thin. It had stains in it and was unraveling on the edge of each step. The walls were tan, yet, certain spots were darker. The light fixture didn't have a light bulb in it. The mailboxes were broken, with black scuff marks across the metal frames. The banister was splintered and I remembered the last time I had caught a splinter in my palm and about freaked out and fainted. I thought I had been contaminated with diseases from the junkies that seemed to lurk nearby.

Seth was a crack dealer. He made his wealthy living from it. He may have lived in the worst building in Pierre, and lacked furniture in his house, but, Seth had bank loads of cash on hand. He spent all of his money on attorneys and court fees. He wore expensive jewelry and clothes. He drove nice whips. He gambled his life away by making bets that, if fell false, would run him dry.

The door knocker was hanging by one screw. His wooden door was wearing the first layer of wood away. His silver doorknob was smudged with fingerprints or whatever filth was caked on it. I refused to lay my hand on it. I knocked hard as the music was too loud to hear me.

The place smelled stale. Cigarette smoke filled the air. Weed hit my nose the minute I entered. Ammonia or something powerful as such was also in the air. I wasn't about to find out what it was.

"What's up with ya? Come in, make yourself at home." Seth answered and stepped back letting me through the doorway.

I glanced around. It was the same old shit. He had an old blue couch with a worn down coffee table in front. Super big gulp cups were spread throughout the place. He had a fold out chair and a recliner missing a cushion. A big console TV was sitting on the floor with another one on top, a bigger one with a coat hanger sticking out from the back.

I couldn't figure out where I wanted to sit. Dewey's room may have been trashed like this, but he was my cousin. His shit was new shit and dirty, not old shit and dirty. There was a difference.

"You look beat, dog. Have a seat, take off you jacket. Kick off your shoes, get cozy. I'm about to fire up some Ganja." Seth sat back down.

Foster was sitting next to him rolling up a blunt. He wasn't like Seth. They may have been brothers, but Foster had more common sense than Seth. Foster only fucked with marijuana. He didn't smoke cigarettes or anything else. He's never been arrested and never sold drugs. He was his father's favorite, being the basketball star that he was.

I decided to go with the fold out chair. I turned it around and sat backwards in it. I rested my arms on the back. "What's up with your scholarship, dog? Why ain't you away by now?" We all knew that he had got that shit. He was accepted to UCLA.

"Because he wants to be a fucking cop, can you believe that shit? He passes up an opportunity to go pro and he declines to go into the police academy!" Seth didn't hesitate to share his opinion on his brother.

"A cop, dog, come on." I smiled lightly, still not feeling like interacting like I usually did. My heart wasn't in it. Two of my bitches weren't mine, anymore, and that sucked dick.

Foster laughed and licked the paper. I was getting second thoughts about smoking it. I was the one who rolled 'els. It was my saliva that everyone touched, not the other way around. I could bypass Brian and Cardy and sometimes, J.D, depending on what he was eating at the time, but, Foster…I didn't know the history of Foster's saliva.

"One day, dog, I was just chillin' in my room, listening to my girl singing in the shower, and I started thinking…what if I don't get anywhere with my basketball career, you know? And, my dad, you know he's a sheriff. I don't want fame or fortune. I just wanna get people like this motherfucker off of the streets. I want a family and shit." Foster was deep in thought, more than I had ever heard him think about.

"That shit's wild, dog. I don't know. It's good, I guess, but, a cop?" Foster had the discipline in him, that's for sure. He wasn't as wild as even I was. But, a cop, couldn't he choose something else, something that gets more respect?

"I'm a cop killa," Seth sang to his brother.

"Yeah, and I'm gonna bust your ass." Foster threw back, playfully.

"Oh yeah, you gonna do that to your brother, your own flesh and blood?" Seth leaned over on him and lit the blunt. Foster pushed him away.

"Hey, what's up with your brother, dog?" Foster raised his eyes at me in concern.

He caught me by surprise because I had never told him that Cardy was my brother. "What do you mean, you mean Cardy?" I stuttered wondering if I could admit it to everyone, now.

"Yeah Boo, who else is your fucking brother, you got two out there or something, your daddy getting freaky with all the women around, or what? Come on, we both know he's your brother." Foster was smart. I don't know, Foster was…

"Who told you?" I took the blunt from Seth and inhaled.

"Man, you did. Back when we were at St. Paul academy, dog. You don't remember coming to class and telling me that shit, that Christopher was your brother and shit? Then, when we met up in Pierre, you said you found him, again. I always knew."

I had forgotten. I had gone a good six years of school with Foster at St. Paul Academy in Cheriton. It was a private catholic school. He had moved first when his father had accepted the sheriff position in Pierre, and then, I met back up with him when we moved. I didn't realize that I had spoiled my dad's secret way before now.

"I never showed him to you, though." It was puzzling me.

"You didn't have to show a motherfucker your damn brother. He looks just like your mark-ass. All that shit you did for him, who would do that shit for just anybody? I didn't remember you letting Wes kick my ass, or J.D. Nah, you had my back on that shit. But, Cardy, Cardy was different. You sided with *his* ass. Now, that's some shit, huh?" Foster had a point. Foster had good common sense. It made me think. Did he *let* Cardy beat his ass for the sake of mine? I wouldn't doubt it. Foster had brains and fight in him. He had a good loyalty to him, as well. I still couldn't get over the fact that my little brother had got the best of him, twice.

"Alright, dog, he's in the I.C.U. I don't know what's going on with him. His bitch ass mom has a restraining order and shit." I didn't feel like continuing the conversation. So, I changed it

"What girl you with?" I didn't want to talk about Cardy. I was there to forget shit.

"The girl of my dreams, dog. She's perfect. She's five two, slender ass waist, with a big ass juicy ass romp. She was a senior when we were juniors,

dog, on the cheerleader squad. Fresca might know her." Foster leaned back in some odd obsessive daydream.
    I double blinked. I didn't want to think about that bitch, either.
    Fresca, that bitch.
    "Want some Grey Goose?"
    That's all I needed to hear, to think about.

Chapter Ten
Cardy

"Mom, I don't like this motel." I sat on the queen size bed. It was too firm. The comforter was a fuchsia pattern with bright green leaves. The vertical blinds didn't open. The television set was glued to a turn table that didn't turn towards my bed. The bathroom was smaller than the hospital's.

"What do you expect, a mahogany bedpost with strippers on them? I paid thirty dollars, Cardy. We're only staying one night." She wiped down the toilet seat with one of the washcloths and flushed the toilet. She ran the water for a bit and then shut it off.

"Easy for you to say, it's not your last night out of captivity." I pressed the power button to the remote that was screwed to the night stand.

"Did you read the pamphlet? It's sixty five thousand square feet of land. There's two tennis courts, a full court for basketball, a running track…it's paradise." She opened the night stand drawer and set out the bible. I hadn't seen one of those in years.

When she walked away from it, I picked it up, flipped through it. "What if this shit isn't real?" It wasn't that I didn't believe in it. I was raised to have faith. I was guided to put my life in God's hands. But, what if it was a bunch of morally correct stories to scare people into doing the right things? What if my life wasn't in God's hands, and I was alone?

"Don't refer to it as shit, Cardy. It's not shit. It's God's word. And, it IS real. Why are you questioning it?" She stood before me as if I had become a stranger to her.

Honestly, she didn't know me. Hell, I didn't know myself. I questioned it because I *hoped* it was real. I wanted God to protect me and make me feel better about my life and my future. With someone above me, making choices for me with a mapped out destination, then why did I have to try so hard? It was going to happen, anyways.

"I was just thinking that's all." I sat it back down and gave it one more glance. I knew the stories by heart. I knew my saints and my prayers. I knew the psalms and the songs. What if Abraham sacrificed his son from insanity, rather an act of faith? What if Jesus was a man who didn't do miracles, yet, he was great in many things in his day and it seemed like miracles? I was just saying, that's all.

"Well, you need to be thinking about your stay at Safe Haven and what you're NOT going to do when you get out." She lit a cigarette and quickly put it out in the sink. It was a non-smoking room.

"I'm already bored." I admitted after flipping through the channels and finding nothing to watch. I was tired of Baywatch re-runs, even if Pam was running across the beach.

"You wanna walk over to that McDonald's and grab us some cheeseburgers? It'll give you something to do and you can get some fresh air." She took out her wallet, handed me a twenty and expected me to jump for joy.

"Not really." I took the twenty and waited for her to turn her back. I pocketed her wallet and her cigarettes. If I was going to walk over to McDonald's, then I was going to tour the whole block. I'll be back when I get back.

"When you get back, you can do this crossword puzzle with me, I suck at that stuff." She smiled, as she knew I was good at it. Yeah, when I was what, ten?

I scoped out the street. It was a busy little main street, with motels taking up half of the block. Fast food joints and bars came second. I didn't remember the town I was in, or why it was a place for a strip of motels, but, it had a bar. That was a plus.

Alright, so I wanted to get fucked up before I got so clean that I became dehydrated. It was my LAST NIGHT, for fucking sakes. Sure, I was too young to buy cigarettes, let alone a beer, but, with the right conversation and the right girl, some bitch would spot me some liquor. It helped to offer up money, which is why I brought my mom's wallet.

I didn't look too young. I was tall enough, at least. I opened the door and didn't get one look...good sign. I headed over to the empty pool table and stuck in some quarters. If I didn't get drunk, tonight, at least I was playing pool. It beat playing fucking puzzles with my mother.

"Hey, baby, want to throw down some money on a game?" She leaned in closely as soon as I started to rack the balls. Perfect.

She wore a short black sleeveless button-up. It was tied above her pierced navel. Her jean shorts were high risers, showing off her cheeks. Her hair was feathered blonde, with pink dangling earrings that touched her shoulders. On her feet, well…they were cowboy boots. Amusing.

"Fifty dollars, no special rules." I couldn't win if I had to choose a damn corner for the eight ball. It was too hard.

"Okay, buddy, fifty it is." She withdrew a wad of bills from her chest and pulled out a fifty. What the hell was she, a cowgirl hooker?

"One condition," I smiled. I edged up close to her, smelling the perfume my mother used to wear, White Diamonds. I was good on distinguishing that kind of shit for some reason. I touched her pink earring with my fingers and slid through. "You have to buy me a bottle of Tequila. I'll pay, I'll share."

She seemed thrilled on the encounter. "Tequila with the worm?" She smiled back. It wasn't the prettiest smile, but it would have to do. Her teeth needed some work done.

"Whatever suits you." I laughed, lining up to break the balls.

"Good deal, youngster." She knew I was under age. I didn't give a damn.

"Youngster…alright then girl," I had the charm and I knew it.

Somewhere in my head I knew I had it. For some reason, I had requested Tequila and couldn't wait to taste it on my tongue. I knew I was being cruel to my mother and ruining her last night with me, but…but, I was compelled to misbehave.

The alcohol hit quick and I was feeling good. All I could think about now, was getting that ugly girl up against the back of the bar. She wasn't very pretty or worth my time. I knew I could get better if I had worked the bar a little, but, this one came to me. I didn't have to try.

Some pool, Tequila, and a bitch were worth spending my last night away from the hell I was going to visit, tomorrow.

"Okay, slow down commando. Take it easy." She laughed a drunken slur into my ear. I wasn't about to slow down. She called me Commando because under the sweats that my mother had given me, I didn't have boxers on.

I had lost the game of pool on purpose and ended our night on the side of the building with her hoisted up around my waist. I wasn't about to take it easy. I wanted this over and done with so I could get back to my mom and go to sleep.

"What's your rush, cowboy?" Her nicknames were getting on my nerves. I pushed into her briefly and decided that she was older than I thought. She was probably older than I had ever messed with. She could have been my mother's age, come to think about it.

She shrilled and got to the point. My mind wasn't on getting pussy, now. That thought erased when she was too damn dry to fuck with. Now, I needed to persuade her to go down on me.

I pulled out and shoved her to the ground. I wasn't nice about it because I was in a hurry. My mom could have called the cops. I didn't think about that until now."Just do it," I snapped. My frustration and guilt was rushing in. I had to hurry up or it would catch up with my pride.

The rush and release that I got from it was too much to take in. I was wasted and fucking up, already. Something in me was messed up. I felt it. Suddenly, I didn't want to be doing what I was doing. The little boy in me wanted to rush back and hide under the covers. Hide from who I was becoming and who I was at heart.

When it was all over, I had to get her away from me. I had to leave. I pulled her off and turned away. Feeling guilty, I pulled out a twenty dollar bill and tossed it upon her. Before she could stand, I was gone. I didn't look back. I heard her yelling after me, explaining that she wasn't a prostitute, but, I didn't care.

My head was aching. I felt it throb and swell from the Tequila. I had smoked more cigarettes than I had planned, and now, my lungs felt congested. I was drained of energy. I needed to get back to that motel and rest.

But, I was hungry, too. My mom wanted me to go to McDonald's and I couldn't come home without it. So, that's where I went. Eleven o'clock at night, five hours after I had left, I was standing at the drive-thru lane, without a car.

"Can I take your order?" The nice lady's voice snapped on the intercom.

"Uh, yeah, I need a Big Mac and some fries, a large Dr. Pepper," I spoke into the speaker, laughing at the fact that I was standing there ordering on foot. "I, also, need a…I need something for my mom. Just put anything in the bag, I'm sure she'll be fine. How much is that?" I couldn't think straight.

I pulled some change out of my pocket and dropped about three quarters, maybe they were pennies…who knows. When I bent down to pick them up, headlights scared the shit out of me and about knocked me over. I covered my eyes and walked on down the line.

I must have caught the girl by surprise because when I popped up into the window with another twenty dollar bill, she screeched and dropped to her knees. I stuck my head in the window and stared down at her.

"Hey, girl, give me my food." I thought I was hilarious, not an idiot.

When she realized that I was drunk and not robbing her, she stood up, patted herself down and proceeded.

"Where's your car?" Her face was round like a bubble, red and swollen. She had to be around my age, covered in skin blemishes. She handed me back the bills and a receipt.

"Why is your door locked?" I wasn't aware of the time, in all reality. I knew I was late and I knew I was in the wrong.

"You mean the lobby? Oh, that's because we close at ten. I'm not supposed to serve you like this, you know." Her red shirt was tucked into her kaki colored pants. Her hips reminded me of the legs of a nervous mammal, drawn inward and abnormally bent. I couldn't think of the right name of the furry animal in my head, but, there was one. I was too drunk.

"Did you put a cheeseburger in the bag for my mom?" I leaned over the edge and glared up at her.

"No, you didn't say a cheeseburger, I'm sorry." Now, she was looking like the lady I had left on the side of the bar. Maybe they were related. Maybe I was seeing things.

She continued. "I put a side salad in there."

I rolled my eyes. "Did I say a side salad?" I couldn't remember.

Fuck, I was walking back with a side salad, five hours later. What the hell was I doing? I knew I didn't need to be out here. I knew I had just had a head injury from drinking. My impulses were getting out of control, all over again.

It scared me.

Chapter Eleven
Binderman

"Why the fuck did you let me do it, dog?" I whined. I tried sticking the keys into the ignition. I couldn't get it right. I was eight sheets in the wind and my heart was racing from cocaine. I don't know why I did some lines. It wasn't my style. I think I did too much.

"Boo, I went to the fucking bathroom to take a piss. When I came out, you were bent over doing the shit. I didn't know." Foster pulled my arm until I was sitting on the pavement. I was too drunk to drive home.

I didn't argue back. I knew better to fight to drive home. I was glad that Foster was with me. "Dog, I'm sick. I feel like running around the block with this fucking energy rush *and* barfing, dog. My stomach hurts." I held his wrist for support as my head hung towards the ground. My body was doing spins and butterflies and heat waves. I was about to pass out or something.

"I'm don't know what the fuck I'm doing anymore, Foster." I wasn't speaking right.

"Chill, calm down." He tried to pull me up against the door frame but, I was limp. "I knew you should have never gone to Seth's, dog. I can't drive, either."

We battled our way through Pierre on foot. I don't know how many times I fell over on my knees. I was ready to give up and give in to sleep, all the while laughing from the cocaine. I began to sweat, not knowing what the hell I was doing.

"Dog, I'm telling you, I'm going to have a heart attack." I held onto my chest for dear life. I felt like I had run a hundred mile marathon or some shit. The liquor had drained me, yet, the coke had given me a boost. My body didn't know how to react, since I wasn't used to it.

"No, you're not, you're just wiggin' out." Foster reassured.

We made it to the front steps of my house. I sat on them staring down at the sidewalk. Millions of shoes had walked on this path. Millions of different kinds of shoe soles should have worn this concrete thin. But, it didn't. The cement was stronger and can withstand many heavy bodies. I wish I was concrete, able to withstand all the burdens on my back.

"Mr. Sox, he's right here," Foster had brought my father into this situation. He thought that my dad would be able to carry me to my room or something, I don't know. I didn't appreciate it.

"Binderman, get up. What the hell is wrong with you?" He stood behind me embarrassed that Foster had to witness my weakness. He knew that Foster was the son of the sheriff. Hell, Foster's dad and my father went way back. They were friends.

I smirked at the Irises that seemed to sway with my posture. I never looked at those damn flowers. They blew with the wind, yet grounded to the earth. Why couldn't my roots ground me? Was I grounded? Did I have roots?

"I'm talking to you, Bin, look at me. What's going on with him, why isn't he responding? Did he take something? Is he just drunk? I need to know my son's condition and whether he needs to go to the hospital." He hadn't dealt with me this way.

Yeah, my face was soaked in sweat. My mind was racing with empty thoughts. My eyes were glazed over with a sugar rush and my head swam in a lake of Grey Goose. My palms were clammy and my feet had given up on moving. I wasn't about to admit that I did cocaine. I didn't want him thinking that I did it all the time.

"Um, I think he'll be alright, sir. He just needs to lie down. We walked from the east side, that's where his car is parked." He wasn't going to rat me out, that's for sure. We were boys. Foster gave me one last glance before he headed down the drive way.

"Bin, this shit ends tonight. I keep telling you, things are going to change around here and I mean it. It's three thirty in the morning." He went to grab my wrist and attempt to bring me inside before the neighbors heard a scene. What he didn't know was that they were used to scenes in front of my house. I had parties and fights and loud noise almost every weekend.

"It's early," I laughed to myself. Three thirty was a good time to call it a night. Sometimes, I wouldn't show up until six or seven. He was lucky.

"Don't be ridiculous, get up." He slapped the back of my head and I tensed up. "Don't make me move you because I will." He grabbed the hand that I offered and forced me to stand.

I leaned on him. "Dad, I fucking hate you." I laughed playfully, yet I wasn't very far from telling the truth.

"You can sleep on the sofa," And he balanced me to the damn couch.

Sometime after that, I had crawled my way up into my bedroom. I lay on the floor and cried. My emotions were fucked up on this combination. I knew all the meds, coke, beer and liquor were a fucked up mixture, not to mention the budd I smoked. Hell, the budd could have been laced, too, knowing Seth. I had never felt so alone and fucked up.

"Dad?" I yelled into the carpet. I didn't know why I was calling him, I just was. I propelled my body upright and stumbled across my room for footing. I fell against the window and instantly wanted to feel the wind. I raised it sticking my head out. It was a cold dreary night.

Not using logic or physics, I sat on the edge of the window pane. The air was crisp and cold like it usually got around this time in Pennsylvania. It was misting and the smell of rain felt refreshing. I closed my eyes for only a minute.

And, then…bam. I fell out of the window and down into the bushes below. It was so fast that I couldn't scream. The scream came after when I fell on my wrist. The pain was delayed.

Unfortunately, I had to scream for my dad.

I guess my cries for help were louder than I had heard myself, because…all at once, lights from each house on my block turned on. People came outside in their robes and night gowns. I was the center of attention at the worst of times.

My dad followed with Bobbi close behind. They found me on my side rolling with tears. My wrist was broken, I knew that much.

"What on earth did you do, fall out of the window?" My father wasn't serious until he saw the curtain blowing outward. He sighed and knelt beside me. "You have to be kidding me, Binderman. This has gone way too far."

Blurry images of Basia and Kyle's little brother, his name escapes me, stood to my right as my dad placed me in the backseat of my Expedition. Everyone was talking and asking questions. My father's grunts didn't want to answer them.

He didn't speed like he should have. He didn't ask me if I felt okay like he should have. No, the motherfucker took advantage of using this as an example of my out of control behavior. If he wanted to witness out of control behavior, he should have been around when his other son was popping Tylenol when he had no Xanax and sifting through empty ash trays for any remnants of marijuana residue when I wouldn't give him an 'el. He should have been there when Cardy overdosed on shit, when he drank Oxy and shit liquor…yeah, he thought I was bad.

"What am I missing, Binderman? What do I need to know or do, to help you? I come home and find my only son trying to commit suicide by jumping out of a two story window? What if I wasn't home, what then? Is this normal of you? Bobbi, is this normal of your brother?" he was way out of his league of parenting skills. He knew nothing about nothing.

"I'm not your only son," I mumbled, holding my wrist against my chest and trying to recall any last minutes of our conversation. I had a migraine. My heart hurt. The pain I felt was coming from all directions…my wrist, my body, my brain…all from thinking too damn much.

"No, daddy, he doesn't do anything like this. He's usually very good. When he drinks, he comes home, cleans his car…he's always in a good mood. I don't know why he's acting like this." Bobbi didn't seem to acknowledge me in the car, nor the groans that I was giving her for talking about me.

"Well, I don't like it. Something is wrong with him. He needs help. Has been going to that shrink lady, the one he's supposed to see?" My father wanted to hand me off to someone else, instead of fixing shit, like always.

"From what I know, yeah, she gives him medicine." Bobbi was ratting me out. I didn't want him to know anything about me.

"I didn't jump out of the fucking window." I spit as I talked, letting the tears fill my mouth. I was crying harder than I thought was possible. They had me all wrong. I didn't want to fucking die. I didn't mean to fall out of the fucking window, either. I wasn't thinking right, that's all.

"Doesn't matter, something is wrong with you, I can see it. You're different. I can't talk to you anymore. I can't reason with you, I'm afraid that Christopher has affected you the wrong way." He was blaming this shit on Cardy.

Maybe it was Cardy's fault. The minute that he moved in with me, I became a brother to a brother. It was different than being an older brother to Bobbi. I had to show him how to be a man, yet I didn't know too much of that shit, either. And then, when it came down to it, he was a baby sibling all the same. I had to protect him like I did Bobbi. It was weird.

X-rays confirmed that I had a wrist fracture. I didn't need surgery, just a cast. Luckily, the bushes had broken my fall and saved more bones. They kept me over night to watch my behavior. My father forced them to. Apparently, he thought I was suicidal. It was going to take a lot of convincing in the morning to explain my drunken story.

"I'm not that person, lady. My dad has me all wrong. I may be fucked up in the head, but I'm not suicidal." I watched on as Bobbi signed my cast.

"Have you ever had suicidal thoughts, maybe thoughts to hurt other people, yourself?" The hospital psychologist was evaluating my state on mind.

"Yeah," I swallowed, wondering what the hell she was going to say after that shit.

"So, you have considered suicide?" Her rephrasing had made Bobbi stare me in the eyes.

"No, fuck no," I jerked my arm away from my sister and felt like hurting the psychologist with it. "I felt like hurting people, doesn't everyone? Fucking shit," I was getting nowhere with her. She was hearing what she wanted to hear.

"Look, can I just talk to MY therapist? Her name is Cynthia Roma, she makes house calls. I don't feel like starting over with your ass." My life was complex. Given the time frame, I didn't have weeks or months worth of time to explain myself. It was worthless to try.

"Alright, Mr. Sox, I'll let her know of this incident and she can follow up with you. It was a pleasure to meet you." They all said that. Was it a pleasure? Did I please her in some fucking way? Cause they really needed to rephrase their departure. It sickened me in knowing that it was a polite way of saying goodbye.

"You never thought of suicide, did you?" Bobbi shut the door behind the therapist and took a seat next to me.

"No, I mean, maybe when mom died, when dad left. I don't know. I was never going to do it. I just thought about it. That shit's old. I wasn't trying to kill myself last night, Sissy." Sometimes, I called her sissy. It was what my mother had called her when I was little.

"I thought about it." Her eyes wouldn't find mine. She worked her fingernail into the groove of the table following the line to the edge.

"When?" It was news to me. It scared me because if she was thinking of killing herself, what if she had? What then, would I do?

"I used to think about it all the time. It was mostly when I was little, right after mom died. I thought that if I swallowed poison, I might wake up in heaven and see her, again. I thought about it like that. It was a fairy tale. Don't you remember me collecting apples and taking one bite out each one? I was acting like Snow White, only trying to go to sleep for real." Her pride in that story was a sick one. She was eight when our mom died. She was eight when our mother KILLED herself. Maybe we were all fucked up. We all needed help.

"But, you've never thought about it more recently? You're happy with everything?" It never dawned on me to question Bobbi's mental status. I had assumed that she was well cared for and had everything she wanted. I didn't stop and think that maybe she felt the way I did about things.

"I was happy, yeah. But, when Cardy came, he kind of took you away from me. I was a little jealous. Not really jealous, like I didn't want to die or anything. I thought it was cool to have two brothers, but I felt left out. I felt bad for you, for what you did for him and he walked all over you. I wasn't happy because I knew you weren't. Like now, I'm worried about you." It was one of our first real conversations in a long time. It felt nice.

I smiled at her. She looked just like mom with her rosy cheeks and big blue eyes. She may have had my dad's color, but my mom's eyes were magical. They were filled with hope and dreams, no matter what you told her. "Don't worry about me, girl. I'll straighten out. I just need to get it all out of my system, trust me. It's only for a little while."

I was serious. I wanted to get so wasted that I hit rock bottom. Once there, an idea would pop up and shit would be fine. That's how I fixed shit. I'll know when I'm there and I'll figure out what to do about it. It was the only way I could appreciate what I had and what I lost. I was close, but not close enough.

Chapter Twelve
Cardy

The motel room was locked. I had to bang on it. With the McDonald's bag in hand, I crouched down to level out my headache. It was on fire. My eyes felt like they were burning flames and as dry as a fucking desert.

My mom flung the door open, grabbed the McDonald's bag and slammed the door in my face. Uh oh, she was pissed. I knocked, again.

"Mom, I'm sorry! I got side tracked, honest! I'm back, and now…fuck, mom, open the door, I don't feel well, please!" I rested my head against the door frame.

"I thought you ran away, Cardy! I almost called the police! I can't believe you did this to me! I don't know you anymore!" The latter part of her sentence hit me in a memory.

"I don't know you, anymore," Basia screamed in my face.

Basia. The lump in my throat thickened and my stomach tossed. Within minutes, I was puking up the Tequila. It splattered between my feet as I forced my last memories of her away. I didn't know what I was going to do if my mom didn't open that door. I may have heaved until I passed out.

What was going on with my head? I couldn't control my actions or impulses. I knew I needed help as I crouched in front of the motel door, tears pouring. I still didn't recall my past, but from the feelings that I was getting, I had to stop before I started.

It was a pressure that I didn't like. Something inside of me was trying to get out. All my energy was bottled up, ready to be released in any way that it could let go. It was increasing, as my control was fading.

"Mom, come on, please. I said I was sorry. I need help, I know it. I'm drunk, I'm fucking drunk and I don't like it." My voice cracked with my emotions.

I heard the latch unlock. The knob turned and I fell into the doorframe at my mother's feet. I felt her kneel behind me.

"I don't know what to do with you. You steal my wallet, you take my cigarettes, you don't tell me where you're going, you just disappear. What's become of you, Cardy? Never in a million years did I think that you would be like this. I can't believe it's you, my little Christopher." She was soft spoken, trying the best that she could to control her own anger and disappointment.

I turned towards her with open arms. I needed her just like I had needed her, before. "Mom, don't leave me, please don't leave me. I'm sorry. I'm sorry I hurt your feelings, I'm sorry I took your wallet and squares. I don't know what I'm doing. I didn't mean it. Let me come in, I just wanna go to sleep. I'll pay you back, somehow. I promise. I won't do it, again." I said everything that I could think of to apologize for my behavior.

I mean, I didn't mean to hurt her in the process. My intentions weren't to hurt anybody. I was…bored.

She cried out of desperation. What could she do? She held me against her tightening her palms against my shaven head. Her wet tears dripped onto my scalp burning fresh reminders of the pain that I had caused her…the pain that I had caused everyone, or at least, that's what it felt like, I couldn't remember.

"Of course I won't leave you, baby. I will never leave you, again. I'm sorry I ever did. It's my fault you're like this. It's my fault, I'm your mother. You hear me? I am your mother and I am here for you, no matter what." She squeezed my cheeks at her face to imbed those words into my memory.

She was my mother. She was the one who tucked me in bed at nights. She was the one who held me against her, singing 'You are my Sunshine' when I was sad. She had read me stories, fed me, changed me, rocked me to sleep.

She was my mother.

"Mom, help me," I gagged. The vomit rushed with burning stench into my mouth. I panicked not wanting to puke, anymore. I scrambled around her and crawled onto the carpet. I wouldn't feel safe until the door was closed. With it open, I could be kicked out.

She was my mother…and I didn't trust her.

She grabbed my arm and tried her best to pull me up off of the floor. Together, we walked to the small closet of a bathroom. I fell into it, heaving my head into the bowl.

"I'm sick, mom," I managed to mumble as my saliva dripped from my lips. I didn't know if I meant sick in the head or sick in the stomach. It could go either way, I suppose.

As I wiped the drool with my forearm, another piece of me came back. It was the stomach clenching and head jerking headaches that I used to have. The alcohol had triggered a craving that I had temporarily forgotten about.

I wanted heroin.

"Mom," My legs jerked as they ached to move. My arms twitched. I wanted to throw them in the air to rid me of the adrenaline rush that I received from that memory. "Mom, help me, I'm cold. Get me a blanket."

I was scaring her. Her eyes widened as if I had just injected heroin into my skin, possibly while I was away from her. She did as she was told, dragging back the ugly fuchsia colored comforter. She kept quiet tending to my every move.

"What the fuck?!" I spit. Vomit had covered my jogging pants, or Jeff's, however I looked at them.

I was a mess.

A new problem was rising in my mind. How was she going to keep me in this room, when all I was thinking about was dope? For a second, her purse screamed out to me. She might have had Advil or my pain reliever in there.

She did, I saw it.

My thoughts were strange. I felt like someone had crawled into my body and forcing me to do bad things. My body ached for the urge to run the streets. Yet, my mind wasn't attached to it. I knew it was wrong. I knew I had to stay put and go to that facility.

I was battling myself.

"What is wrong with you?!" My mom's tears pleaded with me. I didn't want her to have to deal with me or see me in this position. I was awful, even to myself.

"Mom, just hold me, just hold me. Don't let me go." I cried. I was afraid that if she let go, I would find a way to run. If she held me, I was reminded that she existed, that I existed. It was some kind of grounding that needed to bind me to the floor.

We stayed like that, all curled up together. When my mother felt that I was okay, she helped me to the bed. She took off my shoes, tucked me in, and kissed me goodnight. I lay awake against the pillow, staring at her face.

I was in my own world, trapped within my thoughts of good and evil. I knew I wasn't a bad kid. I knew I wasn't supposed to be a junkie. I wasn't supposed to feel the way I felt or act the way I did.

My past was crawling out of me. The lies that I had become was turning true. If I was to escape the person that I was…

I would have to want to get help, and help I needed.

I didn't get up. I didn't leave the motel room. I was too frightened to experience my next move. I was a good kid. I was where I should be, with her, with my mother. I let sleep take over and persuade my subconscious into better behavior.

Another dream took place, instead.

The car was blue. The upholstery was grey. My nails dug in deep as my body swerved with the current of the car. It floated and soared along the street, yet not touching the pavement. It was a shooting bullet, faster than lightning, faster than the speed of light. The only thought that I had was turning my head and waiting for my brother to save me. He would be here for me, soon. It was a waiting period as I shot down an empty road.

It was an odd dream. I didn't wake up with sweat. I wasn't scared shitless, as the other nightmares had made me do. I was peaceful, feeling the need for my brother increase inside of me. As I lay on my side of the bed, I called out to my mother and said the words I had been dying to say since it had happened.

"I miss Jeff, mom."

The problem was…was that I don't think it was Jeff that I was missing, I just assumed it was. I had no other brother that I knew of.

Chapter Thirteen
Basia

"Get up, Basia. You need to take a shower, you stink." Amanda yanked on my arm as I wouldn't open my eyes.

"It's been three days since you walked around the house. Why don't we go to the mall, I'll buy you something." Darron did his best to persuade me.

Life hurt so much that I refused to do anything. "You don't have any money." I mumbled, giving them my back.

"I do. Come on, I'll *drive* you there." Amanda sang. She was insinuating that she had a car or that she had her license or permit or whatever made her happy in saying such a thing. It didn't do me any good. It didn't bring Cardy back from dream world or drug heaven.

"Basia, you can't do this to yourself. I'm going to kick you out. You want that? You want to live on the streets with Jasmine? Then, you'd have to deal with her. You'd have to comb her hair and tie her shoes, let her *bite* you." Darron wasn't being so nice to me, lately, but he wasn't fully serious, either.

I drew my body up like a puppet on strings. My arms fell to the side and stayed there. My posture slumped over and my face felt like a zombie's, crusted and drooping. I pried my eyes to slice open. "You wouldn't kick me out, you love me." I meant it as platonic as I could only he loved me in another way. I always knew that Darron loved me.

"Yes, yes, I do love you. That's why I'm dragging your ass out of bed and into the shower. I swear to God, Basia, if you don't do it yourself, I'm going to strip you down and sponge-bathe you." He smirked at Amanda knowing I would jump up as soon as I heard it.

But I didn't. He didn't have the guts to see me naked. "I dare you." I dropped back and kicked out my feet.

"Watch me!" Darron grabbed the edge of my sweat pants and jerked them down to my thighs. I was being playfully attacked and couldn't help but smile from his bold move. I twisted around to hide my underwear, only given him full range of my bottom."Darron, you jerk! Stop it, I'm going, I'm going!"

I fell to the floor, on my knees. I had to watch it from now on. I think Darron was getting rather feisty, nowadays. "I hate you. All of you." I stomped to my feet and threw my body every which way to get to the bathroom.

I wasn't happy, and if I wasn't happy, nobody was going to be. That was my new motto in life.

"Hey, Amanda, can you get Jas and make her a juice cup?" I wasn't about to ask Darron. He had filled it more than enough times, today, and she kept throwing it at his head.

I stepped over the doll that lay in the hallway, walked through the pile of dirty clothes, spread them all over again, and into the bathroom that lacked a light bulb. Great, the light switch flipped off and on and there wasn't any light. How was I supposed to take a shower in the dark?

"Darron, is your electric on?" I screamed down the hall.

"The TV's working," He yelled back, snatching Jasmine up by her arms and swinging her into Amanda's embrace. Jasmine was part their family, Uncle Darron and Aunt Amanda, not that they went out. For goodness sakes, Amanda wouldn't dare go out with scrawny Darron, no sir.

I thought they were a perfect match. They BOTH thought I was wrong.

I ran the shower and sat on the toilet. I thought of all the times that Cardy had barged into the bathroom to sneak a peek of me peeing. It was ridiculous at the time, but now, funny. I missed it. He never succeeded even though the door didn't have a lock. No lock in Darron's house actually worked.

Most of the time, I'd have to make Amanda come in here with me just so she could barricade the door while Darron and Cardy would throw their shoulders into it. Jeesh, boys were weird. I never wanted to see a boy pee.

I stared at the water as if I had never taken a bath, before. I didn't want to feel clean. I wanted to sit in grime. I wanted to appear the way I felt, awful. I shouldn't have to clean up for Amanda or Darron. Sure, I'd go to the mall, but maybe I wanted to look like a bum. Didn't they care that I had my own fashion to state? Maybe I could get the zombie look going, oh…maybe that already started without me, only they wore a white mask and black makeup.

I tested the water. It was perfect. It was another good reason to stand in there and get clean. It was just my luck. I stripped off my clothes and slowly but surely, jumped in. the water hit my face.

Ooh, I needed to shave. My armpits would scare the devil out of anyone, ha, ha. Boy, I was in some kind of mood, wasn't I? I had run out of razors like a month ago. I peered around the shower curtain and caught my eye on one of Kyle's. Being the mean ass that I was turning into, I decided to use his. It served him right for leaving it in here. While I was at it, I'm shaving my legs. It serves them right for forcing me to shower. They wanted it, they're getting it. I'm not even picking up my towel.

"Hey, Basia?" Darron interrupted my daydreams of Cardy's pre-gone wild kisses.

"What?!" I snapped as snappy as I could.

"I didn't mean that, literally. I wasn't going to kick you out." His voice was soft, yet deeper than just a month ago. He was changing, changing into a little man. He was barely taller than I was, and I was five six.

"Ya think?" I jerked my head at him as he used his x-ray vision on the curtain. I wasn't in the mood to be serious or nice or just polite. I wanted to be a brat.

"You don't have to be so rude about it. Ever since Cardy's been in that accident, you've been a different person. I don't like it." He sat down on the toilet and wanted to boyfriend-girlfriend talk. There in the bathroom, he wanted to talk to me as I stood naked on the other side.

"You know what I don't like? I don't like little boys talking to me while I'm shaving my legs. It's perverted." But, I gave him a sly smile to let him know that I wasn't being literal, either.

"Fine," I felt him roll his eyes as he sighed his way out of *my* bathroom.

I *have* been a different person since the accident. I couldn't help it. I was so angry that life was lived the way I lived it. Enough said. Yeah, Jasmine's hair was knotted up. Yeah, she was going through a biting stage and I wasn't with her enough to get bit. And sure, those damn shoes wouldn't stay tied. Why did they make little shoe laces too long in the first place? Infants and toddlers couldn't tie shoes. They should be Velcro, all of them.

I gave up crying a few weeks ago. It was useless. God didn't hear my tears. God didn't pay attention to my voice. God, it was always about God, wasn't it?

Well, I'm going to stand up for what I believe in. I believe in myself. I had gotten this far without Cardy and my parents and GOD. What did I have to be ashamed about? A lot of teenagers had babies this young. Ricky Lake proved it. She had little girls on her talk show with babies and the girls couldn't figure out which man was the daddy. At least, I knew her daddy. At least, I had a good three years with her daddy before we broke up.

Yeah, I should stop crying and go to the mall. Cardy was getting better. I didn't have to slump around feeling sorry for myself. Sooner or later, he'll come around and wish to see me. Soon enough, we'll be together. It was just a waiting game, now.

Wait, wait, wait. That's all I ever did. Wait for God to hear me, Wait for Cardy to live, to get better, to recognize me. Well, I'm not waiting for them to get ready to go to the mall. I've had it. I was ready and that was all that counted. I just wish that I didn't have to take along Jasmine. I went nowhere without her.

"I'm ready, are you?" I ran my fingers through my wet hair. I hated to wash it. It frizzed out if I brushed it. It stood up if I didn't put products in it. It was useless to even try to get it to do right. I'll just go to the mall like a wild woman.

"We've been ready, Basia. We've been waiting for you." Amanda sighed, raising Jasmine up on her leg, over and over, again.

"It's about time." Darron grabbed his black GN'R hat and stuck his chain into his pocket. GN'R stood for Guns N'Roses. They weren't a band, anymore, because Axl decided to quit. Well, I didn't know the entire story, but Darron and Cardy used to love them.

Honestly, they were a group that was banded from my cassette library because of the explicit lyric label that my parents despised. Thanks to Tippy Gore, we owe her our gratitude, sarcastically speaking.

"Hello, Basia? Can you climb off your stupid little cloud and get with the program? My sister is outside, she's my licensed driver. I only have my permit, so we should be going before she drives off without me." Amanda stood holding Jasmine on her hip. I loved it when she was over. She took control of motherhood.

"Why didn't you say that in the first place?" I rushed off not wanting to displease Angie on my account.

"She did, twice." Darron shoved passed me to beat me to the door.

Well, her sister wasn't being impatient. She loved the time it took me to take a shower and walk downstairs. She was sitting on Boo's front porch steps smoking a cigarette. I wonder if her mother knew she smoked. Amanda could use that as blackmail if she wanted to.

Boo sat next to her. His hoodie hid his head and the hat shielded his face. He wasn't looking so good, I heard. He was in a sweat outfit without shoes. He took the cigarette out of her hand and puffed on it. They were sharing?

"What took you so long?" Angie stood letting her Nautica shirt hang out of her pants.

She had started to wear bigger fitting clothes ever since she had Devon. Her butt was gigantic and her thighs rubbed together. Secretly, Amanda made fun of her and called her thunder-thighs. It was hilarious.

"Uh," Amanda pointed over at Boo. "Don't act like you're bored. You know you'd rather be there talking to him than riding us around."

"I thought you were driving." Those two sisters bickered all the time. They never truly argued, but the words they exchanged were far from what I would be saying to my sisters. It was disrespectful.

"Not the point...hey, Boo." Amanda took out her keys and sat in the driver seat.

Boo waved and disappeared in the house. He didn't say one word. That was odd. He usually had a smart come-back. He'd smile, wave, ad say something awful, anything to be talking.

"What's up with Boo, Angie?" I squeezed behind Amanda as Darron got behind Angie. It was their mother's old car, a Dodge Escort, small and compact.

Boo had fallen out of his bedroom window, the day before. It was supposedly by accident, but people were wondering if he was so drunk that he was trying to jump out. I saw the aftermath of it all. His father scolded him, Bobbi cried, Boo being forced in the backseat by his dad. It was a crazy night.

"Oh, he's been really down, lately." Angie didn't or wouldn't give me more details.

I didn't know too much about Boo. I knew he drank, smoked, and partied. I knew every girl dreamed of getting with him. I knew he was Devon's father and a good one, but that was all. He was Cardy's role model, a bad one.

"He's just as upset as you, Basia." Amanda glanced back before she suddenly stopped at a stop sign.

"No way, no one's as upset as Basia. Basia even overdoes it." Darron realized who we were driving with and strapped his seatbelt in tight. He jerked on it making sure it would catch and then held onto the back of Angie's seat.

"Why would he be as upset as me? Cardy wasn't anything to him but a friend. I was the one who knew him, the real him. Cardy was fake with Boo. Boo doesn't know what he's talking about." I was rambling more to myself.

"They were like brothers, Basia. He cared a lot about Cardy, whether you believe it or not." Angie defended her mythical God of a creature.

"Or not." I added. I wasn't about to believe anything about Boo.

Chapter Fourteen
Binderman

I was piss-ass drunk with my left wrist in a cast. What the worst part of this shit was was that I was left fucking handed. Thankfully, I wasn't in school. Thankfully, I didn't depend on handing out checks as a form of payment. Fuck…how was I going to roll a blunt?

I was done with my house.

I wasn't about to cramp up my style with a father up my ass. I couldn't bear enter my room after I foolishly fell out of it. It reminded me off the stupidity of my life. Shit happened, right?

Fucking wrong, shit happened to me. That's what it was.

I wanted a blunt. That was all I thought about. I needed more shit to drink and I wasn't about to go hunt down some poor ass motherfucker so he could beg his stupid ass brother into getting the shit for me.

In other fucking words, I drove my drunken ass back through Casa to Dewey's house. I hadn't been there since I gave Dewey a concussion, serves his ass right. He should have recognized my little brother from the beginning. He met him, he was there.

It was *his* birthday party that Dena showed up at. I introduced Cardy to all three of my cousins, right before we chased invisible goblins. It was all fun and games, back then. Was I the only one who fucking remembered his ass?

Wasn't Cody old enough to distinguish Christopher as one of ours?

I'll find out. I'm letting it spill. Fuck this secret crap.

I struggled with the side entrance into their kitchen. It was the only door that I had a key to. Unfortunately, I was greeted by my Aunt Cathy, holding a paring knife, carving an apple. God, I didn't want to talk to people right now. My intention was to apologize to Dewey and force him to roll me a blunt.

"What are you doing?" She stood in front of me hesitating to carve anymore of the red lining.

Don't get me wrong, my Aunt Cathy was a good mother. She was involved in every sport that Cody and Wren was a part of. She cheered them on, head of the P.T.A. She belonged to a lot of high end charities and hosted many festive parties.

She stood by her son's side when everyone else scolded Cody for knocking up a stripper. *Force an abortion,* my family insisted. Not Cathy, no, she wanted a grandson. She wanted a bigger family if it wasn't for my Uncle Brody shrugging it off.

"I'm wasted." I slurred, barely able to stand.

"That's not what I asked." She set her knife down and rinsed off the apple, partially skinned. Her eyes never left mine.

She was perfectly built, toned, with all the benefits of being married to a plastic surgeon. She worked out, always dieting. She loved to wear athletic gear, Nike and Reebok stretch pants with a matching cap. Low-key, she was a sports mom. Cathy was a busy housewife, striving for perfection in every possible way.

"I'm drunk," My comprehension was faltered. I couldn't understand a word she cared to share.

"Okay, you're wasted, you're drunk. I got that. It still doesn't answer the question on why you came here after what you did to John Stuart." John Stuart was Dewey's legal name, only used by his mother.

Today, she wore a grey pair of exercise pants bunched together at the shins and a baggie t-shirt that once belonged to Wren. She could be the most beautiful lady in the most down to earth clothes.

"Yep, uh, what? Oh, that. I was…I was mad. He shouldn't have messed up my brother." The sight of Dewey's thin face was scarred into memory. He was surprised that I had chosen Cardy over blood, or so he thought. He was upset that I had scolded him and wouldn't hear him out.

I didn't care.

"That was no excuse to hurt my son. And, you need to stop referring to Christopher as your brother. Blood or not, he wasn't raised as your brother. He doesn't *see* you as his brother." She opened a cabinet, took out a mug, and attempted to prepare two cups of coffee.

"Bullshit." I shrugged, refusing to grasp the warm ceramic against my palm.

"Excuse me? How many times have I let you curse in this house? And, how many times are you going to try to come over here without permission? I told you that you weren't allowed back, not until you apologize to the appropriate people. Since when do you come here to pass out?" She rinsed her hands at the sink and dried them on a dish towel. She leaned against the counter and expected me to fully understand the questions set forth.

I fumbled for words, forgetting the million dollar answers that I was good at giving. "Catherine," I laughed in mockery of my uncle's tone. "I am sorry...for the inconvenient time...that I beat the shit...Out of your weak ass son, but...If it hasn't occurred to you, yet...your sweet John Stuart...is fucking with heroin. I don't know how that...plays into your master plan of things for your baby boy, but I...think he's way in over his head...just thought you should know, that's all." Every other second I had paused to swallow. I was smashed and feeling the revenge of the liquor.

Her face drained. I hit her emotional core. Her eyes watered and her body began to unravel. "You think it's heroin?"

I lowered my chin against my chest trying to stop the backflow of the contents of my stomach. "I know it's heroin. Dr. Garosi found it in Cardy's system."

Her hands shook. She bit her lip as the tears poured. "I don't, I can't. I'm a good mother, Binji. This doesn't happen to good mothers. This can't be happening to me!"

I never meant to go there and cause trouble. I thought she was aware. After all, she was involved in his life. She saw him every day. Didn't she see the signs of depression in him? Could her denial overlook such obvious factors?

I suppose that things don't exist if denial is stronger.

I didn't have time to waste in consoling her. She had a husband for that. She had two other sons for that. They needed to call a family meeting, the way they did on a monthly basis.

"I'll talk to him." I stood up and held my stomach. I wasn't about to stall and vomit in the kitchen. I'll detour and head for the bathroom before I do my good deed for the night.

She had crumbled to the floor breaking down in front of me. She should. It was her baby son who was weak enough to intoxicate his body with filth.

"He's not up there. I don't know where he is. He left, like a month ago. I thought he was at your house. But, then again, I assumed he was at his girlfriend's house. I hadn't checked up on him. What if...what if..."

I vomited in the doorway.

"Who is his girlfriend?" I was on my hands and knees as Cathy crawled near me.

"I barely met her. She was a little blonde. You can tell that she's still in high school. I thought she was anorexic because she was so thin. But now, come to think of it...it had to be the drugs...oh my goodness, Binji, what have I done?" She sat next to me, palms on the floor, eyes blankly staring at nothing.

It sucked how reality clenched the pit of your stomach and forced its way out like an iron fist. As I threw my guts up, Cathy's reality was slicing the lining of her silver cloud. We were both drowning from the sickness that we endured.

"What the fuck is going on?" Cody appeared behind me carrying a bottle of Crown Royal. He was as shitfaced as I was, only standing.

Cathy clawed her way up his pants leg in tears. Cody could only grip her elbows and lift her to eye level. "John Stuart is on heroin, Cody. My baby is gone."

"What?" He glanced down at me as I wiped my mouth for the fifth time.

"Yeah, you gotta find him."

It seemed as though the worst could get worse and it wasn't going to stop until people got their head out of their asses and opened their eyes. Everywhere I twisted, lives were spiraling into dramatic episodes of hell.

I wasn't going to ask "What else?"

Because a million things could unfold and hammer into my skull like a rusted screw gone astray. Have you ever tried to hammer a screw into the wall? It caused little cracks around the hole until the entire drywall crumbled to the ground.

Our lives were drywall. We could paint it, patch it, nail it up in a way that served well, but...in the end...

It was fragile. Anything can tear it down. The most cautious approach with all the right angles and tools were necessary. And even then, shit just crumbled.

Chapter Fifteen
Angela

It was four in the morning. Someone was knocking on our door. I hurried to the window but because of the dim lighting, I couldn't make out who it could be. My mother didn't get home until five. She worked the graveyard shift at Cheriton Hospital. Her car wasn't in the driveway, either. So, it wasn't her.

My eyes were barely open. No matter what I did, I couldn't force them apart. I was tired. Devon had been teething and I had been up all night. I finally found sleep and now this.

I thought about waking up Amanda for some back up. It could be a serial killer or rapist or some kind of no good criminal looking to hurt me. It was the only possible explanation. I grabbed the cordless phone on our end table and considered running to the kitchen for a steak knife.

The knock hardened. I jumped at the sound. I would rather pretend that I didn't hear it and hide under my covers until the noise went away. The counterpart to that idea was our windows. If a criminal wanted in, he'd break in.

My hand idled on the doorknob, too shaken to twist the lock and pull it open. What if it was Basia? She came over once before in the middle of the night in hysterics. I never found out why, but Basia could be a possibility. I ran my hands over my loose ponytail. God, if it was her, then I looked hideous.

"Angie, open up the fucking door, I know you're right there. I'm not a fucking predator, fuck!"

Boo. Oh my gosh, what the hell did he want? How did he know I was there? I didn't make any noise.

I tugged on the door, listening to the creak in the hinges. It sometimes stuck and my mom always wanted to put some W2-40 or whatever that grease stuff was to make it sound better. She never got around to it.

On my door step, in my doorway, stood a disgruntled Boo Sox. A couple of years ago, I would be falling at his feet and inviting him in. Unlike then, I didn't appreciate the disturbance. He had frustrated me enough to the point of annoyance. He was too stubborn to deal with, too demanding to put up with.

He liked things his way. He wanted Devon to wear *his* clothes. He wanted Devon when *he* wanted him. He expected me to drop what I was doing and hand him over. He even has the nerve to enforce meatless meals upon the little baby. I had refused, of course. Babies needed their protein.

The last time I had saw him was when he shoved me back into his guest bedroom at his house. It was an awkward situation. His father didn't know that Boo had a son. His father, apparently, didn't know anything about anything. And now, he was home.

Boo didn't look like himself. He had let his hair grow out, curling up in every direction and reminding me of Shane Williams. It wasn't as big and thick as Shane's, as it had only a month's worth of length, But overall, it was about to be a replica of a perm.

He looked rather rugged with his facial fuzz thickening up around his jaw line. His eyes were red and inflamed, either from lack of sleep or his obsession with alcohol. His posture was slumped using the doorframe for balance.

He gazed on, exhausted and cold. "Can I stay with you?"

His car wasn't on the street. His hoodie was soaked from the rain. Raindrops were rolling down his cheeks. He had walked, four in the morning, in the rain…to my house.

What for?

"Are you drunk?" It was my first impression, my only impression. He wasn't there for Devon that was for sure. Did he mistake my stay at his house as an invitation for more?

It wasn't like I was giving him reason to expect sex from me. The whole time that I had stayed, while my mom was on vacation, I slept fully clothed and far away from Boo. I didn't want him to think that I wanted to do anything.

He smirked out a sound, but didn't respond. He slumped forward with a smile and proceeded to push passed me. He was way out of line…and, drunk. I smelt it as he brushed by me. He reeked of liquor.

"What are you doing?" I rushed after him with irritation. He was headed to my bedroom. "I'm not sleeping with you, if that's why you're here!" I wanted to make that perfectly clear.

He turned in disgust but held his silence.

"Aren't you going to ask me if you can stay the night? There isn't someone else you'd rather be with, tonight? My mom is going to come home, soon. She won't let you stay, you know." I watched him, cautiously.

Confusion filled my head. If he wasn't here to see Devon, and he grimaced at the thought of sleeping with me... what the hell was going on?

He pulled his hoodie up over his head and off of his shoulders. He dropped it to the ground. His shoes kicked off. He was undressing. Oh my gosh, I didn't know how to handle this situation.

He continued to take his shirt off, leaving him in his white muscle shirt. His tattoos were bright against his skin. His muscles were perfectly contoured. He had once been the man of my dreams, right up there with Brad Pitt and Ryan Phillippe. But, that was before. That was before he had shattered my hopes of a relationship with him.

He went as far as to slipping his cross necklace over his face and placing it on my dresser. When he went for his belt, he turned and stared at me, finally acknowledging my presence. He grinned, taking amusement in my discomfort. He ripped it out of his jeans and slapped it to the floor.

"I'm not here to fuck you." He laughed, leaving his hands on the button to his jeans. He retracted his fingers and swayed above my bed.

"Then, why are you here?" I felt totally taken advantage of, whether or not he was here for sex.

"I'm here," He shifted in stance for the right words. "I'm here, Angie, because I have nowhere else to go. I'm here because I don't know what the fuck I'm doing, anymore. I'm fucked up and I need a place to crash."

He crashed right on top of my twin size mattress, stomach first. He crawled up to my pillows and hugged them against his chest. He stared up at me, challenging my approach to his behavior.

"You can crash at Fresca's. She's your girlfriend. I don't want any more trouble with her. Do you know I ran into her the other day and she refused to make me a sandwich?" I had assumed that he knew she was working at Subway.

I thought it was odd. Fresca had fake nails and everything. Her reputation didn't call on her to be some servant at a deli place. She was head cheerleader, Boo Sox's girlfriend, friend and foe to many, but... not at all someone to wait on you.

"What the fuck are you talking about?" He altered his position in my bed to get my full explanation.

I sighed not wanting to go into detail. It wasn't the point that Fresca was denying me service or that she worked where she worked. It was about her damn boyfriend who wouldn't get out of my house.

"Go to Fresca's, Boo!" I snapped, tugging on the pillow under his head to reinforce my order.

He wouldn't let it go. Instead, he held on tightly. "I don't go out with that bitch, anymore. I can't go to Teesa's because she's fucking pregnant and getting married! I wanna stay here, Angie! Let me fucking stay!"

His demeanor was more than confusing. He looked desperate and depressed. I tried to take that into consideration. I mean, Cardy did just have a life threatening car accident. His girlfriend is obviously gone. His father is giving him grief and his part time girlfriend was…pregnant?

Hearing that Teesa was pregnant would be some juicy gossip to spread around…hmmm. And, who would want to marry a skank like that? Did she know who the father was?

I kept quiet. It wasn't the time to ask questions. It wasn't the time to start shit, either. Boo had come to me out of desperation. I should be flattered that I was in his mind, at all. Boo and I shared common ground on one thing and that was Devon.

In fact, I didn't know much about Boo. All of my information had come from gossip, sources that couldn't be trusted in a time of need. Sure, I had spent an entire week in his house, but he was barely home. If he was home, he was up Cardy's ass. And, Cardy wasn't sane.

Devon was already a year old. People would think that I knew a lot about Boo Sox. I never had the time to sit down with him and talk. He never tried to listen or be concerned with me. It was as simple as 'hello, goodbye, where's Devon?'

I kept my distance as I spoke. I wasn't about to share a bed with him. I guess I'd have to sleep on the couch, now. "How's your hand?"

"Fine," He mumbled into the pillow. His eyes were closed. He wanted to sleep.

I couldn't get over the fact that he was in my bed. He was defenseless without smart comments or some kind of negotiation terms. He was in my bed expecting me to let him go to sleep.

His hair was curly. I didn't know that. His mountain man appearance was attractive, even though I had always considered myself a 'clean cut' version of Brad Pitt type of girl. Okay, I could get through this. He was Devon's dad in need of a place to sleep at for tonight. It wasn't that bad.

The longer I stared after him, he didn't move. He was falling into a faster sleep than I thought he would. What was I going to do? Was I supposed to grab an extra pillow out of the linen closet and lay down on my sofa as if this was normal? And, my mom…what was I going to say to her?

My mother didn't allow boys over. Sure, I had a baby, now. But, her rules were still the same, if not stricter. I was on birth control and she knew what not to let me do…no boys in the house.

"Boo," I whined and stomped my foot. I shouldn't have to be put in this position. Why couldn't it be like it usually was? I didn't want to have him come over in all hours of the night expecting me to give in to him. It wasn't right or fair…to me.

His eyes peeled back. Even in the moonlight, as it shined so lightly above my headboard, his eyes were a bright blue. They were the lightest shade of blue that I had ever seen. They twinkled when he smiled. They haunted my dreams. They pierced through every girl that ever looked him directly in the eyes.

"What? I'm sorry I'm here." He assumed that it was enough to let him fall back asleep.

But, it wasn't.

I retreated to the linen closet. I grabbed a blanket and pillow and headed back to my bedroom. If I slept on the floor and locked my door, then maybe my mother wouldn't be bothered with my disobedience. I mean, it was for one night, right? It wasn't like I was having sex with him.

Chapter Sixteen
Binderman

I didn't want to be at home. I couldn't stand seeing my room after I had fallen out of the damn window. I didn't want to deal with my dad. And, I could give a fuck to spend time with any of my stupid ass friends.

They weren't my friends, anyways. After Brian left, I had no one I trusted. They hung around me because I was something they weren't. I was confident and arrogant. They were weak and misguided.

Hell, they were little followers who copied off of me. They idolized me. I didn't know why. Ever since I came to Pierre, they saw me as something special, someone to respect. I guess because back in sixth grade, right after my mom had passed away, I was going through some kind of transition.

I hated the world and took it out on everyone. I didn't respect teachers, didn't listen to adults, I fought everyday for a year, just because I could get away with it. The little kids were afraid of me.

Nevertheless, my consequences came. I was put in a residential facility when I was thirteen. It was a behavioral modification institute to discipline my out of control actions. I assumed that my father was waiting for the day that I turned thirteen in order to send me away. That's the way I took it.

It was that place that diagnosed me with Bipolar. I spent a few months there. It was called Safe Haven, the same place that my father had persuaded Judge Calhoun to do with Cardy. I knew the steps all too well.

When I had returned to school, word got out that I was sent to juvenile. Someone said that they couldn't handle me and gave me back to my dad. I didn't justify the rumor. The kids didn't bother me. Soon, I had a group that did what I said. Girls were dropping at my feet.

I think about this from time to time. If I had stayed in Cheriton, going to St. Paul Catholic Academy, would I have this same fortune? I doubt it. I was nobody there. I did what everybody else did.

I was an altar boy. I sang in the choir, played piano. I wore suits to church and volunteered at the retirement home that was funded by St. Paul. I walked and talked with aristocrat style. I followed my grandfather around to political meetings and hosted sock hop birthday parties until my mother died.

I was an average little kid who did what all the little kids did in Cheriton. I wasn't something special or something to consider as cool. When I was shoved into Pierre, I realized that I would never have to be the person that knew my mother. I could be whoever I felt like being.

The same went for Cardy. I knew what he was doing to himself. He needed to intercept the changes before he lost his identity. I don't know where he stands, now...but he had changed into something else after his brother died.

In other words, without Tequila or bitches, parties or being the center of attention, I didn't know who I was. I was already lost.

Take my liquor away, keep me at home during the night, take away all my bitches that meant something to me...what was I left with?

I was left with being a vegetarian. I was left with a memory of music sheets that became useless when I broke our piano. I was left with a phobia of being alone, of hearing my mother's cries in the middle of the night. That's why I couldn't sleep. That's why I cleaned so frantically.

It was an obsession to keep my mind hard at work. If I kept things in order, if I struggled to control the things that I could control, then maybe, I wouldn't have to think at all. I'd be on automatic response, flowing with the current of the day.

But, my cool response wasn't getting me anywhere. It was harder to do now that I had a brother who needed help. It was harder to do when I had my father at home pointing out the flaws in my life. It was getting more frustrating by the day to know that what I had worked hard at avoiding, was now attacking me by the minute.

I couldn't be me.

I wasn't about to stay here and deal with my dad. I needed a place to crash. If I couldn't crash at Teesa's because of her narrow-mindedness, and Fresca was out of the picture, and Brian was fulfilling his stupid ass dream to be killed in war, then I was left with my last resort.

I swallowed my pride and brought nothing with me. I had never spent time at Angie's house in the way that I was planning on doing. It was going to be hard, but I was willing to sacrifice what I called daily necessities.

She didn't have cable or big screen TV's. Her house wasn't as clean as I was used to living in. Her mom liked to cook family meals and expected them to eat at the dinner table. They lived in a three bedroom house, but the rooms were so small that everyone knew what everyone was doing through the thin walls and close quarters. It was going to suck.

I was desperate to get out of my house. I was desperate to feel what everyone else felt in a family. I needed to give up my luxuries and see what I was missing in my life. I was so depressed that I had resorted to Angela.

There was one good thing I could say about Angie. I trusted her. Out of all the bitches in the world, I trusted Angela and my sister. I used to think I could trust Fresca, but in all reality, I had burnt the connection with her. She didn't trust me and now I couldn't trust her.

Chapter Seventeen
Cardy

I had been sick for the entire morning. I didn't know if my head was hurting from the head injury or from the hangover. It was pounding, even after taking Advil. My eyes burnt and my cheeks were inflamed from the pressure of vomiting. My heart was racing with the sickness.

"Can't we call and reschedule?" I hung my head in my hands and closed my eyes. I wouldn't let her turn on the lights or raise the volume of the TV in fear that it would cause my migraine to jump up a few notches.

"No, Cardy, we can't. As you may have noticed, you're getting more out of control by the minute. You need this program more than ever, now." She decided to ignore the no smoking signs since last night's drama. She lit a square and passed one on to me. It was good parenting, huh?

"I don't even remember last night. I know I got drunk and shit, but fuck, I wanna go home and go to sleep. I don't feel like dealing with people, today." I let the nicotine relax my nerves. "They better not try to fuck with me, I swear. I'll knock their fucking teeth out."

"You and that dirty mouth, stop it! I can't wait to get you there. I hope they do you some good. And, I'm definitely going to talk to a therapist on staff. They need to prescribe you something more powerful than Ritalin. I think you outgrown that." My mother's words of wisdom didn't even make it through my ears. As soon as I heard therapist, I blocked it out.

I didn't need a fucking shrink prescribing me medicine. I didn't need medicine. I was fine all those years without Ritalin, I'll be fine without shit else. It was all a big joke, medicine. It didn't work.

"Give me that brochure. I wanna know what the fuck I'm getting into." I held out my hand as she retrieved it.

Safe Haven, a stupid ass place built for rich ass people to send their petty little kids so they didn't have to deal with them. That's where I'm going? Fuck, they ain't going to know what to do with me. I wasn't like the rest of them.

"Mom, why doesn't it say co-ed?" I was starting to panic. I flipped through the pamphlet looking at all the fucking motherfuckers with cocks. I didn't remember the judge saying it was for boys.

"It's not co-ed." She simply commented.

"How do you know?" I skimmed the first few lines of their philosophy, but I didn't feel like straining my brain power to read.

"Because I read it, Cardy. It's a male facility that houses thirteen through twenty. It's more like a high school." She was already tired of dealing with me and we just got out of the hospital yesterday.

"A fucking dick camp." I set the brochure down and couldn't read on. It was that moment that I had decided that I wasn't going to stay. I wasn't going to follow directions or finish the program or anything else to the extent. I was angry.

"No, it's not, Cardy. Girls are a distraction. It used to be co-ed and it was split up six years ago because something happened to make it that way. I think they caught someone having sex." She sure knew a lot about Safe Haven. She was such a bitch.

"How do you know?"

"Because your brother went there. Get up, we'll get breakfast and head out." She tapped my foot and grabbed her purse.

"Jeff? I don't remember Jeff going anywhere," I searched my memory banks for a time that I wasn't around my brother.

"Your brother, Cardy, your brother. It doesn't matter." She snapped, counting her money and shoving it back in when she realized that I had spent too much of it.

"Was he there when it happened, the kids who got caught?" It was amusing because I would be the one red handed in that situation.

"I don't feel like talking about it. It's not co-ed and we don't have to worry about it, do we?" She pulled out her keys, locked the motel door and headed for her car.

"How old was he when he went in there? What did he do?" I was interested in the whole ordeal. Maybe someone would remember the details at Safe Haven.

"Drop it. It's enough. I don't feel like talking about Jeff, alright?" The ignition came on and she was off to the highway.

Silence. I hated it.

"Stop playing with the windows, Cardy. And, stop changing my station, I like this song." Her hands were all over me as she was trying to slap me away from everything. Fuck, she was a control freak. I couldn't touch anything. I couldn't change the radio, roll down the window, open the glove box, or anything. Fuck!

I bit my fingernails. They were getting too long anyways. When they were bitten down, I smoked a cigarette. When that was over, I sat on my hands, counting the telephone poles along the side of the road. It was bad enough that I had to listen to a fucking Michael Bolton song after Elton John. Who listened to this shit, parents? Don't get me wrong, they were the shit with older crowds, like my mom's age and shit…but did I really have to be part of this serenade?

"I wanna go home." I blurted out. We crossed the border to New York and I was already homesick. I was a state away from my hometown. I was a state away from my life and what was left of it. I wanted to go home.

She ignored me.

"Turn around." I stomped.

Fine, I had it. "Mom, I'm going to open this fucking door if you don't pull over. I'll fall out, I swear on Jeff's grave!"

She swerved to the side, breaking so hard that I almost hit my head against the window. I could die, that way. She knew better and she felt stupid for doing it. She'd feel pretty awful if I died after recovering from a head injury and then she jerked me into another one.

"Don't you dare swear on Jeff's grave! Do you hear me!!!"

I crossed my arms and hoped to die. I didn't want to ride with her anymore. I hated her.

Chapter Eighteen
Cynthia Roma

Binderman Sox. He was on my list of appointments, today. This should be interesting. I loved talking to him, loved to spend an hour staring into his beautiful eyes.

What, psychiatrists shouldn't be attracted to their patients? It wasn't like I was going to sleep with the kid. Jesus, I was turning thirty eight, next month. He was what…twenty, now?

"Did Binji say why he needed to see me?" I hooked the buckle to my heel for the second time as I leaned up against the reception desk. These stupid things were getting on my last nerve. Why I was wearing heels in the first place was something I wasn't about to analyze.

"No, Dr. Roma, he just said he wanted to talk to you." Kirsten, my secretary, was told time and time again that she could call me 'Cindy'. Dr, well, I thought that the title was too intimidating. If people referred to me as 'Cindy', I was their friend.

"Well, cancel my lunch with Stephen. Bin likes to go passed an hour. He cancelled last month, didn't he? Yeah, we need to catch up on some things." I took his chart into my office and dropped it on my desk. I had a good ten minutes to do some reading before my next patient showed up.

Binderman Sox, Jr., this kid had some heavy issues. I met him at Safe Haven, my other office up in New York. I traveled two hours there, and on Mondays, two hours here to Cheriton. Thankfully, I lived in between the two businesses, or I'd have to give up one.

He was thirteen years old when he became my patient. His mother had just committed suicide and his father was in denial of the burden it left his family with. Binderman, or Binji, as his family liked to call him, didn't really grieve.

He was sent to Safe Haven for his out of control behavior. His juvenile record consisted of arson and assault. He had become obsessed with flame.

He had a total of three fires that he had started. One was the boy's locker room. With a lighter, his school assignments went up into flames. He said he was done with schoolwork, but he didn't mean to set the whole room on fire.

He was expelled from St. Paul Academy at age twelve. He strangled a friend, choked a teacher, and ripped down a Catholic banner. He refused to pray or go to church. He spit in the holy water and urinated in the confession box. I knew this because he told me. He was amused by it, almost as if he was proud.

At Safe Haven, he fought his way to isolation. I still remember his eyes, wild and fierce, ready to dagger them into anyone who stepped close. It was those eyes that I held dear to me. They were full of rage, yet sorrow. I had the position to break the ice and calm the tide.

It was hard at first. He hated everyone.

But, I had an unorthodox approach that seemed to work with most. I wasn't like the other "shrinks." I belittled myself in so many ways to conform to what they needed me to be. If they were afraid of authority, I wore sweatpants and came late to my own appointments.

Nobody is perfect. I wanted my patients to be aware of that.

If they were shy, I was outgoing. If they were outgoing, I was timid. I balanced out the equation to form a bond. Bonds were important. Bonds told stories that normal strangers like us "shrinks" wouldn't hear, otherwise.

And, most of all, I was all ears. I listened and asked questions. I gave opinions, honest criticism that most doctors steered clear of because it was an insurance policy to protect doctors from lawsuits. If we gave too much of an opinion, then we were at fault.

That's why most of us nod and say the universal "How do you feel about that?" It's a safe question that leaves opinions out of it. I get his emotions on paper, yet make the patient seem like another checkmark off my list.

I don't like it. I never followed directions to the "T." I had problems with doing things the same way that other people did. Even in Algebra in high school, I somehow managed to get the correct answer in a way that the teacher didn't teach. My brain didn't work in the order of everyone else's.

The first twenty years of my life, I conformed to my cohorts in order to be like everyone else. I pleased my parents, my teachers, my friends, and my family. I was what you called an "ass kisser," an adapter to society. This is why I was able to be timid and outgoing, all in the same day.

But then, one day, it hit me. I was good at being myself. I was good at doing things in an odd way, still getting the same results as everyone else. So, why couldn't I use this approach in my therapy sessions?

That's why I get top dollar for my services. I am unique in my approach and it works. I have a waiting list of patients, waiting a year to see me. I stand out to the public with a raw honesty that people look for.

"Alright, Bin, let's have it. Where have you been?" I lean back in my chair, chew on the cap of my pen, and twist. My legs are crossed and the notebook is in my lap. I am in no way of being perceived as a doctor, which Binji hates.

My first observation was his hair. It was everywhere, on his head and on his face. His bright blue eyes were weakened and exhausted. He didn't smile, nor give me a compliment. He always gave me a look-over and commented about my hair or new earrings. It was his natural charm.

His posture portrayed defeat and his lack of any words whispered turmoil. He bit his lip, rubbed his curls, and sighed. There was a lot on his mind, or a lot going on in his life. Maybe, both. When he pulled the collar of his shirt to his mouth, I had to cut in. he did this when he was thirteen, his sign of scared shitless.

"Tell me about your brother." I snapped, knowing that it had to deal with Christopher. We had many conversations about the love child that his father hid from the world. I knew that Christopher had been living with him, unbeknownst to his father.

The last time we had talked, Christopher was doing cocaine. He referred to him with another name, a nickname, but, the title escapes my conscience. Bin wanted to detox him, his way. I tried to talk him into rehab, but Bin, like me, wanted to try his idea. It must not have worked.

Bin dropped his wet collar and leaned on his elbows. He held out his hands as he talked. His eyes pleaded for my assistance. "I don't know what to do, anymore. I don't want to be here."

I sat down my pen and picked up a pencil. It was easier to gnaw on the wood. I had realized that by doing this, it made him feel like I was expressing his own nerves. Ironic, but yes, it worked. It drove other professionals crazy because I picked up the habit when I was off duty.

"Here as in this office? Here as in a certain position, or here as in alive?"

Bin liked eye contact. In fact, he expected eye contact. If I wouldn't look him in the face, eye to eye, he wouldn't comprehend a word I said.

"All of it."

"I have some reports that say you fell out of your window for attention. What's up with that?" I handed him the hospital documents. In that way, he read what I read and can make assumptions along with me. He liked to be included.

He rolled his eyes, like a long blink. "I didn't try to kill myself. I was drunk and sat on the edge of the window sill. Nobody believes me. My dad thinks I did it for attention. The fucking shrink at the hospital was on his side."

"Are there sides?" It was an easy enough question.

He snarled his lip in defense. "Why would you ask that? Of course there are sides." He stood and walked behind his chair. He wanted to smoke.

I did the most sensible thing. He wanted to smoke, I appreciated smoking, myself. I hadn't had a chance to stroll outside today. I slid out my drawer and withdrew my cigarettes. If Larry caught us, I'd be in trouble.

Larry was my partner in this little private business. He said it was a no smoking office and would reprimand me any chance he got. But, as weird as I was, and as defiant as I was getting, I loved the idea of getting under his skin.

See, I was close to forty. I hadn't married, hadn't had kids. I was all about my career. When my father passed away last year, I realized that he had something that I wanted. He had a life with a family. I wanted a life with a family.

"You need to live, Cindy. Take some risks. Forget about your job, for once." Those were my father's words on his death bed. I thought I had made him proud by being the first in our family to hold a doctorate degree.

He had been referring to my sister, Mary Alice. Mary Alice was my counterpart twin. She did everything wrong in spite of me. I blamed it on her name. Mary was such a good Christian name. Mary Alice hated it. What my father said, well, it propelled me into thinking like her. All this year, I smoked in my office with my patients. All this year, I was having a hidden mid life crisis.

He smiled and took out his green box of smokes. "Squares" he called them. I wasn't updated on teenage slang, but squares were an ironic word to call them. They were circular and long, thin and round. Nothing made them a square. Back in my day, a square meant you were a dork. To be square was to be un-cool.

He was elegant in his movement. His right wrist, unlike his tightly bound left one, would flex as he walked and talked. When I first carried on our sessions outside of Safe Haven, my initial thought was that he may be homosexual.

I laugh at this now because I was never more dead wrong in my life. He was what you called a rich spoiled brat. He was extra clean, scared of germs because of his trip to Mexico. He wouldn't eat meat because of this trip, either. Well, his mother didn't eat meat, but it made her stand correct in issues. She had warned him, didn't she?

He was very feminine in all his approaches. He resembled his mother because his father wasn't around to tackle him to the floor every chance he had. Oh, he played football alright. Right up to the point that he had asthma attacks and had to be rushed to the hospital. He forced himself to prove masculinity.

I watched him, even now, as he slumped back into his chair. He wasn't sitting proper or looking clean cut. Something had altered his existence.

"How are you and father getting along?"

He inhaled, deeply. He actually twitched at the sound of that question. "We never get along. He thinks he can come into our fucking house and control things. He doesn't control shit, Cindy. I do. He took my credit cards. He's making me send back my cars. He wants me to go to college and he wants me to forget about Cardy."

Cardy was his name. That's right. I tried to spell it on my notes. Was it with an "i" or "y." Where did that name come from?

"So, he stripped you of everything that you know? He's turned your life upside down because he feels like making amends with you?" I uncrossed my legs and inhaled my cigarette myself.

"Yes! And he can't go back to his job because he quit!" Binderman was more than pissed off.

I tried to put myself in his shoes. With a father always around me, I couldn't imagine having to grow up without one. Let's see…He was around, but he made it apparent that his job was more important. When shit got rough, he worked longer hours. His mother paced herself into schizophrenia. If I grew up in a house full of misfiring neurotransmitters, who would I be?

Would I know? I would have been pleasing my mother, avoiding my father, and taking care of my little sister. When peer pressure was at its peak, I would want to be on top, in fear that I would have to repeat the same existence in my household as a pleaser.

"You are losing sight of who you are, now, aren't you?"

He closed his eyes and refused to open them. He bent over his knees and held his face. He wanted to cry. "Tell me what to do, Cindy! I'm a fucking alcoholic and I don't want to be. I don't want to live in Pierre. I hate it. I don't want bitches to love me. I don't want friends. I don't want my dad home. I don't want to be anything that I was."

"What do you want?" Everything was 'don't.'

"I want my fucking brother back."

"What is different with him? Why have you attached yourself to him? Does he make you feel different about yourself?"

I wasn't going to control this conversation. He had set his mind into venting and not analyzing anything. He used to be good at self analyzing. We worked on that.

"I feel like a fucking brother. He does what he wants to do. He's the first motherfucker who goes against what I tell him. He thinks I don't have bipolar. He doesn't care what a doctor says."

I didn't know how all of that tied in, but…it was a start. Bin admired his brother for his stubbornness. It was something they both shared as a trait. Bin felt equal to him no matter how he tried to oversee Cardy's behavior.

"He's just like me."

"Do you think he has bipolar?"

"Do you think I give a fuck?"

"Alright, Binji, settle down. Talk to me."

"When he started coming to me for advice, I thought that was the shit, you know? But then, something just happened where he would battle everything I did for him. I don't know what the fuck I want. I just want him back and safe." He was confused.

Brotherly love. What was it with brotherly love? Is it the same for sisters? Two men connecting behind the scenes, where nobody but them around to witness, were they like little boys? Did they wrestle still into their twenties? Did they find manhood through the eyes of their brothers just by merely analyzing each other's actions? If they had a brother, did they need a father?

I loved the idea of brothers. I never had one. I was intrigued by the connection they shared. And, if they connected on that level with their brother, and their father entered into their lives, did the bond between brothers overpower any say over father and son?

Bin had connected with Cardy, that's for sure. They lived similar lives, yet with different approaches. They learned from one another. They needed one another. They were each other's father, in a sense.

Bin jolted me right out of thought. "Why don't we talk about you, for once? I'm tired of talking about me."

I frowned. "Me? No, we don't talk about me, Bin. You pay me to talk about you. Let's keep it simple. You can't seriously tell me that you drove all the way out here to talk about me." I glanced at the clock and knew that I was right. Bin liked to stall and keep things complicated.

"No, I drove all the way out here to get away from me, Cindy. I wanted to get out of Pierre for the fucking scenery." His sarcasm was amusing. When he argued, I felt like I was connecting with him on his level.

"Fine, Stephen and I hit our six month check point. It's our six month anniversary, today, actually. We were going out for lunch to celebrate." I closed his chart and eyed him, giving him the hint to get to his point of seeing me, today.

He glanced at the clock with me. "Then, why are you still here?"

"Because there are a million more important issues at stake than a stupid anniversary. He knows what he got into when agreeing to this relationship. We can go to Calgerio's later." Calgerio's was a high-profile restaurant that takes months to get a seat in. Calgerio's had delicious crab cakes and steaks to die for.

He smirked and played with his fingers. He shuffled his feet, well aware of taking up my time. "He knows he's at the bottom of your list of priorities, yet he's so infatuated with you, he abides."

"Sounds correct." I smiled back knowing that I would get an earful when I called Stephen to apologize. Sometimes, my work carried over into days. I never had time for him and this is what caused me to be husband-less.

"You know, Fresca broke up with me." He grabbed the single frame on my desk and stared at it. It wasn't of my husband or kids. My father or my mother wasn't framed, either. No, it was of Sampson, my Bischon Frise.

Now, we were getting somewhere.

"I'm sorry to hear that. What caused the break up?" I took out an orange and began peeling away at it. He wouldn't mind. I was hungry and he liked me to be rude. He loved it.

"Cardy."

I dropped the orange and it rolled onto the ground. It rolled under the desk and sat there, staring for me to save it from the carpet fuzz. I bent down. "How did Cardy break you guys up?" When I returned, he was on the side of me. "What are you doing?"

"I'm watching you. It's funny. You're so retarded at times." Binderman was attempting to change the subject with his body. He actually talked with his bodily gestures. It was something I had to be careful about. He could make people forget what they were saying, all in a brush of his hip, or curl in his lip. He had charm. And with that said, sometimes, I hated Binderman Sox.

"What are you talking about? My orange fell out of my hands." I didn't understand how the word "retarded" could explain my lack of grip.

"No, you're lame, actually. You have a picture of your dog on your desk. You eat oranges. You seem excited to be with this Stephen, but when you actually have a chance to clarify your relationship, you peel a fucking orange and talk to your patient like he's your only friend."

I was baffled at the accusation. "What do you mean?" I was offended. "How can you say that it's funny, retarded, and lame? And, what do oranges have to do with any of this?" He had lost me.

What did he have against oranges?

He sat on the edge of the desk and took the orange out of my hand. He dropped it in the waste basket. "You're funny because I think you're a retarded psychiatrist. You don't have the professionalism of a real therapist and that's why I come to you. You're lame because you occupy yourself with shit you can't fix, and whine about things you can, when you don't."

I was still at the word "retarded." I have never been called retarded.

He leaned into me, face to face. "Go to your fucking boyfriend, Cindy. I can take care of myself. I came here to amuse myself with your behavior."

"Excuse me?" it wasn't what I expected from him. I was concerned.

He stood up, pointed at the clock and headed out. What the hell was going on with him? Was this just a waste of my hour?

I had to follow up. No, I needed to give him a visit, that's what was in order. Sometimes, a house and its very essence spoke more than words.

Chapter Nineteen
Binderman

I had been drunk since Cardy's accident. I had drunk myself into misery. And now, it was time to set shit straight. As I keep saying, I couldn't do it at home.

Cardy was going to be okay. With that said, I would be okay. After a year's time, I would reunite with him. I had a year to get my shit together.

I had lived and learned. It was time to make those lessons well earned. It was a turning point for me. I couldn't get worse and I was going to make damn sure that I wasn't about to go backwards. It was time to make all of my horrible situations worth living through.

What could I do to make a mark in this world, if only something small?

I was old enough to make my own choices in life. I had do start dealing with my consequences. I was smart enough to do something great, if just good. I needed a new plan, a new existence and purpose in life.

It started with Angie.

I don't know what I would have done if I didn't have Angie to turn to.

The smell of bacon gagged me awake. I hated breakfast time. Breakfast was full of sausage, bacon, and eggs. Breakfast had grease-thick plates of meat that started my days off feeling gross.

"Who the hell is cooking?" I wanted to leave. My head was swishing with Vodka, my father's choice of alcohol when he didn't care to spend more money. Maybe this was a bad idea.

I knew Susan, Angie's mom, made family meals and shit, but I didn't know she made breakfast. If I had to smell this shit every morning…the fucking toilet would become my best friend.

I don't know why the smell of meat turned my stomach sour. I guess because of the association with bacteria. It was what I thought of when I was forced to be around meat. I didn't used to be this way.

My mother was a vegetarian. I was raised to despise meat and meat products. It was the only thing that I kept about me that I grew fond of. Meat was disgusting.

There was this one time when I ate a piece of meat in Mexico. I was with my father. We were in Mexico City to meet a man. I don't know the details because I was only five. Hell, he could have been there to meet a woman. I was only five and didn't know of his affairs at the time. I was the only one who went with him.

He offered me to try meat explaining that I should at least try it. I wanted to show him that I wasn't scared of anything, even if my mom had scorned me to save the animals. See, she was into the environmentalist shit, where I didn't eat meat because of this incident.

I might have changed my mind about being a vegetarian if it wasn't for Mexico City. When I ate it, it gave me food poisoning. I was sick with a stomach virus for an entire week. I was hospitalized for unknown parasites invading my damn five year old body.

I didn't know what I had or cared to ask about it at a later age. The fact was scarred into my head. Meat was poisoned. Meat had bacteria in it. If I smelled it, I tasted it. If I ate it, I'd surely die from the shock of doing it. I was *that* paranoid about it.

Oh, it sent my parents into an argument. My mother was angry at my father for letting me try it. She said it served him right to do it in Mexico City, behind her back. He apologized and bought her the house in Pierre as a present. Sure, it needed to be rehabbed, but she loved all the Victorian Carvings that it came with. Only, she never made it there when it was fixed. She died too soon.

"My mom," Angie sat up in the floor.

I had already forgotten what I had asked her. My mind was trailing my past with scrutiny. I was in a slump and depressed about everything that I had become. I needed to figure out everything, about every situation that had taken place within my childhood and come to a conclusion. Although I had a hangover, I wanted to fix shit, soon.

Angie made me nervous. I don't know why. I didn't know what to say to her. I didn't know what she was about or how to act around her. Usually, I would work my good charm on a female, get them to do whatever the fuck I wanted them to do. It worked on teachers, too.

But, Angela was different. I didn't want to touch her. I didn't want to make her fall head over heels for me. I wanted to be her friend, as I had no one.

"Do I have to go outside and smoke?" I knew this from the summer that I was with her. Even then, her mother knew someone had been smoking in the house and grounded the poor girl for two weeks.

"Yeah, since you just barged in here as if you owned the place, can I have one?" Her sly comments weren't going to get the best of me. I handed her one as she snuck me to her back door. There, I could stand on her patio and assume I was just visiting. That's if we got caught.

"So, tell me what's going on." Angie shielded Devon from exiting to the yard with her leg. She knew all the right ways to keep him from doing things that I had no clue in doing.

I respected that. When he would cry, she'd rub his back and comfort him. When he was teething, she'd hand him a cold washcloth to bite on. I didn't know these things. I learned from her.

I shivered as the cool wind that rushed against me. I was still in my wife-beater and regretting it. "I don't know. I had everything figured out, what I was going to do with my life, and then, I don't know. Shit just popped off."

If I could be honest, she'd be the one to admit things to. I didn't care to put a front on, even though I never cared to confide in her, before. I continued, without giving her the time to question more. "I needed to get away from shit. I don't want people to bother me."

I was still sidestepping my biggest problem. I was ignoring the fact that she existed.

Fresca.

"So, you come here?" Angela was eyeing me in disbelief.

I exhaled. "What the hell can I do? There's a lot of shit going on and I don't want to be a part of it. I don't know who the fuck I am, anymore."

She was amused. She inhaled her cigarette with a smile. "You are Boo Sox. You are Prince of Pierre. What more do you need to be?"

I didn't like her response. I wasn't shit, that's who I was. I stepped closer to her. "No, I'm not, Angie. I don't know why people think I'm this big bad ass. One minute, I'm the new kid, the next, I'm popping bitches left and right. Who am I to you? I party, I drink, I fucking cheat on my girl, and I have a kid that

I don't even know what to do with! Take that shit away, and who the hell am I? Tell me *that* shit."

I was more serious than she had expected. She leaned back to absorb the spotlight. "I don't know," She laughed, uneasily. "You're whoever you are. What do you do when you're not doing those things?"

I needed a shrink, that's what I needed. I was using Angela as a fucking substitute because I didn't feel like having my crisis on paper.

I mean, I saw Cindy, yeah. But, she was far from a person that I felt safe to confide in. who knows, the bitch could go as far as confronting my dad. My dad had that certain charisma to persuade the smartest people into believing him, hence the judge and all the fucking people I had to deal with when my mother died. He was good at that shit. He could turn her against me. I might as well leave her out of it.

"I don't know." I left it at that. At least, she knew where I was coming from. It was more serious than any fucking party I threw. It was more important than figuring out which bitch to call back so I could fuck them.

Angie picked up a piece of bacon that sat on a pile of napkins. She crunched it and my stomach cringed. I followed her back to her bedroom, passed her mother's doorway. Susan was asleep. Her night job had caused her to sleep during the day.

"I'm fucking serious, Angie. I don't wanna go back to my house. I want to stay here, for awhile. I'll pay for cable and organize your room or something. I don't know. Just let me stay." I glanced around her room and it was tedious.

She had a small boom box of a stereo system. Her CD's were few and laying on the floor with the radio. Teen magazines were halfway under her bed. A pile of clothes, dirty or clean, who fucking knew, was in front of her footboard. A pair of shoes sat on top of her dresser. And the bottom dresser drawer was out on the carpet.

Devon's baby bed was shoved in the corner with a pack of diapers inside of that. Devon had spread each one out onto the mattress. Baby toys lined the bottom of the crib. The changing table was aligned next to the chest. Her room was so squeezed together that there was barely any room to walk freely in.

It was getting on my nerves.

"You want to stay longer? I thought you wanted to spend the night, last night, not a freaking week or something." Her attitude was disheartening.

I couldn't take it. I was desperate. I grabbed her by the arms and pushed my body into hers. I wanted her to take me serious. "No, I wanna stay longer. However long it takes me to figure shit out."

A year would be good. In a year, Cardy would be out and I could go home with him. I'd feel connected to that house, again.

She tensed up as I expected. She wasn't used to me conniving her with my very essence. "I'd have to talk to my mom, Boo. I don't know. Where would you sleep?"

I thought hard, harder than I really thought at all.

"Go out with me." It was more shocking to listen to my own words than I had thought it through, which was spontaneous in asking.

"What? You're kidding. Oh my god, you better be kidding me." She twisted out of my grip to head to the corner of her room. She analyzed my expression for some kind of twisted joke.

I smiled, knowing how stupid I was being. Of course, she thought I was faking. Why would she think any other way? She wasn't my type. I didn't make little girls like her my main bitch. There wouldn't be any use for them.

I headed towards her. "Angie, I know shit between us..." But, she ran across her bed to the other side.

"Fucking stop and listen to me! I want to make it work, alright? This ain't a fucking bet or prank. We could at least try for Devon's sake." It had never dawned on me, before. But, I didn't want Devon to grow up in two separate households.

I never planned on having a fucking kid with Angie. It was supposed to be with Fresca. We were supposed to get married and have a bunch of kids. Fresca had it mapped out. But, what was done was done. I had a fucking kid with Angie. Maybe, I had it all wrong. Maybe, it was Angie that I was supposed to be with. She had more sense in her head than Fresca did.

"Why are doing this, Boo? You can have any girl out there in the world. We don't need to be together for Devon. He's fine."

"Look at him, he's not fine. He knows when I'm not there. He knows when you're pissed off at me. He knows everything." I stared at my son, who was only one. He may or may not know of these things, but I did. I remembered when my father wasn't home. I knew that it pissed my mother off.

Devon was in a purple Barney sleeper. I begged Angie to throw it away. He carried a bottle in his right hand and a piece of bacon in his left. His hair was darker than mine was at that age and it was straight. Angie's stupid ass genes were kicking in. I think Brandon, Cardy's kid, had lighter hair than my kid's.

Angie picked him up and hoisted him onto her hip. "Yes, he is. Get real, Boo, I can't go out with you."

I wasn't used to rejection. "Why not?! Any other fucking girl would die to be in your position." What the hell was her problem?

"Oh yeah? I know a lot of girls who wouldn't dare share the same room with you." She walked away.

I followed her. "Who?"

She placed Devon on the ground and took another piece of bacon from the counter. God, this was going to irritate me. She snapped it in half and chewed a piece, talking while chewing. "Amanda, Basia, all of my friends."

Basia.

"Why bring up Basia's name? She has nothing to do with us. I would never in my fucking life try to get with her. You're naming bitches that I could care a less about." Not now, anyways.

Basia was something, alright. If it wasn't for Cardy, I would have already tapped into it. I may have not noticed her before, but lately…fuck, she was hot. She would have been perfect to work with, too. It never dawned on me that I hadn't been with a black girl, or mixed girl, or Asian or Mexican or any other race other than white. Was I missing out on something? Were they different? As many bitches that I had fucked with, fuck…they better not be different.

"I'm just saying, you shouldn't expect everyone to fall head over heels for you. There are certain types that you need and certain types you shouldn't bother with." Angie stood her ground smiling at her ability to refuse me.

"And what's that?"

"You need stupid little tramps that think you're all that, that way, their little airhead brains wouldn't question your faithfulness. You can walk all over them without feeling guilty about it. But, no, with me…see, I wouldn't even attempt to be your girlfriend. I won't even consider it. You'd cheat on me, lie to me, and I wouldn't be able to handle it. I'd kill you." Angela didn't know who the fuck she was talking to like that. It was pissing me off.

"Kill me? You're a psycho bitch? Please. You're just scared. You wouldn't kill me." But, I didn't know her. Maybe she was a psycho bitch.

"You didn't say you wouldn't cheat on me. See there? I'm right, again."

She walked her little confident ass out of the kitchen, apparently trying to lose me in her own god damn house.

"I don't want to go out with you, anyways. You're lucky that I'm even here."

"Leave, then." Angie thought she was something, fucking bitch. She was always ready to contradict whatever the fuck I wanted to say. Whether it was Devon's outfit, or food, or being my fucking girlfriend, she was ready to shoot me down.

"No." I lay back down on her mattress. "I like it here. I don't have a girlfriend to bitch at me, I don't have to answer to a bitch, you're right, you know. If you were my girlfriend, I'd probably leave."

I was satisfied.

"Oh really?" Angie yanked down a big t-shirt from her closet and pulled out a pair of sweat pants from a drawer. She tried to conceal a pair of her underwear in her fist. She was about to take a shower.

I sat up. "Yeah, I'm only nice to bitches who don't own me."

But, it won't stop there. I already made up my mind. Angela Debrowski was going to go out with me because I wanted her to. It would be easier to explain Devon to my dad. It was a perfect plan.

I didn't need bitches. I didn't need Fresca. I had Angie. Angie couldn't hurt me. She had my son. She was the perfect girl to bring home to my dad. He wouldn't try to fuck her. He could respect her. It was a great little plan of mine. And, who knows, maybe Angie could work out for me. I could adapt to her ass. I was good at adapting.

Chapter Twenty
Cardy

We had been driving for miles and miles, which felt like hours and hours. I was punished with The Grease Soundtrack that my mother so happened to have in her glove compartment. Oh, and Kenny G and Elton John. Let's not forget the easy listening station and the good ass oldies. Make me fucking sick, will you? I needed to get out of this fucking car.

"I'm hungry."

"No, you're not, Cardy." My mom sighed. At every intersection, I had a reason to stop at a gas station.

"Then, I'm thirsty." I kicked the Mountain Dew bottle with my foot, hoping it wouldn't swish too loudly.

She ignored me. She loved to fucking ignore me.

"I'm gonna piss in a bottle if you don't pull over. I swear to God. I'm sure you need another pack of cigarettes." I refrained from stopping the John Travolta wail of a song. I refused to let my hands scratch my arm or my nose or any other part of my body that decided to itch. No, my palms idled underneath me, waiting to let loose in a gas station.

"You can pee on the side of the road. I'm not stopping at another gas station." She was in a hurry to throw me out of the car into the hands of the experienced.

We had stopped at five gas stations. I stalled longer at each one, grabbing shit, reading magazines, talking to clerks, anything to pass the time to being late to the stupid institution. Only twice did I take a piss.

"Can we at least listen to some decent music before I'm banned from existence? They probably make you listen to AM radio. Or better yet, Christian talk shows. It would keep my mind busy, mom." I ejected the cassette since her Taurus didn't have a CD player.

"Whatever, Cardy." She had to be ragging. Her fucking mood was getting to me.

My last forty five minutes was nothing but guitar solos and drum beats alongside of my synchronized fingers. My mind was swept away to the music, the lyrics drowning out my fate. It poured the rage out of me, draining the adrenaline with each guitar prick. I don't know what it was about music, but it filled me. It crept under my skin with each vibration. It was a slight heroin sensation, riding my veins to a bliss otherwise unknown.

We pulled up to a fifteen foot iron gate. Tall pine trees blocked the view of everything else. Large stone pillars bordered the gate. A security guard approached us.

My mom leaned her head out a ways to greet him. "Hi, we have a meeting with the Dean."

He checked his list. He confirmed her driver's license and glanced over at me. The electronic gates retracted back to a black top road. She was ushered to proceed.

The black top opened up to a vast field of trimmed grasslands. Young oak trees were freshly planted with the dirt still mounded up high. In the distance were numerous buildings. As we got closer, I saw a tennis court and a basketball court. To the left of me, there was a football field. It was busy with people. Everyone was occupied with some sort of sport.

My perception of this place became clearer. Not happier, just clearer. It seemed like a boarding school. A male boarding school for the little criminally challenged. They wore uniforms. Not suits and ties like the Catholic schools up in Boston. But, certain colored shirts, if I didn't perceive it wrong.

I saw a lot of the same shade of greens, blues, and grays. All were polo shirts, like a fast food restaurant's attire, kaki and colored polo's. Was I going to have to wear that shit, too? Did we get matching hats and jackets, hold up slogans for brochures, "Safe haven is Safe?" How about name tags? Did they have a mascot, like a fucking taco or jack ass? Jack ass would be great, a bunch of jack and no fucking ass. How about bull shit?

We drove around the circular drive way alongside of a stone water fountain. The Safe haven logo was the centerpiece. Flowerbeds surrounded it. Everything was perfected to resemble peace and relaxation. Well, I knew better. This was a sucker's paradise. Not me, not at all for me. I'd rather stay in the hospital and get doped up all day. At least I had my mom to wait on me.

My mom parted her lips. I heard her do so as she clicked her tongue at her ability to read my thoughts. "Don't start, Cardy. This is your home, now. Respect it."

"I ain't respecting shit. I'm here because I have to be, doesn't mean I'll make it worth my time." I opened the car door for fresh air and nothing else.

And like being late for class, the patients, kids, what the hell do I call those motherfuckers? Well, everyone stopped and stared at our car. *A new visitor, another fuck up, huh?* Five staff members, all in white, came rushing out to greet us. Bullshit, better not put their hands on me.

"Be nice." My mother's favorite words of the day rang in my ears. No, *they* better be nice.

She got out, gave them my paperwork, my death sentence, my "go directly to jail" card. *Do not pass go, do not collect two hundred dollars.* Fuck you.

"He's being very defiant, today. Don't let him fool you; he's a good kid, really. He's just not being himself, lately." It was more of a warning that she didn't want any more trouble from me, not on the day she had to say goodbye.

I bounced out, preparing for a battle of opposition. "I'm cool, mom, really I am." I eyed them up…sized them up. My head filled with anxiety, but my body ached for physical contact with at least one of them. *Fuck with me, really, come on.*

"This is where the goodbyes are handled. We like to leave the lobby with good memories." A tall thin man, obviously in charge of the others, had to enforce.

My eyes searched my mother's for some compliance. I dreaded this moment. I didn't want to leave her and I would have given her a big hug and kiss like a good Cardy would have done. But, in the middle of the open public, with white uniforms observing every movement I made, in fear that I would make a run for the gates, I had to hold my own.

"Alright, mom, see ya." I rolled my eyes with attitude. She wanted this shit, not me. I gave her all the time to turn around and head south for the border, or north to Canada or west to California. She had all the necessary maps to get there.

She squeezed me with tears. I didn't absorb it. I kept my body tense and my eyes locked on the staff members waiting to whisk me away to my dark hell. Let's get this shit over with. Make it short so I had preserved energy to fight my way to freedom.

"I love you, Cardy, Christopher. I love you no matter what, you hear me? You behave. The judge said you have to comply to be released. You'll be out before you know it, alright? Just be nice." Her fingers formed over my cheeks wiping away invisible tears that never came.

"Yeah, mom, me too."

And, that was that. She strolled around the car, waiting for me to cry or show some sort of emotion that I needed her. I did need her, but…I wasn't about to show it, not in front on them. Her car disappeared gradually down the pavement. All the while, I felt her looking in her rearview, tears burning into my eyes as if they were my own. She cried for me and that was enough.

I wouldn't see her for a year. The pamphlet said that I wouldn't have visitors or receive phone calls or letters. I wasn't going to be distracted by the outside world. Okay, what if I was distracted from *not* seeing my family? Did they think of that?

Fuck them. Fuck all of them.

The five white polo's walked me to the reception desk. The lobby was huge with a ceiling that echoed and a polished floor great for break dancing. I wasn't any good at break dancing. Who was good? Darron was decent. He could walk on his hands and balance his weightless body on them in a sitting position. Try doing that at the height of a tree, hence me.

"Your name?" A round plump lady asked behind her bifocals. Her hair was dyed red with long pink earrings hanging from her stretched out ear lobes. Her blush was a heavy pink as was the rest of her clown makeup. She probably needed to add some digits to her prescription, since she couldn't see how many layers she caked onto her skin.

Her glasses had a purple string attached to them. Her name tag read Ruth. Her arms were short and stout, flabby at her sleeves. Brown specks covered them. Did that come with old age or from the sun? Are people born that way?

When she talked, her words struggled with each breath. She had trouble breathing, possibly from being overweight.

Stan, his name tag read, decided that I didn't have a voice. He spoke for me. "His name is Christopher…"

I raised a strong hand to shut his ass up. I leaned on the counter. "Ruth, my name is Cardy Deburke, legally named Christopher Viscardi Deburke." Stan wasn't about to consider me shy or non-complaint when I felt in the mood of being otherwise.

As I replied, I gave the lobby another look over. It was mostly white with white tiles and white walls. A few plants were shoved into corners. Gray chairs were aligning the walls. Posters were taped up with all the inspiration needed to host a "You can do it" seminar. You can do what? I wonder. Sink deeper into depression because all you see is white fucking walls?

A drinking fountain sat to my right. Two elevators stood at my left. A long corridor went further down from the water fountain. Some of the staff was standing around, whispering, about what, me? Come get me, motherfuckers. I'm waiting.

"Christopher Deburke," She said to herself, typing my name into a computer. She bit her thin lip for concentration. She typed with her two index fingers, slowing the pace even longer. She wasn't very professional. Next to her computer was a pink haired troll. On the side of the computer was a prayer, Our Father, to be exact.

The words began to float in my head by reflex. Too many days in church did this to me. I knew the shit by heart. I didn't want to know it by heart. Hell, I could recite most of the bible if given the chance. Hell…I shouldn't rack that word with the same sentence as the bible, should I? Oh, what the hell, why not? Let God come down here and make me stop. I invite him to show his face to me. I needed to see the proof.

She seemed to be having trouble with something and adjusted a small picture frame back in place. It was of a girl. Her daughter, I assume. She was a cheerleader with pom-poms at her feet. It was a universal pose with that same universal smile, fake and sweet. Innocent, yet…in my eyes…ruined before she graduated. Why did I know this?

"It always does this to me, I don't know why." Ruth gave the computer a little pat. I heard her feet shuffle and her face blushed darker than her makeup. She was getting frustrated. "Oh, I didn't spell your name right." She leaned her face into the screen. I couldn't help but smile.

"There you go. You are on fourth floor, in room 407. Here is your schedule. You are to meet with Dr. Roma as soon as you get settled. Tomorrow, if you like. The Dean will meet you by the end of the week. He's off on the weekends. Stan is your floor manager. Any questions can be directed to him. If you have medicine to take, he will be in charge of dispensing it." She closed her mouth to wait for questions.

I didn't have any. I didn't want any. I took the schedule, flipped it open and pretended to skim it. I closed it and tapped the counter. "Okay," I didn't anticipate seeing my room or being in it for a year. So, I did the least I could do.

"Alrighty, the elevators are over there. You seem right enough to find it. If you have any problems, the men in white attire will attend to you, oh and welcome to Safe Haven." As she said the latter part, she raised her arms in a weary fashion. She grinned as if she said it a million times before. *Welcome to Safe Haven.* The repetition was already exhausting to me and it was one of the first times I heard it.

Stan smiled, knowing he got me on his floor list. Tall thin man, alright, if I had troubles, he'd be the first one I could pound on. He was little enough to take my aggressions on. Good. It was better than the bigger Italian one popping his knuckles, wishing I was with his group. What was his name? Oh, Sal. Sal was a brute of a man, stout and hairy, gold chain around his neck, chest hair pouring out over his collar. How much hair can a man have to come out of a Polo?

Stan followed me to the elevator. He was a good distance away, but enough to let me know that I couldn't turn around and head for an escape. Escape, was it possible? Could I make it out of the doors, down the winding driveway and to the open road before hitting the security guard with a rock and passing the gates? Could I make it back to Pierre, walking more than double the hours it took me to get here? Would my mind co-operate well enough to do this frustrating ordeal?

I think not.

I could if I wanted to, though. I had to keep that in mind.

For now, I did what I was told. I went to the fourth floor. I trailed the wall down the long corridor. Images of a dark one with candles lurked in the back of my mind. It was a more familiar hallway, one I couldn't recall if I tried.

I stopped in front of room 407. Great, the doors were white metal. A glass window was in the center of it. It resembled a jail cell. A light was on and everything seemed white in there, too. I hesitated on the doorknob. I looked around. Nobody but Stan was in the hallway. He preoccupied his suspicions with a small wooden desk at the end of that hallway. It was his work station, a center to watch all the doors. Was he a resident or did he go home to a family?

I tugged on the door. Silence. I walked in. All white. White tiles, white walls, white sheets, white everything. Sick. It made me feel like I was in a mental facility. What was up with all the white?

I noticed the bed and headed for it. Face first, I was preparing. I could use some sleep. Hangover like a bitch, a freight train roaring louder through my head, I needed to pass out. With Stan out of sight and Ruth down under, my body retrieved the rest of my state of a hangover.

"Hey, what's up?" a voice caught me off guard. I twisted around to the other half of the room that I had missed because I had focused in on my bed, my white bed, my white twin size bed.

A kid sat on another mattress with a notebook on his lap. His hair was like Darron's, parted in the middle, hanging level to his ears. He had Darron's body frame, too, small and frail. Only, he had tattoos up and down his scrawny wired arms.

"Are we roommates?" I flatly stared at him with regret. I didn't want to share my space with anyone, by all means. My disappointment was too apparent.

"Yep," He flung his little legs off the bed and set his notebook aside. He held out his hand for a shake. Sissy move. "I'm Brett, been here for four months." He wore a green polo tucked in kaki colored cargo pants. His belt was a dark brown, too big with the excess length sticking out. His shoes were white. Of course, more white. But white shoes were perfect. I liked white fucking shoes.

I didn't shake his hand. In doing so, I would have submitted to this idea of being his roommate. In doing so, I would have submitted to agreeing with the terms of this facility and all that it possessed, good or bad. Did I have to be nice to this guy? I wanted to ignore him for a whole year.

He withdrew his hand. "I'm in here for grand theft auto and smuggling cocaine into my school. My parents thought it best to put me here. It wasn't my choice. What are you in here for?"

He thought we could share some common ground. Yeah, okay. He had nothing in common with me.

"Everything, or that's what I'm told." I gave him my back and slumped down onto my bed. I bounced on it and laid back. I stared up at the ceiling. This place wasn't going to work out. It was too silent, too friendly, too…white, right down to the people. I mean, didn't they have some quota to account for? Where were the black people, the Asians, the Mexicans? What happened to diversity?

I mean, Pierre was ninety six percent white, too, but not this white. At least in Pierre, I had multitudes of color to go around. If I had to stare at white people too long, then I had flower gardens and hues of paint on colored walls to make up the difference. I was by far not prejudice, just to remind you. In fact, my ex-girlfriend was bi-racial. I loved the difference in our skin tones. It was beautiful…the abstract, the connection, the uneven shades of life.

My mind drifted to all the famous actresses that I obsessed over. It was a good wheel of color going on, with abstract personalities to go along with it. My favorite at the moment, the one I would die to be with, to touch, to lick, to suck on, was Beyonce Knowles. I saw her on TV in the hospital. I tried to force a dream out of it, but no such luck.

And then, Gwen Stefani's sweaty pushups drew me in. I loved her approach, her personality to not be "just a girl." She was opposite of Beyonce, but only the best of opposites. Let's go on, because I would rather think of her than the stupid ass talking my ear off about a car he had stolen.

Penelope Cruz, Selma Hayek, those sweet talking princesses could whisper in my ear every night if they dared. Oh and, I didn't know how popular she was in United States, but she was a favorite on that Spanish channel. Her name was Shakira. (Remember that this is 1998. My obsession with her will continue for life, as she did become famous in the U.S, later). That bitch could rattle her hips on me anytime, anywhere.

"You don't know what you're in here for or you don't want to say?" He wouldn't give up. He ruined a good dream about to attack me.

I was rude. I was cock blocked from my dream of bitches. I jumped up giving him the impression not to fuck with me, anymore. "Motherfucker, I was court ordered here, for one thing. I didn't have parents shoving me in here. I ain't like you. I was fucking with heroin, fucking with shit you know shit about."

Intimidated as I towered over him like a fucking willow tree not giving him space to breathe, he backed up, hands raised in defense. He didn't say anymore. He didn't have to. I was somebody to fear. Motherfucker, so fear me.

Chapter Twenty-One
Binderman

I couldn't get my mind straight. I had all these ideas twisting in my head and I didn't know which one to follow. Usually, it was one idea. It was easier to comprehend and see the consequences at stake. But…a few, several…I was impulsively doing them at once without any clear reasoning.

For once, I couldn't keep my feet planted at home. I was driving all over St. Paul. I had gone to Dewey's, only he wasn't there. I had wondered to Seth's and fucked myself up on cocaine. I had found myself at Teesa's bedside, only to be belittled by Roger. And here I was, stranded at Angie's, asking her to go out with me.

How fucked up was I?

Life should still exist for me without Cardy. It should still go on with my dad at home, too. I had done this before. There was a good decade and a half without my brother. There were a few good years with my father at home, also. So, what the fuck was my big deal?

I was losing my self control. I hadn't taken a shower in three or four days. Usually, it was three or four times a day, not the other way around. I hadn't had my hair cut since the accident, which was going on three months, ago. Hadn't shaved, since, either.

Today, I was sober. Today, my head was spinning with a to-do list to get shit straightened out. I thought Angie could help me. Obviously, she was stupid. I shouldn't put my trust in an eighteen year old girl who just graduated this May. She had her own agenda to deal with.

"I can't stay here if you won't go out with me." It was my only excuse to run away, yet again. Yesterday, it seemed to fit and fall into place. Today, I was sober. Shit wasn't feeling the same.

"Fine." Angie crossed her arms in agreement.

I wanted her to plead with me. I didn't want it to be that simple. "It's not fine, Angie. Shit's not fine."

I grabbed my hoodie, threw it over my head and walked out of her house before I had it over my stomach. I didn't know what to do. I wanted to lay low, somewhere. I wanted it to be Angie's, yet I didn't want to deal with her mother or Angie's mouth.

Later that night, as if my life wasn't turned upside down, I did what I would have done, any other night.

I went to a party. I needed the release and the familiarity. I needed the crowd to drown out my thoughts and the liquor to wipe away my increase in anxiety.

I took a long hot shower. I had Bobbi clip my hair like I had done to Cardy's. I shaved my face and brought back the man I didn't care to look at anymore. The man who resembled Cardy, who represented Pierre, who devastated so many lives while living his…I went back to being Boo Sox.

My resolutions were put on hold…for now.

I called up Kyle, Terrance, and Wes. I called Taylor, Tyler, and Leslie. I made sure that every bitch that I knew was going to be at the party. The party was at Frankie Mercini's house who was kin to little Anthony.

Little Anthony was nothing more than a punk out of Jersey or New York, or wherever his family came from. He walked around like he was the shit. He talked like he was me. He assumed he would own a piece of Pierre by the time he was a senior, and unfortunately, that wasn't the case. He was in Angela's grade, which now is done with.

I never liked him.

Now, Cazaro Mercini, he played defense with me in football. We were cool. Frankie, he was Cody's age, Seth's age, an era that left me out of the mix back in the day. I didn't know too much about Frankie except that he was more the shit than Anthony. Frankie hung around Seth, most times.

A party was a party, I guess. That's the way Cardy saw it. All my people would be there. They wouldn't be pampered with the best stereo equipment or the never ending supply of liquor that I was accustomed to, but a party was a party. I tried to tell myself that.

Everyone that wasn't going was now going because of me. I hadn't been out in awhile. Let's say three months. I hadn't hung around my friends for three months. I needed to get away and get fucked up with a bunch of losers. I needed to fuck a bitch, that's what it was.

I pulled up, same fashion, careless and parking my Expedition in front of many. I didn't give a fuck. They knew who it was and nobody would force me to move it. I hated to travel around and find a fucking spot. There never was any.

I checked the rearview and stared at myself. Was I ready to enter a world that I knew I was drifting out of?

I had to.

Instantly, I was greeted by bitches and skanks and hoes and little girls that knew nothing about me. I barely got out of my car, let alone stand. I was suffocating from the mixture of "bitch." It was that smell of perfume and lotion, shampoo and hair spray. Laundry detergent and house scents. Not to mention, gum and ashtrays, sweet liquor and marijuana heaven. Some even gave off the smell of being in-heat. Not like I could decipher which bitches were giving off too many pheromones, but it was there, too.

I was always greeted like a rock star handing out autographs. It was insane, really. I needed my fucking body guard, Brian. He would push the bitches back, shove them to the ground, purposely by accident. We'd wade through the crowd and somehow, manage to escape injuries.

Bitches, well, they weren't so lucky. I cherished those moments where one was too close to me and the other wasn't. Hair pulling and shirt ripping would go into effect. It was like watching a hockey fight in your face, only the participants would soon be naked and offended. I didn't know why they were fighting, I'd fuck them both. I wasn't picky.

I mean, I was in a sense, but if I hadn't fucked her, I'd fuck her for the sake of it. I wasn't fucking these hoes because I liked them. I fucked them because I wanted to say I fucked them. If it was all about busting a nut, then I'd rather stay home with Fresca.

Wonder if she'd be here, tonight…

Okay, here's a confession. It had nothing to do with Fresca.

I did what I did because I could. These bitches walked around asking for it. I wasn't proud of using and misusing these little girls. What could I say? They were more than willing to lose their virginity in the spur of the moment to be with me, to say that it was me.

It was stupid, really. I didn't respect the girls I was with. How could I? They thought it was cool to sleep with me as their boyfriend was in the next room. I didn't care. It was pussy to me. That's the only way I saw it. Pussy.

What guy wouldn't? Of course, those bitches weren't the bitches to make a girlfriend out of. They were tramps, part of our game.

Our game? It was officially a game.

"Dog, you back in the game, or what? Anthony might have you beat by now." Terrance did the pushing and shoving, not even making eye contact with the broads as he did it.

I waded through, following him to the porch. "I never left it, dog." Lighting a cigarette and observing the scene. Girls and guys were already drunk, kissing and dancing to the music coming from the house. It was pathetic, but nevertheless, my kind of shit.

"Never left it? What do you call your vacation these past few months? Anthony, shit, you should see him, he's creeping up in the world." Terrance. I never liked Terrance.

He was a follower, an ass kisser. He wore what MTV wore, whatever was in style. To me, he dressed like he was from Casa. That sunvisor shit was getting old, upside down and sideways. Sure, it was his trademark, everyone knew he was Terrance. A little rich boy, he was. Not as rich as me, but quick to flash some floss of it.

"What do mean, give me the books…" I didn't know if he had them or if Brian gave them to anyone before he left. He didn't give them to me.

"Kyle has them." And Terrance did the scoping for Kyle.

I wasn't at all feeling threatened by Anthony Mercini. I had enough bitches on those pages than anyone put together. Anthony couldn't win. Shit, Cardy had more bitches than the rest of them. He was the motherfucker than I should be scared of. He was seventeen, close to reaching my numbers. But, I won't give him credit where it's due.

He was my brother. Of course he'd come in second place. It was in our genes to manipulate women.

"Hey, Kyle!" Terrance shot out into the grass to grab him.

Kyle yelled his famous "Dude!" and hurried up the steps to pull out a folded notebook of scores. Virgins were ten points. Anyone's girlfriend was worth twenty, and that motherfucker who got played loses fifty. It was all second grade math, really.

"Leslie fucked Anthony last night, dude. We gotta beat his ass in this shit."

Plus twenty for Anthony, down fifty for Terrance.

Fresca wasn't in this shit…although Cardy, that punk motherfucker, played me. Fortunately, no one knew this. I wasn't about to admit it, either. It would remain between the three of us for now.

Understand that this is for real. Shit like this happens. Bitches are nothing but a number in our game. Leslie Brande was, is, and always will be a number. It's stupid punks like Terrance who keep them as girlfriends.

Oh, strippers are ten, too. Not prostitutes, they don't count. Strippers are paid to take off their clothes and dance, not fuck you. If a stripper fucks you, it's some good shit. Mikayla was ten, twice. Cody was down a hundred, but, he didn't know.

"Give me the digits." I flicked my cigarette to the ground and squinted at the chicken scratch of Kyle's, the bookkeeper of this game.

"You stand at 2460," He went on to announce the others…

"Dog, how am I at 2460? I was 2500 something the last time, maybe even 2600, I don't remember. It wasn't 2400 something. What's up with that shit, don't be erasing shit." I took the book and read what it said.

It didn't say much. Kyle wasn't good at jotting down names next to the scores. When I had it, I had the bitches next to the numbers for definition. Brian did the same. Kyle was lazy.

"Dog," Terrance took it and tapped it towards me. "Your bitch is pregnant. Roger took her. You had to drop in numbers, dog. Get with it, understand that you can be played, too." Those words were harsh.

I shoved him back. "Fuck off, motherfucker. Teesa ain't in this shit, anymore. He's marrying her." It was the only excuse I had.

Teesa had become my girlfriend only on paper. Everyone knew that I wouldn't play if Fresca had been entered into the deal. My numbers would rocket if they couldn't fuck her. Not that Teesa gave it up, either. My competition, like I said, was Roger and Cardy. And Roger wasn't anywhere near Cardy's digits.

"No shit, really?"

Did they not know this? Where have they been? Where had Teesa been to announce the engagement?

"Dude, I'm knocking Roger out of the game. He doesn't need to be cheating on his wife." Kyle drew a line through his score and name. We all agreed.

Marriage wasn't something to fuck around with. It was over between Teesa and me and that fucking sucked, worse than the scoreboard.

"Roger's going to miss out."

"Roger's going to get an ass beating, that's what's going down." I cocked.

"Dog, don't do that shit. Just cause you got played doesn't mean he ain't your boy. They're all fucking hoes. Bros before hoes, dog." Terrance thought he had a phrase going. Bitch. He couldn't stand there and assume he wasn't heartbroken over Leslie Brande. He had been messing with her since ninth grade.

"Fuck that." I lit another square.

Chapter Twenty-Two
Cynthia Roma

A week went by and I didn't hear anything from Binderman. It was time for a visit. After my rough day at Safe Haven, his normality was appreciated.

This new kid, Christopher, was kind of getting to me. I had no background on him. His hospital records stopped at fifteen and picked up in the emergency room, a few months ago. There was a big gap between the two. He had never seen a therapist, let alone a psychiatrist. His mother was missing information and his father, let's says his mother's husband, well, ex-husband, jeesh, was NOW out of the picture. Long story.

His real father is halfway in the picture, maybe a toe nail or so, I don't know what the deal is with him. Well, the point was clear. Nobody knew this kid and couldn't give me a briefing to what he was about. His mother, Dena, spoke to me on the phone and that was after a good twenty rings to her house.

No wonder why he did drugs. He had nobody to show they cared or to stop him, for that matter. Of course, that was the assumption. I had no paperwork. I had nothing to go off of. His mother sounded drunk and depressed. She said he had run away to his real father's house, only he never knew it was his real father. He stayed because he was friends with his brother, yet had no clue that his brother was his brother.

This gets confusing, I know. I am trying to figure him out. The best part to this entire puzzle is that he has amnesia. The very patient with all the information I need has forgotten what went on in the past two years of his life. Or, and I mention a mild "or"...he may be hiding from the truth. He may not want to admit it or explain it.

He, very well, might have amnesia. He suffered a head on collision with a truck. The driver flew out of the window and broke his collarbone, the driver of that truck, I mean. Christopher, the reports say he slammed against the steering wheel and windshield with so much force that it knocked him unconscious. He was in a coma for the rest of the evening. When he came to, he had a seizure and was put in a drug induced state for a few weeks until the swelling went down. It was a critical state to be in.

I think of all of this as I drive to a young man's house without giving him a call. He may or may not be home. Knowing Binji, he most definitely wasn't home.

My goodness, I couldn't get over this new kid. He wasn't like the usual ones. The other ones are younger than him, maybe thirteen or fourteen, rebelling against a family rule, like curfew. I don't get the privilege to challenge myself with someone of Christopher's status.

My facts were small. Christopher was on drugs. On many drugs. The doctor said he had everything in his system. Heroin and cocaine were two of them. A hair sample proved that it was routine, not a onetime ingestion. In his pockets were containers of Oxycodone and Ativan. None of which were prescribed for him. And, his alcohol level had sky rocketed passed the normal limits. All of this concerned me.

His forearm proved that he was once into self mutilation, a common symptom of being under immense pressure. Many patients cut themselves to relieve the pressure they feel, a release. Sometimes, it's for a pinch of reality, to feel *something*, kind of like pinching when thought in a dream state.

His weight was the same as when he was fifteen, which meant one thing. Maybe it wouldn't have meant anything if his height had stayed at 5'10, but it didn't. This kid had grown a good four inches and stayed the same weight? Bull-crap. He dropped weight because of the drugs.

I didn't ask him about any of this.

Oh, I had a good five hours of dwelling on this kid. It took five hours to Pierre from Safe Haven. I already popped an Aleve. It had yet to work.

I shouldn't be thinking of this one. I should be thinking of my next one, of Binderman. I was worried about him, too. He never looked so down and out. Falling out of the window, accident or not, shouldn't be overlooked and undermanaged.

My cell phone rang. I glanced down and saw the number of guilt. I wouldn't answer. I couldn't dare to admit that I was going on another mission of saving the world, one poor soul at a time. And, I wasn't about to deny or lie about it. He had heard enough these past six months.

Okay, okay. I was great at what I did. And that was work. I excelled in dishing out advice and patching up people's mental states. I sucked at relationships. I knew Binji Sox like the back of my hand. I knew him more than Stephen what's-his-middle-name? See there?

I yawned. My goodness, I was tired. I should stop for that extra cup of coffee, maybe a soft drink...maybe...should I dare...a candy bar?

I detoured off of '79 and down the exit ramp. I had a right to caffeinate myself. All of this driving was wearing out my brain. Sure, I was on a diet. I was watching my weight. I was caffeine free, like, yesterday. I wasn't smoking last night, either. I had refrained from the cravings long enough to eat five yogurts. That was a start.

"Will power, you wanna talk to me about will power?" I said this to myself as I unbuckled my seat belt. "I'll tell you where to shove that will power of yours." I smiled, happily giving in to the devil on my shoulder.

Just this once.

As I grabbed a Snickers candy bar from the shelf, I stopped and stared at the wrapper. It wasn't to reconsider my chocolate craze. Nuh-uh. An idea was forming.

I wanted to bribe this kid. Chocolate was a good substitute for drug cravings. When I was assisting a former boyfriend at the rehab facility, he wasn't the advisor, mind you, he carried a bag full of bite-size chocolate candies. He gained a good five to ten pounds from it, but...Christopher needed some weight.

Yes, perfect. I'll be the chocolate lady. I'll feed my way into his trust. I grabbed the entire cardboard container of snickers and then another of Reese's. What if he didn't like peanut butter or peanuts? Damn. I carried them to the counter and then walked back for Three Musketeers. This was good enough. I can stock up at a wholesaler's, later.

For now, I will deny the fact that I was addicted to chocolate. Psychiatrist or not, I had a sweet tooth-caffeinated crave that I swept under the rug from time to time, not to mention the refreshing buzz of a morning cigarette burning into my lungs. Hey, I was human.

Yes, I told myself. I was definitely human. I didn't contaminate my life with troubled teens for the mere fact of not facing my own reality. No, I was helping those who couldn't understand peer pressure. I was asserting myself in every which way to save someone's life, any way possible.

Chapter Twenty-Three
Cardy

I slept in a small white bed surrounded by white walls. The ceiling was white and the tiles were white. The only color came from my hands and my clothes. Oh and, my roommate's side of the room. I wouldn't dare give him the time of day.

I was dreaming of big buckets of ice cream, rocky road and fudge brownies all piled into one. The chunks were so big that the fudge filled my mouth with one bite. The container was big enough to sit on my lap, like a box. Basia had a blueberry syrup bottle and poured it into my perfect mix of ice cream. I was stunned and couldn't figure out why she thought blueberry was an additive to chocolate. It had ruined my perfection.

As I chased her freely and happily down the road to the crash scene, she was hit by a car, a blue one…with grey upholstery. I froze. My eyes couldn't peel back the hands of time and wouldn't retract from death. I was devastated. Her screams echoed my own, over and repetitively.

Every dream I endured followed a nightmare of that night, that night I refused to remember. I wanted to, believe me. The only memories came in my subconscious. I was haunted by the death-grip of it being there…in the back of my mind.

When I arose, a lady with auburn colored hair stood before me. She was asking permission to sit on my bed. She was calling me Christopher, to which I didn't understand her. That's why I slept passed her intrusion. I didn't answer to Christopher, ever.

She seemed rather tall or she did as I lay down. She wore a skirt, long and wavy, black with blue printed flowers. Her sweater was small and black, buttoned to her chest. Her shirt underneath was blue. She was perfectly color toned, right down to the shoes I saw as she sat without my permission. She wore black sandals.

Her hair seemed on fire. The edges flew back from being windblown. Her headband was blue, adding to her color choice of the day. I didn't like it. I hated long skirts of trying to look pleasing. Her eyes matched her outfit, deep dark blue.

Her skin was of pearl, shiny and untouched. If she wasn't so old, I would mark her off as a virgin. But, she had to be in her thirties, young in her thirties, at least. I didn't know any virgins in their thirties. She sure dressed the part.

I wasn't about to sit up. My head hurt. I didn't care to know who she was, but she told me, anyways.

"My name is Dr. Cynthia Roma. I am assigned to you while you reside at Safe Haven. And, your name is Christopher Deburke?" She sat so pleasantly. I wish she would give up the act. People don't sit pleasantly, not behind closed doors, anyways.

I nodded, grabbing my thunderous beat of a headache.

"You come from Pierre, Pennsylvania?" The questions were ridiculous. Everything she asked, I nodded a yes. They were all simple pieces of confirmation.

"Do you have a nickname, like Chris or Topher, or something like that?" She thought she was being funny, but she wasn't.

"No."

Now, began the disagreeing. Everything she asked from then on, I denied, even if it was a lie.

"Were you born anywhere other than Pierre?"

"Did you live anywhere other than Pierre?"

"Did you runaway when you were fifteen?"

"Have you ever met your biological father?"

I was born in Cheriton. I lived in Cheriton until I was three. Did she need to know this? No. I met my father once that I could remember, and I didn't remember that. I just knew of it.

She stood with a sigh. "Okay, alright. Would you like a tour? Did Stan give you a tour?"

"I would like to fucking sleep, thank you. I have a hangover." I shoved the pillow over my face and retraced my dream of ice cream.

"Oh." Her sandals flapped against the tile and stalled at her exit. "Hey Cardy, come by my office if you care to talk between sessions."

I tossed the pillow to the floor as soon as I heard my name. Did she know all of this information and was she testing my lying skills? What the fuck was that shit all about?

I chased after her.

"If you knew the shit, then why did you ask me?" a confrontation was in order.

"I only know your nickname, sorry. I wanted to get your permission to call you that. Apparently, you didn't want me to say it." She was sly, alright. I held it against her.

"Apparently you're pissing me off. I don't need someone to talk to. I don't need anything except sleep." Apparently, I was going to have to deal with this bitch for a year.

"Okay, okay. I know we started off on the wrong track. I shouldn't have begun with all of those questions. You're crabby and you have a right to be. Next time we meet, it'll be on your terms, alright? Does that sound fair?" The bluebell of bitches brought it down a notch and began treating me like a child.

"Who the fuck gave you a degree? I'm seventeen, not five. I didn't skin my fucking knee, I'm on heroin. I wasn't placed here by my parents, either. I was forced here. Don't think I'm going to be brainwashed with this shit 'cause I'm not." I felt the anger rise to uncertainty. I was spitting fire against a narrow-minded wall of steel. Shrinks have one way of looking at shit and that's a text book piece of crap.

"We'll see, Christopher, we'll see." She left me with that and headed down the hall.

I didn't trust her. I didn't trust anyone. Having a roommate and shrink at my disposal was going to be hell. Being locked five hours away from Pierre was going to be hell. Not being able to slumber my way into nirvana…the picture paints itself neatly in hell.

I paced the hall. I wanted to smoke. I couldn't smoke. I wanted to leave. I couldn't leave. What the hell was Stan looking at?

"Do you have a problem with me?" He was the only one there to take my aggression. He may or may not have been looking at me. But, he was looking at me, now. I raised my arms out, ready to fight.

Stan stood. He checked his watch. "No Deburke, I really don't. The question is rather, do you have a problem with me?"

Punk ass.

I strolled my way towards him with a ready smile. "Yeah, I do."

I don't know where this part of me came from. I didn't remember being so defensive or aggressive. I knew I was way out of line for no reason. I knew that my attitude sucked and needed an adjustment. I knew all of this, but it felt good to release the unknown anger onto something.

"Step back, Deburke. I don't have time for this. My shift is almost over and you can handle Pete. Pete likes assholes like you." Stan made the wrong assumption that I would stop in my tracks and turn around. He had assumed I would agree and wait for Pete.

Well, I hadn't met Pete. I might like Pete. As for Stan, I didn't like Stan for the mere fact that he was Stan and he was there in front of me. Pete might not be in this position with me, depending on my mood.

"Are you calling me an asshole, motherfucker?" There went the papers on his desk. There went his arms up to block me. His mouth screamed for security and he didn't hold back from manhandling me.

The rooms piled out like army ants being called to duty. All of them in green aligned the walls with structure and whispers. They weren't security, no. they were my cohorts, my colleagues, my enemies for the next year.

I pushed Stan down to the ground and wailed my fist into his head. The chair scooted back and Stan stumbled for his footing. I shoved into the desk, knocking over the phone. I wasn't trying to start trouble. I mean, I was starting it, but I couldn't control myself.

Even while I struggled to get a good shot at his face, my mind raced with the idea of how crazy I was. I wanted to hurry up and get it out of my system. I could face the consequence of this, but not with the pressure built up from not finishing.

"Deburke, I don't even know you!" Stan could hold his own. He picked me up and slammed me down. As I fell, my head hit the desk. The fight had to stop, for now. I had a migraine like a bitch. Quickly, I realized that my head injury was at stake. I could damage myself even more.

"Alright, alright, stupid motherfucker, get off of me!"

By then, the security guards came up and hauled me away. They wouldn't let me walk. My feet drug the ground as I tried to gain balance, but they drug on. I was shoved into a room, similar to mine, but with padding on the walls.

Great, a real insane asylum room, this place was for crazy ass straightjackets. The door slammed, locks echoing down the hallway. My eyes danced to each wall, bouncing my vision from side to side. Nothing. I was in here with nothing but pads.

I could go crazy just from looking at this shit. What did they want me to do? Unfortunately, the shrink was not off of duty, yet. She paid me another visit.

"You know, if you wanted a tour from Stan, pounding his head wouldn't have guided you very far. You're lucky he's okay. Do you know what happens to people who hurt our staff?"

I thought of chains and electrocution. Maybe whips and belts. Better yet, I thought of being expelled. I didn't answer.

"They add onto your sentence, Christopher. You don't get kicked out of here, by no means. For a court ordered teen such as yourself, you are demonstrating that one year isn't enough time to assist in your disruptive behavior. The next time you decide to go into combat, I'm sure Dean will have a few allocations up his sleeve." The doctor hovered near the door with her arms crossed.

She wasn't playing around. In fact, I think I pissed her off and stepped on a few nerves along the way.

"How could you attack Stan? He did nothing to you. Am I going to have to watch my back around you? Can I trust you?"

It wasn't that she was concerned for my behavior. I had frightened her. She was scared for her safety. In all reality, I didn't think I was intimidating enough to be accused of such a thing. Stan was asking for it. He called me an asshole.

"You know, he called me an asshole." I stood as she backed up flush with the door.

"He said you were already on your way to attack him before he called you that. No, he shouldn't have provoked you, but…that didn't justify your behavior."

I paced and paced. I felt my eyes wired with indecision. They burnt for something to focus on. I crossed my arms not knowing what to do with them. "Since when does my behavior have to be justified? I don't have to give you an excuse or reason or any fucking explanation for why I do what I do. He was pissing me off."

"Why?" It was more like a plea, a whine to understand me.

"Because I fucking felt like it. He should have left me alone. He shouldn't have been there." I knew it was stupid. There, I was wrong. Fuck it.

"I'm going to let you leave, now. I want you to think about this fight and use it for future references. When you get an urge to hurt something just because you feel like it, come get me. We have punching bags and running tracks for ventilation. It doesn't always have to resort to this. I want to help you, not provoke you." She remained at the door, too frigid to give me a pat or touch on the shoulder for support and comfort. She knew better.

"Bullshit." I brushed passed her long enough to absorb her atmosphere. It was a breeze of fresh linen, something that reminded me of yet, something else white and sanitary.

"Cardy, I'm serious. I'm not like anyone else around here. I keep my promises and drop everything that I'm doing at the slightest whisper of need."

I turned back for half a second. "Don't call me that!"

Chapter Twenty-Four
Basia

Slowly, gradually, at the pace of a snail, as deep as the ocean and as high as Mt. Everest, I was making some sort of progress. I opened my eyes every morning. I hung my legs off of the bed. It took me another hour to step down, but I did it. I was taking a shower and keeping the drool in my mouth when I chewed.

My tears had dried up. The trench of an empty canal stayed on my face. A permanent frown appeared with it. I still couldn't get up enough nerve to bounce up my curls or hydrate the roots, but…a pony tail was good enough. At least it wasn't in my face or matted to my cheeks.

I actually cut my toenails and shaved half of my legs. I didn't care to shave my thighs. Who would see my thighs? On a sunnier day, a feel good day, maybe I'll work the razor against my skin. Until then, nobody was going to make me strip my thighs of hair.

Life seemed to go on with or without me. I figured that much. Why be a part of it if it didn't want you? Why head out into the world with all the protective gear strapped to my back, when all I needed was a raincoat?

I thought metaphorically, lately. Who cares?

The summer was a hot one, yippee. The sun loved to glow into late evening and attempt to singe me through the shades. The moon liked to hide on every day that I attempted to search for it. The clouds seemed to get thicker and grayer and closer if it rained. On foggy days, I felt that death was surrounding me, knocking on my door. Death as in depression not the actual reaper, get with it.

But, I still moved about like a fat squirrel, ever so quietly, gathering up little tidbits here and there, getting ready for something colder. Had to do my duty. Had to protect my child. Had to cook her soup and smack her hand and tie her damn shoes.

Thankfully, I had Amanda and Darron. Amanda loved to take her fingers and stretch my lips out to present a smile. She'd pull back my eyebrows and force my eyelids to open. She'd drawback the curtains and shine my face with her tiny mirror. Amanda was there for me.

As for Darron, I couldn't ignore him. He was the loud mouth, the bass that kept his mouth open too long. He'd jump on the bed, stomp around like a giant that he wasn't. He'd sing even louder, songs that he knew I hated. He'd make Jasmine sing with him in spite. They were a team, Darron and Jasmine. The "I bother Basia" team.

My spunk was gone. My bounce had flattened. My bowl full of jelly became crust.

"God help me." I muttered too low for anyone to hear. I wasn't asking for God's help. I was figuratively speaking. You know, metaphorically, figuratively, not matter of factually, or literally?

"Basia, here's your plate of food." Darron dropped the yellow ceramic plate onto a TV tray that kept me company. He wasn't polite. I had worn him thin. I grew on him like a tumor, growing, growing, until...burst!

I curled my lip in a thank you way, or, telepathically, I was hoping he got the message. I wasn't hungry, anymore. An hour ago, when Darron was above me, drilling scrambled eggs into my taste buds, I was hungry. But now, my stomach had adapted on a few crackers that crumbled on his night stand. I deserved crumbs.

Darron unfolded his card table chair. He sat it down precisely in front of me. I couldn't see the TV, anymore. He began to hum a tune that I hated, tapping his foot to the beat.

"Excuse me, retard, you're in my way."

"Don't start this shit, again." Darron shook his head in disbelief.

You wanna know something? Lately, his vocabulary has included "ass," "damn" and "shit." He hasn't worked up enough nerve to shout out the "f" word, or dare call me a "bitch," but, it was coming.

His leg was getting longer. I guess the other leg might have been, too. That's how it usually works. Only one of his feet was on the bed, the other was grounded to the floor. I think he might be catching up with puberty. His voice has been cracking for the past two years, now. Wouldn't by now it would get deep? I mean, how deep can little Darron's voice get? It was amusing. Even when he tried to mock deep voices to Jasmine, I could get deeper than him.

"Uh oh," I smirked, pointing at his face.

He grabbed his chin as if he had some food particles still on it. "What?"

"I think…" and I got just a little bit closer to observe what was invisibly there. "Yep, I think I see a hair…right there, next to your lip!" I was joking, of course.

His eyes widened. He so wanted to grow something there. He was dying to reach manhood. He jerked up to look into the mirror. By that time, I had jumped up, folded the chair and tossed it out into the hallway.

Now, I can see the TV.

"Oh my God, you get on my nerves!!" He screamed and stormed out of his bedroom.

I only smiled in accomplishment.

That was how my days went. I had only Darron to bother. I did a good job at it, too. Everyone has always said that if I put my mind to it, I had the creativity to be productive in the best sense. I used to use that on my school work. Study, study, study. Think, think, think. Now, all that energy was put to some great use. I bothered Darron.

Amusing, isn't it? All my days focused on how to ruin Darron's good nature. A part of me wanted him to hate me as well. Throw me out into the snow, if only it had been snowing.

Oh, why was I self indulging? Where were manners? Darron had put up with my nonsense for a good two years, now. Maybe more. I forgot to keep count on how many days turned into weeks that turned into months and years. Where did the years go?

I'll tell you where my manners went. Right up Cardy's ass as soon as he got hit by a car. That's where. I was tired of being a good girl. I was tired of praying to a God who didn't listen. I was exhausted from being a mother and being cooped up in this house. How would you feel?

My parents. Oh where do I start? Did they not think of me? Did Cardy not think of me? Where was I in all of this shit? Where was poor little church bitch in all of this chaos? At Darron's, that's where.

"Look at her, all she does is lay there while I do all the house work." Darron had someone beside him, talking about me, in front of me. He was standing in his doorway, in MY doorway.

Kyle, his stupid big brother, poked his head in. Dreadlocks. Kyle was sporting dreadlocks. Good word, huh? Sporting, I can pick up a few words here and there, watching TV and listening to Becca and Loren ramble on about yet another teen party.

"Dude, she looks depressed."

"Ya think?" I cocked, giving him my biggest frown of the day.

Kyle took it upon himself to enter my heavenly abode. "Why don't you ride skateboards, anymore? I thought it was kind of cool to see a girl on one."

Silly Kyle, boards are for happy people.

"I have mine, if you don't have one." He offered. I saw Kyle's skateboard. It was in the hall closet next to the knickknacks that we used to bowl through. It reminded me of Cardy.

"No." not even a no, thanks.

He pushed his dreadlocks behind his shoulders like a girl would do if she had too long of hair getting in her eyes.

"Who does your hair?" I finally asked, too bored with coming up with my own answers on it.

"Oh, you like? Sherrice does them." He seemed proud in it. I wasn't.

"You don't wash them, do you?"

"Can't."

"He's gross, Basia. Don't admire disgusting fashion. He has none." Darron commented. Who wanted his opinion? Certainly, not me.

I stretched my legs down and arched my back. Apparently, my shirt had risen above my navel and it caught Darron off guard. He rushed passed Kyle and pulled the cover up over my body.

"What the hell are you doing to me?" Offended, I jerked the cover back down.

"You're practically naked!"

Okay, I was in Amanda's night boxers. I was in a small pajama shirt that used to be Angie's when she was twelve. Before she got fat. Didn't matter. I wasn't showing off any skin that any other girl wouldn't have strutted around in the mall. Jeesh, Darron was jealous, wasn't he?

It gave me an idea. "Hey, Kyle, where would I go if I wanted to get my belly button pierced?" It was a simple answer and it wasn't like I wanted one. I just wanted to know. I raised my shirt, patted my stomach and wiggled my finger into my navel. I wanted the attention, sorry if that's surprising.

Darron "hmmpf,'d" and paced out of the room.

Kyle got closer. "I don't know, the girls go somewhere outside of Cheriton.

It's a small run down town where people go for tattoos. If you trusted Boo's cousin, I bet he could do it."

Boo's cousin. Hell no. I didn't know him, didn't want to know him, and never heard about him. No, thanks.

A girly thing happened to me, right then. My body was on fire for no reason. I didn't like Kyle at all. But, when Darron had reacted the way that he did, I liked it. I felt alive. I felt like I was purring like a cat. An internal purring had taken over my body. I wanted to sleep with Kyle, just for a flash of a millisecond.

I didn't feel ashamed. I felt on fire. I wanted something so badly to penetrate me. Something to wake me up and bury into me like a big fat…

"Basia!!" Darron jerked me out of my daydream as I stared directly at Kyle's you know what. Darron caught me looking, but Kyle did not, thank the lord.

"You have to go!" Darron shoved his palms into Kyle's chest and guided him out to the hallway where the chair sat.

He slammed his door and slapped my face. "What the hell were you doing?!"

Shocked, I fell silent. I didn't know what came over me. I couldn't believe that Darron had slapped me. I couldn't believe that for that millisecond of thought, I was thinking of someone other than Cardy's you know what. Even then, the thought of Cardy's was rare.

I burst into tears. "I don't know, Darron, I swear. I really don't know."

"Were you really looking at my brother like that?"

I could imagine the curiosity in my face. I had never seen one, not even in books. Those things were hidden from me. Kyle's may have been covered by his pants but, I knew what was behind it. I knew the bulge of fabric was cradling something that was forbidden.

I was only sixteen. Many sixteen year olds had seen them, but I didn't. I may have been with Cardy and felt one. I may have gotten pregnant by one, but in all honesty, I had no idea of what one looked like. The thought was getting the best of me.

"I don't know." I felt my face turn bright red and in an instant, Darron knew the answer. I had to justify my behavior. "I don't like your brother. I wasn't thinking of him like that! It's just that, I never…I don't know. I never saw one, Darron. He was close enough…I was sitting down, he was standing…"

"Oh, shut up, Basia! You act like it's something interesting. It's not! What if he saw you? Your eyes were staring hard. It's sick. You can't stare at my brother like that! It's disgusting!" I think he was more jealous that I never stared at his package. Well, for one, he was small. His pants didn't push out or bunch up around that area. Kyle's did.

And yeah, it wasn't anything special. Kyle had just been there and sparked an interest. Whoever it would have been, I would have looked. It wasn't like Kyle was…what was the nicest word for it? He wasn't…erect or anything, not that I knew of.

"If you wanted to see one, I could show you…"

I closed my eyes before he continued. I squealed a quick no before he said more.

"I was just saying, Basia. I don't ever want you to look at my brother like that, again!"

Later, as I lay on the bottom bunk staring up at the ceiling of it, I imagine if I hadn't stopped Darron. What would have come of it? Would he have taken it out and pointed to the different parts of it? Were there different parts of it? I felt ashamed to even think about it.

It was a taboo in my household. God would strike me dead if he knew that my mind was at work with dirty thoughts. But nevertheless, my mind was hard at work. I wanted to see one, at least on paper. I didn't want anyone to show me or explain to me, either. I wanted it to be my secret.

Of course, I had seen drawings that little boys drew in fifth grade, large ovals with two circles underneath. It never got more detailed than that. Was that how it looked? Was it curved like a baseball bat?

I shoved the pillow over my head. Dirty little Basia. I shouldn't be thinking of this at all. My mind was being controlled by the devil and I knew it. The devil had forced himself into my conscience and was planting bad seeds in it. I forced the pillow harder onto my face. I squeezed my eyes until I saw black spots.

Temporarily, I had overpowered the devil. The thoughts were shamed away.

Chapter Twenty-Five
Binderman

"Roll me a blunt, dog. I hadn't smoked since I got this shit on." I tapped Terrance in the arm with my small cast to usher me into the house. Frankie's house was a brick one with a covered porch and swing. The swing was filled with teenagers drinking and swaying it into the others behind.

What I hated the most was the space. People didn't have the rooms I had. People squeezed about a hundred or so bodies into little 12' by 12' rooms. The air was always thick with sweat and breath. This was the case, tonight. Any other night, I would have turned around and left. I didn't have time to waste a night on shit like that.

But, the last time I left a party, J.D had died. It had been awhile since I thought of J.D. I missed him. He was crazy and tempered, but he was as close as a best friend I had. Brian came second, until J.D wanted to compete against me with Cardy.

Terrance pushed through the barricade to the blunt station. Frankie stood with Anthony rolling the night's supply of budd on the kitchen counter. The counter was small and in the corner. It was the only one in the kitchen. It didn't help to be behind the refrigerator. Next to it were the baggies of cocaine. Anthony and his cousins, his brothers, his entire family, were cokeheads. They did more coke than anyone I knew. Well, J.D was a close second.

"Hey, baby. Here, on the house." Anthony grinned his thin lips up like the joker. He was quick to act like a big shot. Everyone knew that he wasn't shit. I was the shit.

I took it without gratitude. I didn't owe him shit. I turned around with a nod and headed back through the crowd. I was getting claustrophobic. Too many people being too close to me. I liked my space. I liked my wide open space.

"Dog, I don't know. This shit is pissing me off." I was referring to the constant sway as people knocked into me. I lit the blunt, inhaled, and relaxed. It hit me, instantly.

Terrance huddled near, hunching his shoulders as if it would help keep people from pushing him farther away. "No shit, I should have thrown a party."

His house was bigger. It was two stories, brick and open. His rooms were giant with raised ceilings. It was clean and straight. New shit in and out. His parents were older, retired actually. He was an only child and given the world. I wish the party was there, too.

"Is that Ashley Pitt?" I noticed her from afar. She stood near the bathroom talking to a girl. She didn't really show up at parties.

She stood smiling with her bright white teeth. Her hair was naturally curly, puffed up and all over the place. Her face was fresh, round and bright. Her cheeks were tinted pink as her smile never faded. Her eyes were big and blue, always grinning with her smile. She was curvy, partially from the cheerleading influence of her last seven years. I heard she went to Cheriton University, cheerleading still.

She had stayed on our hit lists, but out of grip. No one had banged her. She was worth fifty good points because of her dignity. She went out with Steven Stone, who now plays at UCLA. When Foster declined, they picked Steven up.

Ashley was a good girl. She veered away from the cheerleader group and worked with the yearbook committee. She was a straight A student. She didn't party. Every now and then, she'd show up with Steven who rarely partied, as well. They were a couple, a good solid couple.

"Damn, dog. Tonight's the night. Fuck a party at my house." He knew exactly what I was thinking. Steven Stone was out of town, out of state, rather. It was worth a shot, a shot of Tequila.

I pried my way towards her with Terrance trailing close. Motherfucker, he wasn't about to compete with me. I chucked him back a few feet.

"Dog, chill, I got this, you don't."

Terrance froze in defeat. There was nothing he could do. Cast or not, I'd knock him out, especially over Ashley Pitt. I'd break my whole hand if I had to. I had been drooling over this girl before she grew tits. I'm sure everyone was.

She eyed me, saw me coming. She nudged Delilah. I think that was her name, one of Angie's friends. Delilah smiled, too. They were happy to see me.

"What's up, ladies? Need a drink?" I leaned against them, palms against the wall. I was pinning them from the people, from escaping.

Ashley smirked with shyness. "No thank you. I had enough." She was beautiful, more than sexy, more than something to just fuck the shit out of.

Surprisingly, I noticed that they *were* drunk. Their giggles were rewarding. It was easier than I had envisioned. Ashley was drunk. Ashley was wasted. Ashley was there without Steven and giggling at me. It was a triggering pleasure.

"Ah, come on. It's never enough. If you say it's enough, you gotta keep drinking. Come on," I took it upon myself to walk Ashley, and only Ashley, back to the kitchen. Willingly, she went. I couldn't believe it. She held my hand, warm in my grip.

What the hell, it was exciting. I hadn't been this thrilled since…I can't even remember a time. I was taking her straight to Anthony…to rub the shit in his face.

"I don't usually drink…" She started to announce over the crowded voices.

"I know, what's the occasion?" I smiled back, realizing I knew nothing more about her.

She came to a pause and stood still. "I'm single." She didn't smile, but there wasn't a frown. I kept note that there wasn't a frown.

"Single?" I imparted my full attention on her. Rebounds were grand, but…six years in a relationship? Was it really cool to step over Steven and fuck her? And the impossible was becoming more possible by the minute. I had the biggest chance to fuck Ashley, tonight. I couldn't pass that up.

"Yeah," She shifted, uneasily. "We broke it off like a month ago. He's at UCLA, I'm here. It doesn't work out very well. I mean, we still talk and all. We love each other. It's just that…We think it's better to see other people, until college is over. What do you think?"

Little girls and their questions…In my eyes, she was a little girl, unaware of the intentions of others. She was sheltered from the party life. In my eyes, I saw the opportunity of a lifetime. In hers…well, I didn't know what was in her eyes.

"I think we need to go somewhere more quietly and figure this shit out." I detoured from Anthony and headed towards his basement. Down there, a sitting room with a couch awaited. Sure, people may have filtered down there, but…

"Get up, motherfuckers. Go somewhere." I flicked the light off and on for attention. A few strays had wondered down there smoking their joints and using a water bong in peace. They knew who I was. They weren't going to do shit. Like I said, I ran Pierre.

It was time to bust a move, bust a nut, rather. Pardon my coarse sense of action. I had to have this bitch. Her name had outlasted all the other females on my list, leaving her the most unfinished goal in my life. It was important.

"Now, what were you saying? Steven and you are finished?" I sat her down like a princess, fingers in the air. Bitches loved that shit and I didn't know why.

She sat on the edge facing me. Her hands hit her lap, palms up for explanation. She was drunk, still smiling, still giggling a bit, but trying to be serious. It was amusing. I loved when girls did this.

"Yeah, we…we broke up. It's not over, I'm sure it's not over. I mean, we need our space. We need to go out with other people. We never dated anyone else. At least, we'd know how much we mean to each other, you know?"

By then, her heartbeat was against mine. As she talked, I listened, right at her lips. I tasted her breath, the sweetness of the liquor rising off of it. She didn't smoke and that was a relief. I hated bitches who tasted like fucking squares. I didn't kiss her…but, I was ready.

"I just want to…" She was eating her words as her eyes watched my lips come closer. She didn't back away. She was unsteady in her reaction…but ready, all at the same time. She was preparing her lips for mine, drawing them into her mouth and wetting them.

"It was his idea?" I mumbled, feeling the softness of the skin on her cheek, warm and silky. Her eyes sparkled with curiosity, eyeliner thinly aligning them, glitter on her eyelashes. I could taste her…I wanted to taste her, her mouth, her skin…everything about her.

"Yeah, he said things were more important than us right now. We needed a break…" Her lips trembled with her words. Her shoulders shifted. She was nervous, not prepared.

I closed my eyes.

I took a deep breath and withdrew my body. I didn't kiss her. She said what I didn't want to hear. She had given me a reality that I didn't want to have.

Fresca.

I was thinking of Fresca. She *reminded* me of Fresca. Soft and sweet, too innocent to fuck with someone else's girlfriend, whether or not they were broke up.

I had put Fresca aside because our relationship wasn't as important as other issues in my life. And Cardy ran game on her. I couldn't return the favor. It was an imposition I couldn't get out of my head. Would Steven feel the same? Did all the motherfuckers feel this way when I fucked their girl?

I leaned back against the sofa. My eyes were still closed. I reached for her hand and raised it to my lips. I couldn't fuck her. I couldn't. I wanted to, badly. Cardy had done something to me by fucking my girl.

He had opened my eyes. He had fucked my girl. He had changed my entire thinking process.

"You still feel like you go out with him, don't you?" I knew the feeling.

She nodded in agreement. Her eyes fell to the floor. I think she wanted to break that heavy chain and kiss me, but…it was an anvil, too heavy to lift. She didn't cheat.

"I'm sorry. When we walked down here…"

I patted her leg. It was an odd move, but I did it. "Don't say it. I don't want you to do it. You belong to Steven." I was disappointed in this realization. Certain girls at this party belonged to certain friends of mine. Steve may not have been my friend, but…we had mad respect for each other.

What the hell was going on with me? I didn't like it.

"Ashley…" I started, but something hit my lips from continuing. It was Ashley ramming her lips onto mine, forcing herself to like it.

I kissed back because I wanted to. I stopped her because I *had* to. "Don't do this to yourself. Go home, call him. Fuck, fly out there. You don't belong here."

With that said, I stood. I didn't look back in fear that she may call me down to her. I left her alone for the sake of Steven, for the sake of my apprehension.

I shouldn't be here, either.

But, I didn't go. I couldn't go. Where would I go if I did leave…home, Angie's? No, I came there to get fucked up, just not with Ashley. I had another reason to drink…Fresca.

Frustrated, I headed back to the kitchen. I grabbed the first bottle out of the ice box and took a swig. It was already open, but I refused to think of germs. Not now. It was Jack Daniels, J.D's drink.

Shit, I was depressed. The shit wouldn't get out of my head. J.D was dead. Cardy almost died. Fresca is gone. My mother…

It wasn't the place to grieve. Not now, not ever.

"Dog, you look like shit. You see a ghost down there or what? You sick?" Roger's hands rested on my shoulders as the bottle hit my lips. Just what I needed…more shit.

I dusted his hands off of me. I didn't acknowledge him. I kept drinking, barely taking a breath. That was hard to do with J.D, (A.K.A Jack Daniels, the reason J.D drank the shit).

"Dog, I'm sorry about Teesa." Roger was pressing on.

I twisted around and shoved the bottle into his stomach. I pushed my body passed him and headed out of the house. I didn't feel like fighting even though I wanted to kick his ass. Not tonight. Tonight I wanted to drown in liquor, not Roger's blood.

He ran after me. "Dog, we're boys. Come on."

I shot around. "If we're boys, then why the fuck did you ruin my bitch? She's pregnant, motherfucker!"

It was causing a scene. Groups stopped talking and dancing and watched us. Roger and I had been boys since sixth grade, since I came to Pierre. We had been fighting over Theresa Gardeeni just as long. People knew this.

"I know. I didn't plan on it."

"No shit, motherfucker. Now, you're marrying the bitch? Do you call that being boys? I don't." If it was Fresca…Fresca, I hadn't seen that bitch in a few months, either.

Paranoia was setting in. what if…what if Cardy fucked up? He was always fucking up. He had more kids than my bitch ass…what if she was hiding from me? Hell, Basia did it to Cardy…why couldn't or wouldn't she do that to me?

It couldn't be the case. But I couldn't forget about it, either.

"You're mad at me? You act like you wanna fight me!" His arms rose out in defense.

"I don't want to fight you!" Although, I did.

"You know what, fuck it. You want the bitch?" He paced in front of me. "It's not your kid, dog. We know that for a fact." He was trying to justify or clarify or whatever the fuck you wanted to call it.

"It's not yours, either, motherfucker! We know it's a twenty percent chance that it's yours!" I knew who it could have been, and it wasn't Roger.

That girl was at my house every other night. If she wasn't there, then she was at Dewey's with Cardy. Yeah, the kid wasn't mine. But it could be my brother's.

"Bullshit. It's more than that! She never fucked you around that time!" Roger argued.

Did he know about Cardy?

This shit was getting out of hand. I had to control it. "Fine dog, marry the bitch, you have my blessing. But, if the kid comes out looking like me, don't come running to me with a DNA test, cause we both know it ain't mine, right?!" I was referring to Cardy…but, he assumed it was me.

"Yeah, whatever, dog. I'll see you around, she just called." He shoved his cell phone in his pocket and headed towards his car, headed towards his bitch.

"Later," when I feel like fighting, I guess.

The night didn't end there. I had a lot of more shit to get into, a lot of more shit to fill my head.

Wading back into the crowd, Jenna Williams, Fresca's cousin, hurled herself into my chest.

"I thought you were in Florida?" I cocked, still pissed at Roger.

"I was, but it's summer. I'm not taking summer classes. I'm here until August. Kind of cool, huh…like old times?" Her slurs were familiar, hiccups between words, her back stiff as she moved in too close to talk, like always.

I was glad to see her. I could ask her about Fresca. I had a million of questions to throw at her, but…not all at once.

"Come drink with me." I offered pulling her into the house.

Jenna was always cool to hang around. She knew me like Fresca did, as my secrets were always spread to her, either from Brian or from her cousin. She was the middle man, the messenger, Brian's girlfriend.

"You know, I broke up with Brian."

No, I didn't know that. Fuck.

We drank for a good three hours, passing up midnight and creeping towards dawn. Most of the crowd had slimmed down. We sat in a corner in the basement, too wasted to crawl to the couch. We played stupid drinking games that didn't make sense, making them up as we went along.

Astonishing as it was, I hadn't fucked a bitch, all night. That wasn't very usual of me. In fact, it wasn't usual at all.

But, my luck was about to change for the worse.

Jenna was stripping. I didn't remember why.

"What the hell are you doing over there?" Even though she was inches away from me.

"I'm hot, so hot. These clothes have to come off." Her shirt peeled away. Her bra came second. Her tits popped down and perked up. I don't remember seeing Jenna in that way, before. I felt myself rise.

"Do you see these boots?" She tugged on them. She couldn't get them off. "They were a present for Christmas. Hey, help me."

Together, a shirtless Jenna and I tugged on the zippers of her boots until they were both off. By that time, I found myself on top of her. Somehow, her skirt was gone. Her underwear was gone. She was completely naked underneath of me. I don't recall helping her out of her clothes, but maybe that's why all the zippers seemed to appear on her boots.

I never had sex with Jenna. I was never left alone with Jenna. Wherever Jenna was, Fresca was sure to be. Not tonight. Jenna and I were about to embark in something dangerous, dangerously erecting.

I kissed her, harsh and invading. She did the same. Our hands clashed against each other as we scrambled them to each inch of our bodies, intertwining our limbs. She managed to pull my shirt off and now…we touched, skin to skin.

I was too drunk to think. She was a bitch. She wanted me. My dick wanted her. That's all that mattered when the situation lines itself as it did.

My jeans were unbuttoned. My zipper was down. My boxers were expelling, and now…I touched her skin with my shit on her thigh, waiting for the cue. The cue was not now.

Jenna's name alarmed my conscious. My alter-ego tried to chase it down with an eraser. I knew this was wrong. It was a matter of will power. My body wanted to be inside her body. That's all that mattered.

Or did it?

"Fresca doesn't have to know about this. It'll be our secret." Jenna whispered the fatal words to my erection and I went flat. She didn't have to say her name. She didn't have to.

"Fuck!" I screamed into her ear. I'm sure it damaged her ear drums because she held them closed for a few minutes, later.

I rolled off of her. I bent my knees up to calm myself down. This was bullet number two in one night. I was shot down, twice. First, Ashley. Now, Jenna. I was thinking too much, even overpowering the liquor.

Jenna did the unthinkable. You would think that my shout would have turned her deaf, made her ears bleed. But, no. she climbed on top of me.

"Get it out, Boo. I need it."

Her face spun before me. It took awhile to understand that this shit was happening and real and not a fucking dream. She was definitely Jenna Williams, Fresca Taylor's cousin, Fresca Taylor, my girlfriend, whether or not we were going out.

If this happened...I would never be able to be with Fresca again. She would make sure of it.

"She doesn't have to know." Jenna repeated, rocking against me to work up my third erection of the night.

I tossed her off and sat up, wiping my face. Fuck! I couldn't believe this shit! Not in a million years! "*I* would know what we did!"

Now, that's all that mattered.

I would know.

"Get away from me!" I stumbled to my feet only to go back down against the ground. I couldn't get my footing. I was off balance and drunk. I was shirtless, too, but I didn't think of grabbing my shirt.

I fell, over and over, until I was crawling up the stairs. I fell against the walls, back and forth, until I was out of the house. I fumbled for my keys, but knew I couldn't drive. All the contents in my pocket, my chap stick, my wallet, my phone, my money, my half smoked blunt, fell to the ground. Fuck, I fell with it.

I sat on the sidewalk and stared at the gravel. I rubbed it against my hand, feeling for my keys. I touched my phone. I picked it up and dialed her house.

She didn't answer. The bitch wouldn't answer. I threw the phone down the street only to wonder after it. It was probably an hour later that I found it. I dialed, again.

This time, she answered.

"What do you want, I'm sleeping. It's five in the morning."

Her voice never sounded better. It was dry because she was asleep. She needed a drink, a Gatorade, like I was in need of. No, I needed coffee. I needed that cup of coffee that my Aunt Cathy had offered me, the other day. When was that?

"Baby, I need you to come pick me up."

She was offended. I hadn't talked to her in more than three months. And, I called for a ride, a ride from a party. It was definitely bad on my part.

"I don't drive, Binderman." She never called me that. It was a bad sign.

I laughed, but not happy. "Don't call me that name." it meant that I was in trouble.

"Well, I don't. We don't go out. I have no obligation to do anything for you." I heard the pause in her voice and then the click.

"Fuck!!!" I screamed in desperation. I patted myself down for my squares, but realized that they were not in my pockets. They were…where the fuck are they?

I dialed again. "Baby, baby, baby, don't hang up. I need to talk to you."

"What?"

"Your fucking cousin just tried to molest me, that's what." I needed to get it off of my chest before it got back to her. I was offended that Jenna tried to take advantage of me. That's what it was. The bitch wanted to maul me for the sake of mauling.

"What are you talking about? Jenna is in Florida!"

"No, no, no, she's not. She's here, at Anthony's. She tried to fuck me, Francesca. She got naked and was kissing me and tried to fuck me. BUT, I didn't fuck her, I'll have you know, that I didn't fuck her!!"

She hung up again.

This time, she called me back before I could recall her number in my soggy brain.

"What are you saying? Are you saying you fucked my cousin?!"

I laughed, uneasily. If I was sober, I would have worded it better. "No, no, baby. I didn't fuck her. Aren't you proud of me? I didn't fuck her. And I didn't fuck Ashley Pitt because she wanted to fuck me, too."

Click.

She was getting the point. She called me back, thank god.

"Why didn't you fuck her? We don't go out, anymore. You can fuck her, Boo, if you wanted to. She's yours, have her!"

"Baby, no…" I whined. I wanted to cry. She was enforcing our break up like it was nothing to be concerned about. "No, I didn't want to fuck her. I never fucked her before, and I'm not fucking her, now. I want to fuck you, baby, not her."

Click.

"FUCK YOU!!!" I threw my cell phone down the street and couldn't find the motherfucker. I wondered around aimlessly, watching the sun rise in the distance to a bright beam of light.

Fuck it. I'll walk. And I knew who to walk to.

Many scrapes and bruised later, I ended up on the doorstep of the place I needed to be in the beginning. I hit my head on her concrete step, fell into her wooden door, but pounded my knuckles wildly against it.

"Fresca!!!!"

I was too drunk to think about pride. I had to see her. It has been too long. We were too distant from each other. I'm sure…I'm sure if she saw me…

The door flew back and she kicked my head as she stepped closer. Fucking bitch. She didn't mean it, but still.

I was curled up on her little platform of a porch, too drunk to even sit right. I smiled, slyly. I held my arms up for her to prop me up. Like a fucking baby, I was.

"Hey, baby." I welcomed her anger. At least, I was witnessing it and not half a mile down the road to wonder what the hell she was doing with herself.

"Why are you here? I said you can fuck who you want. Go down your fucking list, I give you permission. Just get it over with. You don't have me standing in your way!"

She looked different, but good. I wanted to hug her, hold her, feel her existence against me. I needed her to help me, love me.

I needed her to love me.

I pulled myself up. I met her eyes. "Baby, Fresca, please. I'm sorry. There, I said it. I'm so fucking sorry. I don't want to break up with you. Just let…let me in. your cousin is a stupid whore. I hate her. I didn't fuck her. Ask her, I didn't fuck her. She told me to not tell you 'cause she's stupid, but I told you because that's what I'm supposed to do. Please, baby, please." I rambled as fast and slurred as I could, trying not to forget to say something, anything.

The tears came fast. She began crying. Instead of letting me touch her, she pushed me away. "I don't want anything to do with you, anymore, Boo. We're over. That's it. I don't love you. I can't."

It was my turn to create tears in my eyes. I didn't want to. But, they came. "Don't say that." I whispered.

All of my reality was gone.

"We're over, just like that?" It couldn't be true.

"Yeah, so I don't know why you're here. I want you to leave me alone."

My depression tripled, quadrupled. And then, it turned to anger. I couldn't help it. I closed my eyes. I exhaled.

It was all because of Cardy. He did this to her.

"It's Cardy, isn't it?"

She looked confused, but I knew to undermine the expression.

"What are you talking about? It has nothing to do with Cardy, Boo. It has everything to do with us!" she wanted to shut the door in my face, but I wouldn't let her.

"You fucked him, didn't you? You fucking fucked him. He told me about it. That day, that day he crashed, he told me you fucked him. You know what? You wanna know what the fuck you did to me?" I slammed my fist against the doorframe less than an inch away from her face. I wanted to crush her, if only.

"You fucked my brother! But, I didn't fuck YOUR cousin, did I? Fuck you, Francesca. Go have a happy fucking life!"

I forced my body upright and propelled it down the sidewalk. I was too off balance to walk the streets. I had to keep on the pathway or I'd surely pass out and get ran over.

I left the bitch to think about it, to weigh the options of us being brothers…I didn't look back. I was too fucked up to look back. I was too depressed to think about shit.

I even thought of death.

If I didn't have that bitch in my life, I wanted to die.

As drunk as I was, I wanted to commit suicide over a bitch, a stupid ass bitch.

Chapter Twenty-Six
Dr. Cynthia Roma

It was late evening when I arrived at Binderman's house. I didn't know what to expect, as he usually called me for house calls or made appointments. I had never forced my services when it wasn't on his terms. Today was an exception.

I knew he needed my help. It was obvious. And, I wanted to meet his brother, offer my services. He talked about his brother so much that I needed to put a face on him. If not my services, then at least I would have a good understanding about him. We could figure out a plan for his brother. Bin would appreciate that.

I had to park across the street. As many cars as there were in the driveway, it seemed as if they had company. I knew this was a bad idea.

I knocked on the door watching the sun set behind me. Sunsets were pretty. They could be taken any which way…the end of day, the beginning of night. The time where shadows crept out and the haunting began. It reminded people of being alone, of being cold. Or, it was all about hope, for the sunset brought another day to an end. Tomorrow may be better.

I always appreciated the concept of sunsets.

His sister answered the door. I never had the chance to chat with her. She had grown since the last time I came here. Her hair was still the same, long and thick, untouched and unprovoked. She was interesting, to say the least. Here, Binderman fancied himself with materialistic things, with stress and issues galore, yet…Roberta Sox seemed to be captive to his luxuries. She was always upbeat, unharmed, unaffected by life.

"Hi, I'm Dr. Roma. I hope I'm not intruding. I'm here to see Binderman."

Roberta stepped back and held the door open. "He's in there on the couch. He's not much of company, right now. I think he has alcohol poisoning, if you know what I mean."

I smiled, knowing exactly what she meant. Binji had another hangover. The boy loved to live with hangovers. "It's not serious, is it? Does he need to go the hospital?"

"I think he does. He doesn't. He had a rough night. He didn't come home until eight this morning. He walked home. He's been sick ever since." Roberta escorted me through the foyer and into the grand family room.

I had always loved their house. They spared no expense to create exquisite surroundings. It was Victorian with maroons and warm hues, lace, and roses. The wood carvings were remarkable, right down to the marble fire place that was incased in it.

There he was, wrapped in a couple of blankets, head barely visible under the thick fabric of comfort. His eyes were closed, his body elongated. He took up the entire sofa with his head on the arm rest and his feet smashed somewhere beneath the other one.

The cocktail table had a box of Kleenex and wads of used ones. A paper bag sat crumbled in the floor. An ash tray was overflowing with cigarette butts and a cup full of chilled coffee sat untouched. A Gatorade bottle was on its side. A small waste can was to the side of the sofa, I'm assuming to catch the vomit, if there was any.

Roberta left to retrieve her father, although, I didn't know that she had. I assumed she had left to read books or draw horses, which are the only pictures in my head that Binderman had shed light on to who his sister was.

I squeezed my body onto the edge of the sofa. Seated at his chest, I tapped his shoulder.

His eyes broke open as he adjusted his vision at who I was. He rolled them when he recognized it was me, his shrink.

"What are you doing here? Did my dad call you?" His lips barely opened as he mumbled. His voice was dry and exhausted. He kept his body still, not moving at all.

"NO, actually..." I was about to inform him of my objective, but his father stepped in.

I hadn't seen his father since Binderman was thirteen. Mr. B.J Sox was a man of irrational decision, quick to temper and cause distress. I remember this from my notes back in 1991. He didn't want to hear what he considered to be misbehavior. He wanted it fixed and fixed fast, as he had a flight to Belgium in two days. He wasn't about to grieve over something that wouldn't resume his wife's life.

He expected the same from his children.

"Hello, Doctor, fancy meeting you, here. You came just in time. Would you like a glass of wine?" His charm was never off.

In fact, I would appreciate a glass of red wine, but my circumstances were not the case to think selfishly. "No, thank you."

I stood to shake hands. It was the professional in me to do so. I hated hand shaking. It was under false terminology. I agree, you agree, we are friends. We were not, indeed, friends. I didn't approve of this man.

"He came in here, last night, this morning rather, like he usually does. He thinks he is old enough to drink, but not too old to be babied with the consequences. Imagine that." He chuckled politely, although, his next order was in my head.

Fix him.

"Well, let's go over a few things, first. You came home because of your other son, he needed you, correct?" I picked up my brief case, sat in on the cocktail table. I unlatched it, withdrew a notebook and hoped that my memory served me correct. Binji's chart was back at my office.

He did not like the information Binderman had given me. He sighed heavily and stood like a rock, a broken rock, fused together with mortar. "He told you about Christopher?"

I knew about Christopher since Binderman was thirteen. It was a constant conversation between him and me. He had a brother and he knew about it. He had never forgotten about his blood, so close in age, so far away from him.

"Well, yes." I admitted. His facial expression was firm and unwanted. He did not want me to know these things.

"Christopher has nothing to do with his behavior. He is a spoiled bastard who needs discipline. I don't know what to do with him." Or ever, I wanted to say. He never knew how to raise his children.

He continued. "I came home because my son, my *only* son, needed me. I came home for Binderman and Binderman only. He was crying. I obviously knew that something big was going on over here, but I didn't know the extent. Now that I know that he's spent up much of my accounts and wrecked my house, not to mention exposing Christopher to our affairs, he's completely and utterly ruined his future. The boy drinks himself to death, every day. He yells at me like we're enemies. He hates me."

My pen flew from side to side against the paper. This would have to be a family session, as B.J needed therapy, too. And Roberta, who stood in the doorway not wanting to disrupt or participate, must have feelings of her own. I needed to make her an addition, if not now, another day.

"I don't hate you, motherfucker!" Bin shot out from under the covers. He flung the quilts back and sat up, grabbing his head in doing so. He couldn't stand up if he wanted to.

The tension was thick. Too many things were going on at once, maybe not in view, but in the minds of the Sox's. There was a lot to settle and decipher. It could take months, maybe years to get to the bottom of this and iron it out like wrinkles on silk. I refused to think that this family was ruined. After all, I was an optimist, or I wouldn't enjoy my job.

"Are you alright?" I directed my attention to my patient. It was most important to let him know I cared, if only I.

"No, I'm not. I don't want to be here with this motherfucker. All we do is fight! I don't want to fight. I want to leave. I can't stand this fucking house. I can't stand anything right now." He leaned back against the sofa. It was the first time that I had seen him without a shirt on.

He had numerous tattoos. One was above his stomach, like hip hop artists liked to do, what was it called? Representing? That's amusing to me. Although, Binji's was of something I couldn't make out. He wasn't sitting straight enough. Three letters, but in Old English, was it a gang, did he belong to a gang? Did they have gangs in Pierre?

I wish they were in separate rooms. They wouldn't admit more if they had the other in ear's range. I had walked in on something great, something horrible. And it was the beginning of everything yet to come. I didn't know if it was for the worse or better. It was yet to be assumed.

"What happened last night?" I wanted to start from the beginning of this episode and work my way backwards after the current issue was resolved and out in the open.

B.J was about to speak for his son, but I raised my hand. B.J wasn't appreciating my conduct. He shouldn't be silenced in *his* house. But, maybe…he should. You hear more when quiet.

Bin swallowed hard. He squeezed his head together for thoughts to form. He groaned from pain, internal or physical, maybe both. He wiped his dry eyes, red and swollen. "I don't fucking know. I'm sick, that's what's happening now."

"Mr. Sox, can we have a moment alone?" I glanced over at Roberta who picked up the hint and disappeared down a near corridor. B.J huffed away. Soon after, I smelled the burning of a cigar.

"Binji, what is going on? I thought we talked about your drinking. Didn't we agree that you were going to jog through this weakness? What made you change your mind? You were doing so well, weren't you?" My disappointment was showing, but so was my desperation.

He leaned forward, glanced around. He wanted to talk. I saw it in his despairing blue eyes. "I was, but shit changed. I can't figure shit out, anymore. My head's all fucked up."

"Try again. What's going on?"

"I'm going to be sick." And he gagged as he reached for the waste basket. He vomited. His fingers gripped the upholstery as he couldn't stop. I felt awful for him.

"What are you thinking about?"

"Right now? I'm thinking about all the shit I can't control." And this is why he was puking, not only because of the liquor, but because he couldn't have control.

He dropped the basket and lay back down. He rested his hands on his stomach. He took a big breath. "It's over between me and Fresca. She won't take me back. She cheated on me with my brother."

"You know how it feels, now. Don't you?"

He compressed his tears away. "I want it to go away. I don't wanna feel like this. I don't wanna be like this. Everything is fucked up, everything. I can't even fuck a bitch, anymore!"

"Erectile dysfunction?"

"No," He laughed. "I can't get the stupid ass thoughts out of my head long enough to do it. I second guess myself. I stop."

"Maybe that's a good thing, Binderman. Did you ever think of that? Maybe, you're growing up. What was important yesterday might not be as important as today. Do you think you would stop if it was your girlfriend?"

"I don't have a girlfriend."

"Does that bother you?"

"Yes, it fucking bothers me! My other bitch is pregnant by my boy and they're getting married. All these fucking bitches are begging me to fuck them and I could, but I can't. Something won't let me. I don't like it. Tell me what to do."

"Is this the problem? You want to have sex with all these girls and something is refrained you?"

"No, that's not it. I don't know what it is. I don't like anything that's going on, right now. Nothing is in my hands."

"Your father…"

"He's a big part of it. I wanted him home, but now, I want him gone."

We talked for a good hour, going over a list of "fucked up things." We went over reasonable ways to cope and deal with these things. We set a new list of goals and what he looked forward to. We did this a lot, him and I. We lived off of lists. He liked to see the facts on paper.

My next conquest was B.J.

He sat with his head hung low. He may have heard every word that was spoken, yet he kept quiet in the kitchen.

"I think the three of you need time together, away from Pierre. I think you guys need to pretend to be a family and see how it makes you feel. As long as you pretend, then your feelings won't have to interfere. It'll be a test of strength, to use your will power to try to get along. Things can resume with your arguing when you enter this house, if it must, but…on vacation…no one, and I mean no one, will contradict any one's actions. Do you understand? Can I get you to agree to this?"

"I have been thinking…if I had stayed, who would he be? Would he be in college, a football star, someone who I would admire and be proud of? And then, I get to the point of rationality. My son is my son, no matter what he does. I love him. I'm proud of him. I want what's best for him. Because of my mistakes, he shouldn't have to be punished. I will do whatever it takes to mend our faith in each other." His voice was as deep as a bear's, loud and fierce, yet slow and steady like a midnight train. It was soothing, and full of bass…like a long drive in a car, humming profusely.

I hugged him for the confession. This man was wrong in his ways, but loved his son. It was enough to induce a goodbye and head to my office. I had to add these notes to his chart. I wouldn't get home until midnight, but…my job was my job.

What I had forgotten to do was get a view of his brother. I had no idea what came of him. Was he there in that house, somewhere? Did he runaway or go home?

I didn't have time to go back…another day. I could work for them and them only, and still not come up with the perfect antidote.

Chapter Twenty-Seven
Cardy

The lights automatically turned off at ten. A dim one replaced it in the center of the ceiling, dim enough to find the way to the door. Brett was already asleep when I turned around. I jumped up, aware of my new surroundings. I was scared of the silence that was even heavier with the lights out.

What was I afraid of? I couldn't possibly be afraid of the dark. My heart was racing with an uneasy feeling. I didn't like it here. The impact of reality was growing stronger. I wanted to cry. I didn't comprehend on how my life ended up being so screwed senselessly.

One minute, I had the girl of my dreams (Basia), a best friend (Darron), and a future in basketball, and then BAM! I wake up from a coma and with addictions and consequences. Maybe if I could piece together what I had been doing for the past few years, things would make sense. I could sort out the demons within me and I could clean myself up. But I couldn't even start, I…

For some reason, out of the corner of my eye, a shadow lurked. It scared the piss out of me. When I turned my head, it was gone, or never there. What the fuck was I doing to myself? I was paranoid about nothing. It was the silence, the newness. It was the cold hard fact that this was my life. It was shitty to look forward to.

I crept up, scared to wake Brett and afraid to frighten myself by any noise I might make with my shoes. I tiptoed to the door and pulled on it. It was locked. Oh no. I tugged on it harder. I looked out of the small window and down the hallway. It was lit by the same lighting in this room. It was the kind of light that made shadows out of nothing. It was scarier than Boo's hallway.

Wait, what the fuck did I just say? The thought was quickly replaced by anxiety of looking down the hall. What was I thinking about, just a minute ago? It was something about the hallway being dark. I continued to stare, to recollect that triggering piece of information to my past.

In the middle of the corridor was an intersection to another hallway. There to the right, sat a guard at Stan's desk. He had his feet propped up and his arms behind his head. That must be a boring job, scary, too. He was sitting out there in the middle of four dark hallways. Immediately, I got goose bumps and a cold chill. I looked away.

There was no way I could sleep, now. I was too paranoid. I paced awhile, until I decided to go over my schedule that they handed me a bit earlier. I took it out of my back pocket and squinted at the small print. It was too dark to read. I carried it to the window, the window with bars. This was a fucking prison, I'm sure of it.

Damn... group sessions, anger fucking management, life skills, and the regular academics, math, literature, science. What about history, didn't I have time for history? An hour for each, talk about throwing me into shit. I didn't want to go to any of it.

It was more disappointment. I couldn't even call my mom and complain about it. I was in the rehab's hands. I was turned over to the staff.

I gave up and slid my shoes off. I decided not to dress down to my boxers. I wasn't that comfortable. I eased under the thin blanket, the thin white blanket. I bit the inside of my lip and closed my eyes, forcing sleep.

As I did, vivid visions of skin flashed before me. A certain giggle lingered in my head. Some girl was coming back to my memory. I couldn't give her a name or see her face. She giggled faceless, shirtless. Her thighs straddled me. I shrugged off the thought. I still didn't want to think about sex.

Her bright smile kissed me. Her breath was warm against my neck. She said my name in a whisper, but suddenly disappeared. She was replaced with a different girl. This girl was in front of me, pulling me down the school hallway, giggling too. I was trying to get away, over towards yet another girl that I had my eyes on. This one seemed not up to the challenge, whatever the challenge was.

The memories seemed useless. As I lay on my bed trying to figure out any reason to be dwelling on my daydream, I bit my cheek so hard that I drew blood. Why was I remembering all of these girls? I could recall every kiss, every hug, every perfume that they smelled like. It was weird. They were all over me, hands, tongues, and...and...shit. I had to stop thinking about this stupid crap. All it was doing was frustrating me.

My fingers ached to touch. I had a problem with that shit. I rubbed my thumbs against the rest of my fingers, trying not to think about shit. Soon, my arms started in on wanting to sway. Soon enough, I wanted to stand and walk around, pace and bite more of my lips. I walked a couple more times to the door, as if it would open. Then, I pushed my face against the window, just to feel the coldness of the glass.

I was fucking bored with this shit, already. How could anyone sleep with the quietness in this fucking place? I needed a radio, a TV on, some kind of sound to drown out the obsessive deadness. I sat back down on the edge of my mattress, rubbing my thighs like I had obsessive compulsive disorder, maybe that's what it was. I couldn't sit still.

No, I had A.D.H.D, that's what it was. I hated feeling this way. I remember being younger and not being able to sit in my desk. I would raise the back of the seat up and down, rocking my idleness. I'd tap my pencil, bite it. Sometimes, I'd throw it at Darron. I'd open and close my text books, flip the pages, stand up too many times.

I learned to ask questions just so I could talk. I was a talker, back then. I wouldn't shut up. During an assignment, I'd turn it over and draw, because drawing kept my mind busy, my hands busy. Then, I'd flip the paper back over and finish before anyone else did. My mind was fast and smart.

At home, before my medicine, I drove my mother crazy. I was the kid who slid down the carpet staircase on her cookie sheets. I tried to swing off of the chandelier, breaking it twice. I drilled holes into her walls with forks and ruined many doorways by climbing to the top of them. Once, I climbed the roof and jumped with no hesitation. I was eight. I wanted to attempt to fly, and if I didn't fly logically (I knew I wouldn't) I wanted to feel the freedom against my skin.

I was always taking risks. I knew the consequences and still, needed to feel the adrenaline release it gave me. I was always coiled too tightly, wound up too strictly. I was a spring bolted to the floor, a hinge that never opened. I was the wheel that didn't roll, the strap that stayed locked. I couldn't get the pressure out of me. I didn't even understand this, until now.

Then came the Ritalin, my life seemed to go normal from then on. Sure, I was still energetic. I was up most nights, listening to my parents argue. I was up each morning, ready for the new day, never tired.

I thrived in sports.

I strived in everything that I did. If my mind was in it, I was a quick learner. I caught on and completed complex things at a faster pace. Spelling bees, math contests, band concerts, I was there, and head of most. And mostly, I was conceited. I knew what I did was good.

Where did I go wrong?

What the hell happened to me? Clearly, I was off of Ritalin. I would have never risked my life doing drugs if I was calm and clear headed. But, without my medicine, my thoughts spun out of control. Impulsive, compulsive, obsessive, and attracted to risk, I was a danger to myself and society.

Now sitting here, all I wanted to do was break out. White made me sick. White made me feel trapped. Locked doors made me feel coiled, again. Someone had to give me medicine. I couldn't live a year like this.

I lay back down and stared at the painted cement blocks. I traced the edges of each one with my finger. The cement was just as wide as my fingertip, flat yet rough. The blocks had small air holes in them, either from being made or from the paint not covering them, who knows. I imagined staring into Basia's eyes…I formed her on the wall and touched her face.

I didn't feel close to her. Did I see her in the past two years? Something about her brought a sickening feeling in the pit of my stomach. Something wasn't right. And, it made me not want to think about her. I rubbed the imaginary borders of her face off of the wall.

I thought about the rest of this program. Each week the students, patients, or whatever we were called, would take turns doing chores. Chores, I hated chores. What would happen if I declined such an offer? Would I get thrown into that padded room until I obliged? Would I get a day added to my sentence? Did I care?

My father's fumed face popped in my head. When I wouldn't take out the trash right after dinner, I'd get a beating. If I was in charge of dishes, he would inspect them to see if I left any marks. He wanted to beat me. He was looking for any reason at all to let out his frustrations on me.

Those were the days, huh? I was a good kid. A little high strung, but a good kid. I took out the trash, I washed those dishes, I cleaned my room every day. I finished my homework, hung up my coat and put away my shoes. I made good grades and made the honor roll. I won trophies and did my best in sports. All American good kid, I was.

But, it was never good enough.

Jeff was praised for his bad behavior. He came in all hours of the night. He drank, partied, and brought girls into our house at midnight. I'd hear them in his room, making a bunch of loud noises. His room was at one end of the hall, opposite of my parents. If they would look out of there door, they would notice that he wasn't asleep, but sleeping with girls.

Did he get in trouble? My mom sure tried to whoop him. She was alone when it came to his discipline. My father said he was a growing boy and needed to learn the hard way. He was just living his life, getting the best out of being a teenager. He was in high school. Oh, the excuses for Jeff's behavior were plenty.

So, why was I getting a beating for being good?

Because I was Christopher, that's all that mattered to my dad. I was the boy with blonde hair and blue eyes. I was the kid that didn't belong to that family. I was the reminder to my father that my mother had once had an affair. I was the consequence he had to look at for just being married to her sorry ass.

I squeezed my eyes shut. I didn't want to think about those days and my dysfunctional family. Jeff was dead. My parents got a divorce. My mom hadn't spoken with him since the night of Jeff's accident. He was out of our lives forever. He had no reason to stay around. I wasn't his son. His wife wasn't his wife.

The anger filled my lungs like heavy helium. Ironic that helium is light weight, but still, my anger floated with a heavy lift, tugging me to react with force. I never liked my dad. I loved my mom, but never respected her decisions.

That was that. I was filled with heavy helium, coated with titanium. Whatever the metaphor, combustion was about to strike fire. In other words, I was a ticking bomb, erratically inclined.

My reverie started off fine. My last thoughts for the night hadn't triggered a nightmare, not yet, anyways. I was in a field, lush and tall. I ran with full force, maybe five years of age. My head poked just above the tips of needle thin grasses. I wasn't the only one with blonde roots. To my surprise, even in my dream, I was joined by four more pale colored tops. We laughed and rolled on top of each other.

The daisies swayed with the wind. My cheeks grew red, as did the other boys. I was at peace, for the cold didn't match the fun I was having. I kept giving chase to these nameless friends of mine.

One stuck out more than the rest. His eyes were as crystal clear as mine, full of admiration as he stared at me. He grabbed my hand and pulled me up, brushed off my shirt. His cheeks were round and cherry, like he had them stuffed with food. He laughed lightly, guiding me back to my mother in the distance. Our play had ceased. And he was gone.

The wind picked up. Tree branches tumbled to the ground. The lightning struck across the sky like wild electricity, looking for its next victim. The sky darkened, the rain poured. My friends had vanished. The storm raged on.

My mother's yellow hat blew off of her head and she didn't dare give chase to it into the field. The ground became muddy sinkholes, as my shoes submerged halfway down. We trudged, alone, back towards the car, but the car was gone.

We hitched a ride with a stranger, driving a blue mustang. You know the rest. Except, my mother lay on the hood in Jeff's place, her blue eyes piercing into me. That was odd because my mother didn't have blue eyes. In my dream...they are dark blue.

In my dream, my memories could twist and turn as they must, fabricating potholes and unearthing vivid hallucinations. I didn't know what my dream had meant. It was only a dream. Early morning or late night, whichever it was called once you went to sleep and then woke up and the sun wasn't around. Whatever...I saw that little boy on the ceiling.

His face was still fresh in front of me. He seemed real, as if I had met him before. I saw the curve in his eyelids, thin and moist. The tips of his eyelashes curled out, dark and thick. His blue eyes were the same as mine, connecting with mine. I couldn't get him out of my head. I can see him whispering my name.

A memory.

I tried to think of a time that my mom had ventured us into a field, possibly with daisies. I tried to recall a blonde boy, or boys, but...I didn't know anyone with the golden locks I was cursed with.

He was a memory, indeed. He was so clear and certain that I had to have met him. His cheeks were fat, swollen like someone had squeezed them that way. His lips were small and round, red as a cherry-popsicle. He curled them as he spoke. He spoke with proper syllables and pronunciations, too mature for his age.

Why did he come to me in my dream? He held a purpose, that I was sure of.

I even tried to close my eyes and follow him, for he was trying to lead me somewhere, somewhere before the storm. Instead, he took me to my mother. The clouds darkened to grey. Who was he?

I missed him. I knew I missed him. I felt so alone without him.

Chapter Twenty-Eight
Binderman

I was sick to my stomach. I had been since that night at Anthony's. Maybe Bobbi was right, maybe I had alcohol poisoning.

No, maybe it was Fresca's fault.

Either way, I was far away from Pierre, cooped up in some "supposed-to-be" cozy cottage that my dad owned. It was in a valley, below the mountains. It was secluded and wild. The trees hid the sun and the bushes hid the road. The grass was thick as fuck and I couldn't see where I was stepping.

No phones, no electric, no hot showers. No television, no bed, no peace of mind. I was sick, remind you. I didn't want to be there. My dad drug me into the car, didn't pack shit and forced me to this piece of shit hellhole that he referred to as relaxation.

Bullshit.

I had no energy to fight back. I had no motivation to speak above a whisper. My throat felt too swollen to open. My migraine wouldn't vanquish. I felt hot. I was nauseated with a sickness that no antibiotic would fix. Everything was hitting my nervous system at once.

The air was too cold and crisp. The trees were too tall. The damn birds were too loud. The gravel was too rocky. The cabin smelled stale and rotten. All the old blankets had rat holes in them. The floor creaked when we walked over it and I swear it was about to drop a few feet to the left. I didn't like it.

My dad's face showed disappointment, immediately. What did he expect? Maria, our nanny, didn't travel all the way out here to tend to the shit. But, did he complain? Did he pack his kids up and say "No, this isn't the place for my family to spend a few days…"

Fuck no.

"It'll be great. Remember when we used to come out here? We can rough it like we used to do."

Even Bobbi knew better. She wasn't the slightest impressed with the situation as she dusted off the spider webs in her hair. She hated spiders. "We had electricity back then, dad. And we had mom."

My dad grunted and began opening all the cabinets for pests. Thankfully, nothing flew, sprung, or jumped out with bloody fangs. Instead, remnants of their existence were the only thing left behind. You can imagine the worst of animal fur and feces.

It was contaminated. I took one glance around and detoured back towards my truck. I'd rather die of carbon monoxide poisoning, or pneumonia, a snake bite, a lost bear wanting to eat me. Whatever the circumstance, I wasn't about to stay in that germ infested cabin.

"What are you doing?" My father followed me onto the front porch. His footsteps were heavy on the wooden planks. He better watch it, six four and a couple Hundred and a half pounds wouldn't be supported for long…not by the way that shack was holding up.

Cozy cottage my ass. It was a death sentence, a death trap.

I stuck my hands in my hoodie after readjusting my cap. "Nothing, chillin', and don't think I'm going to spend the night in there. I'm sick already as it is."

His feet hit the gravel, shuffling with frustration. "Don't be a pussy. Be a man. If you're sick, which I doubt, you can sweat it out by helping me clean this place up."

He was full of frightening hope. It didn't persuade me at all. "Bullshit, I am sick. I think I have a fever."

He laughed, then. He pulled out my keys and locked the doors of my Expedition. "Sorry, son, It's time to rough it out. You kids are too pampered as it is. You don't know the real meaning of living until you sacrificed everything you think is dear. So bullshit on the bullshit and get your ass in gear."

Get my ass in gear, I couldn't even argue, I was that sick. I closed my eyes with regret and headed back to the porch. He wasn't about to force me to touch anything. I'll supervise…if that.

I dropped into a wooden chair and slouched. I covered my face with my cap and tried to relax my aching muscles. No use, they were sore. They felt like tight knots, twisting and grinding against each other. My head did the same. It throbbed my vision to blur.

He seemed pleased enough to vacant my space and join Bobbi as she clanked shit inside the cabin. I couldn't believe she was actually considering on staying. This was a nightmare. It was my punishment for the anger I had for that man.

Not long later, he reentered my atmosphere with a bow and arrow. "Remember this? I taught you how to use one of these. Your mother sat on this porch holding Bobbi. You and I demonstrated our skills. I know you remember."

I remembered.

"No, it's too long ago. I can't remember shit before mom died." And I wasn't about to share any memories with him about her.

His heavy breath exhaled. I glanced up long enough to see the desperation in his eyes, searching the thick woods ahead of him for something in common with me. Guilt crept close, but didn't overcome me. I had to keep alive the fact that he abandoned us, right when we needed him the most.

He stayed away long enough for the memories of him to fade with my mother's face. I had once shared a bond with him that many boys couldn't because their father's were gone or too busy. I once had him all to me, him and me, me and him, together as men, talking and walking as father and son. He loved me…once.

Now, all he wanted to do was corrupt my lifestyle. Take back the years of desertion and fix shit. Pretend shit…

I shifted in the chair, too ill to yell at him to leave me alone, or too ill with my own mistakes to bother with his. Either way, we had our burdens on our backs, together, as father and son…a distant father and son.

His hand gripped the wooden post, as tough as his outer skin was, I imagined him crushing the splintered beam with one squeeze. He was always a man with power, a cowardly power, a rough outer shell with a weak heart.

Charming and arrogant, strong and naïve, brutal and crude…that was my father. Selfish and full of pride, victim of death's toll, a soldier he was no more. Now, he stood on his last rope of hope, wanting his family back. Trying with all his ability to hold strong with attitude, with gratitude, and ignorant to anything I can come up with.

"I miss her, too, you know." Words given more to the wind, so it may rise up to the heaven and have her hear him. It doesn't work to speak to the air. She doesn't answer because she doesn't hear. I've tried. I've tried for many years. I stopped the effort the day I took in Cardy.

I still didn't answer. I heard him loud and clear. I had ears, unlike her. But, he didn't need me to answer. He knew I was listening under my cap.

"I wasn't going to marry her. I think, now maybe I shouldn't have." His conscious was unwinding. His secrets were ready to be released upon his son…me. He wanted to confide in me, tell me things that I didn't know, and would rather not understand.

I lowered my hat to my mouth, pinching the back of it with my lips. "What are you talking about? You didn't want to marry mom?" as much as the question was worth avoiding, I had to know why.

His cold eyes met mine, which in return, I closed them. I couldn't look him in the eyes. Too many connections were there. He could see through me, and I could see through him. It wasn't right to share such a connection, not when I wanted to hate him.

"She was pregnant with you. I had to."

Sixteen. My mother got pregnant with me at sixteen. She was still in high school, down in Texas. She told me the stories. Her prince charming rode in on a white horse with a key to another world. She ran away with him, pregnant with me. She left her family, her life, to end up with a man who cheated on her, day and night.

It was an awful existence. He drove her to suicide. She was twenty eight when she did it. She couldn't stand him, couldn't bring herself to leave him. She was held captive in her own home. Couldn't party, couldn't have friends over, couldn't do anything that a normal twenty eight year old would love to do. Her life ended before it began.

I jumped up. I had enough. I walked around the cottage to the back and dropped onto the wooden steps to the back porch. I wasn't thinking, wasn't sulking. I wanted to be left alone, to feel sick.

He came through the house and out the back door. He dropped the bow and arrow behind me. "Maybe later we can practice."

And, he left me alone.

If I wanted to, I could shoot his ass with it. I grabbed the bow and stretched it. I took the arrow, lined it up, and fired it in front of me. I missed everything. It landed a good fifteen feet to the left, not even straight ahead. The grass was too thick to retrieve it. It can stay there.

What the hell was this trip about? It wasn't going to solve anything. It was another premature idea of his. He was impulsive, like Cardy, quick to get shit in his head and do it, without analyzing the situation at stake.

In fact, he was probably the one with Bipolar, him *and* Cardy. Cardy seemed to have a lot on common with my dad. They were both arrogant and naïve. Both were confident and impulsive about everything. They reacted, destructed, and expected shit to change without adjustment.

Cardy, he was more like my father than I was.

I was like my mother.

Maybe he didn't quit his job. Maybe he was fired. F.B.I agents couldn't drink, could they? Could they have mental problems? My dad sure had one. Maybe he was fired because his evaluation failed. Maybe he was forced home.

Chapter Twenty-Nine
Binji Sox

1991.

My mother had been away for six months. She wasn't coming back. I knew this, but still waited up for her return. I couldn't go to sleep. When I slept, I saw her body. When my eyes closed, I heard her voice. She was gone, but she was there, everywhere I looked.

We moved to Pierre to get away from her memories. I welcomed the change. Still, she followed. I couldn't get rid of her face and I wanted to.

My father was distant.

My sister wouldn't speak.

Our cat was dead.

I killed it.

My life was over.

Within six months, I had transformed into a different person. I was no longer a son of Cerinda Sox. I had no one to please. I took that as it was. I was no longer her son. I belonged to nobody, especially Binderman Sr.

Pierre was going to be different. I had no mother. I had no father. My sister was a mute. My cat was dead. And that was okay. It was all okay.

I didn't cry. I was thirteen, well, about to be thirteen. Everything will be different at thirteen. Just wait and see.

I met someone at school, someone who thought it was cool to fight with the other kids. Someone named Jeffrey Deburke. He was the same age as me. We had something in common. And it wasn't age.

It was my brother. I knew this because he had the same last name as him. I made it certain that we would remain friends, so I could watch my brother grow up. It was the only thing that made me wake up in the mornings after my mom died.

I had a brother, someone who wasn't my mother, who wasn't my father, who wasn't my mentally challenged sister without a voice. And he wasn't my dead cat.

He was my brother, the brother that my father assumed I had erased from my memory along with my mother.

Well, I didn't. I remembered every detail about him. Every visit we had together. And, Jeffrey Deburke will stay my friend as long as I can force the issue.

Jeffrey Deburke introduced me to his group of friends. One, Kyle Sorum, was my neighbor. He was the kid I hung around the most because we were three houses apart. His little brother was friends with my little brother. Kyle and I had something in common, too.

My brother.

The other kids were followers. I could tell by the way Jeffrey ordered them around. They did what he said, when he said it. I thought that was awesome. He controlled a bunch of little kids.

I wanted that power. I wanted that control over people. My house and my life lacked control in it. I needed something in my hands, something to have "cause and effect" in.

That's how it started, my life in Pierre. It was because of Cardy, because of Jeffrey, or J.D is what we called him. He gave me the idea of control. He gave me the window to see my brother from afar, yet, in the same house. J.D gave me all the possibilities to live for.

"What does your house look like? Why can't we ever go over there?" J.D stuffed a handful of Doritos into his mouth and spit as he talked. He didn't care how rude he was. I was envious at how he could care less about what people thought.

I shrugged my shoulders. I never wanted to stay in my house, that's why. But, I never said it. I was the new kid in town. I hadn't the ability to do what I wanted to do. So, I let them come over.

"You have a piano?" Brian, a chubby little Mexican screeched.

"Not just any piano, dumb ass, it's a grand piano. Those things cost a fortune. Are you rich, Binderman?" J.D shoved his palm into my chest really hard just to get an answer out of me. In those days, I barely said anything. I talked with my fists.

I tightened my jaw as he touched me. I let it roll off of my back since he was my brother's brother. "No, I don't think so."

I didn't know what being rich was. A millionaire was driven around in limousines. I wasn't driven around in limos. Billionaires had people shining their shoes. I did not. So, from my perspective, I wasn't rich. I would find out, however, I was richer than them. And, that meant more to have a friend around who was rich.

That kid was me. I was the rich kid that people mooched off of. They wanted to come to my house, play with my crap, watch my televisions and play with my games. It was a luxury to them. What they didn't know was that it was hell to me. I hated that house.

What was more bizarre was that no one ever asked about my mother. My father was always away, working late nights or going to business meetings or fleeing off towards another country. He always found crap to keep his mind busy.

But, no one cared to ask why my mother was missing from my house. Did they not care? Were their mothers gone, too? Was it not important to have your mother waiting at the front door when you arrived home from school? My mother would have met me in the foyer. My mother would have offered me cookies and give me a giant hug. Did their mothers not?

There was this one girl who finally asked. Her name was Fresca Taylor. And when she asked, I wasn't prepared. I didn't know what to say or how to react. It was the question that brought my sister back to reality.

"Where's your mom at?" Fresca stood at the bottom of my staircase. She was already a cheerleader with scrawny little legs. Her mouth was full of metal, too big for her smile. Her hair was pulled back in a pony tail with barrettes at each side.

The color in my face drained as she said it. I watched her mouth say it over and over. I zoned out, going into a trance. I felt myself getting dizzy, head spinning. I was close to passing out…until Bobbi spoke for me.

"She's dead." It was the first phrase she had spoke since my mother had died. She stood at the top of the staircase like a white ghost, no expression.

Fresca's smile faded as her eyes widened to connect with mine. She was about to place her hand on my shoulder, giving me sympathy that I didn't want.

I jerked up the stairs after Bobbi. I wasn't proud that she was talking, again.

I wasn't going to congratulate her on her progress. No, I wish she had never learned again. I wasn't ready to hear those fatal words.

She screamed another victory towards her accomplishment in verbal expression. I gave chase, grabbing the scissors that somehow sat on a table in the hall. I think she had them out earlier to cut paper dolls. The shrink said it was good to shred paper when she couldn't use her voice to be angry with. Well, now I was going to get revenge.

I pulled her back by her hair and kicked her in the stomach. Horrified, she covered her face and begged me not to do it. But, I did it anyways. I stretched out her long blonde hair and chopped it off.

It would teach her not to speak when not spoken to.

I tossed the loose ends at her chest and stomped to my room. I shut the door. I was done with my friends. Bobbi had embarrassed me and now I couldn't bear to see them. See what she caused?

I still didn't cry. And I didn't feel sorry for Bobbi. I flipped on the TV and started watching music videos. My friends, my sister, my father, everything melted off of me as I stared at Run DMC and their Adidas shoes.

They had cool shoes.

Soon, I heard a knock. I ignored it. I figured it would be Maria, our nanny, waving the hair in my face, scolding me for my behavior.

Instead, it was Fresca Taylor. I just rolled my eyes.

"My mother's dead, too."

I refused to hear her, but she continued. "She died of cancer. She lost her hair and her chest and her life. She was always sick and in treatment. I didn't get to say bye to her. She died in the hospital. I was at school."

She sat on my bed giving me a good distance away from her. "So, I know how it feels to be alone, Binderman. You don't have to be embarrassed to have feelings. It's normal."

What did she know? She was just a dumb cheerleader.

My body went weak, again. A stray tear formed in my eyelid. I stiffened. I wasn't about to cry in front of a girl. I hadn't cried yet, and I wasn't about to do it, now.

"Did it just happen?" Her voice was soft and comforting. I didn't know what the hell she was doing to me. I didn't appreciate it. She was breaking my barricade.

I frowned, hiding my face towards the wall. I nodded, quickly.

Before I knew it, she was hugging me.

And I was crying.

Nobody knew of this moment, no one but me and her. It was first of many that she was there for me. And when word didn't get around about my episode, I figured I could trust her.

Fresca Taylor and I had something in common, too. We had no mothers. We were victims of our mother's death. We felt what no one else felt…alone.

I guess that's why we became boyfriend and girlfriend, not too long after that. We shared secrets and memories. We talked about the women that we couldn't talk about to our fathers. We talked and that's what mattered most.

My life had soon evolved. My first girlfriend and my new best friend had taken up my time to dwell. It was the beginning of a new life. I was happy with this life, this life without my mother.

In all honesty, Fresca had replaced my mother. Twelve years old, she would sing me to sleep. I'd sneak her in my house just for the occasion. She said that it was what her mother had done with her. And I loved it.

I fell in love with Fresca Taylor at only twelve years old. The problem was that I didn't know what love was. I didn't know that I loved her until seven and a half years later, when I was sitting in the cottage dwelling on, yet, another female ripped out of my life.

I loved her. Those words gave me pain because I didn't want to love anyone, especially a girl with so much meaning to my existence.

Sure, I could say I loved Teesa for the very same reason…

Late 1991

I personally met Theresa Gardeeni at Safe Haven, back when it was co-ed. I knew of her, before, at St. Paul. She was the girl who got sent home for wetting her pants in the library. She was the one who got caught smoking at recess. She was the girl who shoved me into mud because I called her a stupid little slut. She was Theresa, only known as Teesa in Pierre.

It was only a matter of time before she was sent to Safe Haven. The signs were everywhere on that girl. She was trouble the minute she entered class. And, she continued to be trouble when she wound up with me at Safe Haven.

The girls were in the same building, but shared different floors than us boys. It didn't keep us apart, nevertheless. When she recognized me, we joined forces. It was always her and me, me and her against this crazy insane asylum of hoodlums. She liked to call them that.

I was already going out with Fresca. I was already used to Fresca sleeping in my bed, singing me to sleep. I was already used to sharing my life with a girl. In fact, my entire life was surrounded by girls…my mother, my sister, my girlfriend, and now, Teesa.

Safe Haven was an awful place: Schedules and procedures and strict discipline, padded walls and tranquilizers and straightjackets, medicine and therapy sessions. My head had enough in it to have to deal with. I didn't need another list of shit to follow through on.

That's where Teesa made my stay worth the while. When I wasn't in a straightjacket or locked away with padded surroundings, I was sneaking around with Teesa Gardeeni. It was Teesa who gave me my nickname and the possibility to control Pierre.

I was sent back to Pierre with a reputation. Teesa spread the word at how crazy I was. I wasn't anyone to fuck around with. It was all bullshit, but it worked. I don't know how it worked, but it did. Teesa was only in Pierre for a short while, going to school with me. When she left, it was just me and Fresca.

But, if it wasn't for Teesa, I would have had nightmares in that place. She had taken Fresca's spot temporarily, singing me to sleep with her body.

I guess you can say that Fresca was my emotional back bone, there when I needed a hug, a shoulder, some company. But Teesa, Teesa gave me the possibility to release my anger in a different way, a sexual way.

And that started another piece of my life, sexual healing…getting out the stress in my head and letting it go out of my body…replacing the tension with something pleasurable.

I may not have deeply loved Teesa, but I was attached to her. She meant more to me than she did to Roger, that's for damn sure. She had been there in the beginning, a part of my legacy.

Chapter Thirty
Cardy

Gum after gum, caramel after caramel, water after water, my hands still felt crazy. I needed to chew something. My nails were bitten off too short as it was. My lips were raw. My tongue was sore from my teeth grinding it to lose this energy.

I had been there for a week and it was already starting to wear me out. I didn't see the shrink because I refused. I didn't go to my classes because I couldn't take the social atmosphere. Every class was boring, too. I kept to myself in my room, forcing Brett to find another place to write whatever it was that he wrote. He respected my intimidation and left me alone.

God, with nothing to do, I was bored out of my mind. I was hyper by nature. Didn't they understand A.D.H.D? They wouldn't give me medicine until I showed necessary need of it. Ha, if they only knew what the hell I was thinking. I was about to go ballistic. I needed to be running and spinning and smoking down this inner compulsion. I felt like a lost lightning bolt needing to strike something.

They denied me access to the outside. They said it was a privilege to be outdoors. If I didn't attend my classes, then I didn't need to join an activity. Well, fuck them.

My veins vibrated every second. Stop it, stop it, stop it. It wouldn't stop. I could feel the vessels in my brain beat with my pulse. I could imagine the blood flowing through, rushing with rabid fear.

Anxiety.

What to do? What the fuck to do with my time?

Everyday was unsettling. I knew nothing would happen. Day in and day out, I expected a crazy kid to try and run wild on the teachers. Rebel against routine. But, everyday was the same old shit. They walked, talked, and acted like zombies. They were all being controlled by a higher hierarchy.

I was sinking deeper into a depression. I was becoming less and less of a person. I was invisible to my own self. I knew nothing would change around here. I was tired of waiting for my year's end. Yeah, it had only been a week. I kept reminding myself that. I couldn't even stand a week locked away.

My thoughts collided with each other. I had so much to look forward to. I had been given a second chance at life. I could be drug free and sober. I could be nicotine free, too, for an entire year. By then, I won't want to do it again because I had been taught other options. It sounded too perfect.

On the other hand, this boredom shit, all these steps and rules to follow were eating at me. I wanted to be good, but then again, I wanted to make shit happen. And I mean bad shit. I had this never ending impulse to start shit because shit wasn't happening around me.

Everything was flat, dead, flat-lined. Whatever it could be called, my life was at a complete stop. I was wasting my time, here.

No familiarity. That was another thing. I knew no one. No place, nothing. I was desperate to get a piece of my past back. I wanted to cry, everyday. But, I knew I couldn't. I was a man, about to be eighteen. It sucked knowing that my eighteenth birthday would be passed up sitting in this hell.

Finally, I met with Dean. Dean was what people called him. He was the dean of Safe Haven. His real name was Dwayne something or other. But, he liked to be called Dean. He was a short man with a blue buttoned shirt and tie. He wore glasses and his face reminded me of Steven King, the king of horror stories. Dean was a fast talker and vigorous in action. He shook my hand quickly and abruptly. He offered me a seat and adjusted his tie.

"Mr. Deburke, I see you have made yourself right at home, here. You haven't been to any of your classes, stay to yourself, and won't give Dr. Roma the hours she needs to assess you." He was right to the point since I was taking up his precious time. He was more sarcastic and rude, rather than just plain honest.

I shrugged and leaned in his chair. I chomped my gum and glanced around his office. He was yet, another war fanatic. It made me wonder if he was related to Judge Calhoun. He had war modeled tanks and planes on his table. He had black and white pictures of war world one on his walls. A soldier's hat hung alone on his coat rack.

"Were you in the military?" I asked, flatly. I needed to know if he was going to drill me out, one day. I didn't want to be called out and spit in my face for not chewing my food thirty two times.

He adjusted his glasses in confusion. I seemed to confuse everyone, lately.

"No, no, actually, I was not. My father was in the air force. I took over this facility when he passed. The memorabilia is his. I kept it up in honor of him."

Well, what belonged to Dean, then? I didn't see anything that represented him. Did he not have a hobby? Or better yet, did he not have a life?

"So, do you want to tell me why you were skipping your classes this week? I know some of you like to take a few days to adjust to the schedule, which is always nice to ease into new situations, but, an entire week has been long enough. You see, Christopher."

That did it.

"Cardy," I mumbled.

"You see, what happens is when you don't finish the program in the set amount of time, it gets added on to the end of your stay. You wind up staying longer. You have a year, or twelve months, rather, to complete the treatment for you. This is what is recommended for your recovery. If we don't meet the deadline, you are not fully recovered. Therefore, you see, we must get you through the program for as long as it takes. We have a couple of kids here that use us as a hotel. They've been here a couple of years and don't see a reason to leave. They get room and board, hot meals…why not? They can't cope out in the real world. And, as long as someone pays the bill, we don't mind it. We continue their sentence and add on as long as needed. Do you care to join that crowd, Christopher?" and he purposely emphasized my name to enforce that he was the boss.

"No," I huffed out of his chair and out of his office. I was pissed.

I wanted to punch the motherfucker. I wanted to kill him, really. He knew how to crawl under my skin and piss me off. I didn't want longer time. I didn't want any class schedule. That's why I dropped out of school in the first place. Fuck damn rules, nobody controlled me.

What I had realized as I was walking back to my room was that I uncovered a small memory. I actually remembered dropping out of school. I remembered sitting in my room, on my bed, rolling a blunt, and feeling bored. It was the same feeling I was getting, here. I remember that all my friends were in school and I had no one to socialize with until they got home. Did I live with a friend? Did I live with a couple of roommates?

I tried to recall what my room had looked like. Just remembered my bed. The comforter was thick and cozy, some kind of expensive fabric, so soft that I was drooling for it, now. I had tons of pillows and no head board. I could see my face in the mirror across from it. My walls were…were…

Damn, I lost it.

Later that night, I had a dream, another one. It was a nightmare. Another one. It was that car scene, again. Only this time, I felt high and drunk, higher than high, drunker than drunk. My body was limp and I couldn't grab the steering wheel. A girl's scream was echoing in my ears. Her name was Lynn. Within an instant, I was having sex with her. She was crying because it hurt. The car was driving by itself, as fast as lightning, headed towards a lake filled with blood. A baby sat in the middle of the lake, screaming and wailing because it was drowning. I wouldn't look at him. I kept forcing myself deep inside this girl, even though she was crying. And then, all of a sudden, she was gone, and my brother Jeff was thrown through the windshield. His blood was all over me and I couldn't breathe. I started to convulse and the car flew up into the air and down again, into the brick wall. I felt the impact and immediately began screaming out a name.

When I came to, out of my dream, I was in the floor being rocked by Brett. Quickly, I shoved him off and hurled my body away. I was mortified and humiliated.

"Dude, you were having a seizure or something. I tried to hold you down, but you were fighting me. Don't think anything else, dude." He was embarrassed, too.

I wasn't having a seizure. I was having a nightmare.

I caught my breath and tried to calm down. I couldn't. I was replaying the scene repeatedly, in my head. Lynn. I was having sex with Lynn. She was my girlfriend. That baby, the baby in the lake…ah fuck, Brandon, Brandon Deburke, November 12th, his birthday…holy fucking shit!

I began to shake. A tingling sensation went through my body as more of my past was coming back to me. Tears swelled up in my eyes as I was realizing who I was.

Cold chills wouldn't stop. I was sweating all over. I wanted to puke. I was so nauseous. My stomach began to knot and toss. Finally, as I realized that I had a son, I hurled onto the floor. I was freaking out so much that Brett started to bang on the door. He hollered for Pete to help us.

I was having a panic attack. I couldn't catch my breath. My vision was blurry and my face started to numb. Flashes of Brandon were getting stronger. Memories of Lynn arguing with me started to hurt my chest. We no longer went out. I had fucked it up, somehow. And, now, this kid was out there, somewhere. He existed all because of me.

My tremors came back. It was the first time that I wanted to smoke anything and everything. I wanted Tequila. I needed to drink. The need was causing my body to tighten.

As Pete and the security guard came rushing through the door, I was horrified at my recollection of the past. I didn't want to be disturbed. I was angry at the world. I was intensely mad at myself. I began to battle my thoughts by hitting Pete in the mouth. Brett stepped back, out of the way. The guard tackled me and I threw him off. My tears were coming faster as my fear reached a new limit. It was now or never to escape.

I didn't care if I ever got better. Just make this feeling go away. Make the pain subside. I threw my fists wildly in every direction. I bowed my head to hide my eyes, forcing my body into them. The guard called for backup right before I slammed him to the ground.

Don't fuck with me, motherfucker. I was Cardy. Nobody fucks with Cardy!

I blacked out from reality. All I saw were my targets. I could actually kill a man. And, it scared me. I had forgotten the treacherous way that I felt, not too long ago. The crash had temporarily numbed my feelings. But, now, now I was back with full force. No one would get me that vulnerable, again. No one.

I ran down the hallway passed Pete's desk. My body slammed into the wall next to it as I ran top speed. I refused to slow down. Seconds later, I was flying down the staircase, two, three at a time. If I made one wrong step, I would fall to the bottom. But, I didn't have time for safety. I had to get out of this place.

I couldn't believe that I let myself think that my mom actually cared about me. I was a fool to go compliantly with her. and how fucked up it was to have to stay here, locked away, far away from what I craved on the outside. I needed shit. I needed that shit pumped into me to erase the memories. I didn't want them.

I had indeed, flipped into myself.

My memory was on fast forward, replaying the last two years in my head, as I ran. Flashes of Fresca, Jenna, Teesa, Brian, and most of all…Boo. I paused at the exit door as I thought of him. Boo. I had done him the dirtiest, fucking his bitch and all. I rubbed it in his face, that night.

Damn.

I heard the doors open above me. Heavy footsteps came after me. The chase was on. Alright, cause my fists were on fire and ready to break jaws. I stormed out into the lobby and was met by police. I didn't even hesitate. I charged the barricade as their hands gripped my clothing. I had made it to the front doors, but then stopped. They were locked.

"FUCK!!!!" I screamed. I had been defeated and now, being held against my will. I twisted, turned, used all my force to break free from their grips.

No luck. I was tranquilized.

Chapter Thirty-One
Basia

"Hey Basia, just hear me out, alright? I have an idea." Darron walked into the kitchen as I decided to play mommy and make Jasmine a bottle. That's what it felt like. I was in a never ending cast on Broadway, playing house. I was tired of it. I wasn't even getting paid.

I shook the formula and tested a drip on my wrist. It was warm and ready. There, I did my good deed for the day. She can say I gave her a bottle.

I'm sorry. I was just drained of life.

Everything was the same. I was a mother. I wasn't Cardy's girlfriend. I was living in Darron's house without my parents. I couldn't stop thinking of my problems. It was a constant battle in my head. It was over and over, obsessively thinking of the same things with no outcome.

Sure, I wanted to say that I do my best for Jasmine. But really, I wasn't doing anything for her. I'm sorry. I am so sorry for everything that I was doing to myself and my baby girl. Things were supposed to be different.

Maybe I should have gone to England, maybe I should have aborted...

There I go again, getting sidetracked.

"What, Darron?" I snapped myself to reality.

"Okay," His arms were already out for defense mode. He was only offering a suggestion and didn't want to ruin my mood for the day. I was also sorry that I caused him so much stress.

"What if I dropped out and took care of Jasmine? I already do most of the things for her, anyways. School just gets in the way. When school starts, I think I'm going to quit. You can go back if you want. You're better at that kind of stuff, anyways." Darron seemed sincere in his plans.

I didn't blame Darron for wanting to quit. Ever since Cardy stopped hanging around him, all he had to look forward to was the teasing that people gave him for his height. He was still frail, small wrists and legs like a pelican's. His mouth got him black eyes and harsh shoves in the back of the head.

Last year as a sophomore, it didn't get any better. His lip ring didn't prove a thing. Secretly, I think he did it to bring attention to himself, to get friends. It did nothing. And with his big brother out of high school, Kyle couldn't protect him, either.

But, for me to go back to school? I couldn't do that to Darron. Jasmine was my responsibility. He had done enough to last a lifetime of favors from me. I couldn't possibly owe him more.

"No way, I'd have to be a freshman, again. I can't do it. I wouldn't know where to start. And, besides, you do enough for me as it is. I can't make you drop out of school. You need to graduate. I'll…I'll manage."

He sighed. "It'll give me a reason to quit. You know I hate it. I'm flunking."

I cut him off. "You're flunking because you won't let me help you."

"I'm flunking because I don't want to be there, Basia. My mind's settled. I'm not going back. You can do what you want. It's on you. I think you need to take advantage of this opportunity. It's not like she'll miss you. She misses me. I take care of her." He was offended that I was interrupting his little scheme of things.

Yeah, she missed Darron, alright. Sometimes, I was a little jealous of him. She cried to him. She whined for his attention.

But, what can I say? I was too depressed to be there for her.

"Just think about it, Basia. It'll give you something to look forward to." He disappeared into his mother's bedroom, probably to tell her his idea.

How could anyone just throw away their education for no reason? At least, I had a reason not to go to school. How could he just sit at home, in my position, and assume his future would be alright? Of course, he wasn't thinking about his future. He was thinking about not getting up at six in the morning. That's what it was.

My eyes still popped open at that time. I may not have gotten up and did anything that early. I may have stayed in bed all damn day, but…my body was still in habit of school mornings.

I came to a conclusion when Jasmine wouldn't sit still for her bath. I was easing into doing motherly things, but…I hated it. I didn't appreciate her.

The water was still running. After scalding her little feet, I tested it and shoved her to sit. She quickly stood, grabbing the open bottle of shampoo. It went into her mouth and then poured out into her bath. I jerked it away.

Her hair was a mess. It was wild and twisted, knotted up good. It wasn't black like it was when she was a newborn. It was gradually fading to a blonder tint. Weird, I know. The ends reminded me of bleach tips, shading upwards to brown, then to a darker brown. I wadded it up and poured a plastic cup of water over it. It barely dampened the thickness. Unfortunately, she had my texture.

Her skin was a lighter version of mine, yet darker pigments around the creases of her elbows and thighs. Her eyes of course, were as crystal blue as a clear sky, shining with each sunray that struck through Darron's torn shade. Those, I know, belonged to Cardy.

In fact, her smile was his. Her chin was his. Her beautiful blue eyes were the giveaway. Maybe, down deep, I knew who she reminded me of. Maybe, that's why I couldn't bear to hold her. She smelled like him. Her breath, her skin…her chipmunk roll of laughter. She reeked of Cardy.

Her temper wasn't mine, either. She wouldn't sit still at bath time. I tried to avoid this time of night and let Darron do the dirty work. But, with him wishing he could quit school, I didn't want to burden him for much more.

Her hands grabbed everything in reach. The soap already had tooth marks from last time. The wash rag that plugged up the drain was already wrapped around her small fingers. Her smile widened because she knew she made me mad.

I shoved her back down, too impatient to get this over with. Her legs kicked out, her arms grabbed the sides of the tub. She made it seem as if I was drowning her, which I wasn't. I wouldn't dare. But, her reaction was accusing me of such wrong doings.

I tugged her out. Soap was still on her back. Forget it. I'll dry it. It won't hurt. She took off before I could catch her, down the hall, passed our bedroom and straight into Kyle's. She never got to go into Kyle's. She knew that.

Oh goodness. I needed a vacation.

I picked her up and she bit me. I screeched in alarm and from pain and hurled into the doorway for Darron to help.

"That's it!!" I heaved her into Darron's stomach and threw my hands in the air.

"If you want to deal with her, then do it! I'd rather go to school and do a hundred tests!! I can't see how parents have eighteen children!!"

Of course, I was exaggerating. What I really meant was I couldn't believe how people had two kids. I couldn't stand to have two, even if they were ten years apart.

Oh, yeah, Jasmine didn't dare bite Darron, her mother hen. No, the stupid boy had her spoiled rotten. He cradled her naked body and wrapped a small infant blanket around her butt. He started humming stupid little tunes that annoyed me and rocked her to sleep. Within fifteen minutes, the mean brat was passed out.

"I hate you." I mumbled, stomping back to the bathroom for my own bath. I was going to take an hour, no matter what. Even if it ran cold, I was going to take an hour away from existence. I wanted to sink and soak. I wanted to relax and think of a new beginning.

A beginning with books. A beginning without Jasmine biting me. Darron could have her. I didn't want her. Not right now, anyways.

Yes, school seemed like the only option. Maybe if I got away from her, and not around her twenty four hours a day, I'd miss her. I'd want to see her. I'd want to hold her and sing stupid Aerosmith songs to her, myself.

Chapter Thirty-Two
Binderman

I fell onto the pallet that Bobbi had made me on the ground next to the campfire. I watched her stick a marshmallow on a stick that she had found in the grass. It was sickening. With all the damn bugs around there, flying around, crawling, leaving sticky shit all over the place, ugh, it had to be contaminated. I winced.

My stomach was still knotted. My forehead was still hot. My chest still ached. My nerves needed a blunt. My head was trying to dry out from the liquor, but, I wanted some more. It was hard to cope with this illness being sober, whether or not it was from depression.

The fire was crackling, the smell of wood burning was rising up in thick eye-burning smoke. My dad poked at it, maneuvering some branches deeper into flame. He sat on a wooden chair, leaning over as far as he could to reach the fire pit. Mosquitoes hummed, softly. He smacked one away. He was peaceful, at least. Or, he seemed relaxed without worry to me.

I remained quiet, as I did on this entire trip towards nothing. I observed, and only observed. If I said anything, it may lead to something, and something may lead to an argument. Arguments weren't on my agenda, as I was too sick to bitch. So, as I said, I remained silent.

I watched my sister and my father share the bag of marshmallows. They were back to normal. Their eyes smiled with each glance. Their faces were full of happiness, the way a father and daughter should be.

Well, I wasn't going to let him get to me. She was soft.

I was tougher.

"So, tell me about Christopher, Binji. Tell me everything you know about him." His hand reached out towards the flame and let the marshmallow blaze into black. He waited for my gaze.

I leaned back on my elbows, looking to the black sky for something neutral to respond with. The stars appeared brighter, tonight. The sky was clear and black, shining its glitter upon the ruins of my life. It wasn't a good night for stars. Not when I wasn't laying next to Fresca, or my mother. It just wasn't right.

This whole situation wasn't right. I shouldn't be here with my dad and my baby sister. I should be out partying, pissing in the street with my cell phone in my hand. I shouldn't be dwelling on shit that I couldn't change or accept. I should be giving a fuck about the fucking stars.

"What do you want to know?" A counter question was always worth throwing out there.

I picked up the Hershey candy bars and ripped open the pack. I withdrew one and peeled the paper down, ever so gently. My fingers were stiff. My hands were shaky. But, chocolate was always worth the effort.

"I wanna know about my son, Binderman!" His voice could scare away the owls if he screamed any louder. He was firm and frustrated.

Now wasn't the time to be either. So, I took my second bite of the Hershey's. I wasn't about to talk with my mouth full. It wasn't my style.

"He's just like Boo, dad. I mean, Bin…" She corrected herself, biting her fingertips to get the sticky shit off of her fingers, even more disgusting and rude.

"So he's a stubborn spoiled brat?" This time, my dad grinned with his irritation. He thought he was something, calling me out like that.

"He ain't shit like me." I sneered at Bobbi for even referring OUR brother to be anything similar. "He's like you." This time, I waited for his expression.

"And what would you consider to be just like me, a coward, a traitor?" His eyes lightened with disappointment, as he assumed that I thought of him in such a way.

Coward and traitor, he said. Did I think of my father as a traitor?

He was naïve, yes. But, could I think of him as a back stabber?

"No, he's stubborn as fucking fuck! He never took my advice. He contradicted everything that I said, wanting to argue. He was against me. He was too quick to react, rather than chill and think of prevention." This conversation was already going sour.

I didn't feel like talking about similarities or personality traits, or anything that could give my dad more reason to apologize or hear me out. I just wasn't wanting to converse about shit.

"Then he's like the both of us."

"Bullshit, motherfucker!" I snapped.

Bobbi, ready to avoid conflict and end the tension before it flickered with the flames, she just had to add her two sense in. It wasn't for a better conversation, even though she thought she was doing well. "Cardy's a bigger alcoholic than Boo, I mean, Bin."

Jesus, holy whatever.

"I'm not an alcoholic, fuck!!" I was tired of motherfuckers trying to blame that on me.

My dad's hands went up to settle down. "Chill."

Whether he said that shit before or not, I didn't feel like hearing him say "chill" one more time.

"How many D.U.I's did you get this year?"

See? Here we go.

"None."

I wasn't lying. I didn't get any. I was too busy fucking with Cardy. I was too scared to drive too wasted, since J.D, Amy, and Wes caused me to be more cautious. Sure, I drove drunk, but…I was more aware.

Alright! I shouldn't be driving drunk at all. FUCK! I know this.

"Did you tell him about Devon, yet?"

I remember a time when Bobbi couldn't speak. It would have helped me out a lot right now if she never regained that part of her abilities back.

She was a fucking bitch!

"Devon, who's Devon, a new girlfriend?" His eyebrows raised in surprise.

"And he doesn't go out with Fresca, anymore."

I was about to cram all those fucking marshmallows down her throat. I felt the urge increasing. I should remind her who I was before dad left. Before we had to defend for ourselves and I would chase her around the house with whatever was in my hands at the time.

"Shut the fuck up, right now!!" I ordered, just as loud as my dad, earlier.

"Alright, alright. Chill out. Is that it, is she your new girlfriend?"

"No, I don't want to talk about it!" I scrambled to my feet and was going to make a mad dash for the filthy cabin.

Thankfully, my dad didn't follow. No, he drilled Bobbi for all the answers, which was worse. She didn't tell a lie. The fucking bitch wouldn't lie for me, not to our father.

"He's the one you should be asking about, dad. He's just as much as a mystery as Cardy. There's a lot he hasn't told you about." Bobbi's voice was about to betray me. I wasn't about to stick around to witness the consequences.

The floorboards creaked and screamed from the pressure of my weight on them. My footsteps were heavy and fast. I didn't know what to do. I wanted to hide or run, or anything that got me away from his angry face when he heard the news.

He shouldn't be hearing it that way. Bobbi should have known better. What the fuck were sisters for if they didn't protect your secrets? I couldn't think of anything Bobbi was good for. She was always a damn thorn in my fucking back. I had to consider her, I had to feed her, give her money. I had to make sure no one touched her, harmed her.

No, sisters were a burden. Little ones were, at least.

My hand froze on the back porch door knob as my father's voice echoed through the air. "What do you mean he has a kid?! What the hell is he doing having a fucking kid?! Why didn't he call me?!"

I hurried back to the front door to watch his next move. As scared as I was of him, my curiosity only urged me to stall. It was dark in the cabin. I'd have enough time to duck out of sight, right?

"You're telling me that this happened last year and I'm just getting word of it, now? What the hell, Roberta, you could have called me. You could have told me! This can't happen." He was beyond angry. His face was red and fuming. His stance was deciding on whether to walk towards the cabin or calm down. He shifted in posture too many times. He lit a cigarette and stared directly at me, although he didn't know it.

"Binderman!!! Get your ass out here, right now!"

I jerked back and took in a deep breath. I was never afraid of anyone...unless he was my father. I swallowed, but the knot wouldn't go down. I shook my arms to calm down. Inhaled, exhaled, nothing changed. I even closed my eyes in hopes that I would wake up somewhere else, anywhere else. But, miracles didn't happen like that.

I tried to hold in the tears. I tried to keep my pride from backing down and running. I wanted to confront him and explain. I wanted to be a man and take responsibility on my mistakes. I wanted to...

But, I couldn't. He would have to drag me to him. He'd have to force me to speak to him, cause I was now rushing to the back door. I flung out of it and almost fell onto the gravel. I refused to dash into the woods, where he wouldn't find me. I couldn't face that situation, either.

I was a fucking coward. That's what I was.

I ran to my truck, considering on busting out the back glass. There was a spare key in the glove box. It was on the extra set of car keys for the eclipse. Why I put it inside that damn truck, I don't know. But, it was there and it was an option. I was about to break in my own god damn truck and drive away from all of them. Fuck it.

But, he caught me.

"Don't you walk away from me, boy. You think you're a man, then talk to me like a god damn man, for once!!" He tackled me to the ground like I was being raided by the F.B.I, like I was some fugitive on the run. He jerked my arms behind my head in an awkward position. The sharp pains shot through my shoulders. I screamed in torture, but he didn't stop.

He even went as far as patting me down for weapons, maybe a habit he did when he worked for the damn government. I don't think he meant it. But, still...he handled me disrespectfully.

He turned me over and got in my face. His eyes searched mine for the boy from before...before my mother died. I saw it in his expression. He was now realizing that I wasn't Binji, his son. I was someone else, someone who made a mistake and now running.

I was still a boy. Not the one he knew, but...still a boy. I couldn't take this shit like a man.

I cried.

His fingers imprinted themselves into my cheeks, almost digging for me to reveal myself. He was desperate for an answer, desperate for the truth. I smelled the after shave lotion on his skin, the warm scent of the ash and smoke that the fire breathed onto him. I sensed everything that he was feeling, as we were too close...

"Why didn't you tell me?" His voice was a whisper, a plea. His hands were still pinning mine back. His knee was in my stomach, forcing me to stay against the ground. With all this pressure, I was lost with words.

"I don't know," I tried to avoid his eyes. I needed to avoid his eyes.

He jerked my face back to his. "What do you mean, you don't know? You can tell me anything, son. You know that. You could have..."

But, I couldn't.

My heart was racing faster than I can keep up with. Fear was staring me dead in the eyes. Fear had me pinned down against the harsh gravel. Fear was making my desperation cry out.

"Dad, I don't know! I don't fucking know!! I'm sorry, alright?! I'm so fucking sorry!!! Get the fuck off of me!! Please, you're hurting me!!" My pride was humiliated.

His huge hand let go. He crawled off of me. He sat to the side, defeated and emotionally crushed. I couldn't run…not now.

I sat up. "Dad," I rubbed my wrists as if they were just in handcuffs. The tears were still coming. "I'm sorry. I couldn't tell you…"

"Why?"

"Because I didn't want to disappoint you."

"Well, that's not the point. The point is that you have a fucking kid…Jesus Christ…Binderman, you have a fucking kid. You're just a boy, yourself. You can't raise a kid. Hell, I can't raise my own children and I'm fucking forty five years old!" Crouched down, one knee on the gravel and one balancing his large body upright, he lit a cigarette.

He handed one to me.

I stretched my back as best as I could, as it was stiff and bruised from the rocks beneath me. "Fuck…I'm sorry…"

"Don't say sorry to me, Binderman. It's not me you have to worry about. Get up…" He held out his hand and pulled me to stand. As I started to brush off my clothes, he decided to help me do so. My anger was gone. It was replaced with guilt and hesitation.

"Come back to the fire, it's cold out here. We can talk about everything," He proceeded to head back, and then turned to see if I was following. "And, I mean everything."

Fuck. I wiped my eyes and puffed on the square. My body shook. Not just from the cold, but from the fact that the hardest part was over. I couldn't believe it. He didn't beat me. He didn't hurt me…that much.

It didn't matter. I still shook. I didn't feel sick from breaking up with Fresca, now. I was sick because my father was about to show he cared. My fever was gone. My stomach was knotted with a basketball size tumor. Something great was going to happen tonight and I wasn't ready for the connection.

Chapter Thirty-Three
Cardy

"Christopher?" Dean's voice came from a speaker from an intercom next to the door. "You're on lock down for a week. You're not allowed out until we decide that you aren't a threat to our facility. Oh, and congratulations, you just earned yourself another three months."

I spit on the intercom. "Fuck you! Come in here, motherfucker, so I can kick your fucking ass!! I'll give you three fucking months! I ain't got shit!"

I paced that motherfucker for hours until I gave up and slid down the padding. I hung my head between my arms and began to think of who I could call if I got close enough to a phone. Someone had to help me. Who can I call? Who did I want to call?

Boo.

No, I was done with that bitch. I was done with my mom, too, putting me here, how fucking could she?! It was all her fault that I was like this. If she wouldn't have kicked me out, then I wouldn't have lived with Boo and be a product of my situations.

Oh my God, my life was a living hell. I wiped my face and rubbed the top of my head. What the fuck do I do, now?

"Cardy?" A lady's voice shot through the silence after it seemed like hours of captivity. It was the shrink. I didn't respond.

"I'm going to try a different approach with you, okay?" She walked in wearing a jump suit. It was another odd piece of clothing she presented herself in. She carried a chair, while two security guards came in with a fold out table.

She placed a photo album on the table and proceeded to sit. She opened the first page and gestured for me to have a seat.

I just stared at her. I wasn't about to cooperate. I still sat against the pads, knees bent, arms drawn upward. She was insane to think that I would express my feelings.

She sighed, but didn't give up. She stood, flattened out her pants, and grabbed the pink book. "Then, I'll sit next to you." She came closer.

She squatted and plopped down with a smile. She smelled like vanilla. It reminded me of Boo's house, his cars. The bracelet on her wrist dangled, and it reminded me of Fresca. Her hair was long and thick. Her cheeks were rounder than I had first remembered. That in turn, made me think of Simoine Adams, one of Bobbi's friends that I had my fun with.

Those three things triggered memories. They were racing around my head. I was subtle and quiet with each flash of reminiscence. I couldn't believe how much I had done within two years. I was still taking it all in as she began talking.

"I want to show you my pictures. We'll talk about me, alright? This is Stephen, my boyfriend. Here I am on our cruise, early spring. Have you ever been on a cruise, Cardy?"

She was small talking for a bigger purpose. I knew the drill. Any comments I would give her, she'd hold them against me. It was some kind of analysis. Fuck that.

"No," and I stared at two pictures sealed behind plastic coverings.

The man had aged lines on his skin. As he smiled, the creases formed deeply around his mouth. He was red skinned, almost sunburned from the spring sun…holding a glass of champagne in his hand. The other hand was wrapped around my shrink. Their distance wasn't close. It was a spur of the moment kind of picture, not really a pose. I could read more into that pose than she realized, but I wasn't about to criticize her life.

"Well, it's a beautiful place. Blue ocean all around you, perfect skies, a cool breeze," She was drifting there in her mind.

She flipped the page. Four more photographs stared back at me. It was more of the cruise. She wasn't in most of them. It was of Stephen. I looked on with my own perception of their relationship. It wasn't hard to figure out. He was conceited with his crisp look and perfect smile. He wore a gold watch and a small gold chain around his neck.

There were other girls in the background. Most of them were hotter than Dr. Roma, wearing skimpy bikinis over bronzed abs. Some of their eyes glared at Stephen with admiration. Some wore flirty smiles and big hair. I wondered about them. I wondered about this lady sitting next to me.

Did all men cheat? Was it a natural thing to do? Was that why Boo did it...Was that why I did it?

I swallowed that thought harshly. I didn't just say that. I couldn't have done that to her...not to Basia. Could I?

Did I?

"Who are they?" I tapped the women with the teased hair, three inches too tall and standing too close to this lady's man. It was apparent to me, was it to her? Did it matter to me? Why was I thinking of this shit?

"Oh, it's his friends from the office. It was their cruise and I decided to go along. We spent two weeks in the open sea." No, she didn't notice. She was oblivious to the obvious. Or was it denial?

I made a sudden move and took the album from her. I sat it on my lap. I flipped through most of it. She didn't get offended or shocked at my approach. It was her lack of confidence showing. She was letting me do whatever.

"So, these people are co-workers?" I let my attitude subside for the moment. As long as I had HER life to sort through, I wasn't thinking of my problems.

I analyzed her as another Fresca. I didn't know why girls put up with the struggle. In the end, it would only mean heartache and depression. With this said, I took a liking to the shrink. She showed lack of character, low self esteem, and nowhere near professional.

Doctors were supposed to show structure and confidence. Their lifestyles should coincide with the professionalism of their workplace. Maybe I was wrong, but...the wrong choice in a decision outside of work, showed signs of concern on how well they can do their job.

Take Bill Clinton. I loved the man. I loved him because he showed a human side of him and proved that even presidents fucked up and made the wrong decisions. But, did that cause some Americans to disprove of him...trust him, when his own wife couldn't trust him? Of course.

Could I trust this shrink to make a better judgment about me than myself? Can I amuse myself with her wisdom and take what I felt like taking from her?

Yeah and no. No, I didn't trust her. I wouldn't. And, yeah, she was good company in this stupid shit hole because she was humanly naïve.

"Oh yeah, we're a big family. We go to all sorts of functions together. This one, I watched her ten year old son while she went on a business trip with Stephen. He's such a little ham."

Ten shouldn't be considered a "ham." At ten, I was riding my skateboard in the street and climbing in sewer drains to get our tennis balls. Ten was too big to be considered a baby, a ham, or anything cutesy to that matter. She didn't know anything about kids, either.

And, she obviously didn't know that she was watching that lady's child so she could sleep with Stephen, huh? I had my mind set, that man was no good.

"What does he do?" I eyed him more suspiciously. He was all about the show. The evidence was written right between his eyebrows as it creased down with greed and mistrust.

"He's a stock broker. His father owns a law firm and all his brothers are lawyers. His cousins are in the stock market, too. It's a big male competition, with his family, that is." She said way more than what most shrinks, that I assumed, would have said.

"How long have you been with this guy?" I didn't want to look through the pictures again, but if I put it down, I'd have nothing to do with my hands. Therefore, my fingertips idled on the plastic covering, tapping lightly, as this conversation was going deeper and making me feel awkward.

"Only six or seven months. It hasn't been long. I seem to go head first in all of my relationships. I'm getting older by the minute, I don't have time to tiptoe around first dates." Her smile widened to become friends with me.

"Oh." My boredom was causing my eyes to shift around the room. I focused in on the table legs, how thin they were. Four beams held it up. If one was gone, like Darron's tables in his house, everything would fall over. It wouldn't be stable, anymore.

That's how it was with family. One parent disappeared, the whole bunch fell and begged for support. Sure, another leg can be added. Something can prop the motherfucker to stand. And a shop can fix the leg and cause it to work like new. But, we all knew…

It once fell.

"Do you have a girlfriend?" Her knees bent like mine and her arms rested against them. Her socks explained everything…they were fuzzy polka dots. What was it with her? Did she roll out of bed and throw on just any type of clothes?

I kept my eyes at the floor, wanting to feel the texture of those socks. I wanted to slip off her shoes and look at them. I don't know. I was bored. I laughed in response. "No, I don't have a girlfriend."

"You're not..." Insinuating that I may be into guys.

Quickly, I got sour. I stood. "Fuck no, I ain't a faggot. I got plenty of bitches back home to fuck with. I ain't gay. I just don't need a girlfriend." I tried to calm down, but I was tired of motherfuckers calling me gay. My dad did plenty of that shit when I lived with him. He's lucky that I wasn't brainwashed from that shit.

"Okay, alright, I'm sorry. Sit back down." She patted the tile with a frown.

I wouldn't. I couldn't. We sat still long enough. I was good for a good half hour. I did what she wanted me to do. Now, I needed to smoke. Needed to get outside. I needed something other than questions and white bullshit.

"You're so...antsy. I didn't mean to call you gay, Cardy. Really, I'm sorry." She knew she had lost our connection.

I twisted around as if the room would change its appearance or something by the time I turned back.

It didn't. Miracles were fake. "I just need to chill...I need to get out of here." I squatted in front of her, looking for patience. I didn't feel like losing it, again. "I need a cigarette, that's what I need."

"Oh, you want some chocolate? I have tons of candy bars back in my office. I bought them because it helps keep the addiction crave down. I think it has something to do with the dopamine, maybe the caffeine. And, it always helps the mouth to stay busy. Gives your hands something to hold, too." I think her assumption was bullshit. Maybe SHE wanted a candy bar.

"I don't care. I really need a cigarette."

"I'll tell you what, I'll give you a cigarette for each hour you spend talking to me. You have to answer my questions, and not get offended. Is that a good compromise?" She stood, too. Her hand went to her hip, waiting for me to comply.

I smiled in disbelief. Was I just bribed?

"You're telling me that if I talk to you, you're going to let me smoke, even though I'm seventeen and this place is smoke free?" It was unbelievable music to my ears.

She grinned with accomplishment. "I never said it was a smoke free facility. We can smoke in the teacher's lounge. But, yes, I am agreeing to give you a cigarette for each hour that you talk to me. It has to be an hour and you have to keep your temper down. You can't tell anyone because I can lose my job, do you understand?"

I held out my hand. "I'll start, now."

She clasped her hands together for the project ahead of her. "Okay, let me get them out of my purse. I'll be right back."

Jesus, she was not a doctor. "Cool."

It was the only thing that I had agreed to since I was there. Me and the shrink would do just fine.

Just fine, thank you.

Chapter Thirty-Four
Angie

Where was that jerk? I called him about fifty times and he never returned my calls. He knew I was going to Cheriton University, today, with my sister, to check out their classes. What the hell was he thinking, standing me up like that?

Just a week ago he was trying to go out with me. That boy has his head on backwards. Surely, he wasn't thinking about me, now. And what about Devon? He didn't want Devon growing up in a single parent household, then where the hell was he at?!

"Amanda, I don't think I can go, Boo hasn't answered." I untangled myself from the telephone cord and headed for my sister's room. Amanda was jumping on her bed, making Devon laugh below her.

She was such a corny sixteen year old, I swear. She was so immature, yet mature. She didn't date boys, didn't want to go to parties, didn't drink, smoke, or have sex. She barely said a curse word, and never argued with me.

She was my corny sister, my best friend.

"Why not? We can drop Devon off at his house. Just because he has a hangover or something doesn't mean he can't help you when it's very important. He can manage that much." She halted her jump-a-thon and picked Devon up.

Where I had *wanted* to go to parties and dabble in some things, I wasn't good at standing up for myself. Where Amanda avoided the party scene, she was good at making a point and forcing people to take account for what they should.

This subject always brought tension. We never argued, I'll give her that much, but Amanda couldn't stand the fact that Boo walked all over me. I considered on going over there and sitting Devon at his front door.

"You're going. You were planning this meeting since the end of twelfth grade. He knew that. So what if he has a headache, he can cope, Angie. You cope with Devon when you have a headache, why should you be easy on him?" she wouldn't think about postponing our appointment with the advisor for one more day. She was stubborn.

"Fine." I let Amanda grab the diaper bag and her nephew. I followed her out of the front door and towards mom's Corolla. Sometimes, I felt like she was the bigger sister, telling me what to do and carrying around Devon like he was hers. She was an awesome backbone.

When we got to Boo's, he didn't answer the door. Instead, Maria, his maid did. She was an older Spanish lady, still with a heavy accent. She was always very kind, letting me enter and find Boo.

"He's with his father. Come in, sit. I'll make you something to drink." She was a short lady, plump around the middle. Her face was wrinkled, eyelids sagging over her eyes. Her cheeks drooped, too, reminding me of an old bulldog.

I liked Maria.

"When will he be back?" Amanda took charge and stood in the foyer. She was looking for a reason to complain about Boo's house, even though there was never anything worth complaining about. It was always straight, clean and elegant, especially when Maria was around.

Maria turned around for a second. "Oh, he won't be back for the rest of the week. Do you need him to watch baby? I can watch him so you can go off and do something. I don't mind."

I glanced at Amanda in disbelief. He was on vacation? He never mentioned a vacation to me! See how much we communicated? We definitely wouldn't make a good couple. God, I was so angry at him.

In the meanwhile, Maria was an option.

"Are you sure? I don't want to bother you…" I slid Devon down my leg and he ran off to the living room in search of his daddy.

"In this big empty house? I'd love to. Leave, go have some fun. You need it. Baby will be fine." She took the diaper bag from Amanda's hands and wouldn't take no for an answer.

She never referred to Devon by his name. It was always "baby," not "The baby" or anything else.

Amanda clapped her hands together. "Well, that's settled. He better give her a raise!"

I knew Maria would take care of him. I knew Devon was comfortable around her. I just…I don't know. She wasn't supposed to stand in for Boo. She was a maid, not a nanny.

"Are you sure, I can postpone…" I reconsidered taking him back while she lightly shoved us out the door.

"Never…go do what you have to do. I've been watching Binji since he was an infant. I changed diapers longer than that. Go, go…come back later."

The door closed.

"Who's Binji?" Amanda asked as we headed for the car.

"I think she meant Boo. You know, I don't even know his real name?"

"Sounds like it's Benjamin. That's funny, he doesn't look like a Benjamin. Well, maybe. Benjamin Sox." Amanda was more talking to herself.

"No, It's a weird one. I heard it before. I think he told me when I had Devon, that's how Devon got his middle name, I just…it's too weird to remember." I refused to let Amanda drive to Cheriton, so I sat in the driver's seat. She wasn't that good at driving, yet.

"You should have known more about him before you spread your legs, Angie. I tell that to all of my friends and they don't listen to me."

Preacher.

"I know, Amanda. I tried to get to know him. Remember when he came over all that summer? I tried to figure him out. He's just…private, he keeps to himself." I lit a cigarette and blew the smoke out of the window. It should be a long enough time before my mom got in and smelled it lingering.

"You mean sneaky. He's sneaky, Angie. He didn't tell you anything about him because you didn't need to know. He didn't want to make you his girlfriend, you were his side project, his toy." She was set on a lecture…an old one that she had brought up too many times before.

"He just asked me out, last week. Fresca broke up with him. He wanted to move in with us." I brought it up because I was wondering what it would be like to have Boo Sox as my boyfriend.

Would he treat me different? Would it make me popular and make all the girls jealous of me? Would they confront me and try to steal him from me? Could I handle the heartache of breaking up with him after he cheated on me?

"What? No way, he didn't! Angie, why didn't you tell me this when it happened? You're not going out with him, now, are you? Is that why you're so paranoid at where he's at? You can't possibly still like him, he wanted you to get an abortion, remember? Remember the mean Boo Sox, the one who wrecked all of Devon's furniture?" She was appalled. She rolled down the window so the smoke would rise out. She waved her hand but didn't complain. No, she wanted to complain about bigger issues. About Boo.

"I said no, alright? We wouldn't work out, anyways. I told him he needed an airhead, someone who would let him walk all over him."

"Good for you!"

We talked about Boo Sox for as long as it took to get to Cheriton U.

She said that he was polite and charming. He knew how to treat "The lady of the hour" like a queen, but knew exactly how to ditch her, too. He was a heartbreaker, a backstabber, and not worth my time. If he was any other, then she would be rooting for me to get a spotlight in his life. As for now, she didn't want me to like him.

Boo Sox, he was a mystery, even after all these years of knowing him. I wish I knew more. And Amanda was right. He wasn't worth my time. He was a waste of time. I could do better and I needed to think of Devon. Being with Boo because of Devon would only cause more grief when it was over.

No, Devon knew what to expect, now. If his daddy was in my bed one day, and in a few months gone, he wouldn't have that routine, anymore. He wouldn't know what to expect. It would strip him of his security. No, I couldn't think of myself, or of Boo. I had to be a mother and do what was best for him. And only him.

"Ready for your future?" Amanda smiled as we approached Cheriton U.

"Yes, I am." I had always been eager to go there. I wanted to graduate college. I wanted to become something of myself. What, I didn't know. But, to be here, with all the opportunities knocking on my doorstep, I think I wanted to be everything. Leave nothing out.

I wasn't like some people around here. I didn't need a man to support my life. Boo may have had money to give Devon and then some for my own keepings, but I wasn't about to let that spoil my chance of meaning something to myself.

Chapter Thirty-Five
Binderman

"It's not what you think, dad. I tried to get rid of it, I didn't want it, believe me. There was nothing I could do." I knew this day would come. My dad was the main reason I wanted Angie to get an abortion. All I heard in my head was his voice, that disappointment ringing in my ears.

"She wanted to keep the baby." My dad's head bent forward, understanding the facts. He twisted a small twig between his fingertips. He focused on the fire and tossed it into the blaze.

The glare from the flames cast an awful glow to his face. His features were rough, stubble already, and older. He was still young, but age was creeping. I could tell his misery just by looking at him.

"Yeah." I glanced over at Bobbi, who was still stuffing her face with blackened marshmallows. She listened, carefully, but pretended to be invisible. I wanted her to leave us alone. I didn't feel like she should be a part of this stupid confession.

"Women and their stupid nonsense." Somehow, he had taken it to heart. "You know that's what happened to me, with Christopher. I tried hard as hell to get Dena to have an abortion. I bribed the shit out of her. But, she was certain that she wanted to go through with it. I told her if she did, I wanted nothing to do with him. When that didn't work, the damn woman was paid to keep her mouth shut. You know the story...hell, you're living it, aren't you?"

Maybe we were alike, after all. He had affairs, I had affairs. He didn't want the mistake that he made, and I didn't either. Circumstance had risen.

But something else was different. I had to make that clear. "Yeah, but dad, now that he's around, he's cool, ya know? I actually like spending time with him." I wasn't going to be like him. I wasn't going to pretend that my son didn't exist.

My dad grunted. Then he chuckled. "Babies are amusing, I know.

Especially your first one. You make all your mistakes with the first, find out the hard way. I was twenty five when you were born, I couldn't imagine having you any younger. I don't think you would have survived."

He was calmer than I had imagined him to be. He was taking it in stride, swallowing his temper. I appreciated that. So, I continued…

"His mom's great. She breastfeeds and takes good care of him. I don't have to worry about anything. She does it all." It was easy to talk about Angie being a good mom. That shit I knew about her. She was perfect when it came to Devon.

It was the other shit that I knew nothing about. I didn't know her birthday, barely knew her age. Back when I was messing around with her, I didn't have time to figure her out. It was more like a hit and run, only stopping to charm her for more…later.

God, I was pathetic, come to think about it.

"A grandson…I can't believe you made me a grandpa at forty five. Most men are in their sixties, Binderman. Most men."

I thought about telling him about Cardy's kids. Biologically, he had three grandkids. That could be another time.

"I thought you knew better. I told you about condoms, Bin. We had that talk the first time, remember?" He warmed his palms above the fire, staring at me.

Memory lane…Fresca.

I was fifteen when Fresca found out she was pregnant. My dad was still around and I was prepared to face the consequences and fess up. I had told him about her. Fresca was so scared, she'd do anything to keep her father from knowing she was having sex.

My father sat us down, told us our options, and she wanted an abortion. We were so relieved that it could be erased.

"Yeah, but that was Fresca, dad. She was down for that shit. Angie, she…she didn't believe in abortion." I didn't regret Devon, anymore. I was glad that Angie let it happen. He was my son. I had a son…

"Dena didn't either."

Dena. Dena Deburke. I hated that bitch.

He leaned back in his chair and sighed. "That's why I bought you condoms, Binderman, all of this shit wouldn't be happening."

I thought about Cardy and how I threw the motherfuckers in his face. I knew the consequences, but I was a hypocrite. Cardy tried to call me out on that shit, too. He knew I wasn't taking my own advice.

Fuck, condoms were hard to deal with. I hated those things. In the heat of the moment, I'd have to stop and strap up, taking up precious time. By then, the bitch might not want to go through with it.

I know better, now. It was that or a fucking kid.

My dad didn't know that Fresca got pregnant a second time. Only, she had a miscarriage. That was one day I'd never forget. I won't even think about it, now. Even though we were going to go through with an abortion, again...having it taken away before that decision only made matters worse. I was scared to fuck her for a long time. I was scared that she was extra fertile and I'd get her pregnant even with a condom on.

"Dad, I'm happy to have Devon. I'm happy to have Cardy around, too. I just wish you would want to be around him. Cardy belongs with us, no matter how much you deny it. He's ours." As if he belonged to me.

"I've been thinking a lot about him, lately. Dena named him Viscardi because she thought it would change my mind and I would divorce your mother. Viscardi is your great grandfather's name. She knew I wanted a son with that name. Imagine hearing that shit. That woman was hoping that I would leave my wife for her and that boy." He paused and then opened his mouth to say more...but didn't.

Viscardi was Cardy's middle name, that's how he got the nickname "Cardy." I only knew him by Christopher until I met Jeff. He was Christopher Viscardi Deburke. His last name didn't even belong to him. He was supposed to be a Sox.

The conversation ended up being three hours long. Not about Devon, but about everything. I told him about my break up with Fresca, and how I cheated on her. I told him about the game J.D started with the point system, how I managed to outdo all of the others. I admitted how I quit football because I didn't want the responsibility, anymore. We talked about J.D's death and how it affected Pierre, how it affected me and Cardy. And most of all, I told him about Cardy sleeping with Fresca. That had been dwelling on me and I didn't know how to take it. He was the first person I had admitted it to.

We talked, he teared, and he apologized for everything that he put me through. He regretted everything. He didn't want me to live the lifestyle that I was living. And, he took all the blame for it.

He took back the responsibility that was handed down to me.
And, you know what?
I forgave him.
I felt many years younger, giving up my responsibility of control. I didn't have to worry about Bobbi or the bills to that house. I wasn't in charge of Cardy.

I could be a son, and only a son.

It felt good.

While I was at it, I didn't want to run Pierre, anymore, either. I was done with that shit. I wanted to live my life in peace, with my family. With Devon, and my dad, and Cardy in rehab.

My dad talked me into going to college, which I had wanted to do in the first place. Now that I had time on my hands, I had a chance to rediscover myself and my options. Maybe I would continue football while I was at it. It would make my father proud if I did.

I don't know.

We bonded that night, as I knew we would, once I got everything off of my chest. We got shit out in the open and became tight, again. That was cool.

I had a father in my life.

Now that everything was smoothed out…I couldn't help but think of her, again. I didn't want to move on without Fresca.

Everything would add up and feel perfect if she wasn't missing in my life.

Chapter Thirty-Six
Basia

School started and Darron hadn't quit, after all. It was his first day of being a sophomore…for the second year. The day drug on and on for me. I couldn't wait for him to get home.

As soon as I heard the front door fling against the wall, I launched myself down the stairs to greet him.

I was in a better mood, for a better purpose.

I barreled into his body, causing him to fall to the ground, book bag and all.

"What the hell, Basia?" Frowning for like days, now.

I helped him up, said sorry, and gave him a giant hug. "I'll do it, I wanna do it."

Confused, he frowned more. "What are you talking about? Do what?"

I grinned from ear to ear, flashes of blue lockers and dirty mop buckets filled my head. "I wanna go to school. You can quit, now."

I hadn't seen Darron happier in years. He dropped his backpack for the final time. "Thank you, God!" He glanced up at the ceiling. His prayer had been answered.

"I already called Amanda and told her the news. She is so excited for me." I rambled on and on with all the possibilities ahead for me.

I kept talking as he climbed the stairs. I held a one person discussion as he turned on the Super Nintendo. Over and over, I explained about how thrilled I was to get back into the world. I was going to learn everything that I could. I was going to be a sponge of knowledge, knowing that education was taken for granted, now.

He stopped listening to me as soon as I gave him the green light of quitting. But, I didn't care. I was going to be a student. A freshman, nevertheless, but a student given a second chance.

I kissed Jasmine's Kool-Aid lips and swung her around. I fed her supper and gave her a bath. I took a hot shower and shaved my thighs. Yes, this year was going to be perfect. I felt it.

And, after high school, I was going to go to college. Maybe I'll be a nurse like Amanda's mom, or a doctor, like Cardy once wanted to be. I could find a cure for cancer or AIDS. I could be a chemist and work with chemicals. I could be a journalist and write reports for newspapers or magazines. Oh, I could be something political…or work at the clinic and help people like me.

Oh, the possibilities were unlimited. I saw them ahead. I was going to be something great, something big and bright. I wasn't going to quit. I was going to go for my master's degree in something. I don't know, I'll figure it out. My head was spinning with all this new adrenaline and motivation.

It was what I needed to get out of the slump I had during the summer. Cardy's crash was a setback, but he was alive. Who knows, maybe I'll do something dealing with drugs and keep kids off of them, so there wouldn't be good kids like Cardy resorting to them. That sounded good.

Who knows, by the time Cardy got out, maybe I would approach him and tell him that I forgave him. I forgave him because he made me realize that I had taken everything for granted, before. I struggled and now I see what I needed to do with myself.

I don't regret my mistakes. I cherish them, like I cherish Cardy.

Oh, Cardy, I wish I could write you and tell you my news. You'd be happy for me, I know it. I wish I could write my mom and tell her, too. She'd be so proud to know that Jasmine hadn't harmed me, after all. She made me appreciate everything.

So, by the middle of the week…I was enrolled. I was a student at Pierre High school, again. It felt…perfect.

"It's going to be so great having you back, Basia." Loren walked beside me as we entered the school doors.

The noise was rewarding. The smell was enticing. The kids were pleasing to my eyes. Finally, the pressure of mommy-hood had lessened. Basia Brahm was back.

"I know, I still can't believe I'm here." I beamed as I followed Loren to her locker.

Loren didn't look like the Loren I grew up with. She had dyed her hair red. She wore thick black eyeliner around her eyes. She was into the punk scene, wearing red and black, spikes and chains. She even dared to wear black lipstick to school. Was that allowed?

"Yeah, now I have a friend that I don't have to feel embarrassed to hang around." Amanda smiled, glancing at Loren's appearance.

Amanda was always the same. Her hair had always been between her shoulders, brown and untouched. She didn't wear makeup or jewelry…maybe a necklace I would share with her every now and then, but, usually, she was earring-less, too. She wasn't about to alter her lifestyle for anything less permanent than education. Becca and Loren, however, were just the opposite.

"I haven't seen Kayo in awhile, where has he been at?" I started searching the hallways for one of the only three Asian kids in our school. Kayo Ching was always a blessing to have around. I missed him. He was the comedian of the group, the ice breaker, the dearest of souls.

Loren and Amanda traded glances. Something was up with him, I suppose.

"What?"

"You don't want to know, really." Loren added and left it at that.

If Amanda had been more of the gossip type, I would have known more about the past two years. If Becca and Loren had ventured over to Darron's more and not strayed to every single party that Pierre could think of…I would have received the news.

Now, I was just finding out.

"Where is he? Is he okay?" If something had happened to Kayo and I wasn't around to console him, I would be so mad at myself…and those girls.

"He hangs around a new crowd, nowadays." Amanda stretched her lips out so she wouldn't say why or how. She didn't smile or didn't frown. It was her neutral way of acting when she was saying the least she could.

"He's gay, Basia. That's old news." Loren lit up a cigarette as soon as we entered the girl's restroom. She made it sound like it wasn't something uncommon, like it was okay to be gay.

Don't get me wrong, I didn't dislike homosexuals, personally. I was just raised to believe that God preferred that a man stay with a woman and so forth. I was raised by the bible…it was a sin to think different. It was a sin to be gay. I would never hate anyone who was gay, especially Kayo, my friend, but…gay?

Could he actually be gay? Why would he choose to be gay?

"No way, are you serious? How could that happen?" I stepped back from the smoke, but more from the reality of Kayo taking the path of the devil. How could he let that happen? He was a Christian!

Loren rolled her eyes. "It wasn't a choice, Basia. I wish you would understand that everything in the bible isn't true. He IS gay and it wasn't what he planned on being. He was *born* gay, okay? Can we just drop the whole thing?"

"How can people be born gay?!" I never understood why people would come out and be gay when they were ridiculed for it. And I didn't believe that people were born gay, like it was genetic or something. It had to be a choice. It was natural to be attracted to women, right?

Right?

"Cause they just are, Basia. You think Kayo wanted to be gay? You think he would rather be with the crowd and marry a girl and not want to be with a man when everyone made fun of him? Don't you think he tried to be with a girl and maybe he realized that he was gay because he wasn't attracted to them? Jesus, Basia, you need to get with the program. Gay people are born gay, okay? It's a fact!!!" Loren snapped at me like she wanted to fight me. She even had the nerve to blow smoke in my face when she spoke.

I couldn't believe that Loren was so outspoken and mean. I mean, she used to be the nice one. Now, now all she cared about was proving me wrong.

Amanda pulled me back and eyed me to drop it. I had more questions than answers on the subject. Of course I couldn't see Kayo wanting to be gay. Nobody should want to be gay, right?

There was a lot I needed to figure out when it came to the bible and the world. Did that mean that I couldn't be friends with Kayo? Did it matter to me that Kayo was gay?

Certainly not. How could I judge him? God judged people. Not me. It made me want to see him more. My curiosity was brewing, as I never met a gay guy before.

"Here, have a smoke, calm down. Everyone can't be perfect like you, Basia." Loren sneered, offering me a cigarette.

What nerve she had!!!

I winced away. "No, thank you."

I didn't like Loren, anymore. She was rude.

"Suit yourself…" Loren puffed away as I left to my first class.

What have I missed? I felt like the world had changed while I was gone. Everything was different. Every ONE was different. They spoke different, they acted different…hell, some liked guys!!!

Did I really want to join the world, again, or stay in my little bubble of a house and pretend the world was just as sane as before?!

Chapter Thirty-Seven
Angela Debrowski

I was a freshman at Cheriton University. It was so awesome. If it wasn't for Maria watching Devon for me, I would have put it off until next year. I thanked her and thanked her. I don't think anyone ever thanked her as much as I did. I hugged her and squeezed her. I ran back to her and squeezed her, again.

I had to buy her a gift or something. I bet no one in that house ever thought about giving her a present. She deserved so much more than that. She was the nicest lady I have ever met, besides my mom, that is. My mom was great, too.

Oh, I was just so exited!

And who would ruin my biggest smile of the year? Who was good at ruining my life?!

No one other than Boo Sox, of course…

He came over the weekend before I started class. It had been a week and a half since I enrolled. It had been longer since I had talked to him.

Bastard.

Could he come over in the evening? Could he come over bright and early in the morning? Could he be descent enough to call me, first?

Never in a million years.

He showed up at two in the morning, assumingly drunk off his ass. That was my first impression.

"Angie, I'm so sorry…" He pushed his way into my house and headed for my bedroom. "My dad had this stupid ass plan to get us out of that house and talk to me about some shit. When I left, I was too drunk to bring my cell phone and we were miles away from a phone."

He didn't smell like liquor, for once.

As he stood above Devon's baby bed, touching Devon's little fingers as he slept, I realized that Boo wasn't drunk...just stupid.

"Why are you here, two in the morning? Why do you wait until it's pitch black outside to come disturb us? I am so mad at you, whether or not you're sorry!" I was fed up with his shit and crossed my arms.

He surprised me, then. He twisted around and grabbed me by the shoulders. He shoved me back and pushed me down to sit on my bed. My heart was racing in fear, as I felt I was going to have to fight him off of me. He may not have been drunk, but I was expecting some kind of rough kiss or...

"I'm sorry, I'm sorry, I'm fucking sorry, Angela. What do you want me to do? I didn't have a phone, my dad didn't know about Devon until last week and my sister sure the fuck wasn't going to remember to bring my cell phone because she's a bitch!" He whispered as harshly as he could without waking Devon.

He was too close to me. He didn't smell like liquor. He smelled like soap, a lot of soap, maybe aftershave and a little dab of cologne. His eyes were wide open and he was alert.

Something was different about him. What was it?

Was it maybe because the last time I had seen him he was all scrubby and looking depressed? Was it because he wasn't asking to go out with me or yelling at me for letting Devon sleep with his favorite pink pacifier? He did see that thing in his mouth, right?

"Ever heard of a pay phone?" I sneered. I wasn't going to give in and forgive him. I heard Amanda's voice in my head, shaking her finger, and reminding me that he was the one who trashed my room, a year and a half ago.

"Are you serious? I'm not touching a fucking pay phone! Think of who touches those things, all the fucking germs and shit on it?! You want me to get a disease just so you know where the fuck I am?!" He still sat too close, leg touching mine. His eyes locked in on me, waiting for my next accusation, ready to give me bull-crap.

"I could care a less where you are, Boo! I had to enroll in school, remember? I needed you to watch Devon. It was important and you were nowhere. The least you could have done was let me know that you couldn't do it so I could have found someone else!" I didn't mention the fact that Maria was my savior. If I did, then he would feel that he had some kind of help in the matter, as she was HIS resource.

His eyes widened more as he realized our earlier agreement. "Holy fuck, I forgot! You don't know what kind of shit I had to put up with since I was over here, last. I totally forgot. I'm sorry, okay? I was too wasted to do anything…I've been sick, I've been doing a lot of thinking, I've been talking to my dad…"

"That's just nice, Boo. Why don't you go back to your dad and tell him about Devon, for once? Take responsibility for something!" He could talk his way out of anything if the right person let him do it. Well, I wasn't about to be pulled into his lies.

"You're not listening to me, Angela. I told him. I just said I told him. And I do take responsibility. What the hell do you think I've been doing the past fucking years at my house? I had a lot of shit to deal with. Now that my dad is home…" He wanted to argue, or converse, or whatever…but I wasn't down for any of it. I wanted him gone.

I jerked away and stood. "Why are you here?!"

He rose too, this time getting in my face, trying to hold eye contact. "I wanted to see him."

I pushed him back. The warm cotton of his t-shirt pressed against his abs. I had to refrain from admiring the firmness. I had to remain strong, think clearly. This is why I gave in so much, because he was Boo, he was what everyone adored. He knew this. He used it against us girls.

"You could have seen him in the morning!"

He was too much!

"Angie, stop fucking with me. I wanted to talk to you, too." His eyes were pleading, now, baby blue sparkles in the moonlight.

I hardened. "About what, Boo? What the hell couldn't wait until tomorrow?"

He swallowed. I saw it as he paused. He was without words for a minute. "Can you just sit down, you're making it harder."

"What?" I slumped down on my bed so he could get out what he felt was needed. I'm sure I looked terrible…eyes still half asleep, ridges on my cheek from the wrinkles in my sheets…I felt them as he stalled.

He sat next to me. "I can't go to sleep."

"Is that MY problem?!"

He sighed. "No. I just thought that I could stay here, tonight. I want to be here when Devon wakes up."

I stood, again, like musical chairs…a rise in one of our voices was the cue to stand. "I can't believe you. You think that because you've been away for awhile and you can't sleep that I'm just gonna let you waltz in here and sleep with me?!"

We were doing pretty good not to wake Devon. Our voices were argumentative, but in a deep daggering whisper. Boo stayed seated. Instead, he pulled me against him.

"Listen to me, I'm sorry for everything, Angela. I know it's not enough. I'll sleep on the couch if I must. I just don't wanna be alone." He was whining. The stupid ass was whining to me.

"Fine, just get out of my room!" I gave in.

He stepped over to Devon and glanced down. Then, he headed out of my room and threw himself onto my sofa. He tossed and turned, tossed and plopped. Even though I had slept plenty of nights on my couch, I'm sure he wasn't used to the cozy positions that I had found peaceful, given the fact that he had a giant mansion to lay his head in.

Minutes later…

"Angie!!" He moaned.

I gave him a second before I answered. I wasn't his maid. He had Maria to call out to for that. "What, now?!"

"I can't sleep."

"Good!" Although I got up and stood above him.

I don't know why.

He smiled when he saw me. He rolled over on his side to watch me steam. "I can't sleep because I can't stop thinking about things. When I close my eyes I think of being alone. I don't like to be alone."

"That's tough, you're not weaseling your way into my bed, even though it's warm and cozy and nice." I couldn't think of better terms, as I was too tired. I just wanted to rub it in, for once I had something better than what he had.

"No, I'm serious. When I lay in bed, alone, I think of my mom."

He never talked about his mom. He continued…

"I used to sleep with her until she died. My dad had to sleep in another room. I think that's why he cheated on her, because I took his spot."

Why was this happening to me? Why did he have to confide in me? I didn't want to hear it. That was for a psychologist. I wasn't a psychologist. I didn't want to feel sorry for him and didn't want to comfort his loneliness. I wanted…I didn't know what I wanted.

I sat at the foot of him, distant enough, yet there. "Don't be telling me lies just to get your way, Boo. It's very cruel if you're using your mom like that." I was cautious enough, scared to believe him.

He sat up on his elbows. "I'm not fucking lying to you! I would never use my mom like that. I DID sleep with her up until I was twelve. And when she died, I had Fresca. She would come over and sing me to sleep. She lost her mom, too."

I didn't know what to say. What could I say? I couldn't be mean, not when he was being so vulnerable. I couldn't make a joke, because it wasn't a joking matter. I couldn't get up enough nerve to hug him or tell him everything was okay because he was Boo Sox.

I didn't know how to react.

He sat up and grabbed my wrist. "I'm telling you this because you didn't know. You don't know shit about me and I don't know shit about you. The least we could do is get to know each other."

I jerked it back, frightened of what that may mean. "And you want to sleep with me because you want to know me?" Sure, that made sense.

"No, I want to sleep with you because I don't want to sleep with anyone else. And that doesn't mean I want to fuck you, either. You're safe. I don't fucking bite."

What were the odds?

"You're really pushing your luck, Boo." I let him follow me into my room.

"You know my real name is Binderman. You don't have to call me Boo."

I glanced back in amazement. What the hell was going on with him?

"I only know you as Boo, I can't think of you as anything else."

"Yeah, I know, nobody can."

Chapter Thirty-Eight
Cardy

After a week worth of padded walls, I was sinking farther into insanity. All I could do was think, think, fucking think.

I repeated my name in my head, over and over.

Cardy Deburke. That name meant so much to so many people. I no longer identified with that name. Who was I really? Where did I belong in this wide world of society? A name was supposed to give history, a background to your bloodline.

But my name brought distortion, remorse. I had to make sense of who I was, what I've become, what I've done. What did my future gravitate to?

Fate, it rested in my hands. It was such an invisible force that I couldn't grasp. What was my destiny? What was I supposed to foresee? I had a second chance to make my life right. But, it was so easy to corrupt the smallest chain reaction. One false blink or swallow, then I was shoved inside a pinball machine to ping along with my consequences.

My memory was back. I remembered it all like it was yesterday. And...

I was left with nothing. I had a sea of memories that twisted into nightmares, each night. I had no ambition, no motivation. I had no inspiration to move me forward. Everything that I had was depleted. It was gone. And, I knew I wouldn't get it back.

Boo was dead to me. It was never going to be the same. As I thought about everything that he had done for me, I had taken his friendship for granted. I knew that, now, with my head being sober. I had taken the coolest kid in town and turned him into a pussy. It wasn't very nice of me. It was degrading.

How could I live with myself, knowing that I had used up all his money on drugs, fucked the love of his life, and ruined his reputation by making him look like a fool?

I had to shove those thoughts deep into my subconscious. I couldn't think like that. I couldn't think of him. It was in the past, he was history.

This is now. I had to be sane. Even if I was locked away in this white walled cell, held captive against my will, I had to remain sane.

I was a junkie.

I couldn't believe that I was heavy into drugs. I remembered...I kind of remembered, all this time, that something was lurking in my head. I just didn't want to acknowledge its existence.

It fucking sucked, my reality.

Being hit with who I was, I didn't want to remember anymore. I wanted it to stop. I took advantage of him.

Stop thinking of him.

I couldn't help it. He was a big part of me, a big part of my past. I kept seeing his face, that night, sheer panic and the tears in his eyes as he fought with me. I had scared him. I had always scared him.

I don't even know why. No one intimidated Boo Sox. No one.

But, I did. Somehow, I had managed to get to him, to persuade him, to conquer him. He was nothing but a big fake. If people knew that, they wouldn't be so frightened of him. They wouldn't be all over him like they were.

I knew Boo Sox for what he was. He was lucky. On pure luck, he was able to control the world around us. Ha, that was a joke. Pierre was full of ass kissers, pleasers, low self esteem little kids who needed that direction he gave them.

Boo Sox was a kid who ate peanut butter out of a jar because he was too scared to eat meat. Boo Sox was a baby who was afraid of germs and had compulsive problems with order. Ha, Boo Sox was easy to control behind the scenes.

All I had to do was confront him. No one confronted the motherfucker. He wouldn't even hit me, that night. Don't get me wrong, the asshole could fight and fought with hard fists. He dominated because he had the strength to.

No, Boo wasn't weak when it came to a crowd of kids.

But, he was weak around me. I didn't understand it.

The guilt in that rationalization was supreme. If Boo Sox controlled Pierre, and I controlled Boo, then what did that make me to Pierre? The higher power?

If only.

Ahhhh...I can't stand this shit! I stood from my corner of guilt to pace in a ten by ten foot square. To think…it was killing me. I didn't want thoughts. Who needed thoughts? They collided with any new ones. They attacked me. They mauled me when I wanted to sleep. They…

I wanted it to stop. I was going crazy. I didn't ask for this shit. I wanted to stop my mind from this shit. Now, stupid Safe Haven was making me face the shit that was going on in my head. I didn't need that shit.

Drugs fucked me up. This is true. It took my reality and my existence and created a new storyline of behavior. I was false, yet I was being me. How could that both be true?

It was.

Now, I was reliving the pain of addiction. I had to filter the disease and nit-pick the lies, the truth. My gut instinct had been slaughtered. It was ripped right out of my peritoneum.

Now, how the fuck do I know that word?

Dewey, that cock sucker. He knew all those stupid ass words. He was another smart ass kid with a brain the size of a genius's, but flushing it down the toilet seemed to make him feel better about himself.

Arghhh…I hated how I felt! My wants, my needs, my greed, my thoughts, my pain…I wanted it to subside…just so I could sleep. Sleep would be nice. But, then again, my ever growing fucking aggression to the never ending mood swings in my damn head was pissing me off. I couldn't sleep with all this tension.

I wanted to bust something up, like a window. Kick in a door. Hit a security guard. Do something in this motherfucker!!!!

Why won't they let me outside?!!

I squeezed my cheeks together as my tears decided to dry. This has got to stop. I can't flip into madness like this. I needed someone to say "Hey, this is you, this is who you are, this is what you did, and this is where you belong…"

Why was I thinking of this shit?

No one comes. Of course not. Who is supposed to? They all hated me.

I hated me.

The shit you think of when forced to…

I tried to think of a time that wasn't so pressured…a time when all I felt was happiness. When was that? Even before I met Boo, I wasn't great. I hated my life, then, too.

My parents were only good for arguing. They argued about me. They argued about shit in the past that they couldn't change. They held grudges against each other. Who the hell did it hurt?

Surely, not them. No, divorces made it final to their fights. They could go on about their fucking lives as if they survived decades of torture. But, what about me?! What if you are raised in the hellhole and that's normality for you?

Then what? How the hell am I supposed to feel when shit IS normal? It made me want to ruin it, that's what.

Fuck normality. I piss on normality. I spent so many years trying to be normal, live a normal life, be like everyone else…and all it got me was padded fucking walls. Normal is what you're used to.

The problem with me is that I didn't know where that normal laid…was it with my mom and her overbearing need to suffocate me, 24/7? Was it with Boo and partying? Was it with Basia and her infatuation to save my soul at all times? What the hell?

The only time I felt normal was at Darron's, when I played Super Nintendo and hid myself away from society. That's accepting to me. Just get the fuck away from everyone and stay in my own zone.

Darron hated me. Basia hated me. Boo hated me. Fuck, the whole town of Pierre hated me.

Jeff hated me.

God dammit!!!!! Get it out of my head…if I wasn't thinking awful thoughts already the vision of Jeff's wreck was still fresh in my mind.

Nobody but Boo knew that I was in that car. It was a secret from my own conscience to keep quiet about. Nightmares told otherwise.

Fuck…what the fuck am I supposed to do for a damn year in this place?

White walls…white pads…white polo shirts with needles…white tile, white bed sheets…white people. It'd be nice to see a little red on my knuckles…that would be a sight.

When Cindy, the shrink, approached me, she had a bigger smile than I wanted to see. I was mad at her, too. The last time she visited me, I had refused to talk and she wouldn't give me a cigarette. Fuck her.

"It's day seven, Cardy. Ready to behave?"

I mocked her in my head. No, I wasn't ready to behave. "Yeah," I gritted such a lie.

I pushed passed her before she changed her mind. "Give me a cigarette…"

I demanded. I didn't care to be nice or polite. She did nothing for me to offer such kindness.

"Give me an hour." She firmed her tone. Her notebook was against her chest, ready to talk.

"Take me outside." Another order or I wasn't going to do shit.

"After lunch." She gestured for me to follow her.

"Whatever." And I did follow because I was hungry. In lock down, you got a sandwich and a bag of chips. I didn't get a choice on a beverage and sometimes ended up with Apple juice. If I was lucky, I might be able to sue for starvation when I got out. If I was anywhere near under a hundred a fifty, I just might.

"Have you been in our cafeteria, yet?" Her voice was enthusiastic as she twisted around to see my expression. Today, she wore a business suit. Black with thin pink stripes, it looked good. Her hair was wrapped into a bun, pins on the sides. Her black dress shoes clicked against the tile. Hmm, I guess she didn't know who she wanted to be, either.

I couldn't figure her out. Her outfits were obtrusive, chaotic and indecisive. One day, she resembled a virgin. The next, straight to the point. She worked long hours. That, I knew because I saw her all the time. She smiled a lot, even when I was giving my all to hate her. Optimistic, or so, she tried.

"Are you going to give me a cigarette outside, after lunch?" I trailed her backside as it swayed lightly in front of me. Women, they didn't know that a walk meant something. Today, her walk was determined. Tomorrow, it might be frustrated. Never know.

She stopped at some huge double doors, hand ready to tug on the handle. "Maybe."

Maybe wasn't good enough. If I wasn't starving, I would have turned around and headed up to the fourth floor to my room, sulking to get my way with her. She seemed the easiest to cave when it came to me feeling pressured.

"Are you going to eat with me?" I grinned, wanting her company, as I didn't know how to behave in such a noisy ass atmosphere, anymore. I don't know, one wrong look from somebody may send me back to the pads.

"Sorry, no," She checked her watch. Bitch. "I have other plans in the teacher's lounge. I'll give you a half hour. Then I'll come back and give you a tour, outside. A half hour, Cardy. Remember to be nice, I know you don't like isolation."

Bitch.

FINE.

Colored metal picnic tables were lined up in rows. Hear me? I said colored. It was relieving to know that someone in this bitch had enough decency to decorate the cafeteria tables with some color. Green, blue…wait.

The kids were color coated…or color coded…whatever it was. The green polo's sat at the green tables. Green was fourth floor. I was green, although I still didn't agree to wear the required uniform that they gave me.

I was still in my white t-shirt that smelt like a three week old prostitute without a shower. Imagine that. And, remind you…I haven't taken a shower, either. I was filthy because I was defiant. I was being defiant because I could give a fuck about impressing any motherfucker in this bitch. Maybe if I was dirty enough, they would expel me for contaminating the staff with whatever lurked underneath my clothes.

That would be the day.

Most of these kids were around fourteen and fifteen. Their polo's were neatly tucked into their pants. Their pants were creased and straight. Their shoes were bright white and their shoelaces were actually laced up and appropriate.

I already knew that I didn't belong here. These kids parents' considered them rebels, but for what? Back talking? Skipping school or missing church?

Give me a break. Maybe I needed to be in jail. This wasn't the place for me. I towered above most of them. My voice was deeper than the rest. I walked different, I acted different. I had character. These kids…these kids ate what was fed to them.

Not me.

I stood in line behind a fat kid. This kid had an afro bigger than a rapper's. He was white, with pimply skin and freckles. His armpits were wet from sweat and his pants were a bit too tight. Still though, his appearance was accepted, tucked in, strapped up, and obedient.

His tray was red, matching his shirt color. I watched him closely as he grabbed chocolate milk and headed for some nachos.

The food was fire. Not only did they have chocolate milk, but cans of soda and Gatorade. Nachos and pizza and salad…chicken patties and fries…god damn, they had everything all at once. My stomach growled, intensely.

I was stalled by the fat kid. He was puzzled on what to get next. He stared at the nachos and brought a shaky hand towards a piece of pizza. Then he stopped.

"Ah, come on, dog, grab both of them, will you? Get the fuck on with it." I tried not to shove him because I wanted to stay in line and eat. I wanted to watch my temper and eat. Eat, eat, eat...it was my main objective in life.

He gave me a frown. "Easy for you to say, I bet your mom doesn't give you twenty bucks to eat on each week." His cheeks were so fat that it sounded like he had food stuffed into them.

We had to PAY for this food?

"What if we don't have money?" I was getting worried, as I didn't have shit. Couldn't call my mom for shit, either. What the fuck did they expect me to do?

Now, I was really suing over starvation.

"It gets billed to your account at the end of each month. That's what my parents have me do." A razor sharp kid behind me added. His hair was greased back like the fifties did. What, sixteen, maybe my age?

"Cool." I mumbled. I grabbed the nachos and a slice of pizza...AND a thing of fries, AND a bowl of salad, and a bag of chips. I took a cookie and a bowl of chocolate ice cream and a small thing of pudding. I put a carton of chocolate milk and a can of coke on my tray, as well. Fuck it. It was time for that father of mine to get some payback.

"Are you kidding me? Are you going to eat all of that crap?" Razor guy announced to the world. A couple more kids looked on with hunger pains.

"What, ya'll can't pay for all this shit?" I smirked, knowing that I wouldn't finish half of it. Well...maybe I could. I was hungry enough.

"No, a slice of pizza alone is two dollars. You probably have about twenty dollars of food on your tray!" Razor guy wasn't too sharp in math, I guess.

"So, I ain't paying for this bullshit."

I think I started a trend...already. Razor guy and tree-top kid behind him piled food onto their blue trays. Parents couldn't yell at you until the program was over. Glad I thought of it.

I strolled over to the green table and stayed clear of Brett, my roommate. No need to spend more time with his stupid ass. And, I wasn't about to sit alone. Fuck that.

There was one empty chair between a two guys talking. They weren't just normal conversationalists, either. They laughed, they glanced at the others, and they shifted in ways that portrayed that they were the shit.

Well, they weren't the shit, anymore.

"What's up?" I intruded their space, took a seat and opened my carton of milk. I waited for a remark…I wanted to start shit.

Intimidated, one guy spoke for the whole group. This kid looked like a fucking Nazi. His head was bald and it pointed up in the middle, like a bullet. His eyes were cold blue and he had a tattoo on his wrist. Prejudice pansy.

"Uh, new kids sit down there…" He had the nerve to point down towards Brett, who sat with maybe about five other loners. No one down there was talking to each other, just eating in peace.

I didn't want to sit down there. I wasn't *about* to sit down there. Fuck no, I was there to be known.

"Nah, I like it here." I slumped down into the green chair and picked up a nacho. I smiled to myself as I swallowed. Then, I took a bite of my ice cream, swirling my plastic spoon around to piss them off.

Cold blue Nazi eyed the others with indecision. Others searched for clues around the blue tables. They were confused on how to handle me, as most people were, when you fuck up there routine.

"Well, I'm saying I don't like you here, so get the fuck up and move!" He snapped his fingers and pointed, yet again.

I scoped out the scene, the other kids. No one looked like the Nazi I was sitting by. Maybe he was the cool one at Safe Haven. Maybe he was one of the hotel rats that Dean couldn't get rid of. Hmmm…

I bit my pepperoni pizza and cherished the greasy cheese that hung down like a torn rubber band. It was so fucking delicious. I hadn't had pizza since…

"Are you fucking deaf? Charles just told you to go away, when Charles tells you to go…"

I turned my head towards the squeaky follower of *Charles,* the Nazi. "And, I said that I wasn't going to sit anywhere but here from now on because I don't give a FUCK what Charles has to say." I blinked with a challenge, ready to get out my aggression…

Just needed a few more bites of this heaven…

"Christopher Deburke! Get over here, right now!!!" A familiar tone echoed into the air over the crowded voices and directly centering my ears with nonsense.

It was Cindy the shrink, the bitch who wanted to overdose me with nicotine if I fed her my life story. She was fifteen minutes early and I wasn't happy about it.

"What now?!" I pushed the chair back and sighed like she was a problem to me. I could feel their eyes on me as I did this. I didn't think much about it until later...nobody was rude to Dr. Roma.

She was too nice to be rude to. Well, I didn't care. I had lost everything but my pride. I wasn't going to lose that.

"Do you know who you were talking to?" She headed through the double doors and down a long corridor to the fresh wilderness that awaited me.

I grinned in disbelief. This kid did have a reputation for something. "Charles the Nazi?" I laughed harder.

"Yeah, Charles Dunmore the fifth, actually. He doesn't like strangers and is one of the only problems we have at Safe Haven. He was sentenced here, three years ago, and still manages to screw up so he can stay longer." She assumed that she had said enough and I would leave him alone.

Fat chance.

"Is fourth floor where you put all the kids who are sentenced? All the convicts, the fuck ups?" I was laughing because it was too funny to disregard. Charles the fifth didn't mean shit to me.

"No, it was coincidence, but now, I may have to move you." She opened the electronic door to the outside world. A breeze of fall hit me suddenly in the face and I swept away by nature.

God, I loved the outdoors.

"Move me? Why me? Why can't you move him?" I was getting rather fond of Stan and Pete. No better way of getting acquainted than a physical greeting with fists.

"Because we've tried every other floor and this one is a good one for him. He hasn't had a fight in over a year." She guided me around a wall and towards a bench. A sign that read 'staff only' was posted at the entrance.

Smoke time.

"Come on, I was just about to be friends with him." I smiled, knowing that he was about to be friends with my knuckles...the kind of red I was looking forward to seeing back in my white walled cell.

"Oh, yeah, friends alright. Don't start trouble and then there won't be trouble, okay? Here, smoke fast." She handed me a Marlboro Light and a purple lighter.

"I wasn't going to start trouble with the guy. I was mingling."

Chapter Thirty-Nine
Angie

"Angie, why did you like me?" His voice drifted in the air as I drifted off to sleep. I heard him, slightly. Sure, he was right up against me, I felt him. But, it took a minute before I registered his words into my reality.

I shifted my head against the pillow. "I don't want to talk to you, Boo. Go to sleep."

"Why do all the girls like me?"

Realizing that he wouldn't shut up, I turned over and faced him…the clock flashed three in the morning. How rewarding.

"I mean, what the hell did I do to get like this? What makes me so different than everybody else?" there went his soft irises, throwing questions at me that I had nothing to reply with in return.

"Why do you care?" I countered it.

"Because I do. Why did you obsess over me?"

Those feelings were long gone. I didn't obsess over him, anymore. But, I remember it like it was yesterday. He was the cool one, the one that every girl was talking about in the restrooms. He was the one girls wrote about in their letters. He was the one my friends had crushes on and would kiss their pillows and fists in honor of his lips.

He was the Brad Pitt of our generation. He had charm, the look, the athletic ability to be great. He sweated testosterone and smiled perfection. He was everything, "it," the "one." He was the challenge to get with and the gossip to spread about when it happened. You were something if you got with him. You were envied if you slept with him. You were the talk of the town.

"Because everyone did." It was that simple. I crushed on him because he was the trend.

"That's not what I think." He was starting something with me. He wanted to keep me awake.

"Why do you think, I'd love to hear it." He had no fact to think otherwise. I challenged his knowledge of me.

"Because you wanted to break me. You wanted to change my ways and make me fall in love with you, that's why." He smiled, confidently.

"Yeah right, whatever makes you feel better." That was a lie if I ever heard one.

"Oh really, did you ever find your diary?!" He chuckled as if he knew more than what I knew he knew.

Oh my God!!!!

Within half a second, I hoisted up the pillow and slammed it against his head. When he tried to jerk, he fell off of my small mattress. He tumbled to the ground in shock.

"You didn't take it, Boo! Tell me you didn't! I lost that thing before I even brought you in my house!!" I stood on my bed, bewildered. I tried to recall the last time I saw it. I had accused Amanda of taking it. I imagined running across it someday, maybe in the couch or behind my dresser, something of that sort. I had never imagined Boo taking the damn thing!

He jumped up with a wider grin. He got me awake, alright. "No, you left it out on your night stand when I came over. I took it the first time I was here. I assumed you knew it was me."

"Why would you take something so personal from me!!!?" I grabbed the other pillow and continued to hit him, along with slapping his arms as he blocked my blows.

"Was it more personal than what I already took?"

Oh, the bastard, the stupid conniving jerk! I was so embarrassed. What did I write in there? What the hell was in there about him, I couldn't remember!! Oh my God, I should have never let him in. I'm never talking to him again. He could kiss Devon goodbye!!!

"I hate you!!" I screamed in tears.

"Don't cry about it! It was nothing, really. I was amused, that's all. Is that what all the girls do, write about me in their stupid diaries as if I'm some God to them? Why the hell would they ever think that?! That's why I brought it up. What the hell did you girls think when you got with me?!" He still thought it was something to laugh about, something to tease me about.

Oh, I hated him.

And he wouldn't drop it. He wouldn't leave!!

"Get out, Boo Sox! I hate you! I never want to see you, again!!"

He deflected every blow I struck. He pushed me against the doorway and pinned me there. "Don't say that. I'm sorry. I'll give it back to you! I was curious. I used it to show that I had you, that's all."

My eyes panicked. My heart broke in a million pieces from humiliation. I cried louder. "You showed it to everybody? How cruel can you be?!"

"No, I never read it to anybody! I swear. I swear on my mother's grave that no one else read it. I was going to give it back to you at the end of the summer but then you pissed me off. Come on, I liked it." His body was all over me, hands on my arms, chest against chest, heart against beating heart.

I still hated him.

"Get away from me. I wanna sleep with my sister. I can't stand to be around you." I freed my fist and jammed it into his stomach. I wasn't playing around.

He coughed and hunched over. "Fuck, Angie! I'm sorry! You don't have to be embarrassed about it!"

He chased after me as I dashed into Amanda's room. She was already standing and wondering what the hell was going on.

"He read my diary, Amanda. He stole it from me!" I was in tears.

It was Amanda's turn to hit him and cuss him out. I shriveled into a ball and soaked my sister's bed with tears. I was mortified.

"Why don't you leave her alone and go home! Nobody wants you here, anyway!" She tried to slam the door in his face, but he wouldn't let her.

"Amanda, tell her I'm sorry. She shouldn't have left it out in the open. What the hell did she expect! Come on, I like your sister. I want her to talk to me. Just as friends, alright?" He still smiled. It was the smile that made Amanda hold her ground and defend me.

Then, I decided to team up with her and get him out, together. We both might be able to take him and shove him into the cold. He was too strong, too tall, too...everything.

"Ah, fuck, come on, stop being bitches!" He realized that we were both charging and about to hurt him. All the while, he smiled.

To tell you the truth, after my tears had dried and the anger had dissolved into battle, I was having fun. It was fun to push Big Boo around with Amanda. He was having fun, too, as his grin and chuckles to overpower us were contagious.

"You're never going to get me out of this house!" He held onto the doorframe to the kitchen. We were forced to get him out the back door since he ran towards it. His fingers held tight to the border. Our bodies shoved into his stomach…those tightened abs that were now working to his advantage.

"Ya'll girls are weak, I swear." Every now and then he would make a smart comment as a tired Amanda and I tried to tackle him down. It was useless.

"Oh, I give up!!" I was the first to.

"You good, girl?" He grinned at Amanda.

"I'm gravy, Boo, let's go." She smiled back.

Oh, Jesus. I pushed Amanda away from him. "Just go to sleep, he won't stop. He's too stubborn to stop!"

He laughed all the way into my room. He smiled all the way to my bed.

"I'm still mad at you."

"I don't give a fuck." He lit a cigarette after he knew he wasn't supposed to. Knowing his hardheadedness, I didn't bother to scold him. I sat next to him with my hand open.

He gave me one.

"You know who you remind me of?" I sighed, inhaling something that I rarely did unless he was around me.

"Who?" he leaned back against my mattress and eyed me. He still was too alert and awake. It made me mad.

"Cardy, Cardy would come over here and fight with us. He was just as stubborn as you are. He never gave up and would drive us mad."

God, that boy was insane at times. Sometimes, Cardy would jump on our counters and kick shit at us, whatever it was, sugar, paper cups, whatever was handy, he would kick it. He'd jump out and tackle us, even though we were girls. He played too rough, but it was fun. I hadn't had that fun since then.

"Hmm." He was thinking. Instead of speaking what was on his mind, he leaned over.

He kissed me.

Oh my god, he kissed me. Where were my defense mechanisms? What the hell was going on with me?

I kissed back, cigarette falling to the carpet, probably burning a hole in it. Did I shove him off? Did I make sure I didn't burn the house down?

Unfortunately not…

His mouth covered mine and laid my body back with ease. His breath was soft and sweet. I don't think he even took a puff of his cigarette, as I didn't taste it. His heart raced, waiting for me to stop him.

I didn't…I couldn't. Something was wrong with me.

His fingers laced through my hair and pushed it away from my face. His lips were tender and smooth. His tongue was perfectly manipulating. Every touch from him was relaxing. My muscles eased. My mind erased. My skin itched for his hands and my body yearned for his contact.

"Angie," He mumbled through his teeth.

I didn't care what he had to say. If I spoke, I may have stopped him. I refused to. I ignored him.

"Angie," He said, again. His body was warm, too warm for me. I felt the heat of his skin against me.

Again, I didn't speak.

He knew not to go further. He knew it.

But, he didn't listen to his thoughts. And, I was glad.

"Angie, we need a condom." His breathing was fast and his heart pounding. Mine was racing with anticipation.

My hand went into the air and I felt my finger point to wherever. I was trying to show him where they were, where he had left the box when he was around before Devon.

Then, without my response, he threw himself away and sighed, heavily. "Fuck, Angie, talk to me!"

I blinked and focused in on his face. I was already in dreamland, drifting somewhere between reality and bliss. I licked my lips for more and found my voice.

"They're still where you left them." I cracked.

He laughed. "The same ones?"

"Yeah," I barked, impatiently waiting for the outcome, the best and worst part of Boo Sox.

He wiped his face and paused. What the hell? I tugged on his shirt so he would get the hint. It was only a small reaction to get it going, but he got the point.

He pulled his shirt over his head, and reached over me. His skin smelt like heaven, a mixture of man and cotton, soap and cologne. His skin *tasted* sweet as it touched my lips. His long body hovered over me as his arm reached down to the floor and under my bed.

When he wasn't fast enough, I pulled him. He lost his balance and fell against me. He came back to my face and ripped the wrapper only inches from my mouth. Then he kissed me. The wrapper was tossed to the side.

I had forgotten about Boo Sox and what sex was about. Quickly, all the memories came back. This time, I didn't feel ashamed of my body. I didn't have time. My concentration was on him, his movements, and his breathing.

Oh, his breathing was something. I didn't remember how eager he sounded, before. This time, it was all in his voice, his sounds, his silent but moving desire for me.

And then, the fatal words of the moment were…"Go out with me, Angie…"

And I had to say yes.

Immediately, fireworks blasted against my eyelids. Rockets screamed in my ears. It was magnificent and miraculous. No words could describe what my nerve endings were feeling. It was like I was turned inside out, thumping and sparking new waves of emotion. My lips trembled from the reaction. My legs had gone numb and my whole body was tingling.

What the hell just happened to me?

I was frozen. I was replaying the last few sparks of pleasure throughout my body. Could it always be like that?

Boo was quiet, now lying next to me. He was deep in thought, maybe regretting me. I didn't know…and I didn't care.

"I didn't mean to…" He started to say, but I stopped him.

"It's okay, really…" I had to admit it.

I had wanted him. It was awful to say, but I wanted to be his girlfriend, too. I was so ashamed in feeling that strongly about it.

I was weak.

"Good," He smiled, kissing me lightly on the neck and fading asleep.

It was my turn to be alert. I stared at him…all night long. I tried to figure out why I wanted this, why I liked him all of a sudden.

I was confused.

Chapter Forty
Binderman

I had a girlfriend.

"Angie!!" My voice shot through the silent morning like an avalanche. Fuck, it was so quiet around here. I didn't even raise my voice.

"Angie, girl, come on, get up." I tapped her cheek, lightly. Her eyelids were closed. Her mouth was parted. Some of her hair was tangled against the pillow. It was a rough knot that needed to be cut off.

If she was my girlfriend, then she needed to be girlfriend quality. No girlfriend of mine was going to drag herself around like she hated her body. I was tired of seeing pony tails and sweatpants. Angie needed a self esteem lift.

I couldn't bring myself to kiss her awake. A thin line of drool had dried near her lip. Her untamed hair was getting on my nerves. I could have easily rethought my decision and changed my mind. Last year, I would have.

Last year, I had Fresca.

And Teesa.

No, what Angie needed was a makeover. It was time for her to feel like my girlfriend...

"Angie, get up, it's time to get up!" This time, I tapped her forehead.

She bolted upright. "What, what's wrong?"

I leaned back to stare at her. She was so...average.

"Aren't you going to Cheriton?" I smiled with bigger intentions to the question.

"Oh my gosh, no!" She jumped up, lost her footing and fell onto her floor. Without rationalization, she threw herself into her dresser, withdrew out a pair of jogging pants and bounced a leg in.

"What the hell are you doing?!" I was confused at her erratic behavior. Did she always act like this in the morning? Was she crazy?

"Boo, it's eleven thirty! I had to be in class at nine!! Why didn't you wake me up, earlier?" Her hands were all over the place, giving me gestures, patting her wrist, pointing to the clock...just chaos spewing.

I laughed, now realizing that she was dumb and mistaking my question as something else...like today being the first day of school. "Angie, calm down. You don't have school, today. I was asking if you were enrolled. I guess you are." I couldn't hide the grin any longer.

Her face froze until she huffed. Her eyes squinted and her hands came after me. "What the hell, Boo!! I almost died getting my clothes on!!!"

I grabbed her wrists in defense, all the while, laughing at her misjudgment. "No shit, how's your face?!"

"I don't have time for your games! You know I'm enrolled!! And don't poke me to get me awake, I hate it!!!"

Why did girls think that they knew how to break out of a guys grip? She couldn't do it no matter how much she groaned and moaned. It wasn't going to happen.

Instead, I let her go. She flung backwards and landed on her ass. I think the girl was born with one side of her head filled with lead. She was so fucking clumsy.

"I enrolled, too. That's what I was getting at. We can ride, together." I rubbed a cigarette between my fingers, ready to smoke.

"Really? Nuh-uh! That would be so cool if you're serious, Boo. What major did you choose?" She sat at the foot of her bed, giving us some distance. Maybe she didn't understand the word "girlfriend."

A girlfriend sat next to me. My girlfriend sat on my lap. Whatever the circumstance that made her sit away from me...it wasn't going to be because she didn't mean what she said, last night. She was keeping her word.

"Architecture or environmental design, I don't know which one, yet."

Who was Angie's last boyfriend? When did she ever have a boyfriend? Did she not know how to act around me? These were important questions that I needed to know.

No, I already knew the answer.

I had been messing around with Angie since her junior year. She didn't have a boyfriend, then. The way she acted that summer was obvious that she didn't know what she was doing around a boy.

Damn.

"Wow, are you sure you're up to the challenge?" It almost felt like she was reading my mind. Was I up for the challenge of dealing with an inexperienced little girl?

But, she meant my major. Her eyes widened as if she was shocked to hear my degree of choice. She didn't think I was serious. Her eyes said so.

"What's there to challenge? The only thing that I'll have trouble with is attendance. Girl, I make good grades. You don't even know."

My words made me remember what Cardy had said, years earlier. He had made good grades, just didn't feel like doing so. Hmmm…was he good in math? Did we get that from B.J?

She smirked like I had the charm but not the brains. "Okay, but I'm not book smart, Boo. I can't help you if your life depended on it."

I stood with a smile that turned into a laugh. "Trust me, I don't need your help." I unlocked the latch on her window and began to raise it. I wasn't about to run into her mother while trying to smoke.

Finally, she joined me for a cigarette. When her hand opened for one, I gave her mine just to see what she would do with it. Smoke it all, share it?

"Boo, everyone knows that you made little girls like me do your homework. That's why you came in with the second highest grade point average. You're such a cheat." She was confident in her accusation. She was so confident that she wasn't nervous around me, as her elbow touched mine and she handed back the square.

"Wanna know a secret?" I whispered in her ear, too eager to pass up intimidating her. "I never cheated on my schoolwork in my life. I swear on my mother's grave. That was a rumor or cover up, however you look at it."

Her eyes stared at me, then. The dark blue became aqua with the sunlight. Brown sparks danced their way around her pupils, as I noticed her shade more clearly. She let her voice fade into a whisper, too. "Why would you want to cover up something like having good grades?"

"Because people expected me to be stupid. It's cliché, I know. You don't know me, at all, Angie. I barely know myself." I tapped the square until the cherry fell onto the windowsill. Instead of smashing it back in place, I tossed the rest of it to the patio, outside.

Cigarettes were a cliché, too. If I was smarter, I would have never started.

As serious as she could be, and as serious as she could ask me, she went on. "Who are you, then?"

I had asked her that very question a few weeks ago, looking for an easy answer.

At that moment, I didn't care if she had indention marks on the left side of her cheek from lying on her sheets all night long. I didn't care that her hair screamed for repair mechanisms or that her cuticles were swollen and peeling.

I didn't care because she wanted to know me.

The real me.

My eyes softened. My lips melted for confession. "I'm from Cheriton. I'm smart, I can speak four languages, I play piano, I sang in choir for twelve years…I read, I ride horses, I'm Catholic. I can recite most of the bible, I took etiquette classes…I know my manners. I'm everything that tells you I'm a Cherry…because I am."

I think she swallowed the smoke that she tried to exhale. She was dumbfounded. Her eyes desperately looked for a hint of exaggeration, a grin to let her know I was joking.

But I wasn't.

It was a long time since I had been my mother's Binji. It was time to recollect those days.

"And you came to Pierre with the knowledge to rule it…" She was reciting her own storyline…but seriously…yeah, I knew how to persuade the hardest of hard.

"I had no idea that I would wind up being this way. I never said that this is what I wanted to do and how and why…it just sort of happened. People around here are cheap. I bought them with my money. That's all they needed to know." My heart raced ten times faster than it did when I saw Devon popping out between this girl's legs.

My heart fluttered on the verge of ceasing as I was in a territory that I was scared of. I was admitting to secrets that only Fresca knew, that only my family knew…my mother, in particular.

"Boo…" She whined a desperate realization. "You have so much going for you! I can't believe you know all that stuff! I mean, I really can't believe it!!! To be from Cheriton…that's like coming from another country, with a gold spoon in your mouth! What languages do you know?"

She was intrigued, if not obsessed, over what I might say next. It amazed me that she accepted the lies I had lived with over half the past decade.

"German, Russian, French, and Spanish. We had accelerated courses at St.

Paul and I used to travel with my dad, a lot, so that helped, too." My arms still shook with uncertainty. I was waiting for her to ridicule me or say something awful.

Then it was a game to her.

"Say something in French…"

"Vous aiment aller faire des emplettes pour l'universite?" I smiled with confidence. I'm sure the pronunciation was rather weak, as I hadn't spoke French since I was sixteen.

She giggled with excitement and applauded. "No way! What did you say?"

I lit another cigarette, as I was too nervous to go on without one. "I asked you if you wanted to go shopping for college. So do you?"

"Oui!" She exclaimed…and she hugged me. She fucking hugged me.

"Ce qui sont nous achetant?" She tried hard as hell to ask me. (What are we buying?)

I guess she took a French class in high school.

I beamed at her with anticipation. "Everything…" No need to say it in French. I didn't need to boast about my talents anymore than I already did.

Soon enough, I gave her the luxury of being a Sox. Being a Sox meant getting what you want, when you wanted it, and all the luxury in going overboard. That's what being a Sox meant to me, that is.

"Oh no, I couldn't possibly…when you said shopping, I thought you were talking about getting you…" Her speech was jumbled up with anticipation, opportunity, and excitement.

I encircled my arms around her chest and let the necklace drop into place. I don't think she ever owned a necklace. I didn't see a single jewelry box in her room, let alone her house.

The necklace wasn't anything to call home about. It was just a diamond one, a simple piece on a string…I wouldn't be proud of it. Shit, Fresca had dozens of those misplaced around her room. I used to find them under her bed, that's how careless and abundantly supplied she was.

It was nothing, really.

But, it was everything to her.

"Okay, take it off. I can't keep it." This time her tone was firm as she tried to undo the back.

The jewelry store worker eyed her, suspiciously. Angie stood in the middle of the floor, sweatpants and all…refusing a gift that I wanted her to have. Angie made it so obvious that she wasn't used to this attention. Her posture was off. Her stance was poor and defeating. Her attire…well, I was about to work on that.

I smiled politely, but disregarded her attempts to take it off. Aback, I grinned more. "You can't give it back, I bought it. I give a no return policy, warranty included."

"What do you mean you bought it? I just put it on!" Her lips frowned like she just signed her life away without warning.

"I buy a lot of things without trying them out, get used to it. Here, it matches."

Unfortunately, I didn't rip the sales price off of this one. Angie was a bargainer, someone who bought during sales, and that's if she bought at all. "Oh my gosh, Boo. No, no way! There's no way I can accept this! Look at the price!!! It's ridiculous. I can pay all my books with this!!!"

I wasn't used to arguing with a bitch…girl, rather…over a price. Usually, she took it before I would change my mind. Angie…Angie, fuck…

"Don't put it back, I swear to God, Angie. It's nothing…it's cheap, that's what it is. Do you know how many bracelets Fresca has that can pay for your entire college tuition? That girl could buy an island with all the jewelry I bought her."

Which reminds me…somehow, I needed to get it back. That's why my dad was bitching. All the fucking necklaces that girl had…the rings, the earrings…I'm sure that's where most of the money went to.

He didn't even check *my* account. My inheritance account was drained from Cardy. That motherfucker was about to pay my ass back for that shit. Just wait…just wait until I inform him about his money…he's cutting me a check.

"I can't believe people like you waste your money on things like this. Do you know how many people are starving? Do you even care?!" Oh the bullshit she was into!

"Fine, Angela…I want you to keep the fucking necklace and I'll never buy you another one. Just take it. We'll feed Africa, later!" I was fed up with her bullshit. I was pissed that she could deny me like that.

I left the store, letting her wonder after me.

"Kids are starving!!" Her save-the-world-bullshit continued.

"Then do something about it!!!" I snapped, heading directly towards the double doors to have a cigarette.

"I can't, I don't have any money."

"You wanna save the planet? You really want to feed motherfuckers?" Her honesty and commitment, the dedication in her fucking eyes…God, what the hell was I getting myself involved with?   "Fine. Do what you want…feed them. But, you can't go around looking like you crawled out of a fucking zoo. You need a haircut…and some clothes." I doubt she got the picture, clearly.

I meant that she can use my money for whatever she wanted, if she presented herself better.

"What are you talking about?" So clueless.

I grabbed her shoulders. "Angela, you're my girlfriend. You can do what you want with my money, I don't give a fuck. It's just money…just let me buy you some clothes." Her sweatpants were going in the garbage as soon as I got my hands on them.

She smirked in disbelief. "Yeah right."

I flicked the cigarette out into the street and pushed her back towards the mall. "Get your ass in there and find something to wear."

I thought it would go peaceful. I thought that the girl knew what she liked and had an idea to what size she was.

But she didn't.

She was worse than Fresca when it came to clothes. Fresca just collected shit, tried it on later. Too many bags, not enough time, arms full of jeans after jeans. *Angie,* on the other hand, couldn't decide on anything!

"You are killing me, girl. Pick something, anything, out! You don't have a single thing." I wasn't used to this behavior. I wasn't used to Angie, period.

"You don't seem to understand, Boo. I am so many different sizes, it's crazy! That's why I wear sweatpants. Nothing fits right. If you haven't noticed, I'm a bit bigger than most girls you see!" She was just as frustrated as I was.

"Then pick a bigger size!"

"That's not how it works. Look," She grabbed a pair of jeans that Fresca would never be caught in. I laughed at that rationalization. Fresca wouldn't be caught dead standing next to this girl, either.

"See, I may be a size nine, here," She held the waist of the jeans at her hips.

"But, I have a size twelve in love handles and probably a fourteen in my thighs. Then you get to my calves and I can wear a size seven. All the butts in these things sag, they're too long…"

"Jesus Christ, Angie…" I think I was just spoiled with Fresca Taylor, I don't know. She was a size five at her biggest, thick thighs and all. What the hell was up with shit like that? Shouldn't there be something for everyone?

"What?" She snapped. She dropped the jeans back on the rack and headed towards the back…where shelves stocked bigger sizes.

"I'm just saying…fuck, I don't know. Remind me never to go shopping with you, again." She could go with her sister, someone who was used to her erratic indecision making.

Angela broke down, then, right in the mall. God wasn't making this light on me, I swear. "I just want something that looks right on my body, Boo. Nothing ever looks right on me. It's not fair. Every other girl can wear what they want, eat what they want. But, noooo, big fat Angie has to be a whale!!!"

I couldn't help but roll with laughter. A whale? She considered herself a whale? I lifted up her chin and let the nasty tears touch my fingers. "Angie, baby, you're not a whale. We'll find you something that fits. Come on, you can do it. Fuck these jeans…"

It was all I could do. Angie was crazy.

And whale? What the fuck was she talking about? Yeah, she needed to tone up and work off her stomach…but Angie had thighs, maybe not firm thighs like the cheerleaders, but they were definitely worth holding onto…

"Where are you going?" I redirected her away from the jumpsuits and guided her out of the store. Apparently, this place wasn't where bigger people (with thighs) shopped at.

Chapter Forty-One
Cardy

Day two in the cafeteria: nachos, pizza, fuck the salad, fries with chili, and a hot fudge sundae. It was all I had to look forward to. Tomorrow, I'm adding that country fried steak smothered in gravy. God, I was so hungry!

I didn't bother Charles the fifth Nazi generation of his kind. No, I had better things to do…like eat.

I even checked out the breakfast platters, this morning. The last time I had everything on my plate like that was when I lived at home. It was back when my mom would slave all morning trying to get her family to have breakfast, together. The only one who ate it was me, me and her.

Jeff.

Why the fuck did I bring them up for? Anytime I thought about my mom or my family, I thought of Jeff. In turn, I thought of my nightmares of that wreck. It was in the past and I wanted to forget about it.

But, I couldn't.

Obsessive thoughts led a long ways. Jeff turned into the wreck. The wreck resulted into Boo, and Boo resulted in my life. It was never ending. If I was good on my word, I should have been cured by now. If Cindy was good on her word, I wouldn't have a cigarette to smoke, after lunch.

I saw her an hour a day, every day, except for weekends. I said as little as I could to get her to hand me over a square, nodding and agreeing, shaking and smiling. She seemed please with what little progress I gave her to work with and that was that.

Nothing really amounted to anything. She didn't really know me. And, I wasn't about to admit that I had any ties to my past.

I didn't have heroin cravings. I didn't think of sex. I didn't think of Basia or Lynn or any other bitch, for that matter. I didn't masturbate. I didn't overly masturbate. I didn't do shit. I didn't think shit.

I didn't have reoccurring dreams. I didn't miss my mom...or my dad, Jebb. I didn't think about my real father...who I hated with a passion. I didn't want to die. I didn't think of suicide, everyday.

I didn't deserve to live.

Nope. I didn't think of shit like that. Because Cardy didn't think like that. Cardy was invincible. Cardy was some kid with supernatural powers who didn't feel shit at all.

Okay, I was in denial.

Who fucking cares?

"Gimme a cigarette." I plopped down into my chair for the hour. I grabbed her name plate and huffed on it, polishing it because it was smeared. It bothered me like my thoughts did.

She rolled her eyes. And I mocked her.

I liked Cindy. Cindy was cool. I could get away with murder if she was around. She was so naïve. She was so trusting.

Okay, but I didn't want to commit murder. I already slashed the throat of Cardy number one and decided to hold his body captive to drug infested dreams. Ha, that was funny.

I was in a foul mood, today, wasn't I?

"Can we start over, Cardy?" she insisted and dropped, rather slammed, the yellow pad of paper onto her desk. She was in a foul mood, too. I can tell.

I leaned forward with annoyance. "Fine..." I stood and circled the chair. I repeated myself.

"Gimme a cigarette," And plopped down like before.

She smirked. "You know better..."

"Oh, I forgot." I grabbed her name plate and huffed on it, again. I was so fucking cocky...

She decided to snap to the point. "Dean is breathing down my throat to get something more on you. If I can't crack you, then he's transferring you to Dr. Godfrey. Trust me Cardy, Dr. Godfrey will evaluate you in a way that's not amusing. He gets right down to your childhood and yeah, he may help you...but, not when you *feel* like talking. I like to let the patient decide, he doesn't."

I frowned. No Cindy?

I frowned worse...no cigarettes?

"Well, you're just gonna have to do your job, then. Crack the shit out of me!" I encouraged, although it wouldn't be what she wanted to hear.

"I'm trying, Cardy, I'm trying! Tell me something I didn't know, yesterday…like how do feel about your other brother?" Her hair went behind her ear and she pulled out a pencil.

My what?

I was puzzled. My other what?

Brother, brother, brother…what the fuck was she talking…

"I hadn't seen him since I was five!" It finally occurred to me that she knew more about me than what she was leading on. I didn't like the lies. I felt betrayed.

"But you remember him?"

"I was five!" I shouted. No, I didn't remember him…

"What do you recall about him?"

Blonde hair, blue eyes…a smart mouth, a fast runner…someone to look up to rather than Jeff, someone to want to see and play with when I saw him next time.

"Nothing."

She scribbled on her notebook. "Nothing? You can't recall a single detail? He may have walked right beside you and you wouldn't recognize your own brother, your flesh and blood brother? You wouldn't know him enough to say 'hey, he looks like me, huh?' nothing of the sort?" She was getting impatient with me. I didn't like it.

"I would have recognized him, Cindy. If I saw him before, then I would have noticed him, again. I fucking played with his ass when I was little, of course I would know him."

Oh.

Fuck.

"So you do remember him…you know what he looks like, you've played with him before, enough to say that you would recognize him later?"

What the hell was she getting at? Why would she ask me something so stupid, so wasted…

"You act like I'm on trial, Roma!" I stood, opening the palm of my hand. Sometimes, I liked to call her Roma, just Roma because it pissed her off.

Quickly, she recovered her purse from the floor and unzipped it. She was pissy and full of piss and just pissed off. She threw a pack of cigarettes at me and jerked her purse at her feet. I smiled, widely.

"Why does it even matter, Cindy? It's not like I'm going to meet the guy when I get out. I'm not going to some family reunion on some motherfucker's side that I don't even know! The motherfucker doesn't want me, Cindy. He made that perfectly clear. He's bullshit. I mean fucking bullshit!!!" I argued my case in front of her desk, not taking my eyes off of her, not lowering my hands for one minute. The bitch needed to know how serious I was about that motherfucker being in my life!

She sighed and leaned back in her chair. "That wasn't so hard, was it? All you have to do is vent, Cardy. The honesty is in there. You just have to get it out of you before you explode, right? Am I right?"

I was pacing. I didn't realize I was pacing until she repeated herself at the end. I stood still, thoughts brewing. "I need medicine."

"Excuse me?"

"I said I need some fucking medicine before I go insane, Roma. I can't take this shit, anymore. I can't sleep, I can't stop thinking. I don't know if I'm scratching because I'm nervous or if I need a fix. I can't take this fucking shit!!!" I hit her wall by reflex, shocking myself in the process.

I was flipping out.

I didn't want to think about Binderman. I would admit to anything if I didn't have to think about *my other brother*.

He didn't exist, he wasn't real to me.

"Alright," She did some more scratching with her pen. "I will fill this prescription, personally. You will have your meds, tomorrow. What else is happening to you that I need to be aware of?" It was a side of Cindy Roma that I never met.

She could be business. She had the doctor tone and direction about her, when she used it. Naturally, though, she was a friend…a dedicated someone who sacrificed her life to save that one person that could sum up her entire career.

I sat back down in consideration. What should I say, where should I start?

I inhaled a breath that I didn't feel like letting go with. "Did my mom tell you I have A.D.D?" I didn't say A.D.H.D because I abbreviated the abbreviation. It was all the same, right? I mean, all the H meant was hyper. She could get the point.

"Your records explain that, yes. You were on Ritalin. When was the last time you took it?" The Cindy I knew was missing. Dr. Roma was sitting in her chair. I didn't know if I liked Roma.

"Fifteen." I smirked, knowing that my mom had been right about my behavior. I didn't think about it until now. I had so much adrenaline in my body that it needed to be idled down, somehow, someway. If Ritalin didn't do it, then street drugs were the substitute.

It figures.

I bet most people out there didn't know that. I bet most criminals needed Ritalin. There was some times where I just wanted to destroy for the sake of destroying…because it felt like a release. It made me feel good, ironically.

Did I relay this feeling to Cindy, I mean, Roma?

Fuck no. if she didn't know what I would do without Ritalin, then it was on her. She was the damn doctor.

"Where were you getting the drugs, Cardy?"

Interrogation, is that what this is? Were they looking for a name, was that the deadline Dean was talking about?

I wasn't a nark.

I folded my hands on my stomach. I bounced my legs. I twisted my neck and arched my back. I was getting uneasy. I was getting unhappy. "What drugs?"

"You know what drugs, Cardy, don't play around with me, anymore. I'm talking about the prescription meds you were popping, the Oxycodone, the Percocet, the Ativan, the Lithium, um…what else was in your system, Heroin, by chance? Cocaine, marijuana…the list can go on and on, Cardy." She arched her back, too.

Something was going on with Cindy. I'm not talking about with me, in this office. I'm talking about outside of this place, her personal life. She was getting impatient with me because of something else. I felt it. I knew all too well when it came to people taking shit out on me because of someone else.

I'd rather bring Stephen, her boyfriend, up. Let's figure Roma out.

"What's up with Steve, huh, troubles?" I tried to grin the bad feelings away. I tried.

Her head tilted to the side in disbelief. Her hair followed, red and thick. "You know what, that's fine, Cardy." She bent down, came up with her purse.

She wrapped her fingers around a yellow lighter. "You wanna smoke?!" She threw the lighter at my head. "Do it on your own time!"

She didn't stop there. Her lipstick, her sunglasses, her eyeliner...all went towards my direction.

I was stunned. The bitch was just as crazy as her patients.

Then she cried and apologized. "I am so sorry...oh my God, I can't be doing this. I need a vacation! I really do! I try so hard to be there for my patients...but no one cares how much I try...I really do try...I had it. I just had it with everything..."

Mid life crisis?

Rag?

Stephen troubles?

What the fuck?

If she was insane, then who was I supposed to impose on?

Dean?

I jumped up and ran to her side. I had to. I needed her to be there for me. I was just warming up to her.

"You're lucky it's me you're having a fit with. You'd scare the hell out of a little kid..." I wrapped my arms around the lady and held her against my chest. Her hair was soft...and sweet...and beautifully pleasant to smell...

Like fresh soap, downy sheets...linen, again.

She surrendered for only a moment. It was enough to know that even a doctor, professional or not, was able to break down from life's obstacles.

Even then, minutes after my aggression had startled me...I was shocked to feel my next move. So opposite of my temper, I swallowed my pride and hugged her. I would have with my mother, so long ago.

A woman was crying. A woman needed me. I could have easily shrugged her off and laughed her away, because I was feeling selfish and angry. But, did I?

My moods were so off balance that I reacted before the thoughts arrived. I reacted to instinct...to a woman crying...like long ago.

She lightly pushed me off of her, appreciating that I did it, but nonetheless, embarrassed. Still in tears, "I should have never...I don't know what's gotten into me. I'm sorry, Cardy, today's one of those days. It's so wrong of me to...well, it's not your fault. I...I need to go home." She stood, backing me up, once more.

I sat on the corner of her desk, still too close to her. I felt awkward, too. The twisted vibe of confusion was upon both of us, rising to the air like a thick fog, lingering between our bodies as we figured out what to say, what to do.

It, indeed, was not about me, today.

I played with my fingers, trying not to swing my leg as she picked up the contents of her purse. I was quiet. Too quiet, wanting to say everything to her, wanting to give her more reasons to stay than leave me.

My temper was gone. I was not feeling selfish. I wanted to hear her thoughts, her worries…her plans.

"Stephen broke it off with me. He told me last night. I should have stayed home like my sister said, but…no, stupid me goes to work and pretends that I'm not bothered by yet, another failed relationship." She said this, aloud, but mainly to herself.

"Do you have to go?" My eyes absorbed her sadness, her movements, her tears as they dripped onto the yellow notepad. My leg didn't listen to me and decided to swing, nervously.

She glanced at me like a person, now, not a patient, a kid, but of another human being, who wanted her to stay and join the world.

That connection was a lot to me. It told me that there could be more of those, later. We could share thoughts about relationships, her and I. I had plenty of observations to go on…me and Basia, mom and dad, Fresca and Boo…me and Lynn…

And then there were all the relationships that didn't mean anything…like all the girls, all the guys…and friends. Friends made certain connections, too.

All I know is that Cindy Roma and I connected that day, on another level. I touched her and she let me. I hugged her and she needed me. She was about to confide in me…it was a lot.

I felt special.

She grabbed my shoulder and squeezed."Thank you, Cardy." She left me to sit in her office, on her desk swinging my leg. Instead of running after her, I quickly closed her door and smoked two cigarettes, back to back.

God, it felt good.

"No…thank *you*, Cindy." I smiled. I was satisfied with a full pack of Marlboro Lights.

Chapter Forty-Two
Basia

From school, I detoured to Amanda's house. She was going to quiz me on a test we were having in Algebra, tomorrow. I wanted to make sure I would get an A, not an A or a B…a specific A, if not an A+. It was important to me. And, Amanda was great in math.

I hadn't been over at Amanda's house in a few months. And it was even better because I didn't have to bring Jasmine and keep my eye on her. Angie and Amanda had a lot of clutter going on. It was hard to keep little hands off of knickknacks and such. I don't know how Devon didn't break more things.

"You probably don't need me to help you, Basia. You were good in that class when we had it, together, remember?" Amanda took a good five minutes looking for her keys, when all she had to do was turn the knob. It was unlocked for a change.

She sighed and gave me that look. Angie was home. Angie was home with Boo. I didn't know the scoop, yet, until she filled me in.

She walked straight to her kitchen, dropped her book bag and opened the freezer. She took out two strudels and tossed them in the microwave. While she watched the glass plate make its turn around and around, she had some gossip to share.

Amanda never gossiped. But, she liked to clue me in on Angie, her sister, at times. This time, we were both concerned.

"Angie's going out with Boo. Can you believe it? She dyed her hair…it looks good, but…she's turning into one of them…" When Amanda, or I, say 'one of them', we mean one of the cool kids, one of the popular people who follow the trend.

"He bought her new clothes…he spends the night, which mom doesn't know about. He's all over her like she's something. I'm just afraid that she's gonna get hurt. I mean, she's his girlfriend, Basia. Or that's what he tells her, that is. If she's Boo's girlfriend, that makes her his number one girl. I don't believe it. I don't believe it for one second!" She wrapped a paper napkin around a strudel, handed it to me, and repeated the sequence for herself.

I was surprised, like completely shocked, to hear that. I thought Boo was a thing in Angie's past and now she was smarter in making boyfriend choices. I thought that she knew better than to trust Boo. I thought she *hated* Boo.

"Why would she do that? He cheats on girls, Amanda. He's going to hurt her…" As soon as I closed my mouth, low and behold, Boo Sox came strutting into the kitchen. I slouched in a chair at the table and hoped he wouldn't dare try and make conversation.

"Who's going to hurt whom?" He let the question mingle in the air with the breeze, not caring to hear an answer. He opened the back door and lit a cigarette. He was shirtless, mind you. I didn't appreciate men walking around without a shirt on.

That's why they made shirts…to wear them.

His eyes danced over Amanda and then to me. He was being nosy and intrusive. He stood at the back door, leaning his shoulders against it. His body was a landfill of tattoos, carelessly placed around with colored ink.

I tried not to stare at him when he looked the other way. I tried not to be impressed with his chest, or his stomach, his biceps, or the groove in his hips as it dipped down. No, he was full of toned muscles that didn't deserve to be talked about…or thought about. I didn't care that he had an athletic body like Cardy…or forearms like Cardy, or hips like Cardy.

No, I didn't care. I didn't notice anything.

I didn't glance over every time he made a sudden move, because I didn't care. When he blew smoke out of his mouth, and the sunlight hit his eyes at the perfect time…I didn't pay attention. I didn't care to think about the curls in his hair and wonder why he didn't shave it like he used to.

I didn't notice Amanda doing the same thing because "us" girls, didn't think like that when it came to Boo Sox. He was off limits even in our minds. He was something that ruined little girls and Angie, for that matter. He was anti-boyfriend material that didn't need to be appreciated…perfect abs or not.

And a quick thought of his lips, how perfectly bowed and soft, didn't plant onto mine, locking in the sweet satisfaction of bliss. His arms didn't imaginarily wrap around my body in a heavenly slumber and spoon me the way Cardy did.

Boys should keep their shirts on, that's what I think. Then unpleasant thoughts wouldn't be a hassle to deal with. It went for the same for girls…guys and this sort of stuff didn't come up in parent teacher conferences. Guys shouldn't get double standards. It just isn't fair.

"Basia!!" Amanda's tone reminded me of Darron's, not too long ago.

"What?"

She nudged me in the arm to stop staring.

When Boo disappeared, Amanda had a lot to say. "What were you doing? I know he looks good and all, but he's a jerk. You can't look at jerks like that. And, he's my sister's boyfriend. What if Angie looked at Cardy like that? I wouldn't be hearing the end of it for like…forever. You'd hate my sister!"

I didn't understand what she was talking about. "What was I doing?"

"You're eyes were all over him. It was so obvious, Basia. You have a crush on him, don't you?" How dare she accuse me of liking Boo freaking Sox. It was so wrong of her!

"I do not! I was just looking at him. I don't like-like him. He reminds me of Cardy. Don't tell me that you don't see it. It's all over his face, all over his body. There's something to him, that's all. He could be Cardy's twin." It was odd to me.

They were so similar that, for a moment, I saw Cardy in that doorway, smoking a cigarette. Why did they look so alike? I mean, yeah, some guys had blonde hair and blue eyes, similar characteristics…but, those two…if Dena wasn't married to Jebb, I would swear that Cardy belonged to the Sox's. It was that apparent.

"I think you just miss Cardy and see Cardy in everybody. Just last week you said that the way that one kid in your class wore his hat like Cardy reminded you of him…and you even said that the way Bobbi laughed reminded you of Cardy…you really need to get your head away from Cardy. He's making you crazy. He's making you look at Boo Sox, Basia!" Amanda was right. I was thinking too much about Cardy, too many times.

"Yeah, but if Boo was Cardy's twin, then Bobbi would be his sister…" It made sense to me. I of all people know what Cardy looked like. She should understand the knowledge I had and the assumption that was taking place.

Amanda laughed and headed for her room. "That would be crazy, Basia. Do you really want Bobbi Sox to be your future sister in law? Think about family get-together's, you'd never feel comfortable around her."

I know it was stupid of me. "You're right." But, as I walked out of the kitchen, I couldn't help but turn my head left towards Angie's room. Boo was throwing his shirt on over his head. I swear I smelt the pure skin smell of Cardy, lingering and lacing my thoughts with curiosity.

Boo looked like Cardy. If my nose wasn't deceived…Boo smelled like Cardy.

So, I did what I would have never done before. I had to find out. I had to put out the flame that sparked my interest, and quickly. I didn't need to go back to Darron's and wonder about this theory. I didn't need Boo dreams interfering with my Cardy dreams.

I walked into Angela's room and stood, nervously. They both looked up at me like I was an idiot.

"My book bag didn't wonder in here did it?" It was the only question I could come up with in such a short period of time.

Boo smiled and slipped on his shoes. He probably knew I had no reason to venture into this room. He knew better than that.

"It shouldn't have. Did you touch her book bag?" Angie, her hair long and dyed with thick blonde highlights, sharpened her eyes at Boo.

Boo shook his head with a laugh while he tied his shoelaces. "No, it's probably in the kitchen. Did you even *look* in there?" his eyes met mine and I held my breath.

Oh my gosh, his eyes were crystal blue like the ocean, not original at all. I knew those eyes. Those eyes were Cardy's eyes, my daughter's eyes. I knew those irises well, that sparkle and gleam, that mesmerizing glare into my own.

Stunned, I stepped back, almost falling over a white statue of a dog, so carelessly misplaced at the wrong time. Why did they collect statues of dogs? Why did it have to be there, next to the doorway, just so I could trip and look more like a fool?

Boo stood, so tall and lean. So muscular and built…so Cardy-like and intimidating. He rubbed the top of his head, the way Cardy did. His curls were small, yet thick. They bounced so lightly with his fingers. Just like Cardy's.

Nobody had hair like Cardy. Cardy had his own wild mane of curls that grew to unearthly measurements. Cardy had to straighten them. Cardy had to add so much gel and hair spray into his locks to get it stiff and spiky. No, no one on this earth had hair like Cardy.

Except Boo.

Why did Boo have to resemble him?

Is that why Boo buzzed them, because they were a hassle to deal with? The more I thought about it, Boo was a lot like Cardy, maybe not in personality because Cardy was sweet and charming. Cardy was down to earth and didn't expect women to fall at his feet.

Amanda's hand jerked me back to reality and pulled me away from the torture that my mind was creating. "What are you doing? You're book bag is in my room. You tossed it in there when we walked to the kitchen!"

"See?" Boo had to add as I was hauled off. Nobody was talking to him. Nobody needed to hear his opinion.

Now he was sounding like Cardy, with his deep voice. Oh, I was stupidly dumb and insane. I was crazy and hallucinating.

"How can I concentrate when he's in the next room?" I forced myself onto Amanda's bed and slid my book bag to my feet. I unzipped it on a subconscious level. I wasn't thinking of homework or studying.

I was comparing two boys for no reason at all.

"I don't know what's gotten into you lately, Basia. Darron said you were staring at Kyle, and now you're staring at my sister's boyfriend. I think you're boy crazy in a weird way. Cardy needs to come back and put you in your place." Amanda took out her own math book and pencil. She sprawled across her bed behind me.

"I wish he would." I mumbled.

Before I had the energy to lift my great big Algebra book into my lap, Boo appeared in Amanda's doorway. It was his turn to give into curiosity.

"How's that baby of yours?" He leaned into the doorway, letting his weight be supported by his fingers that gripped the doorframe. His hat was on, now. His eyes pierced mine with infatuation.

Oh, those beautiful blue eyes…no wonder why people drooled over him. It was one characteristic that I missed of Cardy, his translucence into my soul.

Stuttering with my nerves, I froze. "Good, I mean, great, I mean, whatever." I wanted to pound my forehead with a stupidity stamp. I was nervous. I was nervous because…

Unfortunately, I liked Boo Sox. No, I loved Boo Sox.

But, only because he reminded me of Cardy. It had to be the only reason.

He laughed, again. His chuckle was amusing. It was a relief to hear. "The last time I saw her was when Cardy stole her…" It was a memory that I didn't want to remember.

I stiffened with confidence. "Oh, well, she's at Darron's if you ever wanted to see her, not that you have a reason to, unless you have some ties with Cardy that I don't know about."

As I said this, Amanda shoved me hard, so hard that I almost fell off of the bed. What? He wouldn't know what I was talking about unless it was true. And I highly doubted that I was right.

His eyebrows rose with interest. "I'll visit Kyle, then. I hadn't seen him much, either, lately." And he left.

He left.

Chapter Forty-Three
Binderman

Basia Brahm. What do I say about Basia Brahm?

She was a little girl with a beautiful smile. She was Cardy's ex-girlfriend that had my niece. Baishee, I used to call her. It was a funny name to me. It rhymed with Asia. Basia, Asia. Why was I thinking of her?

Because I just left Angie's house and that little girl was over there with Angie's sister, that's why. She was perfect for Cardy to come home to. I wish he would know that. She was everything that shouldn't be taken for granted.

I took Fresca for granted.

Basia was a church girl, born and raised. She respected people. She did the right things, like keeping Jasmine away from Cardy when he was sick.

She was a good girlfriend and I respected her.

My head was filled with thoughts about her as I drove home. I wish I could help her, somehow. I wish I could give her money for Jasmine. I wish I could tell her about Cardy being my brother. I wish…I wish…I just wish I could approach her and tell her everything.

I never meant to harm Cardy. It wasn't my fault that he was the way he was. I know she blamed me. Fuck, I blamed myself for exposing him to that lifestyle. If it wasn't for me, then she would have him the same way that he left her…untouched by partying.

I don't know, maybe it was my entire fault. I was his big brother. I should have known that he wasn't used to the things I was used to. I should have known better than to let him smoke and drink. J.D knew better.

J.D told me not to do it. I think, in his own way, he didn't want Cardy to be like us. He knew he was doing wrong. No big brother should want that for their siblings. Only, I wasn't thinking. I thought I was being cooler than J.D.

I was wrong.

I pulled into my driveway and noticed more cars than what should be parked there. It was my Aunt Cathy's car and Cody's Lexus. Fuck, what kind of family affair was I walking into?

Nobody looked happy. My Aunt Cathy was slumped over her knees in our recliner closest to the fire place. A mug shook in her hands. My cousin Cody was on the edge of his seat, drinking a beer. Wren was there, too, sitting on the arm rest, hand on Bobbi's shoulder. Bobbi had tears in her eyes.

My father stood, too nervous to sit. It made me think that something had happened to Uncle Brody…or Dewey. Brody and Dewey were missing from the group.

"What's going on?" I dreaded those moments. I *hated* those moments.

My father spoke, first. "Cody needs you to get Dewey with him. He thinks that you two are the only ones able to walk in there and get away with it."

Before I could question everything that was now filling my head, Cody continued. "We found Dewey. He's at Seth's. He's been there for a couple of months, now. If B.J or my dad would go in there, they'll start trouble. They'll think he's a cop, which he is…it's not safe. I figure we can get in there and drag Dewey out without some crack heads starting shit with us. And Dewey would be more willing to come if it's us…if it's you."

Dewey had been my sidekick since we had been in diapers. In the past recent years, I had traded him for Cardy and partying. He wasn't the partying type, too shy and reserved. He was mainly anti-social, mixed up with some head drama that made him feel different than other people.

I don't know. Dewey had issues, too. I think we all did.

"Why didn't you check Seth's before?" If he was living at Seth's, then he was worse than I thought. Yeah, he may have turned Cardy into a junkie, but I thought Dewey…I just wasn't thinking.

"I didn't think Dewey knew Seth, Bin. I only took him over there once. I had no reason to think that he was getting shit from Seth."

"Bullshit, Seth supplies everybody, motherfucker! If shit's going around, it's coming from Seth. Someone needs to do something about him. I'm tired of his ass fucking with my family. Dad, you should do something about him. Stake him out or some shit." I was serious. Seth Bryant needed to go to prison.

"He's that bad? What does he do?"

It was Cody who clued him in. "Seth controls most of the Northwest. He deals heroin, coke, whatever sells. He's been in and out of prison, already.

Nothing sticks because his dad's the sheriff, you probably know him, Bryant, I think."

"Bryant? His son is the reason that my nephew is the way he is? He's the reason why my son is the way he is? I *will* put a stop to it." and he headed for the kitchen to make the appropriate calls.

I felt like a nark. I hated to be a nark. But, Seth brought it on himself. He should have never fucked with my family.

"So, what, are we gonna drive over there?"

"You be careful, Binji, Cody. If you have any problems then call B.J. Don't hesitate. I'm going to tell your father the news." She took out her own cell phone to make the appropriate calls.

"Yeah, grab him and go."

Brandon Deburke sat in his diaper, in his playpen, in the corner of a room. He no longer cried. He was exhausted from the energy it took to wail for his mother. He no longer looked from side to side in search of a body to pick him up to comfort his saddened soul. He no longer sucked his bottle because it was a bitter sour curdle of a taste. Although he didn't know his colors, he knew it didn't look right, anymore. It was a thick layer of chunk, browned at the edges and broken off into the watery stained poison. It was awful.

He was starving and dirty. The diaper was unhooked on the left side. Feces had seeped out and dried to his thigh. His fingernails were long and caked with the diaper contents. His hair was matted to his head, no longer blonde, but muddy from the formula and stench he slept with.

The only toy was a metal spoon, rusted around the handle. There was a dried puddle in the center of the spoon where the heroin had been. Brandon could reach out and grab more interesting objects, such as syringes and pipes, toilet paper tubes with burnt aluminum foil taped into it. He only tried five times, but gave up because his body gave into sleep.

Every now and then, he would hear his mother's voice trail by. But to her, he stopped existing. He was a burden. He was a bad seed that rooted into her stomach and wouldn't die. If he talked or comprehended, or thought logically, he would be able to escape the torture of neglect. But, he was only ten months old. It was only a matter of time before he gave in for good.

It was in God's hands, now. It wasn't like he was the only one going through this hell. Many babies have crack head mothers. Many die. And if that was what God had intended, then so be it, right?

Maybe he was supposed to be a statistic. When the time came, the numbers would prove a reason for serious action. Maybe this tiny innocent baby was supposed to die and never understand what love and happiness was about. Could God be so cruel? Or was there a God?

And just as his eyes were falling and peace was taking over…he was gripped up by two strong hands. If he was older, he'd feel like it was God, a blurry image outlined in the dust, taking him to the heavens.

But, it wasn't God and Brandon wasn't dying. He did all he could do to smile up at his savior. And for once, a smile was returned.

"It's okay, baby, it's okay." I cradled Brandon in my arms and lashed out at Dewey, again. "How the fuck could you let this happen?! Look at him!!"

I didn't want any part of Dewey. He had let Brandon die. He didn't care that Brandon sat in a filthy cracked out play pen in a room he shared with Lynn. He didn't give a fuck as long as he got to fuck Lynn.

Stupid bastard. I hit him again with Brandon in my arms.

Cody did a fine job at hitting Dewey, himself. Dewey was getting hit from all angles, as we defended this little baby on the verge of death.

Seth was trying to collect his things for a getaway. He knew he did it, this time. Well, Seth wasn't going to get away with this place. One number and he was just as good as dead. I had dialed my dad and shit was about to pop off. I didn't even have to say much, just "call the cops, now."

Lynn stood naked in the corner, hands over her mouth with wails for forgiveness. I had hit her, too. I had slung her off of Dewey so fast and hard that her body flung across the room and into the broken dresser. Her body was skin over bone, flesh hanging and sagging off of her arms, ribs protruding at her chest, stomach sunken in too deeply. Her hair looked as if it was falling out.

Cody and I had walked into this house with no expectations. To our fucking surprise, Lynn was sitting on top of Dewey, fucking him…all the while as Brandon sat in the same room in the corner, dying.

Cardy's son was dying. My nephew was dying. It was all I could think about. It was all Cody could think about. Fuck saving Dewey. Dewey didn't deserve to live. We had to save Brandon, this baby that had nothing to do with Heroin addiction, yet everything to do with it.

"Dog, come on, just leave. We'll handle this. We'll figure it out. We'll take the motherfucking baby to the hospital and help Lynn. Come on, dog, don't bring the cops here. Tell them it's a mistake." Seth pleaded with me to cooperate.

Like it was an option to consider…

"I'll give you all my money, all my dope, whatever you want!!" Seth held onto my arm and squeezed it like he was going to hurt me if I didn't do as he said.

I jerked it away. "Don't fucking touch me!"

Cody had other plans. Cody stuck his hands behind him and withdrew a gun. I had never saw Cody with a gun. I wish I never did.

"Get the fuck away from my cousin, motherfucker. Step back, right now. You think you can let this shit happen without consequences? You think messing up my brother and my cousin's kid is okay? Well, fuck you, you fucking bitch! Fuck you!!" He was trigger happy. Cody's arms were shaking. He was actually thinking of shooting…

"Cody, come on. Don't do that shit! I have a fucking a baby in my arms!!"

Everything was happening so fast. Dewey with Lynn. Dewey fucking Lynn. Lynn was a crack head. Brandon was dying. And, now, Cody was about to make the biggest mistake of his life by shooting Seth.

And he did it. My eyes squeezed shut to shield out reality.

Seth fell to the floor. Blood splattered my face. Blood hit the baby. My knees buckled and I dropped.

Cody cried out in horror.

All I remember is that I didn't drop the baby. I held onto Brandon like it was the death of me. I didn't see more, didn't feel more, didn't think more. I just didn't drop the baby.

Even when my dad tried to peel Brandon away from me, I held on for dear life. My dad didn't know who he was, but knew it was a fucked up situation.

Watching someone die…it doesn't really register in your brain, yet. It's like watching a movie, being a part of a movie…

It was like seeing J.D, all over again. I never thought I would have to deal with another dead body in my life. Seth was dead, or dying. Whatever the different, I couldn't do anything about anything.

Cody was arrested for murder.

Lynn was arrested for child endangerment and possession of a controlled substance, and everything that goes along with being a Heroin addict in a Heroin house.

Dewey was taken to the hospital.

Brandon was ripped from my chest by the paramedics.

The cops did their usual with questioning and I could barely speak.

My eyes never left Cardy's little boy.

Besides that…I felt numb inside.

Chapter Forty-Four
Cardy

Their showers were stand alone stalls, like you would see in a gym. No curtain for privacy, but at least there were walls. The water got hot, quick. I liked hot steaming showers.

The stalls were white, the tile white. The bars of soap were white. The towels were white. What else was new?

After my shower, I decided to wear the damn uniform. I was agreeing only because I was tired of standing out in my dingy white t-shirt that I tossed in the trash can. The green polo wasn't the size that I would wear it. It was a size too small. It was too short for me, as well. I had to tuck it in to make it look right.

The pants fit too perfectly. It was the kind of perfect that I didn't care to appreciate. They fit, unlike the saggy way I liked to sport them. With a belt, I felt like I was from Cheriton…in a cheap, copy cat way. Even Cherries wouldn't wear this crap.

I felt plain.

I didn't have cologne or deodorant. I didn't have a razor, which meant that the fuzz on my chin was getting thicker and disgusting. They didn't give razors to anybody. You had to earn a shave…like it was a privilege to hold a razor. They didn't trust me and assumed that I could kill someone…or cut up some coke.

Now that would be amusing. Like I knew how to break the piece of shit and find some cocaine in this bitch. That would be the day.

Not that I would do it. Maybe I would, maybe I wouldn't. It depended on my mood.

It was time to venture outside.

Green, blue, and red polo shirts scattered around the vicinity like dropped M&M's. Everyone was everywhere. They were playing tennis. They were playing basketball. Some were standing around observing, others reading on the benches. Some were writing under trees. Wherever they were, they were busy.

I had nothing to do.

I strolled near the basketball court and leaned against the fence. Charles the Fifth Nazi was playing and missing the net every shot he took. It made me smile. The boy wasn't good at anything I bet, but running his mouth. At least he was trying.

He played against another one of his friends, who seemed pretty good. The boy was tall and had his shot position down. He curved his feet, arched his arms and got all air into the net when he tried.

Charles didn't look like a player of any sport. He was short and bald, dark and evil. I saw him collecting Nazi signs in his room. I saw him leading a group of misfits into war. I saw him killing his classmates for mistreatment.

Yeah, Charles didn't look like an athlete. Looks may be deceiving, but his skills proved me right.

"What are you looking at?" Charles noticed me and held the ball against his waist. It was exactly what I wanted him to do…stop playing so I could show him up. I needed to work on my shot, anyways. It had been what, three years or so?

"Wanna make a bet?" I smirked, coming onto the court and stopping in front of Charles.

"Yeah right, with what?" His words lashed like it was a sword he was swinging.

"I don't know, what do you want from me? I don't have money and I can't get money. So, money's out." My head was working fast, as I wanted to play so badly. A bribe seemed only fair to get him to play me.

"How about your lunch…for a month. And, you'd have to do my chores for a week." Charles stood before me, maybe to my shoulders. He spoke like he could talk down to someone as tall as I was.

"Motherfucker, I'll buy your lunch for a month, but I'm eating too. Fuck that shit. And, I'll do your chores." He wasn't about to ruin my love affair for food.

"Cool, let's play." He bounced the ball to his friend and smiled."You have to play him."

"Alright, cool." His friend had nothing on me.

As soon as the ball hit my grip, it was a feeling of ecstasy. I hadn't touched a basketball in three fucking years. All the memories of playing came back to me. The voice above the crowd chanted in my head, recalling all my past shots of victory.

I loved it. I loved the sport, the adrenaline rush and release, the jumps, the dodging and dribbling…oh, I was in heaven with this game.

Damn, I was rusty. I didn't make a basket within five times of trying. I was disappointed in myself. It only made me try harder. I was a competitor at heart and I loved a challenge.

I loved the fresh air, the noise, the sound of my feet against pavement. This is where I belonged…on the court, outside. This was my terrain…my turf…my sport.

By the time I got my jump shot back, the asshole was winning. But, that was okay, because I was back. Cardy number one was back in my body and making a point to win.

I felt free.

I felt victory on the tip of my fingers as I made a comeback. The final move felt awesome. I pump faked to the left, power drived, and…

"Aw, I banked it, motherfucker."

But, I won. That's all that mattered. I didn't want to bank it off the backboard, but what the hell. It made me win.

Charles wasn't happy. I had caused a crowd to form, as we were playing to win and not just to play around. Most of them were talking about me, not Charles or…

"What's your name, dog?"

"He isn't your dog, bro." Charles snarled.

Bro. I hated when people said "bro." I guess "dog" could go the same way.

"Well, I ain't your bro, either, motherfucker." I snapped back.

"People call me Billy." The tall guy smiled, willingly ready to play, again. We slapped hands with respect.

That's when Charles had to crawl under my skin and ruin my good mood. "You just got lucky. You're not shit."

I guess he was looking forward to eating on my bill…

"Back up," I pushed him away from me because he was too close, asking for an ass beating. I didn't even mean to piss him off. It's just what I do when people get too close to me, when people step in my boundary of space.

I should have known better.

He shoved into my chest and that was that.

I knocked his ass to the ground and felt my knuckles hit his face. Over and over. His bald head was covered in his own blood. His lip swelled with pain. His eyelid bruised with defeat.

He wasn't shit when it came to fighting, either. He was just a fucking mouth and I was disappointed in what he had to offer. It wasn't worth a week behind padded walls.

And that's what I got. Stupid ass. Next time, I'm really pounding his face in the pavement, just for causing another week of hell for me. Another week of sandwiches…ugh.

I won't go into the details of Dean. Dean wasn't happy. He gave me three more months to prove his point. That meant that I had to stay eighteen months instead of twelve.

All it did was make me mad. I was so fucking angry that I didn't give a fuck anymore. It was a setback. I regressed and decided not to do shit for anyone, anymore. I tried to accommodate. I tried to adjust.

It wasn't working.

Just when I was getting accustomed to this routine…I wind up losing my temper.

Chapter Forty-Five
Dr. Cynthia Roma

I don't understand Christopher Deburke. He's been here for a couple of months and I still don't comprehend what makes him tick. Maybe I'm not doing a good enough job at encouraging him to talk. Maybe I should be more assertive and not just a friend.

It was important for me to gain trust in him. If I wasn't hounding him for information, if he learned to rely on me for friendship, then maybe he would confide in me without the reinforcements.

Maybe my personal life was getting in the way of seeing clearly. I've done this before. I wasn't cut out for balancing out the two. I couldn't hold a relationship and career if it was the death of me. It was one or the other.

However, when I had my nervous breakdown the other day...

I saw a new light in this boy. Something amazing happened to him when I cried. He lost his pride. He came to me and comforted my tears. It was a step in trust. He cared about my emotions. He didn't want me to cry.

I obtained all of my data on Christopher. I scattered it across my desk and stared at the words. It wasn't much. It wasn't like Charles the Fifth's chart. His chart was about three inches thick, with medical records, juvenile records...a long list of interviews with his parents about the behavior of a misguided child.

But, Christopher's, hmmpf, there wasn't a juvenile record. There weren't handfuls of interviews from his family and friends. In fact, there wasn't one interview about him. I had doctor notes of A.D.H.D.

Which reminds me...a lot of times, A.D.H.D was misdiagnosed in a child. A.D.H.D is the first diagnosis of Bipolar. It is commonly assumed that a child with behavior problems had an attention disorder, rather a mood disorder. They carry the same characteristics, but on different levels. Bipolar is more extreme.

It's like a flip of mood…one day he'll put all of his energy into behaving and controlling his highs and lows. Then, suddenly, he explodes into a manic episode, tantrums and fits to get his way. Or, depressive episodes of tears and sensitivity to trust the world.

Yes, I was on to something, here. Bipolar could be genetic. I needed to talk to his family, someone other than his drunken mother. What I really needed to do is get in touch with his biological father, see what he was about.

Bipolar couldn't be diagnosed over night. It's a long list of therapy sessions to come to that conclusion. Lithium couldn't be taken for just anything. Lithium was a very powerful drug, able to drain your salt intake and cause kidney damage. It could be deathly if combined with the wrong meds. It could affect so much more if I misdiagnosed him and put him on the wrong prescriptions.

No, Christopher needed attention to the fullest degree. There were other issues there, too. I know that there was a divorce. His brother died in a car accident. He was living with a secret brother that he was not aware of. His biological father was missing. OH, Christopher, you have been through some things…haven't you?

I stared at the thin pages…Bipolar…was he one or two? Did he suffer from mixed states? Did he have the illness in the first place?

I had to do some research and quickly.

I dialed Ms. McPherson, Cardy's mother. The last time I had talked to her was when she was drunk. It was a crucial piece of evidence to his situation, her being drunk.

Even though Bipolar didn't have a certain cause, alcoholism among family played an interesting role in diagnosing Bipolar. Many children from alcoholic families, with a history of mental illnesses, seemed to add to the cause. Scientists were trying to isolate a certain gene for the illness, however, at this time, it's still in the process.

"Hello?" A tired, weary voice appeared on the line. I made the assumption that she wasn't drunk, today, but rather dealing with a hangover. She was still getting accustomed to her life change…her oldest son, dead, her youngest in rehab, and a divorce. All good excuses to drink into the night.

"Yes, Ms. McPherson? This is Dr. Cynthia Roma, Psychiatrist at Safe Haven. I am working with your son, Christopher. I have a few questions that I would like to meet with you about concerning him. Do you have time, later this evening? It's very critical that I speak with you." I didn't have time to dilly-dolly. I had an appointment with a student, soon. Christopher was just taking up my precious mind, that's all.

"Well," I could tell that she didn't want to meet with me or deal with issues concerning him. I think she was relieved to not have to deal with his behavior, as most parents felt when handing over sons to Safe Haven.

Usually, when we come into the picture, they had their share of bad times and didn't want to be reminded of something out of their control. They wanted them fixed and given back in new condition. Well, I laugh at this because they expect a miracle.

It's not that easy. Children have to adapt and adjust, just as much as the parents have to. It's a cycle of adjustment and adaptation. It will never be the same. It will and may get better, but everyone changes to fit to the new lifestyle.

It's getting there that's hard. It's understanding that takes time.

"I suppose I can make arrangements. I want to do what's best for him." Oh, the dread in her voice...I didn't mean to cause a delay in engorgement. When it comes to Christopher, she should drop everything without hesitation...for as long and as much as it was needed to.

"Good. I have your address here. Should we meet at your house? And if at all possible, why don't you set aside some things that Cardy's into, like old trophies and pictures of friends...things that make him happy. I would like to get a feel to who he was before the drugs." I smiled and jotted down the time in my planner.

It was set. I was going to go into Cardy's past and hunt him down. Who was he?

I was thirty minutes late, a usual trait of mine. I pulled up to a small ranchero house with overgrown bushes below the bay window. No basketball hoop in the driveway. No lingering newspaper on the sidewalk. No sign of life existing on this property.

The mailbox was full of envelopes. It was another sign that things were dead around here. I knocked on the door, letting it echo in this quiet neighborhood of a town called Casablanca. I didn't know much about Casablanca, except that it bordered Pierre.

The wooden door drew back, tired like its owner. A wrinkled lady appeared behind it, eyes puffed and red. She had been crying or drunk, or something of the two combined. She couldn't smile politely.

I entered into the stale room, quiet and dead with nothing to amuse my eyesight. The lights were dim. The walls were bare. One small loveseat sat alone in the living room with a television console on the floor. No flowers or vases or framed faces.

Boxes lined the hallway. In red marker, bold writing proclaimed the contents. Some had "Cardy" written carelessly diagonal. Interestingly, some others had the word "dead" across them. They must be Cardy's brother's belongings. I never thought of a parent advertising her son's things as "dead." What kind of diagnosis could I come up with for her?

I only had an hour.

"I opened up a box of his. It's there next to the table. I was going to take some things out but I couldn't. I got upset. You don't understand what it feels like to know that your son is the way he is." She slouched into her sofa and cradled her chest with her arms.

"Cardy's very bright, Ms. McPherson. I have his transcripts from Pierre Junior High. He was taking College Algebra courses. I'm sure if we get him on the right medication, he would be able to get back on track." It was a distraction that I liked. I brought up his good qualities to overshadow his faults. Parents loved to hear them.

I picked up the box, sat it on my lap and began dissecting the little boy that I knew nothing about. A t-shirt was the first to present itself. Black and faded, he must have worn it a million times. On the front, a band that I knew nothing about…was Pearl Jam.

I knew one song. The music video had caught my attention. It was about a child who shot up the classroom because he was picked on? Was that what happened to him? I don't really remember the reason. I just saw the blood being splattered across frozen faces.

"Was he into music?" I smiled at Dena as if we were sharing teenager stories. I didn't have children of my own, but I dealt with many on a daily basis.

This time, her lips curled upward as if she was recalling a time so long ago. "He was. He still is. It was always about music with him. He did a lot of sports, a lot of activities after school, but his music infatuation never died."

"Rock music?" I bunched up the shirt and kept a tight grip on it. I wanted that vibe she was getting, that feeling of a child enwrapped in his youth, in his music…

"Mostly, he went to so many concerts, watched so much MTV. You know, sometimes I think I was too easy on him. Maybe I shouldn't have let him watch MTV. Maybe I should have paid more attention to his song selection. A friend of mine was telling me the other day that kids get these wild ideas in their heads from songs. Certain bands are satanic and brainwash our children into believing certain things about life. I don't know. What do you think?" It was the first time that she actually wanted to hear my opinion.

I could go on and on about lyrics being too explicit, too vulgar, etc. But, this wasn't Cardy's case. "I think that Cardy's a bright boy with a mental illness. I think that he took to drugs to occupy something that wouldn't go away on its own. It was an impulsive instinct to settle his boredom, his needs, his rage. Does that make sense to you?"

"In a way, he has Attention Deficit Hyperactivity Disorder. Oh, it took some time to get him better. He never sat down in a classroom, wouldn't shut his mouth, couldn't concentrate. He'd go on these little spurts of rage where he wouldn't stop unless he got his way. Kicking and screaming, biting and cursing. I still never got the child to stop cursing, not fully anyways. When I reunited with him, his mouth was worse than ever. I couldn't believe that someone could use such language in one sentence!"

"Have you ever noticed Cardy being depressed?" I wrote down every word that she said, underlining certain key phrases that meant a lot to me. I could have tape recorded our session, but people get nervous and focus more on the tape spinning, rather their thoughts.

"I guess he could have. Jebb used to beat him, I mean, beat the living daylights out of that child. We fought more over Cardy than any other couple. It wasn't right, I tell you, Jebb and me. Cardy knew that's why we fought. He could feel to blame for our arguments, I don't know. I never asked him."

"Did he ever try and commit suicide, runaway? Thoughts about death? How was he around animals?" I know I was attacking her with more questions than she had time to think over. I was getting aggressive because I was learning a lot about Christopher.

In his box, there was a baseball glove, a baseball trophy, a letter from a girl…"Can I take this to my office?" I held up the folded note for her permission.

"Take what you want. He doesn't want any of it. He's so different, now."

A small cigar box was filled with notes, handwritten by a girl, or girls. A lady's man, was he? I took them just for a peek into his history with females.

It was a clue, something his mother wouldn't have looked for because she was too busy drinking.

At the very bottom were a handful of drawings…

"He's an artist, another talent put to waste." She tilted her head into the air with a sigh.

I had to set something straight before she drank herself to her death. "It's not your fault, Ms. McPherson. You didn't fail as a parent. Cardy has a condition, a mental illness that has nothing to do with you…"

If he didn't have Bipolar, then he had something else. I was sure of it.

"His father is crazy, has a crazy son, too. So, it is my fault because I should have never had an affair. If he belonged to Jebb, then he would have only had to deal with a horrible temper, not anything dealing with Bipolar." She pulled her legs up underneath her and held them.

Bipolar, she said Bipolar.

"You're aware that Cardy may be suffering from Bipolar?" It was a huge surprise to me. You would think that a medical condition such as Bipolar would be mentioned in the beginning, possibly to doctors or staff, teachers, or somebody!!!

"Cardy has a brother, an older brother with Bipolar. I didn't think he would get it. I don't know much about it, but I know the boy's crazy and psychotic. It's only a matter of time that Cardy would be just as destructive as Bin." She went through her robe pocket and withdrew a cigarette. She smoked. Nicotine seemed to be a nurtured habit. If one parent smoked, then it was more likely that a child of theirs would. Hmmm…

"When you say destructive, what kind of destruction do you mean? Is he a criminal, is he into drugs?" This was the missing link that I needed and craved to know. Cardy had lived with this brother for some time. Surely, he would pick up some bad habits of his.

"He's been hospitalized for suicide. He's cut his sister's hair. He's into drugs. He's an alcoholic. The son of a bitch used to be friends with Jeff, my other son. I never thought that Cardy would be stupid enough to follow him around like he did. I would have…I should have…"

"Don't blame yourself." My mind was conjuring up many scenarios. Cardy had probable Bipolar.

"Can I get his name? Maybe I can talk to him." My pen idled between my fingers. I was ready to make a house call to whomever I needed to meet to understand to the greatest depths necessary.

"Binderman Sox," She exhaled such an evil fog of smoke that I thought she was on fire. In fact, my chest was on fire…because I knew Binderman Sox.

My eyes almost fell out of my head. My mouth surely dropped. "Binderman Sox, you mean Binji? *He* is Cardy's brother?!" I couldn't believe it.

Of course! Cardy reminded me of him in almost everything that he did!!!!! It was a breakthrough. It was exactly what I needed to hear. Binderman would be a breeze to talk to. And I've been hearing about this so called brother of his for a decade or so. I knew more about Cardy than I had anticipated. This boy had been talked about. I had notes in Binderman's chart about this kid. This kid caused Binji so much grief and pain…

It was only obvious to link the two together. They looked so much alike! They talked, they walked, they acted…oh, this is great. This is so easy to figure out!!

"Ms. McPherson, I am so pleased to meet you. You have been more than a pleasure to talk to. You may have just saved your son's life!" I closed the notebook and stood. Oh, this is so great I could jump for joy.

Binderman was the link. Cardy was Binderman's link. Wait until I explain this to Dean.

Chapter Forty-Six
Angie

"Boo, talk to me, what's going on?" I was standing in Cheriton Hospital without a clue to why I was there or why I was called. I had been standing above him for about ten minutes and he didn't budge.

He was the color of white paste, worse than as if he had seen a ghost. He didn't move. He didn't blink. He had been turned to stone. I couldn't figure out what had happened to cause him to go into shock.

I hadn't even seen shock, before. He was scaring me.

As I took a seat in the chair next to him, his father came into the waiting room. He was a tall man, wide and bulky. His t-shirt adhered to his muscles like a fitness instructor. It was short at the sleeves and tight around his waist. He reminded me of a cop, the way he dressed. Clean and appropriate, clean and off duty. Did he carry a weapon on him? Was it tucked neatly behind his back like the ones in the movie, even off duty?

Boo resembled him with his father's hair color except maybe being just a tad bit darker. Some would confuse it as being blonde. Others would call it a light brown with blonde highlights. Either way, it was buzzed like a cop's. His face was firm and tight jawed. His neck was like a wrestler's or a football player's, as wide as his jaw line. The same blue hue from his eyes, they twinkled no matter what his expression seemed to fall under.

Boo was going to look like this man, one day. It was clear. Like father like son, Boo couldn't deny the relation. His father was handsome and younger than I had imagined.

Boo's father took a seat across from us and cleared his throat. He folded his hands on his lap and leaned forward. "He's been like this since I picked him up. He's been through a lot, today." He didn't know me, but was kind enough to say something, anything to break the silence.

Still confused on what events had taken place since this morning, I sat quietly, staring at Boo for some type of confirmation that he was okay. It had only been five hours since I saw him. He walked out of my house alright. He didn't seem to be having problems. What could have happened within such a short period of time?

Mr. Sox held out his hand as he tried to keep it steady. "I'm B.J, Bin's father. And you are?"

I grabbed it, nervously. "I'm Angela, uh," I gave Boo a quick glance, as I never addressed myself in this way before. "I'm his girlfriend."

Mr. B.J smiled. It was a smile that Boo could do when he was being polite…or when he knew something he shouldn't have known. Maybe it was a sly grin.

"Ah, yes, the one with the baby. He mentioned you just the other day. I wasn't aware that I had a grandson for a good year of his life. It's not the greatest time of circumstance to meet you, but I would like to get to know you and my grandson. Devon, is it?" His tone reminded me of a cop being nice. He said what he wanted to say in a polite manner, but the melody of his voice stayed calm and untouched.

"Yes." Now I was answering like I was talking to a cop. I couldn't think of anything else to say. I didn't know this man. This man didn't know me. Boo, the one who should be giving the introduction and saying everything that he could to make us feel less awkward, was now staring at the floor in a blank trance.

"Um," I shifted in the chair. "Do you know what happened? He was just at my house this morning." My mind tried to think of all the possibilities. Was it Bobbi? She was the only one I could think of.

Mr. B.J rubbed his face with both hands. I could tell that he didn't want to talk about it. I should have kept my mouth shut. Boo had called me for some reason. I should have minded my business and waited until he popped out of dreamland.

"My nephew is a heroin addict. Bin and his cousin picked him up this morning. He's worse than what we expected. Cody, the one who went with him, apparently shot the tenant of that apartment. He's been arrested. I don't know the details. Supposedly, it was self defense. Now, there's a baby in the mix and I don't understand why Binderman is so upset about it. Yeah, he's been neglected, but Bin seems to be most affected by that. Not about his cousin being a heroin addict, nor Cody going to prison for murder. Do you have any idea what that baby has to do with this?" His eyes pleaded for some information that he didn't already know.

A baby, did Boo have a baby that I didn't know about?

"Was he with his mother?" If I got a name of the mother, then I would be able to place a face on her. We knew everyone around here. Certainly, I would know of this baby.

He sighed, once more. He gripped the back of his neck for strength. "He was with his mother but his mother is a heroin addict. I didn't catch a name, I'm sorry."

"Lynn." Boo mumbled, still unmoved, still staring at the floor. At least he acknowledged my presence. My eyes locked onto him for more.

"Lynn Hayes," I questioned him. "Cardy's baby?!"

"Oh Jesus Christ." Mr. B.J stood and paced around the aisle of chairs. His face turned red and he wanted to fume. His hands went up into the air to do so, but dropped back into place like he didn't want the hassle.

Boo raised his head, then. He made eye contact with me and then to his dad. "I was going to tell you…"

Mr. B.J shot a deadly look at his son. "Right, I have to find out by the death certificate?"

It was a cruel thing to say. I wanted to leave and let them sort it out, whatever it was that they were arguing about.

"He's dying, dad. I should have taken him when Cardy crashed."

I didn't understand any of this.

"He is not dying, Binderman! If you would have been paying attention when the doctor came in, you would have heard that. He's not dying, he's dehydrated and malnourished. He has Hepatitis from the fucking shit he was sitting in. He'll make it through. God damn it Bin, why aren't you telling me everything when I ask you about it?!" B.J attempted to lower his temper as he sat back down.

B.J's teeth were grinding behind his lips as they locked in place. I saw the veins in his neck tighten and his jaw turn to chiseled stone. His fists were formed and braced on his knees. He was a lit bottle rocket, waiting for the wick to expire.

"I was going to! You didn't ask about Cardy! You never ask about Cardy! He's your fucking son and you can give a god damn about him! When are you going to care? When he dies? When your fucking grandson dies? Why does someone have to die before you realize all your fucking mistakes?!" It was a stab at his father that I didn't want to witness.

I didn't belong there. What I had heard was enough. The words replayed in my ears, over and over, drowning out any new ones that they traded. Cardy was Boo's brother. Cardy was B.J's son. It didn't seem possible, yet they argued like it was true.

It had to be true.

But why was it true? How could Cardy be Boo's brother when he had a father? What was I missing? Did Amanda know more than I did?

"What do you want me to do, Binderman? What the hell do you want me to do? At this point, I just want you to stop yelling at me! I want you to calm the fuck down and explain to me what you need from me!!" By then, Boo was standing face to face with him, challenging his next move. B.J shoved him to his seat and paced.

"I want Brandon with me." Boo's voice lowered as if he was still thinking about it.

"What the fuck did you say?!" B.J was just as cocky and dirty mouthed as his son. He bent over as if he didn't hear him. Were they always like this?

"I said I want him home with me. I want custody." He slithered those words...

I was...I was in utter amazement. How on earth could Boo take on such a responsibility? He wasn't thinking. His father had to be reading my mind.

He laughed and shook his head. "It's not your problem, Bin. The state will decide who gets him and it won't be you, ha, it definitely wouldn't be you. You're so fucked up, Binderman. I wouldn't trust a baby around you, look at you! Just a minute ago you couldn't speak!"

Boo was mad, then. Boy, he was mad to be told no!

"It *is* my problem, dad! Cardy has *always* been my problem. I'm the one who took care of him for the past two fucking years! I took care of Brandon, too! They're my responsibility! They're mine!" It was Boo's turn to pace, only he stuck the collar of his shirt between his mouth, instead. That was odd to me.

"It's Dena's responsibility! You're just a child!" Head to head, I could have sworn that the two would start fighting in the waiting room.

"Dena doesn't know shit about Brandon! Lynn didn't know shit about Brandon! I'm the one who got up when they were too fucked up on shit! I'm the one who changed his fucking diaper and made sure he had a bottle! I'm the fucking one who deserves him!" This was the first that I knew about those things.

This was the first that I knew about anything…

"Fine, fucking great Binderman, go ahead and ruin your life for that fucking kid! He's not even yours! Do what you want, you do anyways!!" And his father stormed down the hall to who knows where.

Boo jerked himself into his seat and stared at me, studying my face for some kind of reaction. He didn't say anything, he just watched me.

"Are you sure you can handle it?" I questioned. He couldn't even handle Devon, let alone Cardy's baby.

"I can handle everything." He stomped his feet into place and twisted in his chair. "I need you to help me." He just had to add *that*.

What was I supposed to say? He didn't like the word "no."

"Is your cousin going to be alright?" I dared to change the subject.

"I don't give a fuck about either one of them." He crossed his arms and swallowed his breath. He closed his eyes and I felt the prayers in his mind…So still, so silently wishing this would all end.

I wished, too.

Chapter Forty-Seven
Cardy

This is bullshit. This is double bullshit.

The door unlatched and opened. Cindy walked in. I wasn't in a mood to deal with her.

"I'm letting you out." But she stood in the doorway with her arms folded.

I didn't answer. I didn't want to.

Her eyes studied me like I was some lab rat. "How do you feel?"

I paced. "How do you *think* I feel?! Shed some fucking light on me, motherfucker."

"I think you feel afraid of tomorrow. I think you know that something is causing you to make the choices you make and nothing will get better. I think you want to be good but don't know how. I think you have something that requires attention and therapy. I think you need me and know it." She said it as a matter of fact.

It was bullshit.

I edged closely. "I don't need shit!" I wanted to spit in her face.

No, I wanted to play basketball.

"I think you're on the verge of a manic episode. Do you know what that means?"

Do I know what manic is…bullshit.

"Manic is characterized by excessive physical activity, rapid changing of ideas, and impulsive behavior. Would you consider yourself manic, right now?" Her arms didn't uncross. Her tone didn't lighten.

She was verbally abusing me.

"No." I sulked until I got an idea to behave. "Cindy, I feel good. I'm not manic. I'm great, see? I was just playing basketball and I felt great. Just let me out of here and I'll do whatever you want me to do. I'm good, great. I'm gracious, I'm grand. I'm fucking ecstatic and fantastic."

"Hmm," She wasn't persuaded. In fact, she seemed more amused to call me names. "Cardy, I think you're impulsive behavior says something. You may very well have A.D.H.D, but I think there's more to it. I'd like to ask you about the last two years that you stayed at a friend's house."

She shut the door and walked into the center of the room. Her long skirt followed. Today, it was red, a thick plain red.

Her arms unhooked.

"I wasn't starting shit. I didn't mean to do it. He was all over me. He was jealous or some shit. I don't know. I'm not going to fight anymore. I don't wanna be in here. I'll be good, I promise, just let me out!" I ignored anything that she had mentioned a minute ago, on purpose.

"Do you remember having feelings of anxiety, restlessness, being on edge? Do you think that the pills you were taking were calming you down or making it worse?" Her hands gathered behind her back, an approach that I didn't appreciate. It was a gesture of discipline, reassuring me that she meant no harm, yet…still…I didn't like her stance.

"What are you talking about? I feel fine, Cindy. I'm not crazy. I need Ritalin. That's all I need. Ritalin, Vicodin, medicine, whatever you feel like putting me on. I'll even take Valium, or Helium, Maximum, whatever…" I was making fun of the situation. I was grinning widely, avoiding her questions left and right. Maximum wasn't a drug, or I didn't think was a drug, it just fit in there, right along with the rest of those stupid titles.

I did feel fine. I felt like a big ass weight was lifted off of my chest and I could breathe again. I had thoughts bouncing around with the basketball that dribbled in my vision. Yeah, that basketball was really getting to me. It made me free, connecting to a part of me that I had lost so long ago.

All I had to do was behave. I could listen and go to class. I could sit in her office smoking a square and talk about shit. Yeah, it was possible. I could do it. I controlled my behavior before. I can do it, now.

"How is your sleep going?"

"Fine." I slit my eyes at her. I didn't trust her questions. She wasn't hearing me. I didn't like when people didn't take in what I was saying.

"Didn't you just say…"

"I know what I said, Roma. I'm cool, collected. Can we walk to your office so I can smoke?" I shielded the corner that I had stashed all the cigarette butts in.

She had given me a full pack of Marlboro Lights, remember? Late at night, I had smoked ten. I smashed the butts as little as they could go and shoved them into the corner. The security guard didn't pay me any mind and that went to my advantage.

"Is that what you want to do? Will you talk to me, Cardy? I mean, really respond to my questions? I'm willing to work with you. I want to help you. If something gets to feel too overwhelming, we could change the subject. It's okay. I just want to get to know you, the inner you, alright?" She let me open the door and proceed to the hallway.

The inner me...

Who the hell was inside of me?

I can tell you who was there. Christopher was there. Christopher was there holding onto my mother and my brother, Jeff. Christopher was there smiling as his father beat him with love.

Tough love, they say.

I knew my dad loved me. I earned my love from him. He had to love me. He raised me. He taught me to be discipline, taught me about the stars in the sky. He kept me in line and made me do everything right the first time.

He was the one who gave me consequences. I had to obey. Or else.

Dad, where were you now? What has mom done to you?

"What?" My thoughts were colliding with my response. I replayed her questions in my head. "Oh, yeah, I'll fucking talk to you, get on with it." But I didn't know if I was willing to open up my world.

It was hard enough to admit it to myself. I was a stupid bastard that took advantage of everyone. I was a stupid son of a bitch who ruined his life for drugs. I wasn't strong enough to face anything. I wasn't able to commit to anything.

I was nothing.

I was stupid.

I was everything that no one should be.

"Why don't you start with your mom, how is your relationship with her?" She took her seat as shrink and spun her chair in place.

Mom.

"My mom used to be cool." I started.

It was me and her, her and me. It was just the two of us against them...them as my father and Jeff. She gave me the world. Whatever I wanted she got. Whatever sport I felt compelled to try, I did it. Whatever game I was playing in, she was there. And *only* she was there.

Besides Basia and my friends, she was my life.

"Cool as in what, she spoiled you, she played favorites, she let you do whatever you wanted to do even though your father didn't approve? What made her cool?"

I *could* talk about my mom. At least, up until she switched roles on me and turned into an evil wicked witch. I could do that.

I explained our relationship, how I was spoiled. I told her how she would make me sleep in the bed with her when my father was away. How I had to drop everything to watch her favorite movie with her. How I was her best friend, as she didn't trust anyone else to be.

Me and my mother,

I was a mama's boy. Yep, that was me. I can admit it because I wasn't one, now. I was obsessed over my mother and she was obsessed over me. It was a shared commitment. We were there for each other and that caused tension between my dad and her.

I laughed as I recalled the jealousy between my mom and Basia. I decided to share the thought with Cindy.

"My mom liked Basia, my girlfriend…but she seemed to plan things around the time that I was going to see her, so Basia would be pissed. And Basia, she didn't want to cause problems with her, but I knew she was upset. It was hard to be there for both of them at the same time." Oh, that time was impossible to get back.

I used to think that it was the hardest thing in my life, to balance two women who adored me all the same. Ha, at one point, I had balanced so many girls that I had a waiting list for them to get with me. Imagine that.

Cindy had a smile of interest. I was amusing her. "You have a way with women, then?"

Flatter me, will you?

"I guess you can say that. I know how they work, what they want, why they want it. I mean, the other girls, the little ones, I never understood why they needed to be with me. I was shit, really. Everyone knew that I wasn't going to take them seriously. They knew they were being played, but they stayed in the game. I was something to be proud of…like an accomplishment to be with. I don't know. It's all stupid." I was relaxing around her. Not because I trusted her, but because I had enough nicotine in my system to calm me…to be in a state of peace with our conversation.

I could talk about girls. Girls, I knew. Girls I loved to talk about.

"Are you sexually active?"

"Am I sexually active, come on. I'm seventeen, Roma." How could she possible put me down like that?

"Hmm...how was your sex life, then?" Maybe she would start talking to me like I was seventeen and not a child. Maybe she would realize that I wasn't like these little sons of bitches that walk around smelling like little virgins.

No, I was nothing like these kids.

I laughed with my own amusement. What should I say? How should I answer? Should I tell her about all the seniors when I was a freshman? Should I explain to her that my numbers outdid everyone in this school, put together? Or did I want to get into that?

"Cool." And I remembered the game book. Let's flatter myself even farther...

"We played this game with girls. They knew about it. They didn't care. We got points for the girls we..." I stuttered on saying 'fuck' and replaced it with what I should say. "The girls we had sex with. It was fun. I think I came in second, last time I checked."

Oh, the game book. It was a red spiral notebook, folded and stained, wrinkled and falling apart. It was a book of genius, a book of competition. It was my brother, Jeff's, idea. Pages and pages were desecrated with our names of fame. Rows and columns of girls haunted our past achievements.

Our scores were circled and tallied each day. Certain bitches had titles and point amounts. Virgins were ten. The hit list, which was in the front of the book, with lines crossing off the ones already tagged, had the most desired bitches to get with. I went down the list and did my business, making sure that they knew I was number one.

My goal was to pass up Boo, as he had the highest score. My brother fell between the lower ones, like Roger and Brian. I came in second, something that no guy appreciated, as I was the youngest to play.

"What do you mean a game?" Her confusion was expected. She was an adult, an authority figure that did things the right way. How could she possibly understand the nature of this game and think that it was fine to do?

"Just a stupid little game we played." But, I had to explain the whole concept, rules and all. She was intrigued that something so selfish and cruel could be so real and involved. In fact, it controlled all of our agendas.

"You said that your friend, Boo, had the highest score? How many females did he have to sleep with in order to achieve this?"

I shouldn't have told her about the game book.

"I don't know. He was doing it since high school. You figure that St. Paul is divided by three counties and we partied in all of them, I guess you can say it was a lot. Every weekend, for a while, was devoted to racking up numbers. It was insane. We'd go through like five broads a night, if possible. Times that by four years, Boo had the most. It was amusing that I came in second. The others couldn't get girls like us."

"And why was that?" She didn't believe me. I could tell in her mannerisms. She had stopped being interested and appalled, and let the idea fly over her head.

"Because I'm the shit, Cindy, just deal with it. I ruled Pierre." I leaned back into the chair like I would in school. My confidence was showing and I wasn't about to stop it.

"Don't you think that's a little grandiose?" She made a note on her pad of paper.

"Grandiose? Fuck no. It's a fact. The numbers said so. If you would just see them drop at my feet, Cindy. They loved me. I got little virgins begging for me to take it from them. Jeff didn't get that shit." My smile wouldn't fade.

"Do you know a Binderman Sox in Pierre? He seemed to rule Pierre, too. That's what he said, anyways." Now she was trying to call my bluff, although I wasn't bluffing.

"No." I quickly announced.

I didn't know Binderman. I wasn't about to admit that Boo was indeed, Binderman, and no, I didn't know him. Binderman was my brother and Boo wasn't my brother. Let me be in denial. Facing Binderman was facing my life. I was just talking about girls and the game book, not my life.

"You know, it's been more than an hour. Can I go to my room?" I was done with questions. I was done with reminders about Binderman, too.

"Sure. I'll see you tomorrow in class, alright?"

She was the teacher of therapy writing, a class that I didn't attend because I didn't care to write about my feelings. Well, we'll see. I doubt I was going tomorrow.

I headed off to my dorm room. Or my prison cell, whichever way you looked at it. I had been in lock down for two days. It beats being in there for an entire week. Cindy sure saved my ass.

Chapter Forty-Eight
Binderman

I knew Lynn was no good. I expected this type of shit when I found out she was pregnant. She was a no good piece of shit that was tossed from motherfucker to motherfucker back when she was fourteen. Such a fucking whore, I swear.

I never imagined her being that cruel. I didn't think she would take it that far. Brandon, he was...fuck, he had sores all over his body. His hair was caked to his head. His face was filled with dirt. His fingernails were long with who knows what underneath of them.

How could anyone mistreat a baby like that?

How could my stupid cousin let it happen?

I hated Lynn. I hated Dewey. I wanted to kill both of them. I think that's why Cody took it out on Seth. He couldn't kill his damn brother, even though he wanted to. What the fuck, now?

How was this shit going to resolve?

Right when I was feeling good about myself, this shit happens. All I kept thinking about was Brandon. He didn't ask for this shit. He didn't ask to be born or neglected. He was just a fucking baby, not even a year old, yet.

When I looked at him, I saw Devon. They resembled each other, just like Cardy and me. Cardy would have been outraged. Cardy would have killed both of them by his hands. He wouldn't let them live.

They didn't deserve to live.

It made sense that Lynn would fuck with Dewey. I knew the minute that she was fucking with cocaine that it was only a matter of time that she became a crack head. It made sense that Dewey would fuck the first girl that gave it up to him. He didn't get many bitches 'cause he was too damn shy. Didn't give him an excuse to let Brandon suffer the way he did, though.

Fuck.

"Angie, are you still here?" My head was aching from all this fucking drama. I was tired of it. Angie, I didn't know why I called her. Maybe because I would have called Fresca. Right now, all I wanted was Fresca.

She would know what to do and say to me. She knew how to handle me.

"You're dad just left to the hospital. He's meeting your uncle Brody up there. He told me tell you that." Her voice came from a distance. She was in my room, but at the window.

When I glanced up, I wasn't at home. Fuck. I couldn't keep track of where I was. That's right, we went to my grams house when we left Cheriton Hospital because it was too late to drive all the way home. I was in my bedroom at Grams. My cousins and I had bedrooms at her house.

Grams must be having a fit. One of her grandsons is in jail for murder. The other is addicted to heroin. Her great grandson is being treated for everything from neglect, and then there's Cardy. She knew who Cardy was. She always knew of Cardy.

I sat up in a sweat. It was like a heat box in this room. I rubbed my eyes and face. I really needed a shower. No, I needed to see Brandon.

"Do you want to go up there with me? You don't have to. I can handle this shit by myself if you want to go home. It has nothing to do with you." I tried to be as nice as I could to her. She had done more than enough. She had already stayed the night with me and left Devon with Amanda.

She turned around from the window. Her hair had really made the difference with her appearance. It wasn't brown and thick anymore. It was framed around her face with blonde highlights. It made her look better. It made her eyes stand out.

"No, I can go. I'd like to see him. I can't possibly imagine someone doing such a horrible thing to a baby. He has to be scared, Boo. I can't picture…"

Yeah, I zoned out to his thoughts, too. What was going on in his little mind? His own mother treated him worse than a dog. He had nobody to care about him. And, if we weren't looking for Dewey, then he would still be out there, all alone.

What if I didn't go there, that day? What if I would have came next week? It would have been too late. By the look of him, he was dying in my arms. He had no life to him. His body was dead weight, hanging on with no energy.

I stood and patted my jeans for my squares.

I admired Angie. She still stood at the window, thinking about Brandon. She looked good. I was proud of myself for buying her clothes. Even though she settled on jump suits, they fit her. She looked like a hot mom, but mom, indeed.

I hugged her and kissed her cheek. "I'm sorry you have to go up there. I shouldn't have brought you into this. It's my shit, not yours. You have Devon to take care of. Brandon…"

"Has nobody." She finished the sentence for me.

"Yeah, I know. That's why I have to bring him home with me. I took care of him. I could do it, now. I'll keep him for Cardy. When Cardy gets home, he can take him back. It's only a year." My mind was racing with ideas.

I could pull this off. Babies were easy. They were easier than dealing with a teenage sister and a fucked up brother. It was easier than paying the bills to that house and studying for exams. Yeah, I could do this shit.

Brandon just needed diapers and attention, fresh bottles and affection. Money wasn't a big deal. I'm sure my dad could help out if my account runs out. That would be soon, since that stupid bastard Cardy stole my damn card.

No big deal.

"I want to help, Boo. That's why I'm here." Angie was warmhearted like Basia. In fact, Angie was friends with Basia. They had a lot in common and I was glad.

Just then, as if on cue, my grams approached my doorway. Grams, she was eighty years old and still living on. She was something alright. Obsessed with Elvis Presley and still loved to dance. She was the one who taught me to dance. Mostly ball room dancing, but I learned it well and all from her.

"Binji, are you going to save my great grandson?" Her Russian blue eyes softened and her wrinkled lips curled upwards. I loved my grams. I loved her like my mother.

I returned the smile and veered from Angie to Grams. I kissed her cheek in respect, like I did to all my elderly women…Maria, my Aunt Cathy…Grams. I had manners. I knew how to use them when I had to.

"I can't stop thinking about him, Grams. You should have seen him…" I was always a little boy around her. It was just how it went. I grew up around her. How could I not be?

Her jeweled hands rose up to my cheeks. "You bring that baby to me, like you brought Christopher that night. I'll see to it that he's safe. No one will harm him again. I already told your father that he should move in with me, sell that house. I'm getting too old to be alone, anyways. Remember how we used to live here, all together? Everyone will be safe from harm. No worries, no problems. You do that and see what happens. God will have mercy."

My grandmother was Catholic. She went to Mass every Sunday, if not Saturday, too. She said her prayers, every night. She wasn't a hypocrite and did everything she was supposed to do. She didn't believe in abortion, divorce, or adultery. She was a good woman with good Christian virtues.

She loved everyone. There was no room in her heart for hatred. She was the kindest woman I knew, once taking in families of our Parish who needed shelter. Once she took us in when my mother passed away, hiding us from the horrible world that shunned my father for her death. Yeah, my grandmother was great and everything that a grandmother should be.

"I should go to church, shouldn't I?" This was a question that was lying dormant in my mind for some time, now. I felt an urge to sit in that confession box and confess my sins. It had been too long since my last confession.

I had been twelve. Twelve was the year that my entire life had altered. I went through a period of hatred for God. He had taken my mother and it wasn't fair to me. I hated him and everything that the Catholic Church stood for because they wouldn't bury her in their cemetery because she had committed suicide. It was a Catholic rule. She wasn't supposed to be in heaven.

Maybe this was my punishment. Maybe I should be confessing and asking for forgiveness. I knew that it wasn't God's fault. I tell myself this, now. It wasn't anyone's fault. Maybe it was time to grow up and realize that God wasn't to blame for everything in my life. Maybe it was time to believe in him, again.

"Yes, you should." She stood level with my chest, small and fragile in her touch. She hugged me then. I swear I felt the Holy Spirit flutter from her to me. It was a feeling I would never forget. I felt safe.

It was time for the biggest change in my life.

I'm sure my boys would think that I was stupid and turning weak by actually standing up for my belief in God. I knew that going to church, somehow, made people look at you in a different light. Maybe that's why I had decided not to return to church, because it was looked upon as weak.

But fuck them. Who were they when it came to faith? I had something worth praying about. I had a reason to want to broaden my perception of life. No more partying. No more girls. No, I had two kids to look after. I had another life in Cheriton to live.

I was done with Pierre. Moving back to my Grams seemed like the option of choice. I could be me, here. I could be a better me. Go to school, raise Brandon and Devon the right way, and get them out of stupid Pierre before they got caught up in that stupid ass lifestyle…there were so many reasons to listen to my Grams.

If only I had heard her when I brought Cardy there, that night…She had offered us to live there, then. If only…

When my Grams felt pleased with me, she returned to her favorite room in the whole house…the room with the piano…the place with the music. I heard her playing in the distance…something I hadn't done since…I was twelve?

Angie and I didn't share words about my Grams. We drove in silence and I listened to her thoughts. She was seeing a new side of me, a side of me that she didn't know exist.

If only she was Fresca…then Fresca would know that I was changing. I was going to be good, now. She could come back to me.

When we reached the hospital, Brandon was cleaned up. It was a relief to know that his hair was still blonde, his nails were trimmed, and he didn't have a smudge on his body.

Except for the sores on his skin, he looked fifty percent better than yesterday. His eyes weren't sunken in, his skin wasn't as pale, and his lips weren't as dry. He was recovering.

The sores were Impetigo. Impetigo was blister looking sores that became infected with Staph. That's what the nurse explained. She said that he was exposed to a lot of contamination and the blisters spread like a disease. He had them on his legs, around his thighs, and the corner of his mouth. I bet it was from the dirty ass diaper that he sat in.

He had Hepatitis A, which is spread by contaminated food, feces, and water. There wasn't treatment for Hepatitis A and it would go away on its own. The nurse said that he was probably infected by it because someone didn't wash their hands when using the bathroom. It was the most common form of spreading it.

I could only imagine the fucking germs that were in that house. I wouldn't doubt that AIDS was something passed along. I made sure that he was tested just in case. Who knew what Lynn was fucking with? It turned my stomach. I hated that type of shit. I got out my hand sanitizer and tried to stay calm.

He was dehydrated and malnourished. The nurse mentioned something about Scurvy, but that would subside when given Vitamin C. I didn't know much about Scurvy, and she didn't want to emphasize it because it was treatable. I think it was something that would alarm us if she said more. I don't know.

He had a high fever and now, crying. I couldn't take his cries.

"Give him something, anything!!" I snapped at the nurse as she changed his I.V bag. It was awful. No child should have to go through this shit.

"He's definitely a fighter. This morning, he pulled the IV right out of his wrist. The nurse who was here before me had to put mittens on him so he wouldn't do it, again. Last night, he was sedated so he could sleep through it all. But, he's doing fine. You can expect a full recovery." She inserted something into the IV and rubbed the top of his head.

Brandon. He was my nephew. He was Cardy's son. I was never going to let him out of my sight, again. Fuck Lynn. I'm taking her to court if she decides to fight over him. Right now, the state has him, but that was going to change.

He was mine.

"He looks so small, right now." Angie whined, holding onto one of his blue mittens.

"I'm stuffing his ass with hella food when he comes home, just wait." I reassured her.

This kid was going to be spoiled. I'll make sure of it. If I stayed at Grams, then he could take over Dewey's room. It was right across the hall from mine. Fuck Dewey. He wasn't a part of my life, anymore.

Angie and I talked about Brandon's new room and everything that we were going to give him. It excited her. I think she saw him as one of those Samoan children with their ribs showing. She was always talking about Africa and how she wanted to save the starving children…well, here's her chance.

Save Brandon Deburke.

Chapter Forty-Nine
Basia

My classes weren't hard, at all. I was excited to be learning everything, again. The books, the desks, the chalk boards, it was all fascinating to me. What I didn't like, however, were the kids. I couldn't relate to them.

In American History, they would form little regions with their desks. It was like watching small countries form, their backs being the borders. They were full of smiles and conversations amongst themselves.

I was excluded, as I had no friends. I was the only one staring at the black board, paying attention.

The teacher, Mr. Bauer, was lenient enough to let the kids distort the aisles and form these exclusions. He was more worried about reading the newspaper than teaching something about history. At least, he was today. I was disappointed with Mr. Bauer.

I was there to learn.

Eventually, someone did speak to me. He may or may not have been in my class this entire week, I didn't know. Maybe he skipped a lot. I didn't recognize him.

"Hey, girlie, what's cooking, good looking?" He wasn't trying to be cool, he was trying to be funny and get me to smile.

"Hi." I mumbled. I was content on staring at a bare chalk board and recalling the civil war for my own amusement. North and South, something about Savannah, something about Red coats, was I right or wrong?

He scooted his desk closer. "I guess you don't remember me, do you?" He reminded me of "Daniel son" from the karate Kid. I smiled with that thought in mind. Wipe on, wipe off, go on and raise that leg of yours with your arms extended, will ya? That would be funny.

"Should I?" My poor brain was soiled with baby bottles and diapers, how could I remember faces?

"Well, you *were* a little wasted when we met." His smile turned to a grin, an evil grin of pleasure.

"I was only drunk…" And then it hit me.

Anthony Mercini, the senior that drove me home, last year. It was the night that…oh, wow, I almost forgot that I had seen Cardy on my birthday…what did I say to Cardy, that night? God, I wish I could remember it.

"I do remember you." I admitted. I thought he said he was a senior, last year. Was he lying, or did he flunk?

His eyes brightened with interest. "Really, that's cool. Do you still live with Kyle Sorum? You aren't dating him or anything are you?" he knew too much. I didn't want him to know that.

"No, no I don't." I lied. But then, I had to call him on his bluff, too. "Were you a senior last year?"

He blushed and lowered his posture with a laugh. "Yeah, I'm no good with school work. It's my third year of trying to graduate. I suck at it. I don't want to quit, but I'm tired of coming, ya know? I'll be nineteen, soon. But, think of it this way, if I had graduated, I wouldn't have ran into you, again. You don't party much, do you?"

I nodded a quick 'no'. It was an odd occurrence to have a class with him for an entire year. Maybe it was a sign. Maybe we were supposed to meet, once more.

"Here, let me give you my number…you can call me and hang out sometime." He picked up my hand and wrote his digits in ink. Then, he kissed it. Afterwards, he joined a group of girls.

Every now and then, he'd glance over and wave…sometimes nod.

By lunchtime, my head was soaring in the clouds. He liked me. Anthony Mercini liked me. He was someone other than Cardy to think about.

"Uh oh, what's that look?" Loren laughed, smearing black lipstick all over the straw that she was drinking from.

Amanda was proud of me. She grabbed my hand and extended it outwards. "She met a guy today and got his number!" She wanted me to move on…far, far away from disaster.

"No way, that's wickedly awesome, girl!!!" Loren beamed with thick black eyeliner caked around her eyelids. She high fived me and picked up her pizza.

"I know. I keep thinking that Cardy will come back and change for the better. But, if I really consider it, I don't think he wants me back. He's been with so many girls…I have no experience when it comes to that kind of stuff. They still talk about him as if he goes here." And I recalled all the giggling girls in the hallway, *Cardy this, Cardy that.*

"Damn straight, get that boy out of your head. Live it up, be free. Go out with this guy and see what he does for you. Who knows, he might be better than Cardy. You never went out with anyone other than him. Play the field!" Loren chewed her pizza, letting the sauce drip onto her tray. Her lipstick was fading off and the grease was circling the corners of her lips.

"I know you're right. I might give him a call. But, not right away. I don't want him to think I'm easy or desperate." I was considering on Anthony Mercini. I was in fact, fascinated by his approach with me.

The karate kid…hmmm.

We talked every chance we had class, together. He seemed nice, enough. He remembered everything that I had told him, before. And for some reason, he was very interested in my relationship with Cardy.

I didn't give him any details. He knew at one point or other, I was Cardy's girlfriend. He didn't know the extent or for how long. He didn't know why I broke up with him. I made it sound as if we were not something special. And that was because I didn't want him to know I had been hurt before.

I told him about Jasmine and he asked about her father. There too, I didn't explain who her father was. I said that he was someone that I lost touch with, someone he didn't know. He thought it was cool that I was a mother. He said I didn't look like I had a kid, at all.

All of his charm was flattering me. He knew the right words to say and the tone to use them with. I was falling for the guy…the karate kid. It was an awesome feeling to feel. It was awesome that Cardy was put on hold and my life was moving on.

Anthony and Basia sitting in a tree, K-I-S-S-I N-G. And so on. I felt like a kid with a new crush.

Chapter Fifty
Binderman

I brought Brandon home to my Grandma's house at the end of October.

His room was filled with a nautical theme. It was Angie's idea. The top half of the room was painted navy blue, trimmed with a sailboat border. The bottom half was already layered with wood paneling and I had it painted white.

White shelves decorated the walls with model sailboats. Sailor hats hung off their hooks. Brandon's name hung over his crib. His crib was decorated with teddy bears wearing sailor outfits. Angie had done it up right. I owe it all to her.

He was stocked up on clothes for every season, some being from Devon's collection. He had rain boots and work boots, hiking boots, and sandals. He had baby Jordan's and Reebok's. Name a brand of shoe and he had it.

He was a Sox no doubt.

He had a toy box overflowing with toys and a bookcase filled with all the fairy tales that Angie read to Devon. His changing table had too many diapers and wipes, medicines and creams. Our cabinets were stocked with formula and jars of baby food and cereals.

I was prepared. I had learned this from Devon and Angie. Brandon was going to get the childhood that I was too young to give to Cardy…

I had the entire lullaby CD's and necessary baby books…The list could go on.

My dad thought I was crazy. Maybe I was. But, one thing was certain. Brandon was going to have the best life he could possibly ask for and he deserved it. I know Cardy would be proud to know that I was doing all that I could to protect his son and make him happy.

Don't get me wrong, Devon had a room devoted to him, as well. When I moved into my grandma's house, I took over the east wing, the area where all of the grandkid's bedrooms were. Fuck Cody, Wren and Dewey. They didn't need a room there, anymore. No one was going to spend the night, any longer. They were too old.

I had persuaded Angie to move in with me. There was a lot of convincing to do with her mother, but in the end, it finally happened. I had a live-in girlfriend with my son down the hall. It was very relaxing to know and be a part of.

Devon was into wheels. Anything that rolled and spun out of control and took off with speed, he was obsessed with. It was fun to see him chase around a remote control car that I bought for him. He would shriek as high pitched as he could and give chase down the hall.

I was beginning to love little kids. Their curiosity and their behavior was something else entirely. Angie and I would sit for hours just listening to Devon babble on my old cell phone, or carry around that remote control to the car as if he was controlling it.

Since he was into wheels, his room was decked out with race cars. It was similar to Brandon's, only red with cars. He had car models on his shelves, with car shaped rugs on the floor. His toy box was filled with all kinds of wheels, from bulldozers to Ferraris. Angie said that this was a phase and he may not like wheels soon, but… we had the money to change his theme when needed. I was already tired of looking at red walls.

He had a car bed since he would climb out of his baby bed, now. We had to gate him off in his room so he wouldn't run down the hall and fall down the stairs. Most nights though, he slept with Angie, who slept with me, who now had to share a fucking queen size bed with two other people. It was ridiculous.

Sometimes, I'd pass out in Wren's room, which was still set up with all his forgotten baseball trophies. I didn't really want to change Wren's room around. He had pictures of us when we were kids. It was kind of cool to reminisce back to those times, those innocent forgotten times.

Anyways, Brandon came home and was used to me being around him. He quickly attached to me and wouldn't let me out of his sight. Angie thought it was sweet and made sure that I carried him everywhere I went, even in the shower when I took one. I had to sit him in a baby seat that suctioned to the tub. Sometimes, it was alright… but God Damn, I was with Brandon more than I was with my own kid.

Not only was Angie a good mom, she was a good girlfriend, too. I didn't have to listen to her talk about girls she hated. I didn't have to wait two hours for her to curl her hair. She didn't need much affection and could care a less for me to buy her things.

She just wanted me to be a dad. That was odd to me.

She loved my grandma and would take Devon to church with them. Sometimes, I would go. But most times, I would rather avoid large crowds. While Angie was at church, Brandon and I would watch football, together. He liked to chew on the remotes. I don't know how many times I'd Lysol those damn things.

She loved Maria, too. Angie made sure that we made her breakfast when she was over or dinner if she was around late. Angie always kept her in mind. Angie was too damn nice, but it was a good thing.

Bobbi didn't like Angie. Bobbi was used to Fresca and still assumed that Angie was after our money. No matter how I explained Angie to Bobbi, Bobbi wouldn't hear me out. She was calling Fresca behind my back and going out to lunch with her. My sister was becoming the ultimate backstabber. Such a fucking traitor, I swear.

And then, there was my dad. My dad liked Angie, but he didn't get along with my grandma and decided not to move in with her. He said that she was too controlling and stubborn and would expect him to do as she said. So when he visited, he stayed short and flattered Angie with his charm.

I hated when he did that. He used to do it with Fresca. I knew he didn't mean anything by it, but come the fuck on. He didn't have to talk so close to them. He didn't have to hold doors open and stare at them the way he did. It was disrespectful.

I didn't care to see him because of it. It pissed me off.

Oh, and let's not forget school. Living in Cheriton was convenient for school. We went to Cheriton University, Angie and I. We drove together, ate together, and studied together. I helped her with her homework and she quizzed me on mine.

Maria watched the kids. It took awhile for Brandon to let her. He didn't take well with strangers or Maria. I think it had to do with her accent.

I wish I could say that my life was only this. This was the fun part about leaving Pierre. I had Angie, Devon, and Brandon. I had school and my Grams to watch out for us. I was making a fresh start.

But, there was still Dewey to think about. Dewey was in and out of rehab.

He kept signing himself out. My Aunt Cathy and Uncle Brody were struggling with his relapses. Every one of them was in therapy. Nothing was working.

Cody was going to trial, soon. He was out on bail…a rather large amount that my Uncle Brody was pissed about…but, Cody was out. Cody was paranoid as fuck. He stopped drinking, stopped dealing, and stayed behind closed doors with Mikayla.

I felt for the guy, with all honesty. He was talking about marrying Mikayla. It was in consideration as I speak. I didn't want him to marry that bitch because we all ran up in that broad. Nobody wanted to marry a girl that slept with your cousins. Did they?

I don't think Cody cared. He loved her. He desperately, obsessively loved this stripper. What the fuck ever, marry the bitch. I didn't give a fuck. I was done with her. Cardy was done with her. I was tired of lecturing Cody about strippers being whores for life.

And, with Dewey in and out of rehab, Cody about to be locked up…I had other names on the backburner, as well. I hadn't seen my boys for about a month. Even then, I had only run into them a few times before that. I was losing touch with them. They were getting pissed at me.

I was living in a fantasy world, that's what it was. I was in Cheriton, away from the rest of the world. I didn't have the random drop in from Kyle or the others. They were too lazy to drive all the way to Cheriton, so they just called my cell phone and left messages.

One more name sat in my conscience. It wasn't Cardy. Cardy was safe and didn't dwell in my mind. My dad was talking to me about him and we were making amends on the shit. My dad wanted to be involved with him when he got out…all because I had enforced him to reconsider the facts.

No, that name belonged to a girl who owned a piece of me. I won't even say it. In fact, I won't even talk about her.

I missed her…everyday. And I wasn't going to admit it. Or face it.

I couldn't. If I did, what would I do with Angie? I wanted Angie, too. Fresca would just have to wait her turn. No, I have to be done with that girl. She messed with my brother…I had to remember that.

Maybe that's why I was in Cheriton.

There could be many reasons for my departure. One could very well be because I didn't want to run into Fresca. Another could be because Seth Bryant was dead. I didn't want to see Foster, his brother, or admit that I was there when it happened, even though he knew that. Seth had boys. Seth's boys could be looking for me and Cody. I could be shot dead if I stayed in Pierre.

Yeah, I had plenty of reasons to be a fucking chicken shit. Ha, that's who I was, anyways. I was a damn Cherry, born and bred with aristocrat style. I didn't walk around with guns. I didn't stand up and fight with pride, although I did when I was in Pierre, I was done doing that shit, too.

I hid from shit. That's what I did. I took my Cherry ass back to Cheriton so I could be pampered the way I needed to be, away from society and their conflicting consequences. However you wanted to look at it…

I was a Cherry.

Chapter Fifty-One
Cardy

I had this overwhelming urge to do something right. I felt good. I didn't feel depressed at the moment and didn't want to return to those padded walls. I wanted to eat the food that I wanted to eat. I wanted to smoke a cigarette with Cindy when I felt the need to. And, most of all, I didn't want to add to my sentence.

Yeah, I had a lot of rearranging to do with myself.

So, I went to Therapy Writing, first. Cindy was the teacher and I didn't mind seeing what her class was about. To think that I spent the first few months not attending classes, now I had to start from the beginning, as if I was new.

"Today's topic is fear. I want you to write…" She stopped in mid sentence as I entered the classroom. She smiled lightly, but didn't introduce me. She knew better.

When I headed to the back of the room, full uniform and all…she continued. "I want you to write whatever comes to mind when you think of fear. Don't worry about spelling, grammar, or complete sentences. Just write any words that you associate with fear. I'm sure once you start writing, more ideas will come to mind. Don't erase, don't stop and read it over. This is an exercise that we can dissect, tomorrow. I want raw material guys, remember that. If you have to read it over and erase and correct, then it's not raw. It's formed and fake."

She opened a desk drawer and withdrew a red notebook, one that resembled the game book, only new. Her black skirt danced in waves as she strutted back to greet me. She dropped the book in my lap since I wasn't sitting correctly. My feet were in the aisle.

"Remember, don't stop and think about it. I want it to be original. And, I never have to read what you wrote. We dissect them in class, and those who want to share their views with me are welcome to, or if we have a concern with your behavior and need…well, you get the picture. This is your journal. You feel it, you write it. You take it apart and try to understand it. I walk you through the process." She didn't say more and she didn't say hi.

Everyone else had opened their books to a page towards the middle. Their heads bowed and their hands wrote. I stood still, analyzing the room, the atmosphere. I wasn't looking to write and participate in class. I was looking for something to do to say I was cooperating.

The academic part of this program was located in another building. The hallways were not white. The tiles were tan, the walls beige. It didn't resemble an insane asylum, nor or prison with padded walls. It resembled an office, rather a medical one, with upholstered chairs lining the halls with square tables between every five of them. Plants and magazines took up the tables.

Random bulletin boards hung with advertisements. Suicide hotlines and self help programs stood out on them. Tutoring was available and teachers smiled widely on their brochures.

Behind glass doors, trophies and ribbons hung with pride. Some were to honor the school for success. Others were students' personal achievements. None were for sports, which I wanted to see and be a part of. Did they not have a sports program that competed?

Cindy's classroom was gray. It was a soft gray with white shades in the windows. The shades were pulled down to hide the rain outside. The normal blackboard covered the front of the room, and the word fear was written as big as it could be…thick and intimidating.

Fear,

What was my ultimate fear?

I wasn't about to write it in that piece of shit, but I was thinking of it. What did the word fear mean to me?

My first fear was the dark. I was scared of the dark and thought of clowns running out of the shadowed corners of my room, waiting for my mom to close the door and eat me. The fear of darkness and clowns were something I learned from movies.

Any kid would experience that type of fear if they watched movies. It was our imagination that worked its best to create and configure weird shit like that. Freddy Krueger was on my list of fears, Michael Meyers and Jason, too. Let's not forget "It" who lived in the sewers and the Indian grave yards that brought evil children and animals back to life. But again, those work on imagination. It wasn't my ultimate fear.

My dad used to scare me. When he came home from the bar, or from working late, I knew he would want to beat me for not doing something…anything to whoop my ass. But even that fear had dissolved when I towered above him at fifteen. I knew how he worked, what his weaknesses were. I told myself that one day soon, I would be able to take him out. Thankfully, that day never came. I didn't really want to hurt him.

My eyes searched the others who were used to writing this type of shit. It was hard to write. I couldn't write what I felt on paper when I didn't understand what I was feeling in the first place. It was a waste of time. I didn't comprehend what Cindy wanted me to do. I couldn't write like them.

Fear,

I used to feel like I didn't belong to anyone except my mom. I was hers. She was the only one who chose to love me. Even that was a choice. I was supposed to be aborted. Maybe that was my fear. I was afraid that I would never belong to anyone else. I wasn't good enough.

I could easily say that I feared my biological father. I feared that I would meet him and I would hate him. I already hated him, but if I met him, I would kill him. I was afraid to kill somebody. I wasn't a murderer, yet I felt the urge to kill people all the time. How ironic was that? Did that make me a murderer in the making?

I feared being abandoned. That had a chance of being my big fear. I had been abandoned so many times that I couldn't do it again.

Thinking about this was killing my mood. I swallowed hard and joined Cindy at her desk. I sat on the corner of it and held out my hand. "What do I get if I write something in here?" I was stalling. I didn't want to think of fear anymore.

"Can you get off my desk?" As if we weren't cool like we were. I didn't appreciate the superior tone of voice.

I didn't move. I wasn't going to move. "I don't have any fears, Cindy. What do you want me to do with this?" I squeezed the notebook in my hands and wished it was the man who made me.

Cindy stared at me then. "I want you to take it with you and stare at the pages. Do what you want to do with it. But, bring it with you tomorrow."

She knew I was leaving her class. And I did. I wasn't about to waste my time staring at the walls when I could be doing that in my room. I had more important things to do...like sleep and get ready to fill my body with junk food.

I felt stupid carrying around a notebook. Even though everyone else had theirs shoved in their back pockets like it was a game plan...I didn't feel comfortable transporting my feelings around. They belonged under my bed, away from me.

That's where I put the notebook. I slid it under my bed until later that night. When the lights shut off and Brett began to snore...I took it back out. I stared at the pages, white and blank, lined in blue.

My hand shook with an urge. I tore the first page off and began ripping it in strips. Then I ripped them into smaller strips to resemble zig zag papers. I licked them and rolled them. I sat it in my mouth like it was a joint. I laughed at my insanity. I wanted to smoke it, even if it was paper.

Then I was bored. The fake joints wanted me to smoke them. But I didn't try. I knew I would be disappointed. I swiped them off onto the floor and kicked them under my bed. There, I did *something* with the pages. I was being creative.

But I was still bored. I opened the book again. I stared hard at the pages. I wanted to draw. I hadn't drawn in ages. Did I still have the skills?

The pencil hit the paper and I curved a line. The line felt smooth as I drew it. It calmed my nerves, kind of like idling my nerve endings and giving them something to focus on. I liked it...I needed it.

I formed a head, sketching more than drawing it. It was a large oval, staring blankly back at me. The eyes came next, as I needed a face to gaze back at me, someone who couldn't look away in disappointment.

Eyelashes and irises, pupils and shading...there you are, Basia. I see you, now. What the hell are you doing in Pierre? Are you sleeping? Is Jasmine keeping you awake? Or is she a good baby and falls asleep in your arms?

I gave her the lips that once touched mine. Plump and full, grinning as if she knew I was drawing her for amusement. My pencil rounded out her cheeks, raised high and glowing. Such a beautiful face Basia, I swear you broke the mold when he made you...

I couldn't stop there. I drew her neck and her shoulders, shading in all the appropriate shadows that lingered on her skin. And just when I was about to call it a night, I couldn't. I gave her a hand that looked as if she was extending it out towards me, wanting to touch me. I had to. She told me to do it.

I sighed as I knew I couldn't touch her. But I touched the paper and tried. I glanced over at Brett and then pecked her lips, quickly. I laid her next to me on the pillow and thought of all the awful things that I had done to her.

I didn't mean to. I wish I could take it back. "I'm sorry, Basia, I wish you knew that." I whispered through my closed lips. I let the thought of her put me to sleep, recalling the smell of her hair.

I know what my ultimate fear was…it was me. I was afraid of myself. I was scared of who I've become, everything that I was. I am frightened by everything that I *can* become, and everything that I wasn't.

I was scared of me, Cardy Deburke, Christopher Viscardi…

Christopher Sox…

Chapter Fifty-Two
Dr. Cynthia Roma

All I had to do was confront Binderman Sox and ask him to piece together his brother for me. It would be my second interview about Cardy. I really needed this for his recovery.

"He doesn't live here, anymore. He moved in with my grandma in Cheriton." His sister answered the door with a smile. She looked like she was in a good mood, not an act like most of the time. Her face was flushed with happiness. Her hair was brushed and long. Her posture was appreciated and she talked with enthusiasm.

A boy stood behind her, not her brother, but a boy. His hair was so curly and wild that it bounced as he moved. Even a little gesture of movement and it moved. Hmmm…

"In Cheriton, you say? Can you give me the address? I have to meet with him today. It's urgent." I just drove through that damn town. Now I had to drive back? I just wasted an hour.

What made him move out? Was it his father? Did he not get along with him?

I was buzzed through the iron gates and wasn't amazed at the scenery. I expected it from Cheriton residents. Grand wasn't the word for it, mansion after mansion, water fountain after water fountain, and yeah, some personal lakes…whatever.

Oh, there he was. He was outside. He stood in a suit, black tie and everything. I never saw that boy in a suit in my life and I was his doctor for eight years, now. Was it seven years? Who keeps count? He looked sharp. No, he looked like he was rich.

"Did I come in a bad time?"

He smiled with his charm and adjusted his tie, his teeth brightly shining with his eyes. "Why don't you call me, anymore? I'm too busy for you to drop by.

I have to fit you in *my* schedule." He laughed, as sometimes I didn't have time to fit him in mine.

"It's important. It's about your brother, Binji." I fumbled to pull my briefcase out of the passenger seat and carry my purse at the same time. The purse strap was snagged.

"My brother?" He froze.

"Yeah, are you or aren't you brothers to Cardy, or rather, Christopher Deburke?" I knew he was because I researched everything I had on Binderman the day before. It was always Cardy this, Cardy that. The name wasn't recognizable until Ms. McPherson made me acknowledge it.

"Did you meet him? Are you still working at Safe Haven?" His eyes were full of wonder. I had stopped him dead in his tracks. Whatever he was wearing his suit for, he didn't mind stalling and talking. After all, he had been talking about this invisible brother for a decade.

"He's my patient. I didn't put two and two together until Dena, his mother, told me about you. Can we talk?" I jerked my purse onto my shoulder, balanced the briefcase in my arms and approached him with interest.

God, he was handsome.

"Is he okay? What's going on with him?" By now, a girl, suited up as well, came walking out with two little boys connected to her hands. The boys stumbled and waddled, diapers puffing out their pants. They looked like twins.

"We had a little trouble with him in the beginning, but he's turning around. He still won't talk about things. I can't get him to open up about anything. I was hoping you can shed some light on a few subjects. Maybe help me figure out how to approach him." I watched the little boys scream to get away from the lady. They did all they could to break loose.

Binderman glanced back at the noise and picked one up. When he did, the other was satisfied and calmed down. He brought the boy to me. "Did he tell you about Brandon?"

The little boy looked just like his father, blue eyes, puckered lips, chubby cheeks. He was so cute it melted my heart. I would probably never know motherhood.

"No, he hasn't told me about anything."

Bin rubbed the top of the boy's head. "This is Brandon. I'm going to court to get custody over him today, just until Cardy gets out. He's Cardy's son."

"Cardy's son?!" My mouth shouted out faster than I could think it. "Are you sure? He's only seventeen! He's a father?" I was getting to think that maybe Cardy was older than seventeen. I was painting a clearer picture about him with each passing minute.

It was unbelievable. That little boy that I shared cigarettes with was a father? That frightened little boy who wore his dirty white t-shirt for a month just to repulse anyone who walked near him had a child of his own? It couldn't be.

Bin rolled his eyes. "Shut up, Cindy. He's Cardy's kid. Some shit went down with his mother and I had to step in. He's doing well, now. I can't really talk because I have a time frame."

"Does he know about him?" I followed Bin to a black Cadillac as he began strapping the baby into a car seat. The girl did the same for the other one.

"He should know about him." He stood to hold eye contact, to watch my expression as he did. "Cardy has two kids. He has a little girl with a different girl back in Pierre. He hasn't said anything about either one of them?"

"No. I had no idea. Bin, Cardy's just a little kid. He walks around with a teenage attitude. His mind frame is immature. Maybe he's in denial that he's a father…" My mind was racing with new ideas. Did he or didn't he realize he had two children in this world?

"Call me, later. Call my cell phone, I'll tell you everything. But, I want you to keep me posted about his recovery." He walked to the driver's seat and sat down.

"Alright, I will. I promise." I watched the family drive off down the black top…and wondered if his grandmother was home. Was she willing to talk about the Sox's?

Chapter Fifty-Three
Basia

A month into talking to Anthony, I had decided to take him up on his offer. With a little help from Amanda, I was ready for the dating scene. I didn't want help from Loren since her hair was green and she traced her lips with purple eyeliner, now. She was being expressive she said. Yeah, a little too expressive if you ask me.

"I don't trust the guy, Basia. I think he's too old. I bet he has more intentions than just a movie." Darron stammered in the doorway to the bathroom.

I shined the lip gloss across my lips and rolled my eyes. "Oh knock it off Darron. It's a movie. I'll be home around ten. And, thanks for watching Jasmine for me!" I kissed his cheek and brushed by.

"He's creepy. If he tries anything on you…I swear…" But I didn't want to hear him swear. He was being too protective, too jealous. I knew he was infatuated with me and all…but me and Darron…Darron and me…that would never work. He had to understand that I didn't belong to him…or Cardy.

Let's skip a half hour of waiting…

"Wow," Anthony's mouth dropped and his eyes erected out of his skull.

I was flattered to make someone react in such a way. I opened the door and watched his eyes scope me out. Yeah, I know. My legs were smooth and tan. My gold letter anklet was a nice touch. My pink flip flops showed off my pretty little toes…pink, too.

"Damn, I mean, damn! I don't know what Cardy was thinking letting you out of his hands! Holy shit, you're a knock out!" He was more than thrilled to see me. His eyes wouldn't leave my body, up and down, fist in mouth, mouth drooling.

"Let's not bring Cardy up, tonight. I want him far away from my thoughts, alright?" I smiled politely and sat down, crossing my arms. Why did he keep bringing up Cardy?

"I'm sorry. I just can't get over how pretty you are." His face tilted with sincerity. His eyes were brown and did nothing for me. His skin tone was similar to mine and did nothing for me, either. I liked Cardy's pale complexion. I liked Cardy's blue eyes.

You know what? It's not about Cardy tonight. I needed to stop comparing him to Cardy.

He shifted in his seat, a sign of nervousness, I suppose. "One more question…"

I nodded, politely…smiling. My face always smiled when I was around people. It was a natural response, a nervous one at that.

"Your little girl, I know you said that her father isn't from around here…but, are you sure she's not Cardy's?" He never asked me that before. Why did it matter? Why was I going to lie about it?

"Oh no, me and Cardy, we…no, Jasmine isn't his." I let it go with a stutter in response. He could think what he wanted to think. I could be lying, maybe I wasn't. Who cared? The night wasn't about Jasmine, either.

It was about me. It was about him. It was about a movie and popcorn, a nice little get away for Basia. Get back into the swing of life. I hadn't been to the movies since I saw Twister with Cardy. Ooh, there's his name again!!! Stop it!!!

"Alright little mama, you like Mexican food?" And he headed towards Casablanca's Mexican Grill.

Anthony was a talker. He could talk about anything and everything. He fell in love at least once every year. All of them broke his heart and made him depressed. He said he didn't trust girls and didn't want to fall in love again, this year. I felt sorry for him.

That's when I told him that I had gone out with Cardy for three years. I told him how he broke my heart. We had that in common. We knew what it felt to be in love and to be heartbroken. It was so sad.

He talked about popularity and how he didn't let it go to his head. He said he was humble and gracious. He didn't date girls because of their status, but rather their personality. He said he was a romantic. He loved poetry, loved to sing in the shower. The boy just conversed about all of his likes and dislikes during dinner. He was interesting to me.

One time, when he was volunteering at Cheriton Hospital for his mother when she was sick with the flu, he had to use the Heimlich maneuver on this little sick girl. She was choking on her medicine and thankfully, he was right there.

He was so sweet.

And he loved little kids. His older cousin had five kids by five different women. Once, Anthony watched all five of them when his cousin went to jail. I couldn't imagine any one being so sweet like that. It was such an honor to have met him, to go on this date with him.

And then came the movie…oh the movie…we held hands all the way through. He didn't put his arm around me, didn't try to kiss me, and didn't do anything inappropriate because he respected me. I was becoming jell-o in his hands.

This boy had it all. He was charming. He was popular. He didn't smoke, didn't drink, and didn't have one night stands with girls. He respected females. He didn't like how guys thought it was cool to party. He didn't like partying. He liked movies.

He liked me.

He held my hand to the car. He opened the door. He was everything a gentleman should be. You know what? I liked this Anthony Mercini. He was a good kid, even if he was nineteen and I was sixteen.

"Hey, I almost forgot to give my cousin his cell phone back. I had to hold it for him earlier today when we were playing golf. He forgot I had it. You don't mind if I swing by there and hand it to him, do you? It'll only be a second, in and out. And if you want, I can introduce you to him. He's a wild guy, but very sweet. Kind of crazy, but all in all, he's a kitten." His face dropped as if he had no choice in the matter. He seemed rather scared of his cousin.

"Sure, that's fine."

I didn't know that his cousin was at a party.

"Damn, he's throwing a fucking party, shit. I'm sorry, we can turn around. I can hold onto it a bit longer. I know you wouldn't want to go in there and get pushed around the crowd…" His face was full of disappointment as he turned on the ignition back on.

"No, no, you're already here. That's okay. I can stay out in the car…"

"The car wouldn't be a safe place to sit. This is a party. People at parties talk to girls sitting in cars, they might even try something on you, then I'd have to kick someone's ass." He pounded his fists together and opened my side of the car.

My nerves stood on edge. I didn't want to enter the party scene, but Anthony had to give his cousin that phone. Jeesh, how loud could the music get?

"Don't let me go, Anthony!" I screamed into the air as I held onto his hand. My body was already shoved into his as we walked through the doorway. It was so crowded and loud. I couldn't see in front of me or hear my thoughts.

"Hey, Frankie, Frankie, come here, I got something for you!!" His smile widened showing all of his teeth, broad lipped and thin.

A tall husky man appeared. He looked as if he was thirty years old. He had stubble on his face, forming a beard. His skin was darker than Anthony's and he wore a jump suit with yellow sunglasses. The sun wasn't out, but he was wearing them.

"Damn, baby, what's you got with that thing?" He nudged Anthony in approval and stripped me with my eyes. I didn't like his cousin, Frankie.

Anthony stepped back and covered up my chest like a good man should do. "Dog, chill out, stop talking like that. It's disrespectful. This is Basia, Basia Brahm. We just went to the movies and I'm about to take her home."

"Home, why so early? You should stay. Have some drinks…kick back. I got a back bedroom you can use…" But Anthony shoved him with a frown.

"Frankie, come on. I'm not that guy, you know that! Chill out…maybe we'll have a soda. You have a soda around or something?" Anthony walked me to the back of the house to a quieter area.

I was feeling sick to my stomach. I knew Anthony didn't want to be there, either. We wanted to go home. Frankie kept persisting, didn't he? I wish Frankie would take his cell phone and let us leave.

Frankie came back with two red cups. His smile matched Anthony's, wide and thin. I bet his fist could fit in there. He smiled at me like he wanted to kiss me or something. His eyes danced all over my body. I felt degraded.

As I took a sip of the soda, the flat, yet bubbly soda…yuck, what kind was this? I noticed that some of Cardy's old friends were there. I didn't know their names, but I had seen them around Pierre.

"Hey, do you hang around those guys?" And I pointed towards the group of three who seemed to be laughing at Frankie as he danced upon this girl who didn't want him around.

"Yeah, I do. I didn't know they were going to be here, tonight. What do you know, let's go greet them and then we'll leave." He guided me through the crowd and into the circle of guys that I knew nothing about.

"What's up, fellas? Ya'll ever meet Basia?"

I take that back. One of the guys was a regular with Boo. He was some short Mexican guy that helped drag Cardy into their house. He was the one that drove Jasmine home when Cardy stole her from me.

"Basia?" He said it first. "Dog, what are you doing?" He shoved Anthony to the side and they shared some words. The guy didn't seem pleased to see me. I bet he was still mad at me for not telling Cardy about Jasmine.

"Brian, let it go. It's old news." A taller version of the Brian kid said. He looked like a serial killer…a Spanish one with a stone cold stare.

"Nah, dog, I'm calling Boo. She shouldn't be here and you know it." Brian's face was full of anger. He wouldn't stop looking at Anthony.

"Come on, let's just leave." I tried to persuade Anthony to take me home.

Anthony wouldn't respond. "Why you gotta go call Boo for? He ain't Cardy's keeper. He has nothing to do with this. She ain't going out with Cardy. She's my date."

Anthony jerked me away from them as they stared on. He was getting rather mean. He shoved me into a room and slammed the door. I was alone with him, alone on a bed. I didn't know what to do. Maybe he needed to calm down. Maybe he was too angry to drive.

He sat down next to me and held his head. "Basia, I have a lot of feelings for you. I didn't want you to hear that. They're just jealous…I'm sorry…"

I cut him off. "They don't like me. They never did."

"Nah, nah, baby, they love you. Everyone loves you. I love you. You're so different from all the other ones…you have class. You have self esteem. I just can't believe I have you here with me right now. It's a dream come true…" I was getting the notion that he was going to kiss me.

I didn't want to kiss him. In fact, I wanted to go home. My heart was racing. I wanted to go home, home…home…home.

When his face came closer and his eyes closed…I moved away. "Anthony, can we just call it a night?"

He stood, upset. "Basia, I just said that I love you. I've been thinking about you since that night I took you home. I've been having dreams about you. You're all I ever think about. I talk about you to everyone. I kind of told them that you were going out with me. I can't…I can't face them if they know I lied. I don't lie, Basia. I can't…I'm not…why are you doing this to me?"

My mind was trying to figure out the words he was saying. He loved me? He couldn't possibly…dream about…he said we were going…but…"What am I doing to you, Anthony? I thought we were friends. I thought we were just going to the movies…I'm almost getting the idea that you planned this…" Or was I in a lack of trust because of Cardy? What was I doing here?

"Planned this? Basia, you are the most beautiful girl in the world. I would never try to hurt you. I'm obsessed with you. You have my heart, girl…" As he took a seat next to me, he grabbed my hand and put it over his heart.

He was getting the wrong idea. Somehow, he thought that he could get his way with me. He was obsessed with me. I had accidentally messed with his heart. I was so wrong in sending mixed signals. How did I do that to him?

It was just a movie. It was just some popcorn.

"You're just like the rest of them. I saved up all my money to take you out, girl. I spent so much money tonight all to impress you and you can't even give me a kiss? Where's the hospitality?" He stood again and without notice, he shoved his lips onto mine.

I fell back against the bed. Oh this is wrong. I had sent him the wrong message. He expected so much more than what I had wanted to give…

His hands rummaged all over me. He wouldn't stop. His mouth was hot and horrible. His tongue was…oh, I was getting sick.

"Anthony, please!" I screamed, fighting him to get off of me.

"I just want you so bad. You don't know what it's like to want something so badly…" He whined as if it was an excuse. "I need you Basia. I have to have you…"

"I don't want you, I wanna go home!" My fists balled with fire. My eyes wide with fear. I was crying for forgiveness. "Don't, don't you dare!" His hands went for my pants.

"I wanna know what it's like…to be with you. I know Cardy had you. I know someone else had you. Why can't I have you?" He struggled with my pants, already undone and trying to pull them down. His fingers were fighting hard to get under me, to get near me…

"Nobody can have me!!!" I bit his neck as hard as I could. "I'm a fucking virgin!!" I heard myself scream.

I was. I felt like I was. I didn't know this way of life. I didn't know what

I was doing here with him. I didn't ask for…I didn't want…"Get off of me!!" Now I was in complete panic mode.

I was still a virgin. It chanted in my head. Sometime or other, I lost track of myself. I was still a virgin. I knew I was.

He laughed now. My pants dropped to the floor. "You're not a fucking virgin. If you were with Cardy, then you're not a fucking virgin. You have a kid. You're not a fucking virgin! You're a big ass tease, Basia. That's what you are! I want what Cardy had!" He snapped it like a rapist. He shoved his fingers into me like a rapist.

No, Cardy didn't rape me.

I was getting raped…right…now.

"Help ME!!! Please, somebody…help me!!" My body arched up and over. He forced me down. My insides were being scraped by his nails. His breath was hot and greasy…his body…his body…I was about to pass out.

Nobody was hearing me over the music. Its vibration was turning my stomach. I was getting raped. He was going to rape me…over and over in my head. Darron was right. Darron knew.

I didn't.

"Get the fuck off of her!!" And Anthony was thrown away from me, crashing to the floor.

I scrambled off of the bed and into the corner. My eyes were wide with fear. I didn't care what was happening…as long as it stopped. I was dazed. I didn't know who these people were, but they were flooding the room.

I was dying. I felt like I was dying.

Screams and scolds were in the air. Thick voices carried above my ears and I didn't hear a word. I didn't see a thing. I was traumatized by this. I was about to be raped.

I was about to be raped.

"Basia!!" He said. I didn't know who said it. I wasn't going to respond. I hated boys. Filthy little boys…it keeps getting worse. Why did I get myself into these stupid situations…it keeps happening…I keep falling for it…

I was stupid. I was stupid and dumb. I should have known better. My father said so. My mother said so. I should have known…

My body was lifted upward. "You okay?"

Anthony was being stomped on.

"Basia look at me, are you okay?" The voice was in my face. His breath was heavy against me.

I slapped him for being so close. Nobody gets that close to me.

Not anymore. I spit in his face as he picked me up. I was too shaken up to comprehend the difference between reality and this heavy fog that surfaced around my eyes…I didn't know who this boy was that saved me…or if I ever met him before. I just knew that I was saved and Anthony was about to go to jail.

The cops swarmed in, the boy helped me to safety.

The cops took statements.

People went to jail.

That's all I can decipher from this horrible night gone wrong.

Chapter Fifty-Four
Binderman

Sunday was game day. It was *my* game day. My Grams and Angie went to church with the boys, sometimes shopping and brunch. I didn't care where they went. It was Sunday and it belonged to me.

My busy schedule was compiled of homework and bottles, Angie and diapers, playtime and Grams. I didn't get fucking time to myself, not if I wanted to be where I was and with whom I was with. It didn't work like that.

So, I got Sundays.

If I was lucky, I could roll me a blunt, get drunk off my ass, and watch the Eagles game. Angie didn't give a fuck as long as I was home doing it and ready for school the next day. Talk about becoming a kid…I had two mothers in that household. I couldn't do shit.

But I didn't mind, I missed that type of authority. I wanted them to control my every move in hopes that I wouldn't resort back to the old me.

This Sunday, I was about to light an 'el and channel surf until the game came back from half time. I sat on my Grams sofa, feet up, knees bent. The Lysol and cologne was right at my disposal for when Grams would happen to show up unannounced.

I wasn't allowed to smoke this shit around her. She wasn't aware that I did it. My dad gave fair warning that if she caught me, I'd get a three hour lecture and forced to confess to God. Who needed that bullshit?

As soon as the smoke hit the air, someone was at the door knocking. Just my fucking luck, I wait for an entire week to smoke this shit…and someone interrupts me. It's less time I have to cover the evidence up…

I pounded the blunt into the ashtray and slid it under the couch. I sprayed the Lysol and headed for the door. It could have been anyone from a UPS man to a sales person. It could have been a social worker for Brandon, or worse…my fucking shrink.

Smoking a blunt would sure look great in their eyes…

Damn.

I pulled one of the double doors ajar and stood in the doorway, wife beater and all. "What the fuck are ya'll doing here?"

Roger, Terrance, Kyle…and Brian. It was a relief.

"Dog, what the fuck is up with you?!" Roger stormed in and shoved me into the hallway.

"We've been calling your ass all week. What happened to being boys?!" Terrance charged next, brushing passed me.

Kyle didn't say shit. He didn't give hassle one way or another. I bet he missed bumming squares off my ass, though.

And then there was Brian. Brian stared at me with interest. "What's going on with you? Everybody says you ain't been partying for months, now. I got back this week and everybody's hitting me up telling me about your lame ass." He entered and continued. "What happened to Fresca? Who's this new bitch you with? She did shit to you, didn't she?"

Question after question, unwanted and unappreciated.

"Dog, are you on leave or something? Why you back?" I could answer shit, later. I followed them into my Grams living area and pulled the ashtray out. When they saw me light up, their bags came out and they began rolling.

It felt like old times, again.

"Nah, I couldn't take it. One motherfucker was breathing down my back while the other's spraying mace in my face…I couldn't handle it. It's worse than you expect. I was doing too many pushups and laps…they had my ass in this gas chamber…I just quit." He sat down and watched me…analyzing *me* for once.

"Yeah, my cousin went to boot camp…" Terrance began to speak…

But Roger cut him off. "Nobody wants to hear about your fucking cousin. Who gives a fuck about your stupid ass cousin?" He popped a blunt and slid the contents into the small ashtray. I could already see it overflowing. I hated that shit.

"So what's the story, you in or out?" Roger said it for everybody.

They meant the game. Was I going to play these bitches and increase my numbers or was I out? What was I?

I don't know.

"Dog," I rubbed my head not wanting to quit, not wanting to go on. "I don't fucking know." Terrance coughed at the words that flew out of my mouth.

"You don't know? Dog, you still have the highest score. You gotta get back in the game. You have to. You're missing all the fucking action. There's been a fight each fucking weekend. New girls, new places...we got a lot of Cheriton college girls, now. I know you haven't messed with them. People are thinking you don't exist. They hear stories about your ass and you're never around to show them who you are..." Terrance was appalled at my lack of decision.

And I didn't give another fuck.

"Fresca's been asking me about you." Kyle had cut his dreadlocks into small knobs on top of his head. He looked crazy. That and his stupid ass eyebrow bar...what was his deal with that shit?

"When did you run into her?"

Everybody had their own blunt in the air, polluting the atmosphere with thick ass smoke that wasn't going to evaporate by the time Grams got home, fuck. They didn't even ask me if they could do it, they just did.

Kyle leaned forward with no confidence. He never had fucking confidence. "I work with her, dude. I've been working with her at 7-11. I thought you knew that shit."

7-11? I thought she was working at Subway. I knew she couldn't keep a job. She was too much a fucking priss to handle a thing like that.

"He knows nothing, that's what he knows. He won't come back to Pierre. He's a fucking Cherry, now. He thinks he's better than us." Terrance had the balls to say anything confrontational. The problem was that he was a short ass big mouth and thought he was something else. He was still wearing that god damn sun visor, flipped upside down. When was he going to give that up?

"Shut the fuck up, it's not like that. I've been too busy with shit. I'm going to school. I got Devon and Brandon..."

"Wait, who?" Brian was following me. Brian was taking it in for all that it was worth and trying to understand my dilemma. That's what I liked about Brian. He thought of me as a friend and not something to get him bitches with.

"Brandon. You didn't hear about Seth?" I felt my eyes burn and water. My eyelids were slowly blinking and I knew I was high. Fucking shit, I was high as hell.

"Yeah, Seth's dead. I know that part. I know your cousin's going to jail for it. But what does that have to do with Cardy's kid?" Brian didn't know anything…they all didn't know it, did they?

I filled them in with the story, the real one…not the shit that was going around about Cody being hard up for some dope. Not the one about me fucking Seth's girl or shit of the sort. No, those were all rumors that filtered their way back to me. I had to clear it up.

Then I had to admit the truth about Angie. It was something they wouldn't understand for the life of them. They didn't see her as girlfriend material. They didn't apprehend that she was causing me some good in my life or perfect for a mother and shit like that.

They hated the idea. They saw her as someone taking away their boy, an enemy that was controlling me, brainwashing me…

"Dog, come on. You haven't been to a party in a month or more. Get out, live a little. I know you got your shit straightened out over here and all, that's real cool and shit…being a daddy and shit like that…but, come on, dog. Where's the motherfucker that knows how to kick it with his boys? Where's that motherfucker?" Roger had the nerve to bring me down. That punk motherfucker was about to marry my girl, what about that shit?

I know I haven't been around. I know I haven't been with my boys. I know this shit. But, did they understand that there were more important things going on than them? Shouldn't Roger understand that he needed to buckle down for that baby, whosever baby it was?

Fuck no.

"What about Teesa, motherfucker, what's up with her?" I hadn't seen that bitch since she told me she wanted nothing to do with me. She belonged to Roger, now. And Roger seemed to be partying his ass off.

He smiled. "It's a boy. All she wants to do is eat peanut butter."

It didn't say shit. I liked to eat peanut butter. "What do you do with her, leave her home and go kick it?"

"I kick it, dog. But, I can balance out the two. I don't abandon my boys and change my whole lifestyle." It was another shot at my ass and I didn't like it.

"Fuck you, I ain't changed." This was an understatement, as I did change. I changed everything about me and was perfectly content with how I was living.

"Prove it, motherfucker. I bet your ass is too scared to leave Angie for a night. I bet you lost your touch…" Terrance's challenge was pissing me off. The whole situation was pissing me off.

And I was high.

I liked being high.

"Bet. I bet you half of my points that I can still kick it…" I didn't care either way.

Shit. What was I agreeing to?

"Good, dog. Get dressed, we're leaving." Brian stood with his keys and pounded my fist.

I was confused. "What? You're leaving?" Damn, I was lightheaded than a motherfucker. What the fuck was I saying, doing…agreeing to again?

"Nah, you're going with us." Terrance took out his cell phone and began dialing all the bitches' phone numbers.

Ah, fuck.

"The bet starts tonight, dog. We ain't half assing this shit, we ain't waiting on your ass to drive down to Pierre, we're taking you with us and we're starting it, today. Let's go." Roger Stood and followed Brain towards the door.

It was Sunday, game day. It was my day.

But, I had school tomorrow. Angie would be pissed. I was in a situation, wasn't I?

Fuck.

"I don't know," I couldn't think right. I didn't want to think. Any other time I would have followed through and went along. Any other time I didn't two kids to watch and a girlfriend who was strict about shit.

Any other time…

"Fine, fuck it." I heard myself say. I was following the budd. I was following my boys. In fact, I was just following for the fuck of it. I wasn't able to put my foot down, as my foot was already out the door.

They grabbed me with enthusiasm and shoved me all the way down the path to the car. If I paused, they jerked me harder. If I looked back, they laughed and shouldered me to move on. I don't know…I just don't know why I went.

I just did. I was telling myself that I had a right to do what I wanted. It had been awhile and I earned it. I earned a party, didn't I? I was going to school. I was being a good dad, not only to Devon, but to Brandon, too. I was being faithful to Angie, being a good boyfriend…hell, I should get to do what I wanted to do, today.

It was Sunday. Just get my ass back home before dark so I could take Angie to school. I hadn't missed school since the semester started...I earned a day off, too.

Right?

Was I wrong?

I didn't give a fuck at the moment.

We ended up smoking a blunt as we drove back to Terrance's. I ended up drinking a fifth of Tequila, too. I found myself high as fuck, rapping to Bone and Biggie. Only I changed the lyrics a little. I recalled a time where me and my brother did just that.

Instead of Bone and Biggie, it was *Boo and Cardy, let's ride, get high, get high...* damn, those were the days...I was still affected by that shit. Cardy rapped it with me. We never got the words right, as we were too high to hear them correctly, but who gave a fuck. This was our song.

I hadn't listened to Tupac, Biggie, or Bone since he crashed. To think that my boys were still playing that shit...They were stuck back in the day.

The days of partying...

Okay, I was foolish into thinking that I was safe to leave my house and just tip the Tequila and come back home. Maybe I wanted to get drunk. Maybe I missed it.

We arrived at Terrance's just in time to meet the other cars that had pulled up, cars of bitches and more of my boys...and just Pierre punk motherfuckers...ready to party. Remind you, it's mid day.

I was already slopped, falling over with a beer in my hand. How I got a beer in my hand was beyond my knowledge. How many of those did I drink after the fifth of Tequila? Ha...I don't know.

Fuck, I needed a phone. "Dog, dog, give me a phone. I need a fucking phone..." I hung on Brian as more bitches started to approach me, some I knew, some I never met in my life...Cheriton broads...college chicks...bitches up my ass left and right and didn't give a fuck what I was about, as long I was "The shit" everyone was talking about.

"Nah, you ain't getting your phone." Brain admitted. What the fuck was he wearing? Since when did he sport white T's? It wasn't like Brian to downplay his outfits.

I popped his collar and laughed. "What the fuck is this shit?"

He didn't answer. I could answer for him. I stopped giving him shit, that's what it was. He didn't have money like me. No one had money like me. Roger, Kyle, well, not Terrance, Terrance had shit…but no one else could buy the clothes I wore.

Hours flew by. I didn't call Angie, didn't call home. I didn't bother trying to get my ass to Cheriton or anything that I should have done.

I was having fun.

"This is Boo Sox, baby. This is the motherfucker that runs this shit." Terrance threw a bitch into my stomach as I stood on his stairway, bouncing to the music in the air. My Tequila was raised to my lips, my eyes a glossy red. I was stoned, plastered, and feeling good.

The bitch looked up at me with a drunken smile.

Fuck. Triple motherfucking fuck.

The night went on into a blur. That bitch was a blur. The other bitch was a blur. I was cheating on Angie left and right and I am telling you…it was all a blur. I was telling myself that it wasn't happening.

Yes, indeed, it was a blur. I won't think of it as anything other than that. I had broken a promise to myself, a promise to Angie, and promise to God.

That promise was to behave. That promise was being faithful.

And I failed.

I couldn't do shit right, anymore.

Chapter Fifty-Five
Angie

Boo's grandmother and I came home at three in the afternoon. It was plenty of time to give Boo his privacy to do whatever he wanted to do without the kids. We had been gone for a good seven hours, at least.

We went shopping. We went to a small diner that bordered Cheriton. We took the kids to the park. We relaxed. We shared stories about Boo when he was a small child. It was peaceful and rewarding to be so close to his grandmother. I liked her.

But...BUT, Boo was nowhere in sight when we got home. That house was massive when it came to searching it. I searched high and low for him. Calling out loud for him didn't do justice, as the rooms were so far apart that he may not have heard me.

I went to the east wing, where he claimed was his side. I huffed all the way over to the west wing and investigated that region. That part of the house must have belonged to his grandfather, as it was covered with white sheets and dust. Globes and drawings, old canvas, and maps lay throughout each room. Modeled buildings and bridges were assembled on tables. What was his grandfather, a map drawer, Christopher Columbus?

Disregarding the question as to who was his grandfather and what he was about, I searched on. Boo's car was still in the driveway. He didn't leave in it, so he had to be there. It was too far to walk anywhere. But the grounds were extensive. He could be anywhere outside.

Grams had wondered in and out of the downstairs. She said he wasn't in any of those rooms. She had called down into the cellar, where the liquor was...and he didn't respond. She didn't think he would be in the attic, as it was filled with spider webs and he didn't take well to insects. She said no one went up there anymore and she should probably call an exterminator just in case.

Great.

I opened the back patio doors and stood on the stone balcony. Statues stared back. Trees swayed in the distance. The field was empty. The stone benches were bare. The pool glistened with the sunlight, but without Boo in it. I yelled for him and listened…only the birds chirped, the bugs buzzed, maybe it was a frog croaking in the pond that I hadn't yet ventured over to. No sound of Boo.

It seemed as if he vanished.

I dashed back in for the phone. He surely had his cell phone on him. This estate was so big that everyone needed a cell phone when visiting this house. I could get lost if I crossed the field into the woods. I could get lost if I happened to go too far from the front of the house, too. Too many trees and bushes…too many paths that went nowhere but into the woods…too many woods…

"Grams, do have any idea as to where he may be?" I cradled the receiver in my hand, a glass one with gold trim still attached to the cord.

She stood still in her Sunday bonnet, yellow ribbon tied under her chin. "No…" She thought, gripping the armrest to the sofa for support. She was an old fragile lady, all spunk and spirit, yet shriveling before my eyes. "I suppose he could be in the cottage. Did you check the cottage? He used to bring his friends back there when he was younger. I'd catch him and give him a good talking to…drinking and carrying on…that boy, I don't know about him sometimes. He reminds me of his father, so rebellious and stubborn…maybe he went for a walk."

Maybe I'm going to put my foot up his ass. He knew we were coming home. The least he could do is be visible, be around so he could hear me.

I set the receiver back in place when I saw something that caught my eye. His cell phone vibrated on the end table. He didn't take his phone. It was another sign that proved he was somewhere lost in this house or on these grounds…maybe passed out.

I picked it up and let curiosity fill my head. I had never checked his calls. I wasn't that type of girl. I believed in honesty and privacy. What was his belonged to him. What was mine belonged to me. It was out of respect.

Nevertheless, where the hell was he?

He had missed twelve calls. Twelve was a lot. The last one was me, but the next five belonged to a number not listed on his phone. Three had the name "Tay & Ty." One belonged to a "Sherrice" and the other was "Les."

No way.

These were girl names. They were Taylor and Tyler Micks, the twins,

Sherrice O'Reilly, and Leslie Brande, the party girls that I had only heard about. No way in hell was he getting calls from them, was he?

The proof was there, but why?

I closed my eyes and forced the tears from forming. This couldn't be happening to me. How long have they been calling him? Was this normal and he ignored the calls? I know he's been saying that his friends were calling him and he would send it into voicemail, but were they a constant threat, too?

I did some more research. He had over three hundred names in his call logs. Most of them were girls. I checked his outgoing calls and none of them were made to any girls. In fact, the last time he had made a call was to his house in Pierre and that was three days ago.

His incoming calls were much more recent. Brian and Kyle had called around noon. Roger and Terrance had called around two. A couple hours later were calls from the girls…how do you check his voicemail?

Oh, this is simple. He had a voicemail section. I called it. I had to. I didn't want any more secrets between us. This was going to get straightened out. Maybe he was sitting over in the cottage getting drunk. Maybe he was over there with those girls and was trying to hide from me. Maybe I was still going to put my foot up his ass and confront him about these phone calls.

I was getting way in over my head. I knew what Boo Sox was about. I should expect this type of shit from him. He was just so…so different when he was with me…I was being blind sighted by a fairytale. I thought I could change him. I thought he was changing…

"Hey, baby, heard you were at Terrance's. We're coming over. Call us back so we know what to bring to the party!"

"You know what I just heard? I just heard that you were screwing around with that Angie chick that you had the baby with! What's up with that? Where have you been at? You can't possibly be with that bitch!"

"Call me back, this is Leslie."

"Hey, dog, we're tired of being sent to voicemail, we're coming over."

"What happened to being boys, motherfucker! We're on our way over there, so be ready. The bitches are all over my ass, they wanna know what's up with you. Call me back!"

"Hey, Boo, I was just thinking…I think we should talk…"

The last message was from Fresca. I dropped the phone.

I froze. He wasn't here. He went with his friends. He had left me here at his house to go party with his friends. He had left me here with Brandon and Devon with his grandmother…what the hell was I going to do?

I wanted to cry. I was so mad at myself for thinking that I could change this guy. I was so mad at myself for letting it go this far. I should have known better. I thought I had shielded myself enough for preparation of this day…

But I didn't.

I was heartbroken. I was torn apart. All I could think about was attacking him. I wanted to scream and hit him, spit in his face and stomp on his heart. I wanted to go to that party and cause chaos. I wanted to embarrass him. He was embarrassing me for being with him.

God, I was so stupid.

"Grams," I whispered, feeling my confidence drift out to sea. What was worse was that I started to cry. God, I didn't want to cry. "He's at a party with his friends."

Her eyes lit up and then dropped down into a frown. She hugged me and squeezed. "It's alright, dear. Wait until I see him. He will get a piece of my mind, I tell you what. Just go upstairs and lie down, rest…"

I didn't want to rest. I wanted to leave. I wanted to find him and rip his heart out.

"No, I think it's better if I leave. I should go home."

Amanda came out and picked me up. Grams had to explain the directions to the poor girl about five times. Oh, Amanda…I was so embarrassed to admit that I was wrong. He had humiliated me. He had defeated me…

"Don't you dare say I told you so." I snapped.

"I won't. But why did you bring Brandon?" She twisted around and gave a polite smile, although she didn't want him in the car.

"I had to, his grandma couldn't watch him. She could barely watch her sugar intake, let alone pick him up and change his diaper."

The evening went on into the night. I kept waiting for Boo to call and apologize, give me some sad story as to why he left in the first place. I had built up all these words of anger at him, ready to throw it into his face.

I laid Brandon in Devon's crib with him and sang them to sleep. I flipped through a magazine and channel surfed. I sat at the window, I paced the floor.

He didn't show up and didn't call. It was getting ridiculous.

Finally, I had enough.

"Amanda, I can't take it. I have to find him." Visions of girls danced upon him. Visions of his naked skin were against theirs. Even though I didn't feel like he was fully mine…he was still mine. I was his girlfriend. I wasn't a side bitch or mistress or booty call, or his baby's mama. I was, indeed, his fucking girlfriend and I had a right to end his night with hell.

"What are you going to do?" Amanda was concerned that I would make a fool of myself and cause more drama than what was needed. She thought I should stay home, break up with him, and move on. She thought it was so simple.

It fucking wasn't.

"I'm going to Terrance's."

Amanda's eyes widened with fear and her mouth opened to form an O. hell, I knew I was wrong, too. But the impulse was too great. I had to find out and couldn't pretend I wasn't upset.

I drove my mom's car to Terrance's. I parked a block away since there wasn't any room left on the street. I tried to look right with makeup and jeans and jewelry. I'm sure I looked a mess. I didn't know how to wear the makeup that those girls wore. I just didn't want to be obviously "not invited" to the party.

The house was big and the door was open. Girls fell off of guys. Guys fell off of girls. The music was pounding and the screams were fierce. I didn't want to be there. I was a mother and Boo was a father. This wasn't a scene for parents…even if we were teens.

No one bothered to look at me. No, they were busy getting drunker, getting laid, getting high. I didn't recognize anyone. I looked for any friend of his that could point me in the right direction.

Finally, I came across Kyle. Kyle was more down the earth. He was a nice guy who just went with the flow. He didn't start trouble and tried to stay out of trouble. His lips pinched closed when he saw me. He knew what that meant.

"Where's Boo?" I folded my arms and stomped.

He shrugged. His eyes searched the crowd with mine, competing to find him first and give him a heads up.

"Bullshit!" I gave him the coldest stare that I could possibly come across and waited for an answer. No, I demanded an answer.

"I think he's in back, but I don't know. I haven't seen him in awhile." He forced his way out of the front door, far away from me and the tension that I had brought.

I stormed my way towards the back of the house.

Oh, isn't that just dandy. There he was, feeling up on some girl as she sat on his lap. He was shirtless, she was in her bra, and his pants were undone. Oh, motherfucker...

"Boo!!" I screamed as loud as I could.

His eyes jerked abruptly and his hands jumped into the air. "What the fuck?!" He tossed the girl off of him and she fell to the floor. He stood, pants falling midway down his boxers. He grabbed them and stuttered absolutely nothing that made sense.

The dam to my waterfall broke. The tears flooded my face and my hands went to protect what was left of my dignity. This was not what I had in mind to do to him. This was not what I had in mind at all. I wanted to thrash him...hurt him...but crying...crying only made me look weak.

Boo grabbed my shoulders and pushed me backwards. "Angie, it's not what you think. I'm fucking...I'm fucking..." He couldn't finish the sentence because he should be saying he's fucking a bitch.

"How can you do this to me?" I wailed, uncontrollably. Yes, I was making a scene, alright. And right now, I wasn't looking like the girl who wasn't going to take crap. I was just the opposite.

"Baby, I'm sorry." His face bent down to mine, blues pleading with me to ignore what I was feeling. When he put his hand against my cheek, his pants were dipping lower and lower. Whatever he was saying didn't matter. I didn't believe him. I wouldn't trust him.

"What the fuck is she doing here?!" I heard a sneer behind me.

Boo jerked in place. His eyes squinted at the guy, all puffy and swollen from the party. "Dog, don't worry about it. Just chill," Then his eyes fell back on me with a smile. "Go back home, I'll come by when I'm done."

When he's done? Oh hell no. Not with me he wasn't going to say that to. I shoved him with all I could. "What about Brandon, Boo? You're cheating on me and leaving Brandon, who isn't even ours?! How could you be so stupid and inconsiderate?!"

He lost his balance and fell into a crowd of people. He rubbed his head and sighed. "Don't fucking push me, Angela." He stumbled up from help of some girl and he toppled into the guy who had made a rude comment about me. He couldn't stand upright from all the liquor he poisoned his body with. Serves him right.

"You're about to piss me off. I'm just having a couple of beers, Angie. Do you want me to come home with you? I'm not coming home with your ass if…if you…" By now, Boo was surrounded by a bunch of kids who wanted to watch the scene unfold. As he twisted around to see this, he stopped mid sentence.

"No, I don't want you to come home with me. I don't want you to ever come home. You can have your stupid partying and the stupid little tramps you're fucking, fuck you! And, and…just fuck you!!!" I stormed into his chest and shoved him aside. I was headed home.

He waddled after me not caring to hook his pants closed. The crowd followed with their ooh's and ahhh's. "Angela, wait! I'm sorry!"

"Sorry? You're sorry? No, I'm the one who's sorry, Boo. I'm sorry I ever agreed to be your girlfriend. I can't believe I thought you were different." With that said, people started laughing at me. Of course I was stupid. Of course they would laugh. Who would believe that I could be Boo's girlfriend without him cheating on me?

No one. No one but me.

Terrance grabbed him and held him back from making a fool of himself. "Leave her ass alone. You got plenty of bitches here for you. You don't need her ass. Fuck her. She wasn't right for you anyways!"

I turned around and saw my fist flying into the air. It went straight for Terrance's sun visor. I had knocked it off on to the floor. Then I spit in his face. "You don't know what's right for him. Fuck you, fuck all of you!!!"

Boo laughed at my demeanor. He thought I was funny. I'll give him funny. "I hate you! Don't you dare come by and expect to see Devon. And you can't have Brandon back either!!!"

He frowned and dropped to the ground as Terrance tried to hold him up. "Don't say that fucking shit to me! Don't you fucking say that shit to me, Angela! You know what? Fuck you and your fucking fat ass you fucking bitch!!"

Those words…not even the bitch part…but the fat word…the fatal fat word cut deep into my chest and ripped out my bleeding heart. I heard my voice let out a horrible shriek of panic and I ran. I ran from that stupid party and from stupid Boo and from all the laughter that will haunt me for eternity.

Who was I fooling? I was so fucking stupid to think…I wanted to die. I wanted to move out of Pierre that instant and never see another person again. How could he be so cruel to me? He had never called me fat. He had never hurt my feelings so directly!

Girls raised their eyebrows up in disbelief. Their noses flared with laughter. Their teeth shined right through me. Everyone saw me as stupid. Everyone hated me, was laughing at me…was pointing at me…

Oh, what have I done to myself?

Chapter Fifty-Six
Cardy

"Our topic today is father. What does the word father do to you? Do you think of your own father? Do you think of being a father? How does hearing that word effect you? And remember, no erasing or contemplating. I want raw truths. You will come across some interesting words of wisdom if you write what comes natural, believe me."

Cindy's eyes never left mine as I sat in her class for the second time in a row. Somehow, I had got the notion that she was talking directly to me, trying to figure me out with this bullshit. Why didn't she come out and just what her questions were about my father? Why did she want me to dwell on this subject?

I refused to write, again.

I didn't want to think about my dad. And when I say dad, I'm talking about Jebb. Not the other one. Who gives a fuck about…I don't know his name. I won't admit his name. That man is not my father and didn't create me. I refuse to acknowledge that truth. B.J fucking Sox had nothing to do with conception.

Nothing at all. My mom and him were complete opposites. She would have had nothing to do with him then, and nothing to do with him, now. How the hell could the two of them even be in the same room together?

It was just a wild rumor. Boo was not my brother and B.J was not my father.

And here I go thinking about the people I want to forget most.

"Trouble?" Cindy hovered above me like an annoying mosquito, sucking out the life of me.

I stared up with anger. "No."

"Did you find anything interesting when you dissected your fears?" Today, she was wearing a yellow dress, orange flowers pricked themselves against it in a wild outrageous pattern. I smiled only to myself, as her fashion was way beyond ordinary. She didn't know what to do with herself in the mornings.

"Not at all." I shook my head in disagreement. The side of my palm was heavy on the notebook, preparing not to show her a thing. I tapped my pencil nervously on the desk, pounding onto the scrapes that a student had left earlier in the desks life time.

"Hmmm, well I'm curious to find out what tomorrow will bring you. Are you?" Her hands folded behind her back and she swayed with confidence.

Bitch.

"Nope." The pencil went into my mouth and all I could think about is how to shoo her away from me. I leaned back in the desk and stared ahead. God, I should have skipped this one. Why I was hounding her...well, I knew why I was there. I wanted squares.

She tapped her sandals down the aisle and proceeded to her desk. I opened up my notebook and watched the lines make out a pattern.

I saw his face, round and red. His eyebrows were thick and hairy, small hairs gathering in the middle. But only I saw the connection, as no one else was close enough to be yelled at. He had big pores, small black ones on his nose. His cheeks hung down to his jaw line, forming creases into a frown. He was always frowning. He was always unhappy.

My eyes began to close, balancing myself in the air when the desk swayed backwards. I saw him clearly. His round arms raised and clamped around me. My body jerked upwards. I felt his heartbeat against mine, fast and nervous. His breath was full of beer, Budweiser, no doubt. His chest was cushioned by fat, squishing me into his bear hug and holding me into the air...about to slam me down against the floor.

I wasn't scared. Not that day. Sometimes, I liked to be bullied by him because it was our affection, my attention that I got from him. I was used to it. He was used to giving it to me. How could he be any different to a son that wasn't his?

I understood him, now. It was okay. I would give anything to feel that anger against me. Anything to feel the power in his arms to wrap around me and try to strangle my wiry body into formed discipline. Anything other than the feeling I'm feeling now.

"Cardy?!" Dr. Roma shot out into the air and made me crash my daydreaming onto the ground with the desk.

"What?!" I snapped.

"I asked if you were okay." She was about to stand and walk over to me. That, I didn't need.

"I'm cool, girl, chill out." Even though I didn't know what I had done to insinuate I wasn't cool. What the fuck was I doing to draw attention to myself? She already knew, or should have known, that I leaned back in my desk when I was concentrating.

Dad. Where are you now? I'd rather see you than mom.

When the bell rung, I left without asking for a cigarette. I avoided her because I didn't want questions or analysis. To avoid her further, I jumped into the class I had next. She wouldn't think about finding me in there.

It was Mathematics. It didn't say Algebra, arithmetic, or Geometry, just Mathematics. Cool, I could do this shit.

"How may I help you, are you new?" The teacher held out his hand for my schedule. He was a tall slender man with glasses. He sported a mustache and thick sideburns above his ears. His shirt was a plaid button up. The top button was fastened, too. His belt was firmly in place. His pants were tight around his ankles. His boots…well, he could walk home if he must.

I was amused by this man. I liked this man. He was so nervous, so cautious…so…could I say nerdy? Was that a word now-days? It was a sissy term, but it fit him, well.

"Um, I am, I guess." I didn't want to fuck with this man. This man was the kind that everyone fucked with. I wanted to respect him, catch him off guard and be nice, just to be defiant in *that* way.

"Deburke? Okay, Mr. Deburke, we have assigned seating. I will put you here, in front of Everett." He dusted off the top of the desk as if it was dirty.

I sat down and gave Everett a minute of my time. He was a large kid, overweight and overflowing his fatness onto the table top. Hmm. His polo shirt was blue and tightly squeezing the life out of him. He could barely fit into the desk. Why did they make desks so small? I had trouble getting my legs under them. This kid had trouble getting out of them. I could imagine him standing with the desk still attached.

I didn't want to laugh.

Mr.…oh, Mr. Wilson. He fumbled with some paperwork and stacked them on his desk. Then he held them out for me to grab. I stood, stretched, and strolled to receive my assignments.

It wasn't assignments. They were tests. Jesus Christ, they were fucking tests on the first day.

"We start off with multiple number problems and slowly increase the difficulty to find out where you are. Placement tests we call them. It will help us distinguish your future assignments, assessing you at a certain spot and going from there. Where did you go to school at?"

"What math subject were you working on?"

"Trigonometry," I didn't get too far in it. I took it in ninth grade, something not many people do as a freshman. Like I said, I knew my shit.

His eyes rose with shock. "You're kidding?" Now I'm thinking this man is gay. His voice had too much emphasis behind it. Okay, maybe I was being judgmental, and I shouldn't accuse this man of anything. But, I didn't give a fuck if he was gay. I was just stating what I thought. Chill for a bit, will you?

I shook my head in disagreement.

"Lovely," he clasped his hands together and I noticed a wedding band. This man was already sparking interest in me. Some lady out there was with this man. This man was good enough to marry. Weren't all nerds?

I really needed to stop my obsessive collision course of thoughts. Every time I thought of judgment, another thought came and talked me out of it. Fuck, I was going insane.

The first page was addition and subtraction. Second page was division and multiplication. Fuck, now I was correcting the language in my head. A part of me didn't want to cuss, a part of me wanted to scream it.

The third page consisted of fractions and decimals, percentages and equations. Wow, were there kids in here that didn't know this shit? I was in second grade doing long division. In fifth grade my teacher forced me to do algebra. She was amazed how much I could absorb.

Here we go…algebra, geometry, square roots…cool.

I was done in twenty minutes. There wasn't a question dealing with trigonometry. This class would be a breeze. In fact, not once did I get bored and daydream. Not once did my desk come off the floor and cause me to drift out of the classroom.

I liked math. No, I loved math. I don't know how many ribbons I won in math contests at school. I don't know how many certificates I received for the shit, either. It was something my mom was very proud of. She said I got it from my father, as he excelled in math. I thought she had meant Jebb.

I know now that Jebb didn't know shit in math. Jeff didn't either.

I was having a good day. At lunch, I sat with Brett, my roommate. I sat with him just for the change in seating.

He didn't get the privilege to eat whatever he wanted. So, being the nice guy that I was feeling like being, I shared my tray of junk food. He settled on my chili cheese nachos.

We talked about cars, how he stole them, what he used and shit like that. He had never stolen a mustang. He had always wanted to, but never had the balls to do it. When I told him that I owned a 1969 Chevelle, he almost choked on his Dr. Pepper.

He said that a friend of his owned a 1972 Chevelle and he had been dying to drive one ever since. It was the first thing that we shared on common ground...cars. Not that I knew shit about them, but I liked them. I liked that Chevelle.

I swallowed hard when I realized that I would never see that Chevelle, again. I wouldn't have all the luxuries that I once had. Not with my mother, not with Boo. I would have to start from scratch...with nothing.

Ugh. That was a horrible reality. I'd have to get a job. I'd have to work for a living. I'd have to work hard, too. I shoved that thought out of my head. It wasn't going to ruin my good day. Not today, anyways. I'll let that thought resurface when I wanted to get pissed about something.

I went to sleep thinking about fathers.

What is a father? What is his role in life? Was he that alcoholic that sat on his ass at nights, controlling every fucking detail in life? Was he someone who never came home at nights? Someone who beats the shit out of my mom and throws me down the stairs?

No.

I knew what a father was. I never had one.

A father tucked in their fucking kids, kissing them good night. A father comes home happy to greet his family. A father gives advice. He listens, he enjoys...he laughs. He takes you out back to his big telescope and points out the stars. That's what a father does.

I had that chance, once. And I blew it. I was there for Brandon. I held him. I kissed him, I tucked him in. I smiled and I laughed and I talked and I listened. I wanted to be there for him.

But look at me now. I had abandoned him. I couldn't change it. He'll never know me. I had fucked it up and I couldn't fix it. I'm a worthless, useless father. I missed his first step, his first word...hearing him call me daddy.

You can't get that shit back. You can't apologize and pretend that I was around. He knows, now. He knows that I'm a fuck up, even if he was a year old. He knows. Fuck. The thought made me sick.

I didn't write it in the book. I didn't draw anything in it, either. That page was left blank, purposely. It meant that I was nothing. Blankness. Sickness. I piece of blank paper that never made a mark on his child…

Chapter Fifty-Seven
Binderman

Where the fuck was I? What the fuck was on my ass? I was covered in vomit, motherfucker! Did I puke on myself? What the motherfuck?

I was in a corner. I was crouched down in a fucking corner, covered in my own vomit and in someone's living room. A curio cabinet stood a hundred feet above me, towering over me like a fucking tree. Pictures of Terrance stared back at me.

That motherfucker, I was in his house. I was *still* in his house. Why the fuck was I still in his god damn house?!

My hand tried to hoist my body up, but it slid down the glass. I couldn't get leverage. I bent forward, feeling the liquor swish in my stomach. Oh my fucking God, I'm going to be sick. I was light headed and dizzy. My head was throbbing. What the fuck happened to me?!

I crawled out into the open and noticed a slum of bitches passed out on the floor. Plastic cups and beer bottles were slung all over the carpet. A lamp lay on its side. Empty Tequila bottles were near my feet. Did I drink all of those? Was it possible?

Fuck, where's Terrance?

I grabbed the cocktail table and pulled myself up onto my knees. I glanced around for someone I knew. I didn't even know the bitches. They were just sprawled out with their asses in the air, some with no underwear on. That shit made me want to vomit more.

I stood and swayed. I patted my pockets for my cigarettes and realized that my pants were at my fucking ankles. God dammit. I pulled them up and buttoned them. My shirt was gone. My wife beater was gone. My shoes were gone. My fucking socks were stained with mud. What the fuck happened to me? I ask you again, what the fuck happened to me?!

I peeled the socks off and dropped them to the floor. I stepped over the broads and stumbled into Terrance's foyer. I yelled for him. I yelled for Brian or Kyle or Roger. It was starting to piss me off. I didn't want to be here when these bitches wake up and start asking me questions. Fuck these stupid ass girls.

Terrance came to the top of the staircase without his sun visor on. I almost didn't recognize him. "You still here?" He zipped up his pants and came jogging down as if he didn't have a fucking hang over.

"What the fuck is going on?" I held my head and grabbed the banister for support.

He pushed into me and smiled. "Dog, you racked up hella points, last night. Remember that new Asian girl? She was hot, wasn't she?"

"Asian, I fucked an Asian broad? No fucking way." But I wasn't talking about points. I didn't give a fuck about that damn game, anymore.

"No, dog, you did. She goes to Cheriton. She might be here, wait a minute." He jumped off the last step and headed into his pile of bitches. He bent down over each one and viewed their faces. She wasn't one of them.

What the fuck was I doing fucking with an Asian broad? I had a record going. I had to screw it up for that shit? During my entire "fucking" career, I hadn't managed to fuck another race. I wasn't prejudice, or against that shit…I just had a record going.

Cardy, ha, that motherfucker had a different record going. He was out to fuck every race and culture. He liked that shit.

I sighed, heavily. "What the fuck did I do?" I was mainly speaking it to myself. I palmed my eyes for some type of memory and landed on Angie. Oh fuck no. no, no, no fucking no. I didn't want to go there with myself. I had fucked it up. I fucked it all up.

"Wanna see the scores?" He pulled the notebook out from his back pocket. Those motherfuckers never went anywhere without it. I bet he was up in his bedroom figuring that shit out before I called him.

I snatched it out of his hand and tossed it on one of the girls. "Nah, I don't wanna see that shit. I don't give a fuck about that shit. I'm out. I'm done with it." I brushed passed him and up his staircase. I was gonna squeeze into one of his shirts for the hell of it. He owed me.

He ran after me with the damn thing in toll. "What do you mean, you're done with it? Dog, you got fifty points for banging Mai-Lin."

"Mai what? Fuck it, Terrance. I don't wanna play. I'm out. I can't believe ya'll talked me into coming here. I'm not down with this shit, anymore. I wanna go back to Cheriton. Take me home!" I headed straight for his closet which was half as big as mine, but bigger than everyone else's.

I pulled off a white polo from a hanger and threw it over my head. He didn't say shit about it. He was more concerned with me being out of the game. "Dog, you can't bail out. If you bail out then you have to forfeit your points to someone else. And then when you wanna get back in it, you're fucked. You have to start all over."

I stared at him like he was stupid because he was. "Stop calling me dog, motherfucker. Fuck you. I don't give a fuck what happens. I'm out, that's it. Give my points to Cardy."

I didn't even look at myself in the mirror. I didn't care. I wanted to go home. I needed to squash this shit with Angie. I needed to fix it.

"Cardy? Fuck no. Cardy already has the second highest points. He doesn't need your shit, too. We have enough to battle for without your shit added to his. Fuck that, Boo. No, I'm calling Brian. No one's going to let you bail on us." He ran after me as I headed for the front door. He chased me onto his sidewalk.

I was gonna walk home if I had to. No, I was gonna walk to my dad's. He can take me home. "Nobody tells me what to do. I'm giving my points to Cardy. Call Brian, call any motherfucker you want to. They're my points, my choice."

The game was stupid. Who came up with different points for Asians, anyways? Why did it matter? (Oh, Cardy came up with that shit.) It was all stupid. It was a high school game.

I was out of high school.

And then out of nowhere, a BMW swerved onto the curb and parked. An Asian girl jumped out with a wide grin. "I left my purse here, hi, Boo!" She was short and wide hipped. Her hair was long and thick, perfectly straight and perfectly black.

"Motherfucker." I turned around so I didn't have to converse with the bitch. I wish I hadn't done shit last night. I wish I hadn't left my house yesterday. It was all a big ass mistake.

Terrance smiled and abandoned me. He followed the new whore into the house so he could get some play. Probably some head. Fucking cocksucker. Fuck him. I was tired of misusing hoes. I was tired of sluts, period.

What was it about girls that made them feel like they had to put out, huh? We just used the shit out of them until they were so loose and ruined that they couldn't get a decent boyfriend. They were stupid. Didn't they know that a motherfucker can feel if a girl's been with every guy on the block? It doesn't work the same. There isn't enough grip. Yeah, laugh if you must, turn red in the face…but I can tell. We all can.

Everyone was so fucking stupid around here. Go ahead, be stupid. It didn't affect me anymore.

Cheriton broads weren't like that. I don't know about the college girls, but girls I grew up with in Cheriton weren't raised to put out. Maybe it was St. Paul Academy. Maybe the Catholic faith did some good in those girls. They were raised to respect their bodies. They waited for the right time, the right guy to come along. Not that they waited for marriage, but they were an adult, making adult fucking decisions.

Damn. I felt old. Last year I would be kicking my ass if I thought like that. But that was last year. In eight months, I was going to be twenty one. It should be the time of my life. Problem was…I had already partied my ass out. I didn't want to have a twenty first birthday party. I had done everything that I had wanted to do before I hit that age. All I could do now was move forward.

Go to college. Major in Architecture like my grandpa. Be a dad, a good one. Get married.

God, I was so drunk. I'm stumbling home on foot, thinking about this stupid ass shit.

Chapter Fifty-Eight
Basia

Kyle carried me into his house. I didn't know it was Kyle who had saved me until he sat me on the sofa. I never thought of Kyle as a big brother or savior, or as a benefit to know, but there he was…bending over me with full concern.

Darron came rushing, practically falling, down the stairs to my aide. He knew something had happened, but didn't know what. He barged into Kyle and shoved him aside. "What's wrong, what happened?!"

Kyle shoved him back. "Dude, Anthony Mercini almost raped her, she's traumatized. Go get her some water or something!"

I wasn't thirsty. I didn't need water. What I needed was…was…Cardy, my mother…do I dare say the tender touch of my father?

Darron didn't move. "She was raped?!" Of course he didn't hear it right.

"No, I said she was almost raped, I stopped it." Kyle stood in his striped polo shirt, checkered shorts and Sambas. His hair was cut and sectioned into small ponytails, popping up like knobs, wrapped around with colored rubber bands. He had his own style…always did. For some reason, he was always respected for it.

Darron huffed and headed for the door. He was going to give Anthony a piece of his mind. "That son of a bitch!!" His fist pounded into his palm, repetitively.

Kyle jumped in response. He grabbed Darron by his collar and brought him to a halt. "He's in jail. It's taken care of. Everything's okay. He got what he deserved and now we have to make sure Basia's alright."

Darron stared at me, then. He glanced from Kyle to me, back to Kyle. "You saved her? Is she okay?"

"I think so." Kyle nudged his way next to me and rubbed my hair back. He brought his face closely to mine and met eyes. "Are you alright?"

Kyle Sorum. His eyes resembled Darron's, narrow and blue. His lips were thin and looked just like his brother's. I never noticed before how similar the two were. Kyle was wider, bigger, really. Darron was a runt version, small and frail, as if there weren't many genes left to give him.

I nodded. It was all I could do. I felt safe in this house. I felt safe with Kyle and Darron. In fact, I felt safe with Kyle being so close to me…even when he held me against his waist as he trudged out of that horror house.

Kyle wasn't dirty at all. He lived in a dirty room, with dirty clothes and dirty habits…but his skin…his skin was clean and soft. His body smelled like cologne. He was alright…at least, to me.

"I knew it, I knew it!!!!" Darron paced before the coffee table, dropping his arms to his sides for the millionth time. He didn't get me a glass of water, which I didn't want anyways, and didn't leave the room so my shame could lift. Instead, he stared on.

Kyle glanced around the living room for a second until his eyes landed on a knitted throw blanket. He snatched it and covered my legs. I buried my head deeper into the stinky smelly cushion and knew that I wasn't ever going to breathe fresh air, again. I was destined to be home bound.

"Kyle, Dairy, is that you?" I heard Sharon shift her body in the urine stained leather seat. It creaked and moaned from years of torture. She was somewhat of a mean lady, yet, I knew nothing about her.

From the years that I knew Darron, all she did was sit in her recliner, every now and then walk to her bed, which was a hospital bed that moved up and down, but was broke…and screamed for one of her sons to help her. Darron said she was a kind hearted soul that just got stuck in bed from being overweight…that's why she was so angry at the world. She'd watch her soap operas, soak her feet in some type of salt, and cough such a curdling sickness that it made me gag. As of a conversation with her…never had one.

Dairy…I smiled each time I heard her call Darron that. I was smiling, now, with my head like an ostrich's.

"Mama, what? I'm busy." Kyle tilted his head in annoyance, keeping his eyes locked with mine.

"What's going on in there? Did I hear someone say rape? Are they picking on your brother again? No one better have raped my son, I tell you what. I'll get up out of my…"

"Nobody raped me, mom!! I'm right here, like I always am!! Nothing's going on, just go back to sleep! We got it!!" I felt Darron's little fists ball up with his fit throwing voice, irritated that even his own mother thought he was weak and being taken advantage of.

No, Sharon…it was me, Basia, who had been taken advantage of. But, you probably don't even know I've been around for the past five years or so, do you?

Darron's voice lowered. "So, what do we do? What should I do? What are you going to do, Basia?"

Kyle snapped and lightly shoved his little brother towards the stairs. "Go back to sleep, watch Jasmine or something. I said I'll handle this. Dude, you're all over her. She doesn't need to be questioned or worried about what you think, alright? Just go somewhere, do something. Dude, look…I got it!!"

"Is she staying down here or coming…"

"Does it matter?!"

Darron didn't reply. His body jerked with all his might and his feet stomped up the stairs. Was that a cheese puff I smell, or a dirty sock? I pulled my head out of the corner and appreciated the dust that filtered above my nose. Ah, refreshing if you had to smell dirty feet for ten minutes.

"Do you want me to stay down here with you or do you want to be left alone?"

I think I shocked him into using his head. Kyle was never a talker, a questioner, or someone who took action. He was just there…I couldn't even think of him communicating with his friends. He was like a shadow, someone who was given charity to when he hung around Boo Sox.

"Um, you can go upstairs. I'll…I'll be alright." I wasn't going to be alright. If it wasn't for Kyle, I would be dead, maybe not really dead, but dead in my head. I'd be a zombie, knowing that I was raped and I had all the opportunity to see it coming, to predict that a nineteen year old didn't want anything to do with me but to accomplish my body like a trophy…like I was stolen property from Cardy's trophy case.

The room went silent. The lamp was turned off and the moonlight dimmed my feet. Everything else was in the dark. The couch was cold. The blanket was old. The floorboards didn't creak and everything was still, so still that I had forgotten that Kyle was in the room. I thought he had left.

I was soon reminded, though, when the opposite side of the couch dipped down. Kyle was sitting at my feet. The moonlight had outlined his body. I could see his hands wipe down his face and then relax into his lap. I couldn't make out his facial expression. I don't think he was looking at me.

"Kyle?" I managed to break the silence and sit up. What was he doing? I told him that he could leave me alone.

He was full of frustration. "I can't believe he did it! I mean, you of all people. There's certain girls you just don't…I still think of you as a little girl. You're my little brother's friend. It's hard enough that I know you have a baby…but…fuck. It makes me think of all the other girls out there, how old they are. We don't even ask them their age. Motherfuckers just fuck them. I wonder if they feel the way you did and just went along with it, ya know? How many other girls get raped?"

Kyle was thinking. Kyle was considering something not many popular guys consider, or do they? Maybe they don't care like Kyle cared. Maybe, this situation had changed him. Maybe, instead of Kyle saving me…maybe I had saved Kyle. Can I look at it that way?

He turned towards me. "Are you sure you're alright? I don't want to leave you alone. I keep thinking that they'll let him out and he'll come back."

My fingers wrapped around the blanket and my legs drew together. Then I realized that I didn't have my underwear on. Was I naked this entire time? Did Kyle see me naked? Oh my goodness, what was I doing being in that situation and letting the world view me like that?

"I can't go to sleep knowing that you're down here. You don't have to be afraid, as long as you live in this house, me or Darron would never let anything happen to you, hear me? I swear to God, I'm going to kick his ass when I see him and he'll be sorry. I don't care if he's a Mercini. You're safe Basia, I promise." Kyle had said more to me this night than any other night put together.

"Kyle, do you believe in God?"

Darron didn't get on religious conversations like Cardy and I did. He said he believed and that's all he needed to say. At that time, it was all I needed to hear. But, did Kyle?

I felt his smile through the darkness. "Do I what?" After a long pause, he added "Don't blame God for what almost happened to you, Basia. You go on believing that he protects you. Cause he does. He sends people like me and Darron here to make sure of it. And, I will. From now on, I'm making sure you're okay."

"It scared you, didn't it?" I was beginning to like Kyle. Not necessarily like-like, but I felt really close to him. He was a good friend, like an older brother.

"You're screams did. I never heard anyone scream like that. I thought you were being murdered. When I found out that he was trying to…I was so mad. I'm still mad."

"I *was* being murdered. It felt like it, anyways." I dropped back against the sofa and covered my head with the knitted throw. What a horrible, horrible night that I knew better than to follow through with.

Chapter Fifty-Nine
Dr. Cynthia Roma

I was cross matching one fat chart with one paper thin one. It was very interesting. My desk was covered with notes and documentation from Binderman Sox's file. Cardy's folder was open, but starving for information to add to its gut.

I started at Bin's data. I highlighted anything to do with Cardy beginning in 1991, when Binji was thirteen. At first, Christopher was considered an imaginary friend that followed him from childhood. It was the only rationalization I could come up with. One, his father said he didn't have a brother. Two, there wasn't proof that anyone knew a Christopher in Bin's life, not even his sister who was nine at the time.

Many sessions were spent on talking about his imaginary friend, where was he now, what has he been doing, does he talk to him in his room…that sort of stuff. Bin caught on quickly and threw tantrums each time that I referred to Christopher as being invisible. I remember one certain day that he had an outburst.

"I am NOT crazy, you fucking bitch! Christopher is real, no matter what my stupid dad has told you! He's hiding him. He's a secret!" Bin was this chubby cheeked thirteen year old who pinched his lips and squeezed his eyes so tightly that I thought it was amusing to watch.

Nevertheless, his paranoia and conspiracy theory was high at this time. It fit right in with everything else that was going on in his life. His mother had just committed suicide, his father was losing his mind trying to cope, and his sister wouldn't speak. It made sense that Bin would conjure up this old friend of his and blame all his anger on not seeing his brother.

In all reality, I think that Bin was afraid of losing his family. He had lost his mother and he wanted to hold onto who he had left…and that included his long lost brother that everyone but Bin had forgotten about.

Let's see here...I had their first meetings on paper, where Bin met Christopher and Christopher met Bin. Binji wasn't willing to keep anything back. When I told him to talk, oh, he talked alright. He made sure we went passed an hour's time and he had my full attention. When I seemed rather exhausted, he'd jump or startle me. Sometimes, he'd throw a fit and knock over a few of my office things.

It started with the hospital. Bin went with his father to see Cardy in the delivery room, right after Dena had given birth. B.J Sox was friends with Jebb Deburke, Cardy's legal father...which reminds me...I need to track Jebb down.

Anyways, Jebb didn't know about Dena's affair until later, much later. Bin didn't know that this baby was his brother, but he remembers staring down at him and his father turning red with anger. He yelled at Cardy's mother and stormed out of the maternity ward. His father almost hit a car on the way home. Bin wasn't strapped in and hit the window. He was two and a half years old.

He was so young to recall such a memory that I didn't acknowledge the truth about this story until Bin came back at sixteen, telling me that he was friends with Jeff, or J.D, as Bin called him. This is when I started piecing together a truth with having a brother at all.

Those stories had more impact. There was a Christopher Deburke that existed. The problem now was that he belonged to another brother. I didn't have proof that this Christopher had anything to do with Bin except that Bin took a liking to the name and now identifying him as belonging to him, not J.D.

Twisted yes, I still can't get over the fact that they are brothers, that they lived together as brothers, yet only friends...and Cardy didn't know this until the day of the crash?

"He doesn't know about me, Cindy. He thinks I'm friends with J.D because I like the motherfucker or something. I hate his ass. If Cardy was my brother I'd give him whatever he wanted. I'd never be mean to him. J.D takes him for granted. I swear on my mother's grave that I'd never be friends with his bitch ass if it wasn't for Cardy."

Bin had this thing with putting everything on his mother's grave...only if he was telling the truth, like a scout's honor, or hand on the bible sort of thing. He never told a lie when he did that, as he strongly believed in God and that God took his mother to Heaven even after she committed suicide. He *had* to believe that.

Ugh...back then, when his mother died, I couldn't even get him to say the word Heaven. At first, I thought he didn't understand that his mother was dead. He kept telling me she was in Italy. Talk about crazy...I really thought this boy was mental.

Italy = heaven...get it? If she couldn't go to heaven, and she wasn't in hell...where was she? She was in Italy, he told me. She was lying on a beach towel with lemonade in hand, getting some sun like she always liked to do. Talk about odd. I didn't know where he came up with Italy until his father said that they were planning a trip there that summer before she passed. To Binderman, she went without them. It was a safe way of thinking.

I wasn't getting much out of Bin's chart as I had expected. Bin talked about him, sure...Cardy played "Goblins" with him as a child, had a few visits until his father went off the deep end and made Dena stop bringing him around because his mother was distraught and catching on to something.

Oh, this wasn't much. I didn't know what type of boy Cardy was back then.

I picked up the receiver, dialed 9 and called Bin's cell phone. It went straight to voicemail and I hung up, too impatient to leave a message. That boy has been avoiding me for some time, now. Something he doesn't want to talk about, I bet.

I gathered Bin's chart and shut it. I slid it to the side and tapped my pen against Cardy's weak little papers. Nothing, nothing, nothing. I knew he was Bipolar. I didn't diagnose him and wasn't about to label him something without a good evaluation...however, I was doing a trial period with a combination of medicines to see what it would do for him.

I started over on scratch paper.

I made a timeline with what I knew of Cardy so far.

Born 12-17-80. B.J & son meet him in hospital. B.J gets mad. B.J agrees to meet Cardy at his house for visits...why...B.J mad. No more meetings. Bin knows of Cardy. Cardy doesn't know, too young?

Now, I have to intertwine Bin and Cardy, don't I?

Bin's mother dies. B.J moves to Pierre. Bin in and out of facilities. Discovers his brother is in town. He becomes best friends with Cardy's brother to see his own. Bin doesn't involve himself with Cardy and keeps a distance from B.J's secret. B.J leaves country.

Rebellious move: Bin takes action to include Cardy. Does J.D know?

10-05-1996. J.D wrecks. Bin makes move to take over as brother. Cardy agrees because mother is distraught and Cardy has nowhere to go? Does Cardy know who Bin is? I don't think so.

Cardy depressed over J.D…heavier into drugs. Bin can't control him.

This is all over J.D's death, that's for sure. It started there. Cardy has every reason to be depressed. His family is ripped apart and he only has Bin.

Babies…there's babies being born and drugs and alcohol…sex…a game book? Jesus, that was cruelly insane. An actual game book of sex and girls like they were playing a sport!!!

Let's back track. I etched in Cardy's diagnosis of A.D.H.D. oh, wait…what if he knew of Bin and was reacting to losing a brother? He was diagnosed at seven. A.D.D at first, then at ten, it was A.D.H.D.

It's really hard to diagnose Bipolar, this I know. Drugs interfere with behavior, anyway, and a lot of it has to do with dissecting drug induced moods from sincere Bipolar episodes. A.D.D…The biggest question is…did Cardy remember Bin and knew who he was at all times?

Okay, my head is really jumbled right now. A.D.D, Bipolar, separation anxiety…I needed chocolate. Where are my boxes of chocol…oh, no way…who has been eating my chocolate?

Cardy Deburke.

He was the only one who rummaged in my drawers for my cigarettes, that little bastard. I was going to crack his head if it's not his diagnosis, first.

His attitude was…arrogant. He pushed my buttons and everyone else's around here, too.

Fine, I'll just have a cigarette. I lightly tugged open the bottom drawer and lifted out my purse. Underneath it was a faded yellow box with brown lettering on it. Oh…I had forgotten about these priceless little clues. What do we have here?

Love letters, are they?

I lifted the lid and withdrew the first acute triangle shaped note. It was folded tightly, the tip pushed into the side for security. Pink bubble handwriting with hearts and squiggles giggled back at me. Oh, the innocence in this was fun.

I stuck my fingernail into the edge, peeled it open and began straightening out the wrinkles. The page was full of pink handwriting, girl's no doubt, perfectly aligning each letter in the exact same order as the last. It was beautiful in appearance.

4/25/96
Hi, Cardy, wazz up or
D
 O
  W
   N? Are you sick today? You barely ate breakfast and haven't said a thing to me. Are you mad at me for some reason? If it's Darron, let me know, I'll sock it to him. If I did something, I didn't mean to. Is that a new shirt? I like it. Do you still want to meet up at the arcade, later? How late are you going to be up, tonight? I'll try to call you if you'll be up late. By the way, last night I didn't take a bath because I wanted to smell like you when I fell asleep. Is that crazy or what? I missed you. Anyways, I love you so much and hope you write back soon.
CARDY
& forever & ever,
BASIA Basia XOXOXOXOXOXOXO
4EA!

I smiled at this little girl's outlook in life at the time. It was amusing and warmhearted, so simple, yet full of youth and obsession. I remember those days…those days felt like years, never an end to an hour's time. Weeks felt like months and a month meant a year. Now, a day was more like a minute, a blink. Easter, then Christmas, you find yourself wondering what happened to Fourth of July.

I had to read more just for this feeling.

 Dear Cardy,
 I loved the poem. I'll try to write you one, but I'm not that great with rhymes. I'll make you a mixed tape of all our favorite songs, how's that? And you don't need to be jealous of Darron holding my hand because I don't think of him as anything other than a little twirp of a friend. Don't tell him I told you that and destroy this letter just in case. He'd be so mad at me. I love you with all my heart

and can't wait to spend eternity with you. Can you see us together when we're old, holding hands and wearing dentures? You'd be a doctor or famous basketball player and I'd be a famous artist and we'll have a hundred babies and travel the world with all of them with us, right? I know, that's a little much, isn't it? How about fifty? Don't forget to tell your mom that her movie night is cancelled because you want to watch a movie with me at Darron's. Tell her how much it means to you. Be honest, she has to understand. She's nicer than my mom. Anyways, love you so much and forever!
    Basia
    XOXOXOXOXOXO

Perfect.
They were in love. He's a poet, is he? So, he can write? What's going on in my therapy class, then? Does writing remind him of her? What happened to this girl? How do you say her name?
    And there's a clue with his mother. They had movie night. He was her security, wasn't he? Messed up relationships with men and she turns to the company of her son, bonds with him and expects him to never leave…that can fit. I know it fits.
    Here's a different one.

    Cardy, what is up or
    D
     O
      W
       N,
Basia is sick today. She told me to tell you and since this stupid teacher won't let us talk, I'm writing you. What's going on, today? Anything? Have any gossip? Do you want to hear some gossip? Okay, don't tell Basia because she'd be mad. Danah Springs just told Loren that she thought you were cute. Do you think Danah is cute? You can tell me, I won't tell Basia, I promise!?
    Love Becca

I wonder what he wrote back.

Letters and writing, words, and formations with any type of writing utensil had the beautiful mechanism of getting your thoughts out onto paper. It was a positive transition into reality and discovering a pattern to the way someone thought. It relieved many, soothed minds, and let people get things off their chests in a way that speech could not. And, if you didn't like it, erase it…wad it up and throw it away. No one heard you, but you're speaking.

It's great. That's why I'm a teacher in Therapeutic writing. It also occupied my own empty thoughts…the ones that I didn't have because I didn't have a life outside of work.

When was the last time I received a letter from a loved one? Aunt Mildred? Who wanted a letter from Aunt Mildred?

Certainly not me.

Chapter Sixty
Binderman

I found myself at Angie's door before I reached my dad's house. I was determined to plead my case, whether or not I was still drunk off my ass. If I had any sense, I would have changed clothes and slept through this hangover.

I was too desperate to wait it out.

"Angie!!!" I continued to bang on the door, refusing to stop. I leaned my body against the door frame for support while my head was throbbing. Terrance's white polo shirt was clinging to my waist, squeezing my shoulders tighter and tighter, adding to the frustration of my mistakes…my many fucked up mistakes.

I couldn't lose this one, this girl. It was going so well. We got along great. I went months without fucking it up and now this. Now, I fucked it up. I had broken a promise.

After what seemed to feel like eternity, the door flung open and I was bombarded with accusations. Not just from Angela, but along with her sister, Amanda, and her stupid ass mom, Susan.

"You think you can cheat on me, leave me at your grandma's house in Cheriton, and come by with an apology? Like you have any real excuse for what you did to me? You made me look like a fool, Boo! I have nothing to say to you!!" Angie's eyes were full of anger, dark and cold…and…hurt.

I gripped the banister that stood to my left and hung my head in defeat. "I said I was sorry! I didn't mean it, Angie, you have to believe…"

Amanda laughed with disbelief. "She doesn't have to believe anything you say. She saw it with her own eyes. Come on! You cheated on her. It's over. Go home. Nobody wants you around!"

Susan stood in the background, shaking her head and holding Devon on her hip, swaying impatiently. "Go home or I'm calling the cops!"

"Shut the fuck up, I'm not talking to your bitch ass, I'm talking to Angie. It's between me and her!" I snapped at her mother, too drunk to bite my tongue. I was tired of this shit. I just got the girl away from her mother's control…and now, I was proving Susan right from the beginning. I wasn't worth Angie's time.

"Why are you trying to be with her? Go screw around with someone else's life, someone who would take your crap…like Fresca Taylor or some other stupid cheerleader!! Someone who doesn't have a brain!!!" Amanda pushed Angie away from the door so she could close it in my face, but Angie wouldn't let her.

"It's over, Boo. You know it won't work. It was never going to work. I hate you! I hope you're happy." Angie didn't have a plan on what to say, it was just flying out of her mouth as soon as she thought it.

"And I can't believe you did this to Brandon! You don't deserve Brandon! He needs to be with a family who loves him, who can take care of him, someone who wouldn't get a hair up his ass and go party, forgetting about him! It was so convenient, wasn't it? Leave me there as your babysitter so you can screw all those…"

"It's not like that, Angie! Why do you gotta be such a bitch about it? I'm trying to explain…" I couldn't take this shit, right now.

"I'm sending him back. I'm calling his social worker and having him sent to a family he can trust. He can't trust you. Nobody can!" The door forced its way in my face but my hand shoved it back, almost hitting her in the process.

"Don't you fucking do that shit to me! I'm the only one he has! Don't you fucking…" I wanted to hit the bitch for saying stupid shit like that. I said I was sorry. I said I didn't mean it. I was there trying to fix it. I wanted to change…I wanted…

"That's enough. You've done enough to my daughter. You stay away from her. And you won't be seeing Devon until we go to court. I'm not standing around here letting him deal with an alcoholic father. You're just like B.J.!" Susan's tongue lashed out with too many threats…too many fucking threats.

"Fuck you, you fucking bitch! I can see Devon whenever the fuck I want! Stay out of this shit. I'll fucking kill you, bitch! You don't know shit about me or my dad, I'm not like him! Suck my fucking dick!" By now, Angie was pushing me out of the doorway and onto the platform that they liked to call their porch.

Bitch. They were all bitches.

"Close the door, Angela!" Susan demanded.

Amanda didn't allow Angie to decide…she jerked Angie back by her arm and slammed it for her. Seconds later, a cop car hauled my ass away in handcuffs. God dammit, I was tired of going to jail for some stupid shit.

And…of course I called my dad. It was yet, another disappointing move I had to make.

"What the hell, Binderman. This is like the fifth time I bailed you out since I've been home. What was it this time? You get into a fight? You look awful. Who was it, was it those kids with that one guy, the one who got shot? If it was, just give me a name, I'll take care of it. I've been doing some research on that Seth character, anyways. I'm gonna help PD crack the entire drug activity going down in St. Paul, so if you have anything to add…let me in on it." He was taking my arrest too seriously. It was completely off track of what was going on in my life.

"Nah, it has nothing to do with Seth. I didn't get into a fight. I went to a party and fucked it up with Angie. Her mom called the cops on me. I didn't do shit." I watched the trees fly by as we drove home to Pierre. Fuck the birds, the trees, the fucking sunshine. I wasn't in the mood.

He smirked with relief. "Girl problems…this is all over Angie?" He grabbed his squares from the dashboard and offered me a Marlboro. I declined with a sneer. I wasn't smoking that shit.

"I left her at Grams and went to a party. One thing led to another and she caught me cheating on her. I didn't even mean to do it. I was fucking wasted. It's all fucked up."

He thought it was funny, shaking his head with a smile and glancing at me from time to time. "You learn, someday. One day, you'll wake up and be alone, find yourself in Amsterdam, high as fuck, drunk as hell…and nobody to take care of your ass. You'll see."

I frowned and continued to look out of the window. I didn't want to find myself anywhere. I didn't want to learn…someday, motherfucker. I wanted to learn, now. I wanted to change, now.

I didn't know how to control it.

Except maybe…not go anywhere.

Then, what he had said stuck out to me. Not in an important way, "You were high?" But, it was an interesting question.

He parked my Expedition as if it was his. He shoved the keys deep into his pocket and stared at me for a long time. "You try getting out there in the streets, taking down drug dealers, buying shit from them. You learn their ways, son. You get hooked on the shit you're dealing with. It's the way it goes. Can't go undercover and stay clean, that's for sure. You gotta act like them, think like them. Some people get wrapped up in it and turn dirty."

Hell no.

"Did you turn dirty?"

"No, I was always busting them, but I've been through some wild shit in my day. You wouldn't believe it. I've done everything you can imagine, right up there with Heroin."

Hell no, again.

"You fucked with Heroin?"

"I've done it, yeah. Why do you think I told you about all that shit in the first place? I knew what the shit was about. I didn't want my son doing it. It was better that I stayed away from you kids, anyways. I didn't need motherfucker's raiding my family. It was too dangerous." He walked up the driveway, waiting for me to follow.

"Yeah, but you said you stayed away because of mom, that's why you took the promotion." I didn't want to believe that he was doing us a favor and getting lost in the drug scene to protect us. He was never that selfless.

"I did. It was the perfect getaway. I never had to think about her. All I had to do was bust up the drug rings going on and drown my thoughts in liquor." He turned as he opened the door. "I never wanted to be away that long. I never meant to abandon you or Bobbi."

I didn't reply. What was there to say? Sure…I accepted the apology and forgave him. But did I really need to say it? Couldn't he just read my fucking mind?

"I want to help Cardy, Bin. I want to do it for you, for him…for never doing it in the first place, alright? I know he's my son. I want to do everything right from here on out. I want you to help me, son. I need you to help me take down those responsible for the shit going on in St. Paul. They poisoned Stuart and almost killed Christopher. Someone's got to pay." He stood at the freezer, hand on the Vodka. Instead, he smiled and took out the orange juice underneath.

"They did it to themselves, dad. Nobody forced them to do Heroin." I slumped down onto the bar stool at the breakfast table and dropped my head into my arms. I was mad hungry, sick as a fucking dog, and exhausted…mentally, emotionally, and…physically. I couldn't make it upstairs to my room if I tried.

"No, they didn't, Binderman." He snapped and stood still, orange juice still in hand. Why did motherfucker's drink it from the container? Why the fuck was it always the orange juice, too? Did he learn that shit on the job, or were people born doing filthy shit like that?

"You know who's to blame? Do you really want to know who the fuck should be blamed?" He was about to go into a long speech. I felt it. He was argumentative, ready to talk my ass off when I wasn't giving a fuck to listen.

"The government's to blame. Everybody knows that the government has the final say in the drug war. But, that's a bigger issue. I won't get into it. It'll just piss me off. No, St. Paul's problems are these little bastards walking around with their pants hanging off their asses like they're tough shit. It's little motherfuckers who like getting paid for fucking up people's lives. They sell the shit, they profit from the shit…but they're not the ones who are dying from it, are they? No, my son and my nephew have that privilege because we don't have enough education in this fucking town about drugs in the first place. If more people weren't afraid to explain to their kids exactly why they shouldn't fuck with something, then they wouldn't do it in the first place. If Heroin wasn't around, it wouldn't be used. If drugs weren't available to sell, to smoke, to fucking do what it does to you…then…we'd have a better town, now wouldn't we? This is the first time I'm going to admit that I'm happy that this little shithole is a small town. It means that there's a chance to stop what's going on. I'm going to get to the bottom of this shit. I'm going to stop drugs in St. Paul, Binderman. Believe you, me, son…I have the knowledge to make it happen. Just watch."

I laughed into the counter. I can't believe that my dad thought he had that power. Nobody could wipe that shit clean. If he took care of all of Seth's boys, locked them away for the rest of their lives…if he got the Mercini's, and their boys, and Ronnie and Roger…anyone that made a sell…even Brian, or me for that matter…what about the motherfuckers in diapers, huh? What about them? They're just going to grow up and sell it. Someone was going to sell it, no matter what he did to prevent it. It's what happens. Shit fucking happens.

"Dad, it's not that easy."

"St. Paul is easy, Bin." He gripped my shoulder as he walked by and disappeared in the house.

My body lost balance and slid onto the ground. I hit the floor and remained there, not even thinking of St. Paul and drugs. No, I was thinking of Angie…or Fresca…how the fuck do I fix either one of those things?

I had to have one or the other. It's just the way it was going to be. Nobody else was worthy of my time and effort. Everybody else was a fucking slut.

Chapter Sixty-One
Angela

"I'm calling his father, Angela. We're not going to take care of another baby while he's in jail. His father can deal with this." My mother took full control over this matter. She held Brandon like he was Devon. She sat him in Devon's highchair and cut up a hot dog on the tray. She sat in a kitchen chair and watched him stuff his mouth.

I was still angry that she had called the cops. He didn't need to go to jail, again. He already had court dates. "Why did you call them?"

My mom tilted her head, stunned. "Because he was causing a scene, Angela, didn't you see the neighbors? He shouldn't behave like that. If he wanted to talk to you, he could have called. He didn't need to…did you hear what he said to me? Why are you defending him when he spoke to me in such a volatile manner?!"

"I'm not defending him, mom. I'm just saying, he would have gone away if we ignored him. I didn't want him to go to jail. It's my fault that he went to jail, now. And, you don't need to tell him I'm taking him to court because I'm not." Honestly, I didn't know what I wanted to do. I hated him. I felt sorry for him…I wanted to watch him beg me for forgiveness.

"Does he pay you child support, Angela?" My mom picked up a piece of hot dog that fell on the floor and tossed it in the trash can. She picked up Devon and sat him on her lap. She bounced him on her knee, trying to stay as calm as she could.

Devon and Brandon looked similar. Sure, Brandon had lighter hair than Devon. It was curling at the tips, but Devon had the same shade of blue in his eyes. Their eye shape was the same. Their cheeks were puffing out the same. They smiled the same, they laughed the same. Maybe all babies were like that, I don't know. But, I knew something other people didn't. Boo and Cardy were brothers…which made Devon and Brandon cousins, right?

"He pays for everything, mom. He doesn't have to give me money because he buys Devon everything he needs. He buys me things, too. It's not about money, mom. Like he said, it's between me and him, not you and him. He's not dad, mom. He's not gonna abandon Devon like dad did us. We don't need a court order to *make* him pay. He's a good father." I did feel like I was defending him. But I was only admitting the truth.

Yes, Boo cheated on me. Yes, Boo humiliated me, and yes, I hated him for that. But, I wasn't about to take court action on something to make it a bigger deal than it was. Sure, I can get child support on him. I could take full custody and refuse to let him see Devon. I could be an evil mother and use Devon in all awful ways to make Boo comply.

I wanted to do things the right way. Boo and I weren't meant to be together. I knew this when I signed up for the position of girlfriend. I don't know what I was thinking in the first place. If I would have declined, then I wouldn't be mad at myself for getting hurt. It, indeed, was between me and Boo and nothing to do with Devon or my mother.

"Whatever, Angela, say what you want. He's a lying, cheating alcoholic that has no business corrupting my daughter's future. I never understood why you got mixed up with him in the beginning. You're a good girl, Angela. You deserve someone who would treat you like that. Do you really think you deserve to be cheated on? Is there something in your head that's telling you to forgive him because it was something you did? If that's so, Angela, let me tell you something…"

"Mom, please! I don't want to hear it! I can't believe you called the cops on him!!!" I huffed to my bedroom and slammed the door so it would echo and shake the house. Good. I didn't want her to tell me what to do. I was eighteen years old. I can make my own choices.

I stared in the mirror, ready to pity my tears. God, I hated this haircut. Why did I do this to myself? I was never going to look like them. I was never going to have good hair and a pretty face…and these jeans!! I ripped them down my legs and stomped out of them. I picked them up and tried to shred them apart with my hands. When it didn't work, obviously, I slammed them into my trash can. The waste basket toppled over and spilled a can of orange Vess soda into the carpet. It made me cry harder.

What was I going to do? I was so disappointed with myself. I had been conned into believing Boo Sox. I was one of those girls who got trampled over. And the nerve!!! He thought that he can play with my head and apologize?

Oh. Oh, just wait. Just wait. But…wait for what? What was I going to do?

I know what I was going to do. I grabbed a pair of my sweat pants and slipped them on. I needed to talk to Delilah Lewis. She was my best friend and my next door neighbor. She was a good old friend who I can confide in without the hassle of someone calling me stupid.

"Amanda, can you keep an eye on Devon for me? I'm going next door. It won't take long." I hurried passed my mother, who was on the phone with B.J, I think. She was pacing and scolding him as quietly as she could. Hmmpf, my mom knew how to accuse someone, that's for sure. I hope Mr. B.J didn't hurt her feelings in the process.

Delilah lived in a similar ranch style house as mine. We didn't have big porches, but small slabs of concrete with one step. We shared a gangway and used to climb the walls when we were younger. Our back yards were separated by a metal fence and we used to climb over to each other's yard, depending on what we were doing at the moment…swimming, trampoline…you know. It was a constant battle between mom and me…that fence, I mean.

Delilah Lewis had always been my emotional support. She was a good listener and wasn't afraid to speak her mind. In fact, she was always speaking her mind, especially at school. She was an activist, protesting homework to save the trees.

Yes, that's my Delilah. She had this reddish blonde hair that bounced to a different curl each day. She didn't care to tame it. She left it alone, wild and free. That's the way she felt the world should be. A little trim here and there, but let it grow as chaotically as it wanted to.

She had very strong opinions and was able to influence our school to use recycled paper and eliminate Styrofoam from our cafeterias. She didn't litter and was often seen at our small park picking up beer cans and trash with her nifty trash picker upper.

She was the first one that I told that I was pregnant with Devon. Not once did she give me a negative opinion. She smiled her rosy freckled cheeks and beamed with enthusiasm. Of course, she was against abortion and has been known to picket the local clinic about murdering babies. She even thought it was a blessing that I was having Boo Sox's baby.

I remember her exact words. "Oh my gosh, Angie. You are going to turn this boy around!!" She saw it as a plan to save him. Ha, like a baby could do that to him. I didn't believe her from the beginning.

Sometimes, she lived in a fantasy world. She thought that everyone was good, no matter how bad they were. She didn't have the capability to hate anything. In fact, she watered the weeds that grew in her yard. She said that everything deserved a chance at life, even the weeds. My mom thought she lost her marbles, as my mom cut our grass once a week because of the ugly sight of weeds.

I didn't bother to knock. As like most of Pierre, doors weren't locked. I barged in and headed for her bedroom. It was the same as mine, set up and all. Well, except for the peace posters and organic coloring of her room…her room set up was similar to mine…bed in the middle, nightstand, dresser…a little less crowded by a baby bed.

"Hi, Angie!!" She looked up from her freshly painted toes and smiled. She was so cheery that it irritated me like worms under my skin. How dare she be so happy in a time like this.

She continued as she twisted the cap to the glass container. "Do you know that this stuff is organic? Yeah, I bought five shades, all matching my newest outfits. Wanna see them?" She arched her back with her fingers spread out. Her toes were high in the air as she stomped over to her closet.

"No, that's okay." Then she saw my face.

"Oh, Angie, what happened?" She gave me a hug, took in a whiff of my newest vibe of stench and collapsed on the bed with ears. "Tell me all about it."

And I did. I drenched her shirt with my tears as I went into long detail of that night Boo left me stranded. I bawled my eyes out. I sniffed, I snorted, and I swallowed my pride, leading right up to the point of confusion on why I should forgive him.

No, I shouldn't forgive him. He hurt me. But, what if he didn't mean it? What if…I bet Fresca had gone through this the entire time she was with him. He didn't mean it. But, he did. He didn't want to hurt her feelings…but he did. He didn't want to do anything that he did, but he did.

Maybe he wasn't meant to be with anyone.

"Honey, look at me." Delilah Lewis used pet names like that. "Boo Sox is like every other man out there. They make mistakes, especially when they're drunk. They think selfishly and feel bad about it later. He's known for cheating, Angie. You know this. I thought you weren't…"

"I know, I know, I know!!" It only made me cry harder.

"Look, I think you need to let him know that he's not forgiven and give him time to reconsider his priorities…" I didn't let her finish.

"That's just it, Dee. He was being so good. I mean, he's perfect when he's not around his friends and…and when he's not drinking. He's funny, he's thoughtful, he's sweet…"

"Do you love him?" Delilah was always about love. She loved everything and everyone. If love was involved, then love shouldn't be abandoned. Love always found a way. That's what she thought, anyways.

That wasn't the point with me. I didn't love Boo Sox. I was…I was living in a fantasy world with him. I was…I was…I didn't love him, right? I barely knew him. I *could* fall in love with him…it was possible. He was…he was perfect to fall in love with. No, no, not at all. I didn't love Boo Sox. Couldn't at all.

I shook my head no.

"If you give up on him, then he'll give up on himself, Angie. I think he made a mistake. I think you need to distance yourself around him and give him space. I know he's trying. Trust me, I've been hearing good things about him." She remembered her toes and waved her hand in front of them, trying to air dry them as quickly as she could.

"From who?" Who could possibly say good things about Boo Sox?

"Ashley Pitt has been talking nonstop about him. One of the last times he went to a party, he took her to the basement to…you know. She was all for it, after the break up and all. She wanted to sleep with him. You know Ashley, she wouldn't think twice about Boo unless she was desperate to forget about Steven. Instead of going through with it, he got cold feet. Can you believe it? He said she should go home and call Steven. And later that night, she said he was making out with Jenna Williams and he stopped with her, too. I think his head's messed up from Fresca. Whatever happened between them two really made him think about things."

I considered the scenario. Was he with me at the time? No, he only went to one party and I know for a fact that he only went to one party. That party was the one I caught him at. Jenna Williams?

"But Jenna is Fresca's cousin. Why would he even kiss her?" That lying cheating bastard...

"I think it was to get back at Fresca, but then he couldn't do it. Ashley said he was actually scared to touch her. She intimidated him. Now why would Ashley intimidate Big Bad Boo unless he was heartbroken? Boo doesn't pass up the opportunity to be with a girl." Delilah didn't gossip...much. But, she loved to hear about the mysterious side of people. She liked to know that people, like Boo Sox, had good sides to their personalities. She tried to hold onto those as if it meant more than the world.

"Then why isn't he spending the time to get her back? Why did he ask me out?" I have been asking myself this very question ever since I said yes to him.

"Because something happened that he can't face, Angie. What if Fresca hurt him in a way that he couldn't forgive her? What if Fresca was so fed up with his cheating that she doesn't want to go out with him, ever again? Now, here you are, sweet little Angie, mother to his baby...you're safe to be with. Have you ever thought of that? He wants to make it right with you because he can't make it right with her."

"Which makes me second choice."

"But a choice, Angie, he chose you. Now, he's still trying hard as heck to get himself on track. He hasn't been at parties. You said yourself that he's been good to you. What if he really wants to be with you and now you're shoving him away. Don't you think that..."

"You think I should forgive him?" Delilah Lewis was on his side for the mere fact that he was the most popular boy in town with his feelings hurt. Oh, Jesus, I came to the wrong person.

"No, not at all, I think that you should try to understand where he's coming from. I think you should hear him out, keep your distance, take it slow, and see where the river takes you." I didn't understand the metaphorical bullshit.

"In English, please!" I had a headache from the rise and fall of my emotions. One minute I hated him, the next I was actually considering...and now...oh I don't know.

"Don't go back out with him. Do what feels right, like I always tell you...but, listen to him, Angie. Don't bring up things that'll make him mad. Keep your distance, like your guard? Take it slow, as in don't rush back into being his girlfriend...and see where it goes from there. Just do what you really want to do. If you want to be with him, then give it time. You'll know when it's right." Delilah gave me a soft smile and a big hug. She squeezed me for a good ten minutes. It was enough to let me know that she was done with our conversation and needed to paint her fingernails.

"Alright," At least she wasn't trying to get him into court. At least she wasn't telling me what I didn't want to hear, like end it forever. That's why I went to her. I wanted her to say something similar to what she did.

But, did I really need to put my emotions back into the mainstream with him? Well, if I was guarded...but...he seemed to strip me of my guard. It was that damn charm of his...if only...if only he didn't have that charisma.

Chapter Sixty-Two
Cardy

"Today's topic is love." Cindy wrote it across the blackboard and underlined it. She drew hearts and X's and O's around that word.

Bitch.

"What is love? It could mean anything. I won't say what it means to me until tomorrow. Whatever comes to mind."

Love, love, love, every one that I loved turned to stone. Hurt came to mind. I didn't write it. Why should I write it? I didn't love anyone. Why should I?

Love-pain. Love-hurt. Love-

I walked out. I didn't have time for this bullshit. Love was a stupid word. It wasn't real. Love was something you called obsession. It occupied your time...your God damn wasted time.

"Cardy, can I have a word with you?" Cindy, or course, was running after me.

"No."

"Does it have to do with love?" Her heels tapped against the tile, quickly and after me.

I turned around with a smirk. "I don't feel like sitting still, today."

"If you come back to class and try to write something, anything...I'll give you the rest of my candy bars and a full pack of cigarettes. I just want you to try, Cardy, please, for me."

Roma and her damn bribes, what was it with her stupid ass bribes?

How the fuck can I pass it up?

"Fine, Roma, you win." She knew she did before I said it. Fuck, she had me, didn't she? She owned me. She controlled me. It wasn't fucking fair. A pack of cigarettes and candy bars really broke me down.

Cindy smiled to her satisfaction. I sat down and tapped my pencil. I tried to look amused, but I wasn't.

What the fuck was I supposed to write? How was I supposed to write it? I glanced to the side of me and noticed a student's pen crazily hitting the paper. I guess he was in deep thought. He was breathing heavy, back humped over the desk, eyes in a trance.

When he noticed me staring, he covered up his work with his hands. "Ms. Cindy!!! Dr. Roma!! Cardy's trying to cheat!!!"

"Oh, bullshit, like I wanted to write his fucking shit. Fuck you, motherfucker!!" I leaned back on my desk, too pissed off to stare at my own paper. Why would I want to steal his words? They weren't mine. Whatever he thought about love wasn't the same for me.

"Cardy, calm down and relax. David, I'm sure Cardy was just trying to figure out what to write, not necessarily trying to steal your ideas. Right, Cardy?" Cindy narrowed her warning with her eyes.

Bullshit. She's lucky that she was bribing me. I would knock that motherfucker out just for…then I would be in lock down. Fuck!

Then, the guy in front of me turned around and showed me his notebook. Love was written at the top and underneath it was a list of words. I guess he was relating them.

Love:
Live
Life
Die
Death
Family
Circle
Whole
One
House
Brick
Stuck

I laughed and shoved the paper back. "I don't want to see that shit!" Although, it made sense, I didn't want to do it. David pissed me off.

Because I had seen this form, this stupid list, those words *stuck* with me for the rest of the day. In math, one meant whole, whole meant circle, and circles were all around me. One could mean Basia, whole meant us, circle was never-ending...what the fuck was going on with me?

I pushed my desk back by my feet and interrupted the class with its screech. I didn't excuse myself or explain my actions to Mr. Wilson. I left his classroom with pink sidewalk chalk chasing after me. I kept my head to the ground, watching out for cracks, the way Basia would jump from tile to tile in the hallway, careful not to step on her mother's back. When I realized I was doing this in my head...I made sure that I stepped on every crack. Fuck superstition. If you believed in superstition, then you didn't believe in God. But, then Basia believed in God.

Fuck. My mind was going insane today.

My visit to Dr. Roma wasn't helping.

"Have you ever fallen in love, Cardy? Do you know what it's like to love someone? I don't mean your family. Everyone's loved a family member, before. I mean, accidentally crazily in love with a girl that you couldn't get off your mind. We've talked about Basia, haven't we?" I didn't appreciate where this conversation was leading.

Cigarettes or not, I didn't want to talk about Basia or any other bitch for that matter.

"No." Simply said.

"What about puppy love, strongly affectionate with a girl that you cared for? You didn't have to love her, but you didn't want to see her get hurt." Cindy was prying with cold fingers.

Strongly affectionate with a girl that I cared for. I didn't have to love her, did I? Alright, let's swing shit the other way, anything to keep my mind free from Basia Brahm, home of my heart, slayer of everything.

"Sure."

She curled her lips with enthusiasm. "Was she pretty?"

"Beyond pretty, Roma, she was hotter than hell." I lit the stupid Marlboro light, craved a Newport, and continued on with my two year obsession with a girl that I couldn't have. "She would have been the perfect girlfriend. She was a cheerleader and did these cheers. It was hilarious, always clapping and smiling, chanting her heart out."

This was in the early stages of my fascination with her. She had turned into a different person over night. In the beginning, she was so snobby and cruel, thinking she was tough shit. She had the world in her palms and guys at her feet. The minute she touched me, even if it was just a hug, I could easily say I fell for her, head over heels in love, for that matter.

Hell, I knew I didn't really love her. She was just a girl who took interest in me because we knew what her boyfriend was doing at the time. I was better than him. I gave her attention, affection. I knew what she wanted and she deserved better than what he gave her, even if he bought her everything in the mall.

"So, you never went out with her? She wasn't your girlfriend?" Her question was full of confusion. I think she wanted to know about Basia. Maybe it was the time that I mentioned sharing attention between her and my mom…maybe that was why she needed to know more about my girlfriend.

But, I didn't want to talk about Basia. I wanted to talk about Fresca Taylor. I could have loved that girl. I could have swept her off her feet and married that broad. She was marrying material, which was why Boo never let her go. Fresca was everything that was meant for love.

"She was somebody else's."

"Oh…and you liked her. Did she know this?" Cindy's chest was leaning on her desk, full attention, no doubt. Today would have been a good day to wear a low-cut dress. What the hell was under her shirt? She never really showed it off.

"She knew. She let it happen." I could have gotten so far with her. If only…if only I hadn't found myself so drunk and desperate for her, then I wouldn't be thinking about her, now. It ended too quickly.

Sometimes, I would lay in bed at night thinking about her. She was good to think about as long as I kept Boo far away from my mind. Her skin, soft and silky, tan and…ugh, I was getting a hard on just thinking about her. It wasn't fucking right.

"She let what happen?"

I blew the smoke out and leaned back, considering on whether to balance on my chair or tell the truth. "I fucked her, if that's what you want to know. We were very close. Boo never liked it. Sometimes, she'd want me to take her places. Boo was always busy."

Her eyebrows rose with surprise. "Boo Sox? You slept with Boo Sox's girlfriend?" This time, she didn't remind me that Boo Sox was my damn brother. That guilt could pass for the moment.

"I had that girl eating out of my hand, Roma." I would have kept feeding her, too, if it hadn't been for the heroin and the crash. She broke up with him, didn't she? She was missing from the house for a few weeks. Good for her. If I had better sense, I would have found her and picked her up. I would have taken her from Boo and made her mine, although, I already felt like she was mine.

"Hmmm. How do you feel about sleeping with his girlfriend? Didn't you feel guilty? Didn't she?" Cindy wasn't so rude to write all this down. No, I saw the mental picture taking place inside her head. She was categorizing it in sequences, rows of truth outlined with highlighter marker…circling pieces of evidence as I spoke.

"Sometimes she'd kick me out of her bed, and other times…she'd tell me to shut the door. She was upset with him, mostly. I don't think she really liked me. I reminded her of him. I was like his substitute when he wasn't able to be present. It sucked, really. I knew that's why she wanted me. I didn't give a fuck at the time because I wanted her. I had to have her because he told me I couldn't. He said that I could fuck anybody I wanted to, but not Fresca Taylor. Not her or his sister." I remember the strong impulse to touch her, to feel her…to take what wasn't mine and ruin it.

"You never…"

"If Boo Sox is my brother, do you think I would fuck my sister?!" I was appalled by her insinuation. That was bullshit. Bobbi was my sister way before I knew that Boo was my brother. She was too good to mess with. I don't know, if she was a slut…if she was like all those other girls…then maybe…then maybe I would be committing suicide now, thinking about incest.

"When did you know that Boo was your brother? I have to ask you this because it's been bothering me ever since I found out."

How the fuck did she even know this? She knew too much.

"I'm done talking to you, gimme the chocolate." So what if I was bailing and well aware of it. I didn't give a flying fuck. I didn't want to talk about Basia or Boo or Bobbi. I wasn't ready and don't think I'll ever be.

"Did you always know, Cardy? Did something tell you that he was your brother? You had to remember him…"

I let her words play in my head as I headed to my room.

No, I didn't know. I felt like I knew, but honestly, I didn't fucking know. How stupid was I not to? The signs were there.

I remember when I first met him in Pierre. He was Jeff's friend. I was nine, almost ten. He was always so loud and out of control. I knew when he came over because he announced his arrival. The first day, he was riding a BMX bike, chrome and flashy. He hit his breaks on our basketball court, leaving black tire marks in front of me. He laughed and said "what's up?" then he lit a cigarette and threw his pack at Jeff.

I was so mad at Jeff for smoking that I ran in and told mom. Jeff beat me down and I didn't tell on him, again. My mom thought he quit smoking.

Boo was always laughing and smoking and drinking…that's all I ever saw from him. He had a new bottle of liquor each time he came over. Even at twelve, he was wasted. I thought he was ridiculous. I didn't like him.

But he always looked familiar to me. I always felt like I knew him, but didn't know from where. I kept a distance from him up until I was fifteen just because he was so crazy. I watched him from the corner of my eyes just because he was amusing. I never knew what he was going to do, fall over and pass out, or hit Jeff in the stomach for calling him names. I liked when he showed Jeff up.

Now that I think about it, Jeff never let me hang around them. I thought it was because he hated me. Maybe not, maybe Jeff knew who he was and didn't want me around a better brother, not that Boo had good influence to instill in me, cause he didn't, but to Jeff…Boo had everything. Jeff wanted to be Boo Sox from the moment he met him.

Jeff got a BMX bike that summer. Jeff began drinking and smoking. He skipped school, came home with bad report cards…my mom blamed it on Boo and banned him from the house. When my parents were in the peak of arguing, no one cared to pay attention that Boo was in our house, again.

And thinking about it more, my mom had to know all of this. She had to know that Boo was my brother. Was that why he was banned? Who the fuck knew and didn't know? How can I always be so fucking stupid and naïve to see things the right way?

I didn't know about Jasmine. I didn't know about Boo being my brother. I didn't know Lynn was a fucking used up has been slut…and I didn't know that she kept the baby until later. I didn't know shit.

Why?

How the fuck could I talk about shit when I was too stupid to realize it in the first place? Where I was now was because I was stupid. I was blind, for some reason.

I knew not to do heroin. I didn't know it was heroin, but I knew I was shooting something up. I thought it was coke. I thought it was morphine. Well, morphine was similar to Heroin. That's what Dewey said, anyways.

Dewey. I hadn't thought about him in awhile. I liked Dewey. He was so…anti-Boo it was insane. He was taller and lean, like a stick. He was smart and scientific. He questioned the world, made weird experiments and was a bad ass artist. Bad as in good, mind you. His obsession was with needles…with his hands…with his spiritual awakening with life.

He knew the bible forward and backwards. He often recited the book of Genesis to me. He loved the story of Cain. I knew about Cain and Able. They were brothers. Cain killed his brother and God protected Cain from his sin. Ahh, I didn't want to think about the bible.

Thinking about the bible made me think of my faith. I was Catholic. I wasn't being a good Catholic by being me. Religion sucked. It was too hard to be good for someone else. And I was done questioning whether God was real or not.

What did I think? Was I just rambling on and on because I couldn't get obsessive thoughts out of my head? Sure.

I think that God existed. I think he has no plan in communicating with me. I think he can't help me. I think he gave me a purpose in life to learn fucking lessons and here I am, doing my best. My work wasn't done. I was meant to sacrifice everything about me to die with a horrible childhood and lifetime. That was my fate. That's what I had to look forward to.

I thought the medicine that Cindy put me on was supposed to kill those thoughts? How long did it take? Was it working? Was anything going to ever work?

Oh fuck this shit.

Chapter Sixty-Three
Dr. Cynthia Roma

"Hello, my name is Dr. Cynthia Roma, Psychiatrist at Safe Haven. I was given this number by a patient of mine. He said that I can get a hold of a Basia Brahm?"

I had to talk to Basia.

I didn't want to say that I received her number from my patient's sister, who happened to live three houses from them. I couldn't get a hold of Binji. His sister said that he's going through a rough period with girls. It would be really nice if he relayed those issues with someone who could help him out…like me…but Binderman wasn't keen on therapy. I always knew when he was depressed. He didn't call me. He missed appointments.

"This is her." A little voice cracked on the phone.

"Hi, I'm Dr. Roma, a Psychiatrist at Safe Haven, which is a rehab facility for troubled teens. I have a patient named Christopher Deburke and was wondering if you would have a moment to meet with me over him."

"About Cardy, you've met with Cardy? How is he doing? Is he okay? He's not brain dead or anything is he? Can I see him? Is he hurt?" She shot so many worried questions into the receiver that I felt all the love and emotion in her voice. This girl definitely had a thing for Cardy.

"I've been meeting with Cardy for months, now. He's a character, isn't he? He's okay, he's not brain dead, and I'm sorry, at this time he's not permitted any visitors. Are you available this evening?"

"Oh yes, yes, I am." She tried to sound professional, but she was just a little girl. I wondered what she looked like. Was she a cheerleader, was she popular? What was Cardy's taste in women like?

Okay, I had a list to keep to. By early 1999, I should have met with everyone associated with Cardy. I wanted to talk to B.J Sox. I wanted Jebb Deburke. I needed his mother, again. I wanted Binji, for sure…and Fresca Taylor would be a good insight, as well. My list will have additions along the ways, since I will pick up more names as I go down the line. Let's call this my game book.

I wonder how popular their game book is. I'd like to see it. Then, destroy it. How would I get my hands on this treasure?

Anyways, I met Basia Brahm at the park. It was her idea. She said that way Jasmine, Cardy's daughter, would be amused and she can talk freely. She was very thoughtful, even bringing a friend to watch her. His name was Darron. By the look of it, he may be her boyfriend.

"Hi, I'm Cindy. I don't like to be called doctor, by the way." I pushed my hair behind my ear and sat down on the local bench. I admired her, already.

She was a tall curvy girl, with big black curls. Well, it wasn't as much as curly as it was wavy, in a frizzy type of way. I don't know how she managed it. And her ethnicity amazed me. She wasn't Caucasian, as I had imagined her to be. She wasn't African-American, I don't think. Maybe she was in between, interracial, I mean.

Her skin color was beautiful. Like a swirl of bronze and cream, mixed together to form a soft gold, it glistened in the sunrays.

She had long legs with pink faded flip flops on her feet. She wore a pink halter top with white shorts. Her waist was like an hour glass, rounding out at her hips. And the beautiful envy didn't stop there.

Her face was flush with sunshine. Her cheeks were a high rise of cherry smiles. Her eyes reminded me of Cleopatra, naturally shaped. Her eyelashes were long and thick, mesmerizing anyone who glances at her. Oh, she was a beauty alright.

Cardy had splendid taste.

"I'm Basia." She sat appropriately, with her hands in her lap and her back arched. She turned just a little to her side, so she can make eye contact with me. Her legs crossed and I wondered how this sweet little girl, with such etiquette, could have sex with Cardy Deburke.

I glanced at Jasmine, who took off as soon as she saw the slide. Jasmine had soft blondish brown curls. Her skin was olive, darker than white, lighter than tan. "How old is she?"

"She's fifteen months old." Basia didn't give any more detail to anything not asked. Maybe she was shy.

Jasmine was hoisted up onto the slide and shrieked as she slid down. Then, she darted towards her mother. Her curls bounced and her arms flared outward.

The sun was shining brightly this November day. Odd, as it should be a cold day. But, it was fate, letting me meet this little girl in the sunshine. When Jasmine came running, her eyes gave off that cool gleam…that blue hue that has been very popular in my office, lately.

Cardy's eyes, this little girl had Cardy's eyes, his smile…

"She's beautiful. How is Cardy around her? Does she just melt his heart?" I tried to imagine him holding her, playing with her. With his attitude, I couldn't grasp the vision.

"He's only seen her once." Basia's face frowned as she stared at her feet. Oh.

"I never told him I was pregnant."

First, we talked about Cardy finding out, how he kicked Basia and stole Jasmine, how he came back with Boo and how Boo went to jail because he tried to threaten her. Then, we backtracked and she explained how she found out she was pregnant, about running away and hiding from Cardy because Cardy wasn't being himself.

An hour went by and she talked as if I was her doctor. I think she needed me. I wanted to take her in and give her therapy for free. I didn't care about the money. This poor girl needed me, she needed somebody.

"This is my card. Call me whenever you feel like talking. I'll listen, free of charge." I handed her my card and said my goodbyes to Darron and Jasmine.

I had learned a lot. She was definitely a good source of information. I had behavior characteristics from since he was in kindergarten. I had a serious three year relationship to add to his chart. I had betrayal, mistrust, shock, and guilt. I had rape accusations and kidnapping. If he was any older, he could be charged with a lot of this stuff. This stuff wasn't taken lightly if you were an adult.

I didn't need to ask Cardy these questions. I was getting inside of his mind by talking to his friends and family. The more I knew, the better I could approach him.

Fresca Taylor. Where was she at?

No, let's make a house call. We'll get the scoop from Fresca, later.

I heard a baby screaming before the door opened. When it opened, a tired rough looking man stood before me.

"Mr. Sox." I smiled. I was well amused that he had a fit throwing toddler in his arms. The boy was one of those two little ones that I saw with Bin, but I didn't know which one it was.

He returned the smile and extended his arms. He forced the baby into my chest and backed away for my entrance. Balancing my brief case and purse, I didn't know what to do with this baby. He was arching his back, wailing his arms, and trying to head butt me.

"What's going on?" I demanded. The house was a mess. Toys were tossed every which way. New diapers were thrown about on the staircase. The television was hollering out baby tunes and the radio was shouting classical music.

"I'm up to here with this crap! All he does is sleep, mope around, snap at me! I don't know what to do with him! I wanna beat his ass, that's what I'm about to do!" At first, I thought B.J was talking about this child.

But no, he was talking about his son, Binderman. Binderman was here, was he?

"First of all, too much stimulus can cause an outburst, Mr. Sox. Turn things off, dim the lights!!!" Anyone who took a few college courses in psychology should know this. Even child care courses had over-stimulated precautions.

"I don't see how that's going to get his ass up and going back to school!!" He was still set on fixing Binderman, the bigger problem, before conquering the smaller, easier ones.

I shut the radio and television off. I hit the light switch to the hallway. I dimmed the lights in the living room. I did this all while holding onto my purse, my briefcase, and this blonde baby throwing an unnecessary tantrum. I, myself, didn't know how to handle an infant.

"Binderman!!!" B.J screamed up the staircase. In response, this little fella in my arms screeched louder.

I cradled his head against my chest. I covered his ears and walked away from B.J Sox. I rocked him into the kitchen. Maybe he needed security, some grounding to his body. I shushed him, humming a tune that I had forgotten about…Rock-a-bye Baby.

He relaxed enough to hear me. Still uneasy though, he jerked at every move

I made. He had spasms, I think. His nerves were jumpy. He seemed rather paranoid, searching around me, looking for B.J or looking for something.

"Who is this?" I managed to whisper into the other room. I didn't want B.J to near him, as he was certainly frightened of that man. "Stay in there." I warned.

"That's Brandon, my grandson. He has no parents and the son of the bitch who has custody of him is depressed over petty shit. I don't know what the fuck I'm going to do with him. I don't know this shit. My housekeeper is on vacation, go figure." He didn't try to keep his voice down.

You are Cardy's little boy, then, aren't you? "Did his mother do drugs while she was pregnant with him?"

"You got to be kidding me, doctor. Do you think I would know something like that? I've been in Pierre for six months. I don't know shit!!" He met eyes with me in the kitchen and headed for the freezer. "I need a drink." He brought out the vodka and took a nice big gulp.

"If you don't mind, I'd like to pay a visit to Binderman. I'll take your issue with me, if I must." I carried Brandon onto the bigger problem.

Hmmm, I met Jasmine and Brandon on the same day. Were they aware of the other?

I pushed open the door to his bedroom. "Bin?"
No sound.
Instead, he was sleeping half naked in boxers. He gripped a pillow against his chest, head facing opposite of my view.

His room wasn't clean. Similar to downstairs, everything was tossed to the side, piled together, or thrown on top of other things. He wasn't feeling good at all. Bin may have fixed his obsession compulsive need to clean and keep things in orderly fashion, but...

Maybe his head was too cluttered to keep things on his outside world straight. Maybe it was overflowing with unwanted debris, unwanted thoughts...He couldn't slam the closet door on the junk, any longer. It was showing in his lack of motivation.

That sounded about right.

"Leave me alone, shrink." He whined into the pillow.

"I want to talk to you about Cardy, about this baby."

He turned only enough to see Brandon resting his head against my shoulder. After I calmed his environment, his nerves idled low, too.

"Come here," He ordered. He rose up on his elbows, still on his stomach, and ushered me to his bed.

I couldn't help but turn a little red in the face. I never imagined Bin, of all people, calling me to his bed, whether to talk or to…dirty little mind, I swear. He's a little boy, barely a man. Why on Earth would I be thinking of him…but he does have a nice frame to him. Long and athletic…sexy and…

"What do you want to know?" he better keep it covered.

"Everything."

"Like what?" He grabbed Brandon from me, laid him down between us, and eased up on his knees. I turned, just in case something wanted to make an appearance. No need to flatter my curiosity. It would never be of use.

"Just start talking. I want to know about Fresca Taylor, too."

He stood, wiped his face, and sighed. "He was talking about her?" His voice was full of fear.

"Not exactly."

He didn't do me a favor and put on his clothes, no, not at all. Why would he want to lessen the intimidation? He loved to challenge the obvious and make me, the doctor, feel uncomfortable.

"Then what then, Cindy? What the fuck did he have to say about my fucking girlfriend?!" The jealousy went beyond normal limits.

He knew. I knew he knew. Did he want to admit it? That's why they were apart, weren't they?

Maybe I was going beyond my level of work ethic. Maybe I wasn't supposed to make house calls and involve myself fully with this family and their soap operations. Maybe this family took up all my time and I was mistreating the rest of my patients.

Maybe and yes, maybe I was crazy and obsessed, just as well. I really didn't care at the moment. I got to see reactions such as this, something I wouldn't get to see on a normal scheduled appointment.

I needed some spice in this line of work, more than the suicidal tendencies and cheating of dead beat husbands. This family fulfilled my need of a life. I felt a part of them, already.

Chapter Sixty-Four
Binderman

That punk motherfucker, he was talking about my girlfriend. I knew that bastard had something for her, I just knew it. He probably talked her into breaking up with me. He was setting up something, I bet. He just happened to wreck before he got to make a move. He was going to steal that bitch from me.

I swear to God, I would have killed him. Brother or not, he was going to die if he fucked her again. I knew I made mistakes. I knew I deserved to be cheated on, but come the fuck on. You don't fuck with motherfucker's girlfriends…especially…he didn't know. Would it have mattered to Cardy?

I doubt it. Cardy was ignorant like that. He gave no fuck about anything.

Cindy just made me think harder about shit. I didn't want to think about that bitch, Fresca. I needed to call Angie. I needed to talk to that bitch. Fresca…I was done with. Cardy could have her.

If Fresca felt something for that motherfucker, then fine. Fuck it. She ain't worth my time. What if I was right? What if she liked Cardy better than me? What if her stupid ass mind got twisted and she actually thought she loved Cardy? Then what?

What if she's waiting for him to get out?

Motherfucker, I didn't want to think about this shit. Fuck that. Fuck this stupid ass shit. Who needed that bitch? I was fine for seven fucking months without her. I could go on for eternity without that bitch. Fuck it, fuck it, fuck it!

That's what I thought, anyways. I think that talking about the bitch made her think of me. Why she was thinking of me…who fucking knows. Not too long after my talk with Cindy, Fresca showed up at my house.

I was still broken up with Angie. I hadn't talked to Angie since I was arrested. I saw Devon three times since then, too. Amanda was the one who brought him to me. I was on a slope...a dangerous slope to my death. I was too depressed to celebrate Brandon's 1st birthday, which came and went.

It was the day after Thanksgiving, the big ass shopping day. It was the day Fresca had to get up bright and early to compete for things on sale. She was never much of a bargainer, but...shopping was shopping. If people woke up at dawn to fight over things, then she was going to go so she had something to talk about, later.

Thanksgiving was stupid. My dad invited our family out to Grams, which I didn't go to because I didn't feel like admitting that I had lost Angie, too. My dad took Brandon, as they were getting accustomed to each other, by now.

It was too early to be awake. I was asleep in my room, my dirty filthy ass room. Next thing I knew, Fresca was sitting next to me, like a fucking dream.

She was drunk, that much I smelt. I still didn't believe she was there.

"I talked to your doctor." She whispered, touching my hair as if she had the right.

I tensed up. What the fuck was she doing here? I tried to talk to her ass and now, 3:30 in the fucking morning, she wanted to talk to me? Bullshit.

"Don't touch me." I warned, closing my eyes. I'd rather her disappear. I called that bitch too many times to appreciate her presence. Maybe she wanted to admit that she loved Cardy.

She giggled. That fucking bitch was drunk off her ass. "Don't be mad at me, you need to be mad at yourself. I just wanted to tell you that your shrink visited me and we had a long talk."

I sat up. If by cue, she clung to me, wrapping me in her skanky stench...Jagermeister, I suppose. "So?"

If our meeting had been on my terms, when I felt like seeing her, then I would have wanted to react in another way. I would have been pleased to see her. But, she did this shit when I wasn't ready. I wasn't prepared, so it pissed me off.

"So, it made me think of you."

Fucking bitch, she smiled the whole time she kissed my neck. Something was fucked up about this shit, I swear.

"Get off of me. I want to talk to you." I pushed her to the side and stood up. "How did you get in?"

"I climbed through the window." She giggled more, pointing to the open window. Bitch. I know she was lying. She couldn't climb through that window if her life depended on it.

"Doesn't matter, I'm here." She shrugged her shoulders and smiled that awful grin of hers. I didn't want to love her. She was fucking with my head.

The only reason this bitch was over here was to fuck with me, I know. She had to get drunk just to talk to me, just to see me. Fucking Christ, I didn't need this drama.

I thought of Angie. If I wanted to get back with Angie, then I don't need to be fucking around with Fresca. Even though I wanted to talk to Fresca and fix shit with her, tonight wasn't the damn night to do so.

I walked out of the bedroom and into Cardy's room. I found that stupid ass fold out chair and brought it near my bed. I wanted distance. I wanted to stare at her. I wanted to make sure she didn't touch me.

"Come on, Boo, you know you want me. You've been calling me for seven months, now." She was trying her best to strike a pose, to get me to fuck her or something.

"Six months. I hadn't called your ass this whole month. Why are you here? What the fuck are you doing?" I lit a cigarette and wondered if I needed to throw some pants on. Boxers were dangerous around this broad.

"I'm doing nothing. I want to be your friend." Her face was fatter and her hair wasn't fixed. It was flat and down, windblown and without products. The bitch spent hours on her hair. It wasn't like her to look this way.

"I can't be your friend, Fresca. You know that. I want to talk to you about things." I reinforced the subject at hand. I didn't want to be her god damn friend. Fuck that.

"And I said that there's nothing to talk about. Now, you can be my friend, or I can leave."

"Leave." I frowned. My nerves were killing me. There was this wall, this brick fucking wall holding me back from begging her for forgiveness. I was mad at her, mostly.

"Think about it, Boo. I can be your side-bitch. They seem to get more attention, anyways." She was being cynical. I didn't like it.

"What the fuck are you talking about?!" I sneered, standing.

She smiled at my boxers. "Side bitches get everything with no strings attached. I want to be your side bitch, fill Teesa's spot. I heard she was pregnant and marrying Roger, anyways. That leaves a spot open." She was full of shit, I swear.

I didn't like this side of her. I hated her. "Teesa wasn't my side bitch, Fresca. Everything was fucked up. That's what I want to talk to…"

"I don't want to talk about it, Boo. It's over. We're over. Now, all you have left is a side job, so if you want it…"

"I don't want it, motherfucker. I want you. I'm not the same, Fresca." I almost called her Angie. Damn.

"That's good for Angie…Although, I heard you did her wrong, too. You might as well face it, Boo. You can't change. You suck at relationships."

"What the fuck are you doing here, Fresca? You came all the way over here, drunk off your ass, just to accuse me of shit?"

"No, I came all way over here to fuck you, Boo, now do you want to fuck me or not?!" Her mouth was beyond surprises. When she got pissed, she got pissed. Right down to the fucking point.

"I don't want to fuck you, bitch! You're a fucking slut, just like the rest of them!" I was screaming this shit, but my voice was cracking.

"Lay with me and I'll talk to you. I'll talk about whatever the fuck you want to talk about." She snapped, sprawling her body over my mattress.

"I'm not fucking you." I reassured myself.

Jagermeister, why the fuck was she drinking Jagermeister? She reeked of it.

As soon as I climbed into bed, she attacked me. The bitch took my balance and made me fall down against my pillow. Her lips met mine and her hands grabbed my wrists, as if she could hold me down.

Of course I kissed back. All I wanted to do was fuck her. I just didn't want to follow through with that thought.

"Fine bitch, you wanna fuck me? Fine." I hated this bitch. If that's what she came for, then fuck it. After tonight, it was definitely over.

Why now? Why the fuck did she wait until now?…I ripped off her pants. I wanted to talk to her…I threw her on her stomach.

But she had to be drunk, the fucking bitch…I grabbed her wrists and forced them above her head.

Fine, I'll teach her to wake my ass up…she giggled, as she knew this was what I was going to do to her when I was pissed off.

The fucking bitch…she knew what she was doing and I didn't like it.

But I loved her…and I took whatever she was going to give me. Details…you need details? Ah fuck you.

Go somewhere. Get your own details. Next chapter…Chapter sixty two: Nah, just kidding, I'm fucking with you, damn.

Fresca Taylor was everything that I missed. I knew what to do with her, what to expect. I could time that shit out with her because I knew her reaction. Every time she got close, I wasn't going to end it.

If she was going to fuck with my head, then I was going to fuck with hers. I was pissing her off, too. It was great.

"Stop fucking around, Boo!" I heard her say. It didn't matter. She shouldn't fuck with me, I swear on my mother's grave.

I knew nothing was going to come of this. She'd fuck me and it'd be the end of it, the end of us. So I took it slow…medium slow…then slow. I enjoyed every second with her just because I could. She was too drunk to leave.

"Hey," I stopped in mid action. I knew it'd piss her off more. "What the fuck happened to us?"

"Don't you start, Boo." She gritted.

Ha, she thought she had control over this situation. I never lose control over *this* shit. This shit I was good at.

"I wanna know or I quit." She hated when I talked.

"You happened, Boo. You did this to us. Now come on," She slapped my back and I laughed.

"Look at you, you're fucking wasted…why are you drunk?" I kissed her neck, absorbing her smell…never going to smell her again.

"I'm gonna hurt your ass, I swear…"

"Swear on your mother…"

"I don't have to." She balled her fists up at my chest to shove me off, but I wasn't moving. I had her where I wanted her. She couldn't move with me on her.

"Why not?" I continued to ease into her, then out again. Her eyes were beautiful, beautiful and evil at the same time.

"Because I already hurt you." Her concentration broke from me and those blue eyes closed tightly.

"Ah, fuck you, girl. I ain't drunk to hear that shit. You did hurt me…but fuck it. You know what?" And if I said it, she'd try hard as hell to get me away from her…so I tried not to say it.

I wanted to. I needed to.

"Just get on with this, Boo." She whined. She knew what I was going to say.

I didn't say it, not yet, anyways. I wanted this to last forever…and ever and ever. When I woke up tomorrow, I'd be in the same old shit as always…depressed and alone. It sucked.

So I got on with it. No more words. No more thoughts.

When it was over, I buried my head into her chest, knowing she was going to send me far away from her. I didn't want it to be over. She came for this, and this was over. What the fuck, now?

She remained quiet for some time. It was enough to get lost from reality. Her fingers circled the back of my head as she held me against her. My breath was heavy against her skin. I was waiting for that fatal word…that morbid phrase of "get off, I'm leaving."

Why the fuck did I mess this up? It was the best thing in my life…she was the best thing in my life…and I fucked it up.

I held up my head and stared at her. "Don't leave, Fresca…please? Just stay the night. We don't have to talk…whatever you want. Don't go." My whole body was cold…it was tingling on the side of numb. I wouldn't be able to handle her departure…not so soon, anyways.

She didn't respond cause she was thinking. She was considering…God, I've waited so fucking long to know what the fuck was up with her…she was being stubborn. She loved me…or she wouldn't be here.

So, I did what I used to do with her. Call it what you will…but Fresca and I…we said everything with songs…we connected that way…ever since I was twelve.

"Let me take you to a place nice and quiet…" I started with a smile. It was Usher's hit: Nice and Slow. It was the first song that popped into my head. "There ain't no one there to interrupt…"

She laughed lightly, and squeezed my cheeks together. "Stop it, it's not like that, anymore."

"You're going to have to sing that shit, baby, I don't understand you." I really didn't give a fuck what it sounded like, call it stupid, call it whatever. I loved this girl and I really needed to feel some familiar ground with her.

Without her, I was lost.

"Now maybe, I didn't mean to treat you oh so bad…"

I covered her mouth. "Don't sing that song." It was one of her favorite songs when we used to go skating…back in what, 1994? I was sixteen and she dedicated that fucking song to me because it was the first time she caught me cheating. The lyrics meant more to her than it ever meant to me. In fact, I didn't even understand the song. I didn't like rock music.

"You left me far behind." She added.

Fuck.

"I'm sorry, I swear on my mother's grave, baby…I'm so fucking sorry. I don't…I don't want us to be apart…"

"You know, I'm fucking drunk and you know how I cry when I get wasted…but, I really don't give a fuck, right now. You don't do anything for me, Boo. My feelings died for you a long time, ago."

This night just pissed me off and swallowed me whole. I couldn't even remember to breath. I dropped my head once more and held onto her for dear life. "Don't you fucking say that shit. I love you and you love me, don't you fucking say different."

"Shut up and go to sleep, Boo." It took her a long time to get me off of her, but she turned over and decided to stay.

Okay…now what? What the fuck is going on with her ass?! God damn. You don't tell someone you don't have feelings for them and then turn over to sleep. Bullshit. I didn't believe her.

Instead of pressing the issue…I cradled her body and never went to sleep. I couldn't sleep. My mind was fast at work, trying to figure this shit out.

Chapter Sixty-Five
Cardy

It's a ridiculous day. I wake up to the same old shit, in the same damn room, wearing the same old clothes, with nothing to look forward to but the same old shit. I can't even smoke. It's the weekend. I have no squares and no chance at getting them. So, I sit here craving a release.

That's not good. If I want a fucking release and a cigarette had the power to do such a release and I couldn't have one, then what the fuck can I do to get such a fucking release? I couldn't play basketball. It was raining. The staff won't supply basketballs to people when it was raining. It was some stupid insurance policy bullshit.

It was insane. I couldn't focus, couldn't think. I didn't even want to get out of bed all because of a fucking cigarette. You would think that I would be used to not smoking on the weekends. But I wasn't. It was pissing me off.

I thought about searching the grounds for a wet cigarette butt, that's how desperate I was. I wanted to sneak into the teacher lounge and steal a purse in hopes that I stole a smoker's purse. I wanted to do something, anything.

It didn't help that I had obsessive thoughts and now they swam in a field of smoke. I felt the steam rise above my skin to an endless supply of bitter sweet Newport's. Nothing was better or stronger than Newport's. I hadn't had a Newport in months.

It was December. It was a cold, rainy December and we should expect snow by Sunday. I knew this because all I had to fucking do was watch the community television console that sat on the floor in the rec. room. It came from the 1950's, I bet. With all the fucking money this place made, they should afford TV's in every dorm room.

The rec. room was stupid. It had a ping pong table. It had a pool table. It had a dart board with missing darts. It had a punching bag in the corner. A couch sat in front of the TV set and a coffee table had outdated magazines on it. A card table had board games. Another table had checkers, and another had chess. This white ass room reminded me of a mental ward, where crazy ass people joined at the hip to mingle.

Bullshit, bullshit, bullshit. I wasn't playing shit.

I was interrupted by a knock on the door. Stan.

"Cardy, you have dish duty." He swung around my doorway as if it was something worth swinging around to say. He didn't stay to hear my comment. He continued down the hall to call out duties for the week.

Again, I didn't have to do shit. I didn't do chores. Everybody knew that I didn't do my duties. Someone was forced to do them for me. That's just the way it goes.

Bored out of my fucking mind, I followed him down the hall. I let my hand trail the wall behind me, dragging posters and dropping taped documents onto the floor. I wanted to taunt Stan for the hell of it.

"I ain't doing it."

Stan stopped at Charles the Fifth's door. He turned with a quick heel. "Excuse me?" He edged up to my face. "Cardy, we've been doing this crap for you since you came to Safe Haven. It's about time you picked up the slack. If you don't do it, then Charles is going to have to do it. Do you want him to do it?"

Charles peered up from his music magazine. It was a metal magazine, probably years old. He waited for my remark. His bullet head shined in the light. I thought about being a smart ass, but I'd rather not.

"I don't give a fuck who does it." I sneered. I watched Charles drop his shoulders in despair. He rolled his eyes, but didn't say anything.

"You like doing dishes, Nazi?" I smiled at him.

Stan put his hands on my chest and backed me up. Luckily, I was in a better mood. I was bored, but not bored enough to start a fight.

Charles jumped to the occasion. "I'm not a fucking Nazi, motherfucker! Say that shit again!" He was still short.

Still a Nazi.

"Cardy, cool it. Do you know how awful that word is?" Stan wouldn't remove his hands, testing my patience.

Two choices, I had two choices. Which one did I feel like taking today? I *was* a little bored.

"Nazi, Nazi, Nazi, motherfucker." And I ended it, my way. I turned away and headed back to my room.

I heard Stan arguing with the Nazi soldier and I was satisfied. I had started some type of entertainment, today.

Later, I was approached by Stan and Nate, a staff member from second floor. I guess they were boys or some shit. I didn't know, didn't care.

"Hey, Cardy, I have the perfect solution. You have dish duty with Charles, or you can spend a lifetime in lock down." Nate had no hesitation getting in my business. Nate, honestly, looked like a personal trainer, small hipped, broad shoulders, tight little Polo shirt. His crew cut came out of a military magazine, probably the one downstairs in the rec. room.

"I have what? Who says?" I sat up from my lazy day dreaming. "That's bullshit." and decided to approach Nate, size him up…just a little.

Nate had a bullhorn voice, deep and intrusive, whether you wanted to hear it or not. "I say, Deburke. If you don't obey the rules, then we'll take it to Dean and tell him how much of a slacker you really are. You know what he'll do to you. I'm sure eighteen months beats two years in this shit hole, don't you think?"

I thought about it. Yeah, eighteen months were better than two years. Of course I knew that. Did I feel like caring? That was the fucking question, now wasn't it?

"Fine, motherfucker, but don't get in my fucking face, I don't give a fuck who you are." He was as tall as I was which was rare. There were a few kids here at 6'2, maybe a teacher or two, but…not many. The difference between Nate and me…well, he was older…wider…stronger. He was everything that could break me in two if he wanted to.

I still wasn't backing down.

"Good, go to work smart ass!" And he shoved an apron into my chest.

I slammed the door and eyed Brett, who was reading his notebook. "I ain't wearing this shit!" I threw it down and wrung my hands for a square. I paced back and forth, wishing there was something I could do to get rid of this feeling.

"Everybody down there wears one." Brett didn't look up from his book. His hair hung in his face as he read.

Let's get one thing straight. Brett was alright. He was like this little kid who didn't do shit to me. He didn't want to be my friend, didn't even try. He said what he had to so he could live with me, but other than that, he didn't bother me. He kept his head in that notebook, taking him to faraway places, I guess.

Each day, I watched him sit alone at our table. He ate the same thing almost every day, barely anything. We shared some of my classes and he didn't participate in class. I didn't see him interact outside. He didn't show any type of emotion and was just there.

How could I pick on this motherfucker?

"Brett, did you smoke before you came here?" This time, I stood in the middle of the room waiting to hear him out. Usually, I let his words fly over my head.

"Yeah, why?"

"Do you smoke now?"

He thought that was funny. "No, I can't smoke, now." He sat his notebook to the left of him and scratched his arms. Did the cravings ever go away?

"Do you think the Nazi smokes?" I had to go to the cafeteria with that fat ass as soon as possible, anyways.

"Why? We can't smoke and you know it. Even if Charles did smoke, I doubt he'd want to share with you." He leaned to his right and turned on his radio. Ah, sweet music.

I closed my eyes and envisioned a guitar strumming my veins with each prick, with each chord let loose into the air. It was the guitar solos that made me feel like that. It danced inside of me…

No, it was nothing like heroin. But it ran through my body like a heat wave, cooling as it drifted through my ears. I felt each vibration as clearly as the guitarist…someday…I was going to learn how to play.

That was a dream of mine back when Darron and I were going to start a band. I was going to play guitar, Kayo on bass, Darron on drums. Basia, of course, with her choir voice, was going to sing.

That was all bullshit, now.

"If the Nazi smokes, then he just made a best friend." And I headed to enlist in the Nazi army. Okay, that was a little strong worded, but hey…if Charles came with a benefit of befriending…then, I'll squash my attitude with him. I was that desperate.

As I veered towards the steps with Stan and Nate on full alert, word got around that I was going to wash the dishes. I didn't know how the shit spread, but it did. Nobody thought I had it in me to work aside Charles the Fifth of his generation. Nobody thought that I would commit myself to a chore.

I guess I had started a reputation here at Safe haven. Already, people thought I was something that I wasn't. They thought I didn't give a fuck about shit. They thought I expected the world to fall at my feet and do as I say. They expected me to disobey. They expected me to visit the padded walls each week.

It was amazing how people thought. I didn't think I was being that type of person. At least, not until the motherfuckers were crowded at their doorways, watching me head to my duty.

Fuck "them."

Chapter Sixty-Six
Angie

It was like that? A few months with Boo Sox and now I'm just a part of his history? I thought that if I stayed the distance, then he'd come begging me back. I thought that if I gave him the space he needed to figure things out, then maybe he'd call me.

What was happening? He didn't call. He didn't come pounding on my door. Was he mad at me for what my mom did to him? Did he finally realize that we weren't meant to be?

I mean, I knew we weren't meant to be. He belonged to Fresca Taylor. But, was my glory over? Didn't I deserve a little more time in the spotlight with him? If he had any feelings for me at all, then he would call me, right?

What was his deal?

I wasn't about to call him. No, that would be swallowing my pride and doing something stupid. I wanted to call him. I wanted to call him so much. I wanted to head over to his house and have a long talk with him.

I wanted him to be honest. I wanted him to admit that he didn't want me. I wanted to admit that I didn't love him. But something else was there, wasn't it? I wanted to be with him. I wanted him to want to be with me, for the time being. We didn't have to last forever. Nothing lasts forever, right?

As for everything else, it had gone back to the same old thing, like nothing happened. My mom went on working nights. Devon was still bouncing around and getting into things. Amanda drove Devon back and forth to Boo's and never once mentioned that Boo asked about me.

Delilah didn't pry. In fact, Delilah was working on her campaign against oil. She was writing a letter to the president about ocean contaminants. She was busy being herself. She was also waiting to join the Peace Corps. Lucky her.

I was busy doing nothing. I mean, I was going to school. I had to drive myself. I never ran into Boo. I think he avoided me, unless he quit. School was school. The fact was…

I didn't have a life.

After being with Boo, I realized just how happy I was being with him. I liked how he treated me when he was with me. I liked the confidence boost he gave me. I liked the clothes I wore. And, yeah…I secretly liked my hair. I liked being who I was being.

That party night had faded. It shouldn't have, but it did.

Now, each waking day, I see Devon and think of Boo. I didn't use to. But, now…he's all I see.

Devon was big for his age. The doctor said so. Devon was stocky…hefty, no doubt. I had to carry that kid everywhere we went. He didn't like to walk. He didn't like strollers unless Boo made him sit in one. With me, Devon got his way. With Boo, even at a year and a half, Devon knew who to listen to.

Not that Boo disciplined him. He didn't. He didn't know what to do with Devon. Devon liked to bite and pinch and kick shins. He thought it was funny to watch our reactions. Sure, people thought I was a fantastic mom…but, I didn't know how to handle Devon, either. I just read all the baby books.

Oh, I didn't know. I was stalling on what I really wanted to do. I wanted to call Boo. But, what if he didn't answer? I was scared of rejection, too.

See, that's why I didn't bother with boyfriends. They were too hard to deal with. Amanda knew better. We always had talks about stupid boys and how hard it was to deal with their problems…such as cheating.

What was I going to do?

Chapter Sixty-Seven
Basia

It was midnight and I was hungry.

I knew there was nothing in Darron's kitchen to eat. In my head, I went from cabinet to cabinet, searching my memory for that one cracker in its package, an old box of cereal, or maybe a just a jar of peanut butter.

Oh, it was no use in saving me from the disappointment of searching. Even though I knew there was nothing to eat, I got up anyways. I hoped that God had filled the refrigerator with food.

Being midnight, I didn't bother to throw on my pants. It was a two minute ordeal. I'd open the cabinets, understand that miracles didn't happen, and go back to bed. It was that simple.

I crept downstairs, careful to avoid the fifth step to the right and the third step from the bottom. Those two creaked. Darron's mother, God help her, may awake and scream for Darron to help her to her bed.

I didn't turn on the light. I tiptoed to the cereal cabinet and stared at it. Did I really want to skim it for weevils? Oh, what the heck, I'll look.

I reached up and realized that the box was flush with the wall. I rose up on my toes and stretched my arm. I wiggled my fingers as I grunted with determination. I arched and stretched. My leg rose to make me longer.

Within a millisecond, a hand cupped my hip. A body pressed firmly into me. His other hand grabbed the box of cereal. His breath lowered against my neck…spearmint. "I got it." The knobs on his head made me freeze.

It was Kyle. Lately, it was always Kyle…oh God, it was Kyle.

He placed it in front of me and didn't move away. He froze, too. His hand was still touching me. His breath was getting heavier.

"Thanks." I watched my fingers wrap around the box. My eyes wouldn't leave the black letters, bold and straight. I avoided his expression, his mere existence, now against me.

"You're welcome."
This had to stop. What was he thinking?
What was I thinking?!
"Basia?"
"Yes?"
"I'm sorry." And he let go.
I turned. I was met by his eyes, Darron's beady eyes.
I went cold...too cold. Without reason or thought, I barreled into his chest. I pulled his shirt over my wrists for warmth. I closed my eyes as I didn't want to believe that I may be considering Kyle Sorum.

His chin lowered and dropped from my behavior. There was no excuse for my behavior, none at all. His lips parted in slow motion. He was about to speak but then he stopped.

He kissed me.

I was kissing Kyle Sorum.

He sighed and let his body relax against mine. His hand cradled my head and into my hair. The other hand gripped up my butt. Underwear...oh no. I was in my underwear...

"This is wrong, Basia." He read my mind and said it for me.

"I know." I pulled away and glared at the dark floor. All I saw were his sneakers...white ones, too new for Kyle to own.

Good kisser, good kisser...good...Kyle knew how to kiss. Holy crap, Kyle knew how to hold me, to rub me, to touch me...

"I don't want you to..." Kyle mumbled with one last kiss, cutting off the last of his words.

If he wouldn't have stopped, I don't think I had it in me to do so. He pulled away and stumbled back into the darkness. I was left to wonder about him...about this night. I heard him dash up the stairs and then back down. Soon after, the front door slammed shut.

Kyle Sorum had left the premises.

Kyle Sorum didn't know what the hell I was doing to him. Frankly, I didn't know what I was doing to myself, either.

Chapter Sixty-Eight
Binderman

I felt her fingers before I even woke up. They ran through my hair, over and over, again…until she wrapped them around and jerked me awake. Fucking bitch was getting on my nerves.

"What the fuck!"

"Wake up, Goldie locks!" Her voice was still full of liquor. She was still full of fun and games. It pissed me off.

Before I could say anything else, she straddled me. My mouth was covered by her lips. It was a weird ass awakening.

Of course by reaction, there wasn't a way in hell to keep me from being aroused. I wish I wasn't. I didn't want to play her fucking games. She was still angry at me, that much I knew. She didn't want to go out with me. She just wanted to fuck with me…or fuck me, rather.

I felt my hands tighten around her ass, holding her against me as hard as I could. As much as I wanted her to stop so I could be serious with her for a moment, I couldn't. My body was reacting faster than I could think shit through.

I could barely breathe, let alone think. My breath was pounding out of my chest quicker than inhaling it. I couldn't catch it no matter how hard I tried to gasp for air.

This was kind of fun, but still…

She didn't speak, didn't ask permission to use me. She just went on her merry ass way in abusing her privileges. Maybe she was getting me back for last night…as she'd start, stop, and start again. I was about to die from an asthma attack…or worse…a fucking hard on.

It started off quick and was about to end quickly if she'd just get on with it. But, no…the bitch was playing and giggling…drunker than she was last night.

And then, when my mind landed on a certain thought...I knew what she was up to. She had tried to do this shit before. She knew I was too close...too into it...almost to the point of not giving a fuck just to get the feeling...the release of that fucking pressure she was building up.

"Quit it, Fresca, get off of me!" I managed to breathe it out as I exhaled. My eyes were white, not even looking at her. I bit her lip to get her attention. I heard her say "ouch" and laugh.

Fuck! I hated when she did this shit. I had to do what I had to fucking do to prevent what she wanted out of me.

I lifted her off of me and threw her under my body. I couldn't even shove it back in her...it was too late. I was left throbbing into the sheet...relieved that I pulled out as soon as I did.

The bitch laughed and covered her eyes from her crude behavior.

"What the fuck were you doing?!" I squeezed her wrists to the side of her head, ready to kill her for that shit.

She laughed, playfully. "What was I doing?"

"You know what you were doing, motherfucker!"

She came over here to fuck me, alright. She was trying to get pregnant, that's what she was doing. It was just like her...so fucking jealous of Angie.

She thought she wanted a damn baby. Ever since she knew that Angie had Devon, she had pretended to play around to get me to get her pregnant. Fucking crazy bitch, she had no idea what having a baby meant.

She rolled onto her side and covered her face with her arms. "Get off of me, I hate you!" By her tone, I knew she was about to cry...or scream at me.

"Yeah Fresca, you sure hate me. You hate me enough to get pregnant by me? What the fuck is wrong with you?! You don't even know why you want a fucking baby. You just want what someone else has!" I climbed off of her and stood at the foot of the bed.

She was so fucking weak and crazy. I don't know why I put up with this bitch for so long. I couldn't stop there.

"You haven't been with me for seven fucking months and now you come over here in hopes that you can get a baby out of all this?" I lit a cigarette and blew the smoke out harshly.

I began to pace. "Fuck you, bitch. I can't believe you're thinking like you are! You don't want a fucking kid, trust me!!"

Oh my fucking God, I can't believe she just did that shit to me!!

"How could you be so selfish? You think you're sane enough to raise a baby, Fresca?! You think you'd be a good enough mother? You work at a gas station!" All I really wanted to do was knock some sense into her, like physically.

She sat up in defense mode. "Oh, like you're a good father? You just cheated on Angie, Boo. How good of a father is that? I'd be a damn fine mother, if you ask me!"

I held my face until I felt like I turned blue from lack of oxygen…or red from the anger that I wanted to murder her with. "Bullshit! That's fucking bullshit and you know it! You don't know how to be a mother. You don't have a mother, motherfucker!!!"

I knew it was cold. It was so wrong of me to throw it up it her face like that…but fuck! She just tried to rape my ass for a fucking kid!!

Of course her face crumbled. Her lip quivered and she was no longer drunk and happy. She was depressed. "I can't believe…"

"I'm sorry…" I started to say.

"Don't touch me. Don't you ever fucking touch me again!!!"

God dammit, motherfucker!!!

"I won't!" I snapped, grabbing the first t-shirt that I saw. I didn't give a fuck. I was so mad that I was leaving my damn house before she did. If I stayed…I'd kill her. I know I would.

First, she fucks my brother…breaks up with me…doesn't answer my calls…tells me she doesn't love me…then…now…tries to con me into having a baby with her ass?

How fucked up can she get?

I can't respect bitches like that.

She had to have some low ass self esteem to want a baby that bad.

She balled her fists up and dropped them to her sides. "Where are you going?!"

"I'm getting away from you."

"Where are you going?"

"You better be out of my house before I get back, I swear on my mother's grave, Fresca. I can't stand your ass right now."

Holy fuck, I can't believe how mad I am at her!!! I didn't want to be mad at her ass…but God damn…I could kill a bitch!!!

Fresca and I…were over.

Done with…gone…forever…I'll make sure of it.

Chapter Sixty-Nine
Dr. Cynthia Roma

I now understand what is happening to Binderman Sox. Unable to control his brother and girlfriend has caused a failure in his whole approach to his FALSE self. His narcissistic behavior has been diminished and he is trying to balance out his *ideal* self.

He knows he has failed. It's corrupting every aspect of his life. His grandiose feelings of power and control are weakening. He is aware of this. He is in a state of panic, of a paranoid state of mind. He can't be the womanizer, the controller, the idol of everyone.

Not now. Not when his brother had knocked him off of his pedestal and made him realize that he was just as vulnerable as everyone else.

Bin was all about appearance. He never recognized his feelings, his emotions. He was seductive with grandiosity. He was impulsive, a huge gift giver. He has unusual eating habits…always complained and was never satisfied. He never had a good reason for what he did. These were all symptoms of narcissism.

He hated to live alone.

He was confused on love like most narcissistic personalities. But he had to control Fresca Taylor because *she* loved him.

Well Binderman, your grandiosity has been wounded.

Oh, I can go on about his mother. I can go on about Dena, too. These women who raised these boys have created little narcissistic men. They may not have realized it, but they formed their little boys into the exact thing that left them in the first place…their father.

Binderman's mother didn't know what she was doing, as she was young and naïve. But, she had dehumanized and instrumentalized little Binji. She made it apparent that he was the vessel of her discontinued life. He was taught to ignore reality and occupy her fantastic space. He was raised to feel aristocratic with a birth right to get everything he wanted.

And his father…Big B.J, He runs away from what he can't fix so he can still feel like something grand. He seduced Bin's fifteen year old mother for power…and now…as he never came home…she replaced him with Bin…similar to all his attributes.

Twisted, yet it fit. Fresca and Cardy tied into Bin's behavior, alright. I was glad that I knew all of this. If I had to deal with Bin, alone…I would never know what was truly going on with him.

Now, for Cardy…

Cardy prefers to fail as a result of not trying, rather than risk the disappointment of failure after the effort. And just to note…when a child reacts with anger or anxiety to a sincere compliment…there's a special need to fail.

Why did Cardy want to fail? What was he afraid of? What would his disappointment be?

Sometimes, there are defense mechanisms. One is counter phobic behavior. They are fascinated with the object of fear. What did Cardy fear? What was he fascinated with?

Another defense was identifying with the aggressor…he becomes what he fears. Who is Cardy Deburke imitating?

And pain…pain is experienced when there is no outlet for excitement…as in anxiety or rise in fear.

He's proceeded to a certain objective despite fear.

On an unconscious level…he has a means of expressing aggression towards his parents…or acting out a special unconscious fantasy obtaining punishment for sense of guilt.

What is Cardy guilty about?

I'm going to start with that damn game book.

He's obviously obsessed with virgins. What happened to conquer these little girls? Was he intimidated by those popular boys? Did he become his brother out of guilt?

His brother was not able to conquer virgins like Cardy, however. Was he competing with Bin? How can he act so cruelly?

Current behavior: Fighting, argumentative, contradictive.

This is a cover up, no doubt.

His potential: Sincere straight "A" student with a caring heart. (I know this.)

What people need to know about anxiety and fear is that what causes this is a learned behavior. Once the triggering thought is discovered, a new pair can be replaced...We can work on changing that trigger and making it less anxious and fearful. Cardy can learn a new pair by far.

Past Peers: Popular and not popular, two main groups.

Present Peers: Sees them as inferior

Family: No authority, broken home.

School: dropped out before...skipping now...doing the least he can do.

Feeding: engorgement

His mother's second interview was more important to me. Questions were answered.

Cardy was always a bigger child, top of the growth charts, fast in milestones. He was breast fed and weaned at a year's age. He threw fits when she weaned him. He was angered at the sudden change and wasn't adapting well. He used a pacifier until he was four. His toilet training was also a fuss, his mom said. He refused and was angered at the pressure by his mother.

His discipline from his mother was always passive and disregarded. She didn't have a discipline plan. His father on the other hand, was abusive. Cardy learned all his chores and duties as routine from a heavy hand.

It makes sense on why he declines his chores. For one, chores remind him of his father. He doesn't want to think about his father. For another, he's taking advantage of this opportunity of not getting hit for refusal. He was used to being physically forced to do something. And last, he is still rebelling against everything...unless there is a benefit in it for him...hence...bribing.

Cardy was always very verbal from his mother's point of view. He used to over talk. He never kept anything from her. He was honest and curious about everything. He was a Catholic, born and raised, even going to church every week. He did this until he was fifteen years old.

His mother was part of a prolife campaign ever since she refused an abortion. So, Cardy grew up well aware of this. He knew about babies and was good with them...she said.

She never talked to him about the birds and the bees. No one talked to him about sex. This means that he learned it by experience, or mostly from his peers. Now, his peers are the keepers of this game book.

What the hell did he learn?

Chapter Seventy
Cardy

Listen closely, and listen well. I am going to explain something that I should have explained a while back. I zone out when I do a chore. I seem to go into my head and think about shit that made sense to me and nobody else. I think about my life and my dad. I try to understand this stupid life of mine.

So listen closely and listen well. I'm not going to repeat myself.

If the impossible happens, **you learn not to trust the possible**. At a very young age, I learned that my father was less than a father. He was more of a child crying out to the world. This makes the impossible…possible. In turn, that makes possibility endless and shaky.

If something happens that shouldn't, or something that should happen and doesn't, **you learn instability**. Your mind conjures up the impossible at all times, preparing for the impossible…which is possible, now.

Imagine seeing your father trying to commit suicide. He wants to die. He wants to leave you and die. His life is so bad that death is promising. He hates his life. He calls your mother awful things.

He fights her.

He hurts her emotionally, mentally, and physically beats the shit out of her.

If he dies, how should I feel? Should I feel bad and sorry for him? Should I feel guilty because I know it was all because of me? Should I feel happy that this part of my life is over? Should I miss him?

It's all of the above, and the keyword is *should*. Should I?

If she can't protect you, how do you feel?

If this goes on and on for eternity…how the fuck should you feel?

It's worse than the normal emotions than a child usually faces. It's worse than sad, mad, and fearing days like this. **It's worse than fear.**

It's helpless, powerless. **I was unable to control the mood and the events of my life. I was unable to control the consumption of it.**

Helpless
&
Guilt.

It's an emotional pain of destruction. Can I pretend to play G.I Joes with a play date and sleep over at a friend's house? What would I miss? Even without control, I needed the knowledge of knowing what was going on.

I stopped caring about my life as soon as my mom stopped caring about hers. She turned towards alcohol around the time I was eleven. It was such a relief to walk away without a care. It was such a relief to spend the night at Darron's with Basia, without a care about what went on at my house.

I was lost even before my lips hit the bottle. I was lost even before I hit the blunt, fucked a few bitches…I was lost because they lost me. My parents lost me in the beginning. It was only a matter of time before I was aware that I was lost. It was only a matter of time before trouble found me and I embraced it.

And…

It was very hard to make friends when I already realized the important things in life. When I have parents who can't be my parents, I was forced to look at life through different eyes. I used to wonder why other kids could sit there, without a clue to my home life and be concerned with such petty things such as who had the best bike in the neighborhood.

At that moment, I understood the difference between me and "them." The word "them" became a part of my life. It defined everything that normal kids had. I was "me" and no matter what "I" did, it wasn't the same as "them." I felt things differently. I took things differently, even at five years old.

Of course, I wasn't by far a loner. I had a small group of friends. They were other misfits that fit into my pattern of thinking. Each one of them had issues that separated "us" from "them."

Darron was poor. He never had a new pair of anything. When his mom was thinner, she used to shop at our local thrift shop, which now…has closed down because she was the only one who brought profit to the store. Everyone else had money.

Basia was different because her parents were strict. For the first few years of school, she wasn't allowed to wear shorts. Her dresses had to be below her knees. She didn't cut her hair and was very shy at holding hands with boys. It took awhile to break her into our social atmosphere.

Kayo was Asian and overweight. We didn't have many Asian people in St. Paul. In fact, I think there were only three Asian kids in our entire school system. And his parents overfed him out of guilt…I think. Kayo was always eating. His school nickname was "Kayo Mayo."

So, "them" were "them." "We" were "us."

During my childhood, I learned a valuable lesson. I knew how not to be selfish. I was selfless and was able to distinguish the difference fast. **My childhood was never about me and never was supposed to be.**

My mother may have saved me from abortion, but I was still a piece of something else…something more than just a child. I didn't know what that something else was…but I knew I was favored and brainwashed into being her companion.

I learned shame and embarrassment. I learned to lie and hide, think separately from a clique. I had something that "they" didn't, and that was a home life that didn't need to be discovered.

But I wanted normal friends, too. I wanted that simple laughter and fun that "they" seemed to be having. I couldn't be so selfish to think about myself, though. It felt like a sin.

If my mother wasn't in view and my father may have been drunk and hurting himself because I wasn't around to throw anger towards…I still couldn't think about myself.

No, it was never about me. It wasn't about my connection to this world, either. It was about my parents. My life had become my parents' connection to me, that slimy umbilical cord, shaped as a noose, short in length, and able to retract harshly at any given time. One must not think of simple little social gatherings when there are bigger, scarier situations at risk.

I had learned not to care about appearance. I closed my ears to words and whispers, but opened them for the smallest sound at home. I was alert to something else…a vibe…tension. I listened to the walls and the silent frowns of my house and waited to react.

I shielded my eyes from everything, like a second eyelid, able to see, but particles couldn't slip through…like a glass, a window, a telescope…an alligator. Or was that crocodiles?

I watched my classmates, but daydream away from reality. I saw my parents fighting, and alert to jump in…but daydream away from reality.

Soon, my senses were programmed to do so many habits and I was considered weird. My hearing was muffled. I didn't hear what I just heard. I didn't see what I just saw. I guess that's how I was clueless to the truth around me, how I was stupid to understand what was really happening to me, and to Basia, and Lynn, and…and Boo.

My memory was a good data bank, like a detective's notepad, recalling events with clues and keyword phrases, associating faces with feelings. I couldn't remember detail shit, like points that didn't matter…but I had a sight that "they" didn't have. I had an insight, able to feel things out and read people's moods, ready to react. I began to associate music and songs, or whatever my hand was touching, to what happened at that moment. I couldn't remember anything more than that because my "software" wasn't programmed to relay such information. That type of detail was useless in my design.

And guess what the fuck happens when the crisis and the years of reaction are over?

I was left with useless software, programmed for war, equipped for battle, able to flip the switch of auto pilot on…but, now…there was no need to.

I try to shove this reaction to a back shelf, letting it rust to dust and malfunction. Now subconsciously, I still want to fall back on it and actually do…in wrong situations. I won't need it again. It's outdated, discontinued, recalled. But, no…that's my function. I was raised to do this.

I went crazy in one way or the other. I got the normal life that I selfishly wanted, but now what? I didn't know what to do with it. I ruined it, like I did everything I touched. **I didn't know how to react to normal situations. I act on instinct, overriding calmness and relaxation, waiting and anticipating the worse.**

If the worse didn't happen, then I knew exactly how to make it worse. Didn't I?

What can I say? I know now what the fuck was up with me. I was just fucked up. It was my purpose in life…to fuck up, to be a fuck up, and to continue the prophecy of fuck ups. Even as I work side by side with this Nazi, I didn't feel right befriending him, even when he was going to share a cigarette with me. He was ready to squash shit…I…I didn't know why I didn't feel like being his friend.

I was weird that way.

Charles did nothing but smart off at the mouth because he didn't know how to talk to people. I'm sure we had a lot in common…but…I…

I don't know.

I don't fucking know, alright?

Chapter Seventy-One
Angie

"Marry me."

That was the first thing he said when I opened the door. He said it loud and clearly, but I didn't hear him correctly.

"Uh, what?" I laughed in disbelief and stepped back so he could enter.

I hadn't seen this boy in a few weeks and he...did he just say that?

"Angie, I just had a horrible fucking night and..."

I didn't hear anything he was saying. I wanted him to repeat his first greeting. Instead, he was mumbling and wearing a shirt inside out. The tag was bothering me. In fact, his whole demeanor was bothering me.

He was in gray sweatpants and that white t-shirt. No hat, no hair cut, no shave. He wasn't even in Jordan's. They were...wow...he was wearing Reebok shoes. He never wore Reebok's. What's up with that?

Was he always this moody? Did he turn scrubby when he didn't have a girlfriend?

He picked up Devon and carried him into my bedroom, only to stop talking for the second that he kissed Devon on the cheek. When I got back in ear shot, he said it, again.

"Marry me, Angie." He placed Devon in his crib and turned to me. His hands gripped my shoulders like he did when he was being serious. He walked me to my bed and forced me to sit. Then...he took my hands into his, held them in his lap.

"I won't cheat on you if you marry me. I swear on my mother's grave that I would never hurt you if I was your husband. I swear, Angie. I fucking swear. It's the only thing that'll keep me right...I take that shit seriously and I wouldn't ask you if I didn't mean it."

I just zoned out. His face was serious. His eyes were serious. He was seriously asking me to marry me.

No, he was *telling* me to marry me.

I stuttered, at first. "Boo, why are you doing this?" It was the only thing I could say.

He dropped my hands and held his face. "Angie, I wouldn't ask you this shit if I wasn't serious about it. I know I've done wrong…I know I hurt you…I just…I want you to marry me…"

Jesus. He wasn't going to accept "no." He never took "no" for an answer. How was I going to get out of this?

I wasn't about to say "yes."

"Marriage is…it's a little strong, isn't it? We can't even be boyfriend and girlfriend, Boo. Don't you think…I don't think marriage will fix…"

"Angie," He sparked my lips with a kiss and did what he did best when he talked.

He used his body to talk for him…that charm…that stupid body movement that got all the answers he wanted to hear.

I pulled back, hoping that I was dreaming.

I wasn't.

"Boo no, you don't want to marry me." Do I dare say what I wanted to say?

I had to. I had to give this crazy boy back to his owner.

"You belong to Fresca, Boo. We can't get married."

He huffed in annoyance. Then, he stood. "I don't belong with anyone but you, Angie. I'm going to be honest…" He lit a cigarette and paced. "Fresca came by last night…"

I frowned. "See?"

Fate was already trying to set the record straight and force them back together. It didn't matter how I felt about him. It wasn't that I wanted to marry the boy. I never thought he would come to me with this…with this…

"No, I don't see. I don't see the fucking point on why you think that Fresca belongs with me. I don't think…no, I know we don't belong together. She came over and…and…" He was breaking down…not tears…but with frustration and…some type of indecision…tension. He was nervous.

"I don't think we should get married." I didn't want to hear about last night. I didn't care one way or the other. I just didn't want to get married like this.

"I slept with her last night…and this morning…and I don't give a fuck about her. That's what I'm trying to tell you. She did nothing for me. I almost called her Angie. Yeah, a few months ago, she meant the world to me, Angie. I never thought that I wouldn't marry her ass…but, I'm telling you…I'm fucking down on my damn knees…"And he was.

Boo was swallowing the pride that he was known for and knelt on his knees…for me. His head lowered in my lap as his hands grabbed mine.

I couldn't take this…this behavior from him. Boo was…he was…unbreakable.

I lifted up his head and stared into his eyes. His eyes were full of pleas…I didn't like it."Get up Boo, don't do this. Are you drunk?"

"Am I drunk?!" He stood, again. "Angie, I'm not drunk. I'm dead serious for once in my life. This is what I want to do. I want you to marry me. I don't want to party. I don't want to cheat on you…I just want you and Devon. I could care a less to talk with my boys anymore, either." He dropped once more…like a baby he was becoming.

"Marry me."

I was definitely dumbstruck. I seriously didn't want to say "yes." I didn't want to marry Boo Sox. For this moment to be coming true, I think that I was the only girl on Earth that wouldn't say "yes" to him. Amanda might even say "yes" for the mere pleasure of marrying the most popular guy in Pierre…and that money.

"What happened with Fresca last night?" *Something* happened. It was quite clear. I had to redirect this conversation.

He closed his eyes knowing that he wasn't going to get what he wanted out of me. He dropped his posture to the floor like he was drunk and lost his balance. Only, he wasn't drunk.

"It's never going to be the same with her. She's a different person. I don't love her."

"Do you love me?" I knew this answer.

He couldn't love me. Fresca had his heart. I didn't. No matter what he did…he wouldn't be able to get it back. My mom tried to get hers back from my dad. She tried to love someone else…and it ended in break ups. She never recovered from the first break in trust. I don't think anyone ever recovers.

He sighed and thought about it…longer than I imagined he would. "I don't know anything about love, Angie. I just want to marry you. I know I care about you. I know that when I cheated on you, I felt awful and just wanted to kill myself. I didn't want to do it. I was happy with you. When we went out…I was actually happy. You make me happy. Why can't we just get married because we're happy together? We fit and you know it."

I glanced at Devon and back at Boo. I could be the luckiest or unluckiest girl in the world right now. If I said yes, I would be facing more than a break up if something bad happened. If I didn't say it, I'd be wondering about this day for the rest of my life.

I was still undecided.

"Boo, can we try to go back out, first?"

He didn't answer the right way. He jumped up with satisfaction. He kissed me and began to lay me backwards.

I had to stop that, too.

"Wait…did you sleep with Fresca this morning?"

He paused and sighed. "I'm sorry. It's a long waste-of-time-story."

"Then take a damn shower."

He smiled and headed towards my closet where some of his clothes were still laying on the floor. He grabbed one of his outfits and left my bedroom. The confused little boy was about to take a shower because I told him to.

I still didn't understand Boo Sox.

I exhaled for the moment knowing that someday in the near future would be similar to this. He was going to ask me to marry him. It was set in his head.

And I wish it wasn't.

Chapter Seventy-Two
Binderman

"Cindy, I'm on my way to your office, cancel your appointments, I want the rest of your day, no exceptions." And I hung up without giving her a chance to refuse my arrival.

She should be pleased to get an appointment with me.

She met me in the waiting room as soon as I entered through the door. In her arms were patient charts. "I hope you have a good explanation as to why I had to reschedule these poor souls. You know they have bigger problems than yours...hopefully. Am I right? Is this just one of your fit throwing episodes where you think you deserve an entire day devoted to your super ego?"

I sighed and brushed her aside. I headed to her office without her.

"Aren't you cold? It's snowing." Dr. Roma followed me to her office and dropped the charts onto the floor.

I took her seat in her swiveling chair and she was forced to sit elsewhere. It's funny how she wouldn't and couldn't sit in the patient chairs. Inferiority complex?

"Well, what's going on? I've been trying to call you..."

"I don't need therapy anymore, I'm good." I twisted from side to side, unaware that I was portraying an old habit of mine...unable to sit still.

Cindy lowered her head and grinned. "Really? Let's hear the excuse this time."

"Cause I don't need you, anymore. I don't have issues. I'm cured." I bounced my legs and flipped through my chart, not that I wanted to read it...I had already done that.

I wasn't that kid, anymore.

"Bin, we've discussed this time and again. You know how to give fact and example behind your statements, so do it. You are well aware and smart enough to figure everything out on your own, I know. We've been through this, too. But, I want to know what the hell is blinding your good self analysis. You've been in and out of my office with great advice about yourself. Today…today, I think you've gone blind. Have you been to the eye doctor, lately?"

Sinister, I swear.

"What's left to talk about, to analyze? You can write a fucking book on me, Cindy. I need to have a happy ending, sometime. Give it to me." I stood, hands on her desk. I hated when she tried to piss me off.

"Is this about happy endings? People don't get happy endings, Bin. It's never ending. You live life, you struggle, you battle, you accept, you change. There aren't happy endings. There may peace at some time or another, but not an ending. Why are you really here?" She shoved me aside and sat in her chair.

Sometimes, she was like a fucking older sister. I never saw her as a doctor.

"Do you see my chart? I'm fed up with talking to you. I don't need a shrink. I'm over my mom. I've made up with my dad. Cardy exists to the world and he's at Safe Haven. I stopped going to parties. I cut back on drinking. I have a kid and a girlfriend and I just want shit to be normal. If I have to drop shit to talk to you, then I know I'm not normal. I'm reminded every fucking day that I'm not right in the fucking head!" She could twist this shit into every which way to make a point to keep me as a patient. It wasn't right. I knew what she was going to say.

"Where's your mother, Bin?"

Such a fucking bitch.

"She's dead." I gritted. The pain and guilt associated with those words hurt worse than reliving those final moments in Cheriton, walking the lonely corridors of my house and praying she would appear.

"So you've accepted that she's not in Italy?"

"Why are you bringing up this bullshit? I told you, Roma, my mom's dead and I don't want to have to say it, again."

What the fuck did I come out here for, again?

"Your brother calls me Roma. You two are the only ones who call me that. It's weird that you guys haven't talked about me before. He reminds me of you." She opened my chart and skimmed the contents, landing her finger on certain attributes and continuing to pry further into my past.

"I called you Roma before he did."

"Does it matter?"

"No."

"Why do you think he calls me Roma? Is it some form of disrespect when he's mad?" She was redirecting my conversation. She was using Cardy as a deterrent.

"I don't fucking know. Cindy's a common name. Roma isn't. Maybe he likes you." Why the fuck was I analyzing this bullshit with her? I was done with analyzing Cardy. He was in someone else's hands, now.

"Oh! I never thought about it that way, maybe he does. We have grown pretty tight these last few months." And this conversation is going…where? It wasn't about Cardy, today.

It was about me.

I didn't answer. Fuck that. I wasn't going to talk about Cardy.

She circled something in my chart and tapped it. "What about Fresca Taylor, are you over her, too? You don't have hard feelings about her, anymore?"

I could kill her, today.

"No, I don't. And I don't appreciate you talking to her stupid ass, either. She's the one who needs a shrink. I just saw the bitch, yesterday. She tried to rape my ass."

I wasn't going to think about that girl. That girl was history. That bitch was out of my vocabulary, my future…everything.

"Rape you? Are you sure that you're not turning it around because she refused to sleep with you?" She was full of distrust in me, today.

"Ah, fuck you, Cindy. If you knew her, you'd know why she'd try to rape me, alright? The bitch has been dying to have a baby ever since she found out Angie was pregnant. No, it's more like ever since she had a miscarriage. The bitch is crazy. Why don't you focus your efforts towards people like her! I'm happy in my life." I forced myself to sit even though I wanted to leave.

Her eyebrows rose like I assumed. Yeah, write *that* down, would she?

"I thought you were over her."

"I thought you were a doctor." I sneered.

"She has my card. I told her I'd see her." She grabbed her purse and headed out of her office. She wasn't being rude, rather reading my mind. We were headed outside to smoke since I was her last patient of the day.

"I *am* over her, you know. I want to be with Angie." I stopped right under the awning of her office building as the snow was coming down faster. I lit up and waited for her to find her squares. Bitches had too much shit in their bags, I swear.

"Dammit."

"What?"

"Cardy stole my cigarettes." She smiled like she liked that idea. What the fuck was up with that?

"How do you know he did it? Does he do that type of shit?" Yeah, now I was cold. This hoodie wasn't thick enough for a blizzard. I took shelter upon a bench that was against the window. I crouched down and over my knees, trying to preserve the body heat I had under this hoodie and wife beater.

"Oh, he did it alright. He does it almost every day. If I don't give him one, he steals them from me. He's not a thief or anything. He knows I won't get him in trouble."

"He's taking advantage of you, like he does everyone else."

And here we go about Cardy, again. Another hour went by and she told me about Cardy's progress, his regress, his life. I didn't pay attention to anything she said. It went right over my head. Fuck it…I didn't care to talk about me, anyways.

I didn't need a shrink anymore, remember?

When the therapy session was over, I said what I had to say.

"Hey, I came by to tell you that I'm getting married. That's how I know I don't need you, anymore."

I let her dwell on that issue for awhile. She'd call me. I know it.

I was against marriage from as far back as I can remember. She knew this. My mom regretted marrying my father. My dad didn't like being married and that's why he cheated. I don't think anyone was happy to be married. Marriage contradicted everything I was for.

What was I for?

Well, I used to be for partying. I had my good girl…and my bad bitches on the side. I had my tequila, my boys and my budd. It was all I needed in life. And respect and authority went along with it. I had it all. Or so it seemed.

Now, marriage seemed to fix me. If I got married, I'd be forced to change. I had Brandon and Devon to think about. I wanted that family life. It was the only way I could think of getting out of my old existence and making everyone believe how serious I was about Angie.

They had to respect her, then. She would be my wife.

Chapter Seventy-Three
Basia

I woke to the sound of a skateboard rolling down the hall. Jasmine was squealing with excitement and Darron loved the attention.

"Watch Jas, watch this."

She was merely fifteen months old. What did she know about skateboards and tricks?

What did I know about Kyle Sorum and that kiss?

I know I didn't know why I let it happen. I know that my hormones were taking over and causing me to be a kissing whore. Whatever lips came near…I puckered up, that's what. I was admiring the boy physique a little too closely lately, and it got me in trouble.

Anthony Mercini was in jail because of me. Cardy was accused of rape because of me. I kissed KYLE SORUM because of me. Jesus. I needed to get a grip on my priorities.

I wanted to be with Cardy. I didn't want to be with anyone else.

How do I look at Kyle, again?

I couldn't.

Oh God, I don't want to get out of bed, anymore. I was more trouble than I was worth.

I thought Boo Sox was hot!!! Ewwwwww…what went wrong with me?!!!

I lost my marbles. I needed them back. Even in bed, all I was thinking about was Boo's body, Cardy's body, Kyle's body…shouldn't I know better, by now?

Boys are sickening. Boys are gross and only wanted one thing!!!

But still…his lips against mine…his hot sweaty abs against…no, no, no!! I will not allow impure thoughts upon my brain. I was stronger than that. I know how to behave.

Didn't I?

"Darron, get me something to drink, I'm parched!!!" I ordered through my shield of blankets.

The skateboard came to a halt and the tension arose. His feet stomped down the hall and the stairs creaked. The sink was turned on, a glass broke, and the sink turned off. The sink turned back on and then off, once more. His footsteps returned up the steps and back down the hall.

I got water.

Darron was sweating. His hair was growing and some of it was in his eyes. He flipped it back and waited for a thank you. He didn't get one. He smelled like a boy.

"You stink." I sneered. Maybe I needed to be slapped. I didn't care. Darron got the worst of me at all times because he was my punching bag.

"And you're a bitch." He twisted around and grabbed Jasmine before she could hug me.

"You still stink!!" I flipped back the covers and raced after him. Foul mood, foul mood…I'll show him how to skate.

"Move out of my way." I shoved him into the wall, took over his skateboard and rode it.

It felt good to ride, again.

"Uh, shorts?" Darron smiled, relieved to see me on a board, yet awkward to see my underwear.

Where the hell was my dignity? Did it travel to England with my parents? Is it in one of those marked up boxes shoved in some top closet shelf that waits for its owner to claim it?

I think so.

"Sorry." I hung my head so low that it probably dragged the ground.

Minutes later, in Darron's jean shorts with a belt…I barreled him over once more, sending him to the ground. "Let me show you how a girl does it, you stink!"

It was all fun and games up until Kyle intruded. He came out of his bedroom with his hair undone. It was shaggy beyond imagining. He was in a muscle shirt and his jeans were unbuckled. Of course they were.

He was doing this crap on purpose. I think he wanted to make me stare at him.

He rubbed his eyes, gave Darron a little nudge back into the wall and ignored me. He ignored me!

"Uh, hello?" I flipped the board under my arm and awaited my welcome. Jasmine tried to reach for the board and I finally tossed it to the floor. Darron, thankfully, picked it up so she wouldn't fall down the stairs.

"Hey." He gave me. He gave me a 'hey'.

I followed him into the bathroom to yell at him, or talk to him or something…maybe watch him pee, I don't know. He was peeing whether I wanted to see him or not. I didn't see him urinate with *it* because his back was facing me…but I heard it, I thought of it.

"What happened last night?"

He tucked it in, didn't wash his hands, and leaned on the sink. "I'm sorry. It won't happen again."

"Damn right it won't happen again!" And I twirled around like a princess in charge of this house and stole the skateboard out of Darron's alarmed presence.

He didn't ask. I didn't tell.

But he did remind me that Jasmine was wearing the same diaper that she was wearing to bed last night and it was sopping wet.

"I don't have any money." Men vanished from my daydreaming and reality made me frown.

"What are you going to do?" Darron stood there like it was my problem. Well it was, but he was better at being the responsible one than I was.

"I don't know." I wish I could just ride a skateboard.

"Kyle!!" Darron headed for Kyle's bedroom.

"No, Darron, no!!" I tugged on Darron's scrawny little arm and begged him not to do it. I didn't need Kyle helping out.

"He has too!!!"

"I can get a job, we can…uh…maybe we can steal them." A plot was brewing in my head.

Yes, sweet little Basia was dying. I was desperate not to need help. I was desperate not to go to Kyle or my parents.

"What? No, we can't steal. Basia, we can't steal them. Are you out of your mind?!"

We were interrupted by a knock on the door. The door opened and it was Brian. I didn't know Brian, but saw him from time to time with Boo or Cardy…sometimes with Kyle.

"What's up? Where's your brother?" He second glanced at me and headed up the stairs. He nodded when he walked by.

"Dude, hang on." Kyle had heard everything we were arguing about. In his hands he carried a coffee can…a rusted red can that looked like fifty years old…yuck.

"Here, it's all I have." He shoved it into Darron's chest. "Get a job."

The can was filled with pennies, mostly. A dollar bill was sticking out of them. Quarters and dimes were scarce, but there alongside of nickels. Chump change, we used to laugh about. Enough to buy Doritos and a two liter soda…maybe a candy bar for each of us.

Now, it had to buy diapers.

"Kyle, no…we can't…"

"Take it."

Brian looked on, amazed, but wordless. He handed Kyle a pack of cigarettes and they were off. Kyle didn't even change clothes. He didn't buckle his belt, didn't wash his hands, and didn't put his hair back into little twisty knobs of filth. He was dirty and…and filthy sexy.

Chapter Seventy-Four
Cardy

"Imagine a flawless world, everything straight and flush. What would you think about? How would you feel to be equal, to have exactly the same thing as everyone else? What would happen? What would be going on in the world if things were at peace, if everything was the way it should be? Would you be happy? This is an opinionated essay and I will be reading them. There's no right or wrong answer, just an opinion. You will be graded on it for your thoughts, not your answers. If it's one paragraph, then I know you didn't try. If it's two pages, okay, you worked your ass off."

I guess you can call this assignment our midterms, our mid testing for the year. Cindy was piling it on a bit thick, I think. I barely wrote a thing from the beginning.

With nicotine in my system from Charles and Cindy…I felt relaxed. With this medicine working…I suppose…maybe I wanted to behave, don't know, don't care. I was up to the challenge.

Let's see…
Rules
Perfection
Lines
Doors
Cages
Repetitive bullshit

I'd do just the opposite because it's too much control. No originality, no anything. It's just a copy after Xerox copy. We might as well drink with the buffalo. East, west, drink, eat, die…get eaten.

Originality, there's a word I haven't used, recently. Who was always about being original? She stood up and believed in being different from all the rest. She loved to be different.

So did I.

If we were the same, we'd have nothing better to do with ourselves. We'd already be perfect. There'd be no competition, no challenge. We'd dress the same, think the same, want the same shit. I erased *shit* and continued. *We'd want the same things. We couldn't evolve. We couldn't be ourselves. We wouldn't get credit for things that we did because it would be expected out of us. I'd be that person who'd corrupt it just because I could. I'd be the messiah and make sure that people had different religions and different backgrounds. That's what makes us human. We can't have peace without war. We can't have war without wanting peace. If we had peace all the time, then we'd take it for granted. People need to appreciate what we have. If we had everything, what would we be thankful for? I image a colorless world...white walls...white tile...white sheets...color coded shirts...color coded tables...lines of faces that had no expression, like zombies. The zombies would walk and talk the same. They'd play the same sports, write the same thoughts...be here, at Safe Haven. That's what I think.*

I smiled at how I turned it around. I was happy with this essay. It said more than I had started off saying. I was the first to hand it over. I didn't even put much thought into it. I didn't need to.

I lived in a perfect world, all around me. I was always given shit, even Pierre. I had no war in my town, no crime. The only thing that kept me balanced was the war at my house.

Hmmmm...

"I'm going to your office to smoke." And I left her class, once more.

I was getting better and I knew it. I wasn't becoming "Cardy #1" or "Boo's sidekick." I was turning into something else. I didn't know if I liked it. I don't know if I was ready for it.

To be original...

To be with Basia.

No, Basia and I had too much history to together. It'd never be the same. I couldn't be with her. I don't even think I wanted to go back to Pierre.

I chain-smoked two cigarettes and headed off to meet Charles the Fifth. Charles the Fifth was a cool character.

I was starting to like Charles the Nazi because he had some spunk to him. He was different than the everyday kids around here. At least he gave the fourth floor something to think about, like fighting him, fucking with his attitude, or sharing a square.

He was already posted up behind the counter wearing the dreaded apron and leaning over dirty dishes, frantically writing in that damn notebook that everyone liked to write in. fucking sissy.

He slammed it shut and shoved it in his back pocket. Maybe I was wrong about Charles; he was just like everybody else…a writer.

I grinned as I towered above him. "What the hell were you writing about? Anything about me?" I snatched it from behind and became the big bully that people were starting to think I was.

I swear, being here made me feel like one.

Charles quickly turned bull shitter. "Give it back!"

I raised it above his head and smiled more. "Or what?"

"Or I'm not gonna share my smokes with you!!!"

Fair enough. I handed it back and frowned. "What the fuck is with that shit? Everybody writes. It's bullshit. What the fuck do you get out of it?"

"What the fuck am I supposed to do? If I don't write, then all I have are thoughts. I'm tired of thinking. If I write it down, it's out of my head." He shoved the first plate into the soapy water and scrubbed it with a rag that was falling apart.

I guess I was the fucking dryer.

I jerked the plate from his hand and almost dropped it. "What do you think about?"

"Stuff, whatever comes to mind, I just write it down. You try spending a lifetime in here and see where it takes you. You walk around with shit in your head, can't stop thinking about it. I've been here for three fucking years, Cardy. I'd go insane if I couldn't get useless shit out of my head. I hated to write before I got here. I still can't spell. Fuck, you probably couldn't read it if I let you, that's how bad it is. But, I know what it says. I don't even read it once I write it. I just scribble the shit so it's not bothering me anymore."

"So there's shit in there about me." Flattery was always cool.

"Why the fuck would I write about you? I give a fuck about you." He continued on plates as I jerked each one from his grip before it came out of the water.

"Then who the fuck do you write about?"

"There's this girl that…it's stupid, never mind." He retracted his words and left me in wonder, fucking pussy.

"Nah motherfucker, come on, we have an hour with this bullshit, spill it or I'll steal it, again." It was actually pissing me off. I had nothing better to do than hear about Charles's girl fantasies.

"There's this girl that I keep dreaming about. I never met her, I just…I don't know. I have nothing better to dream about, so she's real to me."

I heard enough, but my pride wouldn't let me back down. I wanted to push his buttons. Alright, alright, maybe I was a little bit curious.

"You dream of a bitch that's not real? Is she hot?"

Has Charles even tasted a girl?

"Man, she's hotter than hot. She's always naked and her tits are…"

"Stop it, motherfucker, I'm gonna hose your ass down in a minute." It was more than I needed in my head. I didn't want to dream of this bitch, myself. I had enough naked bitches in my head that were actually real and I didn't need another wet dream to wake up to.

It was bad enough to be fucking celibate. Abstinence my ass, one thought of a naked bitch and it put me in a bad ass mood. I couldn't do anything about it.

"Well, I write about her, about my dreams, about my life before I came here."

I dropped the towel on the counter and stopped. I glanced around for Hobby, the janitor. Hobby was what the others called him; I didn't know his real name. He answered to Hobby, anyways.

"Perfect time to light up asshole, get with it, you can talk your ass off in a minute. Just leave that bitch in your notebook."

Charles lit his cigarette and passed it to me. The towel was our fan. We stuck the butt in the drain.

"You ever wonder what's going on in the real world?"

No. No, I fucking don't. I don't need to wonder about the real world or bitches. Thanks, motherfucker…thanks for the stupid after effects of this conversation.

"Dude, fuck that shit, I ain't trying to think about shit I can't change. What music do you listen to?" I rephrased my "dog" word back to "dude" and redirected this conversation to something less offensive.

He exhaled and stared dead into my eyes. He was ready for my reaction. "Megadeth, Ozzy, and Alice Cooper are top three. Metallica comes close to tying."

I smirked and blew my own smoke out. I crossed my legs and leaned against the counter. "What do you think I listen to?"

"Rap, no question." He took the square back without hesitation. He was set on categorizing me.

"Why?"

"Cause you say 'dog', that's why."

I laughed. "Get the fuck outta here, that's bullshit, Nazi." I didn't give him my top three…not just yet. He could sit and ponder.

"Do you even know who Megadeth is?"

"I know who they are. I don't like them or Ozzy, or Cooper. They suck." I didn't hate them, just wasn't my favorite. And I liked pissing Charles the Fifth off to the third degree.

"That's because you listen to rap. Every true rocker loves Ozzy."

"Oh, bullshit dumb ass. He has a couple songs, but nothing great. If I had to listen to one of his songs for eternity, I'd rather have silence." It wasn't him directly, it was the music. It was…it was too heavy, too…

"Just say it, Cardy, you don't like rock music." He was seriously stupid, I swear.

"Are you fucking kidding me?! Get the fuck outta here, yes I do! I'm just not down for that head banging shit."

"So you're a lame ass."

"Oh motherfucker, I'm gonna kick your ass just for putting my music down, for saying I don't like rock music. Nah, the last rock CD I bought was Limp Bizkit, ever heard of them? Kid Rock, Pearl Jam's fifth album, I bought all that shit before I came here."

"Pearl Jam? You listen to Pearl Jam?" He was making fun of me.

"Right down to the chain and grunge pants, flannel shirts, skateboards…yep. I didn't wear that shit then, but yeah, I was *that* motherfucker." I didn't give a fuck what he thought.

"No way."

"Yeah, dog, I'd show you up on a skateboard, swear to God."

"Do you even believe in God?"

"Do you?"

"Do you?!" He didn't want to admit it first.

"I'm Catholic." I grinned wider.

Chapter Seventy-Five
Angie

Boo came back with Brandon in his arms. He stood him down, dropped Brandon's diaper bag onto my couch and headed for Amanda's room where Devon was. Devon was pulling down all of Amanda's clothes that were hung up and he thought it was funny. Amanda was getting frustrated.

"Take this little midget away from me!!!!" Amanda screamed at him even though she was shocked to see Boo in our house. She kept her mouth shut and didn't give me a good talking to. Good. I didn't want to hear it.

Brandon was dressed well. He had a fresh haircut, buzzed short. He wore a gold cross necklace...yes...Boo put a necklace on him. He had a Ralph Lauren Polo shirt on over some jeans that I bet cost more than my shoes I was wearing. Oh, and little Jordan's never looked so cute.

He was a little Cardy...or worse...a little Boo. He wasn't even Boo's kid.

He grabbed Devon and flipped him upside down. Devon started to laugh and wail his arms at him. Boo was in good spirits, today...I suppose.

He didn't mention marriage and was avoiding his talk with Cindy.

"Um, what did your shrink say?" I second glanced my sweat suit and realized that if I was going to walk around in public with this bunch again, I'd have to resort to jeans, once more. I hated jeans.

"It was whatever." He slid next to Brandon who took a seat on the sofa quietly as he absorbed his new surroundings in. "What's up buddy, say hi to your cousin." He nudged Brandon in the arm and brought Devon on his lap...upside down. Devon beamed with excitement.

Boo was weird. I've made my mind up. Yesterday, he was sobbing to marry me. Today, it was like a continuous of what he had months ago. It was like nothing had happened between us.

"I feel like going to the mall." He added as he placed Devon next to Brandon and sized them up. Brandon was the same height. Devon was fatter, but Brandon was always going to be similar in height…I think.

"They look like brothers." They had Boo's eye color, the same eye shape and everything. Their eyebrows were identical, their little nose, too. Their cheeks puffed out with the same bow shaped lips. If Devon didn't have a darker shade of blonde and straighter hair…I'd assume they were twins.

"I know."

"Are you sure you didn't mess with Lynn Hayes?" I was joking of course.

He grinned with a comeback. "Are you sure you didn't mess with Cardy Deburke?"

"Oh please, come on. That's sick, Boo. He's like my brother." More like an annoying little brother who wouldn't stay off our kitchen counters with his skateboard.

"They look like Sox kids. If you saw baby pictures of my cousins, you wouldn't be able to tell them apart from my pictures. It's crazy. It's like we're pure bred."

Oh, and his conceit was back. "Yeah, right."

"Baby, we can't help the fact that our genes are dominant. It's just the way it is. We got good blood. You're lucky to be a part of it. I don't see anything on him from you." And he rubbed Devon's head because he knew what Devon had from me.

"He has my straight hair and I bet it turns brown when he's older." I was well satisfied with contaminating the blonde gene in their family.

He frowned. "Brandon has my hair."

"Yeah, and he's not yours. Cardy's curly gene is stronger than yours." I grinned and grinned until it hurt.

"Shut the fuck up and let's roll. Change your outfit." He stood and wondered into my bedroom to pick me out something more appropriate.

At the mall, he was all over the place. He wouldn't stay put in any store. He was worse than a hyper kid swinging on a rack.

Baby Gap, The Children's Place, Champs, Foot Locker, Dillard's, Penney's, the Arabic jeweler, every single store that caught his eye…we entered and exited with too many bags to hold.

"I thought you said that Cardy spent up all your money." I didn't believe him when he said he was broke. Boo Sox was always full of money and…lies.

He flashed a card at me and stuck it back in his pocket. "My bank account is low, this is my savings account."

"You said you were broke in that, too."

"No, this is my inheritance account. Baby, I got a lot of accounts. I got a bank account, a savings account, and three inheritance accounts. This is my mom's, which I don't ever spend."

"Why not?" It was just a question out of curiosity. I didn't think it came with a decent answer.

"Because it's death money, that's why. Why should I waste the money I got because she died? I think life insurance is stupid. You get hundreds of thousands of dollars for someone dying and you're supposed to feel good about it? I always felt too guilty using it." He dropped into a chair that was part of the Pretzel Place.

"So why are you spending it?" I never thought about life insurance money that way. He was right. Why should we get a big payoff for someone's death? I wouldn't want to waste my mother's money towards something I really wanted, even if it was a house. It would mean that I got it all because she died. I would rather have *her* back.

"Because it's in the past, she'd want me to buy Devon and you something."

Hmm, did she care that he bought Brandon too many things too? Did they need fifty pajama sets and gold jewelry that they would just break? Did they need a hundred pair of Jordan's when they were just going to scuff them the day they started wearing them?

I think not.

That's why me and my mom bought Devon cheap little Elmo shoes and cute little Winnie the Pooh romper sets. They were babies. Babies didn't know one thing from the next. They scuffed, broke, spit up, threw up, colored on, and ripped apart things that teenagers would die for.

Then he leaned up on his knees. "Hey, let's go in there."

A quick glance in front of me and I was ready to leave. "No. There's no reason to go in there, Boo." I lifted up the brake pedal and began to scoot Devon's stroller far away from Victoria's Secret.

Boo stood too, only Brandon's stroller was headed towards the bras. "Yes there is. Come on."

I stood my ground and rested my foot on the stroller. "No, I'm not going in there. I don't wear anything they have to offer. It's ridiculously priced and too fancy. I don't *need* things like that."

It was another stupid idea of his. "You're a woman, women wear Victoria's Secret. Let's just go in there, come on, chill out." He was there before I could argue.

I stood outside the edge of the store, too embarrassed to be caught dead in it. Yes, women wore Victoria's Secret and I didn't fancy myself a woman, yet. I was eighteen. I didn't have the pleasure of ever wearing one of those bras and didn't care to try one out.

"My *mother* shops here, let's go!" I knew my mom was home sleeping, but still.

He picked up a lacy thing-a-ma-jig and waved it at me as if it was the last piece of food on earth.

"Get over here, Boo. I'm not going in there."

"You'll be fine, baby, come on."

"What the hell do you think I am? I'm a whale, a big fat whale with big fat whale legs and I can't fit into anything that they have. I'm not doing it."

He frowned and left Brandon to tug on some lingerie strings. He approached and began to push me across the invisible threshold that I despised. "We'll buy it and if it doesn't look right, which you're ridiculous for thinking anyway, we can take it back."

I was close to tears. I wasn't a lady. I wasn't skinny. I wasn't fancy or prancy or prissy or anything that mattered to Victoria's Secret. It even smelled prestige.

"I'm not going to look right it in." I uttered as he held up a see through pair of underwear…or shorts, or whatever they were.

"Yes you will."

"No I won't." I crossed my arms and hoped nobody thought I was stupid for being in there with two strollers and a stupid boyfriend who was only thinking of sex.

"I'm buying it, and this, and this, and this, and that." He collected a lot of lacy bras and underwear, and shorts and dress thingies and stupid little things that didn't even matter to wear. Why wear crotch-less underwear?

"You're sick in the head. I'm not wearing any of it, especially for you."

"I'm not buying it for me, Angie. I'm buying it for you. I could give a fuck about what you wear."

"Yeah, right, that's why you changed my outfit before we came here."

His hands went on my shoulders as we stood in line. He pressed himself against me and whispered in my ears. It made me shiver and feel sick. "It makes *you* feel better, not me."

Ugh. And people talk about fat girls wearing skimpy outfits and those girls say just what he said. There are things that aren't appropriate for fat girls, I'm telling you right now.

Later, he sat on my bed after the babies were asleep in Devon's crib. I was dreading this night as soon as the bank card swiped my freedom away.

He was shirtless…and sexy. He could sit there with his shirt off, leaning over without any belly fat. He stretched his long legs down and put his arms behind his head, smiling. He knew what I was thinking and I knew what he was thinking. He was waiting for the tension to build.

"I'm not putting it on and I'm not doing anything with you." I was being stubborn even though I wanted him to leave so I could stress over my love handles, alone. I never wore a thing like those in the bag.

"Then don't." he wasn't arguing, wasn't doing anything, just sitting there, watching me like a hawk. "You're not fat, Angie."

I already had it in my head that he was going to force those things on my body. I had the whole event planned out, what I was going to say and wind up doing…and the aftermath of him touching me even though I was a fat ass whale.

"Fine!" I rolled my eyes as if he was pressuring me to try them on. My curiosity was winning.

He grinned and tried to follow me into my bathroom. I slammed the door perfectly against his face.

"Are you still out there?" After ten minutes of standing on the toilet to see my belly hang over the edge of the lacy thong, I wasn't about to show it off. I wrapped a towel around my waist and was hoping to run into Amanda's room for her stand up mirror.

"No." I felt his breath come through the door.

"Go away, I look hideous."

"I doubt it."

"What are you doing?" I heard Amanda stop short of Boo's position.

"Your sister was dying to buy some lingerie and I told her not to, but she insisted." He lied. I heard the sarcasm in his voice.

"I did not!!!"

"Okay, okay, trust me, I don't want to know. In fact, I don't want to be in this house anymore. I'm going over to Darron's and don't wait up for me because I'm not ever coming home, not with you two around!!! That's disgusting!!!"

When the front door slammed, Boo had to add his two cents worth. "Come out, we're all alone. We can take pictures in the living room."

"You better not have a camera!!!"

"I don't, come on, Angie. I'm just fucking with you; get out here before I break your door down. I will, I promise."

With the towel wrapped securely in place, I unlocked the door.

"Take off the towel, motherfucker!" He was more frustrated than what I thought he would be.

"No, I look obese."

He pushed and shoved me into Amanda's room and slammed the door. He yanked the towel off of me and forced me to look at myself as my hands tried hard as hell to cover my dignity.

His body was glued to my back as he stared along. "Look at that, it's not bad at all." He was already kissing my neck.

The tears came quick. "No I don't. I have stretch marks and this…" I pinched my fat and yanked it all out of place.

"Stretch marks that make you mine; it makes you more special to me." He didn't press the argument, but instead let his hands pry mine away from my stomach.

"I don't feel pretty."

"But you are pretty." His hands weaved in and out of the lace and over my thighs.

"I feel fat."

"But you're not fat." His chest was against my back, the smooth connection of skin sent shivers down my spine. His lips became wetter as he kissed me, making me feel beautiful and skinny. "I think you're sexy." It was all I needed to hear. It really boosted my confidence.

Chapter Seventy-Six
Basia

"Do you think Boo has a good body?"

"Will you stop it, already? I just came from there and I don't care to think about Boo or my sister right now. I think she's stupid and disgusting." Amanda started to pick at a scab on her ankle. It was a small one from shaving. I was told never to pick them, there was a reason it was there. Guess she didn't care if she was ruining new skin.

"I think all girls are stupid." Darron entered his bedroom eating out of a big bag of Doritos.

"When are you going to get a girlfriend, Darron?" I rubbed it in.

"When he can get Gwen Stefani or Britney Spears." Amanda busted with laughter.

He threw a Doritos chip at Amanda and laughed along. "Yeah, I wish."

Darron has been obsessing over Gwen Stefani for three years, now. Cardy and Darron both loved her stomach and her pushups. She was like a tom boy gone girl.

Britney Spears was new. I wonder what Cardy thought about her. I know Darron loved her school girl uniform. Did Cardy?

"Have you noticed how Darron's voice goes up and down? Remember when Cardy's did?" Cardy would crack during each sentence. And when tickled, it was awesome. He sounded like a girl with a sore throat.

"Shut up! I need new friends. You girls are too much."

Poor Darron, he didn't have any guy friends, anymore. All that was left was Amanda and me. Becca and Loren had boys to chase after. Cardy...well, we all know what happened to him. And Kayo...I still couldn't get over that he was gay. Darron had no one.

"We're the best friends you'll ever have, Darron, get real. And, think about it this way, when you get a girl you like, we can help you out. We know what girls like. We can have a Darron make over!" Amanda was mocking Becca and her crazy makeover schemes.

"Who says I need a makeover? I'm perfectly fine with the way I look. I have muscles," And he pumped his scrawny arms up, "I have brains, looks," He flipped his bangs out of his eyes, "And I'm cool." And he stuffed a handful of Doritos into his mouth like a pig.

Yeah, Darron had confidence in his appearance. It was never that. His humor was the best thing about him, and he was sincere. As long as girls liked short little dweebs, he was all set. I mean, I like Darron. If Cardy didn't exist, maybe I would have considered him boyfriend material because he would be perfect as one…but, because of Cardy…he would always remain a friend. No matter what happened between me and Cardy.

"You know my brother likes you." Darron took a seat in his bean bag and turned the Super Nintendo on. "I don't know why, and I don't know why you like him, but he likes you."

Amanda's eyes widened with shock. "Kyle likes Basia? No way, how did that happen?"

"Like I said, I have no clue. Basia's crazy and weird." More Doritos…munch, munch, munch.

"Darron, everybody likes me. Get used to it. You like me. Say you don't, I dare you." It was the quickest way to convert the situation at stake.

"No I don't."

"Yes you do, everybody knows you had a crush on Basia since Cardy claimed her in Kindergarten." Amanda agreed.

"Cardy didn't claim her in kindergarten. We played paper, rock, scissors in third grade to sit by her on the bus when we went to the zoo and that was that. He won Basia, he didn't claim her."

I remember that day. Oh sweet heavenly innocence, where are you now?

"I'm not a prize, Dairy-cakes." I sneered, knowing damn well that he hated that name.

"So what's going to happen now that Kyle likes you?" Amanda rolled her eyes.

"Nothing." I frowned. Who did she think I was? I wasn't Becca. I wasn't going to sleep with him or hang all over him as if he was a tree. Nothing was ever going to happen with Kyle Sorum.

"You don't like him?"

"No!" I was surprised to hear my voice shout in offense.

"Yes she does." Darron shouldn't be in this conversation.

Wow, the arguments I had with that boy. We could go for an hour about me liking Kyle.

"I said I didn't, so I don't, now drop it or I'm gonna punch you." Yes, I was cross enough to hurt him.

He smirked as if I wouldn't.

So I did.

I hit him as hard as I could in his right shoulder and he barreled over with exaggeration. With my hands on my hips, I waited. I was going to give him more.

"You're such a bully, Basia! You know, I could really hurt you if I wanted to." He didn't sidestep the fact that he was indeed angry with me.

"Come on guys, chill out." Amanda wanted to be the middle man and deflect the issue. But the issue had just started. He called me a bully. I wasn't a bully. He was overreacting to my punch. He didn't think I could take him.

I kicked him in the rear, hard enough to mean it. "Hit me."

"What? No." He returned to his game, holding his bruise.

I kicked him, again.

Less than a second later, he jumped up and slammed me to the ground. Amanda screamed his name and I swallowed my tongue…for once. "I am tired of you bossing me around. I'm the only guy that actually cares what happens to you and you treat me like shit. Do you think Cardy would let you walk all over him? No. Do you think Kyle would let you hit him? No. Do I ask you for anything? No. I let you live in my house, eat my food, sleep all day while I watch Jasmine, and you can't even say a mere thank you. Why don't you move in with Amanda or something? I've had it with you!"

When Darron gets angry, you better watch out. He's this firecracker that comes with a long wick. It takes a while for the flame to spark and run its course…but when the wick is gone, he comes with a big bang.

I never saw it coming.

And I began to cry.

Darron stomped out of the room and down the stairs. The front door slammed and opened. Then slammed again. I didn't know whether he was inside or outside. He may have had to slam it twice to get the point across. He's done this when he snapped at a teacher for not disciplining a kid who was picking on him.

Either way…I was kicked out. And if I wasn't kicked out…I wasn't welcomed.

Burn bridge, burn…I didn't know how to put out the flame.

Chapter Seventy-Seven
Cardy

Everything was well on its course. I was taking my medicine…my four prescriptions of peace altering existence. I was going to class. I was smoking with Charles, which made him an associate…not friend. I wouldn't allow him the privilege.

I was going to my therapy sessions. I was able to jog when I needed a fix. I was a regular sight on the basketball court when it wasn't snowing…and I was eighteen. Holy fuck, I was eighteen!

I was eighteen years old. I could legally smoke cigarettes. I was legally considered an adult. I could vote, and I wasn't a minor. I was also old enough to be charged as an adult if I had any other mishaps. And that was put in perceptive.

My juvenile record was supposed to be relinquished, right? Wasn't this the fresh start I was looking for?

It was a huge milestone. I had had a rough year, this year. Too many things had happened to me. Being eighteen gave me the freedom of knowing that I was going to be alright. Maybe it was psychological, but I felt great.

I felt recovered.

I was going to put my past behind me and move on. I was going to take this bullshit asylum in stride, do all that I can do to cooperate and live on.

I didn't think about superstition and the bad luck of mine. My defenses dropped and I felt happy. At least, I was happy for the moment.

Talking to Charles and Brett, I was able to bring up my brother Jeff, share stories of brotherhood. At times, I was more talking about Boo and didn't know it. I'd come to a part of connection, as they had with theirs, and I'd automatically switch to Boo.

I never told them about Boo being my brother. It still didn't sit well with me, let alone admitting it to others. When I talked about him...he was merely a friend that I stayed with.

I'm sure everybody thought I had exaggerated my life experiences. Outside of St. Paul, it seemed as though motherfuckers didn't party as much, or didn't have the advantage of getting liquor and drugs. They barely had sex with broads, let alone my digits in women. They taught me something...

My exposure was fast and harsh. It *wasn't* normal, although it was the norm in Pierre. Taking this into consideration, my perspective about life changed.

Let's try out my eighteen year old brain on a theory...

People base normality on their environment. What they see is what they want to do to be like everyone else...to be normal. What surrounds them also brainwashes them. Makes sense, I guess.

Normal is only a word. It's an average cluster, a medium of a group. Normality of America would be the highest percentage of the public doing whatever was being whatever. The normality of this institute consisted of little boys who did minor things and well on their way of recovery.

I was abnormal in both aspects. I wasn't normal in Pierre. I wasn't normal in Safe Haven.

Once I thought of this, I no longer felt like an outcast. I felt better than everyone else...because I was original. I wasn't falling into the trap of popular demand like "them."

And the more I came to this conclusion, the more I was sparking my mind into someone very familiar to me...

Well, fuck...what's up Cardy number one? Where have you been at?

I sit on the edge of my bed, stripped of my proud attitude for the moment. Everything is quiet. Brett was somewhere outside. Stan was far away. No sound, no life. It was just me and me.

I felt like I had just woken up from a dream. I stared at my hands, opening and closing them. Everything felt like it was in slow motion. My feet shuffled, my legs stretched.

Damn. I seriously felt like my soul was just shoved into my body. I smiled because I knew what that meant.

A part of me was back. A part of my old self wasn't scared anymore. I was alive. That's what it felt like. I was that fifteen year old boy named Cardy Deburke who now sat on the edge of the conviction of the new me.

Ever feel like that?

How everything didn't make sense and you ask yourself 'what the fuck did I just go through?' your body tingles. Your vision gets fuzzy. Your brain spins out of control for a second, going over millions of small memories that didn't even matter. And within an instant, BAM, you wake up and realize that you're alive. You breathe, exhale, and…

Move on.

I was quiet for the rest of the week. I was thinking and thinking hard. Something was changing inside of me. I didn't admit it to Cindy, as I barely confessed anything to her. I just sat alone, thinking. Even if I was on the court, I was thinking, doing my chores…thinking.

I thought about everything.

Secretly, I thought of Boo. I didn't want to think of Boo, but I was. I had to come to terms with what he meant to me.

What did he mean to me?

I can honestly say that if Boo was any other way for the worse, I wouldn't be here to experience any part of my life. He had saved me from further destruction. I could have committed suicide on any given day…but he was there to rip the pills from my hands. Of course not all the times…thankfully, those other times I didn't OD.

I didn't realize his impact on me until now.

He had introduced me to a new way of living…living free, enjoying life. Only I had taken it to the extreme. I went overboard and landed in rehab.

Brother.

I walk like his ass. I talk like his stupid ass. Every time I look in the mirror I am reminded of him. Motherfucker,

Fuck him.

Where the fuck is he now? Why isn't he saving my ass?

Man, fuck him.

I didn't need his stupid ass. Brother or not, I wasn't about to call him up and talk to him, anymore. I could care a less about him. When I get out of here…fuck Boo motherfucking Sox.

I was better than him. I was smart. I didn't need him hanging around my ass and wanting to party or smoke budd…or chill…or jog…damn, I needed to jog. This bullshit was making me anxious.

It was still snowing and pissing me off. I paced in and out of my room.

Boo.

God dammit, why the fuck was he stuck in my head?

Oh, it didn't fucking stop there. When night came, he haunted my sleep.

In my dream, I was back at that house, getting dressed for a party. It felt as real as it could get. I smelled the house. I felt the house. I knew every detail about that stupid ass house.

I couldn't decide on a shirt. I had the hat picked out, but all my shirts were dirty, like usual. I was going to steal one of Boo's shirts, but his door was locked. I jiggled the handle and rammed it with my shoulder. I heard myself whisper 'what the fuck?' I turned around and was greeted by that wicked painting that hung between our bedrooms. It was of a lady, proper and straight, staring her cold grey eyes down my spine.

The hallway dimmed as it extended out to an endless horizon. My bedroom door disappeared and became just a wall. I didn't have a bedroom.

Boo's door was locked.

I dipped my fingers deep into my pocket and found the skeleton key that I usually stole from Boo. That key was like power, having it meant that I could lock and unlock whatever I wanted to.

The key melted into a small black snake slithering across my palm. I dropped it, instantly. I watched it slither under Boo's door and out of sight.

I called out to Boo, but he didn't answer. I ran down the staircase. He wasn't home. Somehow, I knew he hadn't been home for months. He was gone…missing.

A heavy burden fell upon me…I felt lost and abandoned. I couldn't take the pressure and heart ache. My chest hurt, my skin crawled.

I jerked open the front door and was bombarded with sunlight. As soon as the bright lights hit…I found myself in the middle of nowhere, surrounded by desert, with nothing and nobody.

Noise was everywhere. I couldn't see anything, but my ears rang with every noise they ever heard, birds, insects, airplane engines, laughter, screams, cries. I couldn't take it.

I hit my knees and watched my arms turn blue, as if my veins had popped and I was bleeding on the inside. I was about to bleed to death…under my skin.

I screamed and screamed, throwing everything I had in my pockets down a paved road. I was hoping that if I threw a big enough fit that Boo would appear and scold me.

Nothing happened.

I cursed the sky, as if Boo could hear me. I called him all the names I could think of. I cried, begged and apologized for his mercy.

Silence held strong, now.

Boo was dead. I knew this, I felt this. I was alone…forever.

The panic jerked me awake and I was already covered in tears. I searched the darkness for his silhouette, but he wasn't there.

I was at Safe Haven.

Boo was gone.

Both my brothers were gone.

He would have saved me by now if he was alive. He always came. Even if I didn't call, he came. He knew to save me.

So where the hell was his bitch ass at?

What if he was really dead? What if all this time he was dead and I was left with nothing?

Holy fuck, I needed to leave this place. I needed…

What if he was here, now?

I had to find him. I had to tell him…

What if he didn't know I was here? What if no one told him?

Oh my fucking God, this is fucked up. I had all these horrible feelings in me, now. I needed to find him. The need was so fierce that I pounded on my bedroom door.

"Stan!!!" I screamed with terror. "Stan, help me!!!!"

Stan came from his desk that seemed miles away. He didn't pick up the pace and didn't care to really help me. Bastard. His white polo shirt was pissing me off. Everything white was pissing me off.

Stan opened the door when he saw my face. The fucking tears were pouring for no reason. I didn't want to fucking cry…I just was.

"I gotta find him. He's here. He has to be here. I feel it."

Maybe I was crazy. Maybe this was it for me. I was full blown insane.

Stan was surprised and scared to see me this way. He didn't have time to push me back and shut the door. I barreled into him and down the hallway. I wasn't trying to escape; I was trying to Find Boo.

I checked the fourth floor hallways, closets, bathrooms…
Third, second, first…
Elevators, under desks, the lobby…
The main door, the back exit door…
I checked everywhere.
Outside was a blizzard, half sleet, half snow. Lightning was flashing, thunder was roaring. The snow on the ground was thick and…ugh…white.
I felt trapped.
He left me here to die. I can't believe him. He left me to die.
I dropped and screamed, holding my head. "Motherfucker!!!!"
No one could calm me. No one could touch me.
I was alone.
Forever…

Chapter Seventy-Eight
Binderman

I shot up in my bed. What the fuck is going on?

I rubbed my eyes and tried to see straight. The clock said three in the morning. What the fuck woke me up? What was I dreaming about?

Angie was asleep next to me. It didn't look like she moved since she fell asleep earlier. She was still curled around Devon. Devon was fast asleep, as well.

What the fuck?

Maybe it was Brandon. I jumped up to check on him.

No, he was on his stomach and wasn't moving. I paused for his back to rise and it did. He was breathing and asleep.

What the fuck woke my ass up?

Something was wrong. I felt it. Something was going on. I couldn't go back to sleep without knowing what it was.

I stood in the hallway, puzzled.

Grams.

I swear to God it better not have to do with Grams. I rushed down the stairs as fast as I could, skipping every other step. I landed with a leap and almost lost my balance. Big houses weren't good in a time of panic. Too many rooms, too many hallways.

I dashed through the foyer and into the music room, into the other hallway and to the left. It was the fastest way to go.

Her door was open. On her back and eyes closed. Motherfucker, she was so old that I couldn't tell if she was dead or not. She looked too still.

I held my breath and charged in. it wasn't the time to be polite and quiet. I jumped up on her bed and straddled her, ready to slap her back to life.

"Grams!!!" I shouted only inches from her face.

Her eyes shot open and she let out an awful noise of pure fear. She grabbed her heart and almost had a heart attack. "What in the world???"

I grinned out of embarrassment and lifted my heavy ass off of her. "I thought something happened to you."

"So you try to kill me by sitting on me?"

"No, I had a dream or something. Something felt wrong." I grabbed the hand she gave me to sit her up.

"Have you been drinking?" her grey eyes focused in on mine.

"I'm serious Grams, something's wrong. It's the same feeling I had that time at school." I wasn't about to apologize. If something had been wrong with her, at least I was there to save her.

"Well, if you've been drinking, then there's something wrong, now isn't there?"

Motherfucker, I didn't have time for a lecture or…

"Grams, stop, I'm not drinking. Somebody's in trouble." Who the fuck was it?

"Binji, honey, if you ever…ever…do that to me again, you're the one who's going to be in trouble."

"Fine, alright." I had enough of her. "I'm calling dad."

I headed towards the cordless in the music room. Cocksuckers don't believe me when I say that shit. But I'm right, something's wrong. Something was going on.

Of course Bobbi answered, stupid bitch. I knew nothing was wrong with her.

"What's wrong, are you in jail, again?" She yawned like it was no big deal.

"Shut up, where's dad?"

"Asleep, why, are you in jail or not?"

"No, I'm not drunk, not in jail, I'm perfectly fine. Is dad okay?"

"He should be, he's asleep in his room like any other night."

"Go check on him, I'm serious, Bobbi, something's wrong, I feel it."

She sighed as I heard her stomp onto her floor. "You're such a pussy, nothing's wrong."

God dammit, I didn't want to deal with her ass, tonight. "A what?" I never heard her say that word in my life. What was up with that shit?

"A pussy."

"Stop saying that word, Roberta. I'm not a pussy, I'm gonna kick your ass next time I see you."

"Pussy, pussy, pussy." She sang into the receiver.

Minutes later, she yawned again. "The door's locked. He's fine, trust me. He came in here earlier with a girl. I'm not getting the key and opening it, who knows what I'll find."

I sighed, too. I didn't want to think about my stupid ass father getting some. "Whatever." And I hung up.

I sat at the piano and struck a key. Something was wrong with somebody, who the fuck was it?

I hit another key and decided to get up before I found myself playing something stupid.

I paced around, up the stairs, back into my hallway. What the fuck, what the fuck?

Fresca.

I swear to God, girl, you better not be up to something awful.

I cradled the phone and thought about what to say if she wasn't trying to slit her wrists. I doubt she was in trouble, but I needed to know for sure.

I glanced back into my bedroom at Angie. I already felt like I was deceiving her for thinking about Fresca. I hadn't thought about that bitch since I saw her last.

I hated that bitch. I shouldn't give a fuck about what she's doing.

But I was.

I headed to Wren's old bedroom and dropped onto the bed. I stared at the phone and watched my eyes go over her digits. I was such a fucking stupid ass for doing this, I know it.

On the fourth ring, she actually answered. She knew it was me if she checked the caller ID. I was surprised she picked up.

"Hello?" The first word told me she didn't check who was calling.

I bit my lip and spoke, regretting every second of it. "Are you okay?"

"What? Who is this?"

Ah, motherfucking bitch, don't play with me. "You know who this is; you better know who this is. Who else would be calling you right now?"

Cold chills ran down my spine and into a jealous rage. Ah fuck, I didn't even think about arguing with this bitch.

Who the fuck did she think I was?

"Boo? What the hell do you want? Why wouldn't I be okay?"

I was never going to find out what the fuck was wrong with this night. I was wasting my time.

I rubbed my face with exhaustion. "I don't fucking know. I'll get off the phone, fuck it."

"Why did you call me? I told you, we're over."

"Shut the fuck up and go back to sleep, I wasn't calling for that. I had a dream, that's all."

"Oh." And silence held us on the phone.

"What was your dream about?"

I leaned back against Wren's headboard and actually felt like talking to her, even though I shouldn't be. "I don't remember. I just woke up feeling that something was wrong. Remember when I said I knew something was wrong at school when my mom died?"

"I think you're over thinking this, nothing's wrong. It's not like that day, Boo." Her voice was softer and rather concerned. Our past was shoved to the side and I was talking to Francesca Taylor the nice bitch, rather the Fresca Taylor the gone cheerleader airhead.

"It is," I cut myself off to calling her baby and continued. "You know what I just did?" and I told her about Grams and she thought it was hilarious.

"I wish I could have got that on video." She laughed. And silence grew, once more.

It was hard to know it was over with her. Our relationship was more Bipolar than I was. One minute she was a fucking bitch trying to attack me, the next, she was consoling me at three in the morning over a dream.

I decided to 'fess up about Angie. There was no need to keep it from her if we weren't going out…ever again. Not that I believed her…but I was trying to get the picture.

"I'm back with Angie."

"I know."

"How the fuck do you know?"

"Kyle."

"Dog, fuck that motherfucker; he shouldn't be spreading my business around like that. What the fuck?" Kyle Sorum…why the fuck was he telling Fresca that shit?

"Oh stop it, Boo. Kyle's a good friend. He fills me in on you when I ask him. You know I was going to find out, sooner or later."

I dropped it because I could take it up with Kyle. All she was going to do was defend him. "So you were asking about me?"

"Not really. He was talking about some party and was explaining how you stopped showing up at them. He was trying to compliment you, not spread gossip. So then I asked him if you were dating anybody and he said you were back with Angie. He said Angie keeps you on a leash."

Bullshit.

"What the fuck ever, girl. What else is going around about me?"

"Bobbi told me that you're staying in Cheriton with Angie."

Bobbi…God dammit, my sister was really irritating my ass.

"Yeah," I admitted. I still couldn't admit to anyone that I had decided to marry Angie. Maybe I wasn't being real with myself.

I mean, I did want to marry her. If Fresca was serious about never going out with me, again, then yeah…I wanted to marry Angie, who was a better person to be around, anyways.

"Hey, I don't mean to cut you off or anything, but I have school tomorrow."

"School?"

And she explained how she took out a student loan for some cosmetology bullshit. She wanted to be a hair stylist and own a salon. I couldn't see Fresca running her own business with her dumb ass. She could barely pronounce words the right way, let alone read them.

If it wasn't for me, she'd still be in eighth grade. The bitch was dumb as fuck.

"How long have you been going?"

"Since August," Which was four months, now.

"Can you afford it?" Which I should give another fuck about, but I know she's always had money issues with her dad being the only one paying the bills.

"Yeah, that's why I have a job. I'm making payments. I have to take out another student loan for next semester."

"Oh." Since when did this girl make decisions and become so independent? Since she broke up with my ass?

I didn't like it. I don't know. I had been providing for this girl for years, now. I can't believe she was actually considering on doing something with her life. When she was with me, she wasn't going to work…ever.

Her entire future consisted on babies and marriage. That's all she wanted out of life. Well, not to mention the diamonds and purses, and clothes and shoes and…fuck, this broad was expensive to be with.

Angie wouldn't buy Wonder bread, let alone a diamond.

"Alright, baby girl, go to sleep." And I hung up before she could correct me.

I smiled all the way to my bed like a dumb ass I was. At least the girl could take care of herself. I didn't have to be the one making sure she had her head on right.

Although I never found out what the fuck woke me up and why I had that strange feeling of something going on…I was at peace. Fresca talked me into calmness, which was the first reason I ever asked her to go out with me.

She had a way of…I don't know. I was done thinking about her.

I wrapped my arms around Angie and fell fast asleep, only to dream about Fresca Taylor, the brace face that used to tease me about my twelve year old hair cut.

Chapter Seventy-Nine
Cardy

I sat at Ruth's desk, pouring tears into the receiver. I tried not to notice the two Security guards behind me, or Stan and Suavio to the sides of me.

Suavio, just to note, was this Puerto Rican man that had first floor night shift. He was tall and slender, with his Polo shirt always unbuttoned…all the way down. His chest hair eased out from time to time and he talked smoothly, as if he was trying to pull a broad. Suavio was his nickname I gave him because he thought he was suave.

Roma was upset and worried. She was who I called. "You're in the lobby? Cardy, you're not supposed to be out of your room. How…"

"Stan let me out and now I have all the security guards staring at me, Cindy. They're fucking wigging me out. I just wanna go home, I need you to take me home."

"And when you get there, what then?"

"I wanna sleep in my bed, Cindy. I'm fucking tired."

"Cardy, when you say 'home', who's in the house with you?" She was trying to use her wizardry on my ass. I wasn't down for a therapy session.

"My mom, my dad, my brother, Jeff."

"So Jeff would be home when you get there?"

I wasn't stupid…"I want him to be."

"But you do understand the situation?"

"He's in Italy, Roma, yes. I know."

Don't ask me why I was saying some fucked up shit. That dream had my head messed up. All I could think about was Boo not coming to save me and take me home. Now, all I wanted to do was go back to the past and sleep in my bed, the bed that Boo and Jeff used to stumble into so they could blow smoke in my face while I was sleeping.

I wanted to be fifteen, again. I didn't want this life. I didn't want to be here. I didn't want Jeff dead or my mom and dad divorced or Boo giving up on me.

I needed him.

"The first thing you need to understand, Cardy, and I know it's rough to hear this, but it has to be said. Jeff is dead. He's not in Italy, he's not at home. He's dead."

I thought about that stupid ass word as the tears formed a puddle over the keypad. Dead. I know he's dead. I saw him die. He haunts me in my dreams.

And, now…so does Boo.

I didn't answer.

"So that means Jeff won't be there when you get home."

"And my dad won't be, and my house won't be. Everything's fucked up." I didn't care that I was finally talking to Cindy in a way that she had wanted me to. I was so fucking sorry that my life was fucked up. I wanted to stop it.

"Do you miss him, Cardy?"

Do I miss him, what kind of question was that?

"You know, it was all because of me that he died. If I wasn't there that night, they wouldn't have argued over who I was going to drive with and Jeff wouldn't have made Wes try to lose Boo." She probably didn't understand a word I mumbled, but I said it.

There.

I had killed my brother Jeff and broke apart my parents and destroyed Boo and Fresca's relationship and disrespected my only brother left and…and…

"It's not your fault, Cardy." She lied.

"Come get me, Roma, I'm begging you, please, come get me. I need you. I don't want to go upstairs, I don't want to go to sleep, I just want you, only you. If any motherfucker puts a hand on me…I'll kill them, Cindy. I swear to God, I will. You're the only one I want."

Chapter Eighty
Dr. Cynthia Roma

I must be crazy driving out in this blizzard at three in the morning. This is insane. I could be blown off the freeway and my car could be buried with snow. With as much wind and snow falling, I could die, tonight. I really could.

But, Cardy needed me. I had to do this for Cardy. He confided in me and trusted me. He depended on me for support. I couldn't be more thrilled.

This was the friendship I was waiting for. We bonded. I earned his trust. He called me!!!!

He needed me!!!

Sure, he broke rules and expected people to abide by his own…but he cried out to me. The boy was crying as hard as he could into that phone.

This was it. The dam had cracked and there was about to be a flood of emotions pouring out of him. It was starting. It was happening.

Once this happens…the recovery can begin. He had to admit it, first.

Four hours later and I reach the big iron gates to Safe Haven. The weather had caused detours and delays, especially since it was before sunrise and not many crazy cars were plowing the streets for me.

But I made it. I was here. Forget sleep. Coffee, cigarettes, and candy bars full of sugar were doing the trick. I was awake and ready to make the biggest breakthrough in my career.

I was going to save a lost boy.

I was going to save Christopher Deburke come sleet or shine, ice or fire, even if it was the death of me.

The security guards were on full alert to my arrival. The night shift was long over with and the new shift was filling me in on the drama as if I wasn't part of it. It was some night, they say.

Nobody liked to deal with Cardy. What happened last night was one of their fears. Everybody expected it to go down worse than it did. Cardy had put everyone on their toes and they were relieved that they made it through.

Yes, Cardy was stubborn and strong willed. He could out power many of our staff and had taken swings at most of them. He was a child that was going to go down in history as one of their hardest accomplishments, but yes, indeed, Cardy was going to be an accomplishment.

Today, in fact.

"He's not in the Reformatory, is he?" I didn't want to walk into a padded cell and watch Cardy pace like a wild animal, ready to spit at me, again.

Suavio, um, I mean Ricardo, had stayed behind to exclaim his innocence to Dean. He approached me with good news. And let me tell you, I couldn't believe my ears.

Ricardo beamed with a grin, chest proudly protruding with honor. "He went back up to his room to wait for you. When Stan told him that you were on your way but would probably be held up by the snow, he sat on his bed, wrote in his notebook. He passed out about an hour ago. I think he wrote for three hours straight. I bet there's some good stuff in there, you think?"

I couldn't contain myself. I squeezed the thin guy against my bosom and kissed him on the lips. "You're kidding! Oh my goodness, that's great! I can't believe it! I can't wait to read it!!!"

He blushed and grinned harder as if he had talked Cardy out of escaping.

I don't think the boy wanted to escape or he would have. Cardy wanted me.

He couldn't have his mother, his father, his brother…so he wanted me. How awesome was that?

And it was even better!!!

He wrote in his journal. He put the pen to the paper and calmed himself down. He had found a release and used it. All this time trying to drill it in his head and he was actually listening to me. He wrote everything that popped into his mind…I hope.

I was stopped by every staff member that had the morning shift. I quickened my steps, said what I had to say and tried my damndest to get to Cardy, my prized pupil.

Oh beautiful baby, there you are.

He looked like an innocent baby, long and athletically built, but baby, no doubt. He was sprawled out on his stomach, face towards me. His eyes swollen, but shut. He was shirtless, tattoos ruining his innocent posture, but still a baby to me.

Cardy would always remain a baby in my eyes…because I comforted him.

To the side of him lay that red notebook, no longer in perfect shape. For months, now, it looked brand new, untouched. Now, the papers were thick, bulging from ink. The cover was scratched and bent, jagged along the bottom.

I wasn't about to wake him up and ask permission to read it. This was one of those important confiscations. I had to know what went on in his head last night.

I flipped it open.

It was like a scrapbook that a child had used over a number of years. It was more like something a five year old would scribble out their ABC's on, some backwards, some missing. There wasn't much organization to the words. Some were aligned around the holes, causing me to turn it sideways to understand what it was saying.

I knew better to misjudge this masterpiece. This was a work of art, the mind hard at work with obsessive thoughts.

It was his breaking moment of truth, like a raw egg shell that cracked and the contents spilled out causing a sticky mess. It was still able to form an edible egg, nevertheless.

I was more than thrilled. I was honored and relieved that he did this. He had swallowed his pride and let this obsession take over in such a positive way.

I can dissect this egg yolk. I can collect the contents and form a chicken, a chirping, hopping baby chick ready to peck at the world. Yes, indeed, Cardy is recovering.

Here I am, reading every topic that I had mentioned in class. It was done all in a night's time.

Wow, when this boy did something, he was determined to cause an explosion. Sure, it took a lot of prodding and waiting, but…And I knew…I knew within a few encounters with this boy…that he had all the potential he needed. The keywords were "time and trust." Most give up and turn criminal…

But I don't.

Cardy doesn't.

This is proof enough.

He was an artist, a poet, a child at his best. He was a natural writer and full of intelligence undercover. The world had done him wrong and he knew it…but it was time to write it down so it can be stored away and titled "Past."

Time to overcome. All is strong when pushed in a corner. All has the ability of power when pushed towards a cliff.

But who is willing to jump and risk fate?

Cardy.

Fear, he wrote. He listed his fears, ending in his worst fear…himself. *love,* he circled. He wrote all the names of his family, extending outward. Bin was there. Jebb Deburke was there. Basia was there. His children…there.

He never mentioned his children to me. It was Bin who told me.

Pain, he sketched, with all the needles and drugs, knives and guns drawn out. Stairs he drew, looking up from the bottom of them. Broken bottles and lightning bolts, cars crashing into one another…a line at the top and Jeff underlined above it.

His heaven, his Italy.

Fathers, he dedicated an entire page, perfect handwriting and full sentences devoted to a confession from a father. He was sorry. He did exactly what he didn't want to do…abandon.

A Poem was thick upon the next page, so dark that the paper had deep imprints of the pressure of his hand. It was beautiful…a poet, screaming out his pain.

Peel me from the shadow of yesteryear,
It casts an evil glow.
Stretch me from the reach of yesterday,
Because I need to grow.
Strip me of the strings of destitute,
They're tangled above a bridge,
Toss me to the heavens of the present,
So I may have yet to live.

So sincere in the moment, so true in the words, he has a great gift in writing. And I think he already knew this.

He just couldn't get it out.

Hello Christopher, nice to meet you. You can call me Cindy.

Chapter Eighty-One
Basia

"Are you sure you're mom's not going to mind me and Jasmine here?" I dropped Jasmine to the floor and looked around.

This place wasn't like Darron's house. There were rules and guidelines and curfews and…a mother who took charge and confronted the issues at stake. Susan was a good hard working mother.

Susan did what she had to do for her girls. She worked late nights so she could keep an eye on them during the day. Her nursing job paid the mortgage, the utilities, and the car payment, not to mention the insurance bills and groceries. She was a nurse and made good money, but they still had to budget.

Yes, they always had new clothes and shoes and expensive backpacks and things like that. Susan made sure that all her extra money went to Angie and Amanda. Susan saved money and tried to stash away some for Amanda's college. (Angie didn't need a savings account for college, as Boo was paying for her tuition.)

I liked Susan in that sense.

But to be under her roof and following her rules?

What were they again? I tried to remember Amanda's schedule…

Amanda had to be in her room at nine and in bed at ten. She could stay up until eleven on weekends, but no leaving the house or answering the phone. No boys were allowed in the house…ever. They ate at six. Homework was to be done right after school.

Yeah see, I remember.

Do I remember my set routine when I actually had parents?

Not really.

Okay, okay, I can do this. It's been awhile, but I can live by set rules. It'll be good for me.

"Are you going to go back to school?" Amanda broke my concentration as she took my old ninth grade backpack from me. It had all the clothes I owned in it, mine and Jasmine's.

"I don't want to. What if Anthony's still in my class?" Saying his name made me cringe.

"Well, my mom won't let a drop out live here. She's serious about school, Basia. If you want to stay here, you have to go. We can talk to the teachers about having Anthony removed."

I gave her an evil glare. "I don't want them to know. I don't want anyone to know, maybe he dropped out." And I left it at that. No need to think about that, tonight. I had to figure out where I was going to sleep for the rest of my life.

"You can share a bed with me; do you think Jasmine would sleep on the floor? Wait," And Amanda ran out of her room. Minutes later, she drug a folded up play pen through the doorway. She struggled with it to open.

"Devon never uses this. Our house is too small to get some use out of it. When Angie wants to lay him down, she puts him in his crib. I'm sure with the circumstances she'll let you use it. It's just sitting in our closet." The top of the thing stretched upright and the bottom gave a thudding drop. There, she did it. It was set up.

Now where to put it?

Amanda's room was cluttered. She had her twin size bed in the middle, her dresser to the right, and a chest to the left. A stereo rack was on the wall near the door and clothes piled the carpet. A bookcase was shoved in the corner and it housed many breakable knickknacks.

Oh no.

"Jasmine will never stop touching those." I admitted. Amanda was a collector of all sorts of things. Don't get her started. She'll show you her stamp collection that her grandpa started her on. She has a coin collection in her closet. She has a glass pickle jar of bottle caps, a soda bottle of can tops, a gum collection, a sticker collection, and…last but not least…knickknacks of clowns, elephants, and monkeys. Oh, and dogs, she collected little sad puppy dog faces.

She wasn't the only one in this house to clutter her room with junk.

Angie used to collect New Kid on the Block memorabilia. Right before she met Boo was the time she took down the posters of Donnie and Jordan. Talk about late…yeah. She used to collect posters of all sorts of boys…Zack Morris of Saved By the Bell, Cory Heim from Lost Boys, Jeremy Jordan, some singer, Brad Pitt…yeah, that's just a few of her hot blondes. My father would burn my room down with all the papered testosterone going on.

Now…as I grin to myself…all Angie can collect are diapers and toys. I wasn't the only one without a childhood, anymore.

"There." Amanda stuffed the play pen in the corner and it tilted. A bunch of clothes were underneath it. Amanda didn't seem to mind or notice. I wasn't about to complain. There wasn't really any other place to jam it.

I smiled, politely. Amanda was, once again, going out of her way to help me out.

I gave her a big hug. "Thank you, Amanda." I knew it was never going to be enough to repay her with. All I could offer is my gratitude, which I forgot to give Darron.

"If you were Becca or Loren with a baby…I'd say no with no hesitation. Can you imagine them with a kid?" We both snickered at the thought.

Becca would have her daughter looking like a china doll, face painted like a clown and fancy silk outfits that fit snug at the wrists. Loren would dye her daughter's hair purple and braid it like Pippy Longstocking. Remember her?

"But," Amanda hugged back. "You are who you are and I like helping you. You're a good person, Basia. You don't deserve this. You should be practicing medicine by now…with your test scores."

I smiled, again. I was never going to smart enough for that, now. I lost all hope.

"Hey, if I go to school and Darron isn't babysitting…"

Jeesh, Darron did do a lot for me.

"We'll figure something out. After winter break, I'm sure we'll have somebody to watch her. My mom might if it means that you can go back to school. You know how nice she is."

Oh Susan, I'm not your daughter, though. Why would you help me?

Chapter Eighty-Two
Cardy

I found solitude and peace with my next dream. As I slept the day away, I was no longer angry.

Boo and Jeff didn't exist. In fact, my past wasn't real to me. Everything that crossed my dream state was simple and pure…relaxed and safe…nice and peaceful.

I remember the feeling. It was strong and lasting. As I walked down the halls at Safe Haven, my chest was loose, my breathing sublime. My body drifted along the lines of happiness as my fingers felt the textured wallpaper. I was paying close attention to detail in this dream because nothing else was taking up my focus.

The leaves on a plant caught my gaze, simple and green, so perfect in form. The lines etched outward causing a pattern of veins. I didn't once think of Heroin. Or needles. Or drugs…or cigarettes.

I thought of a path where water traveled to and from, giving life to such a beautiful structure. Sure, it was just a plant sitting on a table…but to live, to once live, no matter what it was…to live…was a relief.

I felt alive in my dream. All I did was walk down the hallway and see a plant, but I felt alive. I felt like I was one with that plant…I connected to it. And that's all the matter in the world to me, right now.

To live,
To start over,
To be as simple as a plant,
Live.

As I opened my eyes, Cindy sat next to me. I knew she would come. I knew she would sit there and stare at me…and read my notebook.

I couldn't tell her the things that I wanted to. I couldn't explain the feelings that had been bottled up inside of me for so long.

But I could write.

And I told her in the only way I knew how.

And she read me the only way she knew how.

And for once, I got it across.

She could understand me because she could take my writing and "dissect" it.

No matter what I wrote, she understood it. Don't ask me why or how…but she knew.

I knew she knew when we traded glares.

My eyes found her as I lay silently still. With all that written, I still couldn't speak to her. All I could do is stare. And for now, it was all she needed.

She smiled and rubbed my hair back.

I reached for her hand and held it to my face, so close to my lips. All I wanted to do was kiss it, kiss her. I wanted to thank her for staying with me…not abandoning me or losing hope like so many did.

"I'm so proud of you, Cardy." She dared a whisper into the air.

I squeezed my eyes shut as I wasn't expecting that remark.

She was proud…

of me.

My mom used to say that.

Now we have a problem.

If she was proud…I couldn't disappoint her. I was on a personal level, now.

I never wanted to go there with her or anyone else, again.

And here I am.

Fuck. I can't fuck up, again. I can't disappoint her like I did the rest of my family and friends.

This is my new beginning, my fresh start.

It starts with Cindy…my shrink.

My throat was dry and tight. I forced the words out harshly. "Thank you," I managed to say. *Thank God, thank you, thank everything…*

And then it hit me. The instability that I was cursed with took hold. "I wanna go home." I barreled my face into my pillow as my pride drained to hell. "I just want to be done with this place and go home. I don't care where home is or where it's at; I just want to go home."

It was a horrible confession, a horrible emptiness that replaced my pride. I was no longer angry. I was no longer mad at the world and wanting to fight.

I wanted to go home. That was all there was to it. Home. I found my heart, now take me home.

Cindy cradled my shoulders and laid her head against my neck. "You will, Cardy, soon. You will go home, I promise."

I wish she wouldn't promise. Promises weren't always a guarantee.

"Okay." I sniffed like a damn baby.

"I want my mom."

I refused to say dad.

I really wanted my dad. I was worried for him. If he didn't have Jeff or my mom, he had no one. I don't care if he beat me. That was his way. I don't care if he held a grudge against me.

Somewhere in my childhood, he had been there. And I know that he feels the same way about me. It was that love/hate thing…but it was something.

I wanted my dad…the one who bought me my first bike and telescope, the one who drilled in my head to go to school and get perfect attendance.

You never know how much of an impact a routine is on someone until it was gone.

And my dad, who wasn't my dad…was gone…forever.

Chapter Eighty-Three
Binderman

I was sick. I never get sick. This is the second time in the past six months that I was sick. I don't understand it. I wash my hands, constantly. I use napkins on doorknobs. I wipe shit up, I disinfect. I take shower after shower. I am a fucking clean freak and I still get fucking sick.

"You don't have a fever, your nose isn't running, you don't have a cough, you don't feel hot…" Angie didn't believe me. But what did she know? I wasn't a damn baby. She only knew what to look for in babies.

"I'm sick, Angie. Something's wrong with me. I haven't felt good all week."

"Headache?"

"No."

"Stomach ache?"

"It doesn't hurt, but I feel nauseous."

"Maybe you have the flu."

I rolled my eyes and wouldn't get out of bed. It wasn't just because it was Sunday and I wanted to avoid church. I swear it wasn't that. But she thought it was.

"Can't you just stay behind, today? My Grams doesn't need you. She has all the old ladies to chat with. She'll be fine."

"That's not why I go."

"Fine, go, I'll just die right here in bed while you sing to God. Maybe you should pray for me, go light a candle or some shit."

She frowned in disbelief. "You shouldn't say things like that, Boo. You're gonna go to hell."

"I'm sure I'll be in hell then before you get back."

"Oh come on, you're not that bad."

"How do you know?"

"Because you don't have a fever."

"Oh fuck a fever, I'm sick and something feels wrong."

"Maybe it's your conscience."

"Maybe it's my foot up your ass."

I didn't feel like being nice, today. I was sick and she should stay behind for me. I don't get sick. Something was wrong.

"You're such a baby. You feel like throwing up and everything should stop to hail your every need?"

"Yeah," I sneered.

She sighed and continued brushing her teeth in my bedroom.

"You're disgusting; go do that where you're supposed to." I rolled over and covered my face.

Angie, who came a long way from being the nervous little virgin that lay beneath me, too conscious of her body to move or make a noise…stood there. Angie stood there like the brat I made girls into. I don't know what it is about me. Girls liked to piss me off when they got to know me.

She grinned with toothpaste on the corners of her lips. She opened her mouth and stuck out her tongue. "Make me. You're too sick to do anything about it."

I smiled at her deviant behavior. It was new to me, kind of challenging.

"Angie, I'm gonna fuck you up…" I smiled, jumping out of bed and chasing her back to the bathroom where she closed the door in my face.

I wasn't really sick. I mean, I felt sick…but I knew there wasn't a doctor in the world to cure me. Something else was wrong with me. Something was going on in my head. Maybe Angie was right.

Maybe it was my conscious. Cardy still sat in rehab…alone. Fresca sat in her house…alone. My mom was…alone.

Although I had Angie and Devon…Brandon and Grams…Bobbi and my dad…all the fucking friends that I could need…all the bitches that would drop in my path with a blink of an eye…I too, felt alone.

It made me sick.

Moments later, Grams appeared with Angie backing her up. Devon was in tow and Brandon was attached to Angie's leg, laughing at nothing in particular.

"I don't tell you what to do most of the time, Binderman, but I'm telling you now. Get up off your bottom and throw a suit on. I've been telling everyone how good my grandson is and they think I'm full of it. I told them you go to church in Pierre when you don't show up. Hattie specifically told me that she wanted you to meet her grandson, today. Maybe the two of you can go golfing or something."

Golf.

"Hattie can suck…"

"What?" My Grams interrupted my foul mouth.

"I don't care."

"I'll get out the spatula, Binderman Joseph Sox!"

I grinned wider. Grams never used the spatula on me but I saw her do it to Cody a million and a half times, so long ago. I couldn't imagine her little arms raising it again.

"Fine!" I mumbled and rolled out of bed. "But I need a shower."

"You don't need anything but your grey suit."

"I'm not wearing grey, today." She didn't get the privilege of dressing me. I wore what the fuck I wanted to wear, when I wanted to wear it. People don't understand how important it is for me to feel in my clothes. Grey wasn't doing it, today. Fuck that.

"Put something appropriate on, at least."

"Grams…out!" I pointed at the doorway as she paced her way towards my closet. "I might wear a jersey if you don't get downstairs, I swear on…"

"Uh, uh, uh…don't even say it. Never swear, Binji." Her bony ringed finger waved as she turned.

I rolled my eyes in annoyance. I sighed as the door closed and thought about wearing a jersey for the fuck of it.

This was bullshit, you know. I wasn't used to doing anything I was told. I was never told to do shit. I answered to myself and only myself for the past two years.

I definitely wasn't singing. I'll bend at the pews, I'll flip the pages, I'll stand and I'll kneel. I'm not singing. I don't even want to be touched by all the old ladies who tell me I'm the cutest in the world. I don't wanna hear about granddaughters and their little lies about how sweet they are. I know the bitches. They're all sluts.

Oh.

"Grams…" I ran down the stairs in a fucking black suit and tie and felt too dressed for the occasion. "Hey, do I…" She fixed my tie better as I stopped in front of her. "Do I take communion?"

"What do you think?" Her suspicious eyes warned.

"I think I can, I mean, tell me some things why I shouldn't take it." I didn't want to tell her I was having sex. She already knew it, but I didn't want to say it.

"If you don't take it, they're going to ask me why you didn't take it."

I shrugged. I didn't give a fuck what they thought. "Fine."

Why did shit matter to motherfuckers? I hated having to please people.

"Good boy." She patted my back.

I only grinned at Angie as to what I had to put up with when I came to Grams. I loved her, respected her…I hated to go places with her. She treated me like I was a baby.

I swear she'd dress me and try to control my fucking hair. She used to brush it when I was little. I'd go home and my mom would have to wet it and scrunch it back up to get the curls back. I think Grams knew it made her mad. Grams was annoying when it came to what she liked and what others liked.

Chapter Eighty-Four
Cardy

January, February, March...April, May, June. I watched the calendar of days flip and flip. I was coming around and meeting my prerequisites for discharge. I didn't misbehave and never saw the prison cell, again.

I didn't and couldn't mesh with the others, though. I didn't walk around like a brainwashed zombie, minding my own business and getting to class on time. No...that just wasn't me. I stopped trying to be "them."

I was who I was and couldn't deny it. I had found a routine, one that kept my energy at bay. Even with the medicine, I had this natural adrenaline that needed to be occupied. Every day, at five in the morning, I jogged around the basketball court.

Cindy had bought me a portable CD player and a couple of CD's. They were Limp Bizkit, Kid Rock, and the Offspring. It was by request. Trust me. She had a hard time asking for them at the store. She thought the names were too crazy too ask for, being her age.

I jogged about fifteen laps around the basketball court, listening to music. Then I took a shower and smoked a cigarette in the stall. I was one of the first ones in the cafeteria, too. I got the fresh shit and a big variety of it. Whoever paid for my food should be running low, nowadays. I ate and packed on some pounds.

After breakfast, I went to anger management and controlled my temper fits, lucky them, not me. I went to American History and studied the civil war...etc. etc. American Literature made me read books and Cindy's class made me write books. My math teacher was still in awe and said I need to go to college and use my potential.

Yeah right.

Nah, for real, I was thinking about college. Even though when I get out of here, I'd still have to finish school or get my GED, I was seriously thinking about attending a school out of state. I wanted some place new.

I wasn't much of a repetitive type of person. I needed new challenges and risks. I needed new things to hold my attention and keep me interested. I don't know...I think going to school abroad would be cool.

Nothing was in Pierre, not anymore. Pierre was boring. It was holding me back from what I wanted to accomplish.

Once, Cindy made us write an essay on what we would do if we could do anything in the world. A lot of students had trouble choosing.

Not me.

I wrote everything down. Of course, I couldn't choose just one. Instead of staring at a blank ass piece of paper, I wrote it all.

Skydiving, rock climbing, scuba diving, parasailing, bungee jumping, snowboarding, flying a jet, nose diving in a jet...I'd like to travel the world and see all the cool monuments, too. The Eiffel Tower, the Coliseum, Niagara Falls...I'd like to jump off that...

I don't know what the fuck was up with me and heights. It was a free falling kind of feeling...breathtaking, exciting...I don't know. It was hard to explain. I just loved the freedom to fly and fall...to escape and drop.

Anyways, I was cool with everyone. Everyone knew and respected me. If there were girls here...I'd be "Prince of Safe Haven." But because of no girls, there was no gossip, no competition and no labels. I guess girls made the world turn.

Right now, nothing fucking happens at Safe Haven unless I make it happen. When I come into the room...shit happens. I make sure of it.

I get old Ruth smiling and blushing when I'm around her. She's a widow and lives alone. Her daughter went off to college and all she does is play bingo. I just throw some of my charm on her and she turns red. I do it just because I can. It makes her happy.

I make bets with Stan and Pete on anything, even something little. One of our bets was making Ruth blush within ten seconds or twenty seconds. I had her in five seconds and Stan had to do my chore of that week. One kiss on the cheek did it.

I've made a basketball team that sucks. It's still a team and we play every day, but they suck. Charles can't jump and shoot at the same time and Brett (I got him to play) isn't worth shit, either. But like I said, I got a game going and it gets people playing ball with me. One day I had Cindy playing, but Dean got pissed.

My goal is to get Dean on the court. He's such a tight ass. Stan bet me a hundred dollars that it'll never happen. Yeah, one way or another…Dean was getting on the court. I just needed a plan.

The kids looked up to me for some reason. I don't know why. I'm still stubborn and refuse a lot of shit. Sure, I stay out of trouble, but I'm stubborn as hell. I speak my mind way more than I should and people expect it. When someone tells me what to do, they all stop and wait for my reply.

I'm conceited and flaunt it. I'm competitive and get pissed when I lose. I hardly ever lose. I'm the best and everyone needs to know it.

I smoke a pack a day, which I have to whine to Cindy to give me. See, nothing about me is worth looking up to. Cigarettes play a big role with me. If I didn't have them, a lot of people would be pissed off at me and I'd be a lost cause.

The only thing I can come up with is that I bring character to a classroom. I'm expected to be me, which makes the day worth waking up to…I don't fucking know. People love Cardy Deburke and I'm stumped about it.

I don't intimidate them to like me. I don't threaten or warn or control them. I guess I just keep it real…keep me real. I'm not out to prove shit, anymore. I don't try to make people like me. I don't try to fit in. See, the way I see it, people need to adjust around *me*, or else we're gonna have a problem. That's the way I have to look at it.

And Cindy…ha, this girl is cool. If she was eighteen, I'd maul her. She's so naïve, yet smart and funny, yet corny and outdated…she's just another weird piece of the puzzle to add at Safe Haven. I know for a fact that if she wasn't there, I'd be in prison by now. I would have killed Dean or something.

I cling to Cindy like she's my girlfriend, yet mother, yet my sister. I respect her in all those aspects. Most of all, she's my friend and I can tell her things that no one else can tell their family.

I think everyone needs someone like that…someone to listen and not judge, someone in neutral territory who won't convict you for what you do and say. They just want to understand. That's it. Cindy has made a commitment to understand me, nothing else.

If more people were like her, seeking out an understanding in everything that everybody does…maybe more people would feel safe at being who they really are, no more fake shit.

I don't know. I'm fucking…sorry, I mean, I'm gathering the day's laundry, going down the halls, watching all these mother…fuck, I mean…I'll start over…I'm collecting the kids' laundry for the day and all I have to do while doing this is think…think, think, think. I come up with a lot shit in my head when I'm focused and listening to music in the background…even if it is rock music pounding in my ears.

What I'm trying to say is…I'm adjusting…adapting to this shit hole. Once you get used to it, it becomes more of a playground, a home. I'm trying not to cuss just because it makes people think I'm from a lower class than I actually am.

Cindy likes to say that people cuss because it adds character…attitude. Curse words emphasize your anger and emotions. It draws attention for people to listen to you. A lot of kids who aren't heard say a lot bad words, she says. It starts with your parents. Kids who aren't heard by their parents start to cuss and then it becomes habit. I don't know about you, but it's a harder habit than going a day without squares. It comes natural after a while. I have to listen to myself before I even begin to correct my speech. Listening is pretty hard.

What the hell…

"Why the fuck do you have all these towels in here?" I squinted at Eddie, some quiet kid who just got here a month ago.

I stood in this doorway as he knotted the towels together. I didn't know what the hell he was thinking about, but I didn't feel like picking them up or taking them from him.

"None of your fucking business." He snapped without looking up. He squeezed two towels together to tighten the knot.

Motherfucker.

"It is my fucking business, stupid ass. Put the towels in the basket or I'm fucking kicking your ass." It was a threat that I didn't want to follow through on because I knew I'd be sent to the pads. I was able to use my head and remember the consequences, for once.

"Oh yeah?" Needle nosed prick ass motherfucking jack ass piece of shit said.

"Yeah, motherfucker!" I shoved him back as he approached me like he could do something. I hated little newcomers who did that shit.

His eyes sized me up as if I was smaller than him. He was a small prick, no doubt. I give him credit for not being a pussy, but still. He didn't need to fuck with me. He didn't know me enough to back away. Close his mouth.

I shoved him back with all my force, skidding him across the floor like a skateboard. I laughed as I did it. Stupid ass.

He jumped up and charged, but was intercepted by Stan, Stan my man. He saved my ass from going back to the pads.

"What the hell's going on?" Stan looked from me to Eddie and quickly back to me for an answer.

"He won't give me his towels and I don't know why he has all of them in the first place."

"He pushed me!"

"You started it!" I grinned.

"Finish your job, Cardy." Stan flatly insisted. "I'll deal with him."

I left and made my rounds on fourth floor. That was kind of fun, but dangerous. I was so close to putting him in his place and I knew it was ridiculous.

People don't fuck with me. They know not to fuck with me. People who fuck with me get their ass whooped. That's me…

Cardy Deburke.

Don't fuck with me and I'm all good.

Chapter Eighty-Five
Angie

January, February, March…the months just flew by. I was Boo's girlfriend and Devon's mother. I was Grams partner at church and Brandon's surrogate mother. I don't know anything about Lynn and don't know why she's out of the picture.

Boo said that she never wanted a picture in the first place and was probably slutting it up and OD'ing in the mean time. She had her freedom back and no strings attached to her past. It was an awful way of looking at it.

I felt bad for Brandon. I mean, he was in good hands and didn't know the difference. He didn't miss Lynn or Cardy because he was too little to remember them. Boo treated him just like he did Devon, if not better. But still, I knew he didn't have a mother and no matter what I did for him, I knew he wasn't mine.

And the clothes Boo put him in, my lord!

Brandon was sixteen months old and wearing a necklace that Boo insisted on him keeping. I wouldn't let Devon wear one. See, the issue worth arguing about was this: whatever Boo wanted Devon to wear, eat, etc…and I wouldn't allow it, he had Brandon to do it with. Brandon was indeed, Boo's little doll to brag about.

Boo got his way with Brandon because Brandon wasn't mine. I didn't really care and had no right when it came to Brandon's appearance. Where Devon had a cute boyish "bowl" haircut, Brandon had the all famous buzz cut that Boo had. Where Devon wore cartoon shirts, like Elmo and Winnie the Pooh…Brandon wore Gap and Nautica, Tommy and Ralph Lauren. It was ridiculous and not worth wasting money over, if you ask me.

Brandon was growing like a weed, as tall as Devon, already. One day he wore eighteen months in size, the next he's in 2T. His shoes were baby Jordan's and Boo had to buy three pair because Brandon went from a size 5 to a size 7, skipping a size 6. Did Boo return them like a regular shopper would do? No. He just bought new ones.

People in Cheriton thought we had twins, as they really did look alike. We just dressed them differently. We didn't care to explain the situation because it was an awful situation to get into. What were we suppose to say?

No, Brandon isn't ours, he's Boo's brother's, who's in rehab for Heroin, and his mother is doing Heroin as we speak and doesn't have custody over him, so now we have him. Yeah, people didn't need to know our business. It wasn't right.

Anyways, we were a family of four, a happy family who lived in Cheriton at the famous Lillian Manor with the famous Victoria Lillian as our Grams. It was a spotlight ordeal and I was rather fond of it. Boo…well, he was used to it.

Boo was coming along just fine. He was a good daddy who sat at the edge of the bathtub and watched the boys splash and laugh at bubbles. He tucked them in, walked them to bed, once more, and sang them to sleep when they squirmed to stay up.

We went everywhere together. We went shopping and church. We ate at restaurants and played at the park. We were a very well behaved, civilized family of Cheriton status. It was habit forming to me. I really, really, really enjoyed this lifestyle.

Boo was *not* the Boo Sox that I had met my junior year. Boo was *not* the Boo Sox who cheated on Fresca…or me, even. He was a different changed man who realized his priorities and adapted to his surroundings. Thankfully, he was in Cheriton, far enough away from the influence of his friends.

I felt secure with him. In fact, I trusted him.

It was March…1999…when he asked me, again.

We were lying in bed. We had just put the boys to sleep and Devon for once, had fell asleep with Brandon in his crib. I sank into the mattress with a sigh. My intentions were to close my eyes and fall fast asleep. His…were different.

He stared up at the ceiling for a long time, quietly, patiently, and deep in thought. I found out that when he was deep in thought…or nervous…he bit his cuticles. That's why he had manicures all the time. He bit his nails.

He glanced over at me, who already knew he was up to something, just not sure of it.

He turned to face me and stared into my eyes. He didn't say anything, as he was still biting.

"What?"

"I don't know." He sighed.

"What do you mean, you don't know? You're thinking about something, I know that much." His eyes were searching mine for a decision. His eyes were in a trance, glossy and focused. He wasn't really focused in on me…it was more "through" me.

"Do you like living here?"

Here we go. This analyzing bull crap got on my nerves. He'd start with a stupid question like this, and then more, and then he'd have this irrational idea that didn't make sense.

"Uh, yeah?" I rolled my eyes.

"No, I mean, like forever. Devon could go to St. Paul Academy. They have a preschool. Maybe Brandon could go, too. If something ever happens to Grams, I can take over this place and we can live here, forever. It could be ours." His eyes continued to search and read my inner thoughts.

Ours?

I could have part of the Lillian Manor? This estate was worth more than a million, maybe a billion dollars or so. I could own it?

No way.

"I'd like him to go to St. Paul. It's the best school around here." It was one of two private schools and one of five school districts total in St. Paul. Why wouldn't I want him to attend the top school?

"Everything that I have could be yours, too."

"Okay…" I drained from my voice not understanding the full impact of his conversation.

"So you'd marry me now?"

BAM, I wasn't expecting that. I don't know why I wasn't expecting it, but I wasn't.

I jerked my eyes to the ceiling and thought long and hard about it. I felt his eyes on my every move, waiting for my reply.

What was I scared of? I mean, he was a good guy, now. We worked out perfectly, together. We were a family of four, remember? I was telling me this as I thought about everything.

It wasn't about the money or manor. It wasn't about St. Paul Academy or owning half of everything that Boo owned. It was…it was…

I could easily say no because I didn't love him. I don't know why I didn't love him but I didn't. I tried to convince myself that love was a fairy tale thing and the reality of it was…there wasn't true love at first sight. Love might be something that was made and formed, and bonded together. It was glue; it was…it was…

Oh what the hell.

"Mm' kay." I mumbled through my hands as I placed them over my mouth for protection.

He jerked suddenly, forcing my hands from my mouth and sitting halfway up. "What was that?" I know he was surprised to hear a slight possibility of agreement, even if he was mistaken.

I squeezed my eyes shut as if it would make everything easier to admit to. "I said okay!" I squealed with a little bit more excitement.

He grinned with a small laugh. "Are you fucking kidding me?" Like he never thought I would say yes.

"I don't believe you. Seriously, I don't." He sounded as if he wanted to take the proposal back, as if it was easier to ask when he knew I'd say no.

Did he really mean it? Did he really want to marry Angela Debrowski, the fat chick he knocked up on accident? This is what I was worried about when he didn't believe my answer. I was getting paranoid.

"If you want me to say no…"

He jerked me up by the shoulders with a panic. "No, no, I don't want you to say no. I want you to say yes, but do you really want to marry me?!"

"What did I say, Boo? Don't make me say it again." I was confused on what to do, what to say, how to react, how to respond, all that bull crap that went along with insecurity.

"Say it one more time…please. I wanna hear you say it." He begged, now on his knees…in his boxers, wide grin getting bigger and bigger by the mere on-the-spot-moment.

He was such a kid, I swear.

"Fine," I rolled my eyes with a smile forming in the back of my head. "I want to marry you, King Sox, the high and mighty Boo. I hail you, oh greatness." I bowed down, trying to ruin the moment and break the ice as best as I could.

He frowned and shoved me back against the bed. "Now you have to say it again because you fucked it up. Say it right."

"No, Boo. This isn't a game. I'm not saying it again and if you make me do it, then I'll take it back. I won't marry you. I'll leave you at the altar or something."

"Don't you fucking dare," He snarled it. The thought was now haunting him.

I laughed and hit him. "I'm not gonna leave you standing at the altar, Boo. I swear on my sister. I want to marry you," I sat up rather forcefully and began to back him up. He dropped backwards and watched my next move with raised eyebrows. He was surprised at my boldness.

"I want to marry you and it's not because of what you want to give me, so don't ever think that." For once in my life, I initiated a kiss…and then some. I straddled his boxers and let my new found revelation take over.

"I won't." He tried to say as I kissed him harder. His arms were shaky, his body kind of weak. I think he let me take over that night. I don't know. Maybe I had shocked the shit out of him and now he didn't know how to respond. I was usually rather predictable…and now…well, I said yes, didn't I?

He didn't know how to handle me. He just stopped taking control.

Chapter Eighty-Six
Basia

"Guess what, guess what, GUESS WHAT?!" Amanda screamed and jumped and grinned all at the same time.

"What?" I snatched the snickers from Jasmine's grip and tossed it carelessly onto Amanda's dresser. Jasmine was covered in chocolate, head to toe. It was smeared under her eyes, hanging from her hair, over her shirt, and wedged between her toes. Tell me how this happens, please? I didn't even know she took the damn thing. One minute she was here, next thing I know she came walking into the bedroom with shit allllllllllllll over her.

Amanda had to touch me. She had to hug me, squeeze me, and attempt to twirl me around until I fell dizzily onto her…our…bed. "My sister's getting married, my sister's getting married…and she's marrying Boo freaking Sox and there's going to be a wedding…and I'm the maid of honor, and I'm the maid of honor!!!" She sung her heart out as best as she could.

"What?!" I screeched. For some reason, I was offended that the Cardy look alike was now getting married and legally off limits and that Angie got to live with Cardy's twin and sleep with Cardy's twin for the rest of her freaking life!!!

"Boo proposed to Angie…last night!!!" Her head was in the clouds a little too long. Those clouds must've contained Novocain or marijuana smoke or something. She was high off her high horse and needing to drop to a rocky bottom to get her head on right. Jeesh.

"And she said yes?" I couldn't get it through my thick dumb skull that Boo was getting married. He was the only one I could look at, daydream of, and drool over because he looked exactly like Cardy and I still didn't understand why. I stopped searching for an answer. All I know is that he looked, smelled, walked, talked, acted like Cardy and I was in love with Cardy and he was my surrogate Cardy figure.

And he's gone!!!!!

I wanted to cry!

"Of course she said yes. Why wouldn't she? She's living a dream life! She's in Cheriton, Basia. Who gets to live in Cheriton? And he's so good to her. And he's such a good father and he has Brandon and..."

"Yeah, yeah, yeah, I don't care." I couldn't help it. I didn't care. Sorry, but I didn't. I'm gonna hate Angie all the way up to Cardy's arrival.

"What do you mean, you don't care? You should be happy for her! I know I am. My mom's even happy for her!" I couldn't ruin Amanda's mood if I clubbed her with her curling iron...while it was hot.

"I am, trust me. I am ecstatic about it. Whoopee! Hurray for Angie! She has a bitch of a sister in law!!! Yippee!" Now that seemed like something to be giggly about. Bobbi as a sister in law? On every family get together, Angie had to deal with that...and that didn't like her because that was still attached to Boo's old girlfriend. Yeah, I know the story. Gossip gets around quite well when you're friends with Becca Mantel, not that I see her much, but that was something that was relayed to me.

"OH, Basia, stop it. You're so selfish, lately. Do you want to be in the wedding? I bet Angie would make you a bride's maid."

I bet I get to see Boo more if I was...

"No, no, that's alright. I'm perfectly fine with being plain old me; don't need to get all dolled up for anything."

Although it would give me a chance to show off my curves and...oh, she's right, I'm so mean, today!!

"I'm too shy for something like that, I can't." I said more seriously. No, really...I was shy when it came to Boo or anybody dealing with Boo.

"Well, they don't have details, yet. They need to pick a date. I know it's going to be at St. Paul Cathedral, though. Angie's turning Catholic, she's already been going to classes."

That made me mad, too.

"Catholic? Why does she have to change her religion to fit his?! That's stupid. People should just accept the differences and deal with it. So what if she's not Catholic. Who cares?"

"God cares, for one. The church cares, for two. And I think if Angie wants to be Catholic then she should be Catholic. Boo never told her to convert. It was Angie's idea." Now Amanda was getting a little offended.

Maybe I should tone it down before Jasmine and I are living out of a cardboard box eating out of garbage cans…huh?

"Whatever. Let me know the details when she figures it out."

I shoved Jasmine in the bathtub for the third time of the day and cleaned her off. Scrub, scrub, scrub…that's all I did. If her body wasn't dirty, something she did was dirty. Stain after stain, dirt spot after dirt spot. The girl was the dirtiest girl I have ever met. Now, I had two sisters and I remember them when they were almost two and they were never dirty. EVER. I think she gets it after Cardy.

Cardy was a dirty boy now that I think about it. I mean, he took showers and wore clean clothes, but he was always doing something that got him dirty, that got him sweating. He was constantly playing some kind of sport, wiping his dirty hands on his face, falling off his bike or skateboard because he took it up the slide or ran it off a ramp…yeah, now that I think about it, that's Jasmine, too.

There, Jasmine was clean. For now. I threw on whatever shirt and short set I grabbed for her and headed towards Darron's. Just because he was mad at me and kicked me out, it didn't end our friendship. We were actually closer because we had space.

And Jasmine couldn't be pried away from Darron if her life depended on it. She loved that boy because he paid attention to her. He treated her like a person and not a baby. He talked to her and carried her from room to room. Yep. I could walk over to Darron's and relax a little.

I really needed to relax. And complain about the stupid news I just heard. And complain about Amanda's snoring. And Amanda's giggle. And Amanda's everything.

Don't get me wrong, I loved Amanda so much. I really did. But I needed to vent. I had nothing else going on with my life, might as well complain about something.

Chapter Eighty-Seven
Binderman

"I don't like it." I dropped the pamphlet and picked up another one. Angie had God awful taste when it came to decoration and color and…just everything.

"Why don't you like it? It's a pretty color, Boo. I love this color. And these, and these, I love all of them, really. You haven't picked one that you like at all." Bitch, bitch, bitch, that's all I was hearing from her.

No, I don't like orange…or excuse me, Terracotta. I wasn't having a fucking wedding wearing a God Damn Terracotta vest, she's fucking crazy!

"How about this one?" Another fucked up color.

"This one reminds me of a fucking shitty diaper, Angie. You can't possibly want to wear that shit. We haven't even set a date. We have to set a date before we pick colors. And the people, you didn't pick people either." Jesus, weddings were insane! I can't stand talking to her about this shit.

She set down the pamphlets and sighed like she was gonna cry. "You didn't say who you wanted in the wedding, either!"

"I don't have to say, I already know." Although Cardy was in rehab and Cody was going to jail and my fucking baby cousin was lost to some back ass alley that sheltered junkies, not that I know where he is, but I know he's not in rehab right now, Aunt Cathy said so.

"Who, then?" Her frustration was showing and mine was already on the brink of taking a drink of tequila.

"Alright, I don't know right now. Your friends are weird and mine are fucked up, so I doubt we're gonna have a good pair of any of them. Why do we have to have a big wedding anyways? Let's just fly to Vegas and do it."

Tears were forming in her eyes. Ah, God dammit, she needed to stop this bullshit. "I don't want a stupid Vegas wedding Boo. I've dreamed about a church wedding for all of eternity and I have to have it. I don't really care about color or dates; just let us have a church wedding at least!!" And then the tears fell.

"Alright, alright," I hugged her like I was supposed to do, but just to get her to stop. "Fine, what the fuck ever, but we need to set a date and the colors are gonna have to be subtle. I'm not walking out like I'm a firework display, Angie. It's so fucking stupid."

Setting a wedding was terrible. Too many things came along with it…flowers, cakes, dresses, colors, dates, places…reception halls…I like that one. But was she down for a fucking party or a fucking tea gathering? Jesus Christ, we were two opposite people with clashing opinions and taste.

I know I'm not gonna get a fucking party out of her. She didn't drink, didn't party, didn't know how to have a good time. She didn't know about music or…

"Hey, I'll make a deal with you. You work on the wedding plans and I get the reception. Whatever you say goes and whatever I want for the after party goes, alright?" That should settle that one.

"All you care about is drinking! You only want to party!! This is OUR day, Boo, not YOUR day!!! I can't believe you want to work on the party. You make it sound like it's more important to you!!!"

Oh my fucking God in hell!!!

"Fine, Fine, Fucking fine!" I snapped.

I had to. It wasn't fair. "I'll be in the kitchen if you decide on a color."

"Right next to the tequila." She yelled after me.

Yep.

April was promising. After many nights of hell and Tequila, the date was set, the places picked, the motherfuckers chosen, and the color accepted. The flowers, the cake, the damn thousand dollar dress…all ordered. I wanted this shit done with. It was pissing me off and not really worth the effort.

That's why it was in May.

May 22nd, 1999. She wanted it the last week of May but I threw a fucking fit. She didn't know why I did and I didn't tell her, either.

. May 31st was Fresca's birthday. I didn't want to be married so close to that date. A week before was too close, too, but well enough.

I still had to tell Fresca. Maybe I didn't need to. Maybe she already found out from Kyle. I hope word got around because I couldn't do it. Fresca said we were over and I finally believed her...but telling her that I was getting married to the girl she hated was another story.

I'd rather stay in Cheriton and pretend that Fresca Taylor never existed...no run-ins, no how are-you, nothing.

Thankfully, she didn't call me. It pissed me off, too...which made it easier to go through with everything.

Bitch.

I left my cousins out of it. Cody wouldn't come, anyways. He was still scared to show his face around town, not that somebody was looking for him, he was just paranoid. I don't know the deal with his ass. I stopped asking about him when he did it. Fuck him.

Brian was my best man. He should be honored because there were others knocked out of his spot under the circumstances. Kyle and Terrance were my groomsmen. Fuck Roger and his stupid ass bitch of a girlfriend and their baby...

Speaking of which, Teesa had a boy. Roger and Teesa argue so much that she refused to give the baby his last name. They both knew that the baby was Cardy's, since Roger failed the DNA test.

It had to be Cardy's. I know he wasn't mine.

I hadn't seen him, yet...but I don't want to. I don't want up in their mix. It only meant that if something was to happen and I knew about it, Caleb would come to me. I definitely didn't want to deal with that one. I still had a grudge against that bitch.

I had my own life to worry about, not theirs.

Anyways, I kept my number of people low so Angie wouldn't have a bunch of fucked up girls in our crew. If it was a better mixture, I could pull in a lot of other motherfuckers and have a blown out wedding...but we're talking about Angie. Angie wasn't the type.

She had Delilah Lewis, which I hated because she was so fucking weird. She was too nice to me for no God damn reason, and she didn't know what she wanted to do...save a tree, burn down the white house, or picket abortion rights. She wore cult clothes and said weird words as if it was her own language. I didn't like it at all. Putting her in a dress, a formal gown...that would be hilarious to see.

Amanda, of course was the maid of honor, which was fine.

But the third one...I don't know how she fits in. She never hangs around Angie. She never calls, never visits...what the fuck was that all about? She was Amanda's friend, not Angie's.

I never thought that Basia Brahm would be in my wedding. It was ironic and...weird. I didn't mind her as much, but it's just that...I don't know. Why was she there? Angie was all for it. She never gave me a definite reason on why she chose her. She just did.

Our color was...grin with me...blue and white. I picked the color, she picked the shade. She couldn't go wrong with a shade of blue. I didn't care, as long as it coordinated with something of my taste, not hers.

Oh, the reception hall was at the Cheriton Estates Country Club near the lake. It had this bomb ass balcony that overlooked the lake with all the fucking lights hanging around it. It was an open bar with top of the line liquor, by request. The DJ was a friend of mine out of New York who had DJ'd a couple of my parties, before. He wouldn't dare play something that I could find in Angie's CD player. Of course, I told Angie that I didn't know him and he was some random guy that plays at weddings. I had to, I'm sorry. Angie doesn't know shit when it came to music. If she knew that he'd play my music, she'd never agree.

It was a small lie to get my way.

I rented the spot for all night, since I hated to end a night of drinking at a certain time.

It could hold fifteen hundred people if you included the inside, which was more elegant and formal. Angie's people could stay in there. My people could chill out on the balcony and dance.

Fuck, Angie couldn't dance, either. I had to stay on her ass that night didn't I?

I wasn't down for the wedding part, since she insisted on a Catholic wedding, which takes forever. I'm talking about two hours. Like I really wanted to sit in church for two hours, kneeling and praying and singing and chirping to God?

God knows me by now and he can't fucking make me like it. And I won't. If he's gonna hold that against me...fuck it, I won't say it. I'll be good.

Chapter Eighty-Eight
Cardy

July, July, July, July. I could repeat this month over and over again in my head. This is the month that I was supposed to get out. And I fucked it up.

"How do you feel today, Cardy? You looked bummed out." Cindy caught on to my slump of a mood as I sat across from her without my smart mouth going, or hovering over her just to smell "female."

I just sat there, compliant, ready to fess up about anything she was willing to ask.

"Jogging didn't work, today. Basketball didn't do shit, either. I just wanna go home." I leaned my chair back and put my hands behind my head. This mood sucked.

"You seem rather quiet and relaxed to me. You're not spunky and shooting around all over my office."

"I wanna go home, that's why."

"You know what you need to work on? You need to start wearing your shirt in the halls, then Dean might consider letting you go."

I frowned. Dean has been throwing a fit for months over my uniform disruption. "I get hot. I don't like the tags on those motherfuckers."

"Doesn't matter to Dean."

"Nothing matters to Dean. He hates me and is gonna find a way to keep me here until I'm twenty one. I'm never going to get out."

"That's not true. Dean actually likes you, Cardy. He said for as long as he worked here, you are the only one that he can't stand, yet loves to know your next move. You're interesting to him. I think you're the balls that he doesn't have."

I grinned, as she knew I would. "Dean doesn't have any balls, Cindy. He's been neutered."

"Exactly, that's what I'm saying. You bring life to this facility. You keep him on his toes. If it wasn't for you, he wouldn't know that he needed better locks on every door in this building. He'd think that perfection was acceptable and no reading in between the lines. You gave him better judgment and the ability to laugh."

"He doesn't laugh, I never saw him smile."

"But he does. He asks every teacher about you…every day. He wishes he was like you, Cardy. I know it."

"Bullshit! Dean is full of himself. He thinks he's perfect and that we should live in a perfect world. Safe Haven is his world. He wouldn't last one minute outside of it. He controls this place because he has no control when he walks out of it at night."

"Possibly true, good call. See, you're already analyzing why people do the things they do. It's good, because when you get out of here, you're going to be able to stop and think and attempt to understand why everything works the way it does, why everything happens the way it does. You will want to understand. You'll see that knowledge you need to move on. You won't be hanging onto the past because you understand and accept."

What the fuck is she talking about?

"Whatever, Roma, I think you and Dean are crazy, no offense."

I left her office and headed for class. As soon as I dropped into a desk, Dean's loud annoying voice echoed through the intercom.

"Christopher Deburke, I need to see you in this office, pronto. And I mean immediately. Stop whatever you're doing this instant and get here. No stalling. No stopping at Ruth's desk, no high fiving the janitor, etc. Chop-Chop, Deburke!!"

The class "oohed" and I smiled.

Dean, you cocksucker, I'll give you twenty minutes for that one. What the hell can I do for twenty minutes?

I smoked a cigarette in the bathroom and roamed the halls for another five. I high fived the janitor, kissed Ruth's cheek so she could turn red, and read every advertisement on the bulletin board about fifty times. Then I took the stairs to his office to make it slower. When I approached his door, I stood on the side of it for another minute, just to piss him off. I wanted him to call me again. But he didn't. He knew what I was doing, anyways.

Me and Dean, Dean and me…yeah, we bumped heads, but it was fun. I think he had fun with it, too.

"Christopher Deburke, sit down." He didn't frown, didn't scold me…nothing.

I stood.

"Please, just for today. I have some horrible news."

For a second, my mind raced towards my dad, my lonely dad who nobody thought about anymore. Was he dead? Did he die? What's the horrible news?

"Don't look upset, Deburke, it's not horrible for you, it's horrible for me. Have a seat."

So I sat.

"Mr. Deburke, we have had our differences, haven't we?" I nodded as he continued. "And you came along ways from when you first arrived, haven't you?" I nodded, again. "I have your release date in my hand, sir. You added six more months to your needed sentence and that brings you to a January of 2000 release date, doesn't it?"

I fucking nodded, once more.

"I wanted to say that all your teachers are giving promising results from you. You're showing up to class, turning in assignments, passing all the tests and assessments. Dr. Roma has grown rather fond of you and I can't get a negative remark out of her, so…I think you are on your way to an earlier release date."

My eyes widened with hope. "Really, is that possible?"

He smiled, whether it was fake or not, don't care. The man smiled. "It is very possible, Christopher." Just the name calling was enough to make me cringe. He knew I hated that name.

"You show a lot of character around these halls. You've made friends. You show team work and effort. Your evaluation for the last six months has been much appreciated. Although you still have some quirks about you that are rather disturbing, I don't see why I need to put up with you for another six months. I will lessen your sentence, if you are willing. Are you willing, Christopher?"

Holy fucking shit, my heart was beating way too fast. I gripped the chair and prayed to get me out before my nineteenth birthday. "Uh, yeah, I'm more than willing. I'll do whatever it takes. You want me to do other people's chores, you want me to do extra credit assignments…whatever you want from me…I'm more than down."

"Down..." He considered the phrase and let it go. "I will be having the board of directors coming Friday..."

Okay, okay, okay, get on with it.

"With your behavior..."

Yeah, yeah, yeah, say it, motherfucker, just say it. I'll behave. I'll wear a shirt; I'll give them a tour, whatever.

"I can't have you walking around freely with no shirt on, kissing our receptionist, making bets with our staff, and playing poker late nights with our security guards when you're supposed to be in bed. You're a wild child, kiddo, and I can't control you. My staff seems not to be in favor of making you follow any of my rules. You've been rather spoiled, especially by Dr. Roma. I can't have the board of directors seeing this type of treatment. I want it to stop, immediately."

"Okay." I was on the edge of my seat, heart in my throat, legs going numb from not bouncing.

"That's why I am releasing you, tomorrow. It'll give you enough time to contact your mother..."

I didn't hear shit after that. I froze. Tomorrow seemed too soon...too fast...too much like a dream.

"Are you fucking kidding me?! Are you serious?!" I couldn't hold back my language.

"Yes, sir." He dropped the papers in front of me. Outlined in red was my new release date. Scratched out in black was my second release date. Underneath that was my first one, which is now tomorrow, again.

"I don't believe you." I couldn't.

"Well, believe me, Christopher. I would rather release you than lose my job because my staff decided not to obey the rules. I would rather get rid of you than deal with something I can't get out of once they witness your charm. And believe you, me, son...you have a lot a charm, just like your brother. Boy, I was so glad to see him go. But, I will miss you; I think we will all miss you." He stood to shake my hand.

No fucking way!!!

"Dean, don't be fucking with me. I swear to God if I go back to class and you call me back up here..."

"It would be a great prank, wouldn't it? But, no, Christopher, Chris,

Chrissy…I want you out of my facility by tomorrow, as soon as you can get your foot out of the door."

I let those names roll off of me, as I didn't care at the moment. I wiped my face over and over, sometimes patting it, just to wake me up.

But I was awake. And I was going home…home, home, home. Where is my home?

Mom, I had to call her.

Chapter Eighty-Nine
Binderman

A year ago, I would've knocked anyone on their ass for even bringing up the idea of marriage, especially about me marrying Angie. Ha, I would laugh my ass off if someone believed that I liked Angie in that way.

Never in a million years did I think my life would turn out the way it was. Before, everything was set way before time. I was going to marry Fresca Taylor, I would never stop partying, not even for a minute, I'd never live with my dad, again…I'd always take care of my sister, Jeff would mooch off of me until the day I died…and so forth.

Shit happens…quickly.

I didn't like the curves that seemed to pop up before I knew it. I never did. Everything had to be planned, thought out, secure and lasting. As soon as something changed, I was quick to fix it, alter it to fit into my life. One bitch gone, one replaced. One bottle empty, one replaced. A friend fucking up…one replaced. Dad missing…done and over with.

I didn't sit and dwell over things. I took action and redirected my life to move on. It's what had to be done.

Now, I'm getting married…to a girl that I had never thought of as quality until I really considered her.

Marriage wasn't that big of a deal. I mean, sure, legally I was joined at the hip to Angie for the rest of my life…but it worked out. I never had to worry about replacing her ass again. She was mine…legally. Nobody could say shit. She couldn't even cheat on me without getting in trouble for it. I owned Angie.

I had Angie and Devon. Devon wasn't going to know what it was like to travel between households like most kids. We were going to be a normal family. It was a good plan…a perfect plan of mine.

Now, it was time to swallow that knot in the back of my throat and push back the second thoughts that were draping my confidence. I could do this shit. A lot of people get married. I wasn't being a sellout or anything like that shit…I was doing the right thing…for once.

I had my time in the spotlight. I didn't need to party anymore. I had done everything that I wanted to do, anyways. It was time to settle down…even if I was almost twenty one. I didn't need to be twenty one and hitting up clubs. Fuck that.

So here goes…

Final adjustments on my tie and vest were made as my dad patted me down in front of the mirror. It was more like checking me for weapons rather than brushing off any lent on my tuxedo or shit like that.

"How do you feel?" His voice cracked with those words. Eye to eye, he wanted me to admit that I wanted out.

I grinned with a good word. "Superb."

He smirked back, acknowledging my word of choice. "Superb? You're not nervous or anything? You don't feel like taking the back door to freedom?"

I glanced back to see if there was such an escape. "Fuck no, I'm cool, dad. I want to do this, trust me."

With his hand on my shoulder, gripping with his thoughts, he left me with some advice worth tossing to the wind. "You know, I was extremely nervous when I married your mother. All I kept thinking about was you, how you were going to be born a bastard if I didn't marry her. I don't want you to do this if that's what you're thinking. It'll be better for the both of you if you just didn't go through with it. I don't want you to make a mistake, Binji. If you have any…"

"Quit it, already. I'm cool. I know what I'm doing." I shrugged him off and proceeded to the altar.

I stood at the altar, properly posed and patient. I was able to control my nerves thanks to Tequila and Ativan, all the while clearing any thoughts of bailing. It was still an experience worth going through, whether or not I was making a mistake.

Not that I thought I was making one.

With Brian to my side, more nervous than I was, he was swaying and lightly coughing, shifting his stance…making it obvious that he thought I was in the wrong. I had made the wrong choice.

Kyle and Terrance didn't want to be there, either. All three of them took turns in moving, pissing me off in the process. If we weren't in church, I'd already kick their ass for ruining a perfect picture at the altar.

The girls took their place and there was a moment of hesitation before Angie had her honorable entrance. My eyes shifted around in place of a nervous sigh. I wasn't nervous, wasn't going to be nervous.

Basia looked hot. I tried not to think about shit like that while I was there, but there was nothing really to look at until Angie came into the room. Cardy was lucky. Basia was someone that couldn't be compared to the regular hot bitches.

Her hair was tame for once, bouncing in curls. Her face had all this makeup on and her legs...fuck. I shifted, then.

The dresses that Angie had them wear were slim. It hung to their curves and slid outward around their hips. Basia's dress showed off her ass...rather too well. The back part of the gown dipped to their tailbones and fucking shit...I didn't see any lines or creases of their underwear which only made me think of them, more.

Even Delilah looked alright. I was surprised to see that she even shaved her under arms and legs. I figured she would have protested the razor companies for some reason. I'd...what the fuck was I thinking? I'm at my damn wedding, for Christ's sake.

The music played, everyone stood and turned. Angie, accompanied by her mother, came flowing down the aisle in the most biggest, whitest, laciest fucking dress I had ever saw. Hair up, locks of curls around her face, she beamed with tears and joy.

It was her moment and I was glad. I just wanted a ring on her finger to say she was mine and that nobody could touch her...even think about touching her. She can have all the attention she wanted, the whole damn spotlight...just get this over with.

Father Rizzo raised his bible and began the ceremony. As trained as I was from when I was little, I still couldn't keep my mind focused on his words...God's words.

We didn't have a full house of people in the pews, I noticed. It wasn't the usual of me. Usually, I made sure every space was packed when I threw an event. For some reason, with so late of notice, so spur of the moment, so...secretly...I didn't care to announce this big bash.

Not many people knew of my marriage to Angie.

I don't even know if Fresca knew. Was she sitting at her house this very moment, thinking of me, regretting her decision? Was she crying? Did she want me back?

"In the name of the Father…" I heard the priest say.

I needed to talk to Fresca, tell her what's up. Make sure she'll be fine. It was her decision, not mine. I just moved on, that's all. Could she blame me?

My mind wasn't involved, this day. It was easier to keep it at home, where all the rest of the bullshit sat. I had it in my head to get married and that's what I was going to do, no matter what.

"I now pronounce you Mr. and Mrs. Sox. You may kiss the bride…" Two long hours later.

I kissed on cue, hugged her on cue, and walked my wife out of those doors knowing that shit was always going to be fine from now on. I didn't see the bouquet tossed from the church steps, or bird seed covering our heads…I just felt Angie's hand in mine as I ran for the limo…to the after party…where I could drink.

Chapter Ninety
Basia

I was wrong about Boo Sox. All this time I thought he was selfish and ignorant, self absorbed, conceited, self centered, well…you get the point. I used to hate Boo Sox, the "Prince of Pierre." He used to be this mean overcast of riches, this overshadowing cloud of unworthiness in my eyes.

I remember spitting on his grass, kicking rocks towards his lawn…all from the time they moved in three houses from Darron.

He never did anything to me when I was younger, but he was…he just seemed rather mean, controlling…like a bully. I never liked how people dropped everything to drip saliva from their lips like they were starving for his attention.

I remember when he couldn't drive. He had to ride the most expensive BMX bike, or whatever it was. Everybody loved it. He was this chubby kid who pushed the others around, smoking cigarettes like he was something cool.

It made Jeff get a better bike. It made Kyle get a better bike. They all three rode their stupid bikes to the playground and caused a big scene to take place. We'd already be there, riding our skateboards or swinging…and there they came…taking over the spot like they owned it. It was so rude of them.

Back then Cardy didn't look like Boo. I don't know what happened all of a sudden, but I remember what Boo looked like at twelve and thirteen. He was a fat faced little kid who could bribe anybody out of anything. His mouth was always going. Girls were always screaming his name, hugging him, kissing him…

Ooh, it made me so mad.

But now…now, he was like prince charming, riding in on his black Cadillac, swooping up the little pheasant girl and giving her a throne in his castle. And he wasn't crude about it. He treated her like a lady, held her hand in the air like the princess she had become, wherever they walked.

At the reception, he was a gentleman to her. He never left her backside, cradling her in his arms, sweet talking in her ears, kissing her, holding her...caressing her at the bar...it was just too much.

I had mixed feelings about him. I thought he was very sexy, very amusing to watch, but all the while, it made me sick.

I found my way to an empty table and sat there watching him, closely. I watched him press his tuxedo against her hips, swaying her from side to side...ooh, I wanted a drink.

Yes...I did.

Here I am, all lonely and alone, all dolled up and depressed, all alone...all lonely...all depressed...this sucks.

"Hey, what's up, girl?" Kyle threw himself in a chair next to me with a crooked smile.

He looked very nice today, too. He wore a tuxedo with his hair gelled back. He looked very proper and handsome, like a handsome gentleman.

"Look at them, they look so in love!" I didn't know what else to say to him. I hadn't said much since we kissed and I didn't want to be put on the spot, again.

"You think they're in love? *That* looks like they're in *love* to you?" He laughed and brushed his hair back with his hand. "That ain't love, girl. That's Boo being Boo. He's like that with all the girls. I don't think he loves her. He can't." He said with a matter of fact tone.

Boo was all smiles, bright white teeth shining with the balcony lights. He was so close to her, so touchy, so in tune with her movements. It gave me chills just to see them like that. His hands did the talking, his body moved like a tongue, twining her attention to him and only him.

"He has to love her; he wouldn't marry her if he didn't. Look at them, really Kyle. You can't possibly think they're *not* right for each other." I had made up my mind that they were perfect together. Even though I had an infatuation with him...I knew in my heart that they belonged together.

"If you think that he loves her by the way he's acting with her, then you don't know Boo at all. He'd have to love all the females he's ever came in contact with. Watch, go dance with him, he'll automatically touch you like that. He's smooth, Basia, not in love with the bi...the girl." Even Kyle called girls "bitches," which was disappointing.

I created this whole scenario in my head about Boo dancing with me. He'd kiss me like so, and touch me like that, hold me so gentle and fill up my gap…yes, I wish Boo would dance with me.

Instead…"How old are you, Kyle? Wanna get me a drink?" I had enough.

"I'm only twenty, but I can get you a drink. Boo's bartender caters a lot of our parties, he doesn't ask for ID. You wanna go up there with me and pick one out?" He held out his hand with a welcoming smile.

Oh Kyle, I wish I didn't have a brain to think with.

"What do they have?"

"Anything you want, trust me."

"What's good?" I followed him up to the open bar and waited for him to offer a name, any name, for I didn't recall one.

"Um, you like sweet drinks, kind of like Kool-aid?" He waved over the guy and leaned on the counter.

"Sure." I grinned for no apparent reason. I just wanted to loosen up. I just wanted to end my thoughts over Angie's husband.

The bartender placed a glass on the counter with a pink tinted liquid in it. He carelessly tossed a baby umbrella to the side of the rim.

Hmmm, that was decorative and cute, wasn't it? What was it for?

I sipped it and loved it. I still tasted the alcohol, but the sweet kind of tart taste to it made it worth drinking. "Hey, you wanna dance with me, Kyle?"

He glanced at me twice. He stuttered for a slight second and looked over at Boo. "Um, I guess. It's a slow song. Do you care?"

"I like slow songs." I mumbled around my straw. I already felt a little giggly. I don't know, it could have been psychological.

We stood to the side of the dance floor with my hands around his neck. He didn't know where to place his arms and tried out a couple positions before he rested them on my hips. We swayed, slightly. My eyes were focused on his lips, his chin, the hair that grew between those spots. His eyes seemed to shift from my hair, to my face, and back at the ground.

I made Kyle Sorum nervous.

I bet it was the dress and the makeup.

"You haven't talked to Cardy lately, have you?" That's where his mind was. Kyle was thinking about Cardy.

"I don't go out with him, Kyle. You know that. We haven't gone out for three years, now. We're not a couple." It was easy to say because I didn't want him to disturb this moment with someone like Cardy. I didn't want Cardy to bother me, tonight. I liked dancing with Kyle.

In fact, I liked Kyle Sorum. There, I said it. I like Boo. I like Kyle. Everything was perfectly normal about me liking boys. It was okay.

Within another minute, I relaxed. I rested my head on his shoulder; let the aroma of his cologne creep into me like never before. I inhaled Kyle. I absorbed this beautiful moment with him.

"You make me so nervous." He broke my slumbering wave from side to side.

"What?" I snapped with a laugh. "Stop it, Kyle, no I don't. I can still kick your butt and ride a skateboard better than you and I don't make you nervous. I'm not just any girl. You don't have to feel that way around me."

"That's why I do. You're not just any girl. You're Basia. I've known you since you were a kid. My brother has a crush on you. You're my boy's girl…"

"I'm nobody's girl, Kyle. I'm single. If you want to…"

And the end to that sentence was swallowed by tongue. Kyle didn't hesitate to kiss me there on the dance floor. His hands grabbed my butt and squeezed me against him. He was so close to my stomach.

I got sparks and chills all at the same time.

I think I was in love. I think I loved Kyle Sorum. It had to be. I hadn't felt like that since I kissed Cardy! Well, it's not like I kiss people, either…but still…I think I loved Kyle, too.

Chapter Ninety-One
Binderman

I knew how to behave if I wanted to. Even though I wanted to dance with the other hot bitches I saw, I kept my distance from them and plastered myself to my…uh…wife? Holy fuck, that was weird to say. I can't call her that. She's just Angie to me.

"What are we doing tonight?" I mumbled against her ear as we rocked back and forth.

I knew what we doing, I just wanted to hear her say it. Now as drunk as I was, I wanted to skip this lame ass shit before I was too drunk to fuck her.

This party was supposed to be *my* fucking party and it was turning out to suck. If I strayed too far, I might end up bouncing on another girl by habit. I didn't want Angie to look like a fool. I didn't want to play her…I wanted to be faithful.

But in the meantime, sticking on her ass was boring. It was hard to stay so focused. Every minute I had to restrain myself from making up an excuse to stop dancing with her. I did well. It was the best damn showcase from my ass in a long time.

"Oh, look at Kyle and Basia! I'm so happy for them!!!" Angie whined with some stupid ass joy from the sight.

There was Kyle grinding against Basia, lips locked on Cardy's fucking bitch. Hell fucking nah.

I shoved Angie off by instinct, didn't mean to. I pushed through the crowd of people with my eyes deadset on that stupid ass motherfucking Kyle. He *knew* better. There wasn't a fucking excuse in the world.

I had enough of Kyle. First, he's talking to Fresca and telling her my business. Now, he's fucking with Cardy's girl. Who the fuck does he think he is?!

I grabbed the back of his tuxedo and jerked him a good five feet away. "What the fuck, Kyle?! Get outside, right now. I'm fucking you up!"

"Dude, no, I'm sorry. I didn't mean…I just…fucking shit…I'm drunk, dude. Don't pay me any mind, I know, I know…"

"You don't fucking know, motherfucker. Get outside so I don't have to ruin my party, stupid ass. Go, punk ass motherfucker!" I shoved him back into the crowd, pushing him towards the door. All the while, he begged for forgiveness.

I didn't give a fuck if I was the groom or not. He was at my shit kissing on a bitch that was off limits. It reminded me of Fresca, of Cardy…of all the fucking shit people did to each other that should have never happened. I took it personal.

I had to.

I dropped my jacket, unbuttoned my vest, threw my cufflinks at him, and charged. I was about to hit him when I heard Angie and Basia scream "Stop!"

I slammed his head against the pavement once and stood. I took a breath and glanced at Angie in her dress. Fucking shit, I didn't want to stop.

"Please!" Basia begged in tears.

"Please? Please? You're fucking begging me to stop when you don't know what the fuck you're doing with him? Fuck that! What the fuck is wrong with you?! You're not even supposed to be here. Where's Jasmine? Do even give a fuck about Jasmine or do you pawn her off like Cardy's other bitch just so you can fuck another motherfucker?!" I was too steamed to hold back. I scolded her, face to face, her wrist in my hand.

I humiliated her in front everyone.

It wasn't the best decision, but I couldn't hold back my thoughts. Someone needed to be her daddy and take matters into their own hands. She wasn't being herself.

Angie couldn't get me to stop. All she could do was go back inside to get Amanda.

"Dude, I said I was sorry, leave her alone! I don't give a fuck if you kick my ass, but leave her out of it!" That pissed me off, too.

My wedding, my reception, my fucking brother's ex-girlfriend…this shit was too much to deal with.

"Fuck you! Do what you want, ya'll ain't ruining my fucking wedding night! I'm kicking your ass when I get back, Kyle. I swear to God." I was about to find Angie, but I couldn't resist and walk away.

Any other night...God, I wanted to fight his ass.

"I can't believe your stupid ass! You know better to be fucking with certain bitches! Don't stick up for her like you like her. Tell her ass the truth; tell her what the fuck you do with bitches like her. Show her the game book while you're at it! He doesn't like you, Basia. He wants to play your ass. You're worth points like a fucking game." I couldn't keep my mouth shut.

"What?" Basia glanced uneasily over at Kyle, but Kyle was charging MY ass. Go figure...

"It's not like that with her, motherfucker! It's not like that at all! I like her, I really fucking like her, dude! I don't give a fuck about Cardy. If Cardy has beef about this, then fuck him. I like Basia, Boo, and it's none of your fucking business what I do with her!"

Damn, Kyle had some balls fucking with me tonight.

I couldn't believe what I was hearing, either. I won't believe it.

"Oh yeah? I like Basia, too, but do you see my ass chasing her around? She belongs to Cardy!!" I shoved him off of me. "What about Sherrice?"

"What about her, motherfucker, people think they can get over on me and fuck my girlfriend, but I can't talk to someone I actually like? Fuck you!" Kyle was beyond angry.

It was my dad who finally came to the rescue and made me stop. Kyle and I were trading blows in a playful, but more hateful demeanor. Kyle never challenged my ass like that.

That's how I knew he really liked Basia.

It put me in a worse mood.

I made myself leave soon after that, before I had gone to jail over something stupid.

Minutes later, I had to hear it from Angie.

"What's your problem? You should be happy that Basia isn't crying over Cardy anymore!" Angie bitched as we drove back to my Grams.

"Don't bring that shit up. He's my brother, Angela. She's the only thing that he actually cares about. You don't even fucking know." I had a big ass headache from this whole worthless day. It was a piece of shit wedding with a piece of shit party and a fucked up ending to it all.

I was beyond angry.

Angie didn't know what it was like. She didn't love someone. She didn't come to find out that they fucked somebody else. She had no idea what it was like, no fucking clue.

"I don't know?! Boo, I knew Basia and Cardy way before you did. They were very close. But shit happens and people move on. Cardy doesn't want to be with Basia and it's about time that Basia showed interest in someone else. I'm happy for her. And I can't believe you acted that way. It's our wedding, Boo. Our wedding day was ruined by you, and *only* you."

Where the fuck does she get off blaming this shit on me? Where does she get off thinking she can yell at me that fucking way?!

Fuck it. I'm not saying shit. She can be pissed all she wants. I'm not arguing with her ass, too.

"Are you mad at me?" Angie turned off the ignition and waited for a reply.

"No." I snapped.

"Then why are you so quiet?"

"Why do want to argue?" I twisted.

"How drunk are you?"

"Drunk enough to need more." I smirked only at myself, as I was struggling for the door handle to get out.

She came around to the passenger side and helped me up. "Why don't we drop the attitude and enjoy our special night?"

"Bring the Tequila."

Chapter Ninety-Two
Angie

"Are you coming?" I yelled back at him as he struggled up the concrete steps.

"Is your wedding dress still on?"

Of course he'd say that. He was thinking of sex, wasn't he?

"I just got in the door, Boo. I need you to unzip it." I wasn't in the mood.

My wedding day was going so perfectly until Boo decided to fight Kyle. It wasn't a big deal that he kissed Basia. So what?!

"Find the scissors." He ordered as he ripped the buttons right off of his brand new dress shirt. He had already lost his jacket and left his vest at the hall. Now, he tore his shirt right off of his body...on purpose.

"Why?!" I sneered. He already got the shirt off. He didn't need scissors.

"Cause I'm cutting you out of that thing." He sat on the staircase with his head in his hands, too tired to climb.

"Oh, no you're not, this is a keepsake. I have to pass it down to my daughter." He was flipping crazy if he thought I'd let him come near me with some shears.

"Daughter, what fucking daughter? Devon's a boy, Angie. You don't have a fucking daughter."

"Yeah, but we might, one day." And I carefully watched his expression go from confused to stunned to worried.

He didn't want more kids?

"Baby, I can't make daughters. You want eight boys, then I got your back, but girls...can't do. My shit doesn't work like that. Girls don't run in my blood." He laughed so full of himself.

"Yeah right, what about Bobbi? Everybody can make girls, Boo. Don't you want a daughter, someday?" I hugged him just for the mere fact that he thought his sperm was invincible and indestructible when it came to girl genes.

"Bobbi's an outcast. I don't know where she came from. For...fucking...five generations, there's...there's been nothing but boys. Sox's don't make girls, baby. Get...get fucking...used to it. I don't want any more kids. Girls are...they're too much trouble. Look how you turned out." He squeezed me until I ran out of breath and then let go. He was sober enough to think he made sense, yet drunk enough to be full of shit while he slurred the entire prophecy.

"You will."

"Fuck that, come here." He tugged me closer to him by my dress and twisted me around so he could unzip it.

Then I hit him. "Nothing's wrong with me. I turned out good."

He jerked the dress down, revealing my shoulders, enough to give me a rug burn on my skin. "You turned out pregnant at sixteen, baby."

"Yeah, because of you!"

Oh, wow...what was he saying, again?

His mouth was at the base of my neck, giving me goose bumps. His hands slid my gown over my hips. His lips pressed into my spine as he slid down with it.

"No more talk about babies." He hushed as he pulled me down to his level. "Don't jinx me."

"Con...dom...right?" I was losing track of my thoughts by the second.

He always had that power to do that over me, I don't know why. I'd be saying something and then...forget...what was I talking about?

His fingers pried my garter belt loose as he unhooked it. I went to help him, but he pushed my hand away. "Uh-uh, leave it there."

I couldn't ask why if I wanted to.

The dress was in the floor. Every strap on my body was loose and just hanging off of me, but Boo wouldn't let me take it off. He had some weird thing with lingerie and strings.

Right there as soon as you walk into his grandmother's house, on the staircase, out in the open for people to witness...he wanted to...

"What about..." but he read my mind.

"She's too old to come out of her room right now, shhh..." on his lap, facing away from him, I sat...half naked, straps dangling.

"Open." He forced my legs open like a stripper, like a lap dancer, or whatever they were.

I felt too…too…

"Close 'em."

He was too drunk to treat me the way he usually did. I was getting a sample of his capabilities, witnessing first hand of all of his experience…oh, I can't even think, right now.

"Holy fucking shit, get off." He tossed me to the floor and fell down after me.

"What?" I thought maybe he was hurt or something.

He shoved me on my back and snapped his belt in my face. Then he tossed it across the room. He laughed as if he was thinking on strangling me.

I was full questions. I was too nervous to be fully involved. "Why did you throw me off of you?"

"Shh, it was too good," He smirked. He kissed me, rather too harshly.

"Oh." I was flattered. It wasn't even a minute that way and he had to stop.

"What are you doing?" I continued.

"I don't fucking know." He laughed as his slid his tongue down my stomach. He was going…where?

"You don't know, or you don't want to tell…"

"Shh, I never did this shit before."

"Then why do…" he covered my mouth with his hand.

"Because I want something different…"

"Different like…" I was way too nervous now and he caught on. I wouldn't stop talking.

"Hush up, girl, relax. You'll be fine. You're the first bi…girl I've tried this on, so bare with me."

And that was our wedding night. It was a wide range of emotions…and new things.

Chapter Ninety-Three
Cardy

In forty eight hours…I will be home. I didn't know what home that was or if I would actually like it or not…but it wasn't Safe Haven. Temporarily, that's all that mattered.

Dean released me, tomorrow. I had my discharge papers in hand, tomorrow. Freedom was just around the corner…but another twenty four hours seemed to feel like eternity. Each hour felt like a week, which put me at twenty four weeks left in this bitch.

I swear, each hour was draining my hopes of ever seeing the outside curb to this place. I couldn't be patient. I couldn't stand being still. I couldn't eat, couldn't drink, couldn't sleep.

I walked the halls as if I didn't belong there. I walked the corridors one last time…all of them…roaming…and roaming again. I probably paced the motherfuckers like twenty four times.

A part of me felt like I wasn't done here. I had just got comfortable in this routine. I just found my niche in this shit hole and was able to control what was mine…and here we go, again.

Another transition, another train of thought…another change in atmosphere…

But freedom, at least I was free.

Pending my departure, I detoured outside. I no longer decided to co-exist among fellow cohorts. I no longer cared to follow the rules or anything of that nature. It was my last day here at Safe Haven and I felt like doing what I felt like doing.

And that was sitting outside…

The sky was clear blue, a few cotton clouds in the distance. Birds flapped around every now and then and the wind blew strong. I could see the branches sway back and forth, letting their leaves fall sparsely to the ground. I had always loved the start of fall weather. It was a good gradual transition from summer.

It may rain later on in the night. I could smell it in the air, such a cool crisp breeze, kind of refreshing. I wanted it to rain. I wish they would let me walk in it.

I remember rainy nights back in Pierre, all dark…wet…lonely. I liked it. I'd leave my house from the backdoor, turn on my walkman, flip up my hood to my flannel jacket and walk until I was exhausted.

The rain would eventually soak through my hood and flatten my hair. The raindrops would stream down my cheeks and drip off the tip of my nose.

I didn't mind being wet. It was one way to hide the tears. I could cry all night long if I wanted to…just blame it on the rain.

It was then that my thoughts began to gravitate towards life…what living really meant to me. Being held back at Safe Haven, fucking up on drugs…I didn't have the option of seeing the world for what it is.

Not everything was awful and ugly. I didn't have to barricade myself in this stupid ass environment. I was eighteen, now, mind you. I had many options out there and no one could control my destiny.

Yeah, I had a shitty upbringing. That fucking sucked and I could spend the rest of my life trying to forget it, understand it, and still not be satisfied with what I find and restore. I could snort my life away with the happy buzz feeling that I got from cocaine…a fake happiness that I didn't want back. I knew it was a false feeling. I was tired of superficial bullshit.

I could rebel for eternity and still not be at peace with what I destroy.

I realize now that I was addicted to happiness…I think most people who seek fun in the fast life are seeking a constant happiness. What they don't understand is that it's never enough.

A man once told me that happiness is only for the moment…that its joy we seek and you must find it through God. Happiness comes and goes. You shouldn't pray to be happy and shouldn't be pleased with happiness. What makes us happy isn't worth wasting time in.

It's joy that matters.

This man was a church man. He stuck his palm against my forehead and prayed for salvation. He used to roam our neighborhood, talking to kids about going to church. I never took him serious because I went to church. I didn't need to listen. We used to make fun of him...but now...I don't know where he is. It's a sad thought to think that he may be dead. All his efforts have been washed away.

I do seek joy. I want to be joyous. I want to feel that never ending rise of dopamine and satisfaction in my decisions in life. I don't want that rollercoaster of emotions, anymore. Too many ups and downs...

I just want peace.

I just want a simple fucking life, a simple normal one...where I wake up in my own bed and eat. Where I can go to school and study for something bigger. My main goal: travel and see all that I can see, do all that I can do in the little time I have on this piece of shit Earth.

Okay, so that contradicts my simplicity, doesn't it? I want a simple everyday life with the excitement of traveling around the world. Does that make sense?

It doesn't matter because that's what I have in store for myself. I don't care what you think.

I pulled the red notebook from my back pocket and relaxed against a big oak tree. It towered above me, but it wasn't intimidating at all. Trees may be taller, bigger...but rooted with no place to go. They...were stuck.

I wasn't.

So I wrote my hours away...nothing better to do but to think, to plan...to write.

Whatever popped into my head, I wrote it down. My hands were busy, my eyes pointed towards a destination. My mouth was steady with concentration. I had found a passion worth doing...s simple, clean, sober hobby to pass the time.

It was easy...eyes open, eyes closed. I could release the energy and pain and fear and anxiety by writing any word. No limit on my point of view. No rules, no regulations. No one controlled my writing. No one could tell me what to say or how to say it. It was all mine. If I didn't like it, it was as simple as an eraser top...erasing the past.

I loved it. It let shit get off my chest and not in someone else's head. I didn't have to share my thoughts, my secrets...my own world.

I felt freer to think outside. Who could really think in a tiny white box with white everything else? Out here, I had color. My mind could fly up to the beautiful sky and soar over the treetops, and climb down the trunk of them.

I had the smell of grass, the wind against my skin, the rustling of leaves…and the beautiful hues of autumn. I couldn't imagine a better place at Safe Haven I'd rather be.

"Cardy, can I join you?" Her voice shattered my daydreaming like a swirl of a tornado, wrecking havoc on my thoughts.

It was Cindy.

"Yeah, sure." I stopped writing and fell back against the grass, sprawled out with my hands behind my head.

She barely went anywhere without her clipboard and placed it on her lap. Sometimes, I think it was a defense to protect her body. If she wrote, if she sat in it her lap…then she had a purpose, a shield.

"Daydreaming?" her hands cupped one another and twitched on her notes.

I glanced at her and brought my hands to my chest. "You think they'd let me walk in the rain?"

She laughed and leaned forward, like a child with bad posture. "Since when do you obey the rules?"

I smiled back. Yeah, since when did I obey? It was innocent enough.

She was wearing black trousers, a black blazer…white fucking shirt. There was no personality to this attire. Now her clothes were something to focus attention on because she had some wild taste in fashion. Today, though, she was boring me.

"What's up with the outfit?" I squinted with confusion.

"Oh, I have a funeral to go to after work. Nobody I know, just a friend's grandmother or something…maybe grandfather, I don't remember." And she must not have cared, either.

"Why do you wear all that shit, anyways? All those wild colors and skirts…sometimes you go a little overboard, you know that, right?" I plucked a piece of grass from the ground and twirled in between my fingers. I felt completely relaxed around her to ask such a question.

Her lips curled and her cheeks blushed. It was a shy kind of smile…like a little girl's. "I wear what I feel like wearing. Why should I limit my outfits when emotion is so vast, when moods are so imbalanced? It keeps me free from society, Cardy. I can be whoever I want to be with the mere costume of the day. You should try it sometime. It's nice to grab a wild print and see how kooky I can be just for the hell of it. And who remembers a girl in black? I stand out and people feel safe around someone in a crazy outfit. There's no intimidation, unless they're off they're medicine and I'm over-stimulating their eyes."

I laughed, too. She *was* crazy, in fact. I liked how she was so different than everyone else I knew.

No, I take that back. I know one more girl who was just as crazy...she collected necklaces and stood for what she believed in. if someone didn't like it, tough. She was proud to be original. It's what made her who she was.

With the slightest thought of Basia, I had brought my mood down. I had to get rid of that feeling of loss.

The only reaction to do this was an awful response...and I knew it.

My hand extended to her hair and grabbed the back of her neck. No more thoughts ran through me as I focused in on her lips...her pink fleshy lips that I impulsively wanted to taste...

I felt her stiffen, but she didn't pull back. If she would have retracted like I intended, Basia's memory would have been replaced with angry words and I would feel guilty of touching Cindy, instead of feeling guilty of leaving Basia behind.

But Cindy's response left me confused.

She let me kiss her.

And I did. Because she didn't move back, I went deeper inside her mouth, enjoying the moment of finally kissing a girl since it had been a year before I had the opportunity.

I could have gone further and I wanted to so badly. My body sparked a quick liveliness and impulse to lay her back...attack her...maul her with no consequence to follow.

It was me who decided I was in the wrong. My nerves were on end. My heart was full of adrenaline. My testosterone was bulging my veins, and I was about to hyperventilate into no tomorrow.

But I stopped it before I started.

"I'm sorry." I bit my lips to taste the last of hers and fell back against the grass to wait for a punch, a kick...some spit in my face.

"It's okay. I'm sorry I let you." She propelled upwards and ran off. My gaze followed until the view was impossible from my position.

What the fuck did I just ruin...once more?!

I rolled over and thought about biting the earth. I exhaled all my energy into the ground and hoped that I wouldn't dream of her, later.

Chapter Ninety-Four
Binderman

We were supposed to fly to Greece for our honeymoon.

But we were late getting up. It wasn't my fucking fault. I was awake at 3:30 in the morning, ready to take any earlier flight. I had issues with sleeping and had more energy at night than any other time of the day, drunk or not.

She didn't want to get out of bed. She didn't want to arrive earlier and have more time sightseeing.

Fucking bitch.

I went back asleep…only to wake up to see that it was 11:30 in the morning and we were still in this fucking bed, in this fucking town, next to fucking her.

Our marriage started off wrong. That's all I had to say. I didn't love the bitch, didn't appreciate her taste in shit, and now I wasn't going to Greece. I didn't have a good ceremony because all I was looking at was Basia…my reception was lame and ended with Kyle wanting to kick my ass…and what the fuck did I do last night?

I was so fucking bored with my night, so sober, yet drunk (off of what the fuck was that shit?) that I resorted to doing some crazy ass shit that I swore I would never do with a bitch?

Motherfucker.

"Angie, what the fuck are you doing?" I stood in the bathroom doorway, watching her pace on the phone, sighing as if she was frustrated. I already brushed my teeth twice, but it wasn't enough. I knew what I did and I couldn't brush it out of memory.

"I'm trying to get a later flight, Boo. Don't you want to go?"

No. I didn't want to go with her ass. Her ass was driving me insane. She could have stopped me last night. She didn't have to let me do it. I was more concerned with my stupid ass impulsiveness that I didn't want to do anything other than brush my teeth until my gums bled.

She hung up the phone. She stopped and stared at me. "Why are you still brushing your teeth? You need to be putting your shirt on, your shoes…get ready for Christ's sake. We have a babysitter for a whole week, Boo. We have to do something!!!"

I spit in the sink, wishing it was her face.

"I don't want to."

"What?"

I drank *my* mouthwash and let it drop out into the toilet. Then I spit the rest of it in the bathtub. I didn't give a fuck, right now. I was fucking something up…even if it was just mouthwash and spit.

"I said I don't give a fuck if we do something or not. I'm not rushing around. I was ready last night. Your ass wanted to sleep. It's your fault." It was her fault for me brushing my teeth five times in a row.

She got into stance and crossed her arms. She bit her lips to where they weren't visible. I guess she was mad. "We're doing something, Boo. I don't care if we drive to Lake Eerie…we're leaving St. Paul and taking a honeymoon."

Bitch.

I threw down the towel on the floor…which I don't ever do. "Fine, fuck it, come on." I grabbed her wrist in annoyance and yanked her down the hall.

"Where are we going?" Her tone changed. "Don't you need shoes? Put a shirt on at least!"

I let go of her hand and proceeded down the staircase. I stuffed my feet into the first shoes I saw in the foyer, all neatly aligned because of me. That bitch didn't understand order and organization. She was worse than Fresca.

I snatched my keys and flung open the door. She was left to wonder after me because I wasn't waiting.

No suitcase, no shirt, nothing. I jumped in the Cadillac and turned on the ignition.

"Where are we going?" Angie was inflamed. She dropped into the seat and watched me with suspicion.

"Lake Eerie." She wanted a vacation, she got one.

She can sit her ass at my dad's cabin, complaining of mosquitoes. I didn't give a fuck.

"I wasn't serious!" She panicked.

"Well, I am."

"What about clothes, what are we going to do at the cabin?"

"I packed the fucking trunk last night, motherfucker. I'll wear something in there."

"Can we go fishing?" Oh my fucking God…she likes to fish?! No way.

Chapter Ninety-Five
Angie

I think a retreat to a cabin was rather nice, don't you? I mean, to be surrounded my nature and having a campfire…the owls hooting at night, the pitch blackness…the stars. It could be romantic.

We could get up and fish. I never skinned a fish or fried one, but it sounds very interesting to me. We can rough it for a few days, sleep in sleeping bags under the night sky. We could go on a nature trail and pick up some souvenirs. We can swim in the creek…

This was going to be fun! I never thought Boo was into that sort of stuff.

"Should we stop and get groceries? We can make sandwiches and chips, get some cheap sodas and a cooler…" I was all for the simplicity of camping out.

He just stared at me. "Are you serious?"

"I was…"

"Have you ever seen me eat lunch meat, Angie? Do you think I would drink one of those fucking…ugh, they're nasty. And I don't fish." He was definitely in a bad mood. I think he had his heart set on Greece.

It wasn't my fault. I tried to wake him up at seven. He wouldn't respond. I even pulled his eyelids open and he was still sleeping. God, he took forever to go to sleep, but once he slept…he was out. It was his fault we didn't make the flight.

"Well," Thinking positively, "You can learn something new, then. We can fish. We can sleep under the stars…"

He cut me off. "I am *not* sleeping outside. You want to get eaten by a bear or some shit?"

I laughed at his stupid thoughts. Was he really that pampered? Has he never slept outside and never went fishing and never seen nature the way I've seen it?

My dad used to take us camping. My mom tried to carry on the tradition each year, too. It was one of our fondest memories of our father. And Amanda and I both loved to catch tadpoles with our hands. Every year, we'd bring them back and put them in a fish tank in our basement. Of course, they died…but it was fun.

"You do what you want to do; I'm just going to keep you from complaining." His honesty was starting to disappoint me. He was going for me? He wanted to shut me up?

"You don't want to go on a honeymoon with me?" I wouldn't let the tears come…not yet, anyways.

He stopped in front of the two lane highway that headed towards Lake Eerie. He sighed. "Do you want to go to Lake Eerie? Do you have a better idea?"

"I like the idea of camping. My dad used to camp with us." I lowered my head in hopes that his attitude would change.

"Then we're going to Lake Eerie. I don't camp, Angela. I don't eat sandwiches and I don't go fishing. I hate worms, I hate fish, I hate hot weather. I hate campfires and trees and mosquitoes. I fucking hate nature, period. The last time my dad took us, I almost had a nervous breakdown. The cabin wasn't suitable and animals had raided the place. It was disgusting. I'm doing this for you. You're lucky I'm even considering it. I'm going to rough it for the sake of you. So, are you fucking happy or not?"

If he put it that way…"Yeah, I am." I just wish he was in a better mood, I mean, we *did* just get married.

"I would rather be sitting on a beach in Greece, seeing history and shit…but…"

"I know, I know." What was his fascination with Greece, anyways? I heard that they threw babies off of cliffs if they were ugly. I think Greece people were cruel.

Two hours later, we pulled up into the cabin driveway. I was expecting to see a rundown shack with a broken porch and leaves piled so high that snakes could be slithering underneath…but…

"My dad had it fixed after we left. He said he didn't know it was in bad shape, so he rehabbed it. It should have electricity by now." He smiled.

"See, it's not so bad, is it?"

"As long as I can watch baseball…" He grinned wider, dangling his keys as he approached the door.

Oh, so that's his plan? We'll see.

The cabin was freshly stained…I guess a walnut color or something. I don't know how that works. Flowers were in flower pots near the doorway and a nice little bench was underneath the window. The windows were new. There was a floor mat at the door…and a brass looking doorknob. Hmm…it was very small and cozy. It looked very fake…not rustic and woodsy, but something a little old lady and man might call their home…way, way back in the woods.

Boo shoved the door open and lightly stepped on the floorboards, testing its stability. "Last time I was here the floor was so warped it could of fell in."

Rugs were placed on the floor. A small loveseat near a fireplace…"Does that work?"

"Yeah." He flipped the light switch on and off and ran the water from the sink. "Water, too. I can take a shower."

He was only thinking of himself. He didn't appreciate the cabin life, where you used an outhouse, bathed in the creek, and squatted in the woods with toilet paper.

"Where's the fucking TV?" He paused and glanced around for one. There wasn't one by the loveseat, nor fireplace, nor little fold out cot in the corner. I didn't like that cot. It didn't look very appealing.

"Is that where we're sleeping?" I would rather sleep under the stars, near the fire, and in a sleeping bag…with my husband.

He winced. "I don't fucking know. You wanna just leave and stay in a hotel?"

"No! No, please, Boo, please, we're already here. It's good enough. You don't have to watch baseball. We can manage, please, I'm begging you!!!" I jumped lightly with his wrist in my grip, seriously begging to stay.

He rolled his eyes with a sigh. "Are you seriously sure? You're gonna have to sleep on top of me if we sleep in that thing. And that's if it's clean. I'll sleep in the fucking car if I have to."

"Why can't we just sleep outside?"

His look told me no. He would never understand the meaning of camping…if we had a tent…we could…but no, never mind.

He plopped down into the loveseat and rested his leg on the armrest. He watched me walk around, picking up knickknacks from the past. "What the hell are we gonna do for a week?"

I had an idea. "We could make love under the stars…"

He laughed and then shivered from a cold chill. "Love? Come on Angie, you don't love me, I don't love you. We can't make love. Love is for like old people and shit. I could *fuck* you under the stars. That's about it."

I got the cold chill, now. Why did he have to say the word "fuck"? That word was for strangers, for club hoppers, one night standers…people who didn't care about people. I cared about Boo enough to say I didn't fuck him.

"You can't go all day long, every day for a week, I bet you right now. You'd be crying by tonight."

"That's not what I meant, Boo. Come on. I'm not having sex every night we're here."

"Why not?"

"Because that's ridiculous. Who does that?"

"I used to."

"Yeah right." I didn't believe it for one second.

"You honestly don't believe me?!" This was an argument he felt worth arguing about. Let's not argue about sleeping around the campfire, or not going to Greece…but how many people he slept with in a matter of days?!

"Does it matter?" I was appalled. We were married. We were husband and wife. He wanted to tell me that he had sex every day?

"No." He backed down and changed the subject. "What the hell are we going to do, though? I'm already bored."

I paced into the kitchen with my arms folded. I glanced around. It was cozy, enough. Small dinette, clean and new, the cabinets looked brand new. The sink was there. The counters were good. What was there to complain about?

When I didn't answer, his body pressed up against me. His hands rubbed my arms, up and down. He glanced around, too, his chin on my shoulder. "This place looks a hell of a lot better since I was here, last. It's still not up to my standards, though."

I twisted around. "If you weren't so naïve on nature, you'd be feeling really relaxed, right now. No traffic, no noise…no malls and people…no phone calls or interruptions. It's peaceful. You can learn a lot from me, I'm telling you. Just let me show you how to fish."

He huffed and stepped back. He didn't like my comment. "There isn't even a fishing thing. How can we fish?"

"A fishing what? You mean a pole? We can buy a fishing rod, Boo. We can have a little tackle box and live bait...ooh, I just want to fish. We can fry it up in the fire, like cowboys." The picture was a cool one...me and Boo...camping under the stars...eating fish off of a paper plate.

He cringed and gagged. "Are you fucking kidding me? You want to eat fish that we catch, fish that *you* cook? Oh my God, Angie, you're crazy. I don't eat meat. Even if we buy a stupid pole, I can't stand the sight of bait. What do you use, worms? That's disgusting. Do you know how many parasites are in one worm? I've never touched a worm in my life and I don't ever plan to."

"You never touched a worm, even when you were a kid? Now that's crazy, Boo. Being a vegetarian is crazy. Have you even tried eating meat? You might like it, you're a man! I swear, you sound so much like a girl it's pathetic. Grow some balls, will you?"

He laughed. "Grow some balls? You're fucking out of your mind. I'm not like that. I can't be that stupid ass cowboy type of motherfucker for you. If you expect me to fish, fine...I'll try. But I'm not touching the fucking shit and I'm not eating it. I don't want you to eat it, either. If you get sick, I won't be able to help you. My ass will be puking right next to you. Fuck that shit."

"You're such a baby."

"And you're a lunatic for wanting to fish. I don't see the point."

But we got the poles from the local mini-mart that was a half hour to drive to. I gathered all the necessities of fishing...the tackle box, the worms, the hooks, a net, a bucket, and some bobbers. I bought some flip flops that said Lake Eerie and a sunvisor. I loaded up on lunch meat and bread, cheese and "fake" soda, which is Boo's term for Vess.

His little basket was full of...guess? Twinkies, Gatorade, candy bars, chocolate pudding cups, yogurt, and peanut butter. He had rice crispy treats and licorice. He bought Hershey kisses and a bag of Doritos. No milk, but chocolate syrup...whip cream, a cheese squeezer. He had a case of water. He had hand sanitizer, two bottles. He bought napkins, three rolls.

He had too many boxes of condoms. For what, I don't know. It was just like Boo to keep supplied of something useless.

"Are you done?" I rolled my eyes with disbelief. He had candy and junk food. He lived off that stupid stuff. I'm surprised that he wasn't fat.

"No, I'm not." he snapped with an aristocratic tone. "Shut up so I can think."

"How about a blow up doll?" I sneered.

His expression twisted into confusion and then disgust. "Shut up." He got to the counter and had a long list that he rattled off. "Two cartons of Newport's and five fifths of Jose Cuervo…a bottle of Jack, and Captain Morgan. No, a bigger size, yeah, that's good. I need some Philly blunts and a box of Optimos. Oh, and this shit."

I stood behind him with my body on fire. What the hell was he doing? Was he going to be drunk the whole time he was here with me? Was he just going to stay an alcoholic and a pot head for the rest of his life?

I drilled him when we left…all the way back to the cabin.

"Why did you get all that stuff?!" I was trying to stay calm.

"I don't know."

"You don't know, or don't care to tell me? Why did you buy five boxes of condoms? Why all the liquor? Do you plan of hosting a party or something? Did you invite all your friends here? What the hell, Boo?"

"Will you shut the fuck up? No, nobody's coming. If you don't know by now, the fucking condoms bust, baby. I got plenty for back up." He disregarded the rest.

"Five boxes?"

"Five boxes."

I huffed and puffed, fumed at this horrible vacation.

"I'm not having sex with you." I made up my mind.

"Fine, I'll fuck a tree."

"You do that, then."

He laughed and opened up one of his Tequila's. I guess he didn't care that it was hot. It was empty by the time we got home…or to the cabin.

Chapter Ninety-Six
Dr. Roma

I sit in my office with my head in my hands. I was losing it. Maybe this job was too much. Maybe I needed a home life. Maybe I needed a boyfriend. It was so hard to figure out my own life. Maybe I needed to see a shrink, myself.

He just kissed me. Out of the blue, the boy kissed me. I didn't know how to respond. I wanted him to kiss me. I wanted the poor boy to feel pleased that I didn't reject him. I wanted…I wanted…oh, who cares what I wanted.

I really messed up. He's probably killing himself over it as we speak. Just when things were going so nicely, I go and mess up his head. What if he likes me? What if he thinks…no, it was an honest mistake. Plenty of boys are attracted to their teachers and things…plenty of women are…

I have a splitting headache, that's what I have.

He's going to be released. I wasn't going to have to see him anymore.

But I wanted to see him. I liked Cardy. He was a good person with plenty of character. It made my life easier here at Safe Haven. He was smart and handsome, athletic, talented…handsome.

No, no, no. first, I was attracted to his brother…now…no. it can't happen. I could almost be his mother.

I really needed a life, that's what I needed. Here, I'm resorting to little eighteen year olds because I don't have time to find a man…a good one, at least.

Oh Cardy, what have I done to you? Am I overreacting? Should I pretend it didn't happen or talk to you about it? How will you react if I did?

I sit here for an hour, giving him enough time to get back inside to his room. I stall a bit longer, knowing how he does the same when he doesn't want to go back to his room. He takes forever to do nothing.

He's probably flirting with Ruth.

Maybe that's it. Cardy doesn't have any girls around here. That's it. It was a natural response because I am a female. I feel a lot better.

I slowly approach his room. Brett is heavily writing in his journal and listening to rock music. It's not loud at all. I can't even make out the words. Good, I've had to have too many talks with him to keep it down over the past. Bravo.

Cardy is there on his bed, on his back, staring up at the ceiling. That's a usual position for him. Once, I asked him what he saw and he said the sky. He's a daydreamer, alright. He had a good imagination when he used it.

"Cardy, can I talk to you, alone?" I glanced at Brett and he got the hint. Brett deserted us and walked down the hall.

Cardy sat up and grinned. I didn't know what kind of grin it was. Was he pleased to have kissed me and knew it was awkward to approach him, now? Was he anticipating my move?

"What's up?"

"About earlier…"

"I said I was sorry, I didn't mean to. You were just there, I was there…I just reacted, that's all."

"So you don't have a crush on me or something?"

His laughter was amusing. Soon, I wouldn't get to hear it. It was a roll of chuckles like his brother's. "No, why the fu…why did you get all that from a kiss? It was just a kiss, Roma. You take things too personally, I swear. Think of it as a thank you, if you have to think about it at all."

Oh.

Alright,

"Well, you're welcome, then. Just, don't do it again."

"We'll see." He teased.

Cardy was too confident to feel rejection, right now, I guess. Maybe it *was* his way of saying thank you. He talked more with his body than speaking words, anyways. That's how I'm going to take it. Even if I did appreciate the kiss and needed the kiss to feel alive…it was just a thank you…in Cardy's way.

It was a nice one, a good kiss…an eager need of kiss. He kissed well.

Why the hell was I thinking of it, still?! Goodness gracious, I needed to have a night out, that's what. I think I will. I'm going to get drunk and find myself in a good old fashion one night stand.

I needed it.

I left my office that day, only to embark on a wonderful night of bliss. It was Cardy's kiss that told me to do so. If not, I may have found myself thinking more of him, seeking him out in my dreams…and I didn't want to encounter such horrid thoughts.

He was a mere child.

Here, I met a man. I do not recall his name, but his face was once familiar. I don't remember who he was, or where I found him so intriguingly familiar, but there he was, alone at a bar.

He wasn't my type, but that wasn't the point. The point was to dabble, to dip into the unknown so I may be more familiar with myself. Sounds ironic and contradictive, but it works. To be in one place, not so familiar, not so comfortable makes me want what I have. And along the way, I may find something I want that I didn't know I did. It was my own self antidote.

And my own urge to fulfill the emptiness of my womanly body…I needed to get laid.

Here this man was, short and stocky, stubble and rough looking. He was more my age, possibly older. He wasn't anything that I expected to find, nor go home with, but he, indeed, needed someone, just as well.

No name, not handsome, not even tone. His gut hovered above me in the darkness, swishing with the liquor he embodied himself with. His breath was the stench people avoid, full of the night's worry and drowned in his past sorrows.

I didn't care.

This man didn't have moves or at least when he's drunk, but again, it didn't matter. I was alone and lonely, looking to avoid a lesser crime than being with Cardy.

I was easy to pleasure, as it had been some months before I entangled in bed with some stranger. I could assume he thought he was something, alright. Made me holler and whimper out something fierce, but I knew my thoughts…and they weren't on him.

I didn't even stay long enough to whisper good morning or to let my mind fill with worry and regret. I was gone an hour later, shoes unbuckled and hair a mess. Let's not go into morals. I was a grown girl, able to finish my night with a martini and a cigarette.

In other words, I let shame leave me years ago.

Although the tension had vanished and my headache shoved into the back of my pelvic bone only to rise yet another day, I was still thinking of Cardy, Binderman, and that lovely father of theirs.

I don't know what it was. They had a way with women. Their eyes were like Medusa's. Instead of stone, we women turned to clay…pliable, wet clay.

Now, Mr. B.J Sox would do wonders with me. He was more my age and I'm sure being overseas would give me more than enough reason to cling to his body. Full of experience, full of many different cultures…I wish I would meet him in the bar.

Instead, I am faced with Mr. Gut, which is what I will refer to him as. I don't know anything else from this one night stand. I don't even recall the sex…

Chapter Ninety-Seven
Basia

Boo's words hit home...for the moment. I stood there, stunned that he, of all people, would say something so awfully true to me. I stood there, stunned, that he would fight Kyle to preserve me for Cardy. Was he drunk?

Did he care?

Did he say he liked me?

After their bickering and trading punches, Kyle wouldn't look at me. Maybe it was true. Maybe I was being used for the mere fact of points in a stupid game book. Maybe I was so stupid into thinking that someone would like me other than sex.

Was it always going to be like this? Did all boys want one thing and one thing only?

I thought Kyle was different. But then again, I thought Cardy was different.

I was a stupid girl for thinking stupid thoughts.

I stood there, stunned. I stood there, alone...with Amanda to shield my tears from the crowd.

"Are you alright? Do you want to go home?" Amanda's words didn't do much comfort.

I felt a little fuzzy from that drink. Yes it was only one drink, but I was still shaken up and feeling weird. I don't think I was drunk...but...I don't know. I trembled as if it was cold, and it wasn't. My lips shivered as if I touched ice, but I didn't.

The cold hard truth had bitten me, once more. I was condemned to wait for Cardy and that may never come. I was tortured to think of him, to dream of him, to play prisoner on my own heart and soul.

I *did* believe that Cardy was my soul mate. I *did* believe that one day he would break free from his trance and want me back. But until then...am I forever kept in this box of his, in this small town of boys who wanted to screw me?

Was I only a mother, a friend, a piece of meat?

Did I not deserve more? Didn't I deserve someone to keep me safe?

Or was that only a father's job?

"Kyle?" I pushed Amanda aside to ask him to admit it. I was a big girl. I could handle the truth. I was tired of playing these games. If all he wanted was to *fuck* me…then so be it. I needed to know.

"Basia, let's just go. You can't trust him. You heard what Boo said and Boo was trying to protect you. Let's go home." Amanda tugged on my arm, but I jerked it away.

"Is it true?" I cried, walking slowly towards him as he leaned against his car hood, drinking from a bottle of Vodka…Grey Goose, the label read. Grey Goose Vodka, what, was that supposed to be hard stuff?

"Leave me alone, Basia. Go home. Go to Darron, just leave me alone." He waved me on like I was a fly.

I wasn't a fly.

"No, I need to know, Kyle. Were you just playing a game with me? It's okay, I can handle the truth, I'm a big girl, you know." All the while, I shook in my heels, trembling from an invisible cold storm.

"No, you're not. You're Fresca, you're Jenna. You're every fucking bitch that I can't touch. But they can touch my bitch. They can always touch mine." He slurred this without caring to be polite. He made it sound as if I was a toy, a pawn in his master plan to score.

I pushed Amanda to the side, once more, and stomped my foot at Kyle. "So I'm a game piece for points?"

"Basia, you're asking for trouble. Stop it." Amanda snapped at me.

I didn't know Kyle enough to know his temper, to know his reaction. He always seemed quiet and reserved, possibly a little heavy with a surfer accent…but I didn't know his demeanor, his reason behind anything that he did.

"I never thought of you like that." He circled his hand the way a server would announce a princess's entrance…which was offensive. It was repulsive to me, in fact.

"So I'm branded Cardy's girl for the rest of my life, why?!" I demanded. What was the reason to brand anyone?

He squinted and yelled, shocking me once more with chills. "Because you belong to him, because you have his kid, because he loves you and apparently Boo knows it. I can't touch you. I can't be with you. Even if I tried, I would get my ass kicked for the rest of my life. First, by Boo, then by Cardy."

"And it's not worth the risk?" For once in my life, I wanted someone to say that I was important enough to fight for. My mother refused to say no to my father. Cardy refused to say no to parties. Kyle refused to say no to Boo.

I was never important enough to fight for.

Kyle blinked, harshly. "What?"

"You heard me, don't think you didn't. Am I not worth the risk?"

"Basia, that's enough. You don't like Kyle in that way. You just want attention!" Amanda was now well pissed at me. But I didn't care.

"You're worth the risk, little girl. But am I worth yours?" He grinned like all the boys did when they wanted something. He didn't seem like Kyle...just a boy who wanted to get in my pants.

"Stop it or I'm not your friend!" Amanda threatened.

Kyle opened the driver's side door and waved me in. "Now or never, little skateboarder."

I glanced back at Amanda enough to bare a grin...enough to say goodbye for the night...She'll forgive me, I know it. We weren't friends for nothing, you know. Friends support our stupid decisions.

And this, my dear, was the stupidest decision that I have ever made...and I liked it.

"I'll call you, tomorrow, Amanda!" And I crawled over the seat and into the passenger's side. Whatever happened, happened. I wasn't going to care. I didn't want to be alone, anymore.

"Sweet," He nodded at Amanda and hopped in. "Where do you want to go?"

"Anywhere but Pierre."

Chapter Ninety-Eight
Cardy

The day of my release:
Hot skies, vibrant colors…freedom smelled oh so grand. I was leaving the past behind at Safe Haven. I no longer thought of my life as horrible, but of a vast canvas of white, the ability to paint it whatever thickness I wanted.

Couldn't promise to stop smoking blunts…*that* I was looking forward to. The sweet heavy aroma of cannabis, fresh…fluffy green buds preferably just dried and wrapped up in a fresh Optimo leaf. *That*, my friend, was an addiction that I had to choose to quit…on my own. Of course, I wasn't going to do it every day, wasn't going to do it every weekend…just special occasions…like my release day, every anniversary of my release day…my birthday, every holiday, every fucking day that anyone celebrated that didn't account for me, like Ramadan. Didn't know what Ramadan was, but I was sure the hell taking an 'el to the dome for it.

I laugh at the mere thought. No, I grin at the mere fragment of thought that one day soon I was going to get high for the first time in a year.

Okay, okay, I wasn't going to overdo it this time. I was done with cocaine and oxy and needles. I was definitely done with needles. Pill popping was in my past, for sure. Fuck that.

But weed…chronic, 'els, blunts, Optimos, fire shit, green fluffy fire shit…Oh my God, just thinking about the shit was making me anxious.

And to be drunk, again?

I wasn't an alcoholic, I knew that much. Boo may have been an alcoholic, but I wasn't. I didn't need to drink. But drinking came with having fun, to let lose. I wanted to drink…on occasion. I wasn't fond of beer, even if it was Bud Light. It was the taste of Tequila that called out to my tongue to drown against its current backflow into my throat. I couldn't wait to…

Motherfucker, there wasn't a way to get either one those sweet treats. My ties with the fucking community have been broken. I wasn't friends with any of those people and I didn't care to contact them…not even Boo.

I was eighteen, not twenty one. I could buy a pack of Optimos and sit buddless. I didn't want to make new friends with Casa and I wasn't going to travel back to Pierre for a quick high. I guess…fuck; I guess it wasn't as important to me.

I wanted to be discreet. If I had to live in Casa, still in St. Paul, then I wasn't going to be noticed. I was going to go to Cheriton University and get the hell out of this damn town as quick as I could. Hell, maybe I'll try to do some studies abroad. Stay in some hot London chick's house and fuck the…alright, alright…I'm daydreaming, too much.

What I did know was that I wasn't going to talk to any motherfucker in St. Paul. I was going to be a loner for my own safety. I didn't need friends or popularity to tell me who I was, anymore. I was better than that.

It was about education, now. It was about living and moving on with my life and getting the fuck out of St. Paul. The further away, the less I would have to think about Jasmine and Brandon…Basia and Boo…Jeff and Jebb. They…were all in my past.

It was only my mom and she was just buying me time to get where I wanted to go. I'm sure she'll understand once she knows that I won't relapse. There's a greater cause out there for me.

"Okay, are you all packed?" Cindy, who I had a dream about and couldn't get out of my fucking head and that's why I thought of budd in the first place…decided to drop in and say a goodbye. I wish she would just avoid me.

"Uh, what's there to pack? I can't even find a t-shirt to wear. I'll be damned to wear a polo home." I stood, shirtless.

"Well," she blushed, which wasn't even flattering. She was getting on my nerves. "You can take your notebooks."

"I don't need a duffle bag for that shit." I started to pace, which was a bad sign for her. My head was full of marijuana smoke and I wasn't even around the shit.

"Are you alright, getting a little nervous to leave?" She pushed her hair back behind her ears and beamed on. Her cheeks were flushed, her eyes tired.

"What the fuck is wrong with you?" Something was different about her. Her mind wasn't here.

"Oh, I had a long night, that's all."

"The funeral?" I opened the nightstand drawer and withdrew a notebook. Under my mattress, I withdrew another one. All red, all crumbled and used… I had completed three of them, total.

"Oh, no. I didn't go. I decided to do something for myself, last night. The funeral was for a co-worker, anyways. I was going to give my support, but then I got sidetracked." Then she grinned. "I went to a bar."

"A bar?" Amused and full of interest, I sat. I wanted to know more. Cindy, Dr. Cynthia Roma, didn't go to bars, did she? What the hell was under her shell that I didn't know about? Was I leaving too soon and never going to hear her other side?

"Yes, a bar. I had a headache and needed to get rid of it. It was nothing special, really. Sometimes, I just need a break." Her cheeks were rosier than usual. Her eyes tired, yet…yet…holy shit.

"You smell like it." That's what it was. She reeked of sex, of beer, of a night full of something that she wasn't about. Holy fuck, now all I was thinking about was her. I could just sit against her all day, reliving the essence of pure sex.

"I do not!" She exclaimed with an attitude.

"Yes you do." I stood, again, only to get closer. I inhaled her, gulping in the sweet purity of ripeness. And then I smirk, knowing that this kind of stuff repulsed Boo. He wouldn't be able to be in the same room with her. He'd gag. He'd puke. It reminded him that she needed a shower and fast.

"No, I don't, Cardy, stop it. Just because I went to a bar doesn't mean I slept with anybody."

I searched my memory on what I just said. Did I tell her she slept with someone? Did I say she smelled like sex? I could have meant that she smelled like a bar…cigarettes and beer.

"I think you feel a little guilty, don't you? I never said you smelt like sex. But, you indeed, smell like pussy." I was taunting her because I could.

Now I didn't want to leave. My shrink smelled like some great sex and I had to leave it behind. At least, if I stayed, I could surround myself with her air…inhaling and exhaling what I missed most.

She hit me and pushed me to the side. "Don't say that word, no I do not. I didn't have sex, I didn't…"

"Shut up, yes you did. You came home and didn't take a shower, did you? It's okay. I like the smell." And I sniffed her once more, circling like a crazed animal with only one thing on my mind.

"Stop it."

"I can't."

"Well, you're going to have to. You have an appointment with your mother, who should be downstairs, now."

"I don't want to leave! You smell so awesome, seriously!" I was about to throw a fit. I was playing, yet serious, yet…I don't know. This new side of Cindy that I was leaving was interesting.

"Stop it, will you?! Jesus, do I smell that bad?"

"Who was it?"

"Just a man, Cardy."

"You don't know his name!" I jumped in place and knew that I had her. Shrink, forty something years old, very career oriented…still has one night stands. She had no right; no one had the right to be a hypocrite if they did it too. Motherfucker, I was hell of amazed at this.

I mean, she was forty for Christ's sake. Wasn't that something kids done?

"I'm not perfect, Cardy. Nobody ever said I was. Now, can we get on with it?"

"I did it, didn't it? My smooth move on your ass…I'm good like that, you know. I can't leave here without knowing the details. I gotta hit you up sometime and hear more stories from your ass." Now, respect was gone. She was a little girl to me. I never felt more comfortable around her.

"Well good, here's my card. I was going to give it to your mother for future reference, but I'll give it to you, instead. You still need a therapist after you leave here. I have an office in Cheriton. We can make monthly appointments." Now, she was trying to be all business and ignore the real fact of giving me her card.

"So…"

"Don't even think about it. I don't like you in that way, Cardy…Christopher."

"Alright, alright, fine…"

Chapter Ninety-Nine
Angie

He's a little drunk, great. That's perfect. I'm supposed to teach him how to fish and he can't even make it down the rocky bank.

"Angie, wait the fuck up!" He stumbled over some rocks and almost fell.

I carried the fishing poles and tackle box, the net, the bucket...picture that. Guess what he carried?

Tequila.

"This is some bullshit you got me doing. I'm gonna ruin my Jordan's." His pants sagged and jingled with his keys and coins. His face was scrunched and his eye color was translucent in the sunlight. Poor Boo...poor, poor baby Boo wasn't in his element.

"Motherfucker," He bitched as his Jordan sunk into mud. "God dammit," he almost lost his balance trying to wipe it on a clump of grass. "You're lucky I'm drunk or I'd be having a fucking fit, right now."

"Yeah," I mumbled under my breath.

This wasn't much of a honeymoon. First, he gets into a fight with Kyle over some bullshit. Then, we can't go to Greece because of some bullshit. He bought bullshit at the mini-mart...and now I have to listen to bullshit. Talk about bullshit...he was full of it and I wasn't having fun.

What was our marriage going to be like? Could we not have fun doing things I wanted to do and if we did do things, was he always going to be drunk? Was he always going to bitch about it?

I know we didn't have much in common. I know we didn't have that love that bonded us together through thick and thin. I know that we were married because of Devon. I know that fishing wasn't his deal and drinking was.

Did I make a mistake in marrying this man...this boy?

He got to the edge of the bank where the water was murky and you couldn't see the bottom. The grass grew high in spots and the rocks were full of algae. The trees hung over the creek, which seemed like a river, today. We were secluded, yet heard all the sounds of a wooded environment…frogs, snakes, crickets, buzzing insects.

"The water is dirty." He concluded about to turn back.

"All river water is dirty, Boo."

"That's my point. It's a breeding ground for bacteria." He slurped his tequila with a heavy tilt to his head.

I was pissed. I couldn't take it. I dropped the poles and crap that I had in my arms. "Fine, don't fish because you have a stupid problem with germs. You're so stupid, such a baby. I can't believe you're a weak ass baby. It's just fishing, Boo. People fish in dirty water all the time. But I'm tired of explaining this crap to you. I don't care what you do. Go back to Pierre and live in your stupid mansion. Go get hand fed by Maria all the stupid tofu you want. Maybe we shouldn't have gotten married. We obviously don't belong together."

His face drained and he stood still. "Angela, stop it. I'll fucking fish, alright? You don't need to threaten me with divorce. I'll do whatever the fuck you want me to do. You want me to fish, fine, fuck it. You want me to contaminate myself with bacteria infested water, fine, fuck it. I will fucking get hella sick for your ass just so your stupid ass will be happy. Are you happy you fucking bitch?" he stepped into the murky water, which I wasn't even about to do.

I rolled my eyes. "Get out of the water, Boo."

"Why, you think I'm a fucking weak ass…"

"There might be snakes in the water."

He scrambled up the muddy bank. His white Jordan's weren't white, anymore. Every inch of them were caked with dark brown slop. "God dammit, Angie, you got me down here and I don't know what the fuck I'm supposed to do."

"Good, you'll learn some things, some good quality things, for once."

He was quiet, then. He drank his Tequila, but quietly. He didn't bitch. He only watched and waited for me to tell him what to do.

I baited his hook. I watched his expression of disgust as he held the pole in his hand, careful not to let the worm touch him. He didn't say a word. I don't know if he was scared of divorce or being called a weak ass…but, he was paying attention and being a good sport about it.

He did this for about an hour…and then his Tequila ran out and he was bored. We didn't catch anything, which I assumed before we walked down there. Fishing wasn't about catching fish and that's what people don't get. It's just fun to try, to sit on the bank and relax. It was the fact that you were surrounded by nature.

"You ready to go back and start a campfire?"

"Whatever you want, Angie," He stood, ready to follow my every command...

Another bottle of Tequila opened, we collected fallen branches. Boo had done this before, as he knew that it needed to be dry. That was a relief. He was good at making fires. He poked it, blew it, and kept it in the middle.

Now what?

"We should buy a tent; I don't want to sleep on that cot." I finally said.

"A tent?" I could imagine his disappointment of being outside all day *and* night. But he didn't say anything else.

A tent and another bottle of Tequila later, this was feeling more like camping than ever. I had a drunken husband to deal with, but he wasn't saying much to get on my nerves. I knew he wasn't happy and was way past his comfort zone, but what I had said earlier really made him obey me.

That's what it was. He was doing whatever I wanted him to do. This wasn't Boo, but I wasn't complaining about it. Since he gave in, I'm sure he'll appreciate it later. We'll have some fun in the mean time.

I smiled at his appearance. The sleeping bag wasn't long enough, or wide enough for room for Boo to move in. The tent wasn't tall enough, either. It was a two man tent, but Boo wasn't the average man. Boo was a big one...that liked space. Did he complain?

No. He just lie down, head on a small pillow...watching my every move.

"Do I have to fuck a tree, too?" He slurred. He was done with his bottles...for the night, at least.

"No," I laughed. "I'm very proud of you, Boo. We're having fun, aren't we?"

"Sure." He rolled his eyes and leaned forward to kiss me. "I'll have more fun, now." His kiss turned into a French kiss, and that turned into a brilliant show of talent. Tequila never tasted better.

With the moon light shining through the sky hole of the tent, we made love...a' hem, I mean, we...did it under the moon light...as the stars twinkled in the heavens and my body became one with the universe as I soared like a comet, bursting into flames.

I don't know how Boo interpreted it, as I was selfishly fulfilled. I know when I turned to face him, his eyes focused on the night sky, deep in wonder...or deep in awe. My eyes closed, soon after that.

Chapter One Hundred
Binderman

"What happened to you?" My father so abruptly took notice of my appearance after a week's worth of hell.

"I went camping," My eyes were hardly able to stay awake as I tossed my old Jordan's into the kitchen trash can. I hadn't slept in a week and the shower provided at the cabin sucked. Cold water, low pressure and cheap ass soap from that damn mini-mart was awful to adjust to.

"Camping? I thought you went to Greece." He wiped his hands on a dish towel and picked Brandon up from his high chair.

Brandon seemed to grow since the last time I saw him. He was tall and wide shouldered, face wide awake and anxious to see me. I wanted to hold him, I just couldn't. I needed a shower...sleep.

"We left late and missed the plane. We went to the cabin."

"And camped?"

"And fished."

"My son fished?!" He was full of ridiculed grins and loving every minute of it.

"And didn't sleep and slept in a tent and took a cold shower." It was time to bitch a fit, as Angie was at her mom's filling her in with all the details of a horrible splendid week of torture.

"Good for you." He patted my back and handed over Brandon.

I gave him back. "I can't, dad. I'm going to my room."

"You're room? You shouldn't have a room, anymore. You're married, remember? I thought you two were going to stay in Cheriton with Grams." He followed me to the edge of the staircase as I attempted to drag myself up them.

"I still have a fucking room, motherfucker. Don't you dare change it. I'm taking a shower and then passing out. Just tell Angie to come up here. I doubt she'll get me awake, though."

All I wanted was some peace and quiet. I didn't want Angie telling me what to do or what to say. I didn't want to have to deal with Brandon or Devon, either. I just wanted to sleep.

What the fuck did she expect from me? Didn't she know I didn't do shit like that? I needed time to recuperate. Shit like this didn't come natural to me. I hated it.

I managed to sling myself onto the carpet and into the hallway. I felt like I partied my ass off. If I wasn't scared of germs, I'd kiss the ground for gratitude for being home…my real home, not Grams or Angie's…just here, where I belonged.

My door was shut, which pissed me off.

When I flung it open, already with my pants around my ankles, something was wrong with this picture. No, *somebody* was wrong with this picture. Someone was in my fucking bed, fucking up the covers, fucking up my comfort. Whoever it was is going to have to get out. I was forced to change the fucking sheets…motherfucker.

I walked out of my jeans and over to the bed. A bitch was in my bed. Her hair was on my pillow, her face buried under my comforter. At first, I assumed it could be Bobbi. With blonde hair, who else would it be?

"Get up you fucking bitch," I wasn't about to be nice. This was my fucking shit and I was looking forward to being in my shit, and now my shit was fucked up.

As soon as she stirred and I saw a glimpse of her…I stopped breathing.

I couldn't breathe, couldn't move…couldn't make a sound. I didn't know what to do. My heart sank to the floor and I felt extremely lost in action.

I didn't expect to see her, especially in my bed.

There wasn't a reason for her to be there. I hadn't talked to her, haven't seen her in over a month…I didn't even tell her I was married.

And here she was.

I wasn't happy to see her. She could fuck me up so much. She was dangerously invading my space and my life.

"Fresca, get out of my bed." I felt my own voice tremble with fear.

If she was here, if Angie came upstairs, if…I wasn't going to get accused of cheating when I was being faithful…if Fresca made one wrong move…if she attempted to touch me…I feared it all.

I was married. I had a wife. She was treading on legal documents, now. I couldn't just fuck up and toss the memory to side like I did when I was with her. This shit was serious. I said my vows and I was being serious.

But fuck no, I couldn't believe this shit.

"Hi, stranger, what have you been up to, lately?" She didn't move, didn't blink.

She was beautifully bold and pretty and sweet looking…she was still mine and I couldn't get it out of my head. In my perfect world, I would drop in next to her, wrap my arms around her warm body and fall fast asleep, not worrying about anything outside my bedroom.

If this was a perfect world, I wouldn't be with Angie and Cardy wouldn't be in rehab and Fresca and Cardy would have never met. I would still have Francesca Taylor, untouched and unharmed and we would be married, someday.

That was my perfection.

But shit fucking sucks around here.

"Why are you here?" *Don't she dare say she wanted me back, motherfucker, she better not.*

"Oh, sorry," she sat up, perky tits in her little night shirt, smelling like a field of sunflowers. "Bobbi asked me to spend the night. I didn't like her floor, so I slept in here. I like this bed."

She stood in her skimpy shorts, so short they rode up her ass as it bounced in place. God, I just wanted to bite it. It used to be mine…

I was zoning out, mesmerized by her curves, her thighs as they bulged out from her hips. Her waist was still so small, all from years of cheerleading and dancing. She was a good dancer…we were good dancing, together…we were good, period.

"You know," I fumbled for the words, how to say them right, what to say, exactly…why not to say it and just kiss her…

"I heard. Bobbi filled me in. I'm glad for you. I don't have to worry anymore. I think you made the right choice…" All the while she stood at my chest, small and petite, small and cute, little and sweet, mine and just mine.

"It wasn't a choice," I smirked as I recalled how I used to fling her over my shoulders and throw her on my bed. I was too tired to do this, now. It was the only reason good enough not to.

"Whatever, you love Angie, Boo. It makes sense. I'm happy for you. I won't stand in your way." She waddled carelessly to my doorway and was about to exit my life.

For one thing, I had to make a point. I didn't love Angie and never would. And another, I couldn't let her walk away from me when we seemed to be on good terms for the moment.

"Wait," I stood, puzzled on the fact that I didn't know what the fuck I was going to do or how to explain myself to Angie. This was mandatory.

I continued. "I don't love her."

She smiled, politely. "It's okay, Boo. We've moved on. I am really proud of this, I am. Marriage to you, I mean, I thought you would never…and here you are, and to her…it's really, really…"

By this time, as she fumbled for the same reason, or lack thereof, I made my way to her. "Shut up." And I kissed her.

I just didn't give a fuck. This was where I wanted to be, this was the girl I'd rather be with. Moments like these just don't present themselves quite often and I honestly wanted to feel her against me. It was the only peace I could get out of this hell of a week.

"I didn't think you would come home…"

"Shhh," I had the privilege to carry her back to my bed and claim what was mine in the first place. I took it and it was mine. I don't care if I was married…this girl belonged to me.

Angie, Angie…I could care less of, right now. She should have followed me home. I needed to be supervised at all times, especially if Fresca was going to be my sister's friend.

"I can't believe you, Boo. This is wrong. This is totally."

"Shut up and go home or something. I don't need the guilt." It was all I could say at the end of our union…our unique meeting, our love making. I can, in fact, say that I make love to her because I love her. If I had to say that word at all, I could say it with her.

The only stars I saw on my vacation were the stars in Fresca's eyes. It was a brilliant ending to my time away. A good feeling to replace the awful ones I felt with Angie. Yes, I regret cheating on her. The guilt was eating at me…but, there's really not much left to do about it.

I finally knew what love felt like, what it meant to be in love. As she gathered her pink laced thongs that I had bought her Valentine's Day, her sun dress that was on the floor to begin with, and her flip flops that she begged to get while we were at the mall...there was a sickness within me.

I felt the heave in the pit of my stomach rising to my throat. My skin tingled near numbness as if I was dropping a million miles through a dark sky. A wave of confusion zipped over me. Delirium has never made me dizzier than her, than now.

I had the flu, pneumonia, food poisoning, and heart failure all at once.

Love was like that.

It made me sick.

It made me need to vomit.

To know that we were apart...to never be the same like before...to understand that she was up for grabs because I fucked up...it just paralyzed any good feeling that would ever come from me.

To love someone was worse than hell.

I also figured out why I was so sick this year.

Chapter One Hundred One
Basia

Kyle and I pulled over at a spot near Lake Eerie. He wouldn't stop until I told him to and I didn't know where to go...so we ended up without a road left to travel. It was a gravel parking lot with a wooden fence bordering the bank to the lake.

It was dark and deserted.

"We ran out of road, Basia, what now?" Kyle was only being polite. I think he was frustrated that I got in the car and now, two hours from St. Paul.

"What were you drinking, earlier?" Yes, that little red devil of mine was sitting on my shoulder, whispering should's and could's in my little sweet ear.

He bent forward and pulled out a bottle of Vodka from underneath his seat. "This?"

I snatched it. "That." I twisted the cap and attempted to "swig" it. I liked that word. I had always wanted to say that word.

Yuck. Oh, no, no, no. I couldn't drink this stuff if I tried my damndest.

He laughed and took it back. "Dude, stop trying so hard. You don't need to get drunk."

"Don't tell me what to do. I can do whatever I want to." I pouted in the seat like the child I was.

"What now?"

Here goes nothing...I kissed him, hoping to send the right sparks into his mouth and down his spine and through a more interesting piece of conversation.

His fingertips ever so gently cradled my cheeks. Lips not as thick as Cardy's, but they will do. Beautiful music hummed in my ears. Lip locked and arms conjoined to each other's bodies...we were held apart by the seats...the border that no longer meant anything.

"Get out and go around front," Kyle muffled out loud.

I did.

His jacket came off and dropped on the hood. I stood in front of it as gestured. He lifted me and held me in place before him.

Oh take me now before my mind travels back.

I was on fire. I was in flame. I was flammable and ready to bust. Kissing and unbuttoning, hands and fingers and…and no thoughts…and no worries…no Cardy…and Kyle, and his…

Jesus, I tensed up, unexpectedly. I forced myself to continue.

"Don't do that." He paused into my neck.

"Don't do what?" although I knew what he meant.

"Don't tense up, you're as stiff as a board." He rubbed my arms as my legs took to the sides of his stomach. My body was ready, my mind wasn't. No, my body knew something that I didn't. It was twisted around. My body wasn't ready to be invaded and my mind was ready. That's it.

"Keep going."

"I can't, it makes me nervous. You need to relax." He laughed, uneasily. "You make me feel like you've never done this before." His mouth still wet, still resting on my cheek, waiting for cooperation.

"I really haven't. You have to show me." I didn't think it was anything to be concerned about. Somebody has to show somebody sometime, right?

"What?" He pushed his hair from his eyes and widened them for me to see. "What do you mean, you really haven't? What the fuck, dude? You have a kid, a kid with Cardy!"

He didn't get it. Did anybody?

"Yeah, it doesn't mean I know what I'm doing! Me and Cardy…it was…we did it once!" I didn't know how to explain it.

He backed away and stared me in the eyes. He was mad. "What do you mean, once? You have a kid, Basia. You and Cardy went out for like I don't know, forever. You got pregnant once, or you and Cardy only did it once, or you've only fucked a motherfucker once in your fucking lifetime?" He was utterly confused and pissed off. "Jasmine is Cardy's right?"

"Yes! Of course she is. I only had sex with Cardy once. I never slept with anybody else. Can we just…should we stop?"

"Holy fucking shit, dude, are you fucking kidding me? Dude, come on. Cardy knocked you up the first time? No fucking way! That's why you're like this. That's why you get yourself in this shit all the time! You're a goddamn virgin!!" He jerked his body back to the side of his car, ready to leave.

Okay…fine, I'm going to be mad, too. "I am not a virgin!!!"

"Yes you are! I don't give a fuck if your cherry's popped. You're a little girl, you don't know shit, You get yourself into stupid situations and to me…IS A FUCKING VIRGIN! That's like saying a little virgin who gives head and all that shit isn't a slut! It happens. You're a virgin! I'm taking you home! Get in the car!"

"No, I'll walk."

"You're acting like a bitch."

"You're a bitch."

"See, you're arguing with me like a little girl, a little bitch! Get in the car, Basia, now!" He started the car and followed me back towards Pierre. I was going to walk home…all the way home, even if it took me two days!

I was *not* getting in that car. I hated Kyle Sorum. I never wanted to see him, again. He humiliated me. He called me a virgin and I was not a virgin. I wasn't a little girl. I wasn't…

"I'm going to tackle your ass if you don't…"

"If I don't what?"

"Why do you have to be like that?"

"Like what, a virgin?"

"No, stubborn! You should be glad that I wasn't somebody else. Anybody else would love to get their hands on you. I respect you, Basia. You and Cardy…"

"Me and Cardy are over! I want everyone to know that! Me and Cardy are over!!!!" I screamed at the top of my lungs.

"Get in the car!!"

"You're not my father!"

"Well, somebody needs to be!!" He slammed the car in park and charged me.

I took off as fast as I could, following down the line of light that the headlights produced. Now, this was fun. I was going crazy and it didn't matter.

Eventually, Kyle caught me and threw me down. My dress was ruined, his tuxedo a mess. My elbow was scraped and I was in tears.

"I like you, Basia. I like you enough to say that I don't want to have sex with you, ever. I like you enough to say that you should want to be a good person and be proud of who you are!" He was out of breath and said this in my ear, forcing my face to look at him.

"Take me home!!!" I screamed back, giving in.

"I am."

"Your home!"

"But you're going to your room!"

"Good, I hate you!"

"That's fine with me, hate me all you want."

And that was the end of my night with Kyle. I got what I wanted and that was attention. I got some guidelines and some punishment. I was punished to my room and sent to spend a night with a stupid Darron.

Good…hmmpf.

Chapter One Hundred Two
Cardy

"Mom," I grinned from ear to ear as she came through the lobby doors.

She didn't look like herself. She looked younger. I don't know what it was, but she looked like she did when I was little…young and…can I say vibrant, again?

In the hospital, she had wrinkles that cascaded down around her mouth. Her eyelids were puffy and she could have been a million years old. Her body was fragile and falling apart.

Now, she walked with poise. Her face didn't have wrinkles at all. Her eyelids weren't sagging and she looked happy. Something had happened to her within a year's time…something good.

Her eyes lit up and she covered her mouth. The tears formed and she was more than happy to see me. She ran then, dropping her purse to the floor, only to embrace me in a hug that I thought I would never get out of.

"Oh, Cardy, look at you, look at you!!! I can't believe it! You look good. You're so tall and handsome, and…oh Goodness, Cardy, just look at how much you've grown over a year!!! I can't get over it. Every year you look more and more like you're father!!!"

Okay, now I see what she's been doing…she had breast implants, for sure. Her hug was so tight that they squeezed against me, and they didn't smash.

I pulled away enough to stare at her. "Mom, you look good, too, what's up with that?" Did she really get a face lift? I thought she was against that sort of stuff.

"Oh, well, yeah. I had plastic surgery last spring. They did wonders, didn't they? So how do you feel?" She entangled my arm with hers and turned me around towards the door.

"I feel free." I smiled.

Just when I thought my foot was going to walk out the door for the last time of my life...a voice called after us.

"Ms. McPherson?" Cindy jogged her happy ass between me and my freedom. "Hi, I just wanted to tell you that you have a very talented smart young man at your fingertips. I think you need to guide him towards using his potential. He can be something great."

"Oh, if he's recovered, I know he has a lot of potential in there." She probed my head with her red fingernail. "Cardy was once going to be a doctor, and then a basketball player. Now, I can barely wait to see what he wants to be."

"A millionaire." I joked and she shoved me to the side to shut up.

"His poetry is out of this world...his descriptions when he writes..."

"Ah, come on, Roma, stop it. You make me sound like a pansy, get the fuck out of here." It was my turn to push and shove. If I knew that she was going to tell my mom what I was doing with a pen...I'd never had wrote the shit.

"I remember when he was little; he'd write these little letters..." Yada, yada, yada, do you really want me to relay what she was saying about me? Where was the dignity?

Fuck it. I'm not saying and you're never going to find out. Who gave a fuck about my writing when I was little? I didn't. You didn't. Let's just leave that out of the story...forever.

I tapped my foot, but apparently nobody was paying me any attention. I paced. I paced further away. I walked back to Ruth to kiss her cheek and rub her nest head. I walked back. Oh come the fuck on, will you guys? I was awaiting my release. I wanted the hell out of Safe Haven.

Fuck it; I'm smoking one of my mom's cigarettes. "Mom, gimme your purse." And I snatched it before she could question why. That didn't do it, either. They still chattered their teeth away together, the two of them about stories over me. What the fuck was that all about?

I exited the doors, not knowing whether I was going to enter them again to get my mom out or not. I lit up. I grinned at the security guard because it wasn't his break time. I grinned because he couldn't do shit about me smoking, either.

First thing on my agenda: Buy my own fucking squares.

Chapter One Hundred Three

Do you really want a chapter one hundred? How many chapters do you want to read about me…or "them"?

Okay, fine. Who's left to give a good ending for this second entrance into my life?

Angie…I'll let Angie do it.

No, fuck that. You don't need to know. It's the end of this era of my life and I want to go home, alright?

Just carry on…let me go home to Casa will you, I don't need this bullshit. Let Boo drink his guilt away in Cheriton and Angie could live in denial about what he did. Don't fucking go there with Basia…she's fine at Darron's. And Roma…Roma was weird.

Okay, okay, here's something I can leave you with. No twist or awing satisfaction…but if I write so damn good…here is a poem…take it as you must…

Go ahead…dissect it.

I dare you to try. Maybe it's obvious, I don't know. But it means the most to me. It's Christopher wide open, Christopher baring his scars, his truce, his truths. It's me, Cardy, understanding that there is a God and he has a plan for me. Call me Catholic, Christian, or whatever you feel like…but I have found peace with God, if not with anyone else.

He let me live, didn't he?

Confession of the Crucified

I've kissed death on the tip, a needle well bent, sending waves of ecstasy like a flash of hell well spent. I've sharpened teeth of pain…in my veins and have yet to witness a soft spoken rain. But does that count insane? I've slept wide awake

in a blood ridden lake, rode tides of pure innocent girls with my heart full of hate. Take me now, for I must confess, time to bury the hatchet of inner strength mess. I've sank, I've swam, I've drove by with a slam. No need to think back of a childhood that's damned. I am who I am and need not to land on this selfish journey full of blood thickened jam.

Let my head bow down,
To the gates of his home,
I will sleep once more,
Knowing…
Under his presence I roam.

Forgive me father, for I have sinned, this is my first confession in the past five years.

—Christopher "Cardy" Deburke

Printed in the United States
215783BV00003B/32/P